THUNDER & STEEL

THE WARHAMMER WORLD is a place of unremitting darkness. From the heart of the Empire to the northern wastes of Kislev an eternal battle rages, with each victory only fleeting. Amidst this maelstrom of conflict, every man must fight for his own survival and his own honour.

In *Gilead's Blood*, the elf Gilead seeks revenge on the criminal that killed his twin brother. A quest for retaliation will carry him across the length and breadth of the Old World, but will he find the solace he seeks in hatred and destruction?

In *Hammers of Ulric*, a plot unfolds to destroy one of the Empire's proudest bastions – Middenheim. In the face of this insidious evil the noble White Wolves of Ar-Ulric stand defiant, but they will need more than skill at arms to save their fortress-city.

Riders of the Dead follows an Empire regiment marching to the barren steppes of Kislev. There they will face the twisted hordes of Archaon, a brutal force of merciless warriors. The men of the Empire must hold close their honour and courage, or else they will be lost to the powers of Chaos.

More Warhammer from the Black Library

• THE MALUS DARKBLADE SERIES •

THE CHRONICLES OF MALUS DARKBLADE: VOLUME ONE
by Dan Abnett & Mike Lee

(Contains the novels
Daemon's Curse, *Bloodstorm* and *Reaper of Souls*)

THE CHRONICLES OF MALUS DARKBLADE: VOLUME TWO
by Dan Abnett & Mike Lee

(Contains the novels
Warpsword and *Lord of Ruin*)

• THE GOTREK & FELIX SERIES •

GOTREK & FELIX: THE FIRST OMNIBUS
by William King
(Contains books 1-3: *Trollslayer*, *Skavenslayer* & *Daemonslayer*)

GOTREK & FELIX: THE SECOND OMNIBUS
by William King
(Contains books 4-6: *Dragonslayer*, *Beastslayer* & *Vampireslayer*)

GOTREK & FELIX: THE THIRD OMNIBUS
by William King and Nathan Long
(Contains books 7-9: *Giantslayer*, *Orcslayer* & *Manslayer*)

Book 10 – **ELFSLAYER**
by Nathan Long

Book 11 – **SHAMANSLAYER**
by Nathan Long

Book 12 – **ZOMBIESLAYER**
by Nathan Long

A WARHAMMER OMNIBUS
THUNDER & STEEL

DAN ABNETT

BLACK LIBRARY

A Black Library Publication

Hammers of Ulric copyright © 2000, Games Workshop Ltd.
Gilead's Blood copyright © 2001, Games Workshop Ltd.
Riders of the Dead copyright © 2003, Games Workshop Ltd.
The Warhammer first appeared in *Warhammer Monthly* © 2003, Games Workshop Ltd.
Shyi-zar first appeared in the *Chaos Rising* booklet © 2004, Games Workshop Ltd.
Swords of the Empire first appeared in the *Swords of the Empire* anthology
© 2004, Games Workshop Ltd.
All rights reserved.

This omnibus edition published in Great Britain in 2011 by
The Black Library,
Games Workshop Ltd.,
Willow Road,
Nottingham, NG7 2WS, UK.

10 9 8 7 6 5 4 3 2 1

Cover and internal illustration by Wayne England.
Riders of the Dead illustration by Adrian Smith.
Map by Nuala Kinrade.

© Games Workshop Limited 2011. All rights reserved.

The Black Library, the Black Library logo, Games Workshop, the Games Workshop logo and all associated marks, names, characters, illustrations and images from the Warhammer universe are either ®, TM and/or © Games Workshop Ltd 2000-2011, variably registered in the UK and other countries around the world. All rights reserved.

A CIP record for this book is available from the British Library.

ISBN13: 978 1 84970 023 8

Distributed in the US by Simon & Schuster
1230 Avenue of the Americas, New York, NY 10020, US.

No part of this publication may be reproduced, stored in a retrieval system, or transmitted in any form or by any means, electronic, mechanical, photocopying, recording or otherwise, without the prior permission of the publishers.

This is a work of fiction. All the characters and events portrayed in this book are fictional, and any resemblance to real people or incidents is purely coincidental.

See the Black Library on the internet at
www.blacklibrary.com

Find out more about Games Workshop
and the world of Warhammer 40,000 at
www.games-workshop.com

Printed and bound in the US.

THIS IS A dark age, a bloody age, an age of daemons
and of sorcery. It is an age of battle and death, and of the world's ending.
Amidst all of the fire, flame and fury
it is a time, too, of mighty heroes, of bold deeds
and great courage.

AT THE HEART of the Old World sprawls the Empire, the largest and most powerful of the human realms. Known for its engineers, sorcerers, traders and soldiers, it is a land of great mountains, mighty rivers, dark forests and vast cities. And from his throne in Altdorf reigns
the Emperor Karl Franz, sacred descendant of the
founder of these lands, Sigmar, and wielder
of his magical warhammer.

BUT THESE ARE far from civilised times. Across the length and breadth of the Old World, from the knightly palaces of Bretonnia to ice-bound Kislev in the far north, come rumblings of war. In the towering Worlds Edge Mountains, the orc tribes are gathering for another assault. Bandits and renegades harry the wild southern lands of the Border Princes. There are rumours of rat-things, the skaven, emerging from the sewers and swamps across the land. And from the northern wildernesses there is the ever-present threat of Chaos, of daemons and beastmen corrupted by the foul powers of the Dark Gods. As the time of battle draws ever near, the Empire needs heroes like never before.

Norsca

Sea of Chaos...

Sea

The Wasteland.

Laurelorn forest.

L'Anguille.

Couronne.

Marienburg.

Arden forest.

Gisoreux.

Bordeleaux.

Bretonnia

Grey Mo

Brionne.

Loren forest

Quenelles.

North of Here Lie The
Dreaded Chaos Wastes.
Claws
Erengrad.
Here Be Trolls...
Praag.
Middle Mountains.
enheim.
Kislev
Kislev.
Wolfenburg.
Talabheim
Altdorf.
The Empire
Karak Kad
Nuln.
The
Moot.
Sylvania.
Dracken
-hof.
ins.
Zhufbar.
Averheim.
Black
Water.
Black fire Pass.
Karak
Norn.

CONTENTS

Introduction
by Dan Abnett — 11

Gilead's Blood
by Dan Abnett and Nik Vincent — 13

Hammers of Ulric
by Dan Abnett, Nik Vincent and James Wallis — 205

Riders of the Dead
by Dan Abnett — 467

Swords of the Empire
by Dan Abnett — 685

Shyi-zar
by Dan Abnett — 715

The Warhammer
Script by Dan Abnett, Art by Colin MacNeill,
Paul Jeacock and Adrian Smith — 733

WELCOME TO THE OLD WORLD

COMPARED TO MY Warhammer 40,000 output, which currently stands at a gazillionty novels (yes, that *is* a technical publishing term, thank you for asking), and apart from the *Darkblade* novels Mike Lee and I have unleashed upon the reading public, I have spent comparatively little time stalking the gloomy, blood-dewed forests of the Warhammer realm.

This is somewhat surprising, because I love it. It lights my very particular bulls-eye lantern just about as much as 40K sparks up my glow-globe. Sword and sorcery, heroic fantasy, whatever you want to call it, I adore it, and I especially adore the especially gruesome, hopeless, misbegotten, bubonic, grotesque Chaucer-by-way-of-Terry Gilliam Dark Age vision that is Warhammer.

I think people somehow underestimate quite how... um... *pungent* Warhammer is. If heroic fantasy is cheese (I can't honestly give you one good reason why it would be, but hey, run with it), then Warhammer is Stilton. Or, you know, something runny from Normandy. It is *not* vanilla sword and sorcery. It is *not* interchangeable with other generic fantasy worlds. It is *not* the world of grandmaster Tolkien with the place names crossed out and new ones painted in. It's the sort of place where a brave, fifth-level fighter or magic user from a well-known advanced role playing game system would last about as long as a LARPer at Stamford Bridge (no offence meant to any LARPers.

Or to the armies of Harold Godwinson and Harald Hardrada. Or to Chelsea FC, come to that).

It's earthy and brutal and nasty, it's Breughel and bish bash (Hieronymous) Bosch, it's so raw, dirty and dangerous it's like trying to read *Piers the Ploughman* without a helmet on during the Hundred Years War, and if you're not careful, it'll come around your place, lay siege to your cat, torch your vegetable rack and ram a pikestaff somewhere regrettable.

The gargantuan volume you now hold in your hand collects all of my forays into the Warhammer world, apart from the aforementioned *Darkblade* stories and my 'Warhammer Pirates' novel *Fell Cargo*, which has now, let's face it, been rendered quite uncanonical by refinements in game development (but which is nevertheless entirely splendid and available direct from Black Library Online *plug! plug!*). There are three novels, a clutch of short stories, and even a Warhammer comic strip to round things off with a spectacular visual flourish. As we proceed, I'll even drop in some specific introductory remarks for the three novels presented here.

What more could you want?

So if you *fancy* trying to read *Piers the Ploughman* (not an instruction, as it turns out) without a helmet on, during the Hundred Years War, you've come to the right book.

Welcome to the Old World. Watch your back, and fight well.

Dan Abnett
Maidstone, April 2010

GILEAD'S BLOOD

Apart from one 40k comic strip that I did as a try-out for the newborn Black Library, the original Gilead short story was my first ever work for Games Workshop. This would have been, I suppose, in 1996, when I was approached by Andy Jones and Marc Gascoigne about writing for the publishing arm they were trying to set up. It wasn't simply that they were looking for writers: they were looking for writers who could 'get' the material and capture the flavour of either universe. This was something of a tall order; harder than it appeared. Perfectly talented writers were easily misled into thinking that Warhammer and Warhammer 40K were far more generic fantasy and SF universes than they actually were (and are). Add to that the Inquistorial vetting standards of the Design Studio.

I had recently done a couple of issues of the *Conan* comic for Marvel in the States, and my name had been passed to Andy and Marc by an artist who'd seen the work (take a bow, David Pugh!). The fact that Warhammer and Warhammer 40K would appeal to me became very apparent to Andy and Marc very quickly, as did the fact that I had a long rap sheet of juvenile misdeeds as both an RPGer and a reader of *White Dwarf* in the early years of its publication.

I plunged right in with the character of Gilead (as I did soon after with Gaunt), concerning myself less with accuracy of fluff and more with authenticity of atmosphere, a policy that I believe paid off and endeared me to the masters of the Black Library. Several early Gilead stories were written and published in *Inferno!*, and when the time came and the Black Library was gearing up into the production of novels, these stories became the components of some of the book's early chapters, a process known in the trade as a 'fix up'. The same thing happened with the earliest Gaunt's Ghost stories, which found their way into the second Gaunt novel, *Ghostmaker*. Essentially, the early Gilead and Gaunt short stories set me up with a chance to do my first novel for the Black Library, the first Gaunt book (*First and Only*).

Gilead as a novel came later. It has a co-credit on it. My wife (as she is now) Nik co-wrote sections of the book to help ease the burden of delivering it (my novel writing muscles were not as well-developed back then). It was also great fun working together, and we still do it from time to time. Writing can be a solitary process, and sometimes it's a good idea to bang thoughts together (one of the main reasons I co-write a lot of American superhero comics with Andy Lanning is to stave off cabin fever, have a laugh and generally retain some social skills). By the way, Nik's contributions to *Gilead's Blood* include some of the most brutal and grotesque bits. I don't know why that should be.

I often get asked if there will ever be any more Gilead stories. I wonder if it's too late now. It was a long time ago, and the IP has moved on, leaving this on the fringes of the canon. We'll see.

At any rate, this was my first foray into the Old World, and I enjoyed it very much. Hope you do too.

1
GILEAD'S WAKE

I was anything and everything.
I was a myth.

I AM A poor nobody, so please you, who has crooked his back against the plough for fifty years, and done nothing more heroic than raise five daughters and a son. My whole world is this unremarkable village, in this undistinguished corner on the edge of the Empire. There is nothing in me worth a bent copper.

Except, perhaps, the stories. At hours such as this, when dusk falls and the winter moon rises, you all come to my hearth: the young, the old, the scornful, the curious. And you ask for my stories again.

You call them myths, and the land is full of those. But my stories are not myths. They are something altogether rarer. How many fireside myth-spinners do you know who can vouch for the truth in their tales? I may be a poor nobody, but I have known great men.

The oldest story that is mine to tell begins close to its end, with a lone warrior sitting with his back against the trunk of a tree, trying to sleep. His name, in the old tongue, was Gilead te tuin Lothain, ut Tor Anrok. Call him Gilead, if you please.

Ten bitter years had brought him to that spot.

He tried to sleep, but sleep did not come easy. For ten winters and ten summers in between, his slumber had been troubled and disturbed, haunted by the memory of hoarse cries and the scent of blood.

He sat back against the tree bole in the darkness, at the edge of a campfire's glow, and looked down a long alpine valley. Down there in the night, the fires of a fortified stockade glimmered. It looked so small and insignificant a place to be the goal of a decade-long quest.

Gilead sighed.

This wild place was lonely and remote. It had been several days since Gilead had last passed a settlement – a human village, whose name he had not bothered to learn as he rode around it. There had been a tavern there, where humans gathered and drank and told each other stories. Gilead wondered what stories they were telling this night.

Perhaps even now, some drunken wretch was slurring out a tale of the House of Lothain, of the deathless warrior and his decade of blood-enmity with the Darkling One. Of course, others at the fireside would mock and scoff and claim this was only a myth, for myths are just myths and the land is full of them. They would sneer that no vengeance was ever so pure, and no pain so bright, not even the particular curse of pain that was Gilead Lothain's.

And they would be wrong.

Gilead's mind filled with darkness, burning darkness that rushed in and ignited the papery memories in his head. He remembered, ten years before, on a night far blacker and deader, flamelight that flickered outside a rusty cage door.

Torches raised in their fists, two figures shambled back along the stinking passageway towards the cage.

Is this my death, wondered Gilead? If it was, it would be a relief perhaps. Three days, without even water, chained from an iron rung, suspended like a broken puppet in a cold and airless cave deep in the neglected reaches of the Warrens. His pale skin – for his captors had all but stripped him – was blue with bruises from the regular, gleeful beatings. There was a ghostly, hollow ache of pain where the fourth finger of his right hand had been.

The captors were at the cage door, grinning up at him, their brutish human faces split with feral glee and slack with wine. They had looked that way the first night, when they had come to take his finger.

'A sweetener,' one had called it.

'To jog the memory and open the purses of your kin,' the other had added. Then they had laughed and spat in his face and opened the jaws of the rusty shears.

'They're goin' to pay, elf scum!' one now snarled through the bars of the cage. 'We just had us word. They're goin' to pay handsome for your miserable hide!'

'Your brother himself is bringing the blood money tonight!' chuckled the other.

For the first time in three days, Gilead smiled, even though it hurt to smile. He knew that his brother was doing no such thing. These vermin may have been told a ransom was coming, but a rather different surprise was on its way.

For when they kidnapped Gilead Lothain, this band of carrion had made the last mistake of their lives.

Galeth was coming. Galeth, and five other warriors, the cream of the remaining warriors that the old fastness of Tor Anrok could muster. Even now, they were rappelling down the vent of the brick flues west of the Warrens' main entrance, sooty shafts that had once been the outlet for an old mill forge that some said the rat-kind had built under the earth, ages past. Gilead could smell the air that Galeth and the others breathed, feel the course burn of the rope as they played it out and dropped vertically into the blue dimness.

Galeth Lothain: his brother, his twin. Born a minute after the midnight chime that had marked the first moments of Gilead's life. Born under a pair of crescent moons, within a week of a falling star; born to new snows marked only by a fox's print and the kick of a hare. Good signs, all of them. Good augurs for long, proud, brave lives. Gilead and Galeth, the left and right sides of the mirror, the left and right hands of Cothor Lothain, master of the Tower of Tor Anrok.

Twin siblings are always close; they share so much, not the least being the same face. But Galeth and Gilead were closer still, a fact first noticed by their wetnurse, and then by the ancient sage summoned by Cothor Lothain to school them in physic and the lore. Their minds worked as one, as if there was a bridge of thought between them. In one room, Gilead could cut his thumb on a flensing knife – and in another part of the Tower, Galeth would cry out. Abroad riding, Galeth would fall and soak himself to his bones in a frozen stream – and home by the fire, Gilead would shiver. Their spirits were bound, said Cothor's counsellor, Taladryel. They were one son in two bodies.

So it was, twenty seven winters after the midnight that welcomed them to life, that Gilead knew of his brother's approach.

He could smell the mildew stink in the dark, half-flooded cisterns where Galeth and his men now waded, charcoal-darkened blades drawn ready. He could hear the slosh of the thick, stagnant water, the scratchings of the vermin, the gentle rustle of the wick crisping in the hooded lantern.

And in turn, he knew that Galeth was sharing his experience. Galeth could feel the bite of the chains, the ache of bruises, the throb of his finger's stump. It was that sharp beacon of weary pain that led him on.

THE WALLED TOWN of Munzig lies in the patchwork of Border Princes south of the Empire. You may know of it, perhaps. Surrounded by deep forest and shadowed by the jagged profile of the Black Mountains, it is a market town on the River Durich, and a stop-over for travellers climbing the forest ways to Black Fire Pass. For over a century, it had prospered. But at the time of my story, Munzig had become a place of fear.

In the town, the citizenry spoke anxiously of the Carrion Band. No one knew their faces or their strength, or quite what villainy spurred them on except for a craving for gold and pain in equal portions. Tavern rumour said they made their fastness in the Warrens, a crumbling maze of tunnels and subterranean vaults in the foothills of the Black Mountains, a few leagues from the town.

No one knew who had built those tunnels, or how far they ran. Old myths said they were the work of the skaven rat-kin, but myths are just myths, and the land is full of them. There was, for example, a fine fireside tale of how the settlers who founded Munzig had been protected by elves from the forest, elves who had summoned up their war forces to drive the skaven out and make the land safe. Children liked this story especially, squealing with glee as adults imitated the shrill voices of the rat-kin bogeymen. Another story said there were still elves in the forests, living in a beautiful tower that only appeared by full moonlight and could never be found by humans. Yet another declared that these elves would reappear to protect the land if the rat-kin ever returned. Unless told to wide-eyed children at bedtime, such a tale would usually be greeted by a hearty laughter and a demand for more drinks.

Then the Carrion Band had come, striking for the first time the summer before. Ambushing a wagon on the forest road, they seized the daughter of a local merchant. A ransom was sent and desperately paid. The daughter was returned, dead, by the Durich's autumn flood and the money lost forever. Eight more such crimes followed, gripping Munzig in a tightening band of fear. Loved ones were taken, monies demanded and blood cruelly spilled. In every case, the families had never dared not pay, even though they knew the odds were slim they would ever see their kin again. In the taverns, estimates had been ventured as to the fortune so far lost.

Thirty thousand gold, said some.

And the rest, said others.

Prince Horgan, Elector of Munzig, called town meetings and a state of emergency. Trade, the lifeblood of the town, had all but dried up. Plans were drawn up by the frightened gentry. Guards were doubled, patrol circuits were widened, gratings were made to block the river sluices under the city wall. By now, the old Warrens seemed the likeliest hideout for the Carrion Band, and popular myth spoke of underground passages riddling the town's drains. No one was safe.

Balthezor Hergmund, a merchant whose wife had been the reavers' third victim, had put up a reward and urged the town council to undertake a purge of the Warrens to drive out and exterminate the killers. But even the most willing had to admit the futility of such an act: the Warrens was vast, unmapped and unknown, and the City Militia numbered only four score of irregular infantry and Horgan's own cavalry, a dress unit more used to displays than combat.

What about the elves, the forest elves, someone would surely have suggested? *What about the old pact, the old myth? Wouldn't they help?*

Laughter – nervous but damning – and another round of drinks.

So the fear grew, the cost in life and gold mounted, and the bloody career of the Carrion Band continued unchecked.

* * *

STRANGELY, IRONICALLY AS far as any of the human inhabitants of Munzig were concerned, there certainly was a tower out in the forests beyond the town walls, a beautiful tower never glimpsed by human eyes, magically secreted deep in the wilds of the woods.

Called the Tower of Tor Anrok, in memory of the sunken city, it had for the longest time been home to the House of Lothain, a dwindling familial line who traced their blood back to the ancient, distant kingdom of Tiranoc.

There were only a few inhabitants of the hidden tower now: old Cothor, too weak to stand; a handful of loyal warriors, household staff and womenfolk; and Cothor's twin sons, Galeth and Gilead. Their ancestors had indeed driven out the skaven from the catacombs now known as the Warrens. But that had been in older, stronger days.

When word of the Carrion Band's molestation of Munzig reached the tower, it had been Galeth who had wanted to send word to the prince and covertly offer aid. He yearned to begin his warriorhood with a worthy victory, but old Cothor had been unwilling. The patriarch had decreed that there were too few of them left, their blood too rare, to waste it on what was clearly a human dispute. Human raiders, human prey. Elfkind shunned the company of humans, knowing that men regarded them with fear and suspicion. Whatever had happened in the past, the House of Lothain would not rouse itself now.

Galeth had been disappointed but Gilead, sensing his father's anguish, had taken up the argument and eventually dissuaded Galeth from taking it further. As the eldest, Gilead took his responsibilities to the House and the bloodline with solemn gravity.

It had been a crisp, winter afternoon, three days after this debate, that Gilead had ridden out into the forest with just one companion, Nelthion, the tower's elderly horsemaster, who had trained both youths in the art of riding. Gilead had said they were to exercise the horses, but in truth he had wanted to blow the cobwebs from his mind with a hard gallop through the frosty woodland.

Gilead never knew if it was opportunity or plan; whether the Carrion Band had chanced to hear them riding close and fallen into cover, or if they had deliberately stalked the tower and watched its comings and goings. A dozen of them pounced, dropping from trees or sweeping up from under snow-cloaks, humans and a couple of ugly mixed-blood blasphemies.

A billhook took Nelthion out of the saddle and they fell on him with flails. There was crimson blood in the snow. Gilead turned, his golden-hilted sword loose and scything, but they were many and they were ready. A cudgel smacked him sideways but he stayed up, spurring his mount to bolt clear. Then another of the reavers killed his horse out from under him with a pike and they closed on him with coshes and sacking.

So Gilead Lothain came to be the prisoner of the Carrion Band, chained deep in the Warrens. So, too, did he become their first error, for they had not reckoned with the fact that he, unlike all the others – the humans – they had preyed upon, could lead the wrath of his kinsmen right to their hidden lair.

GALETH AND HIS men skirted the lip of a dirty pool and stepped lightly, like cats, up a buttress twisted by the slow and ancient passage of roots. Gilead smelled the wet soil, felt the weight of Galeth's sword in his hand.

The Carrion Band had not posted sentries. They had every reason to suspect this damp corner of the Warrens would never be located by search parties. Their only concession to chance discovery was a series of tripwires strung out along the slim, natural caves adjoining the vaults they used as a smoke hall and dormitory.

Old Fithvael, Tor Anrok's veteran swordmaster, knelt and cut the trips one by one with his bodkin, slowly releasing the tensions on the severed cords so the bells sagged without ringing.

Seeing this through sibling eyes, Gilead smiled.

Five red-fletched arrows were nocked against five tight strings, the men looking to Galeth for the command. Galeth nodded them in, under a mossy, decorated arch where the features of a bas-relief titan had been all but worn away by seeping surface water. They smelled cook-fires, sweat, blood and swill from where a hog had been butchered, urine from a latrine. They heard laughter and rowdy voices, and a rasping viol heaving out the rough tune of a drinking song.

Galeth stepped into the firelight. Gilead's breath caught in his mouth. They both saw the sweaty, puzzled faces that turned to look. The viol stopped, mid-note.

The killing began.

Like a brief drum roll, five hollow beats in quick series marked the five impacts of elven arrows. Three reavers died on their benches, one toppling into the fire pit. Another was spun round across the table by a shaft in the shoulder, and passed out across the spilled, smashed pitchers of stolen beer. A fifth was pinned to his chair back by an arrow through the gut and began to scream as the pumping blood covered his lap. His screams rose until they and their unnerving echoes filled the vault and the chambers, like a hideous hell-music to accompany the killing.

Across the table in a leap, Galeth met the first two reavers to find their weapons, his scarlet cloak flying. All told there were twelve left alive in the smoke-hall, each scrambling for sidearms and bellowing like stuck pigs. Gilead knew of at least another half-dozen asleep in the cellars behind the hall – and so Galeth knew that too.

The elves put up their bows and surged into close combat behind their young master, who had already sheared one neck with his longsword and was splintering the flail of his second target. Some of the elves had longswords and bucklers, with a knife brandished in the shield-arm's fist. The others swung long-hafted axes. All wore scarlet cloaks and hauberks of glinting, blue-black ithilmar mail. Their hair and their skins were as white as ice. Their eyes were dark with fury. Smoke, and a mist of spittle and blood hung in the damp air. The roar of fighting shook the buried vault.

Fithvael, his axe sweeping, cut through the belly of a visored swordsman and was first into the tunnel to Gilead's cell. As the fighting raged behind him, he pulled the keyring off a nail and slammed open the cage door. Noble Taladryel, Cothor's counsellor, soaked in the blood of others, was at his side a moment later, and together they eased Gilead down from the chains and swaddled a cloak about him.

'We have him! He lives!' Taladryel bellowed, but Galeth already knew this. He and the other three warriors from Tor Anrok cut down the last of the routed Carrion Band. A few survivors, no more than four or five, had fled into the Warrens.

Fithvael and Taladryel carried Gilead out into the vault to a cheer from the bloodied elf raiders. Galeth knelt by his twin and embraced him, tears streaming from both brothers' eyes. Gilead noticed the red weal that circled the fourth finger of Galeth's right hand.

Fithvael put the place to the torch, then they formed up to move out the way they had come, wary of any harrying from the reavers who had fled.

No one had noticed that the wretch brought down across the table by the first flight of arrows was still breathing. No one saw him stir in the billowing smoke and flames behind them as they moved out beyond the titan arch.

The crossbow made just a tiny snap as it fired.

Gilead froze the souls of his kin as he screamed.

And Galeth fell, a steel bolt transfixing his heart.

Gilead woke.

The moon gazed down at him, full and ghost pale. Somewhere in the forest a wolf howled and was answered. The tree bole against his back was hard and cold like iron. In the valley below, the stockade lights had been put out.

Gilead shivered. Even after ten years, the dreams came down at night and fell on him like robbers, murdering his sleep.

He got to his feet and stooped to poke at the thin fire. Pine cones had been the main source of fuel, and a thick pungent scent filled his nostrils as he raked at the embers.

Pine, astringent and cleansing, always made him remember the infirmary at the tower where the veteran Fithvael had nursed him back to health. Fithvael had prepared pine water and hagleaf to clean Gilead's wounds and to soothe his weals and bruises, using the old skills of Ulthuan. His skill at healing was exceeded only by his talents as a soldier and ranger. But he had had nothing to nurse the wound in Gilead's mind.

Gilead had shared his brother's death, a pain that defied sanity. And after it, he had survived the lingering emptiness left in his mind. Some said he was dying too, that the bridge of thought that he had shared with Galeth was allowing the slow, cold stain of death to seep through into his body from the other side.

If that was true, Gilead Lothain had been a long time dying – a decade of slow pain since Galeth had fallen to treachery and spite in the Warrens. Ten years of wandering and blood.

There had been mourning when Gilead left the Tower of Tor Anrok. Ageing Cothor bewailed the loss of both sons to one crossbow quarrel. Was he to be left with no heir? Was the old house of Lothain, which had existed ever since his kind had come to the Old World from Tiranoc, to fall at last?

Gilead had not replied. He had set out. He would return, he told himself, one day when his work was done. But he hadn't returned after five years, when news that his father was stricken with a wasting illness had reached him. Neither had he after nine when a messenger brought word of Cothor's death. His inheritance awaited. Still now he did not turn back.

Fithvael came out of his tent and found Gilead by the fire. The five warriors who had formed Galeth's raiding party had all voluntarily followed Gilead on his mission. Now only the veteran Fithvael was left. Gilead thought of the lonely, godless places where they had buried the others, each one in turn.

Fithvael looked at the sky. 'Dawn in two hours,' he said. 'Tomorrow... that will be the day, at last. Will it not?'

Gilead breathed deeply before answering. 'If the spirits will it.'

Fithvael crouched beside Gilead. Even now, after ten years, it pained him to see his lord's face, pale and cold as alabaster, his dead eyes sunk like glittering chips of anthracite in deep, hollow orbits, his hair silver like frost. Gilead the Dead, they called him, those that met him on the way and spoke of him in taverns. They said it with a shudder. Gilead the Haunted, the walking dead whose mind was tied into the hereafter.

'Can I ask you a question?' Fithvael murmured. Gilead nodded. 'I have never spoken this before, and only now do I feel it. Ten years we've been, ten years hunting the stinking Foe. Ten years, and every second of it your poor brother deserves. But will it be enough?'

Gilead looked round sharply. 'What?'

'When tomorrow comes and your slice your blade through that rat-kin's fur... will it be enough?'

Gilead smiled, but it was not a smile that Fithvael liked. 'It will have to be, old friend.'

THE FOE. THEY didn't know his face. And he had many names – Gibbetath, or the Darkling One, or Skitternister. He had first come to Gilead's attention a month or so after Galeth had been laid to rest in the sacred grove, when Taladryel and Fithvael had captured one of the fugitives of the Carrion Band hiding out in the woods. The human had been questioned, and it was he who told them of the Darkling One and his secret empire.

Gibbetath was a skaven. The rat-kin, his mind as sharp a dagger, was never seen, but his money, his ideas and his schemes orchestrated dozens of clandestine operations that riddled the southern parts of the Empire.

Black market spices ran through his networks and the skimmed revenues filled his coffers. He arranged mercenaries and spies, and dealt in intelligence to the highest bidder. It was said he had started two wars and stopped another three. His bawdy houses in the border towns ran the finest women, and took the fattest cuts. An entire guild of thieves answered to him and his assassins, shadows all, were the finest gold could purchase. It was an empire of filth, a vermin's enterprise, a hidden fraternity of thieves and killers and sinners running scams and turning tricks in a dozen Old World cities to line the pockets of the Darkling One, the mind behind it all.

The Carrion Band and their ruthless cycle of crime had been one of Gibbetath's profitable schemes. He had outfitted the men, furnished them with supplies, presented them with information on likely targets, and took ninety percent of the ransoms. It was his decision that no hostage be returned alive. It made the band vulnerable.

It was said that the Darkling One was most annoyed when Galeth's raiders exterminated his Carrion Band.

So just think, Gilead had told himself more than once, how annoyed he would be when scything elf steel split his head in two.

The Darkling One was his target, his prey. For ten years the elf had stalked him. The rat-kin was ultimately responsible for Galeth's death and Gilead swore he would not rest until the skaven bastard was dead too. He was – and his regret over this was beyond words – fulfilling belatedly the very quest that Galeth had wanted, to drive the evil out of the Warrens and destroy its source. If he had but listened back then, if he had only agreed...

In ten years he had followed every clue to the Darkling One's whereabouts, destroying every one of the skaven's operations he uncovered as he slowly closed the noose on his quarry.

In the last three years the Foe had fought back, sending assassins and war bands to halt the relentless elf avenger. To no avail.

After ten long, bloody years, Gilead was at his door.

Dawn came. Gilead struck.

He had not really been sure of what to expect, but the wooden stockade in the forest was not quite the stronghold he had pictured for the Darkling One. He mused that a surface stronghold seemed unlikely for a creature that dwelt beneath the earth. But the Darkling One had ever been just such a mystery, just such a contradiction... no one had seen him, or knew him, no one even knew what infernal lusts drove his relentless power-building enterprises.

A tub of dwarf black powder took out a ten yard stretch of the timber wall, and Fithvael picked off the sentries from cover with his bow.

Pikemen with mail charged Gilead as he strode in through the smoking gap, but his longsword was a blur. He fought as Galeth had fought. At Galeth's death, his skills with bow and blade had flowed across that cold bridge in Gilead's mind to merge with Gilead's prowess.

One son in two bodies, Taladryel had said. Now, for certain, two sons were in one body.

Blood flecked the avenger's corselet of ithilmar mail. He was shadowfast, a killing wraith that sliced through the defenders without mercy or pause.

The human guards – those that weren't cut to tatters – began to break and flee. Pushing through them, two ogres came at Gilead. Nine feet high, the ogres' great bulk rose like a buttress wall to block him, foam snorting from their flaring nostrils. One had an axe, the other a vicious morning star.

The axe-ogre moved, swinging his huge, flat blade at Gilead. The son of Cothor leapt sideways and, before he could swing again, the hulking beast stumbled back, squealing, a red-flighted arrow embedded in its left eye. From cover by the breach in the stockade, Fithvael loosed two more arrows that dropped the brutish thing dead. The other roared and spun his star at Gilead, but the elf pressed his attack, closing with the huge foe rather than retreating. He let the enemy's charging weight do the work and impaled him on his sword.

Silence. Smoke drifted across the smashed stockade and the twisted bodies. Somewhere, a wounded man moaned. Bow ready, Fithvael joined Gilead and they looked around, their scarlet cloaks fluttering in the wind. The defence was shattered. The doors of the blockhouse beckoned.

Fithvael made to move forward but Gilead stopped him. 'This is the last act,' he said. 'I will face it alone, Fithvael te tuin. If I fall here, someone must take word back to my father's house.'

His companion swallowed hard, but he nodded.

Gilead stepped forward alone.

THE BLOCKHOUSE WAS a long hall and woodsmoke clung to the rafters. The interior was dark, deep and full of dancing shadows thrown by the torches in the wall brackets.

Gilead paused for a heartbeat then entered, his blade ready.

His eyes grew accustomed to the gloom. He saw the empty sacks and coffers that littered the floor of the hall. Was this really the heart of the Darkling One's empire?

As if it had heard his thoughts, a voice said, 'Not much, is it?'

Gilead moved into the gloom, and saw at last the thin, miserable human who sat hunched on a high-backed seat at the far end of the hall.

'You are Gilead, the elf?'

Gilead made no answer.

'My guard said there were only two of you. You and a bowman. You took my stockade alone, the pair of you?'

'Yes,' Gilead said after a long pause, answering in the clumsy human language with which he had been addressed. 'Who are you?'

'You really don't know?' the ragged, sick-looking man looked round at him. 'I am… whatever you call me. The Darkling One. Skitternister. Gibbetath…'

'But–' began Gilead.

'I'm not the rat-kin monster you think you've been hunting? Of course not! Rumours… myths… they help to keep me, and the truth, safer. Or they did.'

The man looked around himself pensively. 'In some towns I was a rat-thing, in others a beast of Chaos, in others still a sorcerer. Whatever suited the local superstitions. I was anything and everything. I was a myth.'

'A myth…'

'The land is full of them.' The man smiled.

Gilead wanted the blood to race in his head, the anger to come so he would surge forward and–

But there was nothing. He felt the emptiness, the dismal finality of this wretched blood debt. Was this what Fithvael had tried to speak of the night before around the fire?

The puny man got to his feet. Gilead could see how the wretch shook, with a palsy or an ague. He was frail and thin, and his limp hair was greying. There were bald patches on his scalp and sores on his skin. He shambled forward and fixed Gilead with rheumy eyes.

'I was richer than kings, Gilead Lothain. My name was just a whisper in the back streets, but for three decades I was more powerful than monarchs. I had palaces, mansions, coffers of gold, an army at my beck and call…'

He paused. 'Then I made the mistake of killing your brother.'

Gilead's hand tightened on his sword hilt.

The man sat down on a stool, his brittle joints cracking. 'We meet for the first time, but you have destroyed me already. When I first heard you were coming for me, years ago, I thought nothing of it. What did I have to fear from a band of elf revengers? You would be dead or tired of the quest long before you came close to me.'

'But you did not give up. I began to spend money and effort hiring men to dispose of you, setting traps, laying false scents. You avoided them. Still you came. My health began to suffer… nightmares… nerves…'

'Do not expect me to feel sympathy,' Gilead said icily.

The man held up his thin hands in dismay. 'I do not. I merely thought you would appreciate knowing how fully you have broken me. One by one, you've burned my palaces and houses, looted my reserves, put my minions to the sword. My empire has crumbled. I have run from fastness to fastness, pouring away my wealth to keep my deserting warriors loyal. And behind me, always, you have come, leaving destruction in your wake.'

He gestured around them at the grim blockhouse. 'This is all that's left, Gilead Lothain. This last humble outpost, those last few soldiers you have killed. I spend half my life scheming my fortune, and then I spend every coin I have trying to protect myself from you.'

He straightened his head to expose his saggy, wizened throat. 'You bastard elf. Take your shot. End my misery.'

Gilead trembled, his blue-steel sword heavy suddenly.

'Do it!' rasped the Foe, leaning closer. 'Finish your revenge and a plague on you! Give me peace!'

Gilead wiped his brow with the back of his hand.

'Do it!' screamed the frantic, wretched ruin of a man, sliding off the stool to his knees.

Gilead stared down at him. 'You want me to end your misery? Cutting your throat won't end mine. Ten years ago, I thought it might.'

He turned and stepped towards the door. Behind him, the Foe wailed. 'Finish me! I have nothing left!'

'Neither have I,' Gilead said simply. 'And living with that is the true price.'

OUTSIDE, THE COLD mountain sun burned down through the stands of pine. Gilead spiked his sword in the soil outside the stockade and sat down on a slanted log.

'Is it over?' asked Fithvael.

Gilead nodded.

'The Foe is dead?'

Gilead shook his head. Fithvael frowned, but knew better than to ask any more.

A meadowlark sang. Somewhere deep in Gilead's mind, a lingering pain refused to ebb away.

I KNOW FOR a fact that the Tower of Tor Anrok stands yet, hidden amidst the forests beyond the town of Munzig, though no one may ever find it. Its grounds are rambling and overgrown, and its windows are empty, like the eyes of a skull. It is just another pile of dead stones in the wilderness.

Some say there is one last Lothain alive, the lost son of Cothor, who will return from the wilds one day and unlock the old doors of the hall. They say he roams the furthest edges of the Old World, a deathless daemon with a sleepless blade, howling out his pain to the moon and warring with the tribes who follow the dark ways of Chaos. Some say that death is in his eyes.

Perhaps it is just a myth. The land is full of them.

II
GILEAD'S FATE

*I will not stir from here
until Death comes for me.*

SO YOU WOULD hear more of my tales?

Well, this land is full of stories, but to be sure most of them are foolish prattle. In Munzig, away in the forests, they'll tell you of a magic songbird that haunts the woodland glades and sings your future in sad trills as it flies from clearing to clearing. If the hour is late, too, they'll speak of a dark shape that hunkers in the graveyard and eats the marrow from bones living and dead. Nurses and watch-mothers, old guard captains and innkeepers, they are all alike. They keep a store of tales to entertain the children, amaze the passing travellers and intoxicate the locals after hours.

Lilanna was wetnurse to the Ziegler family, wealthy merchants from Munzig. A dumpy woman with silver hair in a bun and starchy black clothes, she would tell her stories to the Ziegler children at bathtime and before bed. Gleefully, they would wriggle down and beg for 'just one more'. The best were of the elf-folk, the pale watchers of the forests, haunters of the glades and waterfalls.

Lilanna had two good stories about such folk. The first was of a tower, the tower of Tor Anrok, which was older than time and lay deep in the forests beyond the town, out of reach of man. It only appeared when the moons' light fell upon it, she insisted. She wasn't sure why, to be honest, but it gave the story some charm.

The other was of a pool. Its exact position was not fixed, and that made the details of her yarn easier. The pool was called Eilonthay, she swore, and its waters were still and translucent like glass. In time of need, according to the old woman, the people of Munzig could go down to this pool and beg a wish from the elf-folk of Tor Anrok. They were bound to help, she said. The dwellers in the moonlit tower had watched over the people of Munzig for centuries. They would answer any call, honestly asked. It was their way.

The children laughed. There were four children in that house: Russ, the eldest, strong and firm; Roder, the joker; Emilon, the golden-haired girl; and little Betsen. Lilanna was full of myths and they loved every one.

AS STORIES GO, the fate of these children was better than any innkeeper or wetnurse could dream up, even in their most salacious moments. Russ was found nailed to the oak-beam ceiling with the other adults of his family. Roder roasted on the hearth. All they ever found of Emilon were some bloody scraps of her golden hair. Lilanna the nurse was cut into five pieces, as were the other servants of the house, and strewn indiscriminately with them upon the midden. Only Betsen survived. Thirteen years old, she had been away at court in Middenheim, preparing for life as a lady-in-waiting to the Graf's wife.

She returned for the burials. A pale, silent ghost, she was looked after by Prince Horgan at his palace. She spoke to no one.

It was a summer night when she found the pool at last. Two years had passed and, despite her guardian's repeated urgings, she had ridden out most evening and afternoons, into the emerald glades of the forest. She had always believed the tales her old nurse had told her. Now they were all she had left.

The pool was deep and clear. Translucent. It stood in a glade far off the regular paths, surrounded by twenty solemn larches. She knew it was Eilonthay the moment she came upon it.

Betsen dismounted, pulling her velvet gown close around her. She went to the water's edge and knelt down.

'Folk of Tor Anrok, help me now. I seek vengeance for my family, cruelly slaughtered as sport. Do not turn away from me.'

She knew it was just a myth. But that did not stop her coming, night after night.

HE PUT DOWN his wood axe and knelt. His heart was heavy in his chest. There was the human girl again, kneeling by the clear water pool, sobbing out her wishes. How many times had it been? Twenty? Thirty? How many times before he noticed her?

He coiled himself into the tree so he would not be seen, and bit his lip so he would not answer her as honour demanded.

Finally, she stood again and moved back to her waiting horse. A moment later, she was gone into the moonlight.

Fithvael, last warrior of the tower of Tor Anrok, sighed. It was not right. If he had only been younger, stronger. But he was old and he was tired. Years and years ago, before that decade-long quest and the miserable years since, he might have acted differently. But he was just an ageing woodsman now, haunting the glades, tending the trees, cutting logs to feed his hearth, waiting for a quiet death.

THE TOWER OF Tor Anrok was as silent and secretive as ever. Daylight, stained green by the canopy of leaves, fell upon its high, peerless walls. From a distance, its beauty remained. But close to, its decay was evident.

Since the passing of Lord Cothor, it had fallen into ruin. Briars overgrew the outer walls and lichen discoloured the pale stone. Casements had rotted and fallen in, and birds nested in holes amongst the roof slates. Sections of wall had slumped and spilled exquisite hand-carved sections of translucent stone onto the loam.

Fithvael approached it apprehensively. The many tricks, traps and magical wards that protected the tower glades were still active though the place was dead, but they held no threat to Fithvael. He had lived in this place for most of his life, and as swordmaster had maintained those very defences. His feet knew where to step, what stones and paths to avoid; his hands knew the glyphs he had to make to cancel charms.

His apprehension came from what he might find here. He remembered too well the day when he and Gilead had returned to the Tower of Lothain after their long vengeance mission, and found it derelict. The misery of that day had never left him. Lord Cothor had died – they found his grave in the sacred grove – and it seemed all other life in the tower had vanished overnight. The household staff, the guards, the ostlers, the very life itself had simply gone. He and Gilead had searched miserably for a while, but they had found no trace. The Tower of Tor Anrok was overgrown and empty.

He had not returned there in a long while.

Fithvael set a red-feathered arrow against the string of his black yew bow and crept into the dismal courtyard. He was almost invisible. Long before he had packed away his scarlet cloak in favour of a dull green huntsman's cape. His corselet of ithilmar mail was covered by a moleskin tunic. He gazed sadly around the unkempt yard, where brambles and thorny roots had split the flagstones. He remembered the long ago days when the warriors had trained there; great men like Taladryel, Nithrom, Lord Cothor himself. And the boys, the twin heirs.

'Gilead?' he called softly. 'My lord?' he added cautiously.

Silence, but he did not expect an answer.

He found Gilead in the throne room, slumbering in the great gilded chair that had been Cothor Lothain's. The elf warrior, slim and powerful, lolled in the seat, his longsword dangling from his slack hands. The blue-white steel had mottled and the golden dragon hilt had dulled. Plates of spoiling fruit and meat stood nearby, and empty flasks of wine.

'Gilead?'

Gilead Lothain awoke, shaking off some dreadful dream. 'Fithvael? Old friend?'

'Lord.'

'It's been a long time,' Gilead murmured. He reached for a nearby bottle, realised it was empty, and sank back into his seat.

'Twelve moons since I last called upon you,' Fithvael admitted.

'And how goes your life?' Gilead asked absently. 'In your little hut out there in the forest? You know there is always room for you here in the tower.'

'I would not wish to live here anymore,' Fithvael said bitterly, looking about the ruined shell, seeing the grey daylight falling through spaces in the tiles and walls. Broken glass lay under each window. There was a smell of rot and mildew.

'Yet you're here? Why?'

'True to our old pact, the pact with the humans of the town hereabouts, someone has come to the pool and asked for our help. A human girl. Her plight is great.'

Gilead shook his head. 'Those days are gone…'

'So it seems,' Fithvael said sourly.

Catching his tone, Gilead looked up, fierce. 'What do you mean?'

'We should help her, lord. It was our way, the way of the old pact that was in place before your late father's time–'

Gilead swore softly and waved Fithvael away. 'I have done my work. Ten years, avenging my brother. I will not stir from here until death comes for me.'

'Your brother would have helped. Galeth would have helped.'

Even before the words were out of his mouth, Fithvael knew he had opened the old wound. He froze, ready for the onslaught.

Gilead got to his feet, unsteadily. The dulled blade dropped from his hand with a clatter.

'You dare to speak to me of that?' he hissed. The hiss turned into a cough. It took a moment for Gilead to recover his voice. 'Galeth was one with me, my brother, my twin! We were one soul in two bodies! Do you not remember?'

Fithvael bowed his head. 'I do, lord. That is what they said of you…'

'And when he died, I was cut in two! Death entered my soul! Ten years! Ten years I hunted for the murderer! Hunted for vengeance! And when I found it, even that pleasure did not slake the pain in my heart!'

Fithvael turned. He would leave now. He could not face this.

Then he paused. His heart was pounding in his chest. It surprised him, but there was anger in his blood. He turned back again sharply, fearing what he would see. Gilead still stood, glowering at him, dark sunken eyes glaring balefully from his thin, wasted face.

'I was there too!' Fithvael growled at his lord. 'Ten years I stood with you, till the end of the matter! I was the only one of your followers who survived the quest! Did I not suffer too? Did I not give you my all? Did the others die for nothing?'

'I meant–' Gilead stammered.

'And look what became of this proud house in your absence! All dead! All gone to dust! The pride of Tor Anrok withered because the son and heir was lost in nowhere, hunting his own pain! The line of Lothain, thrown away for your solace!'

Fithvael was quite sure Gilead would strike him, but he cared not. His lord shook, anger blazing in his eyes, but Fithvael strode towards him, snarling out his words.

'I pity you, lord! I have always pitied you and mourned your loss! But now... now you wallow in that pity, waiting for a death that may not come! A warrior of your mettle, indolent and wasting away when others may benefit from your skills? You may crave death, but why not use what life you have to aid others? That was always our way! Always!'

'Get out!' Gilead screamed, shaking with anger. He kicked wretchedly at the plates and bottles that littered the floor around his throne. 'Get out!' He stooped and snatched up a bottle from the ground and flung it at his oldest friend.

It missed by a yard and shattered. Fithvael did not duck or flinch as he stalked back out of the hall.

FOUR DAYS PASSED. Gilead Lothain knew little of them. He slept, or drank, hurling the empty flasks out through the broken windows of the hall, watching them smash and glitter on the yard outside. Pain thumped in his skull, pain that could be neither unloosed or fettered. Now and then, he would howl at the night sky.

Dawn came, waking him. He was lying at the foot of his father's gilt throne, dirty and cold. The pain in his mind was so great, it took a few moments for him to realise that it was not the pale light that had woken him. It was the frenzied croak of ravens.

Unsteadily, he walked out into the tower yard. Ravens lined the walls, dark, fluttering, rasping. Many others circled overhead. Occasionally, one would drop down and peck at the huddled form on the flagstones of the gatehouse.

'By the Phoenix Kings!' Gilead stammered, as he realised what the shape was.

Fithvael was almost dead cold. Terrible wounds had sliced into his ancient armour, and blood caked his body and arms. Gilead drove off the carrion birds and cradled him. The veteran swordmaster's eyes winced open.

'Who has done this?' Gilead murmured. 'What have you done, old friend?'

Fithvael seemed unable to talk.

'Have you... have you shamed me, Fithvael? Did you go to help this human girl?'

Fithvael nodded weakly.

'You stubborn old fool!' Gilead cursed.

'M-me, lord? S-stubborn?' Fithvael managed.

Gilead lifted him up and carried him into the tower.

* * *

THE WALLED TOWN of Munzig, as I may have said, lies in the patchwork of Border Principalities south of the Empire in the forests below the Black Mountains. It is a steep, gabled, timbered place surrounded by high curtain walls. Lofty and proud, the Prince of Munzig's palace stands on a promontory of rock above the market town, commanding good views of the River Durich and the forest tracks rising beyond to Black Fire Pass.

Betsen Ziegler had lived at the palace for two whole years since her return, since the funerals. She had rooms in the west wing, where for months she had done nothing but slumber uneasily and weep. The palace staff worried about her. Fifteen years of age and yet far older in her bearing and mind. Pain does that to a person. Pain and grief.

After a year at the palace, she started to request books to be brought to her, and she would go out into the town and renew acquaintances with those that had known her lost family. In the evenings, she liked to sit in the palace's herb garden and read.

That particular evening, the scents of the garden were thick and heady around her, and her book lay unopened on the bench at her hip. The ancient one, the strange elf woodsman with his kind eyes and soft voice who had appeared to her by the pool, had promised her so much, yet she had heard nothing. She was beginning to believe she had dreamt it all. Another night, then she would slip away from the palace after nones and ride to the pool again.

A breeze swayed the thick lavender and marjoram around her. An evening chill was settling. She was about to rise and go in when she realised there was a figure behind her. A tall, slender form, just a shadow, was watching her.

She gasped and started up. 'Who–'

The figure stepped into the light. At first she thought the ancient elf had returned. But it was not him. Where her mysterious guardian had been kind and unthreatening, this one was lean and powerful, and his noble, pale face was almost cruel. His alien gaze burned into her. He was cloaked in scarlet, and beneath she saw intricate armour. He was truly like a creature from a dream.

He spoke, in a musical language she did not understand. Then he spoke again, tutting softly to himself. 'Of course. I must be employing the leaden human tongue. Are you Betsen Ziegler?'

Despite herself, she nodded. 'Who are you?'

'I am Gilead Lothain, last of my line. I was told you came to Eilonthay and asked for my kind to help you.'

Again, she nodded. 'Another warrior answered me and told me he would render aid,' she began. 'I do not understand why–'

He hushed her. 'Fithvael is a brave soul, but his fighting years are passed. He has asked me to take on your errand and complete it.'

'I– I thank you for it,' she said, still nervous.

'Collect your things, a mount, and slip out of the palace at darkfall. I will meet you outside the city gate.'

'Why? Can't you just–'

'Your quest is one of vengeance, as I have been told it. I know all about vengeance. You must come with me.'

She blinked, struggling to form another question, but he had gone.

IN THE DARK trees a hundred yards from the gate, he was waiting, sat astride a slender warhorse. Betsen rode up to him until they met under the limbs of an old elm that sighed in the night breeze.

'Am I dreaming this?' she asked.

'Humans often dream of my kind because they don't believe we exist. But I do exist. I live. Of that much, at least, I am sure. Let us begin.'

The girl was bright and sharp-witted, and that surprised Gilead, who had never been much impressed with the mental dexterity of humans. Not that he had had much truck with them over the years. When she told him of the crime against her family, of the dreadful murder done, he felt an ache of sympathy that also surprised him. Once she had told of the killings, she was silent for a long while. Gilead found himself watching her. She was fifteen, young even by the miserably short human timescale, but pretty, in that vulgar, human way.

Then she began to tell him what she had found out in the two years since the crime. For the third time he was impressed. It must have taken a great deal of wit and ingenuity, not to mention courage, to tease out this intelligence. These were the facts as she knew them, and as she had told Fithvael, the facts that had sent him off to his wretched defeat. She repeated them now to Gilead.

There was a merchant lord called Lugos, who dwelt in an old fortified mansion maybe ten miles beyond Munzig. He was old and very rich – as rich as the prince himself, some said; richer still, said others. In fact, no one could account for the way a merchant, even a prosperous, successful man like Lugos, could have amassed quite such a fortune. He had ambitions too, courtly ones. The Border Princes could always stand another count, another duke.

The most whispered rumours said that Lugos had crossed into the Darkness. That he had dabbled in forces he did not understand and should not have unlocked. Even that he was a sorcerer, married to evil. No one had proof. No one, except perhaps Betsen herself, had even dared to find any. Lugos was a respectable man, a powerful man. He had a personal militia that rivalled the standing garrisons of some small towns. His mansion was a fortress. He had the ear of powerful men at Court.

Betsen knew that her father, who had been an up and coming merchant, had entered into business with Lugos in an attempt to increase his trade. Lugos had nurtured him, as all good merchant lords do when they find an eager trade partner. Betsen believed that in the course of this business dealing, her father had learned a little too much about Lugos – and Lugos had decided to silence him. And he had done it in the bestial manner his unholy masters had determined.

The mansion was a stronghold indeed; a great blackstone building with good walls and picket towers along the perimeter.

Gilead watched the place from the cover of the tree line. He did not need solid proof of the evil within, not in the way humans seemed to need. He could feel the vile filth of the place oozing out at him. If he had found this place under other circumstances, he would not have needed the girl's urgings to feel the need to destroy it. It was an affront to the nature of the world.

'Stay here,' he told the human girl, handing her a light crossbow. 'I will send for you when the time comes. This device is loaded. Aim carefully and squeeze this if you need to. But I think you will not be so troubled. I will keep them busy.'

'Alone?' she asked.

'Alone,' the elf agreed, eyes dark in the shadows. 'I will deal with them alone.'

'I meant me,' she returned fiercely.

'You'll be safe,' he repeated, catching her tone in surprise. She was sharp, sharper than he expected of a mere human.

He made to ride on, but she stopped him. 'Your... the other, Fithvael? He told me about you. About your pain and loss and... what you have been through.'

'He shouldn't have done that,' Gilead said, his slanting eyes dark and unfathomable. 'It was not a human concern.'

'He told me so I would understand why he was undertaking my quest and not his master, the great warrior.'

Gilead was silent.

'I understand,' she said hurriedly. 'I understand your pain was so great you had no desire to become involved in another's pain. What... what changed your mind?'

'I was reminded of the old duty my kind chose to take up. That changed my mind.'

'He said you wanted only to die.'

'I do.'

'But he also said he thought you should be using your life to help others until death came.'

'He said a great deal.'

She smiled. 'I suppose he did. Are you embarrassed?'

'No,' he lied, hiding his feelings in the lumpen human language.

'I think he was right, anyway. Even a life of pain is not worth wasting. Don't you think?'

'Perhaps... I am here, am I not?' Gilead added after a pause.

'So what will you do with your life after this is ended?'

Gilead spurred his horse on. 'First,' he answered, 'I will see if there is to be a life after this has ended.'

* * *

THE BLADE OF his knife was dulled with ash so that the moonlight would not catch it. It went through four throats and slid in between the back-plates of three cuirasses as his left hand tightly stifled cries. By midnight, he was over the main wall, a shadow running the length of the ditch towards the mansion itself.

There was a high window above the inner dyke. Pausing to hide as another guard went past, Gilead unslung a silken rope and with a deft throw looped its end over a waterchute. The stone of the wall was black and sheer, wet with slime and moss. His feet found every toe-hold as his arms pulled him upwards.

On the ledge of the window, he coiled his rope again and drew his longsword. Below him, in the hall, he could hear singing and merrymaking, the croon of viols and pipes, the clink of glasses.

'Now,' he breathed, and dropped inside. He landed in the middle of the main table. The light thump was enough to bring the merrymaking to a sudden halt. There were thirty in the hall: nobles, women, servants, warriors and musicians. They all stared in dismay at the armed warrior in their midst.

At the head of the table sat Lugos, a withered old human in yellow robes. He smiled.

'Another elf?' he chuckled. 'Two in one week. I am honoured.' He nodded to his men, who were already scrambling up and drawing weapons. The servants and woman backed away in fear. 'Let's see if we can't kill this one outright. I'd hate for him to get away and bleed to death in the woods like the last one.'

Gilead was transfixed by the cruel glee in Lugos's face.

They rushed him. But you cannot rush one who is suddenly shadowfast. Gilead was abruptly in a dozen places, his sword whispering as it scythed. Two dropped, then four more. There were screams and cries, the clatter of falling weapons, the patter of blood.

Lugos frowned, observing the slaughter before him. He turned to his aide, who stood quaking at his side. 'Wake Siddroc.'

'But master–'

'Wake him, I say! This one is a devil, much more than the last fool! Wake Siddroc or we are all finished!'

Gilead cut left, thrust right. He severed a sword arm and decapitated another fighter to his rear. Blades flurried around him like grouse beaten from cover. Some broke against his flashing longsword like shattered mirrors. Others rebounded, blocked, before the ancient longsword stabbed in under loosened guards.

Gilead rejoiced. It had been so long, so long since he had felt fire, felt purpose. His sword arm, his warrior soul, had slept. He spun again, cut, thrust, sliced. And they were all done.

Gilead turned, eyes bright and sword red, and faced Lugos down the length of the long table. The only sounds were the spitting of the logs in the fireplace, the moans of the not-quite dead and the drip of a spilled wine flagon as it drained.

'You are Lugos?' Gilead said.

'I do hope so,' the human said calmly, 'or else you've made a terrible mess in someone else's hall… elf.' He pronounced the word as if it were a curse.

Gilead stepped forward. 'Speak before you die. Confess the nature of your crimes.'

'Crimes? What proof do you have? Believe me, elf, the very best of the Empire will hound you out for this affront to my estate. The White Wolves, the Knights Panther… you will be hunted and torn apart as a murderer.'

'Such things do not scare me. I can smell the evil here. I know you are a dabbler in the black ways. I know your crimes. Will you confess them before I make you pay?'

Lugos raised his glass and sipped. To Gilead he seemed almost supernaturally calm for one of his short-lived, frantic race. 'Hmmm, let's see… as a young merchant, I travelled far and dealt with many traders, dealing in many fine objects. One day, a necklace came into my possession. It was finely wrought and very old, the crafting of some ancient place. Liking the look of it, I placed it around my neck!'

Lugos's face grew dark. 'It was cursed. Cursed by the Dark Gods of Chaos. At once, I was in their thrall.' He pulled open his tunic and showed Gilead the metal traceries buried within scar tissue around his throat.

Gilead remained silent.

'You see, I have no choice. I deserve some sympathy, don't you think?'

Still Gilead said nothing.

'There's more. Since I was cursed I have ordained countless human sacrifices, murdered dozens of innocents, arranged the foul deaths of any who stood in my way–'

'You are a monster!' Gilead said plainly.

'Indeed I am!' Lugos agreed with a hearty laugh. 'What's more, I am a monster who has been keeping you talk–'

The doors at the end of the hall behind the merchant burst open. A snuffling giant shambled in: a huge, inhuman thing clad from head to foot in barbed green armour the colour of a stagnant pool.

Gilead froze. Raw evil emanated from the creature. Its visor was pushed back and it appeared to be eating, its great jaws chewing on bloody gobs of flesh. A rank smell filled the room.

'This is Siddroc,' Lugos said. 'He's my friend. My guardian. My dark masters provided him to keep me safe.' He looked round at the vast creature and tutted melodramatically. 'Oh, Siddroc! Have you eaten another of my aides? I've told you about that!' The creature turned its huge head and snarled. 'Very well… this intruder has caused me a great deal of trouble. Dispose of him and I'll give you all the flesh you can eat.'

With a reverberating growl, the creature shambled forward, casting aside the last scraps of the unfortunate aide. In his right hand he whirled a chain attached to a spiked ball the size of Gilead's head. In his left, he held a curved cutter-blade that surrounded his meaty knuckles with spikes.

Gilead leapt clear as the first blow came down and demolished the table. The elf landed and rolled aside hastily as another shattered the flagstones where he had sprawled. For all its immense size, the abomination was fast. The elf side-stepped another huge blow and cut in with his own, but the longsword rebounded from the creature's armoured shoulder with a ringing chime.

The thing called Siddroc knocked Gilead off-balance with a sideways chop and the flat of the cutter blade sent him flying, blood spraying from a slice to his jawline. He landed hard in the hearth, crushing two viols that the musicians had left there in their haste to leave. He barely had time to get up and clear before the spiked ball destroyed a bench and the iron fire-guard.

Gilead flung himself forward again, trying to find some opening. This time, his beloved blue-steel sword caught against the cutter blade and broke, leaving him with about a foot of jagged blade. The creature started baying – laughing perhaps, it was impossible to tell – and charged the elf.

Gilead thought fast. He faced certain death unless he tried to evade. But death… death was what he wanted! At this moment he could do anything. Even if he failed, he would still be rewarded with the thing he most craved. Calm swept through him.

Gilead did what Siddroc least expected. He met the charge head on. The jagged end of the longsword stabbed into the visor slit of Siddroc's vast helm. There was a pneumatic pop and a crack of bone, and stinking black ichor spurted out of the neck seals. With a monstrous scream, the great creature toppled.

Gilead rose unsteadily from the great, twitching corpse. Once again, he noted darkly, death had chosen to take his side. He looked around. Lugos was gone.

GILEAD CAUGHT UP with him in the main yard of the mansion. The gates were open and the servants were fleeing, taking whatever they could with them in their panic. Gilead ignored the humans as easily as if they were sheep.

Lugos was face down in the dirt, impaled by a crossbow bolt. Betsen stood over him.

'That's him, isn't it?' she asked the elf, her whole body shaking.

'Yes,' he replied simply. 'And that is your vengeance served.'

She looked up at him, tears in her eyes. 'Thank you… but it doesn't feel anything like enough.'

'It never does,' said Gilead Lothain.

AND FOR GILEAD, it truly never would. But for a while, the determination of the human girl, Betsen, had shaken him out of his dark despair. The cold touch of death in his veins had faded a little, driven back by the heat of purpose.

He stood in the ruined main hall of Tor Anrok, alone. It was dawn and the light was watery and thin. He fixed his eyes for the last time on his father's golden throne. A few minutes before, he had lain a twist of thorn-roses, as scarlet as the ancient livery of House Lothain, on Cothor's grave.

He took little from the tower: a few trinkets and keepsakes, three or four of the oldest texts from Taladryel's decaying library, a few last flasks of the rare elven vintage from the cellar. His own possessions were few.

His father's longsword was a regal piece, its platinum guard encrusted with rubies. But it was not for him. He left it, locked in its casket, in Cothor's chamber – where it still lies, so I believe. Gilead chose a more suitable weapon to replace the precious blade he had left shattered in Lugos's hall: Galeth's sword. It was the twin of his own: a long, slim blade of blue-steel with dragon beaks flaring from a hilt set with a single scarlet ruby.

Gilead nodded a last, silent farewell to Tor Anrok, strode out into the tower yard and reached his horse.

On his own steed, to one side, Fithvael watched him, leaning low in the saddle to ease the ache of his healing wounds.

'I never thought…' he began.

Gilead swung up into his own saddle and took the ancient elf's hand. 'The past is dead, Fithvael. It is gone. You showed me that much. I do not know what I have in my future, but I will continue with it… until I find death at last.'

'Then let me ride with you until that day dawns,' Fithvael said quietly.

They spurred away into the morning mist. Behind them, Tor Anrok stood forlorn. Protected by its ancient charms and wards, shrouded by the mysterious forest that only elven skill could penetrate, it would never be seen by mortal eyes again.

III
GILEAD'S CHOSEN

*There is too much magic
in this place!*

What? Where did they go after that?

I've whetted your appetite, I see. Pass me that wineskin and let me think now. The stories have been in my head for fifty years, and they were old before that. They flutter around in the dry attic of my skull, waiting to be let out again. I remember only scraps. Forgive me.

Leaving Tor Anrok for the last time, Gilead and Fithvael set out upon an almost aimless voyage into the world. There was some business with a great, horned beast in the savage wilds to be found to the east of Marienburg, but the details I have forgotten. And raiders too, I recall, practising banditry on the high passes this side of Parravon. They did not live to regret their mistake in stopping two lonely horsemen.

What else? Damn my memory for a musty thing! Wait... wait... two whole seasons below ground? Yes, in lightless catacombs, at war with the rat-kin! Such deeds there, such a tale! But I have sworn never to tell it in full. Some stories carry a curse and that is one of them.

As the tales were told to me, this was a better time for Gilead Lothain, despite the dangers. Consider this much – he owned a wounded life: the death of his twin, the desolation of his ten year quest for vengeance, the misery and gloom that followed. But his companion, Fithvael, had brought him salvation of a kind. First, by spurring him to hunt the damned merchant-lord, Lugos, and then by persuading him to abandon his ruined birthplace where nothing remained save ghosts. Their wanderings gave Gilead purpose, be it bandits, beasts or the foul skaven-things. There was valour and combat and justice enough to stave off the clammy hand of doom that reached for him, across the abyss, that old rapport with Galeth which persisted now and touched his soul with death.

The companions shared a degree of happiness, comradeship, endeavour. A worthy time. But Gilead's heart was still tainted and darkened, and the misery that dogged his life would not remain at bay forever. Ah yes, a good and worthy time. It would not last, and once it was gone, it would never return. Merciful gods, I knew I had it. Now I recall what transpired next. Fill up your cup, sit back, and I'll tell you the story of what followed. But there's no happy ending, I warn you.

First, I must tell you about the voice.

THE VOICE HAD begun to call soon after Gilead had first turned his back on Tor Anrok. Gossamer-faint to begin with, he would hear it fleetingly, just the once, and then not again for months at a time; a very infrequent chiding whisper in the dead of night. Over the months and years, however, it grew, becoming stronger and more frequent. First it seemed to be the voice of his father, then his brother. Then it became a single, crystal-light, intonation in his mind, the voice of an elven woman. Eventually it was a voice Gilead felt he had always known, a voice of the past, and of the future.

Gilead had by then resolved to seek out any remnants of his kind. Veteran Fithvael, at his side day and night, privately believed this to be a fool's quest. The old kind had gone from these shores, its spaces usurped by the crude, short-lived humankind or the loathsome subhuman races. But he humoured his companion. The notion of the quest calmed Gilead, made him eager, curious, determined. It made him alive, and for that little comfort Fithvael was deeply grateful. As I believe I said, this was a good time for them both.

As it started to come to him more frequently, Gilead found himself beginning to follow in the direction of the voice, taking Fithvael with him, until they reached a tangled region deep in the Drakwald where none lived for fear of beastmen. Only now Fithvael faltered, but Gilead was resolved. There was one of their kind here somewhere, one with the power to enter his mind and lead him. He would follow it, to his death if need be.

Now, each long, dark night, her voice filled Gilead's dreams. When she came to his mind he welcomed her gladly. Ever since the promise of his young life had been taken from him, he had seen nothing in his future. It seemed like a lifetime since he had dreamed like a young man; dreamed of desire, dreamed of a lover, a wife, an heir even. The voice in his mind made him feel such things were possible again.

Pressing on through the tangled forest by day, he concentrated now only on following the voice and finding its owner. He thought nothing of what might happen beyond meeting the elf-woman who called in his mind.

'Do we continue eastward again today?' Fithvael dared to ask one morning as they broke camp and made ready to move on.

'Eastward until I learn otherwise,' Gilead answered.

'And what do we seek in the east?'

'A life,' replied Gilead, mounting his steed and turning her head toward his chosen route.

Fithvael did not pursue this conversation, just as he had not pursued so many like it in the preceding weeks. He had begun to mistrust the eager purpose that infused his friend. For so long they had simply wandered idly, sometimes making a little progress, sometimes casting huge circles in one remote area. Gilead seemed now to know precisely where he was going, but he had shared no information with Fithvael. The old warrior well knew the vagaries of Gilead's mind when it was disturbed. Yet now, Gilead had a kind of calm about him, coupled with a channelled energy so different from the murderous frenzy that Fithvael had so often feared to see in his companion.

So Fithvael followed Gilead's lead and waited for a better time to question him.

TWO DAYS LATER, at that time of day when the forest colours became one uniform dull grey hue in the fading light, Gilead turned to his companion. They could not see each other's faces as they sat side by side in the gloom, but Fithvael could sense the thrill surging through Gilead's body.

'We're very close now,' said Gilead, as if this explained everything.

'Close to what?' Fithvael asked.

'Not to what,' his friend said, 'to whom! The voice that calls to us!'

With that, he spurred on through the deep grey shadows of the primeval woodland. Fithvael smelled the churned up loam, the moss, the bark-rot in the trees. He heard the rheumatic creak of ancient timbers, the snuffling of wild boar some hundred paces away, the whirr of glossy beetles in the mulch beneath their boots. Yet he heard no voice, except the one in his own head that told him: *Turn back now and leave the young fool to his insane quest.*

Fithvael stroked his steed's mane, loosened his blade in its sheath and, knowing he was liable to regret it, urged it to trot on after Gilead.

HER NAME WAS Niobe. She made herself as small as possible in the filthy, stinking place into which she had been thrown.

She dared not open her eyes for fear of what she might see around her. She concentrated hard, trying to cut out the cries of her fellow captives, the inhuman wails and screams that filled her ears and echoed in her head. She tried to block out the deep grunts and growls of the bestial guards. She closed her mind to all that she had seen and done.

It was to no avail. The hypnotic, charismatic charms of Lord Ire ran through her soul like poison in blood. She knew what he was doing and why he had brought her here... her and the others.

There was nothing she could do except make herself small, shut her eyes, block out the sounds – and call.

When Lord Ire and his foul beastman brood had first dragged her to this grotesque place, with its sense-churning architecture and its hideous stench, she had set a part of her mind aside. She had locked it shut and poured all the energy she could muster into its solitude.

She knew that Lord Ire was using her magic, harvesting it and putting it to some dark use. And she knew that if he drained away all of her arcane powers, she would have nothing left to fight him with, and nothing left with which to reach out into the world.

Her mind-magic had always been strong, even as a babe in arms. It had made her blessed and special in her father's tower. Now she portioned off a tiny part of that magic and used it to send out a plea for help. If there was any of her kind within a thousand leagues of her, any of the ancient race prepared to listen, then that plea would reach them and perhaps bring them to her rescue. It had been so long now. Months, years even, alone in the darkness, her magic forever ebbing as it was drained away. Yet she called again, knowing it would not be long before she could call no more.

THE VOICE RANG in Gilead's mind once more.

The trees of the Drakwald grew more choked with each passing day. They were in the oldest part of the vast tangle of ancient trees now, a dark, forbidding land that had been this way since the earliest times. An eternal forest, its prehistoric glades undisturbed for a hundred thousand generations, dark and misshapen, with a rank smell and black, twisted trunks and branches that felt spongy and decayed to the touch. Densely overgrown, the pathless depths of the forest might render the most gifted ranger lost and bewildered, and there was a constant scent of subhuman fear on the air.

Yet still Gilead felt energised, invigorated, and ready for anything, the beautiful voice of the elven woman luring him on.

The sky had long since been hidden beyond the tree canopies that formed a heavy, claustrophobic blanket high above. The branches made a vault above their heads, sealing in the moist atmosphere. The air was heavy with dank vegetable smells and the creaking, flexing sounds of the forest. The two riders came to a halt, listening for the familiar sounds of birds and undergrowth creatures. But this part of the Drakwald was dead, and nothing but the most primordial life could survive here.

Fithvael started. Their steeds were suddenly nervous, pricking their ears and flaring their nostrils. The sweet smell of horse sweat rose from their twitching flanks and they pawed the ground, eager to move on.

The riders had reached a dense, high wall of foliage, a heavy hedge of twisted black branches with shiny, dark green leaves that smelled of rotting corpses. They dismounted and approached the barrier. It shivered in the breeze like a living thing and seemed to lean and reach out towards them, almost as if trying to surround them. The rustle of leaves and twigs became a cracking cacophony as the hedge strained to grow thicker and taller around them.

'There is too much magic here,' Fithvael said, trying to dispel his unease.

'And there is elf magic in my mind. We have nothing to fear,' Gilead replied, arming himself with the pair of blades that were always ready at his side.

Gilead struck out at the hedge, both blades whirring through the air, tearing into the leaves and branches before him. As they died, the leaves soared into the air, floating there, drying and browning, shrivelling to dead veins before disappearing into dust. Dismembered boughs screamed and twisted in death throes, spitting sticky brown sap that burned in the throats of the two companions.

Fithvael coughed and gasped, tearing a strip of cloth from his shirt and wrapping it around his mouth. But Gilead fought on, oblivious to the hot rasp of breath in his throat, and to the smouldering places on his attire where the acidic sap had begun to corrode his clothing.

Fithvael breathed easier through his makeshift mask and, arming himself, he ducked under Gilead's scything sword-arm to join the fray. As the pair of them cut away at the dark wall, it twisted and grew around them, until the pair could feel new growth brushing against the backs of their legs.

'Faster!' Gilead cried, slicing and chopping in the confined space.

As the two warriors worked in concert, they began to destroy the barrier faster than it could re-grow. Fithvael struck hard and fast beside his friend, trying to slash away the new growth that burst from the ruptured stems.

They hacked away at the foliage as if it were an army of greenskins, merciless with their elven blades. Small shoots of new growth showed black against the older, dark green leaves, but there were many places now where the sliced and torn twigs remained bare.

'It's working!' Gilead bellowed in triumph and, redoubling his efforts, he forced his blades deeper into the thorny barrier. He strode forward into the breach in the hedge, slicing and chopping and powering his way through. Standing close against Gilead's back, Fithvael kept the new growth at bay as best he could. They were cocooned now in the densely growing wall of vegetation, with barely room to move, but they were still making headway.

Fithvael fought back the thought that they would be suffocated by the noxious plant, walled in by the dark magic that had somehow created this barrier. Then tiny threads and chinks of light began to penetrate the dense greenery before them. At first, pinpoints of light showed through and then stronger bars of sunlight dappled the scarlet of Gilead's sap-bedraggled cloak.

'We are here,' breathed Gilead. He repeated the words over and over to the rhythm of his sword and dagger as he cut away the last of the hedge. It crumbled and broke behind them, defeated, dry and dead. Moments after breaking through, while they were still breathing hard from their exertions, Fithvael and Gilead turned back to the wall. They saw nothing but their own faded path leading back through the dim glades of the forest, their horses nearby.

'It wasn't real!' said Fithvael. 'That hideous barrier… it was just an illusion.'

'Our sweat and fear was real enough!' Gilead answered, turning from the space where the hedge had so recently been. There was nothing now but the sour-sweet corpse smell that had followed them from the moment they had entered the Drakwald, more pungent than ever.

Gilead took a step – then stumbled to his knees. Fithvael hurried to him. 'What? What is it?'

'We are very close, Fithvael te tuin. Our guide awaits us… she just told me her name.'

'Her name?'

'She calls herself Niobe,' said Gilead, drawing his cloak around him and rising unsteadily. 'She is so very beautiful…'

'Of course she is, but–'

Gilead hushed him abruptly with a raised finger. 'We are very close. She is showing me visions. A path.'

IN THE PARTITIONED chamber of her mind, Niobe had stored up a host of images of her prison. Some had collected there unbidden, others she had gathered deliberately, hoping they might be of use to her in freeing herself and her comrades.

She could feel him close to her now, the one whose mind she had reached with her voice. He had followed her calling, he had come for her, and now she could begin to feel his mind and judge his strengths. She probed his psyche, finding many avenues barred and many doors closed. It was as if he was wounded inside, damaged, shut off to the outside. What pain had haunted his life to make him so?

She saw him in her mind. He was fair, tall and graceful, and his sword hand was strong and fast. She encountered both defeat and triumph in the brooding depths of his soul and was satisfied. Despite his pain, despite the soul-deep wounds that laced him, he would be the one.

Her mind burned suddenly with the bright new image of the monstrous living thicket, bursting out its thorny new growth. Niobe knew at once that Lord Ire had also detected the existence of her interloper, of the unwanted intruder into the land he had annexed with his dark Chaos sorcery.

She knew she had to warn her rescuer.

'BE ON YOUR guard, Fithvael. She is penned in by beasts, and a great magic force that is not her own surrounds her. She is warning me this place is evil.'

'Is that so?' Fithvael said sardonically. He had known that for days. Biting back his cynicism, he paused abruptly. 'Do you hear that?' he asked.

'I hear the growl and snort of beasts,' replied Gilead.

Fithvael drew his sword and slung the edge of his moss-coloured cloak over one shoulder, freeing his sword arm from its confining folds. He braced himself.

'Aye, the growl and snort of beasts, where once we heard only the creak and groan of vile, twisted branches,' Fithvael said.

But Gilead did not acknowledge him. He had drawn his own sword the instant he saw Fithvael reach for his. They turned their backs to each other and Gilead shut out the images that were now flashing in his head – images of a huge, shimmering, faceless man in black and grey noble's garb, with pewter and silver ornament; images of a vast, ethereal fortress; images of magic war machines that spewed ball lightning out over the forest. Images surely planted in his mind by Niobe to warn him of his fate.

'On my word,' Gilead breathed to Fithvael as their cloaks brushed close and they moved together. Wary, they stared out into the twilit forest, watching for movement.

When it came, it came without stealth or ceremony. A deep, bellowing howl and a tide of frothing, jeering man-beasts washed down upon them.

They were distorted, mangled beast-things with flattened craniums and dislocated, distended jaws. Many had horns and tusks crowding in amongst crooked teeth and flaring nostrils. Their flanks were naked and hairless, and their leathery hides were the colour of pumice, which lent their skins the sheen of death. Fithvael saw spine pelts and crowns of coarse hair. He saw the grey-white, seemingly sightless eyes of the beast nearest to him and he charged, a war cry on his lips.

Gilead thrust his sword at the grey, hump-backed creature that loomed before him. It was half as tall again as the elf and three times as wide, with massively bulging joints in its stocky limbs, and huge, broad-knuckled hands that wielded a short-handled, double-headed axe. The blue metal of Gilead's sword was met by the crudely hooked blade of the beast's axe. Gilead swung his blade down in a sudden arc, sliding along the curve of the monster's axe and taking advantage of the weakness. He rested his blade momentarily in the curve and then thrust upward. The beast was turning, and took a deep wound to the top of an upper limb that was less an arm, more a living cudgel.

The beast cried out through its clenched mouth, the mandible too distorted to open wide. Gilead saw flecks of spittle hovering in the air for what seemed like minutes. Time stood still for him as, shadowfast, he dived forward, cleaving the beast's face in two across its jaw, severing the monster's jowls. Its exposed teeth flashed through the filthy ichor that gouted from the wound. Gilead made a second thrust through the neck while the beast was in mid-howl, and it fell to earth, dead.

Fithvael drove hard at his assailant, avoiding its blank-eyed stare and slicing with his sword. The abomination parried with the iron-capped club that it wielded one-handed, but Fithvael ducked and swung, side-stepping the heavy blow. Still the beastman stood solid; its weapon whirred through the air, passing Fithvael's head as he bent his knees and drove his blade upward. He connected with the monster's bullish neck, gouging a wad of flesh and tearing through arteries, but still the creature stood its ground.

Fithvael looked once into its eyes and saw his target. Swinging his blade high, he drove it down into the eye socket of his wailing adversary.

'Left!' cried Gilead as a spiked mace sought contact with the back of Fithvael's skull. The veteran warrior did as he was bidden, curving his body to avoid the weapon. Gilead drove his sword through a ribcage and another beast fell.

Gilead and Fithvael fought together in practised unison with little need for words and signs. They swung and sliced, ducked and feinted, taking one beast out at the knees, another through the chest, a third in the gut.

As the day darkened, and the canopy blackened above them, the warriors fought and killed three dozen grey skinned, white-eyed beastmen.

GILEAD WOULD HAVE continued on that same night, but they were both tiring and Fithvael persuaded his friend to rest and take up the quest again the following day. Gilead was unsettled, almost frenzied. He knew that he was close to Niobe now. He could feel her mind probing his and see the pictures she was sending out to him. But he respected Fithvael's counsel. He would rest if he must.

LORD IRE, CHAMPION of Chaos, stood at the top of a steep, sweeping staircase made of sparkling, black obsidian lapped to a mirror finish. Gilead looked up at the man, who appeared far taller than the elf; a statuesque figure of preternaturally perfect proportions. He was dressed from crown top to toe tip in a million shades of black and grey. His cuirass and coulter looked like polished slate and his cloak clasp, buckles and ornaments were pewter and silver. He stood in profile, his head turned away. Gilead concentrated on that profile, marvelling at the perfect tail of blue-black hair that hung in a swathe down the man's shoulder.

Gilead looked on, eyes unblinking, at the giant of a man before and above him, waiting. Waiting for the man to turn and face him. Waiting to look into his eyes and see what horrors lurked there.

It was only as Gilead made to draw his sword that the man finally turned his body toward the elf. The turn was slow. Lord Ire's head seemed to remain in profile for minutes. Gilead watched the man turn, knowing from Niobe's pictures and from her voice in his mind that this was the fell beastmaster who held her captive. Lord Ire finally turned to face his would-be assailant and took his first step down the long stairway.

Gilead used every ounce of his will to rest his hand on the hilt of his sword and draw it, but he could not do it. He stared up at the figure, and into that face as it came closer, trying to quell the terror in his mind.

In profile, Lord Ire's face was pale and elegant with a long straight nose and narrow upper lip over a strong jaw line, appearing more elf than human, though human he was. He was clean-shaven and the perfect arch of his half brow was a work of art in its own right.

But full face there was no symmetry. The left hand side of Lord Ire's face was a very different kind of art. Hair that grew low over this forehead was held back in a silver brace that bisected his head top to bottom and left to right. The upper quadrant was all hair, black and slick and oily. Where a single eye might have shone out between blinking fringed lids there were a series of slots in the beaten silver mask, the spaces between showing a single lidless orb, hard and white like a marble, staring out, unblinking and blind. The lower part of the face was covered in another swathe of the same black hair, straight and glossy, slashed across by a slack purple mouth, slick with bloody spit.

As the elf stared, Lord Ire's sighted eye looked down on Gilead, and the perfect half of his mouth twitched in a wry smile.

Gilead tore his eyes away from the hideous visage and bent to examine his sword hilt. He concentrated for a moment, grasped it and at last managed to free it from its scabbard. As he did so, he looked up again to where the Chaos lord was descending the steps. He saw one footfall and then no more. Lord Ire seemed to disappear before his eyes.

Then Gilead heard the steady, long stride of a huge man above his head but looking up he saw no ceiling. He saw nothing except mist.

Startled, Gilead looked down to see that his beautiful blue steel sword, Galeth's sword, with its ornate gold hilt and elven rune engravings, had disappeared. He was left holding what appeared to be a rough wooden thing made of two laths, the kind he had learned to swing before he had taken his first infant steps. The kind he and Galeth had play-fought with in the main yard of Tor Anrok, under the tutelage of Taladryel and Nithrom, all those years ago. But it could not be.

Gilead ran for the staircase, throwing the toy weapon away. As he reached the first step, he saw that the staircase descended rather than ascended… yet Lord Ire had been above him, coming down these very steps.

Turning about sharply, his stance low and defensive, Gilead found himself by a second staircase. It was straight and the ascending slate steps had no visible means of support. They simply hung in the air. Gilead took the first step tentatively, but finding it firm and strong, he took the next three at ordinary walking pace, then broke into a run, taking two and three steps at a time until he reached the top.

Suddenly there was a wall before him that he had not seen as he ascended. And then the stairs sloped into a new position and locked together in a steep, unforgiving slope. He slid backwards frantically until he found himself at the bottom of the drop and fell over the lip.

Gilead landed on his feet at the opening of a long, arched tunnel.

This place was not real. It could not be real.

He paced forward and found himself in a huge arsenal. Coming through the great portal in the north end of the store, the warrior-son of Cothor Lothain could not see the south, east or west walls, although he knew they must be there. Above him, some half a mile up, he could see that the ceiling was vaulted in a series of gigantic, interlocking domes.

Gilead gasped a horrified breath as his eyes focussed on what was laid out before him. Massed in the otherworldly building were more war machines than he had ever thought to see in a lifetime. Elaborate, multi-armed trebuchets were ranked beside rows of massive war cannons with iridescent barrels that stretched high into the vaulted ceiling. Giant crossbows with ornate winching handles, armed with bolts shaved from entire tree trunks, stood alongside giant catapults which looked strangely fragile and ethereal, like mere shadows.

As Gilead stood in horrified wonder, the machines began to throb and jostle as though wakened from some heavy sleep. Gilead closed his eyes and breathed deeply into his chest. A second breath cleared the elf's mind and a third calmed the adrenaline rush to his body at the sight of so great an armoury.

He opened his eyes and for a brief moment he was surrounded again by the sights and sounds of the Drakwald. He sighed his relief.

Then the arsenal grew up around him once more, as vast and seemingly real as when he had first crossed the threshold. Gilead fled, turning and running desperate miles to reach the door that had been right behind him only moments before.

Stone and wood, metal and mortar had no meaning here. In this place, space was a malleable commodity. The rules of architecture, the rules of reality held no meaning. The rules had been bent until they were so broken and twisted that they no longer existed at all.

FITHVAEL ROUSED AS dawn broke over the forest, to find Gilead already awake and standing beside the remains of the campfire. His friend was fully clothed and armed, but he looked pale and drawn.

'We must leave,' said Gilead. 'We must get the Lady Niobe out of there and we must do it now.'

'There is time, old friend,' Fithvael said in the soothing tone he used when Gilead became moody and obsessive.

'No!' Gilead said in a tone that brooked no compromise. 'My mind is so full of her, so full of the images she places there, I know not what is real and what an illusion. I know only that I must fight for her.'

'I have fought beside you before, te tuin,' said Fithvael, 'and I will no doubt fight beside you again. But if I'm going to follow you, you must tell me what you know.'

'Only that Niobe needs our help. She is in mortal danger.'

'The voice, the pictures in your head come from her? But who is she?'

'My future and my past,' said Gilead, drawing a trembling hand across his furrowed brow.

'You know this woman?'

'I have always known her,' answered Gilead.

'From Tor Anrok?' Fithvael asked, excited.

Gilead dropped his head. 'I don't know. Gods of Ulthuan, Fithvael! I don't know! I only know I have to fight for her!'

Fithvael threw his cloak about himself in resignation. 'I guess that is good enough for me,' he said.

GILEAD STOPPED IN his tracks and took a deep breath as he parted the undergrowth in front of him. What stood in the barren space before them was vast. He could see only the facade of the building, and looking to the left and right gave him no idea of its width, since he could not see as far as its corners. He dropped his neck back and the building curved up and away before him, reaching into the sky so far above that he could not see its roof structures, only great granite and flint walls cut off in the distance by black clouds.

Fithvael pulled up abruptly behind Gilead and looked over his friend's shoulder to see why they had stopped so suddenly. He took two steps back in astonishment, almost falling over a bulging tree root on the ground behind him.

'How... how did we not see this from a hundred leagues away?' Fithvael asked.

Gilead did not answer. He stepped through the undergrowth. The massive, grim structure before them was only a hundred yards from where they stood, but the forest halted its growth abruptly at their feet and nothing grew in the shadow of the edifice. They stepped onto a no-man's-land that looked unnaturally hard, black and level. Gilead lifted one foot suddenly from the liquid surface and Fithvael let out a yelp as his own foot sank into a hot, black swamp.

A dark geyser a thousand feet high suddenly gushed a few hundred yards from them to their right, spraying the elves with hot, murky filth, and the entire wasteland became a bubbling, gurgling quagmire.

Gilead drew his sword and began to wade across the swamp until he was buried in it to his hips, his red cloak wrapped slantwise across his shoulder, clear of the stinking heat and filth of the mire. Fithvael pulled up his boots, tightened his belt, rolled his cloak into the pack on his back and followed Gilead.

'Arm yourself!' Gilead warned, turning to his friend. 'Hurry!' he screamed, surging his way back toward Fithvael.

Behind Fithvael, rising from the mud as though awakened from deep slumber, rose a monstrous being. Huge horns curled downward on either side of a flat, pitted head, and red eyes blinked open as swamp mud trickled away in runnels down a scarred, green face covered in suppurating sores. The monster flexed its jaws and threw its half-submerged body forward, screaming as its paddle-like upper limbs ripped free of the swamp.

Fithvael turned as Gilead threw his dagger by its tip. It whirred through the air, end over end in a graceful arc, and came to rest in the exposed throat of the great swamp beast.

The creature brought one long, webbed hand up to the dagger hilt, but Fithvael was quicker, though still unarmed. He thrust his entire weight against the dagger, driving it deeper and lower into the monster's upper chest. Then the elf heaved on the gore-covered hilt, first pulling it free and then embedding it in the monstrous throat again, lower this time.

The huge, slimy paddles of the beast came around Fithvael's shoulders, embracing him and dragging his feet from the swamp bed. Losing his balance, Fithvael could feel the hilt of Gilead's dagger digging into his own chest. The monster lifted Fithvael with ease out of the sticky mud on the swamp floor. Fithvael pulled up his feet as quickly as the sucking action of the mud would allow and, drawing his knees into his body, he planted his soggy boots firmly in the beast's belly and thrust hard.

Fithvael fell heavily onto his back, creating a slow, broken ripple of mud. The vast thing rose up above him.

Gilead had only been able to stand and watch the action as Fithvael blocked his target, but as soon as the animal's huge bulk emerged, he attacked.

Gilead tore into the lumpy, calloused surface of the beast's back with his sword, hacking through the thick greenish skin until he exposed a cage of heavily gnarled, brown bones. The creature began to convulse and one of its paddle-limbs came floating slowly to the surface. Gilead reached his left hand down into the swamp, found a handhold on Fithvael's jerkin and dragged his friend out. Fithvael coughed and spluttered and took long urgent breaths, as he watched the thing they had killed slide back into the waters that would now become its grave.

As FITHVAEL REGAINED his composure, Gilead sought out Niobe in his mind, latching on to the persistent urge of her call. She had brought them this far and he trusted her to bring them safely to her.

Setting off again in a half-walk, half-swim, their hands paddling the surface of the swamp as it undulated around them, the two warriors made good progress, and soon found themselves within arms reach of the towering, slick walls of the castle.

'Do you see?' Fithvael asked, searching the immediate surface of the wall.

'There are no joins,' answered Gilead. 'The walls are solid.'

Gilead splashed back some way and focussed higher up the wall, looking for patterns that might give him some clues about the structure of the impenetrable wall. He could see reflections on the surface of the ooze around him, forming slanting, rectangular shards of light. He looked up the towering wall again and saw that the reflections fell from windows. They were very high up, but huge. The glass in the windows had a heavy gloss like black mirrors, and they were set flush with the stonework; no frames or sills were visible. Gilead was reminded of the impossible building in his dream and closed his eyes to concentrate again on Niobe's voice.

Fithvael and Gilead sloshed their way along the base of the wall, which seemed to curve gently along its length. Gilead was looking for something, but it was Fithvael who saw it first.

'There!' exclaimed Fithvael. 'Could that be the place?'

Gilead could see nothing ahead of him, though he examined the wall thoroughly.

'Two feet to your right, a hand's-breadth above your shoulder,' Fithvael instructed.

'I see nothing,' answered Gilead and backed away toward Fithvael. Gilead took up Fithvael's old position, and now he too could see the opening in the wall: a kind of grilled storm drain, arched and menacing. The oozing mud of the swamp seemed to lap up to the open slate work of the grille, but did not penetrate it.

This whole thing is an illusion. Remember that! Gilead told himself and then he made his way back to where the storm drain should have been, but again it eluded him. Fithvael was right beside his friend now, but the opening was invisible to him too.

Fithvael turned back and retraced his steps to the position he had been wading in when he had first spotted the drain. It took him several minutes to get the view just right, but he managed it. Following Fithvael's explicit directions, Gilead pulled himself up by the bars of a grille that was invisible to him.

He tried to look beyond it. There was nothing to see. A rush of cold air around Gilead caught the last son of Tor Anrok off-guard. He shielded his face for a moment and when he opened his eyes again he was back on solid ground. The mud and filth of the swamp had disappeared from his clothes.

'Fithvael, we're in!' Gilead said and turned to look out of the grille, but behind him was only a solid wall.

In his mind, Niobe reached out to him, covering his eyes with her hands in a dream tableau that she planted in his waking mind.

Gilead closed his eyes and felt the wall in front of him. It had been hard and shiny to look at, but felt sandy and crumbly to the touch. There was no opening.

Gilead took his cloak from around his body and tore off a narrow length of dense cloth from the hem. He placed this around his face, shielding his eyes in several tightly wrapped layers of cloth. Although effectively blindfold, Gilead closed his eyes once more and reached out his hands.

He could feel the grille before him and passed his hands through it.

FITHVAEL WAS SURE he had not blinked and yet his friend had disappeared through the grille without him seeing it happen. He knew he must make his own way to it now.

He carefully measured the distance along the wall by eye and slowly made his way toward the opening. As soon as he moved it became invisible to him again, but he trusted his mental measuring and carefully walked his hands along the wall, end to end, counting out as he went. Having reached his apparent destination, Fithvael passed his hands tentatively over the solid surface of the wall. He could feel no grille or opening of any kind and he began to despair.

At a distance of only a few yards, the storm drain had seemed overlarge, yet he could not find it even with a hand-search.

Fithvael moved a step to his left and lifted his hand higher on the wall, sweeping across another large area of stone with his open palms.

Nothing.

Fithvael dropped his head for a moment in concentration and then looked hard at the wall, as though he were trying to look into it, or through it.

Fithvael felt the hands on his shoulders before he saw them and tensed in an instant, ready to fight off another foe. Then he caught sight of Gilead's long slender hands, recognising his companion by the missing finger on the left hand. Gilead's arms were protruding through a solid rock wall.

In another instant Fithvael was standing next to his friend, clean of swamp filth, but more than a little confused. He sought Gilead's gaze.

'You must get used to it,' said Gilead. 'I have seen too much of this place already and it is all the same. We are no longer in our world, Fithvael te tuin.'

'I can feel it,' said Fithvael. 'I can smell it and taste it. It crawls across my flesh and penetrates my body. Corruption!'

'Fight it then,' answered Gilead, 'as we have always fought evil… but fight it only for yourself. The evil and the magic of this place are too great for us to fight alone. Our purpose is to release Niobe and then to get out of this vile otherworld.'

Gilead stared hard at his friend, that he might remember the warning, and then strode off down a long, curving corridor, deeper into the alien realm of this huge stone fortress.

NIOBE GUIDED THEM well, yet they were still confused by the architectural deceptions and optical illusions of their surroundings.

Spaces that looked huge at a distance were claustrophobic once they were inside them. Floors and ceilings sloped out and away from each other, lengthening perspective, or simply bulged and flattened, changing shape and dimensions before their eyes. They hit walls they could not see, walked apparently on ceilings, and climbed stairways that seemed flat.

Fithvael peered out from one of the black glass windows that was crystal clear from within. He only did it once. He glimpsed a huge panorama of seething desert with volcanic black sand dunes driven by some abominable sirocco against the horizon. Nothing grew there, but the land was ever-changing. The veteran elf saw a huge sandstorm loom in the distance, turn into a tornado five miles high, and then burn out again in an instant. He had no explanation for what he saw – save that this was truly a realm in which the Ruinous Powers held dominion.

NIOBE COULD FEEL Gilead and see through his eyes. She saw the smaller, older warrior following in his master's wake and she saw the confusion on Fithvael's face when confronted with the trials of the unnatural surroundings. Fithvael, his name was Fithvael. She pitied him.

They were so close now that she could almost reach out and touch them. She had touched no other being for so long. She did not know if it was days or years. Time, like the fabric of this place, was twisted and distorted to suit the tastes of Lord Ire, who dwelt in Chaos.

Niobe knelt on her block, for she was too tall to stand and her hands were tethered by a narrow, near-invisible strand of perfect silver chain, light and fragile looking, but with the strength of links wrought by dwarfs. The block was a narrow column no more than a yard across and perfectly round. It floated less than a third of the way up the steep cathedral-like room that housed all the sorcerous slaves that Lord Ire had collected with such relish.

With every day, sometimes with every hour that passed, the configuration of the columns altered. She dreaded those moves. The way her column floated through the great cavity of the endless cathedral made her sick and dizzy... or was it the knowledge that the higher she rose, the nearer she came to her ultimate destiny?

If she reached the top, what would she feel there? How would she die? She had stopped looking at the skeletal forms that still adhered to the uppermost columns. Those columns had ascended bearing living creatures: humans, dwarfs, elves. All races and species were represented and all were alive during the ascent. Not all the columns descended with their cargoes intact. Many simply tumbled back through the other columns, spilling their desiccated bodies from them. The bodies evaporated into dust and then into nothing before they ever reached the bottom again.

Those columns that descended slowly, bearing skeletons and sometimes rotting corpses, did so only because there was some mote of magic left in the bodies after the life breath had been extinguished. These columns hovered and languished, seeming not to move as often as the others, nor as far.

Niobe could not bear the thought that she might soon be one of them. If she was to die here, then let it be a clean and quick end. For her, there could be no magic without consciousness and no consciousness without life.

Niobe had stopped looking at the other magical beings around her, the living and the dead. She had tried to count them when she had first been chained to her block, but they were countless, numbering tens of thousands that she could see, and she knew not how many lay beyond in the upper reaches of the cathedral. She had stopped watching the new arrivals as they were bound to the blocks vacated by the dead, or to new, white marble columns, fresh hewn, that would be as dark and aged as the others in time.

But more than anything else, Niobe had stopped looking at the altar. It had a mesmerising effect on all that cast their eyes upon it.

The altar was a massive block of solid rock covered in shifting black and grey runes, which would fizzle with light periodically and, occasionally, bleed blue-black viscous liquid. It took up the central position in the elliptical space where a floor would have been – had there been any visible floor. Niobe could see nothing below the altar, yet it seemed to hang in the air, as though hovering, much as the columns did.

Between the writhing Chaos runes that swept across the altar, every inch of space was taken up by tiny pinprick sockets into which silver tether strands were located, tens of hundreds of thousands of them. Many of the threads were silver; some few shone out with the shifting colours of an unlikely rainbow; others were copper-coloured or black and eroded with decay.

Upon the altar lived the Cipher, a being that took no sustenance save what it absorbed from the altar itself. It had no features; no limbs, no eyes or ears, and no voice. It was vast and still, pulsing slowly from time to time, or throbbing a fast spasmodic rhythm of its own. It was changeless and ageless and formless, yet Niobe knew it to be the most powerful element of them all. It was the altar that drained the slaves of their magic while sustaining their physical forms. The threadlike tethers that connected the slaves to the altar were like umbilical chords, binding them all to the will of this place and of this dark thing.

FITHVAEL AND GILEAD wove their way through the structure that had no structure, aware only that they followed Niobe's mind patterns. They looked constantly for an enemy: a beastman, a Chaos monster, even the hideously beautiful lord who Gilead had seen in his dream.

They longed to feel a weapon in their hands, something solid, real, unalterable in this nightmare place. They longed to concentrate their minds in the only truly fulfilling way they knew how; they longed to fight, to shed blood and ichor, to slash and tear and rend flesh, any flesh.

'Where are they?' asked Fithvael. 'Where are the enemy hordes?'

'My sword hand itches too,' answered Gilead, sharply, his fingers flexing less than an inch from the hilt of his sword.

Every inch of this place reeked of evil corruption, and even taking a breath made the elves tense to screaming point.

'Where are we?' Fithvael asked.

'Just follow,' retorted Gilead, flexing his sword hand again and glaring at his companion.

WITH EVERY STEP that Gilead took, Niobe's heart responded with a beat. And as he came closer, his feet beat faster and harder on the floors and steps and ceilings he traversed. She almost filled his mind now. He had forgotten the absent foe that Fithvael still expected at every step, and felt only Niobe. He was moving so fast that Fithvael could hardly keep pace with him without breaking into an aching run.

Niobe's pounding heart beat ever faster and she gasped for breath, trying to pull her hands up to her chest, but having to drop lower on her knees and let her head fall to her shackled hands. In her desperation to maintain the link to him, she had tied her being to his too closely, and now there was a price to pay. Frantic to find her, Gilead was verging on a state of shadowfast. She was weak, at the limits of her endurance. Her body, her mind and her soul were racing helplessly to the rhythm he set, unable to slow down, unable even to break off the link. The mind-magic she had worked to effect her escape was killing her.

Her heart fluttered, failed. She fell.

THE VOICE FELL silent. Gilead winced at the sudden emptiness. He took a last few steps and entered a room vaster than any cathedral.

He stopped, his feet resting on the rock lip overlooking the abyssal vault of the immense chamber. Above, below and around him, the numberless blocks drifted in the cold, crisp darkness. He saw the miserable figures chained to each one, the living, the dead. He heard the moans and distant wails of the captives. Far away, through the litter of drifting blocks, he saw the pale flicker of the altar.

'Niobe!' he screamed. There was no echo. The space was dead air.

The smell had gone. The filthy stench of corruption was completely missing in this vast space. There was no smell at all. Every ounce of power was extracted from the magic slaves; nothing escaped the tethers, no smell, no energy, nothing at all.

Gilead stood hopelessly at the edge of the gulf. Fithvael came up behind him.

'By all the gods of Ulthuan...' stammered Fithvael. His voice was deadened too.

'She's here somewhere,' Gilead stammered.

'Where?'

'I don't know. I can't hear her any more.'

Gilead feared the worst. He strained to catch some trace of her. Nothing. Niobe's voice and heartbeat had fallen silent five full minutes earlier.

'We have to find her...' he began.

Fithvael looked out into the space beyond them. It had no colour, no tone and no shade. There seemed to be no light sources and no shadows. He could see no walls, only sensing that they must be there beyond the thousands stacks of floating plinths that surrounded him on all sides. He looked down.

There was no floor.

'Then we find her!' he snarled, and leaped from the lip of the threshold onto the nearest block. It wobbled slightly as he landed. The wasted, emaciated human-thing chained to it groaned.

Fithvael bounded across to the next, casting his gaze around at the floating plinths and the beings shackled upon them. There were species and races here that he had never seen or heard of, even in legends. Each stood or knelt or crouched or lay dead on a perfect disk of floating rock. Castaways, imprisoned on tiny islands in the darkness. He had never seen so many varied sentient beings in one place, nor had he ever been in one place that was so vast, and yet so claustrophobic – and so cruel.

Filled with a sudden, consuming rage, Fithvael began to move again, leaping from one block to the next, oblivious to the drop below. He started tugging and tearing at the beings, trying to wake them. None stirred, or even seemed aware of him. When he couldn't wake them, the old elf tried to free them. He drew his sword in a grasp that whitened his gnarled but slender knuckles and bared his teeth as he went into a frenzy of hacking and slashing at the delicate threads. He could not break a single one of them.

The sight of his friend moving from block to block galvanised Gilead Lothain. He leaped out too, over to the nearest platform, where a tethered dwarf lay curled in a foetal ball. He tried to shut out the thought in his mind.

She was already lost.

In a bound, he moved on, then again and again. Fithvael was far below him now, almost out of sight.

'Niobe!'

Something made him look over at the body on the block below him, to the right. It was slumped and curled up tight. Long hair draped over the side of the plinth and a hand rested down one side of it. The face was grey, but he recognised it from the images in his mind.

Gilead jumped into space. He almost missed his target, but clawed at the lip and pulled himself up onto the block next to her.

Niobe took two short, gasping breaths, several seconds apart, and stirred slightly. He could hear her inner voice, distant and frail, right at the back of his mind.

Gilead bent to lift the elf maiden. She was light, almost insubstantial. He could raise her only three feet above the plinth before the tethers tightened and would not give. Gilead looked at the tiny silver threads that tied Niobe's slender wrists together then disappeared into the plinth she had been placed upon. He took them in both of his hands in order to tear them. They felt like nothing in his hands and he looked at his open palm to reassure himself that they were there. He made a snapping motion between his hands, but the threads did not break.

'You won't do it,' said Fithvael's voice. He was perched on a block that floated above and to the left of Niobe's. He was sharing the block with the tethered form of a young human male who sat silent and unresponsive. 'Nothing can free these poor creatures,' he said, gesturing around the vast space. 'Nothing will cut those cursed tethers.'

'No! That cannot be true!' Gilead declared. 'She's alive! Very weak but alive!'

He drew his sword and wrapped the slender chords around it twice. He then flicked his weapon hard into the air, but it stopped abruptly before it had formed the elegant arc he had expected. The threads did not break.

'I said–' Fithvael said, his voice dulled by the deadened space.

'Hush!' Gilead tried to think. There had to be a way to break the physical thread that held her mind and siphoned her magic away.

Niobe's voice, broken and fragile, spoke in his mind. 'Do not... cut the threads,' it said. 'Destroy the block.'

Gilead planted his feet squarely, shoulder width apart, and taking his sword in a two handed hold he plunged it down into the rock.

'What are you doing?' Fithvael called.

The blue steel of the blade bit into the block in a flurry of cold, white sparks. Gilead thrust it again. The blade began to take on the same colourless darkness as everything else in the space, and he looked down at himself for a moment. His cloak bore no red colour and the hilt of his sword was no longer gold and gleaming. The vault was draining them too.

Gilead drew a deep, sustaining breath, and Niobe's chest rose and fell in sympathy. He struck again, and a fissure cracked across the face of the block. Shards fell away into the void.

'In the name of Ulthuan, Gilead! You'll fall to your death!'

'If that's all you can say, keep it to yourself.'

With a despairing curse, Fithvael stood up and unwound the long skein of elven cord that he carried around his waist. His practiced hands lashed it twice around his own block, moving around the motionless boy. Then he called out to Gilead and threw the loose end across to him.

Gilead caught it, nodded a curt thanks, and tied it around Niobe's body, under her arms. Then he resumed his rock-shattering blows.

In his hands, Galeth's blade began to take on a hint of its old colour. Gilead was weakening the power. Just here, just in this tiny place, he was cutting through the leeching cold and sparking life and colour back.

His blows became more rapid. As he became shadowfast, the blue steel of his blade shone out and the gold of its hilt became bright and iridescent.

Fithvael watched in mounting alarm, his hands around the lashed cord ready to take up the strain. Even from his vantage point, he could see Niobe's chest fluttering and heaving like the wings of a butterfly. She convulsed in agonising spasms as her heart palpitated at a rate beyond anything Fithvael had ever witnessed. Much more and the strain would kill her.

Scraps of rock began detaching from Niobe's splintering block and became skeins of mist, which floated away into the dead atmosphere of the chamber.

The block shattered. Niobe's limp form pitched off the breaking rock and dropped sharply, her tethers freed from the anchor point. With a guttural cry of effort, Fithvael dug his heels in and dragged at the rope, arresting her fall in an abrupt jerk so that she swung like a pendulum beneath the block that supported him. Teeth gritted, he nearly slithered off the rock himself.

Gilead fell. He spread his arms and tumbled in the cold air, turning like a leaping salmon. He half-landed on a block forty feet below, but the impact twisted it around like an ice floe in fast moving water and he fell again.

Darkness rushed up. Then he landed, square and hard, on a blackened platform, crushing the mouldering bones tethered there.

Fithvael hauled Niobe up and onto his own block and then peered down. 'Gilead! Gilead!'

A moment's silence, then Gilead's voice floated up.

'I'm alive. Take the maiden. Make for the doorway.'

Sparks of light flickered in the icy darkness of the vault. In freeing Niobe, they had broken a link in the magical chain, disrupting the workings of the vast arcane mechanism Lord Ire had constructed.

There was a low rumbling. Screams shuddered across the vastness as some of the enslaved beings woke up and realised their nightmares were real.

With Niobe over his shoulder, Fithvael crossed back from rocking plinth to rocking plinth, towards the doorway. He could almost smell magic now, torn, broken magic. He was breathing hard. Each leap was an effort.

He reached the solidity of the threshold and set Niobe down. She moaned softly in her sickly slumber. Fithvael looked back across the chamber. There was no sign of Gilead. The lights were still sparking in the darkness, and incandescent vapours were pouring from the altar far away.

'Gilead?'

'Your hand!'

Fithvael looked down and saw Gilead scaling the bruised rock face below the threshold, clinging to every scrap of purchase. He reached down and hauled Gilead up over the lip.

SWORDS DRAWN, THE old comrades made their way back through the impossible halls of the fortress. Gilead carried Niobe. Hearts in their mouths, they expected discovery at any moment, but the place seemed empty. No one barred their way.

OUTSIDE, A STORM raged, lashing the ancient forest. The elves could not deduce whether it was day or night, but the sky was mirrored black, seething with curls and blooms of cloud. Spears of lighting jabbed down at the high walls of Lord Ire's bastion. The rain was like a veil. They staggered through it, boots mired in the filthy mud, until they found their terrified horses, tied up in the glade beyond the limits of the stronghold.

Gilead cradled the slender form of Niobe against his chest while Fithvael prepared a bed for her in the shelter of the trees. When it was done, he sought fresh herbs with which to treat her. He could find none; plants of health and healing could not grow in this place, and so he had to make do with the dried provisions he had packed some months before.

After some hours, the rain began to ease off. A pale greyness filled the sky. Fithvael lit a fire and revived the dried herbs in a little of the elven wine they kept in the single wineskin that remained from the stocks they had packed at Tor Anrok.

'You may have killed her,' said Fithvael.

'Not I,' retorted Gilead. 'That terrible place maybe.' He spat in disgust, the taste and smell of Lord Ire's residence returning sharply to his mouth

'Indeed, Gilead te tuin,' Fithvael placated. 'She surely would have perished if she had stayed in that place, but I fear I should warn you that we might have... have hastened her end anyway.'

'How so?' asked Gilead, watching Fithvael prepare his potions in the pestle and mortar that he always kept with him.

'The Lady Niobe sought you out and drew you to her. Her voice, you said. Like a hook in a fish's mouth. She pulled you in, first through this miserable forest and then through the insane architecture of that palace.'

Fithvael rinsed clean rags in a little more wine and wrapped his herbal potion in them to form a poultice for Niobe's chest before setting water to boil for a reviving infusion. He looked up at his companion. 'You and she have become one in a profound way. Because of the link she wrought with you, your hearts beat in time, your souls overlap. What she feels you feel, and vice versa. Your actions affect her life force.'

'And that would kill her?' Gilead asked.

'She's weak, and yet her body had no choice but to mirror yours when you were shadowfast,' answered Fithvael. 'It may have been too much for her. I don't know if she can survive so fierce an assault on her body.'

Gilead slumped to the ground, heedless of where he sat, and dropped his head into his hands. 'Am I so cursed,' he said, 'that I lose one twin and then kill another who twins herself to me?'

Then he looked up sharply. Fithvael was amazed to see a smile on his rain-streaked face. 'No,' Gilead answered himself, 'if my bond with her is so great that my strength injures her... then she has that strength to heal her too!'

Fithvael nodded at the logic. 'Maybe–'

'Damn your "maybe", Fithvael! You know I have it right! If I am calm, restful, if I gather my strength, then by our bond she has no choice but to recover too.'

'No choice?' Fithvael smiled. 'You're going to order her back to health?'

Gilead told Fithvael what he thought of that in no uncertain terms. He rose and walked slowly and surely through the forest, making circles around the camp that Fithvael had built. He breathed steadily, made no sharp moves, and focussed upon the heart of himself. He felt strong. He was strong. He held on to that feeling and watched the day grow dim as he cast his thoughts on Niobe and tried to walk her back to health.

FITHVAEL TENDED THE limp form of the elf maiden for three days, watching over her. Gilead amazed him with his determination to play his part in the healing process. Fithvael found his old friend more eager to take sustenance regularly and exercise gently, although he could not convince the elf warrior to sleep.

By the end of the three days Gilead had almost walked himself into a trance. He tried not to think about the place they had been in or what had been done there lest it affect Niobe.

He tried to think only of Tor Anrok when it was alive with his family, when Galeth had been by his side, and his father had ruled their estate. When Fithvael had been a youthful and faithful guard. When the chamberlain Taladryel had advised and coached the twin heirs of Lothain. When Nithrom, that great elven warrior, had played at sparring with him in the courtyard. He retold the old family stories in his head, letting Niobe into the best parts of his past. He could feel her deep in some recess of his mind, listening.

As they ate by the fire at the end of the third day, Gilead suddenly heard a soft voice in his head again. He pushed away his plate and went across to where Niobe lay on a bed of bracken under his red cloak.

When she awoke, Gilead was standing guard over her. She looked up at him and smiled.

'I know you, Gilead te tuin Lothain, last lord of Tor Anrok,' she said and closed her eyes again.

Gilead slept that night as he had not slept in years. He slept as he had once done after a long day playing and fighting with his brother. He slept like a tired, happy boy.

It was five full days after the rescue before Niobe woke for any length of time. She ate a little, said less, and slumbered a lot, accepting the ministrations of Fithvael with grace and gratitude while watching Gilead's every move with tired, delighted eyes.

TEN DAYS AND ten bleak nights passed without incident. Fithvael became concerned; their good fortune could not last much longer. They were in the dark heart of the Drakwald, the most dangerous and unpredictable region of the lands the humans called their Empire. Why had there been no beastmen? Why had there been no vengeful attack from the Chaos lord? The veteran elf was eager to move on and began to break camp on the morning of the eleventh day.

'She is well enough to travel with us,' Fithvael explained to Gilead. 'And in this place, to travel is safer than to rest in one place for too long.'

'Of what do you speak?' They both glanced around in surprise at the lilting, feminine tones. Niobe was sitting up, regarding them.

'Of leaving this place for another,' said Fithvael. 'It is no longer safe here for us. We have stayed as long as we should.'

'Then it is done,' she said, smiling and lying back. 'Lord Ire is destroyed.'

Fithvael looked to Gilead, and Gilead shook his head and walked away. The older elf made Niobe comfortable and then followed his friend a little distance into the forest. Gilead would not say what he needed to say in front of the elf maiden.

'Niobe called me, and I answered her call. She is released from that disgusting place and we will not return.'

'Then you will deceive her,' answered Fithvael. 'But she knows you, Gilead te tuin. She's in there,' he added, tapping Gilead's brow. 'If she knows you then she will find this deception out.'

Gilead shook his head. 'If her purpose was to destroy this Lord Ire then she will be disappointed.'

'Where are your wits, friend?' Fithvael scoffed. 'I thought you said you knew this maid, knew her by that intimate bond she fashioned. She did not call you for her own selfish reasons, nor would have put our lives in danger simply for the sake of her own.'

'Meaning?'

'She thinks you are a great hero, fool. She called you to put an end to Lord Ire for the good of all those he has enslaved! It's as plain as a rune on a white stone! Rescuing her – only her – was not the point of this.'

THEY RODE THROUGH the morning and stopped by the shores of a dank woodland mere where bottle-green dragonflies shivered between the bone-white reeds. Niobe sat on the salt-grass, twisting old twigs into a bare garland wreath, and told her story to them at last.

Gilead barely needed to listen. The images she shared with his mind had already told the tale so vividly. Gilead felt her revulsion of Lord Ire as though it were his own; he felt her pain as she exposed the fell lord's dark design.

'Lord Ire, who rose to power in some unnameable domain lost to Chaos, where he rules as a demi-god over the subhuman spawn that lurk there, has long looked on this warm, lit world with envy. I think he may have been human once, many ages ago before he meddled with sorcery and forbidden necromantic lore and was cast out into the pitiless wastes of Chaos far north of here. Some vestige of that humanity remains, and it makes him yearn to possess this he left behind. He has but one purpose.'

As she spoke, pictures of the tall man with the mane of glossy hair and the grey garb came clearly into focus in Gilead's mind. He shuddered.

'Ire means to invade this warm world. He has marshalled great forces of destruction in his forsaken domain, raised up engines of war. He has made pacts, I believe, with the true lords of ruin, the foul daemons who fill the outer voids with their insane howling. He is their instrument. His plan pleases them and they have given him power to fashion a gateway, a gateway between this mortal world and his own diseased kingdom. But to keep the gateway open takes power, vast resources of magic.'

'Hence the slaves,' muttered Fithvael.

'Exactly, Fithvael te tuin.' Niobe smiled softly, though her slender face was still pale and drawn. 'Creatures with magic in them, whether they knew it or not. Beings of every race, breed and kind. Creatures like me. He stole us from our lives, often in bloody raids mounted by his bestial warriors, and harnessed us to the gateway. Through the tethers, our magic was milked away to feed the Cipher.'

'What is that?' asked Gilead sharply, but he knew. The monstrous thing on the altar was vivid in his mind.

'His pet, his servant? I don't know, except that, bloated with stolen magic, it keeps the gate open for him. And through that gateway, his invading army will come.'

'None of it is truly real though, is it?' Fithvael asked uncertainly. 'His bastion, all the rest? It was like a dream place. An illusion.'

'It's real enough – in his benighted realm. What you saw, what you fought your way into, was... like a ghost of it, an echo of his fortress projected here into this world through the gateway. It grows more real with each passing day. Soon it will be more here than there, solid, physical, impregnable. Then its doors will open.'

Gilead cleared his throat. What he was about to propose flew in the face of his entire being. 'We... we could warn the humans. Take word to the leaders of this... this Empire of men that claims the land here.'

'And they would believe the words of an elf? A thing stepped from the shadows of their folk-tales?' Fithvael almost chuckled at Niobe's words.

'They have fought off invasions before!' Gilead snapped. 'Their armies are not without strength...'

Niobe nodded. 'Many invasions, indeed. But every one of them assaulted the human territories from outside, from the fringes and borders. This comes from within. Imagine how long proud Tor Anrok would have stood if Chaos had welled up within the throne room itself.'

Fithvael sighed. 'So you are saying that we must go back – and close the gate?'

'Yes, Master Fithvael. That is so. Go back and close the gate.'

Gilead rose, shaking his head. He remembered how hard he had fought to destroy but one plinth out of the hundreds of thousands in that place. He knew that he could not liberate so many beings, even if he had ten lifetimes in which to do it.

'We could not free them all,' said Gilead tersely.

'No indeed,' said Niobe, 'but we could close the gate.'

The emphasis she placed on the word 'could' chilled both the warriors.

She brushed out the creases in her dirty gown. 'In Talthos Elios, my father raised me to honour the old pledge. The pledge our kind made in the last years, as our numbers dwindled and we retreated from the world that had been ours. We may regard them as a crude, ignorant child race, but the humans are our heirs to this land. My father taught me to honour mankind, with my life if needs be. Our time has gone, my friends. The world is newer and sparer than we in the days of our forebears.

'There is a term the lords of Bretonnia use: "noblesse oblige". I see from your faces you know what it means. We owe our heirs. My magic was stolen and used to further the foul strategies of the Ruinous Powers. I would gladly give my life to destroy that gateway.'

'Suicide,' muttered Gilead.

'No, my lord – *honour*. We must honour our legacy. And to honour that, we do not free one slave, but allow a thousand to die if it means that Lord Ire's twisted gateway dies with them.'

Fithvael looked at Gilead, but the elf warrior said nothing.

'You want us to kill them all? All the slaves?' asked Fithvael.

'I do not know,' answered Niobe, looking around at them both. 'But I know that Lord Ire has only one weakness.'

'Then tell us,' Gilead said in a flat tone.

'I saw something in Lord Ire's mind, but I dared not dwell there, lest the Chaos filth infect me. I have no answer except that he knew there was a weakness, and that weakness was his son.'

'His son?'

'He has a son. It is his only vulnerability.'

A long, desolate silence hung over them all.

'Will you help me? Will you do it?' asked Niobe after a while.

Gilead dropped his chin, not wanting to meet her gaze. 'I think not,' he said.

GILEAD ROSE FROM beside his friend and the woman he now believed he loved, and walked away from them. Fithvael stumbled to his feet and followed him, calling out to him as he strode away.

'Gilead! Lord! Will you deny your duty?' he called, but the elf did not turn back.

Fithvael quickened his pace until he was right behind Gilead and, reaching out a hand, he turned him roughly by the shoulder.

'Tell me to my face! Tell me that you are going to walk away from this. Do you not remember Galeth and the ten year quest that brought you to his killer? Do you not remember the years you drank away in the ruins of Tor Anrok, miserable to your marrow? It was your sense of duty that saved you from ruin, your duty to a human. The Ziegler child! Remember her? Oh, I had to punch it into your dulled brain to make you realise… gods, I had to come near losing my own life! But you saw it by and by. Our time has come and gone, Gilead Lothain. It hurts, but it is so. We have nothing left but what we leave behind now. This is your destiny, my friend, our destiny. Don't deny it now.'

'And if I were to lose Niobe?' asked Gilead.

'My friend, if you do not do this thing, then she will surely be lost to you anyway! And if you cannot bear to destroy Lord Ire for the good of humankind, then do it for Niobe and for yourself.'

'And you?' asked Gilead.

'I'll be going anyway. But I'd do better with you at my side. You, Gilead were bred to fight. That's how Cothor raised you, that's why Nithrom trained you. A warrior, of Tor Anrok, of the old kind that is passing away. It is your life's blood. If you deny all else, you cannot deny that.'

Gilead stared at him. For a long moment, Fithvael expected to be struck. Furious pride pinched Gilead's face. The last lord of Tor Anrok glanced away at Niobe, watching them from the water's edge, and then looked back at Fithvael.

'Let us go and do this thing,' he said at last. 'But milady stays here.'

'But we need her, Gilead. Only she can guide us in, only she can trace this son of Ire. If we go... when we go, she surely comes with us.'

NIGHT FELL, COLD and dank beneath the lowering trees. Fithvael checked his weapons and the field pack that he always carried, replenishing what stocks he could and ensuring everything was clean and dry. He also packed restorative herbs for Niobe, whom he recognised was still fragile.

Gilead checked his weapons, ensuring his quiver was full and his bow strung to tension. Most importantly, he spent some time with his sword and dagger, cleaning them and honing their blades to bright, hard cutting edges. He laid his fingers, for a moment, on the elven runes that decorated the steel and thought of Tor Anrok and the ideals his family had always lived by. He wiped mud from his long, narrow warshield. Then he buckled himself into his leather armour and slung the quiver and shield in a cross against his back.

It was time.

Niobe had prepared herself. She had tied back her long hair, and cut off the hem of her gown above the knee so she could run and move without hindrance.

She was so beautiful, Gilead's throat caught.

'Why so sad, tuin?' she asked, handing Gilead back the long leaf-bladed knife he had lent her to cut away her dress.

'Not sad, just... ready. You keep that.'

'I was raised with many skills, Gilead, but warfare was not one of them. Take back your dagger.'

'No, Niobe. Tuck it in your belt. You may have need of it tonight. Thrust with it, don't slash. And don't hesitate.'

She slid the blade under her leather girdle. 'As you wish, tuin. Teaching me now, are you?'

'If it keeps you alive, I will thank myself at least.' He paused. A stale moon had risen, and the trees cast long, mournful shadows across them.

'What?' she asked.

'What happens to us... afterwards?' he breathed.

'Afterwards?' Her vivacious smile lit up her face. She pushed at him playfully. 'Let us pray there is an afterwards.'

'There will be.'

'Such optimism, Gilead.'

'One of my better qualities,' he lied. Nearby, Fithvael snorted.

Niobe laughed. 'Cothor Lothain sired a beautiful son... even when he is lying.'

'You didn't answer my question,' he persisted.

She reached out and touched his temple gently. 'I have been in here a long while now. We are bound together, Gilead. Whatever happens tonight, that bond will remain. I swear to you.'

Shaking, he took her in his arms and as long as their precious kiss lasted, the danger seemed far away.

Fithvael looked away and busied himself settling the horses. They were loaded and ready for the ride out of the forest. He would leave them loose-tethered, anticipating a hurried getaway.

THE THREE OF them clasped hands in the moonlit glade. A silent pact, done in the old manner. Then, side by side, the elves strode away into the whispering forest, towards the great, ghostly bastion of their foe.

An hour passed, and they met nothing. For most of that hour, the three had been able to walk abreast. Once or twice they had to proceed single file and when they did so, Gilead drew his sword and took the lead, with Fithvael bringing up the rear. But even on these narrow tracks all was calm and quiet.

'We must stop,' Fithvael said suddenly. 'Something is amiss.'

Gilead turned to him. 'I hear no threat. All is calm and well. Fithvael, you jump at shadows.'

'No,' replied Fithvael, unslinging his crossbow and winding up its tension. 'Does it not concern you that there are no shadows to jump at? This is the Drakwald, a place of terror, of beasts, and yet we walk through it as though it were the playground of our youth.'

Gilead looked around and into the night sky, through the canopy above them, tensing as he realised that Fithvael was right.

'Do you sense anything?' he asked Niobe.

'The forest is full of menace, but a little mind magic can drive off a legion of ignorant creatures,' Niobe replied with a knowing smile.

Gilead and Fithvael stared at her. It was obvious now: their safe passage had been secured by Niobe, using all the power of her magic to seek out the beasts and monsters of the forest, and to plant images in their feeble minds, distracting them from the trio's scent.

'We are safe because of you?' Fithvael asked.

'For now,' Niobe answered softly. 'When we reach the portal my powers will be exhausted and confused by the corruption there.'

'Lock away your magic,' Gilead told Niobe gently. 'Don't let Lord Ire get a hint of it. What we meet here, we will deal with.'

He took out his blue-steel sword.

'As you wish,' she nodded.

STARLESS NIGHT ENCLOSED them now, cold and murky. They started at every crack and rustle in the thickets around them. They'd gone perhaps a half mile when she suddenly froze.

'To the left! It's... it's...'

As she stammered, Gilead unsheathed his sword in one fluid movement, the rotten stench of Chaos suddenly heavy on the air.

A huge beast charged into the narrow clearing, sheering off lengths of cracking wood from the trees and shrubs as it broke cover. The creature was the size and stature of a stag, with a pattern of mottled grey and black in its coarse fur. Its cloven hooves grew from thick powerful ankles and were a foot across, dividing into dull, horny toes. The back legs of the animal were shorter than the forelegs and the tail was vestigial, like that of a goat. The monster pawed the ground, scoring a deep groove in the rotting ground, while it raised a pair of powerful humanoid arms that grew on either side of a barrelled chest.

Gilead saw in a moment that the beast's arms ended in muscular hands, each equipped with two, single-jointed fingers, echoing its cloven hooves. A black, calloused thumb completed the hand that was grasping a crude but massive crossbow, with a bolt almost the size of Gilead's forearm already fixed in position.

The stag's neck was as broad as a man's chest and above it rose a half-human head, perched there incongruously, narrower than the throat and peaked with a single wide, curved horn.

The beast-thing growled as it made to loose the bolt straight at Gilead, who dived in a feinting pattern first right, then left. The huge bolt whistled a high-pitched scream as it cut the air. It missed Gilead by inches as he rolled and defended his body with his shield.

The bearded head of the Chaos beast seemed to chuckle, making a throaty braying sound as it slid another bolt into the housing on the crossbow.

Gilead's view of the beast was head on and at close range. He saw nothing above its flexed, upright neck and head, concentrating only on the immediate threat.

Fithvael, a few yards to Gilead's right, had a different view, and for a split second he was mesmerised by what he saw.

Upon the back of the stag-thing was a second monstrosity. The beastman sat astride the creature on a bulky saddle made from pitted green leather. Huge, flat stirrups cut from the same material hung right up against the lip of the saddle, cupping the rider's paw-like club feet. Its legs were short and malformed, the thigh bones twisting into the swollen knees.

The rider's body also seemed too short and too wide, consisting only of a torso without waist or abdomen. By contrast, its arms were long and powerful, and its shoulders high and strong. The monster's head was human in form, but ugly and bulbous, covered in warts and almost toothless, and it rested between the bulky shoulders without a neck. The rider held a cleaver in one huge hand and a flail in the other, and its face broke into a grin as it swung the pair of weapons in small, interlocking circles across its body, preparing to bludgeon and tear them all limb from limb.

Gilead ducked the second bolt, which landed squarely in a tree trunk behind him. Two-thirds of the bolt's length protruded from the far side of the trunk. The elf drove forward, low to the ground, and brought his sword up under the stag's chest, using the momentum of his short charge to drive his blade at the creature's heart. The sword penetrated half a dozen inches and then hit bone with a force of impact that made it stop dead. The warrior elf tried to wrench the sword out of the bloodless wound, but the blade was stuck fast.

The stag-thing dropped its crossbow. It reached out for the elf's neck with its huge deformed hands.

Still holding onto his sword hilt with one hand, Gilead grabbed for his long dagger. But the scabbard was empty. He had given it to Niobe. He threw himself down, rolling to avoid the stamping hooves.

'Gilead!' Niobe cried, already knowing what he needed, and threw the dagger across the glade.

He caught it and slashed up into the arm that reached for him. He ripped into muscle and tendons, exposing bone and sinew. There was no blood, no ichor, no body fluids at all.

Drawing two weapons himself, Fithvael drove forward to attack the godless creature that straddled its bestial steed. He struck first with the tip of his sword, swiping it along the creature's thigh and tearing a jagged wound there, which quickly filled with yellowish black, oozing liquid. The downward sweep of the stroke allowed him to drop his head and shoulders, ducking the creature's studded flail as it swept towards his face.

Fithvael took heart that the beast was undisciplined in its use of the flail and kept his position, rising again to drive his sword at the monster's chest. The flail came once more, wrapping its coarse black chain around the blade of Fithvael's sword. With a whipping action of his wrist, the veteran elf freed his blade and sent the flail swinging back toward its master. It thudded heavily against the beast's chest, but the thing seemed not to notice as it brought the weapon over its shoulder in another ragged swing.

Fithvael sliced another chunk from the monster's leg, carving into the knee and almost separating the foot completely. The beast responded by turning its body in the saddle and bringing a heavy cleaver down in a strong, accurate swing that took Fithvael by surprise. The elf fell to his knees to avoid the blade, regaining his feet quickly before the beast could bring his weapon back into play.

Gilead freed his sword and rolled onto his back on the ground, beneath the stomping hooves of the stag-thing. From his new position, he swung his sword again, slicing into the join where the beast's foreleg met its body. The dry wound gaped down at the elf, but the rhythm of the monster's hoof beat did not change.

This time Gilead drove his long blade up towards its chest at an angle, aiming for the throat with his dagger. He found a space between the great, barrelling ribs and thrust his sword home to the hilt, and then he twisted left and right and withdrew the weapon. At the same time, he drove his dagger into the beast's throat, disabling its braying voice and opening a ragged hole in its airway.

His work done, Gilead stepped back and watched the stag-thing trying to breathe through the hole in its throat. The tissue around the tear flapped in and then out again. The monstrosity tried to bring its crossbow up once more, but the hand on the end of the torn arm shook and could not find a place for the bolt.

Fithvael rose to his full height and lunged his sword at the mounted creature's torso. The blade of the cleaver parried Fithvael's lunge and the elf's arms received a heavy jolt before he could bring his sword around. Fithvael cursed, span back and impaled the rider on his sword in a single, fluid motion.

The bloodless stag dropped to its knees slowly and keeled over, still clutching its crossbow in its one good hand. As it tipped forward, its rider was thrown against its neck and Fithvael was able to withdraw his sword and plunge it in again. The rider toppled from its mount and dropped its weapons, lifting itself upright on its fists and using them like feet to make its escape.

Gilead nocked an arrow at a distance of fifteen or twenty yards from his target and finished the beastman off with one well-aimed shot through the head.

Fithvael dusted himself off and sheathed his sword with a sigh of relief. The two elves made their way back to Niobe, leaving the carcasses in the forest behind them.

THE TRIO HAD continued their journey only a few hundred yards further when Niobe brought them to a halt.

'We have arrived,' she said, turning to face Gilead and Fithvael. 'How do you wish to proceed?'

Fithvael looked over her shoulder as she faced them.

'I see nothing,' the veteran elf said. 'Where is Lord Ire's castle?'

Niobe turned slowly until she was facing the same direction as her companions, and in the haze before her Fithvael and Gilead saw the vast outline of the Chaos champion's castle take shape, shimmering into vision from amidst the forest night-mists. 'You see it only through my eyes,' explained Niobe, 'but do not doubt that it is here.'

THIRTY PACES FROM the monumental facade of the castle, a long, low ramp began to rise out of the swampy ground, leading to a portcullis in the centre of the great wall before them.

'A welcome,' Gilead said coldly. 'More than we were granted last time.'

'It's simply an entrance hidden from all but those who have the magic to see it,' answered Niobe. Her light, confident manner belied her fear. The rank stench of Chaos permeated the air they breathed and the earth on which they stood, and she felt it more acutely than her companions. But she had Gilead's strength to draw upon, and in return he had at least a taste of her magic powers.

As they approached the portcullis, Niobe found her way to the head of the group, stopping only yards from the heavy, grilled entrance. The square spaces in the otherwise solid structure began to throb and warp, until a narrow gap opened wide enough for the three elves to step through.

'How do you shift reality so?' Fithvael asked in wonder.

'Because it isn't reality,' answered Niobe, simply. 'Not yet, anyway. It's growing ever more solid, but it's still illusion, an afterimage of the real bastion in Ire's domain, projected here. I can expose it, show it to you. All the while it is insubstantial, neither truly here nor there, I can work upon the illusions and shape them to our own purposes.'

'But this place is evil,' said Fithvael, struggling to understand her skills and how they might be used.

'Evil, yes,' said Niobe. 'This place is thoroughly corrupt because the magic is manipulated by darkest evil, but believe me when I say that magic power by itself is not evil.'

They stepped into a long, wide space that might have been called a great hall. Bolted doors ran along the walls, at a variety of heights, leading, Gilead supposed, into rooms beyond. Passageways led off in other directions, and staircases, ascending and descending at impossible vectors, seemed to add another, unwholesome dimension to the three that were naturally invested in the space.

Niobe made only the briefest examination of the topography before leading Fithvael and Gilead on through the draughty hallway and up a staircase that had seemed a moment before to be plunging into the bowels of the castle.

Another moment or two, and they stepped through into a huge, cuboid area, which appeared to have been wrought from some metal, pewter perhaps. Where walls, floor and ceiling met each other, the joints were invisible. The walls had a beaten, matt finish, without windows or doors, or any other visible entrances or exits. The light that fell across them was even and cast no shadows. Worryingly, there was no obvious light source.

Gilead and Fithvael raised their swords as a foul smell began to leak into the room out of nowhere.

'Ire-' Niobe gasped.

A figure stepped out of shadows and it seemed to grow in stature as it strode toward them. It filled the space, and the space expanded to suit the growing stature of the man. The cube-shaped metal chamber had been perhaps ten paces in all directions, but was now a hundred feet across every measurement.

'More space for me to work in,' said Gilead aloud, staring into the unknowable divided face of Lord Ire.

Gilead and Fithvael lowered their stances in an aggressive posture.

As if mocking the very sight of them, Lord Ire threw back his head and let out a sound that might have been a laugh, but that seemed to echo round his huge body before escaping through his divided mouth.

'Now!' shouted Gilead, his voice sounding like music after Lord Ire's extraordinary bellow.

Gilead and Fithvael circled and lunged around Lord Ire, but as they did so the room began to move on some invisible axis, tipping the floor and turning the walls. The elves were disorientated, and their feet faltered as they looked about them for a solid flat surface.

There was none.

Gilead could no longer see Niobe, but he could hear her sweet tones in his mind. 'Shake off the illusion! It's in your mind. He owns this place and he will use it, but it is as nothing if you deny it!' she instructed him.

He watched Fithvael drop to one knee as the room rocked and turned about them.

'It's mere illusion, Fithvael!' he yelled. 'Block it out!'

The warriors lunged at Lord Ire again. Again the room rolled and twisted, but this time Gilead and Fithvael kept their feet.

Lord Ire drew his sword. It was long and broad, but the Chaos lord held it in one hand, flicking casual figure-eights around his body.

Fithvael stepped in to parry the first lunge of the fearsome weapon, but he was swatted off his feet as if he had been made of paper. Lord Ire swung again at Fithvael, and the elf dropped and rolled. The huge blade struck the pewter surface, sending blue-white sparks flying.

Gilead lunged at Lord Ire, slashing back and forth, but the monster's slate armour denied all his blows with ease.

As the three fought on faster and harder, the room spun more violently, pivoting and wheeling on a set of invisible axes. Gilead and Fithvael kept their feet throughout, both now fighting head on with Lord Ire. The Chaos Lord slipped around their attack and brought his sword down towards Fithvael, slicing into his right shoulder before Gilead could block it.

Slumping to his knees, Fithvael lost his concentration and rolled helplessly around the revolving cube. Gilead watched his faithful friend fall and saw him tossed heedlessly around the metal box.

'Illusion! It's all illusion!' Gilead yelled, but Fithvael still slammed remorselessly around the turning pewter box of the room.

'Fithvael!'

Fithvael disappeared.

'Where is he? What did you do to him, corrupt scum?' Gilead cried, throwing himself at the chuckling nightmare. Lord Ire threw him aside.

But Gilead was not be denied. Suddenly shadowfast, he became a twisting blur, thrusting and lunging, chopping and slashing with his blade. The room spun and bucked but Gilead unconsciously did as Niobe was instructing him: he ignored the illusion and focussed only on Ire.

* * *

NIOBE WAITED IN the small dark space with Fithvael.

It was an antechamber, though beyond that small fact, she had no idea where she was. By force of will, she had taken Fithvael and herself out of the rocking metal cube.

'Hold still,' she hissed.

'It hurts!' Fithvael protested as she bound up his wound.

'Of course it does! Hold still!'

'Where is Gilead?'

LORD IRE GATHERED an echoing bellow in his gut and let it out in a long, rolling sound that filled the space around Gilead. The last son of Tor Anrok had just slashed his blade through the metal guard covering the dead eye on the subhuman side of Ire's twisted face.

Gilead seized the advantage and danced in again, moving so fast now that the room seemed to have come to a lightly vibrating standstill. Whether it was the speed that Gilead had generated or the savage wound that Lord Ire had sustained, the elf warrior began to see something very different before him. The dark champion began to lose his shape and form, blurring at the edges. His form flowed for a split second into an amorphous pulsing mass, before returning unsteadily to his former, humanoid shape.

NIOBE STARTED. SHE had seen Ire as Gilead had seen him, and the truth made her cry out.

'What is it?' asked Fithvael, his voice dulled by pain.

'The son... I have seen the son...'

NIOBE LED FITHVAEL back through a nightmarish maze of passages, until at last they arrived once more at the vast chamber where the slaves were tethered.

'Why have you brought me here?' Fithvael asked as Niobe looked around.

Her voice was assured. 'Do not mourn them, Fithvael te tuin. They will welcome death if it brings relief from this existence. Whether they live or die, you will have saved them. And live or die you will have saved humankind from a far worse fate than this.' She believed what she said and the elf warrior believed it too, but a tear still found its way down the perfect contour of her cheek.

'So which of these poor souls is the son of Ire?' Fithvael asked, readying himself for the most distasteful kill of his career. He had slain many in battle, but to destroy a poor soul tethered lifelessly to a yoke solely to provide magical energy, that was murder and it held only disgust for him.

'None of them,' answered Niobe.

'Then I ask again,' Fithvael said sternly, 'why have you brought me here?'

Niobe turned and looked down at the altar below them, at the innumerable strands plugged into the vast square rock and at the shifting patterns of Chaos runes squirming on its surface. She pointed, for she could barely speak.

'The altar. The thing on the altar,' she breathed.

'What thing?' asked Fithvael, whipping his head around to get another look at the abomination far below.

And he saw it. For the first time, he realised that there was something on top of the altar. The sight of the mesmerising runes and the thousands of glistening tethers had drawn his attention away from the dull shapeless top of the altar, but he truly saw it now. A lifeless mass, amorphous and colourless, entirely without form. He saw it because Niobe had seen it.

'That is... the son of Ire?' asked Fithvael, incredulous.

'The Cipher,' said Niobe weakly. 'It collects and controls the magic.' Her voice was broken and her mouth dry. She tried to speak again, Fithvael bent to listen to her.

'It looks like Ire...' she whispered.

'That is what Ire looks like without his illusions in place?' Fithvael said, already raising his sword.

IRE'S GREAT BLADE cut the air and Gilead darted back. The metal box that contained them continued to spin and roll. Gilead swung again, but the monster's blade tip found his cheek and gave him a bloody gash. Gilead fell, and began to tumble as the box rolled.

It was real now; everything was too real.

LEAPING FROM BLOCK to block, Fithvael made his way towards the altar. He knew he had little time.

He leapt down onto the wide ledge of rock that surrounded the monstrosity and the first of the slave guard appeared. There were four of them, variously armoured. They had stone for skin, cracked along the joints and covered in nicks and scratches made by a thousand blades and missiles. When the creatures flexed their bodies their stone skins moved with them, like the hardening crust of a lava flow.

The mutated hellspawn stood four abreast in front of the altar, holding only batons and whips for weapons. They were the slave guard, and had never needed more than those light arms to control their prisoners.

Fithvael did not hesitate. He flew at them, blade swinging.

It merely sparked and spanged off the impenetrable skins of the Chaos beasts.

IN THE TUMBLING pewter box, Gilead slid down a turning wall and flinched away just in time as Ire's massive blade scored the metal that had supported him.

He tried to gather his wits. Plaintive and far away, Niobe's musical voice still called to him.

'It's all illusion, Gilead... all illusion...'

He rose, his blade clashing with Ire's in a sparking shower of purple light. Again, again a deflection, a parry. Lord Ire's skill with a sword was masterful.

But Gilead had been trained by Nithrom, and the sword he swung had been his brother's. He would not lose this fight.

FITHVAEL SMASHED OPEN the stony hide of the guard nearest him and fell back in revulsion. Underneath the slate armouring the monster's legs was one huge, putrescent wound. There was neither skin nor bone, merely black, decaying flesh and an army of maggots and parasites feasting on the rotting body.

Fithvael drove himself forward, attacking the weakness. He sprayed stinking grubs and ichor all over himself and his blade. The guard toppled and burst at the seams, spewing out a host of foul writhing things along with the decayed matter that had once been its guts.

Fithvael leapt past the disgusting remains, dancing between the slashing weapons of the other guards. Above him, at the summit of the altar, the Cipher shifted slightly, as though uncomfortable.

GILEAD SWUNG IN again, and his blade made a gouge in Ire's shoulder guard.
'Hurting yet?' Gilead goaded.
Ire made no answer.
'No matter... I believe I have kept you occupied long enough.'
Lord Ire suddenly froze, and glanced around at something Gilead couldn't see.
'Yes, I think I have...' Gilead smiled.

FITHVAEL RAISED HIS sword and thrust it down into the disgusting amorphous sack that the Cipher. Rank viscous fluid ruptured out all over him and drizzled down the sides of the alter. The corpse-stench was overwhelming.
'Lord Ire!' Fithvael shouted defiantly, his hands still clutching his victorious weapon. 'Your son is dead!'

THE PEWTER ROOM had gone. Lost in a fortress built solely upon dark magic, Gilead murmured Niobe's name and tried to hold on to the last traces of her voice.

REALITY SPLIT APART. They fled amidst the decaying illusion as towers collapsed and a nightmarish storm erupted in the ravaged sky over the bastion. Spurs of magical energy vented into the sky, blowing out sections of wall that were only half-real.

Heading for the gatehouse, Fithvael almost fell into Gilead.
'Niobe? Where is she?' Gilead bellowed. The abused and frustrated forces of Chaos were stripping the place apart around them.
'Did she not return to you?' Fithvael rasped.
Then, amidst the maelstrom, they saw her slight shape, running and dodging towards them through a storm of exploding magical energy.
But the storm had gathered and fashioned itself into a hideous form sixty

feet long with a comet-like tail extruding from it into infinity. It was Lord Ire, part angelic human masterpiece, part gelatinous, seething mass, part wind, part grotesque noise; all writhing, clawing, vengeful Chaos.

Gilead reached out to grab her and drag her with them. He took her hand and pulled at her with all his failing strength.

Niobe shivered and convulsed under the force of the sorcerous hurricane – then found herself lifted cleanly out of Gilead's arms. She rose and whirled in the current of air that grasped her firmly in a deadly embrace.

Fithvael looked on, only yards away, yet still out of reach. He watched the great raging force sweep Niobe from Gilead's desperate grip and, embracing her, whirl itself up in an energy tornado that whipped out into endless black space and was gone.

Then night itself came down and combusted the ruins of Lord Ire's bastion into a vast explosion of shockwaves and smoke.

FITHVAEL CAME TO his senses opened his eyes. He stood in their last campsite amidst the midnight trees of the deepest Drakwald. Two horses stood nearby, heads bent, feeding on what little fresh vegetation they could find.

Fithvael lowered Gilead gently to the ground and, all his energy spent and his will used up, the loyal elf lay down beside his friend.

THERE IT IS, for all its worth. My bitterest tale. I warned you. No happy ending. But still, I have more heroic stories up my sleeve, more triumphant ones.

But this is the story that matters. He lost her. Gilead lost her. She had bound himself to his mind and he let her slip away.

Few get over the death of a twin, but this...

Words fail me. Yes, that's it. Fill my damn glass to the brim. I'm tired of these stories. They take it out of me.

What's that you say? Did he ever find her?

I'm afraid I do not know. I hope so. All I know is what happened next.

IV
GILEAD'S PATH

*I fear your dreams. I fear we
are too old.*

So, YOU'D KNOW the rest then, would you? The dark times that followed their defeat of Lord Ire and the loss that brought? Gods! Well, then, perhaps another one. I can manage that. Listen well…

From the smoking mere that was all that remained of Ire's illusory bastion, they rode for days, months.

Every morning, they rose to the yellow glow of dawn and directed their course according to the fall of their shortening shadows. At noon, the light was white and clear, and the shadows warm and dappled, and with the light Fithvael's hopes would rise. Then he would see the drop of his friend's head and the white-knuckled grip of his hands on the wear-polished reins of his steed, and he would know that the light would soon fade and the shadows would grow long once more, until there was nothing but darkness again.

Each evening, the diminishing light turned every colour, tone and hue to a dull, uniform grey. That grey was echoed in the pallor of Gilead's face. There was no expression there, save the dark, closed sadness that Fithvael had become accustomed to before, long ago, when Galeth's memory was what drove Gilead. But his friend's blank eyes held a new pain now, a new yearning.

Fithvael kept pace with Gilead, watching him as the heavy blanket of evening sky turned quickly to become a purple night that drove them to a new campsite and the torture of another sleepless, dreamless nightmare.

Weeks passed and, beneath the worn and weary hooves of their steeds, many miles of thinning black forest and tracts of lush green pastureland were crossed. They brushed the hem of the human world. Gilead loathed the crass man-made patterns he detected in the felling of trees, the cultivation of fields and the construction of their despised towns. He hated the humans for their heavy faces and their dull minds. He hated them for their short lives and their hard hearts. He hated them all.

Above everything, he hated himself for coming near them and among them. He had saved them, though they little knew it. He had saved them and it had cost him everything.

Still they continued, daily, southward.

AT FIRST THEY had buried themselves in the deep of the forests, avoiding the humans, keeping to themselves and looking only to the landscape.

'Tor Anrok survived…'

Fithvael had heard Gilead murmur it a hundred times a day.

'Tor Anrok survived, all those years. How many other fastnesses and refuges of our kind might be out there? Niobe spoke of her home… Talthos Elios. We will find it if it still stands.'

Fithvael's brow would furrow with the pain of watching Gilead on his hopeless quest in this human desert. There were no elves here. There had been no elves here for centuries past. This place was human, so human that the elf was almost a myth, a story told by old men to wandering bards, and by bards to taverns full of wide-eyed, incredulous men and women.

In those first weeks after Niobe was lost, Gilead spoke of looking for her himself. Fithvael had barely the heart to point out the futility. Instead, they looked for any and all signs of elven life. Gilead would see breaks in the landscape that reminded him somehow of the trace of Ulthuan. A low, flickering fire would burn in his eyes and he would dismount, leaving his horse for Fithvael to secure, bent only on what he had seen, or on what he thought he had seen. He would trample through thick undergrowth, scarring his boots and gloves on the spikes and thorns that grew there. He would wade to his thighs in heavy, brackish water with its foul smelling blue and green scum. He would study every stone and rock that stood out from the landscape, looking for signs of their kind. Looking for signs that were not there. That, perhaps, had never been there.

Then Fithvael would watch as the light died and the blank, hollow expression returned to Gilead's face.

Gilead ate only when Fithvael prepared food and forced it upon him. He drank only when his friend offered a full flask. He slept not at all. And if Fithvael slept, he would wake to find Gilead staring into the purple night, living his waking nightmare, wishing only for death or for love. Wishing only for an end. It was as if they were right back at the ruin of Tor Anrok, before Betsen Ziegler's cause had roused Gilead from his wasted misery.

They found nothing.

With every day that passed, with every new landscape they searched, Gilead's desperation increased. He no longer simply examined the streams and rocks and changes in the patterns of the land. He tore and rampaged and desecrated and plundered the land for every clue. He ripped his hands and his clothes, covered himself in filth and stench, and time and again he fell to his knees, his lank, matted, sweat-streaked hair falling across his face, his body wracked with fatigue.

'Galeth!'

Fithvael heard him cry the name and a cold fist would clench in his gut. Gilead cried out in his delirium. Only on the best of these worst of days would he cry Niobe's name.

Fithvael watched and waited as Gilead became more distant, more desperate, thinner and increasingly delirious. He watched and he waited for the time when Gilead would open his eyes and his mind and see that there was nothing here for them. There were no elven relics, no elven homes and there were no elves. This was no place for them to find a home with people of their own kind. This was no place for them at all.

Fithvael had seen the decline before. After Galeth, after the decade-long quest, Gilead had returned home to find that he was the last of his people. He had not only lost his brother and ten long years of his life, he had lost a little of himself, a little of his sanity, and the rest he had buried in a thousand indolent, self-absorbed days and many hundred flasks of liquor. Tor Anrok had crumbled around him, crumbled with him, and been lost.

But with the loss, a tide had turned. Gilead had found a new fight and then another, and with every new cause he fought came the possibility of his death and an end to the pain. Gilead had left Tor Anrok and Gilead was the last of his line. Everything was gone.

Fithvael saw now that Gilead's quest was a vain attempt to restore what he refused to see was lost forever. But as he watched Gilead weaken into madness, destroying his mind and body both in his futile struggle, Fithvael knew that there was no turning from this path.

THE TWENTIETH DAY passed, and the thirtieth, and the lush greens and golds of the days changed to the deep, burdensome hues of the dying season. Gilead saw nothing, but Fithvael recognised the pattern as surely as he recognised the lines coming to his own face. The nights fell faster and lasted longer, but it mattered not to Gilead, whose personal darkness enveloped him more with every passing day.

Fithvael reckoned they were fast approaching the fortieth day since leaving Ire's fastness when, riding again, as they had every day, Gilead abruptly wheeled his steed around in the shaded clearing they had reached. Fithvael thought they were to stop, that for once Gilead might ask for food or drink or some other sustenance. Gilead wheeled again... and again. Fithvael watched his friend make small circles, skinning the clearing of its low grey carpet of fragrant sage and camomile. The circles became smaller until Gilead demanded his steed turn on its hind legs, like a show horse in a parade square.

'GALETH!'

The ground shook with the confused horse's heavy hoof-falls. The air shook with the anguished bellow. Foaming at the mouth, the horse began to ooze long threads and patches of sweat along its flanks and down its neck.

Fithvael drew closer, his own horse pawing the earth and tossing its head with a frightened whinny.

That veteran warrior and faithful friend dismounted and, leaving his horse to trot to a safe distance among the trees, he hunkered his body down into itself, making himself small and unthreatening, and took slow steps towards the unified, terrified, obsessed creature that was Gilead astride his steed.

Drawing low beneath the horse's neck, Fithvael reached out a tentative, ungloved hand and began to make soft, reassuring noises. Not to Gilead, but to the horse.

'Hsssst there. Gentle down, gentle down.'

Sliding his feet slowly forward, Fithvael tentatively rested his hand on the damp, cold neck of the animal as it twisted away from him in its ceaseless quest to tighten the circle it was stamping in the earth.

Fithvael ducked as the horse travelled, bringing his hand up again and again to touch the animal. His breath came soft and even, like no breath at all compared to the snorting, flaring hot nostrils of the troubled beast.

Finally, after a dozen or more passes, time began to slow for Fithvael as he focussed on his task. With every pass he rested his hand for longer on the horse's shoulder or flank, until his hand held contact there, travelling over the beast's trembling, flinching muscles. With every turn the tossing of the horse's head lessened, the tension in its neck fell away, and finally Fithvael was able to take the slackening rein and bring the weary animal to a slow, rocking pace, and then to rest.

Gilead sat in the saddle, completely upright, the stains of his own sweat seeping through his heavy clothes and smearing a darkening V down the back of his scarlet cloak. Sweat ran in long runnels down his cheeks and fell in heavy droplets from the lobes of his pointed ears. Everything that made Gilead himself was lost to Fithvael in that moment. He stepped in front of the bow-headed animal that Gilead still straddled and looked up into a face that he no longer knew, into eyes that he no longer understood. Gilead failed to meet the test. Failed to meet his friend's gaze. Failed.

Still holding the reins firmly in one hand, lest Gilead repeat his madness, or find some new horror to perpetrate on his loyal steed, Fithvael moved to the side of the horse. He took a firm grasp on Gilead's boot. He shoved hard, releasing it from the heavy leather stirrup. Then, lowering his centre of gravity, he slid his feet shoulder-width apart, and braced himself.

Fithvael took a deep breath. Holding it, he cupped Gilead's boot in both hands. Gilead did not move. Freeing his breath in a great, resounding gasp, Fithvael launched Gilead clean out of his saddle and onto the ground with a heavy thud and a heavier winding. Standing and brushing off his hands on the sides of his tunic, Fithvael caught his breath.

'That was for the horse,' he said.

FITHVAEL TORE HANDFULS of long feathery grass from around the bases of the trees across the clearing. When he had a generous fistful he folded the grasses over in his hand to form a firm, but gentle brush. He stroked the long, slender nose of Gilead's steed with one hand, while grooming the neck and shoulders of the beast with his makeshift tool. The horse whinnied lightly and thrust his nose into Fithvael's armpit, breathing regularly now after its ordeal. After working his way thoroughly down both sides of its neck and shoulders, the elf cast aside the used grass, now moist and brown, and began the process again. With fresh grasses, the veteran swordmaster worked his way down the steed's slender forelegs, moving slowly, resting one reassuring hand on the beast all the time, whispering soft noises as he worked.

The animal was exhausted and made no protest as Fithvael began to remove the saddle, working straps and the reins, buckles and fastenings. He could smell the sweet elven sweat of his companion mingled with the sour aroma of the horse's fear. As he lifted the saddle, Fithvael sighed. Around thick, whitening sweat-marks he saw deeper, red abrasions. The smell of freshly stripped, raw flesh filled the air and fat, black flies began to swarm toward the bloody, bruised areas on the horse's back.

With two short clicks of his tongue, Fithvael summoned his own horse from the shade of the trees. It trotted toward the elf and beast, ignoring the heap of flesh, armour and rags that still lay, catatonic and foetally curled, in the middle of the clearing.

From the saddlebags on his own horse, Fithvael took boxes and flasks of pungent waxes and oils. He sat on the spongy, moss-covered earth beneath the spreading canopy of a tree and set to work, grinding and pounding using his dagger hilt and a large flat stone he had found in the undergrowth. The two horses stood nearby, nuzzling each other and finding solace in the new-found tranquillity. Fithvael gathered leaves from the ground and scraped the papery red bark from a young tree with his dagger. The air was filled with a sappy fresh smell, mixed with the aromatic musk of well-prepared oils. As Fithvael carried his preparation across the clearing to Gilead's steed, flies buzzed and flitted away from the little wooden bowl cupped in his hands.

Fithvael spread the ointment on the saddle sores, thanking his old gods far away in Tiranoc that his healing extended to elf and beast alike.

The thought made him hesitate and he cast a frown towards the figure that had once been his friend and master, still and broken on the earth.

FITHVAEL SPENT THE rest of the afternoon tending to both of the horses, finding clean water for them and to refill his flasks, and putting them out to pasture among the trees. Relieved of their tack and riders, both horses by turns grazed the undergrowth and paced quietly together. For weeks they had rested only after dark and they felt the relief of a break from the daily monotony. Yet they seemed solemn to Fithvael, watching them at a distance.

The elf warrior made camp, foraged for food and the herbs he would need, roughly cleaned his garments with some of the water he had collected, and as the purple evening spread above him, he built a small fire.

Gilead still did not move. The only sounds were those of the forest all around and the horses resting nearby. Fithvael savoured the solitude all the more, knowing that he must break it soon.

Hours passed and the daylight moved slowly on as Fithvael ate and pondered his next move. He could not go on with Gilead's madness. He needed a plan of his own. The veteran swordmaster doubted, still, that Niobe's home, Talthos Elios, might be found in the south, where for so long humans had lived and reigned. Yet he could not refute that Gilead had sufficient cause, in the first instance at least, to make this journey deep into human territory. If it was so, then south they would proceed, but they must find new ways to trace the old ancestors. The landscape had given them nothing but grief and despair. The landscape had brought on Gilead's madness; a blight consumed his sanity and was never deep beneath the surface of the cheerless, austere elf-lord.

Earlier, in the mauve twilight, Fithvael had thought to leave his master, who no longer deserved his love and trust and obedience. He put the thought from his mind. Their history was too long, too entwined, and Gilead could not survive alone here, not now.

By the last indigo shadows of the evening Fithvael was minded to waken his companion, but the peace was too complete, too sweet without him.

The night came, turning the clearing black, save for the yellow, opaque light around the fire. Fithvael rose and strode over to look down on Gilead, still curled, not moving, but with wide, open, depthless eyes. Old habits and deep-seated loyalty caused the old swordmaster to throw a horse blanket over his semi-conscious friend, but with all that had passed, no amount of fellow feeling could take away the pleasure of his relaxed solitude, and Fithvael left his companion a while longer.

The elf sat through the dark of the long night, watching the fire, glancing occasionally at his friend. By dawn he was preparing the potions and poultices that would bring Gilead out of his strange non-sleep and restore a consciousness that Fithvael could only pray might be undisturbed by the obsessed, delirious behaviour that had grown and matured in the weeks since Niobe had been lost.

WITH THE FIRST strands of daylight marking the horizon with an ochre haze, Fithvael rose and crossed to where Gilead lay. He touched the deep, smooth brow of his friend and tilted his head. He drew his bowl of restorative before Gilead's sightless eyes and then tipped it to his lips. Much of the thick, herbal infusion ran away along Gilead's vice-tight jaw, and Fithvael tilted the elf's head further; if the potion was to work, it must first be imbibed. Two or three spoonfuls made it past Gilead's drying lips, but bubbled back, warm and clear and brown. There was no swallow reflex.

Fithvael began again, tilting Gilead's head on its rigid neck and massaging his exposed throat to promote the swallowing action. Perhaps he had left it too long.

After several minutes, just as Fithvael feared he would have to make more of his potion, Gilead finally gasped a choking gulp. His closed throat gurgled and his neck stretched in a reflexive spasm that showed suddenly in his eyes. Tears came to the corners of those languid, rolling orbs.

His coughing fit at an end, Gilead jumped wordlessly to his feet and cast about him, eyes staring at his unremembered surroundings.

'You are safe, old friend,' Fithvael said softly. 'A minor episode, nothing that a few herbs could not treat.'

Gilead said nothing, but lunged his head and body around in circles, his feet spread apart in an aggressive, attacking posture. His hands searched for the hilt of his blue-steel longsword, which, thank Ulthuan, lay safely in his saddle's scabbard.

Fithvael rose, approaching his over-wrought friend. 'Calm yourself, Gilead. You only need a little rest. Sit with me a while.'

Gilead flailed at him, waving his arms and thrusting one leg out in an uncoordinated kick that all but swung him off his feet.

'Have no fear! It is I, Fithvael, your faithful friend and companion. I would do you no harm.' He stood tall, walking slowly closer, knowing he had nothing to fear from Gilead's exhausted body, wary only of his master's deranged mind. The potion had done its work on the form of the elf, but perhaps not so much on his spirit.

'Galeth!'

With the return of the doleful cry Fithvael's face became stony hard and steel came to his eyes. Enough was enough.

Fithvael drew the short dagger from his belt, the one he had used to collect leaves and scrape bark, and with both hands drawn up and away from his body he made a charge at his erstwhile friend.

'Galeth is dead!'

'Galeth is dead?'

'You are dead!'

'Gilead is dead?'

Fithvael lunged at Gilead with his open, empty hand, more to ward off his friend than attack him. Gilead went wild.

He kicked at Fithvael's open hand, turning his body close to the old elf's. His four-fingered hand struck out to grasp Fithvael's wrist, but his reach was too short, or too clumsy, and he took the blade of the paring knife firmly in his grip. Fithvael looked down as ribbons of blood, seeming black in the dawn light, streamed from Gilead's hand. But Gilead felt nothing.

Fithvael let go his grip of the knife's turned bone handle, brought his arm back in a short but powerful swing, and connected his bulging knuckles with Gilead's jaw. There was a screech of teeth sliding too tight against each other and the harsh sound of bone on bone. Fithvael shook his hand out with the pain of the blow, but Gilead remained standing, whirling rather, dervish-like and manic.

'Don't make me hit you again, Gilead,' Fithvael spoke, almost to himself. 'For I will, if needs be.'

Fithvael had no need to approach Gilead again, for this time it was Gilead that charged, in a bolting, uncontrolled lurch, head down, feet almost losing their hold of the dew sodden ground. Fithvael turned just before Gilead's crown would connect with the veteran's gut. The veteran swordmaster took Gilead's neck in the crook of his elbow instead, wrenching and turning, pulling the elf off his feet and dropping him on his back in the sappy grass. The scent of bruised camomile filled Fithvael's nostrils. Gilead reached out for the older elf's legs.

Finding himself suddenly on his back, Fithvael hollered, 'Enough!'

But Gilead was nowhere close to having enough. He fought as if for his very soul, in a savage, daemonic way that made Fithvael cringe back. Relieved that Gilead was weak and ill-coordinated, he merely blocked and defended himself against the flailing arms and legs. But only seconds into the brawl he knew that Gilead would go on until exhaustion overtook him – or until Fithvael broke him. Gilead had a long way to go to be sound of mind and body again, and exhaustion now might kill him. Yet Fithvael feared that, with just one more blow, he might kill the elf himself.

As Gilead grappled and pawed at Fithvael's cloak, attempting a stranglehold, his companion curled on his side, bringing his knees up to his chest. He pressed his feet lightly against Gilead's sternum, sensing the thrumming, birdlike heartbeat there, and having found his target, he thrust his legs out to their full extent, grunting a deep exhalation as he heaved.

Gilead's body curled as all the breath was taken from him. Winded, he gasped for air, his eyes bulging, his jaw finally slackening. Fithvael waited as several empty seconds hung in the air. Then it was over. Gilead rolled onto his side, his arms folding tight around his knees, and Fithvael heard the first sob, saw the hitch in the hunched shoulders as the elf warrior's body was wracked with the agony of realisation.

Gilead was awake. For the first time in days, perhaps weeks, Gilead was back.

'Now my work really begins,' Fithvael muttered to the whitening light.

GILEAD SHOOK AND rocked as his friend looked on, preparing further infusions and gently warming the poultices he had made the day before. Finally, Gilead was still, and, for the first time since Niobe had been lost, Gilead actually slept rather than lost consciousness. He slept on as Fithvael ensured his comfort, placing a warm poultice on the back of his neck and a cooling balm on his forehead and wrists.

As Gilead slumbered, Fithvael prepared a simple meal – a salad of curative herbs, several patties of unleavened bread, and for himself a pair of small but fat perch lifted in quick hands from a dark stream nearby. When the repast was made and laid out in the small clean dishes that Fithvael carried in his pack, the elf revived Gilead once more, knowing that this time his old master would awaken bewildered but meek and receptive.

FOR ALMOST A week the pair remained in the clearing. They ate and talked and rested, as their steeds relaxed and recovered too. Gilead's horse healed quickly, much faster than his master. On the third day, Fithvael related the incident in the clearing, for Gilead had never lived that day to remember it.

'You did your duty to me and to the horse,' Gilead said sadly. 'I could ask no more of you.'

Gilead's first, faltering words. An apology, perhaps a form of thanks, it mattered little to Fithvael, who had come to expect nothing at all.

'I threw you from your horse for what you did to the beast. And I would do it again,' he answered gruffly.

On the fourth day Gilead was able to walk unaided around the clearing. Reaching full circle he ran a second lap and then a third, exhilarated.

'Sit, Gilead,' Fithvael commanded and the younger elf folded himself back onto the warm ground without question.

'This search. This quest for Niobe, for the old kin, for your salvation – call it what you will. This search: it must end.'

Gilead stared at the veteran elf.

'Or… if we continue, then you must listen to reason. You must begin again, and be led by me.'

SO FITHVAEL VOICED his plan, firmly, without any intention of giving way to the now subdued Gilead. They would continue, but they would find a real trail. They would skirt the human villages and towns, and listen in the darkest corners of alehouses and taverns to the stories of the local people. They would take their lead from the myths and legends that were told or sung in these alien places. And if they found nothing, their quest must end.

Gilead, now both stronger of mind and sounder of limb, did as he was bidden. The two of them spent the next few days eating, sleeping and exercising by turns. Fithvael talked long into the night of reason and rightness and of the possibility of a futile quest. He did what was in his power to prepare Gilead, knowing that this might be his last chance to save his master from the madness of his tortured mind, perhaps even from death by some senseless suicidal yearning to set things right, to turn back the wheels of time, to restore the noble elves to this land.

* * *

On the eighth day, Fithvael and Gilead cleared the traces of their camp, saddled their steeds and left the clearing. They were searching now for signs of human habitation and they found them easily, within an hour of their departure.

They exercised great caution at first, entering the outskirts of tiny villages only after nightfall. They sat in the darkest recesses of tiny backrooms where one tapped barrel of ale served all for a week or more and where the food was meagre or non-existent. They covered or bowed their heads and listened to the humans, attuning their ear to the hard, clipped accents of the south, learning as much from tone and cadence as from the words themselves. They listened without talking, drinking a single glass of ale each and leaving, remarked on only as strangers. None had seen an elf in these parts for a hundred years, and none expected to see an elf, so no elf was seen.

Little by little, as the companions moved from village to village and on to larger towns, they began to pick up a trail. The humans loved to hear stories, often pleased with the same legend repeated over and over. Fithvael and Gilead began to see the patterns in the weaving of the human tales. They moved onward as their ears became attuned to the human sounds and their minds became adept at translating the harsh, quick language. Tales of elf towers and great warriors and noble elves, who had helped avert human tragedies, wove together to create an ever-richer landscape of elf habitation of this land. And Gilead had been right: the further south they travelled, the clearer and more regularly came the stories.

Barely a fortnight later, Gilead and Fithvael entered what might have been their twentieth tavern. A little larger than the last, they had become increasingly confident of their invisibility to these dull human folk. Fithvael strode to the barrel and plank structure that served as the bar, as Gilead, behind him, turned about looking for a safe, dark corner in which to be seated.

As he turned, he almost struck his head on a broad, dark beam that traversed the ceiling of the low, ochre-washed room, and he instinctively took a half-pace back, stepping right into the path of a serving girl. He lowered his head by instinct as she turned to him to apologise, fearing she had been the clumsy one. Only inches from her, Gilead's eyes fell deep into the swollen cleavage, spilling from the girl's too tight bodice. He thought to look away from her vulgar bulk, the very antithesis of elven beauty, but he could not.

Two or three inches of the cleft between bold human breasts fell sharply into focus as Gilead watch a bead of sweat ripen and run down the sweep of creamy flesh, before becoming entangled in the perfect twist links of a beautifully wrought heavy gold chain. The thin line of sweat caught up with itself and formed a bead again, plump and glistening on the link of the chain before falling to the next, clinging and growing and tumbling again.

Time froze in that instant as Gilead's gaze followed the fall of sweat down the chain until it reached the half-buried disc that nestled between the swell of the girl's body and the tight ribbons that traversed the gap where her bodice would no longer meet.

'Ex... excuse me, sir,' she said, trying to turn in the narrow space between stools and tables.

The spell was broken and suddenly Fithvael was at Gilead's side.

'A table, wench?' Fithvael asked, flattening and lowering the timbre of his voice, and using as few of the strange human words as he could.

'Certainly, sir,' she said. Resting her hand on Gilead's flinching arm, she added, 'My apologies, I should had been looking where I was going.' Gilead mumbled something incoherent to her in a singsong tone that made her frown. She removed her hand, looked at him once more as he turned, and then went about her business gesturing at a nearby table as she went.

'Did you see that?' asked Gilead, speaking before he was even seated. 'Did you see?'

'Only that you broke her path and spoke to her. A human. We must be circumspect. We must go unremarked in these places.'

'Fortune favours us now, Fithvael! Did you not see it?'

Fithvael was agitated by the encounter, hoping it had not lasted too long, and that Gilead had not exposed them to recognition. He was eager, now, to leave the tavern at the first opportunity. This was his plan. A plan adopted under duress. A plan that must be followed to the letter, and that meant as little contact with these humans as possible. He looked around him as he sipped at the bitter tasting ale, but very few minutes of surveillance reassured the old warrior that no harm had been done. Cautiously, he turned back to Gilead.

'What was it you saw, old friend?' he asked.

'Around the serving girl's neck. It was the chain at first that drew me, such craftsmanship. But I saw it, I know I saw it.'

'You make no sense. Tell me slowly what it was you saw.'

Gilead took a deep breath and looked solemnly into Fithvael's face, leaning forward across the narrow bench-table, as though telling a secret, or intimating the ghostlier parts of some torrid tale, as the travelling storytellers did.

'I did break the path of the serving girl. And when she turned to me she was standing very close. I cast down my eyes, lest she recognise my race, or question me in any way. And that was when I saw it. I have not seen such a thing these many years. Many times I have thought never to see such a thing again.'

Gilead was in earnest, Fithvael could see it, and there appeared to be no madness in his eyes, only purpose.

'The chain was such as my mother or sister would wear, fine twisted gold links in ranks with gold thread and beads woven between them, intricate as a puzzle. Only one of our own kind would wear so beautiful a jewel. No human would make such a thing, could make such a thing.'

'Such jewels were common among us, but all held a purpose or a promise,' Fithvael said. 'This chain could be a copy of some old design. It has no significance without its seal or talisman.'

'And there it is!' cried Gilead, bringing his fist down, remembering, only at the very last, not to punch the table in his rapture.

Fithvael looked around sharply for the girl, but he could not see her in the now smoky tavern, that throbbed with local life.

'She has a talisman?'

'She wears it against her stinking bosom, tarnishing its significance, as though it were nothing... but that matters not,' Gilead went on, calming himself. 'She surely knows something of us, of our kind. She can help us in our quest.'

Not wanting attention to fall upon himself and his eager friend, Fithvael led Gilead out of the tavern. In the alleyway alongside the rough old building, they talked softly of what they might do to learn where the maid's talisman had originated, but there was no time to decide. Only moments passed before a slight figure, head bowed and covered in a light shawl, entered the alleyway, almost knocking into the elf warriors, then jumping back in alarm. The shawl dropped to plump shoulders and Fithvael caught a glimpse of the chain that circled the girl's short, white neck.

'*Sigmar!*' she exclaimed. 'You quite frightened me.'

'We will not hurt you,' Fithvael said, forgetting to lower his voice, and once again the serving girl frowned and looked harder at the figures before her.

'Who are you?' she asked, taking a pace backwards, pulling the shawl tighter about her neck and hiding again the talisman that lay there.

'We are not what we seem,' Gilead said, stepping forward and making no attempt to hide the cadence of his voice or his alien accent as it rolled over the unfamiliar human words. 'We quest for our own people and we desire your help in our purpose.'

The startled girl tried to back out of the alley, but Gilead was too quick for her, holding her gently but firmly by the arms. The shawl fell away again. Fithvael picked it up from the dusty floor of the alley and wrapped it around her trembling shoulders, taking the chain lightly in his slender hand once it was settled there.

'Where did you find this, child?' Fithvael asked, caressing the delicate chain in his hands.

The girl twisted her fingers into her cleavage and lifted out the thick flat disc that had lain beneath her bodice, brandishing it before her until her knuckles turned blue-white.

'I didn't find it. It protects me from the likes of you. It'll ward off any evils!'

'I know, child,' said Fithvael, losing his hold on the chain and stepping back a little. 'Once, a long time ago, it belonged to one of my kind. It was made for and worn by my kin. A powerful talisman and a great protector, as you say…'

'Yet if you didn't find it, where did it come from?' Gilead stared into the girl's eyes and put a little more pressure into the grip his narrow hands held her in.

'Ouch! You're hurting me,' she cried and tried to turn in what felt to her like a vice.

'Let her go free, Gilead,' Fithvael said in the only language he knew that would ensure his friend did his bidding. Gilead dropped his hands to his side. The girl stood, staring at them both, before looking down at the disc she still held in her hand.

White-faced and trembling, the servant girl hesitated only for a moment before lifting the back of her hair with her short, plump hands, then unclasped the chain and amulet from its place around her neck.

'Th-this m-must belong t-to you,' she stammered, head held low. She held the talisman out, at arm's length, for Fithvael to accept from her shaking fingers.

Fithvael looked long and hard at the disc on the end of its beautiful chain, turning it in his hands and committing its multiple inscriptions, in the ancient script, to memory. Then he placed the talisman back in the girl's hand again and closed her fist gently around it, his long narrow hand with its elegant fingers engulfing hers in one simple movement.

'No. It belongs to you now,' he said, thrusting one hand back at Gilead for him to keep his silence. 'Tell us only where it came from and what you know of it.'

'And never speak of us,' added Gilead.

'None would believe me,' answered the servant girl, looking into Fithvael's eyes. It seemed she had made her decision. 'Follow me, lords. I know a quiet place where I can tell you all I know.'

IT WAS LATE into the night when Gilead and Fithvael returned to their horses and their camp. The grey-black embers of their banked fire reddened as Fithvael stirred life back into it and by its pale light wrote down the inscriptions he had seen on the talisman.

It was the first solid piece of evidence that could lead them on the right track. With the inscriptions and the story the servant girl had gladly told them, albeit embroidered a little and crudely embellished here and there in the human way of telling and retelling, the elves knew all they needed to know to continue their quest with renewed vigour and determination.

IN THAT PART of the Empire, all roads led to Nuln. From your nod, I see Nuln is known to you.

Keeping to the woodland paths to the north of the trade route from Averheim to that old city, Fithvael and Gilead made good time and were unseen by the human traffic that swelled as it approached Nuln. As the city came into view on the horizon, the companions turned to the west, following the course of the River Reik until they discovered what they were seeking.

From the first, the elves were surrounded by reminders of home. There was no need to forage for the smallest sign, no desperate search for a single stone or plant that might signify an elven presence. The landscape was waist-deep in elf design and culture. The plants were right, the ebb and flow of the land was right, and when they came upon the buildings of Ottryke Manor it was clear to them that every foundation stone had been hewn by elves and placed by elves. Fithvael dismounted and led his horse away to a safe distance amongst the trees. All Gilead could do was stare.

Watching Gilead from cover, Fithvael clicked his tongue twice. Gilead's horse lifted its nose, whinnied gently and turned to look at the veteran elf warrior. Moments later Gilead turned his head and responded to the gesture that Fithvael made to beckon him back into cover.

'We have arrived,' Gilead said, dismounting, 'Do you not see? Elves have been here before us. This was once a great elf dwelling.'

'It surely was,' Fithvael replied, and there was an eager look in his eyes. 'The human maid spoke true.'

> *I inherited the talisman. It was a gift to my grandmother, you see. My family worked on the estate of Ottryke, cousin to the Elector of Nuln. My grandmother was a very beautiful woman and a favourite of his Lordship. He gave her the talisman as a forget-me-not, she said, when she married and left his service. In return she sent my mother to work for him in his great house. And she works there still.*

'WE MUST FIND the servant girl's dame,' said Gilead, eyes glistening with anticipation.

'Less haste, lord. Let us first reconnoitre the area. It may be that these humans have no sympathy for our kind after so long a time.'

Gilead demurred, the guilt and shame of his mental lapse still fresh in his mind.

They spent two uneventful nights scouting every inch of the estate, but everything they saw only served to convince them of what they already believed to be true. The humans had built their own great manor on what had once been a large elven estate. The house was oriented in the traditional fashion and even the livestock pens and crop fields followed the classic elven pattern, not to mention some of the architecture – the foundations of most of the larger buildings, external walls, and even some ancient fencing were all elven in design and construction. The signs, hidden in plain view beneath and behind cruder, more recent human constructions, were there to be discovered by any eyes that could see them for what they were.

* * *

The manor was built on an elven ruin generations ago. All the family jewels were said to be elf-made, discovered in the grounds years before. My grandmother always wore this talisman for protection against evil. I did not know if the stories were true.

'How are our visitors?' the lord asked the man who stood before him, his cloth hat being steadily wrung out in his hands.

'The fire has been warm two days now, sire. I haven't seen them yet. They're not there after dark or before dawn, and I dare not seek them in the daylight.'

The audience took place in the lower hall of Ottryke Manor. Lord Ottryke was generally very hard on trespassers and intruders, but the gamekeeper had piqued his interest. These were no poachers – they had killed nothing. And their campsite was too well organised to be run by vagabonds. There was evidence of well tended horses and of thorough meals with elegant cooking utensils. 'Strange and wonderful,' the gamekeeper had described them.

'Very well. You may leave,' said Lord Ottryke. 'Say nothing to anyone.' And with a wave of his bejewelled hand, he dismissed his gamekeeper.

'Someone has been here again. A human, no doubt,' said Fithvael, stirring the fire back to life a little after dawn on the third day. 'We must decamp. We place ourselves in danger here.'

'No, Fithvael, we will remain. Some human has seen this place, but none has hunted us or attacked us. They think nothing of our being here.'

'Perhaps they survey us as we survey them.'

'And if they do, perhaps we can help each other. I wish only to find Niobe or traces of any others of our own kind. We have a duty, you and I, Fithvael. It is too long since we knew what it was to be part of something greater, to have a family and our own people around us. What would you not give to have such a thing again?'

'I fear your dreams. I fear we are too old, and have been too solitary for too long to do justice to women and offspring now,' Fithvael said, so low his companion did not hear.

Gilead slept now, even by daylight, when for months he could not sleep during the darkest of nights. Now it was Fithvael's turn to be wakeful. They were being watched, and he had seen signs that they had been visited; yet Gilead seemed to have no fear of these humans. A character of extremes, the elf felt fear of everything or of nothing, love of life or a passion for death, was shadowfast or comatose.

Fithvael sat beside the campfire, keeping it low lest it give off tell-tale smoke, and kept watch. He spent the day preparing for the next night, without knowing what more there was to find on this estate. He kept watch over his friend and their few belongings. He laid his short sword within reach if he was seated and at his belt when moving around. He lived the day in fear, not of what the humans might do, for they must do something, nor of when the humans might come, for come they would. In his heart he lived in fear of Gilead and of what he might cause to happen to them both.

Dusk drew on, turquoise and amber. Gilead would wake soon, so Fithvael prepared a meal, stirred the fire into fresh life and leaned back against the welcoming nest of roots and bark afforded by the largest tree in the tiny clearing. Gazing into the darkening sky, Fithvael watched blue-grey wisps of cloud crossing the gaps in the leaves high above.

WHEN THEY CAME, as Fithvael had known they would, it was at twilight, that time when a black thread and a white, held equally against the light, both look grey.

Fithvael lay half upright against the tree, his eyelids fluttering and his feet twitching in unquiet sleep. Gilead lay in shelter on his side, well rested, close to waking.

When they came, they did not pour into the tiny clearing on horseback, stamping the ground, rearing their steeds and banging swords against shields.

Fithvael reclined, dozing, nostrils flaring with a new smell, unfamiliar at his time of sleeping. Gilead rolled instinctively onto his back, so that his semi-comatose senses might better hear the new sounds approaching the clearing.

When they came, they came by stealth, parting the leaves and branches of the trees, creeping on near-silent feet into the clearing. They came unarmoured for silence, sporting only the insignia of their lord embroidered on the front panels of their jerkins.

Fithvael took his weight back into his body, breathed one long, slow breath to clear his head and half opened an eye. Gilead gained his feet, hunkered down to keep his shelter; eyes snapped open, one hand, hesitating in mid-air, inches from the haft of his dagger.

They had thought to take the strangers by stealth. But the human scent is strong in the nostrils of an elf, and their footfalls sound loudly in the ears of the ancient folk. Even as an elf sleeps, he hears and smells and feels, and Gilead and Fithvael were no longer asleep.

In the half-blink of a single eye, Fithvael had seen the five men stalking around the clearing, skirting the fire, examining the food cooking there, and looking for the shelter which echoed the shapes of the low canopies of immature trees, and was invisible in the twilight. He knew that Gilead was with him; he could feel his presence, crystal sharp like the edge of an elven sword. Fithvael himself could take out the two men at the west side of the clearing. Gilead would do the rest.

In a matter of two heartbeats, Gilead registered five heavy pairs of feet in his hearing. Two off to the west of the clearing, two more central and one coming closer, to the east of the clearing. Gilead could easily defeat the three humans nearest to him; he knew that Fithvael would be on hand to tackle the remainder.

None of the men spotted the shape of the elf warrior, leaning against the tree, nor could they see the shelter where Gilead lay. The five men thought to wait for their quarry as they skirted the patch of open ground, marvelling at the construction of so neat a fire and the elegant preparation of such a meal. They assumed from this that the men in this campsite would be sophisticated, urbane people; they would be reserved, slow if it came to a fight – and so the newcomers expected nothing more.

Gilead took the first, emerging from the unseen shelter, lunging forward, attacking low. Galeth's sword rested heavy in its scabbard at his side and his dagger was still in his belt. The warrior elf tackled the short, squat man at the hips, below his centre of gravity, and swung him onto the ground on his back, winding him badly. A well-aimed blow to the jaw laid him out unconscious. To his right, Gilead could hear Fithvael emerge into the clearing.

'Do not kill them!' he ordered, and Fithvael automatically put up his sword, always used to taking orders from his faster friend on the field of battle.

As Fithvael floored his first opponent with a flat-handed but powerful blow to the sternum, Gilead was attacking his second, a bewildered young man who instantly dropped the staff he was carrying and waved his arms in alarm in front of him.

'No! No!' he cried, his voice high and wavering.

Gilead squatted, swiftly, and took the end of the staff in one hand, swinging it lightly against the back of the boy's knees and landing him unceremoniously on his rump.

Fithvael grappled with the biggest of the men, but for all the human's bulk he was also fast, and after seeing the fate of his comrades, was now ready for the elf's charge. The guard lifted his axe and swung, but Fithvael was still lithe for an old warrior and, ducking, he caught the haft of the long handled axe below the head and set himself into a spin. The force threw the big man off his heavy feet and into the trunk of the tree that Fithvael had, only moments before, been sleeping against.

As he looked up the last assailant was going down. He was the tallest of them, standing almost height for height with Gilead as they circled each other. Gilead made his move, grabbing his opponent's hand, raising and turning it, taking with it the tall man's entire body. Lifting him almost off his feet, Gilead ducked under their conjoined hands and threw the human over his shoulder. The man landed on his back; his head whiplashed back and he, too, was unconscious before he even knew what had hit him.

'How... how did you do that... sire?' a small voice asked from the middle of the body-strewn glade.

Fithvael and Gilead stood over the only conscious human left in the clearing.

'How? They are all fighting men with weapons. I'm only beginning... but they...'

The frightened boy stammered and chattered, as the elves stood over him, silent.

Gilead pointed at the insignia.

The elven rune, *senthoi*, signifying unity, was newly sewn, on the front of the boy's fresh, starched tunic.

> *My grandmother told me that the lord still uses one of these old symbols on his crest, although none now remembers what it means or signifies. It's beautiful, I think.*

STILL STANDING OVER the jabbering boy, Fithvael and Gilead uncovered their faces.

'By Ulthuan…' Fithvael uttered in his native tongue.

The boy heard nothing more. The two faces and the single, alien voice had taken any remaining sense clean out of his head and he fell backward in a dead faint.

THEY DISMOUNTED IN the courtyard of the manor house and, since the usual watchman for this hour had rode in on the rump of Fithvael's steed, none dared stop their entry. The boy, Lyonen, was white with shock and he seemed in a daze as Fithvael helped him gently down from the horse they had shared.

Lyonen skittered and skipped ahead of Fithvael and Gilead into the lower hall of the manor, as he felt the toes of Gilead's striding boots on his heels. The elf companions made no attempt to hide their identities, and as a dozen faces turned upon them silence fell faster and more completely than it had ever fallen in that room before.

'Guards!' cried a squat, hawk-faced man, his dark hair streaked with silver. 'The rest of you leave, now!'

'You wanted to speak with us?' Gilead asked the lord, who in his confusion and disbelief had risen, although it was his right as lord of the manor to sit in the presence of any but the highest ranking stranger. After a few moments of bustle, the room was empty save for the guards, who looked on, some pale, others openly gaping at the mythical strangers.

'I…' the lord began, glancing behind him to ascertain precisely where his chair was situated, that he might fall into it with at least some assurance. 'I merely wanted to know who was trespassing on my land.'

'You sent five armed guards on a stealth mission,' Gilead observed, a wry smile almost crooking his lips, but kept out of his straight-talking eyes.

'And you return with only one, and the weakling at that,' said the lord, with increasing composure. 'Am I to believe you have killed the others?'

'Since they had no chance of taking myself and my companion, dead or alive, it seemed a little indiscriminate to slay them on the spot. No doubt they will return when they have nursed their sore heads and regained their sense of direction,' Gilead returned, enjoying the sparring.

Usually an elf, when he met with a human, came upon someone in need and in awe of the 'fairyfolk', or someone intimidated and unbelieving, as the lord's guards appeared to be. This human, however, after taking a moment to compose himself, seemed neither afraid nor awe-struck.

'I see what you are, elf. But what brings you to my estate?' the lord came to the point. But Gilead had need of a little more sparring.

'If you know the history of your homestead, then you know why we are here,' Gilead answered, gesturing slightly at Lyonen's tunic.

'Then it seems we both know the legends that surround this land,' the lord countered. 'Perhaps your reason for being here coincides with my reason for sending a stealth party to recover you, rather than killers to finish you.

'Please, put up your weapons and be seated.'

Gilead nodded to Fithvael and they both passed their weapons to the boy, assuring his continued stay in the room, as they took their seats. And thus the meeting commenced.

> *As my grandmother told it to me, the last of the elves that had lived at Ottryke, when they knew their time was ended, took most of their treasures to their family tombs and buried them. But that's just an old woman's story.*

FITHVAEL AND GILEAD were not invited to stay in the manor that night, but their weapons were returned to them and Lyonen returned to the campsite with them. It was he, after all, who had brought the elves to his lord, and his lord had need of their skills.

When they returned to their camp, it was empty of humans and nothing had been touched. Fithvael and Gilead talked long into the night – their youthful guardian watching them solemnly, understanding nothing at all that they said – as the two elf warriors debated the rightness of what they were to do.

Fithvael was aghast that Gilead would dare sanction the plunder of an ancient elven tomb. On Gilead's part though, he argued that the ends most assuredly justified the means. If he could possess the documentary treasures of this branch of an elf family, then the price was reasonable enough.

ANOTHER DAY PASSED as Fithvael gathered herbs, replenished their water skins and tended the horses. Lyonen followed everywhere in his wake, watching each task with wonder and curiosity, asking a hundred questions. Fithvael began to warm to the innocent eagerness of the boy, and his terse answers soon became a commentary on what he was doing, and then a dialogue like that between a mentor and his pupil. Even in such simple domestic matters, the ways of the elf were completely at odds with the crude toil that typified a human's daily labours.

The boy observed the other, Gilead, only at a distance – afraid, not because the warrior was an elf, but because that one kept all and everyone at a distance, even his elf companion. The boy's loyalties were already conflicted between the master he had grown up to laud and observe, and these wonderful elf-folk who knew so much and seemed so complete.

On the second day following their visit to the manor, Fithvael and Gilead received the lord and his entourage in the camp that they had made on these estates less than a week before. Fithvael heard hooves before dawn, as Lyonen helped him to load the horses and check their tack. Gilead stood firm in the centre of the clearing as he was surrounded by the lord, dressed in a kind of hunting outfit, and five of his guardsmen, clad in drab clothes and cloaks, bearing none of the lord's insignia. The armed men fooled no one; both elves recognised them instantly as soldiers of the lord, here to protect his interests against all-comers, including Fithvael and Gilead.

'Welcome, lord,' Gilead said formally, yet without showing signs of obeisance to this dull, avaricious human. 'Do we all understand our purpose?' He did not wait for an answer. 'That I lead you to the ancient tombs of my ancestors in return for any documents we discover there, all other property belonging to you as the current master of Ottryke.'

'We are in full agreement,' Lord Ottryke replied. 'All artefacts of material worth found during this mission belong solely to myself and my family.'

'Then we are agreed. Let us depart,' Gilead said, mounting his horse, Fithvael in concert with his every move.

Moments later, Lyonen, with a gasping clumsy effort, also managed to gain his saddle, accompanied by a glare from Gilead, and a tut or two from the lord's followers.

THE FIRST DAY'S ride was uneventful. The terrain was flat and easy, the steeds sure-footed and confident. If Ottryke's guards were a little nervous it was only because they were in the company of elves, creatures they knew might have existed in the deepest reaches of the world's history, but none that they could believe in here and now. As Gilead and Fithvael rode a little in advance of the rest of the party, six pairs of sneaking, wary eyes watched them constantly.

Lyonen, not quite knowing his place, rode sometimes at the back of the guard, unable to converse with men, who days before had thought him worthless and now only feared his connection to the elf-lords. When he forgot himself and his loyalties he chose to ride alongside Fithvael, causing headshakes of disapproval, even consternation amongst his own people.

After an uneventful night under the stars, the second day brought them to the low slopes that signalled the foothills of their mountain destination and the first expectations of danger. The head of the guard squad spoke to the feared elves through Lyonen, who translated nothing and interpreted nothing, but merely repeated his sergeant's words of caution.

And danger there was.

Gilead came to a dead stop, Fithvael following suit mere paces behind him. Gilead raised his hand to halt the party, but they were only human and the best they could do was shuffle and hesitate and shuffle a little more, coming to a silent stop far too late. Their control of their steeds was clumsy, and it cost them.

The great beast came from nowhere, carried by the scent of human flesh and animal sweat into the rearguard of the group. As Gilead started to turn to admonish the coarse humans he saw it come, shambling, swollen legs bent; huge, hairless paws low to the ground. Ottryke's men grappled with the hilts and hafts of their various weapons as Gilead wheeled and galloped from his turn straight past them. His sword already in his hand, leaving a trail through the air that the humans could almost see, Gilead howled a cry of anger and attack. Those guards who had managed to arm themselves started to raise their weapons to face the elf.

Behind them, the last man was already half out of his saddle, kicking furiously with his single stirruped foot at the broad, scarred, naked body of the monster. The bestial chest was the size of a barrel and as hard as rock, and the guard made no impression on his attacker. A bone-clawed fist reached up at him and snapped at his neck, encircling it easily and wrenching him from his terrified mount.

Gilead wheeled his own horse around and his slender elf sword came down hard, slicing into the beast's back just as he heard the startled cry of a soldier behind him, biting off the barked orders of the sergeant that hung in the air, unheeded. His first blow clove a deep cleft in the brute's unnaturally curved spine, causing the great beastman to turn, screeching at Gilead and spraying yellow spittle out from between its scabby grey lips and rows of broken and pointed teeth. Throwing its head forward, the beast aimed its jaw at Gilead's exposed left leg, but before the teeth could connect with the finely muscled tissue there, the elf had plunged his dagger into the hollow of the beast's broad throat, which spread wider than its narrow, flattened cranium. Black blood spurted from the fatal wound and gushed into the beast's lowered maw, making it wretch in its asphyxiated death throes.

In the stunned silence that followed, the lord and his guard gathered around the fallen, twitching monstrosity. Fithvael alone made to tend the shaken, but only slightly injured target of the beast's ravening hunger. Lyonen's mouth hung open for several moments, and when he finally collected himself he automatically made to applaud the elf warrior, preventing himself just in time.

Gilead dismounted and adjusted his reins. Lord Ottryke remained mounted, looking loftily above him. When Gilead looked up their eyes locked. The guards inhaled a deep breath, as one man, and held it. Brief seconds passed in a slow age.

'You owe me nothing,' Gilead said eventually.

'Indeed,' answered the nobleman, raising his chin as he turned his horse away.

* * *

'That... could have been me!' Lyonen whispered conspiratorially to Fithvael when they had re-formed and were back on their trail. 'If I hadn't been riding alongside you just then...'

'Then continue to ride with me,' Fithvael said kindly. 'I do not anticipate that things will become any easier.'

GILEAD LED FROM the front as the landscape climbed up into rocky lowlands, with the shrubby growth of orange and mauve heathers marking the route. Coming to a stop again by the side of a spring that trickled from between glinting grey rocks, riddled with coppery bright veins, Gilead motioned for the party to gather.

'This is where it begins,' he said, looking down at the narrow stream.

One jump should carry them across the burbling, splashing, clean white water. The gathered group dismounted and stood by the stream, looking bewildered. The boulder above the stream had a barely visible, time-worn engraving on it. Only their lord remained mounted, sneering down at Gilead.

'Is this some kind of elven joke?' he asked lightly, looking around at his men as if expecting them to applaud.

'Cross this stream on that horse and you no doubt find out.'

'Sergeant!' Lord Ottryke started. 'Your opinion?'

Before the sergeant could answer, Gilead stepped in front of the nobleman's horse and took a firm hold of its bridle.

'You pay me to be your scout and the sergeant to protect you from me,' the elf said darkly. 'Will you allow me to do as you bade me, or shall I leave you here for the next beastman to feast upon?'

The lord dismounted, Gilead still holding the reins of his horse.

While the last of the party tethered their horses, a large young man from the centre of the group – Fithvael thought he must perhaps be their corporal, and knew his name to be Groulle – danced on the spot for a moment and then launched himself at the stream before either of the elves could stop him. He could have cleared a small river eight feet wide or more from his position. He was a popular man, making any number of jokes and observations along the way, mostly at the expense of the elves. His laugh was a loud, echoing bray that had startled Lyonen out of his saddle more than once and had caused Gilead to grimace at the human's lack of subtlety.

'No!' Fithvael cried, simultaneously throwing himself after the huge corporal, but it was too late.

Groulle's left foot hit the bank of the stream.

Groulle followed through, hitting the air and paddling his legs in a running motion intended to carry him yards. The rest could only watch, stunned, as the springhead became a boiling, bursting geyser of hot yellow fire. The bank of the stream shook as the others looked down at the footprint Groulle had left in the soft earth. The ground tore apart and collapsed, swallowing the footprint into black fissures that spread fast around them. There was a deep rumbling in the earth, as the rest of the party retreated, still staring at Groulle, who seemed to hang in the air for many minutes.

As he hung there, he could see the bank of the stream push its way outward and the water below him turn bright and luminous as the geyser spat hot droplets of stinging fluid at him. However hard and far he travelled through the air, the opposite bank of the stream moved faster and further from him, until even he did not believe he would make it across.

Groulle leaned forward, thrusting his arms and shoulders as far ahead of him as he could, foolish and frightened and praying aloud to his god in a screeching voice that the others heard only as terrified screams. Finally, his arms made contact with the now steep and cracked far bank. The earth felt hot and dry, but he heaved against it, trying to drag legs he could no longer feel out of the bubbling water. Then there was nothing. As Groulle's feet left the thundering viscous liquid behind, the corporal blacked out.

When Groulle awoke, apparently only moments later, the spring was once again a pretty, narrow, babbling white strand of water that trickled harmlessly away between the rocks.

Gilead nodded at Fithvael and then took in the rest of the group with one glance. He saw faces ashen with fright – and noticed that Lord Ottryke had retreated to the rear of the group and was again sitting astride his horse.

A wry smile passed across the elf's lips as he asked, 'Who will go next?'

SIX MEN AND two elves spent the rest of the day negotiating the rocky outcrop and crossing it above the source of the spring and its dim engraving of the elven rune, *sariour*.

It was nightfall by the time they rejoined Groulle. He was unconscious again. His long boots and leather breeches were entirely burnt away, along with the bottom quarter of his leather scabbard. The end of his sword was blackened with tarnish. Groulle's legs up to the knees were a mass of black blisters and red ulcers, the pus already forming beneath the skin and bloating the sores. Lyonen turned away from the sight as an older guardsman stepped forward. He wore a neat, grey beard and long sideburns, and carried only a crossbow for protection, while the rest of the guard carried at least two weapons, and possibly a plethora of others concealed about their persons. A strap around the veteran's shoulder harnessed a pack to his body; it ran down his left side, tied around his waist and again to his thigh. The pack contained a series of pouches and pockets of various sizes and shapes. Freuden, for that was his name, unstrung the pack from his side and began to arrange bandages and medical instruments on a clean cloth on the ground.

'Human medicines will not work here,' said Fithvael, placing a hand on the stooping man's shoulder. Freuden flinched.

'Then what do you suggest?' he asked.

'Have you a spare pair of boots and some clean breeches amongst you?' asked Fithvael, not looking up from examining Groulle's legs.

Freuden nodded dubiously.

'Then fetch them.'

GILEAD JOINED FITHVAEL beside Groulle, as the veteran began to lance the blisters and boils, releasing a strong and sweet stench along with bloodstained, black pus. Gilead picked up a small, soft wineskin from the ground beside Fithvael, weighing it in his hands.

'You plan to anoint a human with this?' Gilead asked, a hard edge to his low voice.

'It is the only way, Gilead. You know it. The rune showed that our people controlled nature in this place.'

'I also know this man is a foolish, worthless hu–'

'And we may yet need him,' interrupted Fithvael. 'You end life if you have to. I will preserve it if I can. And this is the only decent alcohol we have. It will clean his wounds and begin the healing.' And with that Fithvael took one of the last flask of rare Tor Anrok wine from Gilead's hands and began to pour it, a few drops at a time, into Groulle's wounds.

'It is the last of that vintage,' Gilead said harshly.

'Then it should be used to do good.'

ON THE FOLLOWING day, Groulle's wounds were a little better, and he elected to continue with the rest. Progress was slow as they made their way up the side of the mountain in search of an entrance. Gilead and Fithvael had to stop over and over again to wait for the slower, clumsier humans. The guards surrounded their noble master, guiding and helping him, the slowest of them all, up the ever-steeper incline.

In the middle of the afternoon, having travelled only a few hundred yards, Gilead was growing impatient. He would have been faster and safer alone, but there was a price to pay for everything and today the price was a tomb full of ancient elven treasure – and knowledge.

He shook the thought free of his mind and resolved to concentrate on the job in hand. Reaching a jutting, coppery rock, sticking out at shoulder height to his crouched body, Gilead vaulted lightly on to it and, able to stand, he surveyed the mountain face. A little below him and to his right he found what he was looking for. The rock appeared, on closer inspection, to be a little too smooth and Gilead could see a light, reddish haze around it – and the faintest trace of another elven rune, *arhain*, for secrets. This was his entrance.

He waited for the rest of the motley party to assemble below him.

'This is where we go in,' Gilead said, pointing to the flat, copper-grey boulders below.

'Where?' asked the sergeant, 'I see nothing but rock.'

'Then follow me and you will see all,' answered Gilead, dismounting his boulder with easy grace and stepping lightly down a shallow crease, toward his target.

'Wait!' Lord Ottryke commanded. 'If you go in first, how will we know that we can follow? We do not see your entrance.'

'Then you must trust,' Gilead answered, meeting the lord's gaze squarely.

'No!' argued the lord. 'If there is an entrance then we shall send one of my own men in first.'

'L-lord?' stammered the sergeant.

'What is it, man?' the nobleman spat back, exasperated.

'Two of my men have been injured already... and we do not know what lies behind the rocks. It might be more... prudent if the elf did take the lead.'

'The stakes are high, sergeant,' Lord Ottryke snarled. 'Men will be lost. But if you prefer, we will send in the boy. He has little value as a warrior and I question his allegiance. Yes,' he continued, maliciously, 'let us test the boy.'

LYONEN TOOK ONE last, wide-eyed look at Fithvael, who nodded his head gravely, and then he put his hand out to meet a rock face that did not exist. The boy's eyes grew even wider and he felt the sweat drip down the inside of his shirt, down his sides and back. He shuffled his feet out onto the tiny, solid lip before the illusion – and found that the first few inches of his boot were invisible. In another moment both of his arms had disappeared and then his head and torso. Another heartbeat and the guards looked on in horror and amazement as Lyonen's trailing foot, the last they could see of him, disappeared behind the rock face.

Several silent moments passed.

'He's in,' their lord pronounced. 'Proceed!'

But they all stopped in their tracks as they heard a high-pitched, ethereal scream, muffled in the mountainside. They gasped as one skinny, disembodied hand clawed at the air in front of them.

Fithvael was the first to lunge into the rock, disappearing almost before they had seen him move. Then half of his body re-entered daylight, shouting for help. Then he disappeared inside the mountain once more.

FITHVAEL KNELT IN the dark, surrounded by a hazy red light and a rough-hewn tunnel dripping with dark slime. He could see the boy only as shades of grey on grey in the almost total darkness. He let his hands pass over the writhing body on the floor in front of him, until a shattering cry of pain echoed around the tunnel and the boy became still. His breath was coming in short, flat rasps.

Fithvael found the thick haft of a bolt protruding from Lyonen's sternum. Only an inch remained outside his body. It had penetrated too deeply. Fithvael felt the polished, silken texture of the end of the bolt. It spoke to him like only an elf-made missile could speak to an elf warrior. Fithvael's hand covered the eyes of the human boy, while the heel of the other pressed hard and suddenly against the end of the beautifully-wrought elven bolt. The boy had already met his fate at the hand of an elven weapon. All that Fithvael could do for him now was end his suffering.

Fithvael stepped to the edge of the entrance, thrusting his head and hands out through the penetrable rock, so that the rest could see only the irate expression on his face, and the blood staining his hands.

'He is dead!' he said. 'The first of your men is lost, lord, and there was none more loyal in your guard, if you did but know it.'

'But is it *safe*, elf?' Lord Ottryke called.

Fithvael dropped his hands and they disappeared back behind the rock, a look of disgust on his face.

'Who knows how many ancient traps there may yet be in this tomb? Not I,' he said and vanished.

Slowly and with great caution, Ottryke's men followed Fithvael through the hidden entrance into the elf tomb. They lit small lamps and stood around Lyonen's body. In the light they could see the wire he had tripped and the crossbow that had loosed the bolt that killed the boy. It was crude, by elven standards, and any good human scout would have seen it, but it had been too much for the brave initiate.

The medic, Freuden, examined the body. 'What a waste,' he muttered.

'The boy died in the line of duty,' the lord said pompously.

'His name was Lyonen,' Fithvael said coldly, staring into the noble's eyes.

TENSION MOUNTED AS they continued into the mountain. Fithvael was silent, grieving the death of Lyonen, an innocent lad who should not have been there at all.

The guards had begun to mutter amongst themselves. It was becoming obvious to them that their lord was no leader and they must take direction from Gilead, the elf-warrior, if they were to survive. There were no more traps in the tunnel, but the guards stayed close behind Gilead and watched his every move. When the tunnel opened out into a wider, vaulted chamber, they turned to the elf and none dared move into the open before him.

Gilead took a lamp, adjusted the wick to produce more light and then threaded it onto the barbed end of a halberd borrowed from the sergeant. He swung the light out over the cavern floor, which showed up as a series of worn, interlocking tiles, and then around the walls where he could see five dark openings in the rock. The tiles came in two distinct shapes, larger octagons interspersed at intervals by tiny squares. Although worn, the floor was lustrous and fresh in places, and just as the tiles interlocked, so did the intricate pattern of runes engraved upon them too.

'Do you see the pattern?' Gilead asked Fithvael.

'It is simple enough,' Fithvael returned. 'I will go first.' He had read Gilead's mind.

Gilead made his way to the back of the group, passing instructions along the waiting line of guards. When he came to Lord Ottryke, he said simply, 'Follow in the footsteps of the man in front, unless I instruct you to the contrary.' Then he fell in behind the nobleman.

Fithvael began to make his way across the floor, the toes of his boots falling precisely and lightly, two short steps to the right and then a half-stride backward. He kept his eyes on the floor around him, looking for every trap. Groulle came next, working hard to keep himself from staggering on his seared limbs as Fithvael wove his path. Then came Freuden, the apothecary. When he had led the first two men perhaps a third of the way across the floor, Fithvael turned and called to the sergeant, who was just stepping out onto the floor.

'You can no longer follow my path,' Fithvael instructed. 'Listen,' and he gave the sergeant a whole new set of instructions that seemed to lead him to the left of the cavern and away from the first group.

Suddenly the sergeant stopped, two toes perched, almost overlapping on one of the tiny squares of stone tile. He wanted to wipe his sweating hands on his breeches, but dare not, lest he overbalance in the process.

'Where are you sending me?' he called into near darkness, as he felt himself moving further from the lead group.

'You must trust,' Fithvael replied in a low, soothing tone. The sergeant turned his head slightly, he saw the remaining two of his men following in his footsteps and determined that he would not let them down. Taking a deep, slow breath and steadying his mind, the sergeant called again to Fithvael.

'Lead on,' he said.

For the next hour Fithvael led his party across the void, and guided the sergeant. Only Gilead and the lord remained.

'Why do you lead us like children playing at monsters? The floor looks solid enough to me,' Lord Ottryke sniffed disdainfully.

Gilead looked at him and then into the smouldering grey of the light ahead of him. He took a quarrel from the quiver slung across his back, broke it twice over his knee and wrapped it tightly in a scrap of cloth.

'Sergeant,' called Gilead, 'catch this for me.'

He threw the tight little parcel out over the floor. The sergeant's hand, reaching out to grab at the cloth, was suddenly lit with a deep orange fluorescence. The broken arrow had fallen short and now a patch of floor was lit up and pulsing around it. In a moment the quarrel was smouldering with green light and sending off shooting white sparks in all directions. Then the floor became fluid, like oozing, bubbling-hot treacle and the parcel was swallowed into the viscous liquid. Next to the first tile that had dissolved, a second started to melt away, and then a third.

'You go first,' Gilead told the startled-looking nobleman. 'And step only where I instruct you.'

Only Fithvael and Gilead knew that with every group that crossed the floor, the elven magic became less forgiving. It took an hour for Fithvael and his party to cross, more than two for the sergeant and his two men. Ottryke and Gilead only reached the opposite side of the cavern after five gruelling hours. The journey was longer and more treacherous, and all around him tiles were melting away into the treacle ooze that bubbled and belched in disgust. When he finally reached solid ground again, Ottryke looked pale and was shaking violently. The apothecary came to tend him, but was sent away with an exhausted wave of the hand.

'Give me some of your liquor,' he said to Gilead.

'Elven wine is not for human consumption,' the elf lord answered flatly.

Lord Ottryke insisted on resting in the dark, cramped exit of the cavern. Fithvael changed Groulle's dressings and the sergeant went from one guard to the next, clapping each on the back. When he had spoken a few words of encouragement to Groulle, the man laid his hand on Fithvael's shoulder and held his gaze for a moment. No words passed between them.

FITHVAEL JOINED GILEAD in the dark recess of the cavern, farthest away from the grumbling humans.

'Is this wise, Gilead?' he asked. But he got no reply. 'The men are wasted by a lord who does not lead them, confused as to their duty. Where will this end?'

'All the humans are worthless and treacherous,' was all Gilead's reply.

'Lyonen was a worthy lad and the sergeant seems a thoughtful sort, for a human. I believe he is resolved to follow your direction.'

'It matters not,' Gilead said. 'The end will be the same.' And he turned away from his old friend, deep in his own thoughts, a dark look on his face.

THE LIGHT DID not change in the cavern, although outside the dawn was fast breaking. Gilead and Fithvael were preparing to continue their underground journey, and after watching them for a few moments, the sergeant began to round up his men. They had slept little and eaten less; only the encouragement of their superior brought them to their feet. The lord still slept, slumped in an undignified posture, his drool making clean tracks across his filthy cheek.

Despite some respectful shaking, the sergeant could not rouse him and turned to Gilead for instruction. Gilead sighed and unsheathed his sword, sending it ringing against the rock-face beside the man's head. Spluttering and crying out, Lord Ottryke came round with a start, but said nothing when he saw it was Gilead who had awoken him.

FITHVAEL LED THE party down through one of the recesses in the cavern wall and into a narrow, lightless corridor, Gilead again taking his place to the rear, just behind his lordship. The passage was steep and tall, but only wide enough to accommodate the narrow shoulders of an elf. Soon realising that Groulle was struggling, Fithvael advised he remove first his weapons and drag them behind him, and then, only yards later, his heavy outer clothing. Despite the tight squeeze, Groulle complied without question. But when it came to his lord's turn, Ottryke complained vociferously to Gilead, who could still walk easily in the space.

'Find us another route!' Ottryke demanded. 'This was not the only tunnel.'

'Then take another,' came Gilead's reply. 'But be warned: the elven inscriptions weave intricate spells, and only by studying them for hours was Fithvael able to lead us safely.' Gilead spoke calmly, but when Lord Ottryke became red in the face and began blustering in protest, the elf drew his sword in the narrow tunnel, blocking the lord's retreat. In this space, at this range, the human lord was completely unable to defend himself, or call on his guard to defend him. He had no choice. Struggling to turn his back on the elf and continue up the narrow passageway, Lord Ottryke cursed the filthy inhuman beast under his breath. He had never before been humiliated by a man, let alone by an elf such as Gilead.

As the tunnel continued deeper into the mountain, its narrow walls became smoother and were covered in crisp carvings that looked just as they had on the day they were carved. Progress was very slow; all the humans were reduced to travelling sideways, their backs and elbows against one wall.

Groulle continued without complaint, even though his knees and elbows were scraped with every step, leaving trails of fresh blood, which were wiped away by the shirts of the men behind him. The pain was nothing, but he hated to be in contact with those awful elven runes, the same runes that had almost spelt his doom.

Fithvael, a step or two in front of him, ran his hands casually across the carvings as they passed, marvelling at their beauty and smiling at the welcome they spelled out.

In the rearguard of the company, Gilead's hopes began to rise – but with them, his impatience with the party's patron. Ottryke seemed to stop and inspect every last graze and scratch that came his way, huffing his breath and sucking his teeth, lest he say anything that might cause Gilead to turn on him again. He refused to remove even his outer clothing and kept hold of his weapon, for all the good it would do him, long after his guards had shed theirs. It was plain from his face that only his greed was keeping him going.

Ottryke forgot every complaint in the blink of an eye when the tunnel came to an abrupt end. Below him, as he gazed down from the top of a deeply terraced slope, he could see it all – his new-found wealth was spread below him in a gleaming, glistening mountain of beautiful, elven objects. His men were spread along the top terrace, in various stages of tattered undress, looking down in awe and wonder at the sight they beheld. Groulle's face was pale and grey in the strange internal twilight of the cavern, his eyes bulging, unblinking. Freuden stared wearily, his face a picture of disbelief. Their sergeant stood next to Fithvael, grinning.

'May you find your own riches here too,' he said quietly to the elf.

Then Gilead, the last, stepped out onto the terrace. He watched in disgust as Lord Ottryke stumbled, incoherently down the terraces, taking huge, rambling strides, stripping off his heavy leather jerkin and helm as he went, cackling and screeching. To Gilead the nobleman looked like nothing better than a drunken street brawler floundering after some voluptuous but disinterested whore.

'The documents are mine. The history is mine.' Gilead reminded him in a firm tone. 'Take the gold – but leave me my people.'

Lord Ottryke turned in bewilderment. 'What care I for you or your precious dead?' he said rhetorically, and turning back to his prize, threw himself down the last of the terraces until he was waist deep in cold, heavy gold.

Fithvael and Gilead carefully picked their way through the ancient treasures. The air was dry and sweet smelling, and everything looked perfect. It took some time, but the two elves, searching methodically, finally found a series of leather cases, boxes and cylinders, standing together in a three-sided, stone repository, kept separate from the rest of the artefacts.

All around them they could hear the commands of Lord Ottryke and the bustle of his men as they hurried to obey his frantic commands. They all wandered around, trying to assess the bulk and weight of the relics in order to work out a way of removing them to the lord's manor.

Ottryke himself had given up counting his wealth and had already begun to spend it in his mind, perhaps to oust his cousin, the Elector of Altdorf, from his seat. Wealth and power, power and wealth; inextricably tied in Ottryke's mind they meant only one thing – greed.

GILEAD LOOKED LONGINGLY at the real treasures he had found. He sat on the polished stone floor for what seemed like an age, examining the heavily embossed leather, strewn with golden runes that seemed to flicker and change shape before his eyes. He looked at the great, scrolling gold clasps and hinges. He breathed in the beauty of the craftsmanship and the perfection of the proportions of each piece.

Fithvael stood behind him, not quite knowing what to say, but hoping, perhaps for the first time, that their long quest might finally bear fruit. He crushed the hope before it grew too great for his mind to contain, and closed a mental door on it, for now at least. Between them, he knew that he and Gilead could carry the entire burden of the history held in these sacred books and scrolls. His only other concern was how to safely leave the tomb. They could not return the way they had come. The elves who had built and booby-trapped this place had been far too clever for that. He began to look about him for answers and quickly found them high above them in the soaring, vaulted ceilings. He and Gilead could surely escape, but what of the humans? Would they have the skills or the stamina required?

As Fithvael pondered this dilemma, his eyes were drawn down again by a low, fearful gasp. As he looked down at his friend, he saw Gilead snatch back his hand as if burnt in a furnace, then a tiny cloud of dust settled in a yellowish smudge on the perfectly white floor.

'Too late!' Gilead whispered in terror. 'We come too late!' With these words he rose on his knees, threw his head back and let out a vicious scream of pain and despair.

'What… what is it?' Fithvael asked, after the cry had subsided. 'What is it, old friend?' he asked, his hand hovering inches above Gilead's shoulder, which, as much as he longed to, he could not bring himself to touch.

When he got no answer, Fithvael leaned over Gilead's slumped body to rest his hand on a beautifully tooled leather scroll within his reach. His fingertips had barely rested upon it before it was gone, crumbling into the air. Gilead's second anguished howl did all the rest. All around them, whether because of some charm triggered by their presence or even the new air they had let in to this ancient place, everything was crumbling to nought. Whatever precious knowledge might have been preserved here was now lost.

When the echoes of the horrible sound died, they were followed by another bellow. A deep-seated belly laugh, almost as raucous as the cry had been terrifying, filled the chamber. Lord Ottryke pointed one stubby finger at Gilead, rolled back his head and roared with laughter.

'Your race is dead!' he said maliciously, his mouth wide with laughter. 'I have it all! And you – you have nothing!

'NOTHING!' he screamed, the laughter over. All that remained in the noble's face was triumph and hatred.

Lord Ottryke raised his arms and turned full circle, inviting his guard to hail him the victor. Slowly they too began to laugh and point. Groulle looked ashamed and embarrassed for a moment, but caught the infection soon enough and he too laughed along with the others. Freuden took one sympathetic look at Fithvael's blank, bleak expression and he too began to snigger, almost in spite of himself. At the back of the group, the sergeant sat down heavily. His drooping head shook slightly and he covered his face in his hands. But the gesture alone was not enough to save him when weighed against the scorn and derision of his company.

THE JOURNEY INTO the mountain had taken days. The journey out, undertaken by two lone elves, took merely hours.

They walked away from the mountain, ignoring the faint, distant cries that turned to screams behind them, and retraced their steps to their waiting steeds. Gilead had brought nothing out of the mountain with him. Tucked inside Fithvael's outer garment was a scrap of bloody cloth embroidered with an elven rune, the last remains of a new tabard, once worn by the youngest member of Lord Ottryke's household guard. If Lyonen had survived perhaps Fithvael could have found some way to save all the humans.

When they reached their steeds, Fithvael pulled the scrap of cloth from its place against his heart and stowed it in his saddlebag. Gilead watched for a moment and then caught Fithvael's gaze.

'I have broken no bond,' he said.

'Let me grieve for the boy, at least,' answered Fithvael.

'You must grieve as your heart instructs you,' said Gilead. 'I made a contract with the scum lord to lead him into the tomb, a one way journey. He neither requested, nor paid, for a return trip.'

And with that Gilead mounted his horse and started to ride back down the mountain, away from his people's crumbling past and away from Ottryke Manor.

V

GILEAD'S TEST

*Promise me only this: look into my
eyes and see what I see.*

ENOUGH NOW. YOU'VE had your share of tales from me this night. I'm tired, and the cold gets to my old bones. Sit up, if you will. Drink my wine, enjoy the heat of my fire. My bedroll calls for me and my throat is hoarse from too many stories.

Well, of course there are more. More of Gilead, of loyal Fithvael. More sad and bloody stories of their twilight world.

So they are just myths, are they? Think what you will. I know better. Myths are ten a penny and the land is full of them. The stories in my head are made of better stuff. Truth, for a start...

You doubt me? Well then, hear this one before I retire.

Time had gone by since their dealings at Ottryke Manor. Perhaps a year, maybe two, maybe less. And there was a battle. Bloody, devastating, furious. The hills and woods rang with the sound. Such deeds were done, but what matters for my story happened afterwards.

The battle was at an end. There was nothing more to be known except the dirge of the wind, sighing through the blackened elms that marked that deep tract of the Drakwald.

Fithvael began to rouse. It was cold and lightless as he lay on the dank earth of the battlefield. Yet it was neither the chill nor damp that had woken him. His unconsciousness had been broken by the singular strangeness of a warm, pulsing body lying against his. It was a sensation he did not particularly relish.

Fithvael drew his body carefully away from the warmth. He could sense his own fragility, though he could locate no definite pain. He could feel with every fibre of his warrior instinct the devastation that surrounded him.

But he had no memory of where or how or why.

He cleared his nose of ash and blood and the first invasion of scents brought back stark reminders of the ten-year quest he had undertaken with Gilead, and their continued fight against the darknesses of the world. It was the stench of unnatural flesh. Dead, unnatural flesh. It was the putrefying, astringent odour of Chaos, a stench that could be mistaken for nothing else.

Slowly, the veteran warrior elf allowed his other senses to return. Now he could feel the pitted earth beneath his body and the places where puddles of gore and stale water had formed, soaking into his outer garments and making his joints feel rigid and useless. He wanted nothing more than to move, to release his stiff, locked body and relax the muscles that were tightening with revulsion against his surroundings.

But first he would listen, tune his hearing to this place and discover if his life was at any immediate risk.

The silence was nearly entire save for the pulse and breath of the body that remained utterly still beside him. There was a reassuring taste in his mouth. The sweet-sour taste of sleep and his last long-forgotten meal. The feared metallic tang of his own blood and bile was entirely, blissfully absent. At least he had suffered no grievous injury.

Regaining his confidence, Fithvael gradually opened his eyes. He had hoped against reason that the body beside his own would be Gilead's, broken perhaps, but alive and stable, needful of the elf's ministrations. It was not to be, and the veteran warrior smothered his disappointment.

Fithvael and Gilead could never be as close as the twin siblings, Gilead and Galeth, had been. But the swordmaster had devoted his life to Gilead and to the quest when Galeth had died, and their relationship had become intensely close. On the battlefield, they fought as one and could communicate any amount of information with a glance or the nod of a head. They had one goal, represented one force. Their relationship had long since ceased to be that of master and servant, man and boy, or even companions. They were as much at one as two such singular, disparate individuals could ever be.

Fithvael's elven eyes adjusted instantaneously to the last of the night's darkness. He smiled to himself and moved freely for the first time in hours. His mare turned her head to him, whinnied and then stood up from her resting-place beside her master. Her vigil was over.

As HE FELT the hilt of his sword come into contact with his assailant's sternum, Gilead turned and swiftly scanned the area again. Time was short on any battlefield, even for a warrior of his consummate skill and shadowfast abilities. Yes, Fithvael was still with him, a hundred paces to his right, fighting strong.

The foe were all around them. Tall, darkly noble, yet twisted and corrupt. Elves, kin and yet not kin. Blasphemous parodies of their race, death pale, dressed in reeking black armour, eyes rotting in skulls, breaths foul from black-lipped mouths. Their rusting armour was decorated in flaking gilt, fading silks, worm-eaten brocades.

The last son of Tor Anrok and his swordmaster had penetrated the darkest depths of the southern Drakwald in search of the Tower of Talthos Elios, the birthplace of lost Niobe. They had uncovered recently coined tales that said Talthos Elios stood watch over a foul barrow, an ancient crypt that legend said descended into hell itself. Wars had been fought there, skirmishes of light against dark, until the line of Elios had sundered the spawn of darkness and driven it underground. From that day, their tower had stood, guarding the breach against further incursions.

So the myths said, and the land is full of them. But it was a start, the faint hope of a clue, and Gilead had seized at it eagerly.

Rumours came to them thick and fast as they trekked into the great forest. Rumours of darkness reawakened, of a custodianship long fallen away. And then, all at once, the enemy had been on them. Not beastmen, not bulky warrior clans of Chaos.

Elves. Ruined elves. Broken, twisted, decayed echoes of noble warriors.

Gilead wrenched his blade from a weeping chest. He swung the sword again, in a singing arc, drawing the weight of his body around with it and sinking it so deep into the neck of the assailant behind him that it just stood, expressionless and quite literally dead on its feet.

The stench of the bubbling, tarry fluids that gouted from the fatal, gaping wound would have been more than enough to fell a weaker constitution. It gave Gilead the merest moment to breathe and regroup. The body shielded Gilead from the onslaught of another, which had to tear its own comrade down to lunge at Gilead head on. Its jagged rows of black teeth were bared, and its lean arms, each ending in a mass of bloodied spikes, flailed wildly at the warrior elf.

Gilead took advantage of the fact that he was holding his longsword low, two-handed, in front of him. He simply raised the blade as this latest horror surged forward. It was an easy kill. The tip of the long sword entered the enemy's gut low, the hilt crashing home against a grotesquely misshapen codpiece. Gilead began to pull the blade free, but his adversary grabbed at it with its spike-armoured fists. The warrior sliced upwards, cutting both bestial hands in half, and his sword finally came to rest against the neck seal of the dying enemy's body armour.

Gilead's eyes swept in another arcing scan, once, twice... Fithvael was gone. But the fighting was not over yet.

Gilead had quested for ten long years to avenge his brother's death. The ghost of Galeth had remained with him throughout, but the living twin seemed neither of this world nor the next. Ten years of his life had been spent fighting the forces of evil to bring down one pathetic man. He questioned, often, the value of his task. There was no satisfaction.

Yet his struggle had continued and chiefly because of Fithvael. At first,

Gilead had been compromised into fighting on the side of right. Now it had become his life, he would use whatever force was at his disposal to war against the darkness until the day of his death came and released him from this violent existence.

He had no brother now, and precious few kin in this fading age of the world. But he would fight. Fight on. Against the darkness.

And so he fought now, plunging hard steel into misshapen bodies, severing limbs, scything through torsos and necks, disgorging the foul-smelling ichor and mortal fluids of the things. Gilead abhorred his enemies, bodies corrupted and twisted, infested with evil. From their stench and their symbols he knew them. Bestial, lasciviously decorated devotees of the abomination, Slaanesh.

Gilead fought on as the earth beneath his feet turned to gore-soaked clay. Dark water gathered in the prints left by the heavy footfalls of the enemy. Bodies fell in all directions as the screams and battle cries of the foe became fewer. With every fresh onslaught, with every breath taken after the kill, Gilead's eyes swept the field. Fithvael was still nowhere to be seen.

Then it came. His concentration must have waned momentarily, his thoughts with Fithvael or perhaps with Galeth, instead of with the foe. He was felled. Felled by the last surviving enemy on the field. A foe, fatally wounded, but not yet dead. Gilead's body reeled, parodying his own gymnastic battle-swings, and his startled face watched as his assailant collapsed to his knees. The foe's cadaverous, drawn visage slapped into the cloying mud just before Gilead's head came to rest on its dead back.

As THE SUN began to rise, Fithvael led his horse out of the carnage to a green place with fresh water. He tethered her there and she contentedly began a hearty breakfast. She had earned it. But Fithvael needed more. He needed to find Gilead.

Fithvael did not remember the battle, nor did he recall the last time he had seen his partner. His intention was to follow the course of the battle, mapping its action as he went. He picked his way across the field, no more than a hundred yards or so wide and about the same long. He counted some three dozen bodies, but Gilead's, thankfully, was not among them. The pair of elf warriors had taken on and utterly destroyed an entire band of the foul wights. There were no mounts, so wherever Gilead had gone, his trusted horse had gone with him. A second good omen.

Fithvael began to distinguish his own kills from Gilead's. It wasn't difficult. His own were neat and accurate enough, but Gilead's were a sight to behold. With each group of bodies, Fithvael was able to track every move the elf warrior had made. His mind's eye noted every pirouette, every firm stance. Each lunge, parry and faint came clearly to him. He felt nothing but immense respect for Gilead's fighting skills. Every kill was clean. There were no false starts, no unnecessary swings, no butchery. One stroke, one swing, one plunging blade had destroyed each monster in its turn. Fithvael took in the wide variety of strokes that Gilead had brought to bear in the battle. He could almost hear the whistle of the blade through the air and could even detect where and when the elf had changed hands. His three-finger grip was as effective as the conventional four-finger grip of Gilead's whole hand. Gilead had lost his finger, but Galeth had been there to save him on that occasion, so long ago.

The exercise of dissecting the battlefield began to clear and concentrate Fithvael's mind. He remembered events from the day before and of the week, month and year, but nothing seemed important since Gilead was missing. The veteran warrior spent the rest of that day crossing and re-crossing the battlefield, breaking it down into a grid and searching each sector for clues of his friend. There were no footprints to be found, the earth was a mess of gore and tarry puddles and the enemies' decaying bodies covered most of it in any case. So Fithvael began to look a little deeper.

He found his eyes continually drawn to the corpses of the foe. So like his own kind, so unlike. Elven forms corrupted from within, their ancient armour and weapons tarnished and overlaid with the dank remnants of satin swathes and gold-leaf. What had befallen these... these things? What misery had overtaken their lives, overcome them with rancorous passions and destroyed them?

He set it from his mind.

He could find no shreds or fragments torn from Gilead's garments, no shards of armour, no hair. The elf had left nothing of himself behind in the carnage. Fithvael counted this the third good omen. Even his scent was absent. It would have been hard to detect over the heavy backdrop of malodorous Chaos, but if Gilead's blood had been spilled, his old friend would have found the traces.

With the fall of his second night on the battlefield, Fithvael retired to the green haven where he had left his mare, content in the knowledge that Gilead was alive somewhere. All day he had used physical evidence to work out what had happened. All night he exercised his mind with suppositions and possibilities. He could only conjecture, but the one thing he could be sure of was that something had caused Gilead either to leave his old friend or to forget him. If Gilead had searched the battlefield, as Fithvael had done, he would have quickly found the veteran, in spite of the dark, cold and carnage. He would not have passed the old warrior off for dead. He would have rescued him and ministered to his needs. Of course, the old elf had suffered some amnesia, but his mind had never lost sight of Gilead. Evil was as thick in the atmosphere as the smell of the Chaos spawn, but surely the elf warrior's mind was too strong to succumb to the dark influences?

So, Gilead was alive, unscathed, physically at least. Yet Fithvael knew that he must find his old friend, for something was sorely amiss.

GILEAD'S HEAD NODDED in the light slumber of semi-consciousness. He knew that he was mounted and could sense the reins in his hands, but he was unaware that a rope attached to the bridle was leading his horse. If he had realised, he would simply have assumed that he was being led by Fithvael, for there was no one else. He could not awake, he could not summon the energy to rouse himself. Yet neither could he quite comprehend his own complacency.

He slumbered on, unaware of time and space and unconscious of any needs, desires or appetites. He questioned nothing.

DAWN AGAIN. FITHVAEL had slept little. His mind would not still.

He rose to his elbows on the cold ground and resolved he would begin a new quest. A quest for Gilead, and if it took ten years, as the quest to the memory of Galeth had taken, then so be it. Pray that Gilead was lost to some other fate than death.

THE ROOM WAS softly lit with candle lamps, whose steady flames illuminated wall hangings, depicting epic battles between noble elf White Lions and Chaos beastmen. The rugs that covered the stone flags of the floor were deep and warm-looking in the muted colours of autumn and the heavy, rough-hewn items of furniture were rendered majestic by the gold and silver shawls and cloths that covered them and made them inviting. On a little table by his bed stood a pitcher of water and a bowl of sweet-smelling petals. Soft clothes for bathing his wounds half obscured an ornate little hand mirror in its gilt frame. The soft light of the candles flickered and reflected in the bright surface of the mirror, casting light on Gilead's face.

Gilead rolled lightly over in the warmth of a clean, sweet-smelling bed, and awoke. He suddenly knew the kind of comfort that he had long denied himself. Fully alert for only a moment, he sighed and spread his limbs in the luxurious space.

'Awake, warrior. Your slumber was both long and deep.' He heard the low, soft cadences of his own people, spoken in the lilting, breathy tones of a young woman. Familiar, somehow. 'Awake now and take a little sustenance, sir.' Her voice was so beautiful, and so familiar, that he dared not open his eyes lest he be dreaming.

'Let him sleep a little, daughter. There is time enough.' The same voice, but male and lower, with the slight creak of age, but familiar, and elven – wonderful to Gilead's ear.

He opened his eyes, not knowing how long he had slept, nor how he had come to this place. Comfort dulled his instinct to enquire. He felt clean and could sense the ointment on his bruises. He smelled, not of the battlefield, but of fragrant soaps and unguents and of sweet sleep. Someone had tended him gently and well.

'Father, he wakes!' That familiar voice rose slightly with delight, and a smile showed the neatest row of small, white teeth in a frame of perfect lips. Gilead smiled back and adjusted the sheet around his torso.

'Leave us, child.' Her father dismissed her and she left the room, casting one last gaze down at Gilead. A gaze that showed him her entire face in all its elven glory. The wide-set eyes and lean, straight nose of his kind; the deep, intelligent brow and narrow jaw. Niobe! It was Niobe!

Her father smiled down at him. 'Welcome, warrior. Welcome to the Tower of Talthos Elios.'

'Then... I have found it?'

'You were searching for us? We are... perhaps hard to find. We have secreted ourselves in the darkness of the forest for many years. These are lean, dangerous times.'

Gilead look up. 'Who am I to thank for salvation?'

'I am Gadrol Elios. I welcome you here.'

'Your daughter–'

'She told me how you rescued her, son of Tor Anrok. I am in your debt. I am happy to have rescued you in return.'

'But how did she escape... escape the Chaos scum, Ire?'

'Niobe was never less than inventive. She slipped his bonds after you weakened him, and found her way home.'

Gilead remained in bed for several days, receiving visits from Lord Gadrol, and meals and other necessities from elf servants of the court. On the second day, Niobe reappeared and with her came the reassuring scent of the woods and herbs that she had gathered to tend him with. The same plants administered to his cuts and bruises when he would skirmish with Galeth as a child. The same he had used to restore Fithvael to health after the fool had come to the aid of a the human girl Betsen Ziegler, without Gilead's help...

Fithvael?

Gilead became agitated.

'Your friend fell on the field...'

'I saw him. No, that's not correct: I lost sight of him. I don't truly know what happened,' Gilead interrupted his nurse.

Niobe soothed the warrior's mind with her gentle words and calm, lullaby tones. 'The rescue party found only you alive on the battlefield amongst so many monsters. The carrion beasts had been at work. There was little left of any corpse. It must be your dear friend met a heroic death. To take on so many and to triumph. You two, alone, fought and killed three dozen of the dark ones.'

'And what are they?'

'The old curse. Half-formed ghouls from the barrow it is our duty to guard. Chaos once more raises its head in these gloomy forests.'

Gilead fell silent, not really hearing her as she spoke further. Fithvael was dead. Fithvael was dead.

Throughout the third day and the fourth, the Lord of the Court came to listen to Gilead's story. Gadrol spoke too, in turn, of the rise of the dead things from beneath the barrow, rotting things that came stinking their way out of the earth to haunt the living. Dark beings from a vale beyond. Once more his tower's garrison had armed to guard the land. The barrow-kind held a sway of fear across this region. Raids, murders and the like were common. One of Gadrol's patrols had found Gilead. The warrior had countered a raiding pack from the barrow single-handedly.

He... and his fallen friend, of course.

Gilead was sad, but strong and resolute before the older elf. When he spoke to Niobe as she nursed him, his voice often broke and he openly mourned the loyal Fithvael, the last of his questing warriors. On the evening of the fourth day, Niobe took the little mirror from the table beside Gilead's bed. 'Look into the mirror,' said Niobe, 'see who you are and all that means for the future.'

Gilead looked into the mirror, and was surprised at what he saw there. His skin was clear and bright and he was clean-shaven. He looked like the carefree young warrior who had sparred with his twin and laughed and played and enjoyed life. He thought that time, his quest and the battlefield had aged him and made him cynical, but he did not see life's scars in his face. It gave him hope, brought him calm.

AS DAWN BROKE, Fithvael awoke with a start. His dreams had brought him nothing but anguish. He was exhausted, fatigued by tortured sleep and restless nightmares; wracked with the aches and pains of an agile but ageing body punished on the field of battle; troubled by the ever-present stench of Chaos in the air and by Gilead's absence. All of his faculties were compromised, but he hadn't enough sense left to realise it. His body and spirit were broken and his tired mind increasingly obsessed.

Fithvael contented himself with a handful of clean water for his breakfast. He didn't remember when he had last eaten a meal. He untethered the mare and began to lead her in a wide sweep around the battlefield. She whinnied and snorted and kept her muzzle upwind of the foul arena.

Only hours later did Fithvael find what he was looking for. He had been circling, resolutely, since dawn and must have passed the hoof prints several times already. He and Gilead had ridden into battle and Gilead had ridden out, but these were the only tracks the veteran had found and he would follow them, blind now to reason and probability.

Fithvael sat astride his horse hour upon hour, following whatever hoofprint trail he happened upon, regardless of direction or number. He did not feel useless now. He was on a quest.

GILEAD'S GRIEF WAS sharp and weighed heavy upon him. Heavier because he was surrounded by his own kind. He would see Fithvael's wisdom in the old lord's face, or recognise the old warrior's tone in the words of a servant at the court. His pain dulled only with the kindnesses of Niobe. Her soft words were as effective a sedative as her sweet-tasting tonics. To find her again... it was a victory, a blessing.

A week passed, two, a month. He roused himself, first from his bed and then from his chamber, and soon he began to take his meals with the family and their courtly retinue. They made him welcome and celebrated his recovery, and also talked about the constant threat of the barrow. In turn he recounted for them stories of his quest and of his warriors' unerring bravery. He told how, one by one, he had lost them all and he recounted for them the heroic death of each of his questing comrades.

For Niobe, Gilead saved the stories of his home, the tower he had abandoned before taking up his life-quest. He told her of his dead twin, Galeth, and of how he believed he had taken on his sibling's life force to conquer evil. He talked of Fithvael, of the dead elf's loyalty to the old traditions and ideals of Gilead's ancient family. A family that would become extinct with his own death.

Niobe sat for many hours, head bowed over some piece of woman's work, while she listened intently to Gilead's epic tales. At these times, Gilead's feelings would sometimes catch him unawares and he would find himself searching her face for signs of her response to him.

When he was alone Gilead would lift the mirror to his face and see there something new and positive, at last, for the future. He began to forget Fithvael and Galeth and the hard fight and pain of his past.

THE AIR WAS cold and moist and the dusk a dirty brown. Fithvael could not distinguish the dense, grey cloud from the murky, tumultuous sky. Night was falling, sluggish, heavy and moonless. There were no stars to navigate by, even if the old elf had known where he was or which way he needed to go. Fithvael was so tired that he had long since dropped the mare's reins and was allowing her to meander through thickening woodland. Everything fell into a flat sepia-grey landscape, and he could no longer see colour or judge distance.

Days without food and with little water had taken its toll on Fithvael and his mount, and the mare slowed to an exhausted stop, bent her head and slowly grazed the woodland clearing. Fithvael slumped across her warm neck, then slowly rolled off her back, landing heavily on his empty, aching side. Sleep, he must sleep. Pulling his cloak around his head, Fithvael gave in to his fatigue, trusting that his horse would stand guard for him once more.

Who knows how long he slept? Dull, dark days wove seamlessly into cold, dark nights. There was no sun to wake him. The mare lay beside her master as the old elf sweated and twitched and cried out. Delirious dreams tortured his sleep. Awake, his mind had been full of Gilead, of tracking him, finding him, fighting for him. He'd thought of nothing else since waking on the battlefield, but nothing of his rational mind was left in his slumber, and the nightmares raged.

Gilead was dead. Gilead was dying. Gilead was being torn apart by a horde of cannibal beastmen. Gilead was walking towards him, body slashed open, oozing decaying gore, trying to say something through broken, seeping lips. Gilead was coming back from the dead. Gilead was a monster.

Even Fithvael's dreams did not wake him. He fought his way through them, killing Chaos beasts, reaching Gilead too late. Over and over again the dream circled round in his head and each time the veteran warrior fought harder and dirtier. He needed to get to Gilead faster. Each time he was too late.

Yet again the stench of Chaos was in the air and abruptly he was awake. Fithvael sprang to his feet, knees bent, arms wide. His staring eyes flicked around the clearing, penetrating the foliage, searching out the enemy. A shadow moved and the warrior plunged towards it, a weapon in each thrashing hand, arms flailing, a howl screaming from his dry throat. He threw himself on the adversary's back, plunging twin blades into its collarbone, shoulders, arms, indiscriminately stabbing and scratching at the thing that had taken Gilead. At last the enemy, a corrupted echo of an elf warrior, sloughed off the berserk Fithvael, dropping him unceremoniously on his back and staggered away, trying to staunch a bursting gash in its neck.

Fithvael lay on his back in the failing brown sunlight, awake, breathing hard. The enemy had been real, and, fuelled by his dreams, the old warrior had injured it and sent it on its way. Tired and starved though he was, Fithvael found new purpose. He felt weak and winded and knew he must eat, but he also now had a beast to track. A direct lead back to Gilead. He had a chance. He had hope.

The mare had a full belly and was well rested. The old warrior gathered together some supplies and ate some of the fruits and nuts he had found. He shook out his dirty, crumpled cloak and washed away the ichor that had splashed from the foe's random wounds. He took a little time, knowing that the beast would be moving slowly. He didn't want to catch up with it. He didn't want to have to kill it before he had found his friend. The pleasure of the kill would come later when he was fitter, when he had tracked it to its lair and to Gilead.

THE TOWER OF Talthos Elios was built inside the four sides of a large, open courtyard. It rose into the grey sky, above the drab walls and black-leafed trees, like a finger of ice. A glassy, perfect structure, the work of the gifted and blessed of Tiranoc's dispossessed offspring centuries before. The curtain walls that faced the outside world were thick and solid, without windows. This was a fortress from the outside, but a haven within. The walls that overlooked the courtyard had many windows and doors and even balconies and internal verandas. Gilead began regularly to take up a position on one of the tower's first floor balconies and watch the business of the day unfold below him.

This was where the lord's warriors would practice their combat skills, exercising and sparring with blunted weapons. Gilead began to long for their company and to share his skills with them.

Late one afternoon, Lord Gadrol joined Gilead and they began to talk of the world outside the tower, and the endless duty of the Elios line. The barrow lay in the dark combe beyond the walls and the warriors of the tower patrolled the woodlands. They alone guarded the barrow-breach, an ancient wound in the order of the world and one now recently reopened. It was a hard and unforgiving duty. Gadrol welcomed any help he could get.

Three or four months after being brought to the castle, Gilead was in the courtyard with the other warriors, revelling in the staged battles and the camaraderie. His body had become soft with recovery and with lack of exercise, but his mind was as sharp as ever.

By the half year, he was spending fewer nights carousing with the household and longer days honing his body to its former levels of combat-fitness. He often laughed, in the early days, as he failed to parry a shot from his sparring partner, or lunged too late and fell over his own feet. But as time passed the value of his war-craft came back to him, and with it his old fighting skills. Once more he could wield a sword in either hand, he could move with the kind of dancer's grace that had always characterised his defensive strategy and, finally, late one afternoon, he became shadowfast.

He had spent all day sparring in the courtyard with the Elios warriors who had become his friends and allies. Suddenly Gilead sensed an attack from behind, then another to his left. It was a regular habit of the warriors to ambush each other in this manner, for battle awareness or, at the end of a long day, for fun.

Gilead's adrenalin began to pump hard. He disarmed the elf before him, spinning his opponent's wooden stick high into the air before catching it deftly and boxing the elf on the ears in a resounding double blow. While the practice pole was still in mid-air, he had spun round, dropping the warrior behind him with a swing to the legs. A second blow to the back of the knees sent Gilead's unsuspecting assailant sprawling across the cobbled courtyard, landing him face down with a severe crack to the head. The third elf had no time to fight off the advance of two twirling, spinning staffs. He did not see them coming. One cracked his sword arm at the shoulder and the second beat, point first, hard into his sternum, winding him. Then the first staff came back, wrapping itself around his neck. Gilead had almost strangled the bewildered, broken wretch before he relaxed and let the elf drop, gratefully, to the cobbles.

One moment Gilead had been struggling furiously against one sparring partner. The next he was in three places at once; defending himself simultaneously on three fronts; disarming and felling three fine warriors in no time, with no apparent linear progress. Shadowfast, as of old.

On the ground lay three spent warriors, breathing hard and reaching for the wooden weapon-substitutes that had been broken or confiscated in Gilead's onslaught. He looked at them for a moment, aghast, then began to laugh, throwing his head back in a hearty roar.

He was close to his old pitch of ability. He longed now for more than practise. To face the ever-present incursions of darkness from the barrow, with these brave warriors at his side.

In the meantime he, somewhat sheepishly, helped two of his combatants to their feet. The third was carried away, unconscious. They all took several days to recover sufficiently to rejoin Gilead and their fellows in the exercise yard.

THE SKIES NEVER cleared and the foliage grew ever more dense around Fithvael, but the trail was hot with gore and ichor, and the tracking was easy.

The wounded foe had but one purpose: to return whence it had come. It made no attempts to cover its tracks or move with any stealth. Camouflage was unnecessary for both the pursued and its pursuer, since nothing was visible in the depths of the densely wooded landscape. Fithvael was careful, though, not to be heard and at regular intervals he ate and rested, building his strength.

Fithvael came upon the broken body of the foe less than an hour's gentle ride from his last halt. Cautiously, he dismounted and stood beside the body. He could feel its warmth and sensed that it was still pulsing. If it was not dead, then it could still lead Fithvael to his quarry.

The old elf remounted and the mare took a step or two backwards, then Fithvael reared her, letting out a fierce war cry of his own as the mare whinnied and snorted in surprise and stamped her front feet hard. The noise seemed massive in the still and quiet of the forest, but the wight was not roused. Fithvael reared the mare again, dancing her in a circle around the fallen thing, crashing amongst the undergrowth and clanging his long sword and dagger together over his head. The single-minded elf did not perceive the risk of raising hell in an area rife with Chaos. His only thought was to drag this sorry half-corpse back to consciousness.

The dark one whimpered, then screamed, convulsing in the filth of torn undergrowth and damp, peaty earth around him. Fithvael dismounted, still crashing his weapons together and letting out his ancient war cry. It could feel neither fear nor motivation. It couldn't, wouldn't stand. Then it ceased to writhe. It glared up at Fithvael, ichor still finding an oozing path through the thick, crusting scabs around its dozen or more wounds. He saw it wanting nothing, except to kill him.

It couldn't even do that.

Fithvael turned his back on the beast, bitter and angry that his plan had failed. Then rage crept into his eyes and overtook him. His long sword entered the fallen thing's chest a split second before the dagger reopened the fatal wound in its neck. Death was instant now, but Fithvael took no pleasure in it.

The old warrior had no choice but to continue his quest in any way possible. He assessed, as best he could, the direction the beast had been taking and decided to follow its course. He moved faster now, more urgently. His dream kept flashing in his mind, images of the forest-wights intercut with the knowledge that, in his nightmares he had been too late. Too late to save his friend. Too late to rescue Gilead and renew their partnership.

Fithvael fought his feverish mind… and lost. He began to crash through the forest, heedless of the noise he made and the trail he left. Forgetting that woodland was his natural home, his natural ally, the elf tore a path through the forest, destroying as he went. The ground was churned up beneath the now frantic hooves of the frightened mare, and all but the largest of the trees were hacked aside out of his path.

His mind would not see an end to the struggle, so when the elf suddenly found himself in a steep, sheer pass of black conifers it was a moment before his sword arm rested and he reined in and calmed his mount.

His paranoia turned to glee. In the distance before him, Fithvael could see the tall, glinting sides of a structure. Taking refuge in the lea of the trees, he stopped and looked again. A fortress, a tower, a dank place of evil, this was the monstrous place where he would find his friend. This was where the foe had been making for.

THE TOWER OF Talthos Elios glowed with magnificence. Pennants and banners were raised in the great hall. Gold and silver cloth adorned the benches and grander courtly chairs around the long table, which groaned under the weight of the food that covered it. Meat, fowl and game of all kinds were arranged amongst wide dishes, standing on tall feet, which were heaped with mountains of spices, fruit and bread.

There was to be a grand feast day on the morrow and the Lord Gadrol and his fair daughter Niobe were arranging everything. It was a special occasion and Gilead was to be the guest of honour. He had resided at the castle for a year, so tomorrow was to be his anniversary and his formal inauguration into the court. He was to become one of them and to have so illustrious a warrior join their cause delighted all at the castle. They had every reason to celebrate.

Gilead, too, was ready to celebrate and eager to become a full member of this society. They had so much to offer: companionship, a good cause… and then there was Niobe. The reason he was here. The beautiful elf maiden had restored Gilead's health, ministered to his needs when he was mourning Fithvael, been constant companion and confidante. She had even made a radiant new suit of gold and blue for Gilead to wear on his feast day.

AS FITHVAEL ADVANCED up the pass, coming ever closer to the tower, the last remnant of caution left the veteran warrior. The tower was derelict, dilapidated. Its walls stood tall and square to the outside world, but as he cast his eyes towards the top of the walls, the stone seemed insubstantial. He couldn't focus on individual stones; they seemed to move around each other and he could see the sky through them. The lower walls of the edifice were covered in a brackish black slime of moss and lichens. Fithvael placed his hands on the stone, but felt only the softness of the moss. There was nothing solid there. Working his way around the outside walls, Fithvael found the space where a doorway had once been. One huge, black-studded rotten door still hung from one hinge, the other had fallen inward towards what must once had been a courtyard, but was now a wilderness of rock and dead and dying plant-life.

The warrior elf was confused and disappointed. He had been convinced that this was the place. This was surely where Gilead was being held. Yet there was no sign of him or anyone – until a swift, unseen blow felled him from behind.

GILEAD WAS SPARRING in the courtyard, as usual, when the slumped body was carried in. Patrols left from the castle at regular intervals, but since Gilead had been brought here there had been no new arrivals. He was excited to see that the elf guards' latest expedition had been more successful.

Dropping his wooden weapons and nodding his thanks to his sparring partner, Gilead bounded towards the two warriors who carried another, ragged elf between them. Fithvael was unconscious, one arm around each of the warriors' shoulders, feet dragging across the courtyard and his head down. Gilead did not recognise his old friend at first. He simply wanted to help this newcomer, this stranger like himself. He threw the body over his shoulder and took him up to his own room, the room where Niobe had nursed him back to health.

Only when Gilead had gently laid his burden on the clean bed, did the elf realise that it was his dearest friend who had been rescued.

'Fithvael! Fithvael, my old friend… I thought you were dead…'

Gilead called Niobe and Gadrol and the three kept a bedside vigil for the old elf, while he slowly regained consciousness. Gilead could think of nothing more perfect than to have Fithvael join him tomorrow on his feast day in his new home.

As Fithvael's eyes began to open, Gilead leant over his old friend.

Fithvael sat bolt upright, staring past Gilead's gently smiling face at the room he found himself in. The walls crawled with putrid vegetation and lice. The furniture was black with decay and the food by his bed was rotten and riddled with squirming parasites. The stench of Chaos was all around him, yet this was indisputably Gilead before him.

'Fithvael. It is me, truly. You are alive. You are saved. I want you to meet my great friends and rescuers, Lord Gadrol and his daughter, the Lady Niobe. Gods, you must remember Niobe!'

Two hideous… things stepped out of the gloom behind Gilead, leering at Fithvael and malevolently baring their blackened teeth. Startled and cowering, Fithvael blinked terrified eyes – and saw, in that blink, a majestically magnificent room, decorated in elven style. He saw the beautiful young elf woman, Niobe, and her doting father. He saw fresh fruit and herbs and smelt sweet medicinal potions.

But it was a mere blink and when he opened his eyes again the room had resumed its rotten, filthy demeanour. Fithvael embraced Gilead, closing his eyes for a moment, concentrating only on his friend.

Eyes clamped tight shut, Fithvael felt the syrupy ooze of magic around him. He had seen for an instant what Gilead believed to be the truth. But Fithvael would not succumb. He saw Chaos and realised that they meant not to kill Gilead, but to recruit him, to corrupt him as they themselves had been corrupted. To turn to evil one such as Gilead would delight their perverse minds. The wights wanted to harness Gilead's skill, his knowledge, his tenacity, his bravery. They were elves corrupted by the foul allure of Chaos. To recruit one of their own kind, the best of their kind, was a goal worth pursuing.

Fithvael lay back on the bed, concentrating hard on his quest. He had sworn that he would save his friend, but now he was no longer sure he could. Gilead didn't see what was truly around him and Fithvael could not defeat so many of the dark things without his old friend's help.

He took a deep breath. If he couldn't fight his way out of this situation, he would have to think his way out. He would have to show Gilead the truth.

Fithvael lay in bed, refusing potions and food and talking little. He let Gilead talk. And Gilead could speak of nothing but his feast day on the morrow. His inauguration into the community of Talthos Elios. His new life.

'How long have you been here, my old friend?' asked Fithvael.

'A year tomorrow, Fithvael. I am happy that you will sit by my side at the feast. I have been content here, these are good people...'

Gilead talked on as Fithvael lay, deep in thought. Even time was false here. Fithvael had left the battlefield, where he had last seen Gilead, only a single lunar month ago. And now the old elf had only one short day before Gilead would be lost to him forever, bound to Chaos by whatever disgusting ceremony they had prepared for him.

AT DAWN, THE tower was glorious in the sunlight. Banners streamed in the blue, windy air. Horns sounded clarion notes from the battlements. Gilead woke at their sound and smiled.

The day was full of tournaments, displays of skill, friendly contests. Then, as dusk settled, thousands of lamps and candles were lit in the great hall.

Gilead was dressed in the beautifully crafted suit that Niobe had made for him, but Fithvael saw only the old, worn and dirtied battle garments that were his friend's usual attire. He saw only the filth on his friend's hands and face, smelt only that the elf warrior had missed as many baths as he had himself.

The population of the tower gathered in the great hall, to the strains of musicians in the gallery and took their places at the long tables.

The feast began. Fithvael felt a mounting sense of doom.

He had tidied himself and sat at Gilead's right hand at the head table. He kept his face against his sleeve. The piles of rotten, maggot-ridden food were enough to make him nauseous, but the stench of the gathered host was worse. Fithvael used every ounce of self-control when looking around. He was appalled by the sheer weight of numbers of the dark things; sixty or more, in all their grotesque, reeking forms. He wondered that they could believe they had duped him.

The veteran elf watched as Gilead and his party took their hearty appetites to the rotten food. Fithvael smiled at his friend, but all the food on his plate found its way under the table and onto the floor. He couldn't even bear to sully his clothes by secreting it in his pockets.

Then the speeches began. Gilead stood to toast his friends and his new home with joyous words. Fithvael looked up into his friend's eyes, and by the light of a thousand candles he saw what Gilead saw. He saw the beauty of the sumptuously decorated room and the glory of the feast before them. As Gilead's eyes moved across the room Fithvael saw, reflected there, a large party of elf warriors and then the serenity of a lovely elf woman, as his friend's eyes came to rest on Niobe.

In that moment Fithvael had his plan. He only prayed that it was not too late.

As Gilead resumed his seat, his old friend leaned towards him.

'Gilead, my true friend, it is time now for my toast,' he said softly. 'Promise me only this: look into my eyes and see what I see, see what is reflected there. Be by my side now.'

Gilead looked at him curiously.

'Promise me!'

With that, Fithvael got to his feet and cast his eyes around the room. He spoke slowly of his love for his friend, but concentrated his eyes, first on the decorations, then on the food, then on the Chaos band and finally on the monster that was Niobe.

Gilead looked into his friend's eyes.

Looked…

…*looked*…

As Fithvael came to the end of his speech, he turned to Gilead. The smile had entirely left the other elf's face.

'Now stand with me, friend, and let us raise our swords and salute each other.'

Gilead rose, drew a deep breath and raised his sword to his old friend. Emotions were swirling behind his fixed visage. Rage, disappointment, guilt, horror. But rage was the greatest.

The creatures around them, the filthy, decaying remnants of the noble line of Elios, perverted and corrupted by the baleful influence of the very barrow they had chosen to guard, raised their goblets in mock salute, and the two true elves began their attack.

Fithvael ran through three of his nearest neighbours before any of the fiends had even armed themselves. Gilead, already shadowfast, whirling and slicing in several places at once, had reduced a dozen dark things to a heap of spurting, disgorging corpses.

Then the battle began in earnest as the degenerate court of Talthos Elios fought back.

Fithvael used their weight of numbers against them. Battling on two fronts, he managed to slip out of the fight and turn on a third assailant, as the first two killed each other in their frenzy.

Gilead threw a table over, tipping its contents into the laps of the beasts. They struggled to rise, but Gilead was too fast, attacking them as they lay on their backs in the debris, or were trapped by the heavy dishes that rained down on them. The once-elf things were not prepared for attack and those who wore no weapons fought with their hands, losing their limbs to Gilead's long sword.

Gilead was standing atop the great tables, swinging his great blade and thrusting his dagger into any and all chaos flesh he could find. He fought his way nearer the doorway, taking down half a dozen barrow-spawn with his flailing weapons. The elf-echoes tore at each other in their rage to reach him.

Fithvael ploughed on, slower, but just as efficient. Following the swing of his long sword with a lunge from his dagger, he tore the throat out of one barrow-thing, the eyes out of the next. Here he severed a leg, bursting a great artery and filling his nostrils with the stink of the oozing ichor. He had both strength and purpose and he used them to good effect.

He could not see Gilead, but he could see his work as more foul things fell near to him, their mortal wounds releasing more of the putrid reek of Chaos.

With each blow, each death, the room grew darker, filthier, older and more decayed. The piles of rotten food quickly became puddles of black liquid and then disappeared. The bodies of the foe wept their gory contents, decayed quickly to ugly skeletal forms and then to grey dust.

The elves fought on as the remnants of the foul horde weakened and succumbed. Soon, Gilead and Fithvael stood together at one end of what had been the great elf hall, then a terrifying Chaos gathering. Now it was a ruin.

'Our work is done here,' said Fithvael, sheathing his dagger and leaning on his sword.

Gilead bowed his head. The two looked at each other, then once more at the room, before turning to leave.

As he turned, Gilead saw movement. His sword and dagger were drawn and he spun back into the room, swinging his sword in a wide arc as he spun high off his feet. As he landed he plunged his dagger into the monster that had risen up in front of him.

Fithvael turned as he heard a loud thump. It was Gadrol's head hitting the floor. The lord of Elios's body followed its decapitated head, taking down with it the body of the wraith that had been Niobe. The hilt of Gilead's dagger could be seen sticking straight out from the second barrow-thing's ichor-pulsing throat.

Fithvael stared down at the last two bodies as Gadrol and Niobe twitched in their final death throes. Then they, too, began to decay before the elves' eyes.

'I'm sorry, Gilead,' said Fithvael. He could think of nothing else to say.

'Niobe…' his companion said softly.

'It was not her… she is still lost, taken by Lord Ire. These fiends played upon your dreams, your hopes.'

Gilead looked across at the veteran elf, then down at himself. He was suddenly deathly tired. He had not been washed, nor his bruises tended. He was shabby and dishevelled and the bruises he had received on the battlefield had not yet faded. He raised his hand to his face and was startled to feel the soft stubble that had grown there.

'Time was corrupted too, I'm still bruised and dirty. I dreamed it all, didn't I? How did they do this to me?' There was an odd mix of bitterness and sharp sadness in his eyes. 'I'm in your debt for… waking me.'

OUTSIDE, THE EVENING was slate grey along the pass. Crows rasped from the steep scarps. Two comrades moved out from nightmare into encroaching night.

Their torches lit the walls of the tower with flickering shapes. Fire began to twist and flurry around the desecrated tower. The Tower of Talthos Elios burned, its nobility and its curse sooting away into the night.

'Now the barrow,' said Gilead, ferocity burning in his tired eyes.

Fithvael followed him. There was work to be done.

VI

GILEAD'S SWORDS

*War tends to limit the length
of friendships.*

MY EYES MAY be old and clouded, but still I see doubt in your face. As if all I have told you this long winter night was nothing more than a tale-spinner's fancy. Well, if you ask me, it is the curse of some souls to be born at the wrong time.

Consider this: had Gilead Lothain come to this world a thousand years earlier, in a better age, most likely his life and deeds would have been dutifully recorded and celebrated in the chronicles of his fair people, and earned him fame as a hero even you would have heard of.

But he did not. When he first drew sharp breath at the midwife's slap, in the cold midnight of a bitter winter, his noble and ancient race was already waning. Their civilisation, which once had held the whole world itself as its domain, had become nothing but a shadow on the fringes of life. The elves were beings of the edge places, relics of a brighter time. Their blood was running slower and cooling, their traces vanishing from the land, supplanted by the coarse young tribe of man. The legacy of Ulthuan had been eroded by history, worn away by fate. Even the great elven chronicles were, by then, patchy and incomplete, those that were still maintained.

So Gilead Lothain, last lord of Tor Anrok, was never a celebrated hero. He never became the subject of popular story-songs, or verse cycles declaimed by courtly poets. His deeds were never bound in buckskin to take pride of place in a palace library. His name has never become proverbial, never alluded to in the great poems and sagas of our day. It is his curse to be nothing more than a story. A fireside tale told by old folk to the young. A memory, or the memory of a memory. All that the world has of him now is myth – at worst, ill-remembered nonsense; at best, half-truths swollen by imaginative retellings. The rest is blank, a ghostly trace, like a faint handprint in dust. A life imperfectly and fleetingly glimpsed every now and then in the dim forests of rumour.

Except here, at this hearth. There is truth here, what truth I know. A few fragments of his long, sad life that you can trust to be truer than myths. I have told you most of them.

The last is Maltane, or more properly the Battle of Maltane, also called the Tale of the Thirteen Swords. Or Twelve, or Fourteen, depending on which account you follow. Whatever.

So, if the steward brings me more wine, and my lamp's wick and failing voice last, we'll have that one, and it shall assuredly be my last. The land is full of myths, but few are truer or more worthy than this.

Winter had thawed to spring, and spring had ripened to summer. Gilead and Fithvael, riding as shadows at the edges of the estate of man, had roamed ever southwards, aimlessly, since the murderous deceit of Talthos Elios. Now summer itself, plump and golden on the bow, was about to turn and wither and fall beneath the frosty touch of autumn.

What triumphs and defeats they had braved and shared since the horror of Talthos Elios, it is not possible to say. But there, at harvest time, chance, that most fickle and petty of all divine blessings, led their wanderings to Vinsbrugge, during their festival.

The harvest had been good and the grain towers, beehive-shaped giants of white stone grouped at the lip of the town, were full. The winding streets of Vinsbrugge were decked with corn garlands, linen streamers and crop-gods woven from golden straw. The priests of Sigmar had arranged processions and services in the town basilica, and the guild masters had paid for black powder rockets and flares to light up the night. There was to be a week of thanksgiving, an excuse for revelry and disorder. A merry time to mark the turn of a hard year.

The hostelries and inns of Vinsbrugge were packed with strangers. Many were grain merchants, arriving early for the annual produce markets. Others were travellers and wanderers drawn in by the exuberance of the festival.

Two were not of mankind.

The rockets fizzing and flashing in the late summer evening and the sound of singing had drawn them to Vinsbrugge from a lonely road to the south-west. Fithvael had remarked that the sounds reminded him of victory feasts at Tor Anrok, lifetimes ago. If Gilead agreed, it was not clear. But he did not resist as his old comrade turned their path towards the happy lights of the small town.

They had found lodging, stables for their steeds, and anonymity in the bustling crowds, just two more hooded travellers in saddle-soiled robes. They ate in roast-houses along the main square, drank the night away in taverns at the north end and slept the days out. Fithvael's aching, tired limbs began to ease for the first time in months. Years, he did not doubt.

He hoped, indeed he silently prayed to the smoky, fading gods of Ulthuan, that simply mixing in these hospitable, joyous surroundings would thaw the misery and fatigue in his old friend.

Gilead said little, and Fithvael knew the scars of Talthos Elios were deep in his soul, forming calluses over the ravages of an already unkind life. Fithvael heard him murmur Niobe's name in his sleep more than once, through the hemp-cloth drape that partitioned their rented bedchamber.

Yet Gilead did seem to mellow. He watched the nightly fireworks with alert eyes, and laughed sometimes at the capering harvest fools in the street processions. They were white-faced fools in shirts of woven corn: some on stilts, some tumbling, some chasing into the crowds and beating laughing womenfolk with fertility staves.

Fithvael was simply glad to see a tinge of colour in Gilead's face, some meat back on his wasted limbs, a light in his eyes. It would do for now.

ON THE FIFTH night of the Festival, they found themselves in a crowded inn on Purse Lane, sharing a flask of wine at a corner table. A conjuror had come in off the street and was entertaining the crowd at the bar with sleight of hand. There was laughter and much amazement.

Fithvael was asking Gilead if he had thought where they might go once they were done with Vinsbrugge and the festival. He realised the warrior wasn't listening.

'What is it?' the veteran said.

Gilead looked down at his cup. 'We're being watched.'

'Where?' Fithvael also covered his gaze, pouring more wine for them both, but his eyes darted.

'At the bar, the far end. Ho! Not so obvious or he'll know we've seen him. Drinking alone, clad in a black cloak.'

Fithvael adjusted his boot, taking in the figure as he did so. Tall, slender, with his dark cloak swathed around him and its cowl drawn up to hide the face. The unmistakable shape of a longsword bulged under the folds of the cape.

'I agree. He is indeed observing us.'

'I seem to know the set of him,' Gilead murmured. He shook his head. 'Drink up and we shall go. I'm in no mood for trouble.'

They drained their cups and got up, pushing through the crowds to the door.

Purse Lane was cool and dark. Romping music issued from a nearby drinking parlour and most of the passers-by were laughing and loose on their feet.

They headed down to the north end, near the grain towers, where the air smelled of husks and was heavy with chaff.

'He's following,' Gilead whispered. Fithvael knew it without looking.

At an unspoken signal, they parted company, leaving the cobbled street in opposite directions. Fithvael slid into an alleyway, skirting round a whipmaker's shop to turn back on himself. He drew his sword.

Gilead melted into the shadows, sliding his own sword from its scabbard without a sound. Its weight felt good in his palm. It had been a while, he realised.

The hooded figure passed them. Fithvael stepped back into the street behind it, ready to–

They were gone.

The veteran swordmaster felt suddenly exposed and ridiculous, in the middle of the lane, sword drawn.

'You weren't really thinking of using that on me?' a mellifluous voice breathed in his ear.

Fithvael turned, flash-fast, and brought the point of his blade up to the throat of the hooded figure that stood behind him. Calmly, the figure hooked something over the end of the blade, something that slid down the keen length and stopped at the hilt. A necklace, silver, tied on a leather thong. It was the herald mark of Tor Anrok.

Fithvael gasped. The figure laughed softly and threw back his hood.

'Fithvael te tuin Anrok. I knew you from your gait in an instant. It has been such a very long time.'

'By Ulthuan! Nithrom?'

'One and the same,' said the smiling elf warrior in the black cloak. His long, fair hair was tied back, and under the cloak he wore form-fitting armour of dark green leather. He was still smiling as he whipped around and brought up his long silver blade to block Gilead's longsword. Sparks sprang from the chime of metal.

'Gilead! Put up your blade! It is Nithrom! Nithrom, you hear me? Don't you know him?' Fithvael flung himself forward to get between them, but Gilead pushed him aside with his free hand.

'Something that has his shape, perhaps,' the slender elf growled. 'Something that uses an old face as a mask to deceive us.'

Gilead spun around, circling his long, blue-steel sword in a blur, but again the black-cloaked figure blocked him.

'Ever the cautious one, son of Lothain. That is good. In these friendless days especially.'

Gilead and the stranger shadow-danced around each other. Gilead flexed his grip on the hilt of his longsword.

'Even the voice... you play him well. But the Nithrom I knew is long dead.'

'Am I?' chuckled the other. 'How did I die? I am curious to know.'

'You left...' Gilead corrected himself: 'He left Tor Anrok twenty-five winters past. Never seen again. No word, no message, no trace of his passing.'

'There is a large world outside the tower, Gilead, son of Lothain. To be lost in it does not make you dead. Given that you and old Fithvael are here in this gutter-town, skulking like wanted bandits, I would have thought you would have learned that by now.'

Gilead threw himself at the stranger. Their blades clashed six times in quick succession. Every impact was a parry of Gilead's strokes. The stranger made no effort to press an attack.

'Gilead!' Fithvael hissed at his old comrade. 'I love you as a brother, but you are acting like a fool! This is Nithrom, I would swear it! You were but a youth when he left! I knew him well, hunted in the chase with him, sparred with him, fought alongside him now and then.'

'And taught me all I know of woodcraft and bowmanship,' said Nithrom. 'You were the backbone of the warriors, Fithvael te tuin. What sorry turn of fate finds you following this hot-blood to the ends of the world?'

Fithvael sighed. He sometimes wondered that himself. He said, 'I don't follow... we travel together, as comrades.' It sounded like he was trying to convince himself.

'And how fares Tor Anrok? Your brave brother, Galeth? My old sire, hallowed be his wisdom, Lord Lothain?'

There was a silence broken only by the drunken singing from an inn in the next lane. The crescent harvest moon menaced the hot, dark sky like a goblin's curved blade. The smile on Nithrom's face faded.

'Gilead?'

'My father is dead. My brother is dead. Tor Anrok is but a heap of stones in a weed-choked glade.' Gilead lowered his sword. 'As you would have known, if you had ever come back.'

Fithvael could not see Nithrom's face because he suddenly looked down and the street shadows filled it. There was a dull clang as the silver sword fell from Nithrom's hand. It made Fithvael jump. A warrior such as Nithrom only dropped his sword when death stole him. Otherwise it was brandished or sheathed.

Nithrom walked away from them both, his head bowed. Fithvael stepped forward, picked up the silver blade gently and glanced round at the glowering Gilead with angry eyes.

'Will you put up your sword now, fool?' he snarled.

Gilead slowly sheathed his long blue-steel blade in its leather scabbard. His lost brother's sword whispered softly as it slid inside, like silk against silk.

At the corner of Purse Lane, where it joined the main market street, there was a crumbling pile of worn and fractured millstones discarded by the granaries. They found Nithrom sitting on them, gazing at the moon. Fithvael sat down next to him. Gilead hung back, alone, watching.

'All gone?' whispered Nithrom at last.

'All gone.'

'All of it? All perished?'

Fithvael nodded.

'It is the way of this world that we will all fade and be forgotten,' said Nithrom. 'Our time is passed. I... I always hoped, trusted, that Tor Anrok would stand the menace of time. Away, abroad, following the path Fate dealt me, I cherished the notion that the tower still stood, as I had always known it. Waiting for me even if I never returned.'

Fithvael saw how lined and worn Nithrom's lean face had become. Weariness and care had etched their marks on his once-handsome features. They were about the same age, Fithvael perhaps a few seasons older. Nithrom was of noble blood, the son of Lothain's great uncle. He had been born into the warrior tradition, raised as a woodsman, and had eventually chosen the ranger's path to the outer world, to quest and journey alone.

Fithvael was of lower blood, the eldest of six sons born to the tower court's master-at-arms. But they had been friends, growing up together in the dark staircases and draughty halls of Tor Anrok. A soldier's boy and the son of a noble. Bound to his service in his lord's troop, Fithvael had been destined to stay and serve at Tor Anrok for life, and deeply missed his privileged friend when he left. Missed him and, at the time, envied his freedom. Now he had tasted that freedom himself, following Gilead, and he did not like it much. There was nothing left to envy. He had left Tor Anrok as a dutiful member of Gilead's war-band, and now he was the only one left. And seeing the age in Nithrom's face, he recognised his own. He felt spent, worn out. Regardless of the long-lived nature of his ancient race, Fithvael felt old.

He handed the graceful silver sword back to Nithrom, hilt first. Nithrom took it and set it across his knees.

'When I sighted you and the lord's son in the tavern, I felt joy. It seemed this day would be the happiest of many. But now I find it is the saddest.'

'What are you doing here?' Gilead stood beside them now.

'Mourning,' Nithrom replied, without looking up.

Gilead sat down on the millstones next to Nithrom.

'No... here. In this human nest, mixing with them.'

'The same as you.'

'We have no purpose. No reason to be here. No cause, no drive, no...' Fithvael's voice trailed away.

'Then not like you,' Nithrom said. 'I have a cause. I am here to purchase supplies, collect resources. To collect a few more good swords, if I can.'

He looked round at Fithvael, a smile – sad still, but a smile never the less – forming on his mouth. 'Perhaps the gods brought me here, and you too. Perhaps it is right that our paths cross, no matter the pain that meeting brings.'

'Why?' Gilead asked from the other side of the veteran elf warrior. 'What cause is it that holds you?'

AT DAWN, NITHROM led them down to a livery next door to the Temple of Sigmar. The ostler was just opening the shutters and unlocking the bolts. Early sunlight shafted into the livery barn.

There were three wagons lined up inside, fully packed. Sacks of grain, bolts of white linen, bundles of freshly fletched arrows and a three dozen unstrung longbows, a box of spearheads, two boxes of iron tacks, twenty flasks of lamp oil and twenty more of rubbing alcohol, a drum of pitch, a sack of padlocks, three coils of hemp-rope, five newly struck swords and thirty brand-new daggers, jars of salted figs and olives in oil, ropes of seasoned sausage, sheets of jerk-beef and dried fish, three cases of wine, two kegs of ale... More besides. Boxes, sacks, bundles.

'You're planning a small war?' joked Fithvael, taking in the amount and nature of the supplies.

'That is precisely what he is doing,' Gilead said sourly.

Nithrom looked round at them both and nodded to Fithvael sadly.

'A small war...' he murmured.

Gilead glanced across at Fithvael. His eyes were hooded and dark.

'We are departing now. Farewell, Nithrom.'

'Gilead–' Fithvael began.

'Now, friend Fithvael. Your old sparring companion has run mad and we are not staying to be drawn into his lunacy.'

'Do me one favour, son of Lothain,' Nithrom said. 'Stay until the others get here. Then make up your mind.'

'Others?'

'They are to meet me here. They will be along. Do me that kindness, at least.'

Gilead flapped his scarlet cloak with a curse and sat down on a straw bale.

IT WAS EARLY still, with the mounting sun barely peering through fidgeting clouds, as the first of them arrived. The day was going to be warm, but there was a dawn chill yet in the marrow of the town, and beads of dew winked on every outdoor surface.

A human lad appeared in the livery doorway, framed by the light. He was short and slender, almost delicate, with soft white skin not thus far troubled by a barber's blade. He wore a dark green surcoat and black leggings under a set of oily grey plate mail that had clearly belonged to a father or uncle with a much larger frame. And the broadsword in its sling on his back seemed to weigh him down. His hair was short, fingercut and blond. Fithvael thought him noble looking, for a human. He was reminded of poor Lyonen, the gods rest his soul. There was a fragile grace to him, more reminiscent of an elf than a crude, clumsy human. His eyes were wide and the colour of buffed copper.

'Erill,' Nithrom greeted him, gladly.

'I'm early,' the youth said. His voice was musical, sweet and unbroken, though he tried for gruffness. 'No one's here.' He seemed to deliberately ignore Fithvael and the brooding Gilead.

'I am here,' said Nithrom with a smile and an open-armed gesture that took in the barn. 'Welcome. I'm happy to see you,'

Master Erill seemed pleased by that, and entered the place, sitting down on a mounting block near the wagons, dropping his heavy sword and bulging pack as he did so.

'This is Erill,' Nithrom said plainly. Fithvael exchanged courteous nods with the shy youth. Gilead made no move at all.

A quarter-hour passed, and then a voice spoke from the back of the barn. 'A good turnout, I see.'

They all looked round. Erill got up in a hurry, and Fithvael also rose at the sight of the newcomer Nithrom crossed to greet.

He had come in through the back shutter of the barn, as if he did not trust the thoroughfares of the town, even at this early hour. A lean human, with great power in his long limbs, dressed in tightly bound leather armour and a hauberk of studded hide. His hair was the colour of sun-bleached barley, and he carried his sword, shield and helmet on his back.

'Vintze!' Nithrom said. 'Ever the stealthy one.'

They shook hands. The newcomer cast his hard blue gaze around the stable, eyeing Gilead and Fithvael. He seemed to ignore the lad.

'Who's this?' he asked. There was a twang of the Reik about his accent.

'Companions of mine,' Nithrom replied briefly.

'Elves,' Vintze said, as if he was sniffing a scent from the air. 'Figures. Still don't trust them… no offence, lord.'

Nithrom grinned. 'None taken. I still do not trust thieves. So that makes us even.'

Vintze put down his pack. 'No one else here yet? Madoc? The Norseman? That Bretonnian fool?'

'They will come.'

'Still sleeping off a hard night in the taverns, I'll wager,' Erill said, trying to sound masculine and cynical in the world-weary way that humans found so appealing.

Vintze continued to ignore him. The Reiklander walked over and flopped down in a pile of sacking. 'Wake me when we're ready to go.'

Another thirty minutes passed, and shadows flickered in the growing sunlight outside the stable door. Two riders reined up and dismounted. They entered the barn; short, burly men from the provinces of the Empire, dressed in heavy plate the colour of brass with tabards of black and white. On their shields was the red bull of Ostland. When they raised their visors, in unison, Fithvael saw near-identical, square-cut faces.

'Dolph, Brom. Welcome.'

The Ostlanders greeted Nithrom with nods, and set about bringing their horses into the shade and refilling their waterskins. They moved in the strange, mirrored way only twin brothers could manage. Fithvael saw that for the first time, Gilead seemed vaguely attentive. He watched the twins, as if remembering.

The Carroburger appeared a few minutes later. Tall and dark-haired, with a cropped goatee and a cruel face, he simply strode into the barn and threw his basket helm and huge two-handed sword into the back of one of the wagons along with his leather pack. He wore the slashed and puffed sleeves and leggings – dark red in colour – of a Carroburg man-at-arms, and his black breastplate was polished like a mirror.

'Master Cloden,' Nithrom nodded.

The Carroburg greatsword nodded back and went to sit on his own in the corner of the barn. By now, the twin warriors from Ostland were playing at cards with Erill. Vintze was apparently sleeping. Gilead still sat like a statue near the doorway.

'When are you going to explain the–' Fithvael began.

'When I am ready,' Nithrom answered.

A trumpet sounded outside the livery, a fanfare more noisy than tuneful. Everyone stirred and even Vintze seemed to wake up.

The Bretonnian knight, mounted on his huge white charger, seemed to fill the doorway, his chrome armour glinting in the sun and his helmet's great feather-plume a livid red. By his side, a sullen, balding squire on a palfrey rasped the fanfare again through a sadly buckled cornet.

'His most magnificent and lauded self, the victorious warrior Le Claux! Welcome him, you fine people...' The squire's declaration tailed off wearily.

Le Claux, huge in his gleaming armour, seemed to have trouble dismounting, and the squire had to slide off his squat mount quickly to assist. The knight clanked into the barn as if nothing untoward had happened and grasped Nithrom's extended hand eagerly. He raised his visor, cursed as the heavy thing snapped shut again, and raised it once more. Fithvael saw a handsome, well-boned face that looked tired and bloated.

'My dear Nithrom! I stand ready to ride with you to the mouth of hell and back, for glory's sake! For this, I propose a hearty toast!'

Le Claux produced a wineskin from his harness and squirted a serious measure into his open mouth. They he strode across to the gathering of the others, and offered the skin around. Vintze, sitting up on the sacking, was the only one who accepted it.

The squire stepped forward and whispered to Nithrom. 'Don't even begin to ask how I got him here this early. And for everyone's sake, don't give him anything sharp.'

'The Lady will honour your duty, Gaude,' smiled Nithrom.

Gaude, the squire, suggested something fruity the Lady might do instead and turned away.

'Who, by all that's sacred, are these miserable nobodies?' Gilead asked Fithvael darkly.

A Kislevite warrior-woman called Bruda was next to arrive. She slammed in through the stable doors, dressed in a knee-length chain shirt and high boots, her mane of red hair flowing behind her. She was as tall as any of the men present, and nearly as broad and muscled. Her curved sabre bounced against her hip in its sheath. Fithvael knew that humans had generally a larger build than elves, but he had never seen a female of this stature. She seemed huge, like a goddess walking the land. She stank of sweat and almost knocked Erill flat with a slap to his shoulders. Le Claux offered her the wineskin and she drained it with a rumbling laugh and a hefty belch. Then she set about testing the give of the new bows by bending them against her instep by hand. Biceps like grapefruit swelled as she twisted the sprung wood down. One snapped.

'Not wery good, Nithrom!' she bawled, her voice clouded by her thick, northern accent. 'Wery poor! I think we have trouble if we use these, yes.'

'They'll do, Bruda,' Nithrom said calmly. 'And I know you'll only carve your own from the local wood when we get there.'

'Here he comes!' interrupted Vintze.

A big, black-bearded monster stumbled in through the stable doors. He was the most massive human Fithvael had ever seen, dressed in a dirty bearskin and blue-black disc-mail and lugging his weapons and full-face helm behind him. An old, deep blade-wound dented the left cheek of his rugged face, half hidden by his beard. At last Bruda wasn't the largest in the company. The newcomer was clearly intoxicated and belched freely, leaning on the terrified Erill for support. He clamped his tarnished helmet with its fierce, snarling mouth over his face and barked 'Let's get on with it, shall us?'

He was a Norseman. His axe was huge and he dropped it several times. His name was Hargen Hardradasson, but he preferred Harg.

Madoc, the last of them, rode up just before midday. Blond-haired and powerful, he wore the wolf-pelt of Ulric over his armour. An old warhammer was looped in the thongs on one side of his saddle.

Madoc made no apologies for keeping them waiting. He simply greeted them in the clipped, surly accent of Middenheim. There was something cynical in his bearing, Fithvael thought, more cynical even than the sneering Vintze or the disdainful Cloden.

As the party assembled and made ready to leave, hitching pack animals to the forks of the wagons, Nithrom crossed to Gilead.

'Do you see now?'

'I have waited as you asked. I see who has arrived.'

'And?'

' If you intend to fight a war, even a small war, with them, you're going to lose.'

'That is well said. Why do you think I asked you to stay? Why do you think I need you?'

THE PARTY LEFT Vinsbrugge in the first hour of the afternoon, as the bells of the old temple chimed a single peal. The air was hot and flat and bright, and the sky was cornflower blue and without blemish.

Nine riders on horses, three wagons drawn by packhorse teams, with spare steeds running from the backs of the carts. The lad Erill, the squire Gaude and the beast-like Norseman Harg drove the wagons. The streets weren't busy, and they made their way to the south bridge without provoking much attention from the townsfolk.

Fithvael was the last to leave. He lingered for a moment in the doorway of the livery.

'I am going to go with them,' he said. 'I want to go.'

'You will die and we shall never find Niobe nor our people,' growled Gilead. He stood in the shade of the emptied barn, a dim form like a ghost.

'Maybe. But I would rather die with a purpose than ride on towards the empty doom we're heading for. Nithrom *needs* us.'

Gilead scowled. 'That's not what Nithrom needs…'

Fithvael turned away. He knew the tone, the black mood it signalled. He had weathered those moods once too often.

'Then you should suit yourself, Gilead.'

'I will.'

Fithvael pulled himself into the saddle, and cast a final look back. 'Come with us.'

Silence answered him.

'Then fare well, Gilead Lothain.'

The veteran elf turned his steed's head and cantered away after the others.

NITHROM, ASTRIDE A lean, black horse, was riding at the tail of the party, waiting for Fithvael to catch up.

'I am sorry,' said Fithvael.

'Don't be, Fithvael te tuin. You cannot set his destiny for him. Gilead has his own path to tread.'

They fell into pace alongside one another. Up ahead, Le Claux was trying to get the others singing a round. When no one took up the offer, he sang it himself anyway, attempting to do all the overlapping parts with one voice. Bruda and Harg barracked him loudly and some of the others laughed.

'Yet I feel guilty, Nithrom. It is almost as if I were abandoning him. After all we have been through together.'

'That is understandable. But he cannot set your destiny for you either. He is a stubborn soul, and melancholy. You've given him the best years of your life, Fithvael. But you haven't changed him. Perhaps it is best now you go your own way.'

They were thumping over the boards of the south bridge now. Scintillating damselflies purred among the nodding bulrushes below the rail.

'Maybe…' Nithrom ventured. 'Maybe you are also feeling sad because you know he's right.'

'What?' Fithvael seemed startled.

'He sees this as a fool's errand, that I'm leading this company into a battle it cannot win. Maybe you know he is right, hating the fact that your loyalty to our old friendship is making you leave him to ride to your doom.'

Fithvael frowned. 'I… I don't think so.' A long pause. 'Are we really riding to our deaths?'

Nithrom laughed. 'I don't think so… or I wouldn't be doing so. But many might think the odds are against us.'

Fithvael shook his head. 'I'm with you in this, Nithrom te tuin. It feels like the right thing to do.'

Nithrom nodded and smiled. 'Maybe I was just testing you,' he said.

Fithvael chuckled. He took a final look back down the trackway, past the wooden bridge, into the outskirts of the mill town.

He did not see what he was longing with all his heart to see: a lone rider coming after them.

ONCE THE COMPANY had assembled at the livery, Nithrom had briefly outlined the nature of the venture, though the matter was already known to most of the recruits. They were to ride south and offer protection for a small settlement called Maltane, which every year was raided by Tilean mercenary companies heading home after the fighting season. Most years, Maltane had bought the raiders off with produce, supplies and gold. But this year the harvest had been poor and the town coffers were low. They had nothing to pay off the Tilean dog-soldiers with.

So they had decided to use the little gold they had to hire mercenaries to defend the settlement. Nithrom, selling his sword thereabouts, had undertaken the venture, and travelled north to recruit willing swordsmen. The company and its meagre supplies were the best he could do.

'Barely a dozen warriors against a mercenary company?' Gilead had murmured after hearing Nithrom out. He said nothing more, but shook his head sadly.

'Have you no courage, wood-thing?' Vintze had asked curtly, rising from his sacking bed.

'As much as you, I am sure. However, I clearly have more brains.'

For a dreadful moment, Fithvael had thought a fight might ensue. But Vintze had simply flopped back onto his sacks, muttering, 'We don't need him, Nithrom.'

Others – Harg and the Kislevite goddess – had also simply nodded. They all seemed too weary to Fithvael, as if they would only draw their blades and their anger out if there were money in it.

Le Claux, however, had swaggered to his feet, his armour clanking. 'Braggart! Wretch!' he declaimed at the disinterested Gilead. 'Take back the insult you have laid upon this fair company, or I will smite thee!'

Everyone, even Fithvael, had been unable to resist laughing at the Bretonnian's courtly-phrased challenge. Le Claux faltered at their laughter.

'Sit down and shut up,' Gaude had said cruelly and Le Claux had sat back down with a metallic clatter.

But there was animosity still. Fithvael had seen it then. The dark Middenheimer, Madoc, and the Carroburger had both gazed at Gilead with undisguised contempt. Clearly neither wanted to make a fight out of it either – their mercenary nature was as world-fatigued as the others – but Gilead's insult had rankled.

* * *

Now they were on the track, rising up through harvested fields of golden corn stalks and dry earth. A sheath of deep, green woods awaited them at the top of the slope. White butterflies flickered around them, and across the wildflowers in the hedge-ditches.

'How big is this place, this Maltane?' Fithvael asked.

'Small – a millhouse, a tavern, a temple, fifty families. Three hundred people at most.'

'Defended?'

'They have an outer ditch around the general settlement, and an inner fenced mound upon which the temple stands.'

'Is there a well in the temple enclosure?'

Nithrom shrugged. 'I never had cause to ask.'

Fithvael's unease deepened. If it came to a siege, in the inner fence… without water? 'What size is the dog-soldier band?'

'It varies. Last year, it was two hundred.'

Two hundred… against twelve, if you counted Gaude.

'You can go back any time you like,' Nithrom told him lightly, seeing his expression.

They entered the fringes of the woods. Spruce, laburnum, elm, beech, years old and rich in leaf. Birds called through the sunlight patches under the soothing green canopy. They sighted deer several times, timid and fleeting in the glades off the track.

Bruda pulled out a curved bow and dropped one with swift, experienced grace. They would eat that night, at least.

The track spiralled down through the woods for six leagues. They passed gurgling streams that lapped over mossy stone beds under the bent limbs of twisted elms. Twice they passed groups of ancient standing stones, bearded with lichen, forgotten in the old woodland. Some of the stones had marks cut in them, intaglio carvings almost weathered smooth by years of rain and frost – spirals, sunbursts, stars, goddesses.

Fithvael saw how Nithrom nodded to each stone reverently as they went by. Madoc did too, though presumably for somewhat different reasons.

They reached a wider stream in late afternoon as the shadows began to lie long. Wood pigeons and cuckoos warbled and called in the quiet woodlands. They watered the horses at a shingled ford in the stream. The water was clear like fluid glass and the stones were all polished smooth; dark and shiny under the flow, pale and dry out of it.

Flies buzzed around the drinking horses. The company dismounted and flexed their limbs.

Several of the company were refilling waterskins. Vintze and Cloden both withdrew and lay down on the lush grass by the stream. Harg dunked his huge, scarred head into the water and shook silver pellets of spray from his beard and hair like a dog as he rose.

Le Claux wandered off into the woods. Dolph and Brom, the twin warriors, sat and played dice. Bruda began to gut the deer she had brought down.

Fithvael wandered over to the nervous boy Erill. 'I'll take a turn at driving the wagon, if you like.'

The youth seemed surprised at the offer, surprised that any of the company should even talk to him.

'Thank you. I'd like to ride for a while.'

Fithvael nodded and tethered his horse to the wagon's backboard as Erill loosed his own, undernourished steed.

'A change of drivers!' Nithrom called, seeing this. 'Who else will take a turn?'

Brom and Dolph both volunteered, trading places with Harg and Gaude.

Fithvael climbed up onto the driving seat and untied the pack-reins.

'Do we go on?' he said to Nithrom.

'Wait,' the old ranger said mysteriously, watching the trees around them.

Fithvael sat back and waited, dropping the reins into his lap.

Twenty minutes passed. The company began to collect themselves and return to their mounts. Even Le Claux reappeared from the woods, looking somewhat bewildered, knots of foliage tagged into his armour joints.

Suddenly, Vintze swung around, his sword drawn in a blur. Fithvael started. How could a human react so fast? What had he seen? Bruda and Madoc were also armed suddenly, watching the same part of the tree line.

Am I getting so old, Fithvael wondered, *so old I miss the signs?* Now he could hear movement in the undergrowth, sounds that at least three of the company had heard before him.

'Put up your blades,' Nithrom instructed, his voice commanding but calm, and walked towards the source of the quiet movements.

For a moment, for one wonderful moment, Fithvael thought Gilead had rejoined them.

But the elf warrior, who emerged from the trees leading his beautiful, steel-armoured stallion, was not the son of Tor Anrok. He was an unforgettable figure in polished armour of silvered ithilmar, his plume red and proud, a noble elf, as if stepped out of a myth.

'Well met, Caerdrath Eldirhrar tuin Elondith,' Nithrom said in the high elven tongue.

'Well met indeed, Nithrom te tuin Anrok. I am most pleased you waited for me.' The new elf's voice was musical and soft.

Nithrom looked around at the assembled company and continued speaking in the humans' own language. 'Our thirteenth sword, Caerdrath. He felt it best to meet us out here. Human towns are not for him.'

Most of the company looked on in amazement. Fithvael knew why. It was rare for him to set eyes on a true son of Ulthuan, let alone for this motley rabble.

'Then he's riding to the wrong place,' Vintze sneered suddenly.

Caerdrath looked over towards the lean human swordsman. His eyes, shielded behind their helmet slits, were fire-bright.

'I would not choose to do so ordinarily, rank man. But I owe Nithrom an old debt, and so I am here with him.'

'Elves!' spat Vintze and turned away.

They mounted up and moved on then, crossing the ford and crawling away into the woods beyond. Caerdrath rode alongside Fithvael's wagon for a moment.

'Brother,' Caerdrath said with a tilt of his head.

'I am called Fithvael, also of Tor Anrok. It is good to meet with you this day.'

Caerdrath nodded and spurred his fine steed forward, away down the track.

THE SUMMER NIGHT came down late and slow, and swifts shot like darts against the darkening sky, between the silhouettes of trees. The band made camp in a hollow near a forest pool. Bruda's buck was spit-roasting by the time the stars came out.

Nithrom set a watch rotation, but left out Le Claux, who had been drinking from a wineskin since dusk and was now snoring by the fire. Fithvael fell into a light but easy slumber, his patched, travel-worn cloak pulled around him.

Brom woke him with a shake deep into the night, to take his turn at the watch. It was cool now, and the fire was guttering low. Fithvael rose, stretched out his limbs, took a swig of water from his flask and made a circle of the sleeping camp, silent in the undergrowth. Hunting owls hooted in the dark woods around. The dish of the night sky above was so clear and so full of stars it looked like beaten silver.

Fithvael flexed his aching limbs. The night air was still and without breeze or any sound except the owls, the whisper of nocturnal insects and the crack of the fire. Moths fluttered around the flames like wind-billowed snowflakes.

The veteran warrior noticed that Caerdrath was absent. Somehow that did not trouble him. He had not expected the noble elf to share their camp.

Fithvael knew he was meant to take this watch with the Carroburger, Cloden, and now he saw the human, lurking in the spinney above the hollow. He found a path up to him, through the knee-deep ferns.

Cloden glanced around as he heard the elf approach, a sharp gesture that relaxed when he made out Fithvael's face. The man had unlaced his polished black breastplate and puff-sleeved jerkin, and his greatsword was stuck tip-down in the soil to his left like a small tree. Despite the sharpness of his eyes, Fithvael could see little of Cloden's face; just the suggestion of pale skin between the darkness of hair and goatee. Cloden's eyes were lightless, uninviting hollows.

Fithvael paused next to him and exchanged a nod. Cloden offered a flask of apple schnapps from Nuln, and a sip of the liquor, crude though it was by elven standards, warmed Fithvael's belly.

'Anything?'

Cloden shook his head. 'I doubt we'll meet much out here.'

A short, stuttering cry rose behind them from the camp and they both snapped around. Le Claux called out again in his sleep, wriggled uncomfortably, then slumbered once more.

'He worries me,' Cloden said shortly as they both relaxed.

'Do you mean his drinking?'

'Not so much his drinking, as why he drinks.'

They were silent for a long while.

'I did not expect you to join us,' Cloden said at length. 'Not when your comrade snubbed us so hard. I thought you would depart with him.'

Fithvael looked up into the brilliant zodiac of the sky as if he might read some augury there. 'I thought so too,' he answered, realising it for the first time.

'Why did not you? I thought you were bound and close by tradition, you... your kind.'

It was as if he couldn't say the word.

'We are. Master Gilead and I, bound together for so many years, so many troubles. Have you never had a comrade like that?'

'Never. Never had time for it. War tends to limit the length of friendships.'

'That is true enough. War... and time.'

Cloden nodded. 'So why? Why did you leave him back at Vinsbrugge and take this path? After all those years and troubles?'

'Because of those years and troubles, I think,' Fithvael mused. 'There comes an hour in any life that you need to make an account. To wonder which path to the grave is the best for you. I believe I had journeyed with Gilead far enough. It was an empty road. Nithrom's path has a purpose at least. Besides, I am indebted to Nithrom.'

The Carroburger laughed, coarse and hard. 'Is there anyone of this company who isn't? Isn't that, in truth, why we all ride to our deaths with him?'

'You think that is what waits for us at Maltane?'

'Like enough,' Cloden said. The dark twang of his accent made his sour words more bitter. 'And if not death, not glory either.'

Fithvael was about to reply when Cloden stiffened and plucked his sword out of the loam. It shone in the starlight like ice. He was stooped low, like a stalking wolf.

Fithvael had no need to ask why. He had heard it too: a low, haunting sound that drifted up from the woods beyond the hollow. Not a sound at all, in truth. Just a tremor in the air, a ghostly sigh that trembled the edge of hearing.

Fithvael drew his own blade and they hurried down the far side of the rise, running low, shadowing the trees. Fithvael was utterly silent, and several times Cloden, for all that he moved skilfully and quietly for a human, had to look askance to check the elf was still with him.

The sound came again, and hung on the still night air. It was as subtle and thin as the sound of thawing frost. And just as cold. It came from the watering pool.

The pair moved downwards, through the black trees. There was a scent in the air Fithvael could not place, and a deepening chill.

Ahead of them, through the deep grey silhouettes of the trees, the oval of the pool glowed like a silver mirror, bright with starlight. A white caul of mist hung around the water's sides and drifted like a phantom through the trees. Cloden scrambled round behind an oak's broad trunk to get a better view and Fithvael slid in beside him. He sensed the human was about to exclaim, and deftly clamped his hand across Cloden's opening mouth.

Below them, the noble elf, Caerdrath, stood in the pool, thigh deep, clad only in white luminae robe. The starlight seemed to lend his slender form a phosphorescence. Silver glittered as he raised his ancient blade from the water and held it aloft. Chains of bright water danced off its length and down his arm.

Cloden pulled at Fithvael, trying to break free and advance forward, but Fithvael tightened his grip and drew the Reiklander back, away from the pool.

When they were a good distance back, Fithvael let the human free.

'Why did you stop me?' Cloden hissed.

'Because we should not trespass. Caerdrath is baptising his blade for war, as was done in the old times. It would not be right for us to intrude.'

Cloden seemed dissatisfied with this answer, but made no move to go back. 'Should you not do the same?' he asked with a sneer.

'I find that Caerdrath's ways are as... unfamiliar to me as they are to you.'

Cloden turned and took a last look down the rise to the ghostly pool. Once more, the odd note fluttered the air.

Cloden spat into the ferns and made his way back up the rise to his watch.

Fithvael followed him after a moment or two. He knew he would never forget what he had seen. A sliver of the distant past, of the old ways, of the traditions and lore that he and his western kin had long since forgotten. It made him feel honoured and humble, all at once. And it made him feel older and more worn than he had ever felt before.

DAWN WAS EARLY, and as pale and hard as steel. They woke to mists and ribbons of birdsong. As the sun climbed and steamed the mist away, they were moving again, with Erill, Gaude and Harg driving the teams as before. Le Claux rode silently, lolling clumsily in his saddle as if nursing a black depression or a sore head, or both. Several times he fell behind the main group. At a bend in the track, half an hour after they had set out, Caerdrath rejoined them, armoured again, gleaming and fresh in a way that made them all feel dirty and dishevelled.

They rode up through water meadows and onto higher plains where old vine terraces, weed-blooming pastures and untended lemon groves were returning to the riot of nature. Skylarks, high and invisible, sang above them in the pale blue sky.

The track skirted a small clutch of crofts on the hillslope where a dirty, half-naked child and twenty moon-eyed goats watched their passage past with silent mystification. An hour later, they followed the track in a loop around a ruined broch that had once defended this impoverished scarpland. Defended whom from what, though, none could say.

As they passed the lonely ruin, with its tumble of travertine stones and tufts of weed, Caerdrath rode along past Fithvael. He nodded to the older elf.

'I offer you my thanks,' he said in a low, harmonious voice.

Fithvael shrugged. 'For what, lord?'

'For respecting my ritual.'

Fithvael was about to reply, but Caerdrath had spurred on again towards the head of the column.

The land was getting ever higher now, dry and sparse, with thickets of gorse and thorn, and straggled stands of elms. The sun was still high and hot, but the sky was so pale that the blue was more a grey and stacks of flimsy clouds marched along the horizon. Buzzards and red kites turned and wheeled in the wild air and sometimes dropped like stones into the steep valleys. They saw occasional hares racing in the gorse, but all were too distant for the eager Bruda to take a shot, and had long fled by the time their party came to where they had been.

The track had become a road now, unmetalled but still a worn, wide, marching road cut by generations of migrating soldiers heading north for the fighting season and south again each winter. The bones of horses and mules could sometimes be seen in the scrub of the track. Twice, a lonely grave was marked by a cairn of white stones or a rusting helmet hung on a snapped spear shaft.

This was the hinterland of the great and powerful Empire, the crossing place where one territory ended and blurred into others: other kingdoms; scattered border principalities; loose, casual territories. Here, life was hard and meagre and maintained by ceaseless, thankless toil. They passed olive groves partitioned by dry stone walls, and several terraces of thin but decent vines, neatly maintained. Stringy cattle and lean goats grazed the slopes above the road, but the riders saw no herdsmen.

By late afternoon, the sun was slipped down into the western banks of cloud, as pink and raw as a sleepless eye. The light fell long and low, and their shadows were stretched out beside them. They climbed a last, steep line of flinty hills for another hour, then came out on a broad place where the road curled back on itself to descend again. Below was a wide valley bearded by woods. At its heart, three miles hence, was a mound, fenced and ditched, with a clutch of stone and wood structures nested at its summit. Bare tracks led into the place from the north, east and west, the northern one being the trail end of the road they followed.

Nithrom halted the party. 'Maltane,' he said plainly, with a vague gesture.

There was murmuring, none of it complimentary. All of the warriors, even

Le Claux, stared down to get the measure of the place. Some dismounted. Some shielded their eyes with their hands. Vintze produced a small spyglass and studied the view.

Fithvael took the time to get the lay. At the top of the mound, a good sized building of stone, well roofed, most likely the temple, adjoined a second, larger structure that was undoubtedly the main hall. They commanded a good position, and had a timber enclosure around them, inside a deep ditch cut into the hill's crown. A wooden bridge span crossed the ditch and linked the main enclosure to the clustering homes and outbuildings built ramshackle down the outer slopes. Around them, at the base of the mound, an embankment and another, shallower ditch.

Beyond Maltane, the woods were thick and rose to southern hills with jagged crests. To the west and east, more woodland, following the bowl of the valley. In their direction, rough hills swept down towards the outer ditch. It was obvious their northern approach provided the most expansive clear ground before the town. Anyone approaching from the other compass points would be masked until they were but a furlong from the outer ditch.

Fithvael could see no sign of life in the town. No movement, no figures, not even a stray dog or wandering goat.

"'Tis dead,' muttered Harg.

'More than dead,' Vintze said, closing up his spyglass. 'Not even a hint of smoke. The day's ending. There should be cookfires burning.'

'They're nervous, hiding,' said Nithrom. 'They have every reason to.'

'Did they see us coming?' Erill asked, speaking out loud to the group for the first time since Vinsbrugge.

'No,' said Madoc with utter certainty. 'We would have known of it.'

Nithrom nodded and Fithvael knew Madoc was right. With the likes of Nithrom, Caerdrath and Vintze in the party, no spy could have evaded their notice, certainly not some simple herdsman or vine-farmer.

'Let us presume the worst… that we are too late.' Nithrom turned in his saddle to face them all. 'We shall encircle before we go in. I'll lead the teams down. Fithvael… if you would ride with Cloden and Madoc around to the eastern road and enter that way. Vintze, take Brom and Dolph and sweep to the west. Caerdrath, a full circuit to the south. You can move faster than most and quicker alone. The rest should come with me.'

Most seemed content with this. Bruda readied her bow. Harg eased his war-axe from its loop and set it on the cart bench next to him. Most of the rest eased their blades in their scabbards to make sure they were free. Caerdrath simply nodded and turned his steed west.

'I should go with the outriders!' Le Claux exclaimed, however, pulling out his sword. There was something like indignation in his Bretonnian accent. 'I demand this honour! Am I not a noble champion of the Lady, sworn to uphold good? Am I–'

'Oh shut up!' Gaude spat. 'Do as you're ordered and stop making a fuss!'

'You fiend!' Le Claux exploded and spurred forward. His eyes shone with anger. Fithvael had seen how the lowly squire seemed quite happy to mock and rile his sire, but now he had gone too far. Close to sundown, before a new day's wineskin could be unstoppered, Le Claux was as sober as he was ever going to be. His mailed fist caught the flinching Gaude across the cheek and spun him out of the cart.

'You won't speak to me like that, you offal-hound! You dung-eater! You won't disrespect me so!' Le Claux was snarling, his heavy steed stamping the track dangerously close to the dazed Gaude.

Nithrom rode in smartly and yanked Le Claux and his horse away hard by the reins. Erill and Brom dragged the bloodied Gaude back out of harm's way.

'Le Claux! Le Claux!' Nithrom growled. 'Calm yourself. I need you with me now! Why do you think I did not send you on an outer circuit? I'm driving these wagons down into the heart of what may be an enemy stronghold! I want a noble knight right at my side when I do that!'

Sullen but calmer, Le Claux pulled away and turned his horse down the track, leaving them behind.

'Will you be all right?' Nithrom asked the squire, who was climbing back into his cart. His nose was leaking a thin line of blood and there was a gash across his cheek.

'He gets like this. I should know better.'

Nithrom nodded sadly and then called them to order. Caerdrath was already on his way. Vintze rode off with the twin warriors in tow, also heading west. The wagons and their support trundled off at a lick down the main track, chasing after Le Claux. Fithvael, with Cloden and Madoc at his side, swung east and galloped on, following the lip of the valley bowl.

NONE OF THEM spoke as they rode east, crossing down into the wooded slopes. The spread of woodland soon became too thick for them to see Maltane any more. They took their horses down banks with practised ease, slithering sideways, jerking crabwise down through tracts of gorse, fern and nettle. Cloden checked his position with the sun, half blocked by the canopy. But Fithvael already knew where they were; another mile south and west, and they would meet the eastern track.

Fithvael saw Madoc hold up a warning hand and reined in. He could hear a stream rushing nearby – and the unguarded voices of men.

The trio walked their horses forward in line through the glades, quiet as gliding phantoms. More voices, louder; some coarse laughter.

There were seven soldiers, watering at the side of the brook in the next clearing. All large men, travel soiled, splashing water on their dusty faces or drinking from their helmets. Their steeds, hard-ridden and sweating, drank along the edge of the bank. The men wore light polished plate over grey chain mail, and their long-backed bowl helmets had ragged plumes of blue and white cloth. Tilean dog-soldiers, outriders, scouts by the look of them.

There was no time for conference. As one, Fithvael, Cloden and Madoc surged forward out of the trees and came down on them from the rear. Cloden's greatsword was low against his thigh like a lance. Madoc's warhammer was whirring in a deadly arc. Fithvael drew his slender elven sword and swung it up ready.

Taken unawares, the Tileans had barely turned before Cloden was amongst them. One fell back into the stream with a shriek, his throat torn out, and another dropped and rolled down the back, clutching his shoulder. The Tilean horses started and ran in all directions.

Cloden overshot and crashed into the stream, turning his steed amid plumes of spray to engage another Tilean who waded in and rushed him with a broadsword. Madoc smashed into the water too, chasing down two enemies who ran for their lives towards the weapons and equipment they had left scattered on the far bank. The glade was alive with shouts and curses.

Fithvael reached another Tilean just as the man pulled himself into the saddle of his agitated horse. The Tilean swung his steed around, pulled out his sword and swept a scything blow at the veteran elf. Fithvael ducked low under it and took the human off his mount with a backhanded swing.

Three Tileans dead, now four as Cloden butchered the man with the broadsword mid-stream. Madoc ran down his pair, hammering one sideways into the rushing water and letting his horse's churning hooves trample the other. The seventh, dropping his helmet, ran at Fithvael with a pike. The strike missed, but Fithvael and his horse went over as they evaded, hooves slipping out on the mossy bank. Both horse and elf sprang up unhurt, but Fithvael had no time to remount, and dodged another pike-lunge that came at his belly. He grabbed the passing shaft of the weapon with his free hand and cut it in two with his sword. The Tilean threw the broken wood aside and drew his own sword, slamming it round and down at Fithvael.

Their blades clashed. The Tilean was no mean swordsman. He parried well and managed to wrong-foot Fithvael with his next pass. The Tilean's blade cut a nick from Fithvael's shoulder guard.

Fithvael braced, darted left and then feinted in with a blow that looked like a slice but turned into a thrust. He impaled the Tilean through the gut and lifted him off his feet. Fithvael ripped the blade clear and the Tilean collapsed without a sound.

Stern-faced, Fithvael looked round at the others. Cloden had reached the far bank and dismounted to search through the mercenaries' packs and bags. Madoc sat astride his horse in the middle of the rushing stream, Tilean blood blackening the fast-moving foam around his horse's shins, and glancing back at Fithvael. There was a triumphant look in his eyes, the first real life or passion Fithvael had seen there. For all his sour, cynical bearing, it seemed like this burst of combat had revitalised something in the Middenheim wolf. Madoc grinned at Fithvael and raised his hammer in a brutal, victorious gesture.

A blue-fletched arrow hit him square in the throat, knocking him clean out of the saddle and into the water. His horse bolted, thrashing spray. Madoc's heavy armoured form rocked in the current, half-submerged, but did not rise.

Fithvael heard Cloden cry out as he darted for cover. The air was hissing around them. More arrows rained down. Some hit tree trunks or soil on Cloden's side of the stream. Others shattered or rebounded from the stream's stones or plopped out of sight into the flow. More thunked into the mossy ground around Fithvael, wretchedly close, driving down into the wet ground. At least three embedded themselves into the Tilean corpses littering the banks.

Fithvael ducked into the undergrowth, but not quite fast enough. A blue-trimmed arrow pinned the end of his cape to the ground and the garment yanked him back. He tore it off, breaking his cloak's brooch-clasp, and threw himself behind a tree. By then, his cloak was staked out on the wet grass by four more arrows. Another one smacked into the tree that sheltered him.

The archers rode into view, thrashing through the thickets on light chargers that leapt the fern cover in bold, clear bounds. There were nine of them, more Tilean outriders armoured much like the septet they had slain on the stream bank. All rode expertly, the reins between their teeth, their powerful composite bows raised to fire and fire again. Holsters of blue-feathered arrows slapped at their hips.

They loosed more arrows. Their skill with their bows was notable. Though they rode full pelt and without hands to guide their steeds, they managed a murderous rate of fire. Cloden had scrambled into cover over on the far side of the stream and darts whickered into the underbrush around him.

Now, and only now, was a chance, as the Tileans dropped their bows around their pommels to retake the reins and pull up their mounts before the stream. Three drew swords and galloped on through the water towards Cloden; the others circled around at Fithvael.

A singular whistle had brought the elf's trusted horse to him, traces trailing. Fithvael snatched his half-wound crossbow from his saddle, slapped his horse on and levered the bowstring back fully. There was a Tilean almost on him, but he did not let haste muddy his skill. He nocked a short quarrel, raised his weapon and put the bolt smack between the Tilean's eyes, spinning him out of the saddle.

There was no time to reload. Fithvael flung the crossbow aside and redrew his sword, hastening round behind a clump of willow that shielded him from the next nearest Tilean. He came out round the other side of the sinuous tree, and lanced his sword up through the neck of another mercenary who was charging round to block him. The man fell, shrieking, but Fithvael's sword was lodged tight in him and tore from the elf's hand.

Something heavy caught him across the shoulders from behind and slammed him into the bole of a larch. His vision swam and he could feel hot liquid dribbling down his back under his armour. He moved, slow and unsteady, barely in time to miss a sword stroke that clove into the bark. Then a sword hilt punched him in the side of the head and he went down.

Blood rushed in his ears, like he was underwater. He could hear curt Tilean voices shouting and cursing around him, the stamp of hooves.

A scream.

A cry, in a voice he knew as well as he knew his own.

Blinking, Fithvael looked up.

Blue-steel keening in the close woodland air, Gilead of Tor Anrok exploded into the Tilean horsemen from behind, his white hair and scarlet cloak lifting in the air behind him. Gilead's horse was foaming at the mouth, and its eyes were wild and bright, but not half so wild and bright as the eyes of his old friend. It was times like this that he was afraid of Gilead's warrior soul. The fear almost eclipsed his joy at seeing Gilead here, now.

Gilead severed the torso of the Tilean nearest him and the man's hips and legs rode away on his crazed steed. The son of Lothain churned forward to meet another two, severing the arms of one at the elbows and decapitating the other. The headless corpse dropped out of its saddle and was dragged by one stirruped foot. The other, blood jetting from his jerking stumps, disappeared into the woods as his horse bolted, his screams echoing through the trees for minutes afterwards.

On the far bank, the trio who had chased down Cloden turned and spurred back to the new fight with furious yells and brandished swords.

As they turned, Cloden exploded up from cover and took one off his horse with a massive sweep of his huge two-handed sword.

Gilead blocked a sword-swing from the remaining Tilean on his side of the stream, broke the blade against his own, and cut down through the man's gold-armoured collarbone. Then he turned to meet the charge of the last pair who were powering up out of the streambed at full gallop, cascading spray.

Gilead became a blur, shadowfast. Two riderless horses passed by on either side of his steed and disappeared into the woods. Two dismembered bodies crashed to the ground beside him in sprays of blood.

The elf sat back in his saddle, his smoking sword low at his side. He looked across at Fithvael.

'So you changed your mind?' Fithvael said archly.

'Just in time, so it would seem,' Gilead replied.

Fithvael shook his head at the retort and splashed out into the stream to reach Madoc. Coming from the far side, Cloden reached the Middenheimer at about the same time.

Madoc was alive, but the arrow was buried deep in his thickly muscled neck. Blood stained the rapid water around him. Madoc blinked up at them and tried to speak but nothing clearer than a gurgle issued from his lips.

'That's bad...' Cloden muttered, and looked as if he was about to put Madoc out of his misery, much as a man would a lame horse.

'Help me get him up. Now!' Fithvael commanded, his voice brooking no disagreement.

Cloden shrugged, sheathed his great sword across his back and helped Fithvael lift the saturated dead weight of the wolf. They dragged the lolling Middenheimer back to the bank where Gilead sat waiting on his stamping, wild-eyed steed.

Bodies littered the bank and the moss was soaked with blood. With a grunt, Cloden lowered Madoc onto his back and Fithvael whistled for his horse once more. He had herbs and dressings in his saddlebags, curative miracles beyond human knowledge.

'I thought you said you were done with him,' Cloden remarked, indicating the silent, waiting figure of Gilead with a jerk of his head.

'I did,' Fithvael answered quietly. 'But I don't think he is yet done with me.'

NITHROM'S COMPANY WERE assembled in the main public yard of Maltane, a scrubby area an acre square surrounded by dwellings that lay directly before the main slope of the inner mound. Dusk was falling.

Nithrom rode from the waiting group in concern as he saw Fithvael's party come in through the eastern gate of the town, the elf and Cloden riding slowly and supporting Madoc on his horse between then. Gilead rode in behind, some way back.

'By the gods! What happened?'

'Tileans, dog-soldiers,' scowled Cloden. 'We came upon a clutch and laid them low, but then more came down from the woods. A lot more. Bowmen.'

Nithrom leaned in to scrutinise Madoc's wound with distressed eyes. Madoc, weak but conscious, tried to brush him away.

'That needs attention, and quickly.'

Madoc made a gurgling grunt that was trying to be words.

'You have dressed it,' Nithrom said to Fithvael, who nodded.

'As best as I could. I can do a better job if we can get him to a cot and get a fire going. He is not co-operative.'

'Madoc was always robust.'

'He's got an arrow through his throat. He's sucking breath and he has lost too much blood, and the dart-head is buried in the bone of his neck! I do not care how robust he thinks he is, he will be dead by the time dawn comes, unless we can get that cruel shard out and staunch the flow.' Fithvael seemed far angrier than he had any right to be.

'Fithvael's right,' murmured Cloden. 'Get a dirty piece of iron like that wedged in your flesh, even a mild wound, and the iron'll brew up poison in your blood.'

'We will see to it,' Nithrom said sternly, 'and Madoc won't resist.' He said this last part whilst shooting a warning look at the swaying, sweating Madoc.

Then Nithrom looked beyond them and saw Gilead approaching slowly down from the east gate.

'Gilead te tuin Lothain…' he whispered. 'So you came after all.'

'He... turned the tide, when we were overrun,' Cloden said grudgingly. 'They had us cold, me and the elf.'

Nithrom rode over to Gilead and they regarded each other for a moment.

'Will you stay?'

'Perhaps. For a while at least.'

Nithrom nodded and turned his horse away, riding back to the main group and raising his voice so all could hear. 'Vintze found nothing to the west, and Caerdrath reports the southern edges are also clear of any trace. Only now, to the east, do we have a sign of them.'

'Scouts,' Fithvael suggested, drawing near. 'They had ridden hard, so they were probably outriders probing ahead of the main unit.'

'Usual Tilean company tactics,' said Brom, 'a vanguard pack of fast archers reconnoitring the land.'

'The main force would be but a day behind,' finished Dolph in what seemed the same voice, their words overlapping.

'Did any you met survive? Any ride back to carry a warning?' Harg asked.

'None,' Gilead replied simply, and all understood the truth of it.

'That is really no better,' Vintze said then, wiping a palm across his stubbled chin. 'When the vanguard don't return, they'll be just as well warned.'

'Wery bad...' growled Bruda, scanning the fading light on the northern slopes with hunting glances.

'So where is everyone?' Cloden asked, saying the words for them all, gesturing around the deserted town.

THEY RODE TOGETHER up the steep mound above the main settlement and reached the timber bridge that crossed the deep inner ditch. It was a deep, well-dug fortification, and the low evening sunlight did not penetrate its murky depths. The bridge itself was solid and firm, and built so that a horse team could pull it down from the inner courtyard in the event of a siege. But it was old, and the harness hooks were weed-choked and rusty.

Beyond it, the timber fence was firm and secure, and sat like a crown around the cranium of the hill. Iron braziers on the wall top were cold and dead. The gate itself, a single section of hardwood planks, was sealed tight.

Nithrom looked across at Gaude, who shrugged and pulled out his battered cornet. He blew a loose association of notes, some in the same key. To Fithvael it seemed a sadly appropriate fanfare for their band.

Silence followed.

'Again?' Gaude suggested, gesturing with his cornet and wetting his lips.

Nithrom shook his head and signalled instead to Vintze. Without question, the lean, leather-suited Reiklander slipped off his mount and crossed the bridge to the gate. His long, pale hair and the silver hilt of his sword caught the last of the sunlight as he climbed up the gate, as nimble as a squirrel.

Astride the top, he reached inside with dagger and cut something. Fithvael heard a heavy counterweight trundle to the ground. The gate began to swing inwards and, still astride it, Vintze kicked out at the gatepost, accelerating the motion. He rode the gate as it swung wide and then jumped down, sword in hand.

Nithrom lead the other riders in across the bridge, indicating with a deft gesture for Caerdrath to remain outside on watch. The noble elf turned his steed and sat motionless in the dying light, gazing north.

As they moved in past him, Fithvael saw how Gilead cast Caerdrath a lingering, questioning look. Quite the last being Gilead had expected to find in this ragged human band, Fithvael was sure.

Inside the fortification, it was like black night already. Long bars of golden sunlight raked in through the open gate, but the high fence blocked everything else out. Above them, in a sky as dark blue as the trim of an Elector's cloak, freckles of early stars began to shine.

The main hall rose before them, dark, low-gabled and massive, with smaller outbuildings adjoining it. Behind it sat the narrower shoulders and thin tower of the temple. The party dismounted onto the soft, black marl of the mound's top and, weapons ready, approached the front portico of the hall. Gaude stayed back, watching over the huddled, cloak-wrapped form of Madoc.

Leading them, Nithrom stepped up under the mighty oak lintel. He hammered on the carved doors. 'Ho, within!' he called, in the tongue of the Empire.

Vintze gestured sidelong to the outbuildings with the point of his sword. 'Livestock in there, lots of it, close-packed and agitated.'

Fithvael had already detected the pungent animal smells, the scrabbling shuffle of hooves. 'And in there,' he said, 'I smell humans.'

Cloden and Vintze both shot him hard glances, but Nithrom grinned. 'He has it right.'

Nithrom put his shoulder to the doors, pressing his strength against the bas-relief, weathered image of some insubstantial human god. They did not budge, not even when Brom and Dolph added their weight.

'Barred,' Dolph said.

'From within,' finished Brom.

Nithrom waved up Harg, who hefted his great axe in his hairy paws. Again, Nithrom struck the doors and called out. 'Ho, within! If you won't answer, we are coming inside! Know that we are friends, come to aid you – and stand back!'

He moved aside and Harg, a bestial black shape in the thickening gloom, swung back his gigantic axe. Bruda knelt behind him on the steps, just clear of his back swing, her bow raised ready.

With one single blow, the disfigured Norseman stove the doors inwards. A trio spearhead of Nithrom, Cloden and Vintze led the way inside, with the others in tow.

The hall was high, wide and gloomy, ranged with benches and trestles, piles of sacks, barrels, full skins and other commonplace items. There was a stone-edged fire-pit at the far end, under a horn-shaped chimney flue. The crossbeams of the high roof were hung with salting meat, game and bunches of drying herbs. They scented the still, close air heavily.

A megaron, thought Fithvael, in the old style... a mead-hall, a communal one-room palace, as befits an old, traditional community like this. Rushes covered the creaking boards of the floor.

At the fire-pit end, thirty yards from them, ten men cowered in a tight group, facing them. By their clothes and stature they were farmers, two as young as teenagers, one as old as old men get, the other seven in stalwart middle years. But their faces – they were the faces of cornered killers, ready to fight to the very death, eyes glittering with fear and venom. Several held hoes, threshing flails or pitchforks. Two had corn sickles, one a vintner's pruning knife. The leader had an old, rusty sword.

'Begone!' he cried hoarsely.

'And leave you to the Tilean dogs? I think not.' Nithrom's voice was calm. The elf ranger stepped forward, sheathing his blade.

'In the name of mercy, get you gone!' the sword-wielder called again as the group huddled back against the fire-pit wall.

'Don't you know me? It is I, Nithrom! I swore to bring you defenders, and so I have. Where is Gwyll, your headman?'

'Dead!' spat the leader. 'Dead seven dawns now!'

'How so?' Nithrom asked, genuine surprise in his gentle voice.

'You said you would return, but weeks passed! Then the first of them came, a pack of those dogs, foraging ahead of their army! Gwyll and twenty of the menfolk took arms to drive them off. Four of our kinsfolk were left dead in the outer ditch! We never saw Gwyll or the others again!'

'Merciful gods... and you have hidden in here since then?'

'What choice had we? Seven nights and days, waiting for them to return and slaughter the rest of us!'

'Put up your weapons, men of Maltane. We are here now.'

'You bring an army, elf-who-promises-so-much?' the old man asked with a sneer.

'Those that you see, and three others besides.'

The leader threw his old sword onto the planking with a clatter and sat down on a bench. The cluster of others broke up, lowering their weapons, grumbling.

'Then we are all surely dead,' said the leader heavily.

'What's your name, friend?' asked Le Claux.

'Drunn.'

'Then, Drunn, you are not dead until we declare it to be so.'

'Is that a joke?' asked the wizened old man who had sneered before.

'Enough, Master Swale. Don't goad them.'

'No, I am not to be shushed, Drunn!' The old man strode forward, facing Le Claux, who smiled with slight bewilderment at the hunched, white-haired old man and his rusty flail. 'Where were you a week ago? How can you come here now, promising salvation, when there's but a baker's count of you and an army approaches? Eh? What can you do that twenty of our best could not?'

'We are warriors, old fool,' said Le Claux, his amused smile cooling. 'We know a sight more about the art of battle than a bunch of farmers.'

'Is that right, brave sir knight?' returned old man Swale, his rheumy eyes fierce. The knight took an involuntary step back. 'Oh yes, no doubt you know the delights of war, the glory, the comradeship, the songs, the gold you earn! But I'd wager we of the soil know more about real war! To see our beloved sons killed or mutilated, our daughters raped, our vines torched, our livestock swept away for camp feasts! We know what it feels like to toil a whole year to see it gone in a week, we know how hard it is to till burned soil, or worse, to dig it to make a grave! Don't talk to me about war, knight! You play at it, we live with the consequences!'

With an angry bark, Le Claux thrust his mailed hand out and pushed the scolding old man away. Swale staggered and fell, smashing over a trestle.

'Leave us! Go outside!' Nithrom told the Bretonnian, his voice as cold and hard as steel.

'But I–'

'Now!'

'I'll not be shamed by some–'

'So you would shame us all so we can share it? Get out!'

Le Claux turned and thumped heavily out of the megaron, his ornate spurs jingling against his greaves.

Erill crouched and helped the old man to his feet.

'My apologies,' Nithrom said to them all, his manner respectful. 'For that outburst... and for not being here a week back. It took too long to gather this band. But between them, they are more than thirteen swords. Heroes all, one way or another, from the ends of the land, from triumphs too numerous to count. We're here now, and by my oath, we will stand firm for you. We will protect Maltane.'

'From Maura and his dogs?' asked another of the farmers, his voice weary with disbelief. 'For that, you don't need to bring us a band of warriors, you need to bring us a damned miracle.'

'Then you should think of us as just that, my friend,' Vintze said with a twinkle in his eye. 'A bloody, dusty, mad-eyed bunch of miracles.'

Behind him, Harg chuckled. Fithvael felt himself smile too.

'Where are the others?' asked Cloden.

'Others?' Drunn replied, looking away.

'The rest of the town,' said Dolph.

'The folk of Maltane,' Brom echoed.

'Gone,' Drunn shrugged darkly.

'Run, fled, long departed,' added Swale, pouring himself a cup of wine from a skin hung on the post-end near him.

The elves in the party exchanged glances. Ever so gently, Gilead thumped his foot down on the wooden floorboards twice. The sound it made was deep and hollow.

With a wide grin, Bruda pulled back her bow and shot an arrow into the boards between her feet.

The last six inches protruded from the floor, vibrating. There was a muffled series of human squeals and shrieks from beneath them.

Harg swept back the rushes on the floor with the flat of his axe blade and found the trap door in a moment. Fithvael stepped in beside him and, with Cloden's help, pulled it up and open. Below them, in the darkness, dozens of white, terrified faces looked up. A stench of human misery rose from the cavity.

Nithrom looked over at Drunn. 'How many?' he asked sharply.

Drunn sighed. 'More than two hundred. Mostly women and children.'

'Get a ladder! Get them out of there!' Nithrom ordered, face drawn.

It took coaxing to get them up. Eventually, for reasons that perplexed Fithvael, only he and the formidable Kislevite woman had any success in bringing them out, and only then when Drunn, Swale and the other men of Maltane pleaded reassurance. The floor of the megaron hall lay flush with the flattened crown of the mound, but a deep and massive scarcement had been dug underneath. The townsfolk had hidden there, in the stinking dark, for upwards of a week, huddled between the great earthenware vats of drinking water. As the last of them came up, tearful women with deathly pale, grizzling babes in their arms, Fithvael took a flaming torch and descended the ladder. The scarcement was a large as the hall above, deep and damp, with a floor of oozing marl and walls dressed with travertine blocks.

The stink of human excrement was intolerable. Fithvael found two miserable bodies: an old woman and a girl, crumpled in the furthest corner. He could not tell if it had been fear, hunger or suffocation had done for them. He did not want to know.

He heard a movement behind him and turned to find Gilead standing behind him in the torchlight. Gilead was rapping his knuckles against the bulky water jars.

'Two-thirds gone,' he said quietly.

'There is time to refill them from the streams or the well.'

'No well up here in the inner place.'

'I noticed.'

'Not a good sign if it comes to a siege.'

'I noticed that too.'

Gilead sighed and scratched behind his ear. 'Why did you come here, Fithvael?'

Fithvael cleared his throat. 'Because of Nithrom. Because someone had to. I see that more clearly now I am here. Someone had to.'

He paused. 'And why did you come?'

'Because you did. Because you are usually correct. Because… I did not know what else to do.'

Fithvael smiled, his white teeth glinting in the torchlight. 'Gilead te tuin... you will be the death of me.'

'I've always fancied it would be the other way round... Fithvael of the lost causes.'

'Lost causes?'

'Starting with me.'

'Oh.'

'But if it makes you any happier, I promise I will be the death of you,' Gilead said and clambered back up the ladder.

In the hall, as lamps and fires were lit and food and wine shared out, there was hubbub. The place was suddenly crowded, much smaller and hotter as bodies mingled. The folk of Maltane, mostly women and children as Drunn had pointed out, huddled and grouped, some weeping, some singing, some asleep on their feet. The stench of their inhuman confinement rose from their bodies and blocked out the sweetness of the hanging herbs.

Gilead and Fithvael joined Nithrom, Harg and Bruda at a table where a flask of wine and pottery beakers had been set out. A passing girl slid a platter of husked corn, oil and dried goat-meat onto the tabletop.

'There is water below,' said Fithvael as he sat. 'But it needs refreshing and refilling.'

'So noted,' said Nithrom, taking a swig of wine.

'So... when was you going to tell us about Maura?' Harg asked.

'Aye, old friend, when?' added Bruda. 'When battle commenced? Or before that?'

'Does it matter who we face, my lady of Kislev?' Nithrom smiled, eyes guarded. 'The wars we've seen together, I'm surprised you concern yourself with the enemy's name.'

'When it is Bloody Maura, perhaps.'

Overhearing their talk, Cloden sat down with them, a beaker in his hand. 'Maura's Murderers? Great gods, Nithrom, I'm with the she-bear on this! You should have told us! I thought those were his damnable colours on those men we danced with in the woods. White for bone, blue for blood.'

'Blue?' asked Fithvael.

Harg grinned across at him, the smile ruffling the line of his beard and zagging the dreadful scar. 'Maura fancies hisself a noble prince of Tilea. He's naught of the sort, of course! I'm more a bastard king of the north than he is nobility!'

Nithrom looked over at them both. 'There's more truth in that remark than you'd first know, Fithvael te tuin. Isn't that so, King Hargen son of Hardrad?'

'Bah!' scoffed the hulking Norseman, filling his cup. 'No more of such talk!' He sipped down a big gulp of wine and stared across the table at Fithvael earnestly. 'Maura thinks hisself a prince, and delights in killing to achieve that rank. Hence blue for blood. Noble blood. Understand?'

'Transparently,' Fithvael said.

'And so Maura is the one we face here. Maura and his vermin band. You should have told us, Nithrom.' Cloden's voice was grim.

'Cloden's not been so right since that day at Altdorf field. Then he was wery right.'

'Don't remind me, Bruda. That was another day... and we won, did we not?'

'Just, da.' Bruda smiled.

'He is just a mercenary, a human mercenary, with a band of dogs,' said Gilead abruptly. 'Sell-swords are all dangerous. Why should we be troubled? An armed company returning south after the war season is still an armed company.'

'You've been hiding in the woods for too long, friend,' Cloden said, without malice. 'Maura and his murders are sell-swords, yes, but more than that. Maura takes things... personally.'

'Meaning?'

'Imagine: you're a company of war-dogs. You take coin and assault a town. You fail. You say, "I did my best, goodbye, I'll not waste more trying"... yes?'

'Of–'

'Not Maura. Not "Bitter-End" Maura. Damn that he can't pay his men, damn that it takes three months when it should have taken a week. Victory is all he wants. Victory is all he will accept.' Cloden looked down into his drink. 'A skirmish won't drive him off. He plays to win, and he'll keep sending his men on until he has that victory.'

'But that would break morale...' Fithvael began.

Harg smiled, sadly. 'Not the Murderers. Maura has that, that charm – what do you call it again, Nithrom?'

'Charisma.'

'They're with him all the way. To hell and beyond. He draws to himself the best and the meanest and the most insane. That ogre sergeant of his–'

'Klork,' growled Bruda.

'Aye! The tales I've heard of him. And the leaders of his dog pack: Hroncic and Fuentes! Animals! Bastards! Death-dealers!'

The group was silent for a moment as the sounds of the busy hall washed about them.

'They were good, I will say that,' said Fithvael eventually. 'Those we met in the woods. Just scouts, but they fought like... daemons. Good swordsmen, good horsemen. And their archers, if they were but a taste, I have a dread of what is to come.'

The huddle looked around to see Gaude leading Madoc in. Fithvael stood up, urging the Maltaners to find a cot and heat up some clean water. He still wasn't sure what he could do, but that arrow had to come out. Attended by Gaude and a gaggle of townsfolk, the elf set to work.

Le Claux returned, but paused in the doorway. He glared across at Nithrom.

'Le Claux?' the elf said patiently.

'Caerdrath summons you. There are lights on the northern trail.'

It was truly night now and a loose wind from the south-west scudded rafts of grey cloud against the moons. Leaving Fithvael and Gaude inside to tend Madoc, Nithrom's ragged band emerged from the main hall and crossed to the open gate of the inner mound. Caerdrath, still attentive astride his patient mount, was like a gleaming statue in the half-light beyond the bridge. He heard them approach without looking round and pointed off into the gloom.

On the northern path, the road that the carts had followed that very afternoon to enter Maltane, a string of torches jiggled slowly down. Twenty or more.

'More scouts?' suggested Erill.

Cloden frowned. 'Too many. This could be the front end of the main company.'

'Or an expeditionary force coming to learn the fate of the scouts,' Gilead suggested.

'Aye… and we don't know what numbers lurk just beyond that rise,' added Harg.

Nithrom swung into his saddle. 'We will go to meet them. Make your peace with whatever gods you observe and come on. This may be done sooner than we expect. Master Erill: stay here, watch the gate. Make ready to close it fast if we return in a hurry, and get the townsfolk to prepare torches. Lots of them. Light the tops of the inner fence with as much light as you can.'

Erill nodded and hurried back in through the gate.

Nithrom looked from side to side and regarded the warriors drawn up on horses beside him. 'Vintze, Harg, Gilead… with me to meet them. The rest of you keep out of sight and behind the outer ditch. Come when I call. If it all goes bad, withdraw to the inner mound and close the gate. If my vanguard falls, Cloden has the lead.'

Le Claux started to say something but thought better of it.

Along the line of riders, final preparations were made. Vintze put on his helm and slid his left arm into the loops of his small shield. Harg rested his war-axe across the chin of his saddle as he donned his snarling, full-face helmet. Dolph and Brom buckled on their helms and loaded their long, bulky handguns with synchronised movements, resting the primed pieces across the specially raised rests of their saddle mounts. As one, they closed their brass visors. Bruda placed a fur-trimmed, spiked bowl-helmet on her head, gathering her red hair beneath it, and tested her bow. Cloden adjusted his basket helm and slid on kidskin gloves before drawing his greatsword. Le Claux made a blessing to the Lady and settled a lance across his looped shield. Caerdrath, already prepared, raised up a slender javelin, one of six nested in his steed's saddle-sling, and propped the butt against his right hip.

Gilead, like Nithrom, was bareheaded and carried a long, leaf-pattern elven shield. The rangers of Tor Anrok drew their longswords, Nithrom's silver, Gilead's blue-steel.

The ten riders spurred away together down the mound into the lower part of Maltane. At the main yard, most pulled away to left and right, disappearing into the rambles of huts and dwellings on either side, leaving Nithrom, Vintze, Harg and Gilead riding in a tight pack down to the northern gate.

The torchlights were gathering and milling just outside the outer ditch as they came down. The gathered firelights revealed a troop of more than fifty Tileans, all on horseback, all bearing the blue and white badge.

Some called out and pointed as the four riders appeared on the far side of the outer ditch, emerging from the darkness of the apparently dead town. Nithrom's group reined up just short of the crude ditch bridge.

The Tileans' leader, a thickset man with an eye patch and a long blue cloak, rode forward with six of his men in flank, until they were facing Nithrom's group across the bridge. Gilead took the man in: heavy and muscled, his armour more ornate than his common soldiers. He had no shield, but wore a short sword on each hip. His expression was haughty, triumphant and vain.

'Greetings to you!' the mercenary called out, his coarse voice shredding the soft vowels of the Tilean tongue.

'And to you,' Nithrom replied in perfect Tilean.

'We are but a few journeying veterans, looking for a place to rest.'

Nithrom nodded. 'More than a few, perhaps.'

The commander looked around at the gathered men behind him, as if surprised to find them there. He laughed. 'Aha, yes! My merry band! They wouldn't harm a horse tick, so please you. There's no need for those drawn blades.'

'Is there not?' Nithrom's voice was cool. Gilead was struggling to translate as the exchange continued. Suddenly, he did not need to.

'What is this place, that I am greeted by two noble sons of Ulthuan, a Norse bearshirt and an Imperial swordsman?' the commander asked in perfect low elfish.

If Nithrom was surprised, he did not show it at all. Maura's band travelled the world, Gilead told himself; they have surely mixed with many peoples and places. Just because they were killers did not mean they had to be stupid.

'A peaceful place,' replied Nithrom, switching language himself. 'One that has no desire or ability to harbour a full company of men-at-arms. There are streams in the woods where you may refresh yourselves and fine glades where you can camp. On the morrow, you can get on your way, and we can all be happy there was no… unpleasantness.'

'Unpleasantness?' the man laughed, and a couple of his men cackled with him. 'Who said anything about unpleasantness? Come, Ulthuare te tuin, my gentle friend… all we seek is a roaring fire pit, a sound roof, and hay for our tired steeds. Maybe we could also purchase some game and some ale.'

'I must offer you my apologies, for I must be failing to make myself understood,' Nithrom said flintily. 'Perhaps your fine command of my language is not so sharp after all. There is no place in this town for you.'

There was a long silence. Gilead flexed his grip on the pommel of his sword, waiting. The commander bent and spat dust-spittle into the mud, and then sat back on his steed, gazing absently up at the night sky as he adjusted the fit of his gauntlets. His men waited. The crickets clicked.

'Who,' he began at length, as if patiently trying to deal with a small child, 'who do I have the… pleasure of addressing?'

'I am Nithrom, of Tor Anrok. And you?'

The eye-patched man grinned. 'I am called Fuentes, master-at-arms, colonel. These are my boys and they have ridden long and hard this day. You see, Nithrom of Tor Anrok, I believe you have it about right: we have indeed misunderstood each other. We are peaceful men, the war season is over, we are just going home. All we ask is hospitality.'

'And that, I'm afraid, is the only thing we can't offer you.'

'You know,' said Fuentes, turning in his saddle to address his men in Tilean, 'if that kind of protest had been presented to me by poor, starving farmfolk, I might have seasoned my bearing with respect and humility. But when it comes from a quartet of armed warriors… well, I start to have my doubts. From the likes of these…' and he gestured round at Nithrom and his companions, 'well, it smacks of unfriendliness.'

'Master Fuentes,' Nithrom said in clear, precisely enunciated Tilean, 'we both know that if humble farmers had met you at this gate and denied you access, you would have slaughtered them without a second thought. Perhaps the presence of myself and my comrades will make you think again. You will not cross that ditch unharmed.'

Fuentes shrugged, as if it were nothing. He turned his horse around and moved back through his waiting men in the torchlight.

'We are beaten,' they heard him say to his men, 'fully and soundly by these overwhelming numbers. Let's away.'

Gilead stiffened. He heard Harg curse beside him softly and Vintze hiss the words 'Here it comes…'

His back to them still, Fuentes dropped his hand sharply, and the first dozen dog-soldiers ploughed their horses forward onto the rough bridge, pulling swords.

'Meet them!' Nithrom bawled.

The four defenders powered forward, smashing into the head of the assaulting phalanx as it was bottled by the bridge so only three could ride aside each other.

Nithrom ran the first Tilean through with his silver blade as Harg reaped his way into the thick of them, roaring like a wounded bear and swinging his axe around. Two riders, one missing a head, tumbled left off the bridge into the ditch.

Gilead charged in, deflecting a sword thrust with his shield as he bent low and then ripping the Tilean off his horse with a slice that cut him from belly to chin. Gilead's blue-steel blade had severed the breastplate; the flapping sections of metal fell away with the body.

Vintze was beside him, slamming a Tilean rider off his horse with a sideways blow of his shield, and plunging his broadsword through the eyeslits of the Tilean behind his first victim.

Inside ten seconds, the boards of the ditch bridge were sodden with blood and strewn with the dead and dying. Horses that had fallen into the ditch shrieked and whinnied like banshees. On the far side of the defence, Fuentes turned, his face now shining with rage, and drew two hooked short swords, one in each hand, guiding his horse with his knees.

'On them! On them! Take them!' he screamed.

The main force of the Tileans, forty or more, poured in at the bridge.

'We can take them!' barked Vintze, ducking a sword sweep and slashing out as he fought to control his bucking steed.

'Aye! We can hold this bridge!' Harg added, his axe-blade spraying Tilean blood as it swung.

But already some of the lithe Tilean chargers, under the skilled hands of their sell-sword masters, were leaping the ditch itself and thrashing up the inner slope.

'Break!' Nithrom cried. 'Now! Break and fall away!'

Harg and Vintze, both reluctant, tore away, digging their heels into their horses' flanks, heading back into the compound. Nithrom had to yell a second time before Gilead seemed to hear him.

Then the four of them were galloping back from the ditch into the outskirts of the town, with the main force of Tileans raging after them.

The quartet raced in between the first of the huts, heading towards the public yard and the mound. The first two Tileans on their heels went down hard, horses cartwheeling and crushing their spilled riders as arrows took them in quick succession.

Bruda appeared on the roof of the first hut, drawing her bow with her powerful arms. A third rider went down, a fourth. She whooped.

Several more mercenaries had gone inside past her, and were now cornering in the inner yard. There was a flash and a roar, and one was slammed off his mount. His immediate companion started, tried to turn his horse and died as a lead ball exploded his steed's head, passed through it and punched through his own chest.

Reloading their handguns, Dolph and Brom ran their horses forward. They fired again, and two more steeds buckled and crashed over. Then they were in the thick of the charge. The twins from Ostmark stowed their deadly but slow handguns and laid in with maces. They broke heads, their brass armour flashing in the flickering firelight.

Cloden had dismounted. A greatsword worked better on foot. He came round one of the miserable huts and laid his massive blade into the next few speeding Tileans. His first strike cut completely through man and leaping horse alike.

Nithrom, Harg, Vintze and Gilead turned back to meet the incursion, having lured them into the killing embrace of the lower town.

Le Claux came charging out of the dark and lifted a Tilean off his horse on the end of his lance. He laughed out loud, triumphant.

Like a terrible ghost from distant times, the noble figure of Caerdrath also emerged from cover and charged in, his stallion racing. Each of his six javelins found their mark, and then he drew his sword. He became a steely blur, scything the Tilean cavalry down like corn.

In the thick of the ferocious fighting, Gilead slashed and whipped his sword around, severing limbs and heads, smashing shields and breaking weapons. For the first time in a long while, he felt he had found his place. In a company of proud warriors, however ragged the band, fighting for a cause.

He was still hacking when the Tileans melted back in retreat, destroyed and driven out. Gilead saw Fuentes riding with no more than half a dozen men towards the ditch bridge. Nithrom's warriors had killed almost forty of the Tileans.

Bruda whooped again and Vintze joined her in a cheer, riding around the body-littered street. Gilead lowered his sword and tried to contain the rage inside him.

Above them all, the fence of the inner mound shone with the lights of a hundred torches, suggesting a garrison of massive strength. Erill had done his work.

The first attack had been repulsed.

THE VICTORS, IN exuberant mood, returned to the inner mound and the gate was shut and barred behind them. Dolph and Brom, ever grounded and practical, had suggested their immediate course of action should be to secure and bolster the defences of the lower ditch, for it seemed certain the Tileans would return sooner rather than later.

Nithrom thought this good counsel, but did not take it. Such work by night would be thankless and hard, and difficult to co-ordinate. He wanted to give his warriors time to rest and enjoy their victory. For tonight, they would simply lock themselves in the inner mound. If Maura's men returned, then it would be bad luck but they would at least be fortified.

Besides, Le Claux was already calling for a wine skin, his face glowing with excitement and pride, and Harg, Vintze and Bruda would not need much convincing to join him.

Wine was brought to them, along with hot food that Erill had ordered to be prepared. Minor wounds and scrapes were dressed and bound as the warriors grouped in the inner hall to celebrate. The telling scale of their victory had also raised the spirits of the Maltane townsfolk too. As the middle night passed, a veritable feast was underway with much singing, drinking and general good spirits.

Nithrom watched over it all from the door of the hall, a cup of ale in his hand. He saw Harg and Bruda joking and singing their way through a rowdy, suicidal drinking game, surrounded by a circle of laughing townsfolk. Cloden and the twins from Ostmark were running an all-comers arm-wrestling contest near the fire-pit. Vintze had the utterly undivided attention of several village girls. Le Claux held court, retelling the action like an epic poem for a giddy group of villagers, his metaphors and symbols enhanced by each draft of wine. Even Gaude and Erill were relaxed, flagons in hand.

It would do them good, Nithrom thought. Good for morale. He took a sip of his ale. He would watch the wall till dawn.

Fithvael was suddenly by his side, wiping bloody hands on a rag.

'Madoc will live, for now,' said the veteran. 'The barb is out. He is sleeping.'

Nithrom raised his cup. 'To you, worker of wonders. Your hands are as bloody as ours. You've seen a life or death fight of your own this night.'

Fithvael nodded. 'I don't think Madoc will ever speak again,' he murmured. 'His larynx was torn away.'

Nithrom sighed. 'A tragedy. The tales he can tell, from his time with the Templars.'

'Madoc was a Wolf Templar? A White Wolf?'

'Of great renown. Leader of their Gold Company, doughty in battle. Did you not note his wolf pelt and his warhammer?'

'But not now?'

Nithrom smiled. 'He... acted in a way that brought dishonour to his regiment and was cast from the temple. He's been a sell-sword ever since.'

'What did he do?' Fithvael asked.

'He refused to kill me.' Nithrom sipped again, his mind clearly on distant memories. 'The most courageous thing, to throw away his career to help a friend, especially one of another race. I will tell you the tale some time, Fithvael te tuin. Just know this: though he was cast out in dishonour, I have never known a man more honourable. To his friends. To what really matters.'

Nithrom turned towards the door.

'Where are you going?'

'Someone must stand watch, and I have asked more than enough of this brave band tonight.'

'I will stand it with you, friend, if I may,' said Fithvael. 'We can watch the town and talk of old times.'

GILEAD LOTHAIN SAT alone, oblivious to the merrymaking, gazing into the flames of the fire-pit at the rear of the hall. He became aware of a figure beside him and looked up. It was Caerdrath. The elf carried a goblet of wine in each hand and offered one out to Gilead. The last son of Tor Anrok accepted it with a nod and Caerdrath took that as an unspoken invitation to sit down next to him. The elf had removed his helm but his long hair was still braided up on his scalp. The scintillating sculpture of his armour was flecked with Tilean blood.

'I am called Caerdrath Eldirhrar, tuin Elondith, grandson of Dundanid Flamebrand, of the line of Tyrmalthir and the clans of High Saphery and the Marble Hills.'

'Gilead te tuin Lothain, of Tor Anrok.'

They drank to each other.

'We are alone here,' Caerdrath said, though it was clear he meant symbolically, as the place was crazy with noise and bodies. 'Old world, old blood. Your companion, Fithvael, he mixes better with the human breed, and Nithrom is so worldly, he is neither man nor elf anymore.'

'Do you despise him for that?' Gilead asked.

'Not one scrap. Nithrom is the truest friend I know. He has made a place for himself in this ugly world. Why else would I ride with him?'

'But what finds you here, Caerdrath Eldirhrar, tuin Elondith?' Gilead savoured the chance to use the ancient high tongue, with all its formal modes of address. It was like old music, half remembered.

Caerdrath did not answer directly. 'Nithrom tells me that you and Fithvael are the last of your house. That you have ventured out into this bitter world to find traces of our vanishing people.'

'That is so.'

'Then we are kindred in that also. I too came to the human world to uncover the past. The old realms, the lost cities, most of them now buried beneath the foundations of new human settlements, it seems. I wanted to find traces of the world we had lost. We are alike.'

The notion shocked Gilead. Since, well, forever, it seemed – since Galeth died, at least – he had been driven to seek out the forlorn scraps of the old race. He had also felt himself to be a diluted being, just an echo of elfhood, tarnished by the dull human world. But here was an old one, so much more glorious than himself, an example of the very wonder he had been seeking... who professed exactly the same drive. It was a sobering revelation. So long he had been trying to regain his heritage, and here came a pure, unalloyed part of that provenance, equally lost and equally unfulfilled.

As if sensing the thoughts, Caerdrath said, 'Our age has passed, Gilead te tuin Lothain. Our stars have set. The day fast approaches when we must step aside for brute mankind forever.'

'I have a favour to ask of you,' Gilead said.

'I will grant it, if it in my power.'

'When this is done, this little war, I would see the peaks of Ulthuan before I die. Show me the best way, the routes I should take.'

'I will do better than that, Gilead te Anrok. I have been out in this wearying world too long myself. When we are done here, I will journey with you back to Ulthuan and we will feast together at my father's table in the Marble Hills.'

GILEAD WOKE LONG after dawn. The hall was cool and full of the after-scent of smoke and cooking. A few of the townsfolk were asleep upon the rush flooring and Le Claux was slumbering in a corner.

Pulling off his leather jerkin and his undershirt, Gilead strode out of the hall into the cold daylight. The sky above was bright and grey, with a threat of rain, and the gate of the inner fence was open. Womenfolk were washing pans and platters in a water trough and he crossed to them, naked to the waist, and dunked his head and shoulders. The women huddled coyly as he shook out his mane of white hair.

He nodded a courteous, flirting thanks to them and walked off towards the gate, his jerkin and shirt folded under his right arm.

From the gate, he looked down across Maltane, ugly and stark in the glare of a new day. Smoke rose from the ditch at the north end, black and rancid as the wind carried it back. He could see figures at work in the town below, most of them townsfolk.

Pulling on his shirt, he wandered down the mound into the common ways of Maltane.

Nithrom had roused those he could early and set them to work. Dolph and Brom who, with their artifice guns and tactical minds seemed to Gilead to have almost mechanical souls, had begun to command the defence work. Nithrom clearly valued them for their strategic, engineering bent. Gilead saw townsfolk working in teams to widen the outer ditch, and others who used their spoil to fill sacking to raise an inner bulwark. In the public yard, Bruda was training some of the young men of Maltane – and at least three of the strongest young women – to pull bows. As her pupils flexed, released and missed the straw-stuffed targets yet again, she grinned at Gilead as he passed.

Gilead saw Gaude entertaining a flock of the children, and Erill supervising villagers as they erected tar-soaked bales of straw at the street corners. Down by the outer ditch, Dolph and Brom, both stripped to the waist and sheened with sweat, were overseeing the digging work.

He also saw Fithvael, sat amongst a group of diligently working farmers and crossed to him. The elf was showing them how to fashion arrows, and some were so advanced in this work they were binding the heads with pitch-wetted rags.

'Fithvael,' he greeted his oldest friend.

His companion looked up. He smiled broadly. In truth, he doubted he had ever seen Gilead so happy and carefree.

'The work abounds,' Fithvael said by way of greeting. 'Harg has got a team out in the wood felling timber to shore up the outer dyke. That Kislevite woman is raising a new army of archers.'

'I saw her.'

'Vintze and Caerdrath have ridden out to spy for a sign of our enemies.'

'I had better find myself some gainful work as well, it seems,' Gilead said, and walked on towards the outer ditch.

Nithrom and Cloden, rags tied around their faces, were watching the fire in the ditch pit. Mule-teams guided by similarly masked villagers were dragging the last of the Tilean carcasses, horses and men, to the ditch. The pyre of the enemies they had slain the night before belched black, fatty smoke. A pair of scrawny buzzards circled high overhead.

Nithrom saw Gilead approaching. He left Cloden in charge of the work with a brief word, and jumped down from the ditch head, pulling off his rag-mask.

'What can I do?' Gilead asked him.

Nithrom shrugged. 'Can you cut timber?'

Gilead shrugged back. 'If I have to.'

'Well, you can sharpen blades, at least. From the way your own sword cuts, I can tell you know how a whetstone works.'

'Bring me the blades. I will sharpen with pleasure. I feel almost useless amid all this toiling.'

'Ah, they've done well since dawn,' Nithrom commented, glancing around. 'We've strengthened the inner ditch and raised more obstacles that cavalry won't like. A few other tricks besides. When Harg comes back with the timber, we'll raise a solid bulwark inside the dyke.'

Gilead pointed up along the main avenue that led to the public yard and the mound. 'We should get some barrels or stable planks, and make a few points of cover along there, to the left, you see? The bulwark may slow their horsemen, but a few good nests for bowmen would break the line of the street and stop their vanguard getting up any speed if they make it in.'

Nithrom shrugged and nodded. 'Well said. I will get the elder, Swale, on it. He's a devil with the strength of a giant. Maybe you can show him what you mean.'

'Of course.'

'And I did as you suggested… the water jars in the scarcement of the hall are refreshed and full again.'

'You would have thought of that without my help.'

Nithrom grinned. He took Gilead's hands in a tight clasp. 'By the old gods, it's good to have you here, Gilead te tuin! The spirit of Tor Anrok will keep this place safe!'

Mule-pulled carts laden with freshly cut timber were approaching from the woods. Astride the first, bare-chested, Harg waved his great axe to salute the town.

AN HOUR PASSED in helping to unload Harg's expertly felled timbers and lift them into place, then another teaching old Swale and four of his grandsons to build angled cover in the main street. Passing by, Dolph noticed the defences and nodded in admiration.

Then midday came, and found Gilead up in the cool shadows of the inner mound fence again, sharpening blades. He had acquired a block of spruce as a rest, and a crowd of children as an audience. They oohed and aahed as he unwrapped his whetstones from their oilcloth bag.

The weapons had been brought to him: Fithvael's sword, Nithrom's long blade, Harg's battered axe, Bruda's sabre, Le Claux's broadsword; all of them, and the spare weapons besides.

He set to work, wearing out nicks and gouges, finishing edges, testing sharpness with a few strands of his own long hair, and explaining each piece of work and weapon to his retinue.

'This is a longsword, from an elven smithy. It belongs to Nithrom, the tall elf warrior in the dark green armour.'

'With the kindly face?'

'Him indeed.'

'He's your master.'

'He is my friend.'

'What's an elf?'

'You are looking at one.'

Laughter. Some whispers.

'No, we do not steal away new-borns in the dead of night. You humans have so many wrong ideas about my kind.'

'What's a human?'

Laughter, some playful punching.

'See here, how I make the stone strokes long and unbroken. A little oil… and now the edge comes sharp. See?'

'I could do that!' this from a tall lad at the front.

'Then you may come here and do it. No, let it slope against your leg. That's it. Again, no… against the way of the metal. Like this.'

'Am I doing it?'

'Yes you are. Well done. Now both sides, mark, and both edges of both sides. That is good.'

'It looks easy!' A girl at his shoulder.

'Come around here and try it. Now this is the scimitar of the red-haired Kislev woman.'

'She's beautiful,' said the older boy already at work. More laughter and some jibes.

'She is, and so is her sword.' To the girl now, her hands trembling with the whetstone. 'Long clean strokes now. Careful, do not cut yourself on the edge. And there's only one edge to this blade, so you'll be done in half the time.'

'Why's there only one edge?' piped a small boy in the huddle.

'It's a weapon design for slashing, rather than stabbing or slicing. You work it so!'

Some gasps, some backing off.

'It is very different from this blade. This is my sword. My brother's, in fact. He gave it to me. Taller than you, eh? This is meant both for slashing and thrusting. Ha! And ha!'

More excited yelps.

'Come on now, take a stone in your hand and come here... that's right, some oil... no, not too much... now, along the blade to the tip. Good.'

A little industry around him, small faces concentrating and determined. Gilead smiled.

'Now, the Norseman's great axe! Who's brave enough to whet that?'

A forest of grubby hands.

'You... come on. Here's the trick, rub the stone both ways. Keep the haft wedged against the ground. Yes, good. Back and forth.'

'And now, this is a greatsword, forged in Carroburg! Have you ever seen a sword so big? It'll take two of you at least. You... and you, lad, with the freckles. In you come...'

THE AFTERNOON WAS waning, and all the blades were polished sharp. Gilead was at work on the last – Le Claux's trusty broadsword – with the last of the children grouped around him. Most had wandered away at intervals as more interesting things happened in the town below. A woman had brought him a plate of stew and some ale, but it sat untouched and the food had gone cold.

Thunder rumbled in the cold, windy distance. The summer storm that had been threatening all day was about to break. A first few spots of rain pattered down.

Gilead felt... something. He rose, Le Claux's ornate sword ready before him.

He went to the gate, some of the children scampering after him.

Below, away on the flank of the northern hills, were the shapes of two riders, galloping down to Maltane as fast as they could, kicking dust: Vintze and Caerdrath.

'Get inside. Hurry,' Gilead instructed the children.

Maura was coming.

RAIN WAS HAMMERING down by the time the Murderers appeared in full force. They lined the top of the northern scarp, blue and white banners flopping in the downpour. From his position on a flat roof in the lower town, Fithvael sighed. Nithrom had estimated two hundred, and the night before they had sent forty to their doom. But there was no mistaking the size of the force ranged up there: three hundred, at the very least.

The batter of drums rolled down the valley slope into Maltane, blurred by the rain. The Tilean infantry were beating the march. As Fithvael watched, more drew into view: horse teams, further squadrons of infantry, six-horse limbers that dragged great cannon.

Fithvael looked away, across the rise of rooftops, and saw Nithrom already mounted upon his steed, waiting in the public yard. Le Claux and Caerdrath were with him. Nithrom saw the veteran elf's glance and signed for patience.

Yes, I shall wait, Fithvael thought, though doom itself comes to overlap me.

There was no parley this time. Fuentes had taken word back to his chieftain, and so sealed Maltane's destruction. Fithvael, craning his eyes against the rain and the dying light, could see a brute of a man on a great horse, trotting the length of the escarpment, looking down and issuing orders to the rows of cavalry and foot soldiers that stood around him. The man's silver helmet was plumed with blue and white feathers. That had to be Maura himself.

Fithvael gauged distance and crosswind and knew he had no chance of hitting the Tilean leader, even with his best bowshot. On a roof across the street, he saw Bruda doing much the same. They caught sight of each other and both shook their heads.

What will he do, this Maura? wondered Fithvael. *Lay us to siege? Pound us with cannon? Assault all out with foot and horse?*

Personally, he prayed it would be the latter. He hoped this Tilean doglord would be characteristic of his kind, keen for a swift and arrogantly crushing defeat achieved by force of manpower. That they would greet. But a siege? Such a tactic would kill them, and an artillery barrage would flatten Maltane and leave nothing left standing to be looted.

Though from what he'd heard of Maura, such a punishment would be signature. Fithvael was sure, after the defeat and humiliation of his advance guard, that Maura wanted nothing from Maltane except its death rattle.

A horn sounded. The clear note rang around the bowl of the valley.

Fithvael picked up the human-made composite bow next to him. It had been a while since he'd wielded one of these, and it was crudely constructed compared to what he was used to, but his trusty crossbow's rate of fire was too slow for what was coming.

A wave of Tilean cavalry broke down the funnel of the hill towards them, fifty abreast. Their thunder was louder than the storm rumbling across the sky.

MALTANE HAD NO cavalry force to meet a tide that great, and so, under Nithrom's terse instructions, it did not begin to try. Instead the defenders waited, tensed, as the horse army charged down on them – crossing the low scrub, crossing the slake of marshes that skirted the town, charging up the low rise towards the outer ditch and the bridge.

Which only seemed to still be there…

The weight of the first eight outriders on the ditch bridge brought it down in a tumult. Harg's expertise with a wood axe had severed the beams just to the point of cracking. The bridge falling out from under them, horses and riders, moving at full pelt, cartwheeled and tumbled into the ditch. Those immediately behind were slammed into the gulch by the weight of the charge.

The cavalry broke, moving aside in both directions. But behind them, down the slope, came the infantry, a pouring horde.

Some horsemen tried to jump the ditch, but it was deeper than Fuentes had known it, and the bulwark on the far side was piled up and lined with out-facing stakes. More horsemen foundered in the ditch, some leaping up and calling for the footmen to help them pull their struggling horses free. Others tried the leap and were disembowelled on the timber points.

The first of the infantry were now at the ditch, many clambering over and up the other side. Now Fithvael, Bruda and Erill, along with the half-dozen Maltane folk who had shown any bowmanship, began their work, picking off as many of the troops who crawled over the bulwark as they could.

Fithvael cursed as he saw infantry teams on the far side of the ditch dragging timber boards with them and heaving them out across the mire. They were just out of his bowshot.

A few infantry climbed over the bulwark. Fithvael and Erill picked them off with clean shots. The lad was good with a bow, Fithvael noticed. That plate armour and elderly sword was all for show.

Now the first straggles of infantry were over the ditch, more than the archers could manage. Further bowmen, under Cloden's direction, villagers all, began firing down the main street into the press.

The Tileans had managed to get three boards across the ditch, and that was enough for the milling cavalry. They romped over the vibrating boards, kicking infantry aside as they spilled up into the town, lances and swords glittering.

The first dozen fell on the lethal tripwires that Vintze had fixed across the street. Charging steed limbs snapped as they tripped and went over. Others leapt on, the wires now broken, dodging the sprawling bodies of their comrades and their horses, galloping up the streets.

Now more wires, pulled suddenly taut at head-height by waiting villagers, snapped into place. Tileans cracked back out of their saddles, several virtually decapitated. The horses ran on.

Others assayed the main street towards the public yard, peppered by arrows. Several fell. A quartet of riders made it as far as the town pump, where gunpowder charges buried under a dusting of soil by Dolph and Brom erupted and killed them.

The heat was out of the cavalry now. They fell back, many not even daring to cross the ditch. In their stead, the mass of infantry rolled in, clawing over the bulwarks and the makeshift bridge faster than Fithvael and the bow teams could match.

The infantry seethed up the main street

Fithvael saw Nithrom's signal but he already knew what to do. He lit a pitch arrow and shot it into a tarred straw bundle on the edge of the street. Bruda and the other archers did the same. In a few moments, the main street was a fire-lined inferno that gave the Tilean soldiers little room to move. Gunshots rolled down the street as Dolph and Brom began firing.

But there would still come a point, Fithvael knew in his heart, when all their tricks and skills would be overwhelmed by sheer numbers.

Then Fithvael saw Nithrom, Le Claux and Caerdrath charge into the head of the infantry spread from the main yard, cutting them back. On their heels, on foot, Dolph and Brom, maces swinging.

Cloden, Gilead, Harg and Vintze sprang, also on foot, out of houses further down the street to meet the influx side-on and press them against the horsemen. They had taken the battle to close quarters.

Fithvael realised he had no arrows left. Raising his sword in one hand and his wound crossbow in the other, he leapt down off the roof and charged into the melee.

THE ELF VETERAN emptied his crossbow into the belly of the first Tilean he met, then laid about himself with his sword. It was thick and close in the muddy, wood-walled street, lit by the burning tar-bundles. He glimpsed Bruda nearby, slashing with her scimitar and baying like a she-wolf.

He saw Erill. The youth had come down from the roofs too, his sword in hand, and almost at once had become surrounded. He had killed one Tilean with a lucky thrust, but others were stabbing at him. The lad fell.

Fithvael blundered that way through the press, hacking left and right. Erill was down, blood leaking from a shoulder wound, his aged armour broken and pitted.

Fithvael cut right, removing a head, and then left to open a belly. In the space that he had made, he scooped Erill up and tossed him his short sword.

The lad managed to catch it. It was a pearl-inlaid blade, two feet in length, made by the master craftsmen of Tor Anrok. He stared at it for a heartbeat, flexing it in his hand.

'Don't admire it! Use it!' Fithvael shouted.

Erill swung left, wondering at the lightness of the elven blade, and severed the weapon arm of a Tilean almost on him. The youth laughed with sudden glee, and set into the mob.

Fithvael struggled to join him and set his back to the youth. Murderers, in great numbers, massed around them. They fought like devils, man-boy and elf-sire thrown together by the gods of war.

A figure erupted in through the press around them, swinging his sword and destroying the foe.

The newcomer said nothing, because he could not. It was Madoc. His trusty warhammer lost in the flood of the stream when he fell, he had resorted to the unfamiliar weight of a broadsword, which now he spun and chopped almost as deftly as a great hammer of Ulric.

Side by side, though the hot blood of their enemies covered them, Fithvael, Erill and Madoc held the street.

GORE DROOLED OFF Gilead's longsword. He had lost sight of Vintze and Cloden, but that hacking and splintering nearby could only be the work of Harg and his axe. The elf cut into the press once more, blue-steel spinning, and slit through wrists and windpipes. There was a pack ahead, Tileans mobbing over a victim in the firelight. He sliced them down.

The white warsteed was dead, its eyes staring. Le Claux was trampled in the dust nearby, his armour torn and shattered, two lance heads and a sword thrust through his torso. The knight looked up at Gilead with misty eyes.

'Have we won?' he asked.

Gilead paused. 'Of course, warrior. Thanks to you.'

'I thought as much,' Le Claux mumbled, blood gurgling in his throat. 'I'm thirsty. Have you a drink at all?'

Gilead swung aside and cut down a Tilean who loomed out of the firedark.

Then he knelt by Le Claux's side and pulled out the last of the flasks of elven wine that he had taken from Tor Anrok and carried with him ever since. It was almost empty. The Bretonnian finished the remains.

'Ah...' smiled Le Claux. 'Quite the best I–'

The Bretonnian continued to smile up at him, but Gilead knew Le Claux was dead.

He turned, severing a marauding Tilean from armpit to armpit with his voracious sword before the mercenary could strike him down as the man had intended, and leapt back into the battle.

BLOOD, MEAT, SINEW, flesh, steel, bronze, iron, fire. The currencies of war were played out and exchanged until dawn.

As the sun rose, the Tileans fell back to the north scarp. They left seventy cavalry and a hundred and twenty infantry on the plains before and the streets inside Maltane.

The defenders, many injured, all weary to the point of sleep, had lost Le Claux, and old Swale, and nineteen of the other villagers: four women, three boys, twelve men, all of them fighters.

Yet, by any standards, they had won another extraordinary victory. Maltane had become the Tilean's curse. But it had also become a place of fatigue, of spurting wounds, of broken weapons.

Nithrom called his troops and the villagers back into the inner mound. They had done all they could. They had waged an immortal defence. If Maura now continued, they would have nothing left in them but the pride of denying him the first time. They had nothing left to give.

As dawn rose, true to his nature, the unforgiving Maura began his second assault.

* * *

It was a distant sound at first, like a stick being snapped, then a splash of mud. Fithvael and Vintze were outside the megaron's portico, binding the wounds of the villagers, when they heard it.

Vintze cursed.

Again it came, a sighing cough-crack, far away, then a wet thud below down the slope.

Fithvael grabbed up his crossbow and ran to the wall. He was in time to see two of the nine great cannon on the distant northern scarp puff white smoke. A second later, that cracking sound. Fifty yards below the inner ditch, plumes of wet mud vomited upwards.

'Has he not the range?' asked Fithvael.

Brom was on the wall decking next to him, using Vintze's scope to spot. 'No, he's just getting his aim.'

The man leapt down, tossing the scope back to the Reiklander. 'Get them inside! The villagers all! Get them inside and down into the scarcement!'

Motion seized the throng. Clutching bewildered children to their skirts, the womenfolk hustled them into the main hall. The surviving menfolk of Maltane, some thirty in number, picked up their makeshift weapons and shields. Amongst them were at least a dozen boys who looked too young for combat, and twenty women who refused to hide. Nithrom's warriors, meanwhile, were assembling on the wall.

The first cannon shell hit home, punching through the tower of the old temple behind the inner hall. There was a growl of punctured stone and part of the tiled roof fell in.

A second later, and another shot hit the outer wall, cracking the boards and making the ground shake. One of the Maltane men was thrown off his sight-deck and fell into the mud below.

They have the range now, gods help us, Fithvael thought.

He turned. The gate exploded in, crushing the water butt in a powerfully outflung sheet of stone and water, and killing several goats. The smashed gateway looked so open and vulnerable.

Two more shots screamed in, one tearing through the roof of the inner hall, the other slicing low through the top rails of the wall. Part of the decking collapsed, spilling two more Maltaners. One clambered up. The other, just a boy, lay still in the marl, his left side sheared away.

Gilead and Nithrom ran to the open gate and looked down.

Skirmish lines of Tilean horse were cantering in across the outer ditch and through the lower town. Behind them were infantry files, bearing pikes, halberds and bows.

More shells whistled down, over-shooting the mound and falling in the lower ditch behind.

'We cannot fight this!' Gilead cursed.

'No, we can't.' Nithrom gazed out again and then turned to the defenders. 'Inside! Into the scarcement. They will have to stop shelling before their foot troops get up here. We can ride it out. I ask for two to stand with me, to give the call.'

All the defenders volunteered. Nithrom paused a moment, then made his choices. 'Bruda, Dolph. The rest of you below. Gilead will lead you out when the time comes.'

Even the Maltaners hesitated at this. Nithrom had always given the second command to Cloden. Gilead himself was surprised. If not Cloden, then Caerdrath, surely, before him.

'Do as he says!' Cloden roared, dismissing the slight. 'Get below!'

The defenders scrambled inside and down the ladders into the scarcement. More cannonballs hissed down, smashing the megaron roof and the chancery of the temple. Some struck the wood fence, shattering sections of it.

Nithrom, Dolph and Bruda struggled into cover.

IN THE TIGHT, cloying air of the scarcement, Cloden called for calm. The earth around them shook with the impacts outside, and dust and mud dribbled in between the beams. The Maltane villagers were terrified, and with good reason.

Harg rose, a hefty shaggy bulk in their midst. He opened his arms. 'I've known worse'n this, friends! Much worse! Let's lift our spirits and sing a song!'

He started to sing a phlegmy Norse battle hymn, singing slow so they could learn the words and the return, clapping his meaty hands in time to the song and to the impacts above.

Seeing his efforts, most of Nithrom's band made the effort to join in – Cloden, teaching the children how to clap in time; Vintze, over-enunciating the gristly Norse words; Erill, whispering the words and conducting the womenfolk.

Brom sang too, but Fithvael saw how he kept glancing up at every missile hit. He should be with his brother, the elf thought.

Gilead saw the gunner's nervousness too, and winced. He knew all too well the pain of separation from a twin. He paced through the huddled mass, clapping his hands in time, encouraging them all.

Madoc sat at the back of the chamber, near the steps, his broadsword across his knees, clapping time, mouthing the verse.

Fithvael stepped over to Gaude, who was hunched over the cloak-wrapped corpse of his lord.

'What are you doing?' he asked delicately over the song and the impacts.

Gaude looked round. He had taken Le Claux's sword from his dead hands. 'What I should have been doing.'

Fithvael hunched near to him. 'You're no fighter...' He let the implications hang between them.

'Not now, perhaps.' Gaude cleared his throat, as if nervous. 'I was once... Sir Gaude. I was a champion of the blessed Lady. At Alesker's Field, I lost my nerve and my honour. Since then, I have followed this poor, drunken fool as his squire. Poor Le Claux – he was never made to be a knight.'

'He did us proud.'

'Maybe. The Lady rest him, he never had the spirit.'

'And you do?'

Gaude rose, drawing the beautiful, knightly sword from its scabbard.

'I did. I think it has become time I found it again.'

Fithvael was almost shocked by the squire's raw bravery. He half-expected angelic choirs to begin singing. When they did, he had to shake himself.

But it was Caerdrath. He had brought out an elven lyre, and was strumming and singing along with Harg's rough chant. The Norseman blinked and looked around, but found a smile in Caerdrath's eyes and continued. It was the oddest, most plaintive sound ever heard on the surface of that world. A forlorn high elf of Saphery, with the purest golden music in his voice, singing along with a sour, brutal northman's epic.

They sang it together, in a harmony that none present would ever forget, and now, drowning out the deathly pounding of the enemy's cannon for a few moments, every voice in the scarcement joined in.

THE REPETITIVE THUD of the impacts, always intermingled with the crunch of breaking stonework, the crack of sundering wood and the smash of falling tiles, fell suddenly silent.

They had been holed in the scarcement for two hours. In the gloomy cellar, all fell silent and turned their faces up to look at the roof. Gilead, Vintze and Cloden lifted their blades. Caerdrath wrapped his lyre and put on his helmet. Brom moved to the foot of the ladder, his mace in his hand.

They heard a voice, from far outside. What it said, they could not know. But Gilead, Fithvael and Caerdrath knew at once that it was Nithrom who had called.

'Now!' cried Gilead, pushing up the ladder after Brom, who was already monkeying up to the hatch.

The fighters followed – Cloden, Caerdrath, Harg, Vintze, Fithvael, Madoc, young Erill – and Gaude on their heels, still dressed as a squire but bearing the broadsword and shield of his dead master.

After them, came the warriors of Maltane, the men, women and youths who were able and prepared to fight, farm implements and rusty weapons in their grips.

Gilead and Brom climbed up through the hatch and hurried down the dust-choked hall of the megaron in advance of the others. From without came shouting, the sound of sporadic combat. They barely noticed that the great hall's roof was broken open to the sky and that they ran over shattered tiles and slumped beams.

Outside, the inner fence was a vestige of its former self. The entire north-facing wall and the gate was a splintered ruin. In truth, the entire inner mound had taken a heavy beating, but the north wall had seen the worst of it. Smoke plumed around and livestock loosed from the stables by a series of cannonball strikes ran wild.

Nithrom, Bruda and Dolph filled the gap, ranged side by side, hacking at the Tilean foot troops who even now were forcing entry up the ditch. Nithrom had taken the inner bridge down, but sheer weight of numbers welled up and into the inner compound.

Gilead was with Nithrom in an instant, his sword slicing and slashing a deadly pattern. A moment later, Dolph was joined by Brom and Vintze, and Cloden dove in to support Bruda. Like sword-wielding daemons, they hacked and slashed and thrust and threw the baying Murderers back on themselves.

'Alarm! To the left!' Erill screamed as he and the rest flooded out of the inner hall.

More Tilean mercenaries were pushing in through a splinter in the curtain of timber to their left, where a cannonball had staved in the fence.

Erill rushed to it, Fithvael and Gaude at his heels. The trio laid into the first intruders. Fithvael saw how the lad handled the elven shortsword well, like he was born to its grip. But he lacked skill and experience. His wild, untrained strokes left him open to the dog packs raging in through the fence break, and his wounds did not help him any either. A thrusting halberd mashed into the side of his face, and Erill fell.

Fithvael was surrounded by a thicket of Tileans, swinging his sword savagely. 'Gaude! Get the boy clear!' he yelled.

But Gaude was occupied too. He had cast Le Claux's shield aside and engaged the foe, his borrowed broadsword glinting. It was the most extraordinary display of swordsmanship Fithvael had ever seen from a human. Whether driven by grief or a need for vengeance, Gaude parried, ducked and swung like a master, his sword moving like fluid metal.

Harg and Madoc slammed into the melee from behind, and as Madoc laid in with his own sword, Harg dragged the bloody form of Erill clear. Other Maltaners ran in, joining the fight at the wall's breach.

SWOOPING IN AND out of consciousness, Erill came round to find himself lying clear of the fight by the steps of the ruined hall. He pulled himself up, then passed out in a savage explosion of pain, and then came round and pulled himself up again. The left part of his face was numb and cold, and he knew by the blood on his collar and front that he had a dreadful wound. He couldn't see out of his left eye at all, but he dared not touch it with his fingers, lest he not like what he found.

But through his right eye... by the gods, what legends were being forged.

At the main gate breach, Nithrom, mighty elf ranger, towered over a pile of corpses, his blade slicing back and forth, misting the air with blood. To his left, Cloden, slicing the greatsword of Carroburg into the armoured heads of the scrambling foe... the twins of Ostmark, Dolph and Brom, reunited in combat, maces smashing... Vintze and Bruda, Reiksword and

Kislev sabre, laughing as they faced the endless tide of blue and white liveried soldiers, bathed in blood... Gilead, a daemonic blur, raging his longsword into the foe...

At the gap in the fence to the left, the grizzled elf Fithvael, side by side with Madoc and Harg, slicing and chopping in bloody abandon. Harg's great axe circled and spun as it did its work, Fithvael's sword stabbed and thrust, and Madoc – well, he seemed to use his weapon as if it were a warhammer, spinning and flexing and turning it down at each stroke, trying to use his boundless mastery of the hammer to good effect with a sword.

And Gaude, was that truly him? Almost lost in a thicket of Tileans, revealing a skill with a blade that a humble squire could and should not possess.

Drunn and the impromptu warriors of Maltane were in the thick of the carnage too, jabbing and slicing, pummelling and stabbing. Erill saw several fall beneath the experienced skill of the Tilean dogs, but none died without honour.

He rolled sideways and saw Caerdrath. The elf had seen another hole in the timber fence and had raced across to close it. Four Maltane villagers went with him, spurred on by his cries.

What came through the breach was not a man. Not an elf. Not something Erill ever wanted to see again.

The ogre was three times the size of the largest and most crudely put-together human. He was dressed in rags, tattered blue and white, and he swung a flint-bladed adze in each of his huge fists. Tileans squirmed in through the ragged breach around him, urging him on.

'Klork! Klork! Klork!' they howled to goad him.

The ogre killed the first two Maltane warriors that reached him with a single slice of one blade. The beast bellowed, spittle flying from his broken teeth as his sinewy neck turned his misshapen mouth to the sky.

Caerdrath was there in three paces, a golden blur. His sword prismed light it flew so fast. One of the massive stone adzes fell to the marl, still gripped in the ogre's clawed hand. Black blood fountained in all directions.

The ogre – Klork – howled, and smashed at the elf in return.

Caerdrath dodged the mankiller adze, and as he dived ahead, raked his blade down the flank of the monster.

Klork turned slowly, striking as he went, his remaining adze blade dinting the side of Caerdrath's beautiful silvery armour.

The elf fell, rolled and came up facing the ogre square on. Erill stiffened as he saw the high elf spit crimson blood down his fine breastplate.

Ignoring the pain that lanced through him, Erill clambered to his feet, and found his sword. Giddy, he ran towards the fight, towards the ogre. A Tilean charged him and somehow he side-stepped, slicing the Tilean's head clean off in a single move he did not even think about.

Klork was chopping at the darting Caerdrath, but Erill saw how the elf was slower than before. Blood wept through the cracks in his ithilmar plate mail.

Erill threw himself forward, his sword held ahead of him. The superb elven blade smashed into the ogre's back and the point came out through the huge beast's throat.

Klork vomited blood and fell, crashing down into the ditch like a felled tree.

Erill swayed. He saw Caerdrath smiling across at him. Then four Tilean pikes ripped the wounded elf apart, spitting him from every angle.

Erill dove upon the Tileans, yelling, his sword, stained with ogre blood, flying. He was vaguely aware of Madoc and Cloden reaching him, driving into the breach.

Then the pain of his head wound became too much and the world span about him. Rushing sounds, ghosts in the air, the dying sigh of an elf, darkness.

FOR THREE HOURS straight, until noon had passed, they held the inner mound of Maltane against the hordes that swarmed up from below. Only foot troops could reach the top of the mound, for the ditch and steepness of the slope made cavalry access impossible. Many Tilean riders dismounted and joined the infantry push. The mercenaries harried the space that had once been the gate, and clambered in through punctures made by cannon shells in the stockade. Some even tried to scale the fence. The climbers and the clamberers could bring nothing with them longer than a sword, but at the fallen gate, lines of long pikes and halberds thrust in at the defenders.

Yet at least, as Nithrom had predicted, the shelling had stopped once the Tilean foot had moved into range.

Twice the Murderers broke clear into the inner yard and defeat seemed to be about to overtake fragile Maltane. On the first occasion, at the main gate soon after Klork and Caerdrath had fallen, Cloden, Vintze and Gaude waged a maniacal counter-push from the left side of the shattered entrance, cutting off the harried group of Tileans already inside and closing the breach, driving further attackers back with flailing swords that were so wet with blood they glowed dull red. At their backs, Harg and the twin gunners from Ostmark engaged and destroyed those who had got into the compound in a brutal melee played out on the marl in front of the megaron's portico.

On the second occasion, just short of midday, a new force of Tileans none had seen skirted round the inner mound on the outside of the timber fence, and brought a section of it down with axes. This was round to the west, almost behind the temple, a direction not yet assaulted. The din of the raging combat covered the sounds of their axe-strokes, but a small boy, one of those who had helped Gilead sharpen the blades, saw the incursion from a window of the temple where he was hiding. His wails alerted his mother and an old woman, who darted out through the inner hall and screamed the news to the defenders' line.

Three Maltaners managed to break off and were first to hurry round the mound yard and meet the attack. One was a ploughman called Galvin, tall, with shoulders like a barn roof's tie beam. The other two were a herdsman and a weaver.

There were eight Tilean dog-soldiers already inside the fence by then, and dozens more pushing through the hole behind them. They were all shieldless, and most just had axes and shortswords, all they dared bring on the treacherous circuit of the outer fence. But two had crossbows.

The herdsman dropped, a quarrel through his neck, before the trio had even got within sword-reach. The other crossbowman buried his dart in the meat of Galvin's left thigh, but the doughty warrior did not slow. He killed both bowmen as they tried to reload, with savage blows of his halberd. It was a Tilean weapon he had taken from a corpse earlier in the battle, and he laughed at the justice. Then he and the sword-wielding weaver were in the thick of them.

Two Tileans brought the weaver down with axe-blows, their seasoned experience bettering his fevered eagerness. Then they were all on Galvin, and more came in the breach besides.

By then, Gilead had freed himself from the main fight at the gate mouth, and he ran to the second front by the most direct route: through the shattered megaron hall, leaping out through a broken window at the west end where it met the crumbling wall of the temple. On his way through the hall, he managed to scoop up his black longbow and quiver from the equipment stacks they had carried in on their arrival.

Gilead stood, braced, on the low, tiled roof of a midden overlooking the influx, and began to loose red-fletched arrows into the enemy force. Each draw of his bow sent a long, ash-wood arrow juddering into a Tilean body. He cut down six, enough for the wounded Galvin to barge and hack his way clear of the press of Murderers.

More arrows flew in. Bruda was kneeling on the roof lip of the hall itself, shooting down with her double-curved Kislev bow. Together, the two hawk-eyed archers slaughtered the milling Tileans. There was nowhere to run, no cover from the deadly hail, except back out through the fence. As the last few scratched and clawed their way out, leaving twelve dead or dying on the churned earth, Bruda and Gilead sent more shots into their backs too.

Once they were out of sight, Gilead dropped his bow and leapt down, drawing his gold-hilted sword. He raced to the breach and, with Galvin's help, dragged a haycart in to cover it. Once she was sure no more Tileans would appear, Bruda also lowered her bow and vaulted down to help. The trio wrestled the cart into place, and then used a mattock to stake it firm with broken timbers from the wall. Better repairs would have to wait.

Galvin sat down suddenly, weak from blood loss. Apart from the quarrel wound, he had been gashed and sliced in a dozen places. He was splashed with gore from head to toe, but by no means was all of it his.

'What can I do?' he wheezed to the elf and the Kislevite.

'Watch here,' Bruda told him.

'They may try again. Stay here, rest and watch the breach,' Gilead agreed.

'But I can't just...' Galvin began. He was swaying eccentrically, but the rolling roar of the main fight was too loud to ignore. 'I must fight, for Sigmar's sake! My village–!'

'Then recover our arrows as you watch. We will need them later.'

Bruda quickly showed the ploughman how to use a short knife to cut out the arrows without breaking them.

GILEAD AND BRUDA returned to the fight, barely in time to lay in beside Nithrom and Madoc, who were being driven back by Tilean swordsmen.

'Where's Caerdrath?' Gilead bellowed over the ring of steel and the hoarse yells of pain.

Nithrom glanced at him. Gilead did not know how the other elf had fallen, he realised.

Below, a horn sounded down the valley and drums rolled. The Tileans were signalled to fall back. Even the strongest assault can only maintain its impetus for so long without advantage – and all their advantages had been denied.

Maura's Murderers broke off and fell back down the mound, many running in retreat, for they knew the embittered defenders would not let them leave unhindered. True enough, Bruda and Fithvael, and Dolph with a borrowed bow, fired on them as they ran, dropping half a dozen and wounding more. The inner ditch and the northern slope of the mound were littered with the southern raiders' dead.

The defenders sagged almost as one, overcome with exhaustion. Most of the villagers who had fought fell, weeping or gasping for breath. Women, children and the elderly came gingerly out of the inner hall and the temple to tend those they could help.

Madoc found Erill and carried the lad into the hall. Erill was unconscious and the left part of his face was a bloody ruin.

Fithvael found Gilead standing silently over the mangled body of Caerdrath. Fithvael could feel the pain and anguish throbbing inside his old friend at the sight. It quite eclipsed even the pain Fithvael himself felt at the loss.

'Gilead! Gilead!' The voice rose above the moaning and the weeping, and the distant drums. But Gilead did not turn until Fithvael touched his arm. He swung around sharply, a tall, pale murderous figure in gore-flecked black mail, his eyes as blood-dark as his scarlet shoulder guards and cloak.

It was Gaude yelling. He was on the other side of the inner compound, by the shattered gate. Gilead strode over to him through the press of exhausted and injured townsfolk. Fithvael hurried a pace behind him.

As they approached him, Gaude said nothing more. He turned and looked at the trampled, blood-soaked ground – where Nithrom's body lay.

Vintze knelt down beside the wrecked figure, cradling the elf's head.

Nithrom looked as if he was asleep. A broken Tilean sword blade jutted out from between the ribs of his studded leather armour.

Now Fithvael felt a pang much deeper than he had at Caerdrath's loss. Tears stung his eyes, hot and harsh. He looked around, and found they were all there: Cloden, Madoc, Harg, Bruda, the twins. Their eyes were all dimmed with grief. Bruda turned her face to the sky and began to whimper a Kislev prayer-hymn. Cloden spat on the ground, averted his eyes and shook his head sadly. Harg came forward and knelt with Vintze, meek and gentle as a child. Madoc was silent, like a statue. The twins, in unison, made the benediction sign of Sigmar.

'How?' Fithvael asked.

'In the last moments,' Gaude answered, quiet. 'After the horn sounded, as they fell back. One of the last of them to run, the lieutenant, Fuentes, as I saw it.'

'Fuentes!' Gilead hissed the name.

The villagers were also grouping around now in a silent, disbelieving mass. Fithvael knew this was the worst possible outcome. For all they had done, for the incredible resistance they had put up to defeat the savage enemy, this tore the heart out of them all. Nithrom was their leader, their head. None had countenanced the possibility that he could ever fall, not his warrior band of friends and old comrades, not the villagers who had believed every last one of his rousing words. And not the two elves of Tor Anrok, last of their line, who saw him as a final link to their heritage.

Their morale had died with Nithrom.

The east wind rose and the already dark sky began to weep heavy rain. Down in the valley, the Tilean drums sounded again, and the returning mercenary troops began to reform in skirmish lines around the outer ditch. There were more than ten score still: cavalry, foot, archers, not to mention the gunnery teams on the north scarp.

'We should reinforce the defences,' Dolph said.

'Rebuild what we can before they return,' Brom finished.

'To hell with that!' Vintze snarled, laying down Nithrom's head gently and getting to his feet. 'It is over. We are done. Let's get out, retreat before they can come upon us again. Grab what we can and break through the back of the mound's fence. We can be down in the woods by night.'

'All of us?' Gaude asked bitterly. 'Women and children? The old, the infirm, the wounded?'

'We did what we could!' Vintze cried, turning away. 'We did more than anyone thought we would!' With this, he cast a lingering, contemptuous look in Gilead's direction. 'But it is over now.'

'We leave them?' Gaude pressed.

Vintze shrugged. 'They can come. Whatever they like.'

'And be hunted down in yon woods by the Tilean dogs?' asked Harg. 'Thou knows Maura won't just let us run, Vintze. He'll come a hunting after'n.'

'Without food, provisions, weary as we all are?' Cloden finished the picture. 'And them, supplied, eager for blood? Some of us might get away, the more able-bodied, perhaps. Those that can ride, or fight if they have to. Those who have made a career out of slipping away like a thief.'

Vintze took a step towards the Carroburger and then turned aside. 'Damn you, Cloden!'

'We stay. We fight. We finish this,' Cloden said adamantly. 'We–' He stopped himself short and turned to Gilead. 'Forgive me, lord. I was forgetting my place. Nithrom named you his successor. I… am too used to being his second.'

Fithvael tensed. For a long moment he thought Gilead might not reply. The son of Lothain was an arrogant bastard at the best of times, but now, surrounded by the human chattel he despised, with Nithrom and Caerdrath dead… now would not be a good time to act true to nature, to damn and curse all, to despair and let the black moods overtake him as they had done all his life. But Gilead chose the moment to surprise his companion.

'I am not offended, Cloden. Perhaps it is best if you carry on in the role you know.'

Cloden shook his head. 'Nithrom named you. He did that for a reason. I owe Nithrom te tuin my life three times over in combat and as many times again in word, because I listened to him. Nithrom named you and that's good enough for me.'

Gaude and Madoc both nodded. The twins did too.

'Da,' said Bruda.

'Twas his will thee should lead,' Harg agreed.

Gilead looked at Fithvael.

'Do you have to ask, old friend?' his old friend said.

Then Gilead's eyes turned to Vintze. 'And you?'

Vintze paused, then turned and grinned with a shrug. There was sadness in his face, but the grin was genuine, a scoundrel's look, bright as a clean flame.

'If all these idiots agree,' he smiled.

Gilead turned and looked down the slope through the gateway. Maura's regiment was drawing up behind the ditch. Gilead could see campfires. They would not be coming again until they'd had rest and food, but the cannonballs might.

'Carry the dead in state and place them in the hall,' said Gilead. 'Then everyone into the scarcement. Their guns will speak again before the day is out. You, and you three–' he picked out some of the older children who had worked the blades with him. 'Stand watch up here. Come to us if they fire their guns. I don't want you out here then. But cry out if they move in again.'

Eager, the children ran to the gate.

'What about the defences?' Dolph and Brom asked in one voice.

'There is no point in relying upon them any more. The dogs will break down whatever we build with their cannon. We need a better plan.'

* * *

THE SCARCEMENT WAS as dingy and foul as they remembered it. Now there were wounded down here too, whimpering and stinking the air with open wounds. Water and food was shared out, though the supplies were getting low. Fithvael did what he could for Erill. The lad was conscious again, his face wrapped in dressings.

'A fine scar you will have,' chuckled Fithvael as he wound the bandages off and applied herbal dressings to the wounds.

'Caerdrath is dead. I saw it,' the lad whispered.

'I know.'

'The women told me Nithrom fell too.'

'It breaks my heart to say... but yes. He fell, and gave his life. Valiant to the end.'

'Make me fit. Make me well enough to stand with you.'

'You've got a bad wound, boy, and the eye, well, it–'

Erill sat up smartly. 'I don't care. Make me fit enough to stand with you at the last. I need to do that. If I fall dead a moment after the last of us is conquered or the last of them flee, I don't care a damn. I need to fight now, for my father's sake.'

Fithvael paused. He realised that he had never understood why Erill was with them. The others, all old comrades of Nithrom, who'd fought and warred and drunk beside him, and all of whom owed him a battle debt or a blood-pledge. But this one? Fithvael had always assumed Erill was here because he was trying to make a career as a pay-sword and Nithrom had given him a chance.

'What? What do you mean?'

'Nithrom... was my father.'

Fithvael set down his herbs. Such a thing was not totally unheard of, in the tales, but still...

One of elf kind and a human female? It could explain the boy's fragile looks and his graceful strength. In fact, now Fithvael saw it, he fancied he saw something new in the boy's ancestry. And yet, was it truly possible for the races to mingle so?

'How?'

'I was raised in a village near Altdorf. My mother, always told me my father had died in an Empire war, drafted to the east. But when she died of the fever in my sixteenth summer, Nithrom came. He told me the truth. He provided for me.'

Fithvael sighed. He thought of Nithrom, out in the crude human world, building friendships, fighting wars, finding solace for his loneliness amongst the brief human kind. Nithrom had cast aside the old ways more surely and more completely than Fithvael and Gilead had ever managed. He had become part of what the humans innocently called the Old World, not some phantom watcher on the outskirts. He had lived his life, and raised this human boy to be a son to be proud of, however against the old ways it was.

Fithvael felt the deepest and most starkly hollow pain of his life. It took him moments to speak again. He busied himself in redressing the wound, and turned away from the sprawled boy on the cot, returning a moment later with Nithrom's longsword.

'Use it well, Erill te tuin,' he said as he pressed it into the boy's hands. Whether or not the lad's tale was true or a mere fiction was irrelevant here, with all of them so close to losing everything.

'I already have yours,' whispered Erill, pointing to the shortsword Fithvael had lent him. 'It felt right in my hands.'

'So it should. And your… your father's blade will feel righter. You will live, Erill. If you can stand, stand. If you can fight, fight. I will not stop you. You are owed it.'

'So, ARE WE sitting here and waiting for them to come?' asked Bruda, sharpening her sword with a whetstone. Thanks to Galvin, her quiver – and Gilead's too – was almost full again. Now the wounded ploughman was being tended in the back of the scarcement.

'No,' said Gilead. 'Answer me this…' He looked to them all, the remaining pay-swords sat or stood around him in the cellar. 'How did they hurt us most?'

'With thern blasted blades, damn you!' Harg spat.

'No, worst of all,' the elf replied patiently. 'What made us almost give up?'

Madoc made a sign. He tried to speak first, but his mouth clacked wordlessly. Remembering, he drew in the air with his index finger. The elven rune that was Nithrom's initial.

'Just so. They took our leader. For a while then, we were lost, on the point of defeat.'

'Speaking of points,' Vintze said coldly, 'I'm sure you have one.'

'I can see where he's going,' Gaude said.

'And I,' said Cloden.

'Maura!' said the twins together.

'Maura the Murderer. Just so.' Gilead smiled. It was not a comforting expression to see.

'These filth have been driven at us time and again, and paid the price. Would they come on if there were no Great Murderer at their backs with a whip? If Maura were dead, what would they do? Attack? I don't think so. They would give up and run.'

'So,' said Vintze getting up and sipping from a wineskin, 'your plan is to kill Maura and destroy them at the head. Fine. Let's go. Oh… just one more thing: *how the hell do we do that?*'

Gilead called the headman, Drunn, over to them. 'How old is this place?' he asked the drawn village elder.

'Older than my memory or my family, lord,' the man said.

'The hall, the temple?'

'Have been here years, generations, the town grew up around its skirts. My father's father said that in his father's mother's time, or was it is his great uncle's d–'

'It does not matter right at this moment.'

'No, I'm sure it don't. Anyway, this was once a noble's manor, up here on the mound. Before it was a village, my folk said. The temple, that's from then. The great hall's newer, of course. The Big Winter Fire when my grandgrandfather was a youth razed it and they built another. Looks like we'll have to do the same again, if we have the chance.'

'And this cellar?'

'Oh, that's a relic from the old hall.'

'And this?' Gilead slid behind one of the big water vats and lifted a loose flag. There was a dark, oozing hole beneath it.

'I never knew that was there!' said Drunn, a startled look written upon his pale face.

'How did you know?' asked Fithvael.

'I noticed it that first time we came down here. I was looking for it. Humans who build fortresses never leave themselves without a back door out.'

'Wery impressive,' murmured Bruda.

'But how do you know that?' Fithvael pressed.

Gilead paused. 'Nithrom told me.' He coughed and continued. 'Here is what we should do now: we climb down there, follow it out, we can come out of this mound without the Murderers knowing. That is how we get to Maura.'

'But where does this thing go?' asked Dolph.

'Where does it come out?' added Brom.

Gilead shrugged. 'I do not know that. Away in the woods beyond the village, if this follows the usual way of things. My suggestion, if you are in agreement, is that we get someone who is used to slipping out of things to find out.'

Everyone turned to look at Vintze. He blinked and stood up, reaching for a lamp. 'Oh, it'd be my absolute pleasure,' he said dryly.

He lit the lamp and crossed to the hole without further protest. Gilead held his arms as he lowered himself into it.

Before he broke his grip, Gilead fixed the flax-haired Reikland thief with his eyes.

'You do not want to dream about what will happen if you do not return.'

'I know. Trust me, elf.' He winked broadly. 'Nithrom always did.'

JUST AFTER THE fourth hour of the afternoon, the Tileans resumed their cannonade. The children Gilead had set on watch felt the first impacts rather than saw them. Then spouts of liquid mud shot up from the silt-slope of the mound and they ran inside, yelling at the tops of their frightened voices.

The rain had not let up all afternoon. Now it was torrential and sheeting under the gusts of a blustering north wind. The sky was prematurely grey and opalescent. It seemed the rain showers were but the heralds of a worse storm to come.

Wet through and shivering, the children tumbled down into the deep scarcement, all screeching at once, but their noise needed no interpreter. All had felt the quaking of the mound.

Vintze had still not returned.

Gilead sent Dolph and Brom slinking above to assess the shelling and to discern what they could of the enemy tactics. The storm was darkening the sky to night-pitch and distant lightning was licking the mountains far to the north. The Ostmarkers reported movement in the enemy camp, plainly some form of preparation, but nothing was yet moving their way except cannon-fire. That was, unless the Tileans were using some art of concealment or shrouding sorcery that even their sharp eyes could not make out.

Gilead had just sheathed his sword and slung it between his shoulder blades, about to climb down into the hole below the scarcement, when Vintze returned.

The Reiklander was utterly covered in black mud and slime so only the whites of his eyes showed. Many Maltaners drew back and gasped to see him heaving himself up out of the floor, almost an undead thing covered in mulch from the grave.

He did not speak until he had rinsed his mouth with wine, spat out several gobbets of mud and then drunk properly. He wiped his mouth with his sleeve, revealing it white and stark against his dirt.

'Two full miles, turning west,' he reported, gasping. Fithvael could see he was tired and out of breath. 'Then it rises and turns north and comes out in the woods by the shoulder of the scarp, about half a mile west of Maura's camp by my reckoning, above and behind it.

'And not easy going,' remarked Gilead.

Vintze spat again.

'But it will serve,' Bruda said, eager.

'Who goes?' asked Cloden.

'We all do,' Gilead replied. 'To take Maura in his camp will take all of us... at least.'

'But what if he attacks in the meantime, while we're underground?' Cloden countered.

'Two then, to hold the gate and keep them busy as we move around.'

'Who?'

Gilead faltered for a heartbeat.

'I remember,' Vintze said, 'Nithrom used to draw lots.'

'Then that is what we do,' Gilead said.

They pulled straws from the clasped hands of Drunn. Brom and Gaude plucked out the short ones.

'Then those two it shall be,' said Gilead.

'Those three.'

They looked around and found Erill standing behind them, Nithrom's fine elven sword in his hand. He looked pale and weak, and his lost eye and face was bandaged, but there was a measure of courage in his youthful voice.

'I'll be no good to you down there, but I'll gladly stand here with Gaude and Brom.'

'So be it,' Gilead said, his eyes proud. 'Now, let us about our purpose.'

BELOW, IT WAS far worse than Vintze had described. A ragged chimney of mouldering stone dropped down into the heart of the mound, wet with mud and other, less wholesome slime. They passed into blackness almost at once, feeling their way down. The chimney itself was treacherous, and all quickly realised the extent of Vintze's nimble skills. Hand and footholds had to be made blind in the disintegrating stone. After Cloden slipped and nearly fell, Gilead instructed them to take the chute one at a time and call up once they had reached the bottom. He did not want anyone falling and taking another two or three with him. As it was, if anyone fell and broke bones, he doubted they could be hauled back up out of the narrow shaft. Any such person would doubtless die trapped down there, blocking the passage for them all.

At the bottom, it was lower and narrower still, just a tunnel bored through wet, black sediment. They had to crawl, single file, pushing their weapons and equipment ahead of them. It was humid and airless, and stank of mould and decay. They crawled on, breathless, through the endless dark. Every now and then, there came a distant rumble. None could tell if it was the storm outside, the shelling overhead, or the slumbering growl of great serpents lying far below the earth.

Fithvael cursed each bone-numbing inch of the crawl. He lost all sense of time and position, possibly for the first time in his long adulthood. The depth, the confinement, the blackness, all overwhelmed his natural abilities to judge distance and place. His mouth and hair were full of clammy soil, and he was filthy all over. This was no place for an elf.

He had made his long shield into a sled for his weapons and pack, and dragged it behind him by a long strap tied to his waistband. Every few minutes the shield would snag and stop him and he would have to reach around or kick back to free it. He had no contact with the others. Harg was ahead of him, too far ahead to be seen; Bruda, he believed, was behind. He could hear only scrambling and distant dull curses. Occasionally, a low call would float back down the tight tunnel, from Vintze or Gilead far ahead, but he could not make out any words.

He almost clawed his way into Harg from behind. The Norseman was stationary and moaning.

'Harg? What is it?'

'Who's there?' Fithvael had forgotten how poorly humans saw in darkness.

'It is Fithvael.'

'Have care! Canst thou turn?'

'Turn? Around? No! The tunnel's too tight!' A cold sliver of panic shivered in his heart.

Harg cursed. 'I'm stuck fast.'

Fithvael felt his flesh crawl. He felt the walls close in. If the Norseman was stuck, then there was no going forward... or back. The thought made his head swim.

He peered around the bulk of the big man's legs. The already narrow tunnel was narrower still here, and the roof belled low. He thought of lighting a lamp to see better, but remembered how quickly the flame would use up their scant air. Use up their air... Fithvael tried to bury the fear that clawed at him.

He dug at the mud around Harg and then pushed against him, hoping that the narrowness was temporary. If it wasn't, he was wedging Harg more securely into his grave. The northerner did not seem to move at all. They both clawed at the mud. Fithvael could hear Bruda approaching behind now, panting hard as she made her way.

'What is problem?' she called.

'Harg is jammed tight,' Fithvael cried back, pushing again at the dead weight of the big man. Damn them all that none of them had thought of this! Harg, the biggest and broadest of them, was not made to slip easily where a lean thief like Vintze could go.

'Push him!' Bruda exhorted.

'I'm trying!' grunted Fithvael.

'Let me past! I will push him!'

'There is no room!' spat Fithvael, clearing his mouth of slime. He rolled over onto his left side, braced his legs against the tunnel walls and heaved again with greater leverage.

"Tis no good!' Harg moaned, a note of panic fluttering in the edges of his deep, bass voice.

It would be, by the gods, Fithvael screamed inwardly. He pushed again with all his strength.

The resistance weakened abruptly and Harg slithered away from him with a cry. Fithvael sprawled nose-down in the slime of the floor and heavy gobbets of mud and chunks of stone tumbled out of the roof.

'Harg?'

'I can move... by't blessed worldtree! I can move!' The tunnel had widened again beyond the slump, and Fithvael could hear Harg slithering on.

'Let's go!' he called back to Bruda. As he resumed his relentless pace, Fithvael realised suddenly just how fast his heart was hammering.

FAR ABOVE, IT was approaching the eighth hour of the evening, and the storm gripped the night around Maltane. At every few beats, the sky flashed incandescent with white fire and booming thunder rattled the trees, the tiles, the walls and the ground. Sheet rain had been falling continuously for several hours.

Wrapped in sodden cloaks, Gaude, Brom and Erill cowered by the gate of the inner mound, gazing down through the deluge at the Tilean lines. The shelling had ground to a stop about an hour and half before, and there was no sign of anything in the storm below except the few pot-fires the mercenaries had lit under lean-tos and awnings out of the rain.

'At least they've stopped with the cannons,' muttered Gaude.

Brom nodded. He was sitting on an upturned bucket devouring a bowl of stew that he was keeping out of the rain with a fold of cloak spread like a fisherbird's wing. 'They can't set matches or powder in this. But then, neither can I.' He gestured forlornly to his handgun, shrouded in oilskin, leaning under the lip of the wall.

Erill was watching with the lightning. Every flash revealed the landscape clearly for a second, stark and blue-white. Staring into the flashes made him blink, and hurt his good eye, but each blink recaptured the fleeting image in negative, burned into his mind. The pain in his wounds ached and throbbed intolerably.

'They've been a long time,' said Brom, putting down his bowl. 'Twice the time it took Vintze to scout, and he went there and back.'

'They'll get there,' Gaude murmured.

Another flash and a roar. Even the heavy rain seemed to wince.

'Movement!' Erill barked. They leaped up to join him.

'Where?'

'Inside the outer ditch, in the town dwellings,' Erill said, pointing.

'Just your imagination...'

'Wait for another flash.'

'But–'

'Wait!' The lad's voice was certain.

Lightning shivered across the sky again.

'There!'

'I saw nothing,' complained Gaude.

Brom shook his head.

But Erill knew what he had seen. Dark dots, shiny black in the wetness, glinting in the storm-light below them. And in that latest flash, he realised that some were as close as the foot of the mound.

'Send to the hall. Get the others out here!'

'You're jumping at shadows,' Gaude said patiently, and flinched as another hammerblow of light and noise exploded above them.

'He's not,' Brom said suddenly, drawing his bow.

'What?'

'I saw them too that time. Erill, go and get any of the townsfolk capable of fighting.'

Erill ran off through the storm towards the hall, wading up to his shins in the standing water inside the fence.

Gaude had his sword drawn by now and was looking where Brom pointed. He made some sense of the dark shapes and blotches in the rain. Things that he had taken to be fences and drain-ditches, or hillocks of grass, were moving: scores of armed men working their way up to the mound silently.

'By the Lady!' he breathed, and there was real fear in his voice.

Erill returned with Galvin, Drunn and some twenty-five remaining fighters or would-be fighters; the very last few.

Brom assembled those with bows along the northern fence and around the gate, where the sword, pike and scythe carriers formed a phalanx with Gaude behind the wall of shields they had stuck in the gate-mouth. Water streamed off fists and noses, helmet-plates, weapons. All were motionless and resolute.

There came a hissing, pattering sound as if the rainfall had increased in heaviness once more. But it was a blizzard of blue-fletched arrows slicing up the hill. They thudded into shields, fence posts and soil. The farmer beside Erill fell with an arrow through his throat and another in his hip. The man had never even spoken.

Now dark shapes were running up the mound, dark shapes they could see even without the aid of the lightning. Drawn weapons glinted.

'Stand ready, stand ready…' Gaude cautioned.

Another blizzard of arrows. As they buried their metal heads in the fence, they seemed to make louder cracks. Erill smelt the incongruous scent of smoke.

More arrows came, describing orange arcs in the sky. Pitched arrows set alight, the slick tar burning despite the rain. They hissed and fizzled against the wet logs of the fence, but some caught where the tar spread. Erill knew that now the storm was on their side. Because if the rain let up, Maltane would begin to burn.

COUGHING AND RETCHING slime, Dolph crawled up out of the stone-built opening in the northern slope woods. He was the last to emerge. The opening was overgrown with gorse and bramble, but Gilead and Vintze had cut the worst of it aside to make the way easier.

The last part of the long crawl had been the hardest, negotiating a rising tunnel almost as steep as the one they had descended from the floor of the scarcement, but without the benefit of old stone for toeholds. And they were all pushing or dragging equipment and now were weary beyond measure.

There were no stars to take the time from, and above the rustling trees, the storm was pounding. But Fithvael reckoned it had taken them four or five hours to make the journey. They all stood around, leaning or slumped against tree trunks, breathing hard. Madoc turned his face to the sky and let the pelting rain wash the slime off his features. Harg took a deep drink of wine from the skin in his pack. It seemed as if the last thing any of them was ready for was an armed raid.

Gilead gave them a few moments to stretch out their limbs and check their packs. With rainwater running down his face and arms, he set his red cloak around him, adjusted the sit of his quiver and bow, and slipped his arm in through the thongs of his long, undecorated shield. Everything set, he drew his sword.

He strode over to Vintze, who sat with his back to an elm, his face in his hands. Though better equipped for the journey than any of them, he was exhausted by having made it three times in the space of eight hours.

'Vintze?'

'Ready when you are,' the Reiklander sighed without looking up.

Gilead turned to the others. Bruda was on her feet again, her sword drawn and her small round shield secure on her arm. Harg had his axe ready. Madoc was tightening the leather thongs wrapping his broadsword's grip, and nodded to Gilead. Cloden had stripped the coverings off his greatsword and was testing the edge. Dolph had his shield and his mace, not to mention a bulky shoulderpack that he had dragged from the mound with his handgun in it.

Fithvael set his crossbow, his sword sheathed, his shield cinched across his back now.

'We shall do this,' he said to Gilead. 'We have already come so far.'

Gilead nodded. Fithvael saw a darkness in his look, a darkness that he hadn't seen so intensely since the long lost days when they had quested after Galeth's killer.

It was a look of vengeance. Immediately, Fithvael realised what had driven Gilead this far, what had fired his admirable command of the company. Revenge... for Caerdrath, for Nithrom, for the hope they had symbolised...

And, Fithvael was sure, sheer bloody-minded rage for the pains and agonies of a lifetime. With great sadness and clarity, Fithvael realised Gilead expected nothing out of this venture except the chance to slake his vengeance, to flirt once more with death. He did not need victory. He did not need to save Maltane. He did not even need to live long enough to see the dawn.

He just wanted to send Maura, the architect of all of this, and his lieutenant Fuentes, the scum who had slain Nithrom, screaming on their way to hell.

Fithvael felt ice form in his heart. He had joined Nithrom to find a purpose, and had been overjoyed when Gilead joined them. But it had done nothing except destroy Nithrom and waken in Gilead that dreadful, melancholic urge which had already wasted most of his life.

They were moving off to clash with a murdering maniac, led by a commander who was not a great deal saner, and whose decisions would be clouded by the worst emotions.

THE MOTLEY BAND scurried down the scarp in cover of the swishing trees and the rain, closing on the hindquarters of Maura's camp. The storm did not let up.

As they paused in cover, they saw darts of fire flying up at the distant inner mound, and in the flashes of the storm, saw dark shapes milling on the slopes. One part of the fence was ablaze in patches.

Nearer at hand, just below them and the end of the trees and brambles, lay the Tilean camp: a huddle of tents and larger canopies, lit from within by lamps and small fires. To the west were pens of horse and mules, the pack teams of the gun limbers and pack-wagons, and the steeds of the cavalry. All of Maura's men were moving on foot in the new attack, it seemed.

To the east of the camp, nearest to them, the Tilean cannon were ranged on the slopes, gunner teams huddled under small awnings, smoking and drinking. A few figures wandered about in the main tent camp, and drums beat.

With a silent gesture, Gilead waved his line forward.

They came into the camp from the back. Bruda, Vintze and Gilead, swords sheathed, fell on the gun teams from behind with daggers and silenced them. In twos and threes, the men were left dead without knowing what had befallen them.

Dolph halted them then and, with Harg's help, manhandled several of the squat tubs of black powder from the gun stacks into a pile. Dolph hauled an oilskin over them, and used his flints to spark up a slow-burning fuse string.

Gilead seemed impatient, but he waited until the work was done. Then they were moving again, in amongst the tents.

Madoc cut a slit down a tent's back with his sword and stepped in, surprising two Tilean officers who were playing dice. He killed them both before they could cry out.

Bruda ducked under a guy-wire and waited until a sentry came level with her before sweeping out and slicing him down with a sure stroke of her sabre.

Harg caught another sentry with his meaty paws and broke his neck.

Gilead slipped towards one of the larger tents and burst inside, his sword ready.

It was empty. Gilead re-emerged and looked around, searching for another likely target.

Fithvael, just down the aisle between tents from his old friend, saw the Tilean sentry loom behind Gilead. The man started to cry out an alarm that was cut short by Fithvael's crossbow. But the hasty shot had only winged the man. He went down, shrieking with pain.

Gilead turned and slew him, then snapped an angry look in Fithvael's direction. By then, the camp had already come to life, and blue and white-clad mercenaries were emerging into the rain from all around, weapons in their hands.

The fight began in earnest.

AT THE MOUND, the defenders could only keep the Tileans at bay for so long. Apart from extinguishing most of the flaming arrows, the rain was helping them by turning the mound's slopes into mudslides that caused many of the advancing infantry to fall and slither back. Under Brom's command, the archers of Maltane quickly learned how to pick off an advancing Murderer near the top of the slope so he would fall back and knock some of his comrades down with him in the dire conditions.

But it was not enough. The Tilean bowmen at the mound's foot maintained their rain of missiles, and by force of sheer numbers, the Murderers were reaching the gate, charging in at Gaude, Erill and the Maltane defenders with swords and pikes.

A ferocious melee erupted in the gate mouth. Erill realised how truly disadvantaged he was by the loss of his injured eye. He had trouble gauging space and size quickly, and the atrocious light and weather made it all the harder. He was surrounded by a dizzying, screaming, stabbing, whirling mayhem.

Brom leaped down from the wall, throwing aside his bow now he was out of arrows, and laid into the thick of the attackers with his mace. He smashed his way in next to Galvin, sending Tilean dogs flying, and they drove in at the press, mace and halberd raking and swinging.

Gaude swung his ex-master's sword with the same formidable skill as he had shown before. His armour and clothes were tattered and bloody. With one hand he pulled up a young Maltaner who had been knocked down in the surging mass, hacking with his sword at the same time. He couldn't see Erill anymore. Was the lad down? Before he could look around, another two Tileans were at him with blades.

In a sudden pause in the melee, Gaude realised the rain had eased. Combustive thunderflashes still lit the fight, but the wind was up and the billowing clouds above were spent.

Fanned by the wind, the stockade walls began to burn as another hail of lit arrows thunked into them.

BRUDA, CLODEN AND Fithvael were locked in a hand-to-hand fight in one of the narrow rows between tents. Tileans milled all about them, snarling and yelling. The Carroburg greatsword whispered as it swung and two men in cavalry armour were sent flying backwards, bringing a tent awning down on a pot-fire. Flames licked up out of the collapsed material. More tents fluttered and fell, some dragged down under falling bodies. Fithvael ground forward over swathes of loose canvas, trading sword blows with a trio of brutish mercenaries. His long shield was on his arm now, and the Tileans were gouging ribbons of wood out of it.

Bruda felled a gunner who came at her with a horselance, and then moved in beside Fithvael, spinning one of his assailants away, dead. Fithvael slew another with a jab of his sword, but more rushed in to fill the Tilean's place.

Flailing left and right, Dolph broke skulls with his mace. He was cornered by a row of latrine dugouts, cracking out at anything that came near with his heavy weapon-head.

Vintze and Madoc stood together by the horse pens, blades dancing. Vintze was putting his small shield to good use as an offensive weapon, driving off as many with his shield blows as he did with his sword. The broadsword in Madoc's hands spun and whirled like a hammer, making orbits and circuits in the air, cutting through armour and flesh and sending helmets flying.

With a savage cry, Gilead ripped his way out from a tent that was starting to slump over him, leaving three Tileans dead under its flopping shroud. Through the confused tumult, he suddenly caught sight of Fuentes, Maura's lieutenant, wading in with a hooked shortsword in each hand. Gilead cried the dog's name and hurled himself at him.

Fuentes heard the shout and wheeled his thickly muscled frame around with an answering snarl. His slabby face was sheened with sweat and his good eye was so hooded and dark it matched his eye patch, making his face a death's head in the storm-light. Roused from slumber or a drinking bout in the tents, he had not had time to pull on his rich blue cloak, but his ornate golden cuirass and shoulder guards were in place, gleaming with raindrops like extra jewels.

They slammed at each other like rutting stags, splitting the press aside to reach sword-length. Gilead slashed a dog-soldier carrying a billhook in two as he cut a path to Nithrom's killer. Fuentes showed equal contempt for his own, slaying two more of his own mercenaries who were foolish enough to get in his way, with scissoring blows of his hooked swords. He had taken the first defeat personally, and no doubt had suffered Maura's anger for the failure. Now nothing would stay the blood-rage that drove him after the ones who had bested him. Nithrom had already paid. Now this other inhuman dog was in sight, and Fuentes knew him from the meeting at the outer ditch.

They clashed hard, Gilead blocking one shortsword with his own blade as the other raked a gouge down his long elven shield. Fuentes wheeled and set in again, swinging his paired swords in independent arcs. For all his bulk, he was as swift as a cat, and the twin blades made it impossible to address him in any conventional way. It was like fighting two expert swordsmen simultaneously.

Gilead leapt one scything sword as if he were a salmon, and blocked the other with a downswing of his sword in mid-leap, while turning his upper body and swinging the long shield around like a blade. The tip caught Fuentes below the chin and sent him reeling and choking.

Gilead had seen how well Vintze used his shield as a proactive weapon, but then Vintze's shield was a small, weighted buckler. It took a being of unnatural strength – or of unhinged mind – to swing a long, leaf-pattern shield the same way.

Fuentes rallied and came back at him, chopping down with his right sword as his left dug inwards in a low thrust. That left blade sliced through the edge of Gilead's shield and cut a wound through the ithilmar mail-shirt above his left hip. The last son of Lothain drove in with his shield and slammed the face into Fuentes's chest, before following through with his sword in a side-thrust that Fuentes barely parried.

They broke, circling, for a second. The hooked shortswords spun in interlocking windmill patterns under Fuentes's deft touch. Then the big Tilean lunged in again. His right shortsword buried itself through Gilead's shield, wedged fast, and slashed Gilead's shield-arm. His left ripped through the mail of Gilead's right shoulder, and bit flesh there too.

Gilead wrenched his shield aside, tearing the wedged blade out of Fuentes's grip. The other sword swept in, but Gilead made it rebound from his blue-steel long-sword, angling it vertically. Then he tore downwards with his blade, and cut Fuentes diagonally across the face and down to the chest.

Blood spurted out and Fuentes stumbled back with a howl. He clamped his hands to his face, screaming and cursing in rage and despair as he realised that Gilead had taken his surviving eye. Blind, drenched in blood that pumped out from his savage wound, he slashed and cut frantically at the air around him with his remaining sword.

With a cruel smile on his gaunt elven face that Fithvael knew he would never forget, Gilead side-stepped and placed himself so that Fuentes's next blind lunge carried him onto the elf-blade. Three feet of blue steel jutted from Fuentes's back. Blood gushed out over the gold dragon hilt and over Gilead's hand.

'For Nithrom, you bastard dog!' Gilead spat into the dying man's face in clipped Tilean.

FITHVAEL WITNESSED THE brief, explosive clash from twenty paces away, as he and Bruda battled the scrum of Tileans around them. Bruda yelled out in joy to see Fuentes fall and another, Harg or Vintze, lost in the thick of it, also bellowed.

Meanwhile, Cloden was surrounded by spearmen and halberdiers. He chopped and hacked, urging the greatsword round in circles, breaking hafts and lances, splintering each weapon that jabbed at him. But a pike-tip got through intact, long enough to punch through the Carroburger's left shoulder. Blood gouted and Cloden stumbled to his knees, dragging the pike down with him. He lost his grip on his greatsword and tried with both hands to tear at the lance transfixing him.

Madoc cut his way through to the man, slaughtering the halberdiers who were rushing in to finish the fallen man of Carroburg. Madoc's mouth was wide open in a battle yell that made no sound. The fire of Ulric, the White Wolf, was in his limbs, and his broadsword demolished them. Four Tilean dogs broke and ran in terror. Others, braver, closed in on the silent Wolf guarding the bowed Cloden. There was a loud report, and the first of them fell, his skull shattered. Dolph threw aside his handgun and ran to Madoc's side, mace swinging. Together, they fought off the waves of Tileans, dragging Cloden back towards the horse pens.

Harsh cries came from nearby and another tent frame collapsed. Two battling figures ripped their way out of the flopping canvas, swords clashing and stroking and biting. It was Vintze. He had found Maura the Murderer – or the Murderer had found him – and the pair were now locked in a combat to the death.

MALTANE WAS BURNING. The wooden walls blazed brighter than the intermittent flaring of the storm above. The night was bathed in a hot, flickering flame-light.

Overwhelmed, the defenders had fallen back into the compound, into the ruins of the inner hall, and were making their last stand there against the driving hordes that flooded in through the burning gates.

Just before they had broken from the wall, Gaude had issued commands to those about him who could hear. He sent Brom and three of the remaining Maltaners back into the scarcement with orders to lead any who could still move out through the tunnel into the woods. He knew full well this would leave dozens too sick, hurt, old or young in the scarcement hole, but to save any would be a victory. The rest he would defend to the end of his life.

With him stood Erill, Galvin, two youths called Malkin and Froll, three older farmers named Guilan, Kelfer and Hennum, a drover called Bundsman and an old goatherd that everyone knew as Old Perse. Drunn had wanted to stay, but Gaude had despatched to help Brom evacuate the cellar.

The last ten men used the hulk of the hall against the foe, cutting them down in ones and twos as they pressed in through the open doorways and shattered windows.

Erill kept the main door with Nithrom's silver blade. He had marvelled at the weight and balance of the short sword Fithvael had loaned him, but it was as nothing compared to this longsword. In his hands, it seemed to adjust for his faulty depth of field and inexperience, twisting and writhing like a living thing as it ate into the attackers. Erill knew such blades had individual names. He wished Nithrom had told him the name of this one. He prayed Fithvael or Gilead might know. And he hoped he would live long enough to learn it from them.

Tilean dog-soldiers dropped down into the hall through a rent in the roof, some tumbling, spraying loose tiles with them. They had climbed up to find a way in and brought a section of the damaged roof down with them. Galvin and Bundsman killed the first few with Guilan's help, but more jumped in, deliberately now, and the first to find his bearings lopped Hennum's head from his shoulders with a mighty blow.

Gaude rallied and chopped the Tilean beast in half, bearing down on the next and the next after that. Malkin lost a leg at the knee and fell screaming before another strike of a mercenary's axe silenced him.

More pushed in through a window on the left side, overrunning Old Perse, who fell under their kicking, trampling boots. They did not even bother to finish him. He was left, broken and moaning, under the shattered window frame.

Three Tilean pikemen burst in from the south end, and pinned Froll, twitching like a puppet, to one of the hall's roof posts. Gaude broke to meet them, leaving Bundsman and Galvin to stem the flow from the roof. He saw Guilan lying dead on the soaked boards in a pool of his own blood. He hadn't even seen the man fall.

The whole place was lit by the flickering blaze outside, darting shadows and skirmishing black shapes moving through the ruddy smoke-haze.

Kelfer screamed as a sword took off both his hands. The scream turned to a gurgle as the blade switched back and cut through his neck.

The sword's owner threw Kelfer aside. Gaude recognised him in an instant. It was Hroncic, the other trusted lieutenant of Maura the Murderer. Hroncic was a huge, swarthy man from the south of Tilea, with a wispy beard and bad teeth. The wizened ears of past victims dangled on a thong around his olive neck, bumping on his chest-guard as he moved. He carried a long, curved blade from Araby and a crescent-shaped buckler. His ornate leggings were dressed in gold braid tassels.

Gaude turned on him, cursing foully in Bretonnian. Gaude's blade, the sword that had belonged to Le Claux, was an old one, and had been witness to several crusades into the burning south where it had despatched many of the godless who carried just such curved swords. It felt to Gaude as if it smelled an old foe.

Bretonnian crusader's steel rang against Araby blade and sparks flew in the half-light. Hroncic seemed to giggle in delight as he fought back against the other's frenzied attack. Gaude battled him down the length of the hall in a whirling blur of blades.

At the hall door, Bundsman fell to three simultaneous swordstrokes, and Galvin collapsed as a pike-end smacked into his head. Erill realised Galvin was still alive, just dazed, and stood over him, keeping the foe at bay with Nithrom's sword. He lost count of the wounds he had inflicted. The floor of the hall was littered with bodies and awash with blood.

Hroncic parried Gaude's sword and spun around, coming up hard. Gaude stiffened and froze. Hroncic giggled. The entire length of his sabre had stabbed through Gaude's neck and the only thing keeping the brave ex-squire on his feet was the blade on which his body hung.

Gaude's eyes were wide. Cackling, Hroncic tugged the blade out again.

Gaude should have fallen then. His face was white but the rest of him, front and back, was bathed in gore from the dreadful wound. But the Bretonnian had one last ounce of vengeance-inspired energy in him. Dead by any standards, he swung his beloved sword one last time as he fell. The blow almost decapitated Hroncic. It did not. The brute flinched back in shock and the tip of the blade cut open one cheek.

Pawing at his torn face, Hroncic stepped over Gaude's corpse, dark eyes fixed on Erill. He wasn't giggling now. He spat blood copiously and, slurring from the wound in his cheek, ordered his men back.

The Tilean dog-soldiers fell away from Erill. The youth looked round and saw that Bundsman was curled in a corner with a lance through his chest.

He was the last, Erill realised. A one-eyed lad, the very least of the company that had ridden out to save Maltane, facing a bloodied bastard who had just defeated their best.

Smoke welled into the ruined hall. The flames were now eating at the hall itself. The Tileans pounded their hands together and chanted Hroncic's name. The gore-smeared killer stepped forward.

Erill spat and raised the glorious elven blade.

THE DUEL BETWEEN Vintze the thief and Maura the Murderer lasted perhaps ninety seconds, and in that time, hundreds of blows were traded, faster than most eyes could follow.

Vintze, six feet tall and as hard and fast as a whip's cord, had his basket-hilted Reikland straightsword in one hand, and a foot long poignard held blade up in the other, under his buckler guard.

Maura was a monstrous man, nearly seven feet tall, dressed in heavy golden Tilean plate mail of intricate ornament. His head was covered by a silver hound's-skull helmet, topped with a blue and white plume, visor down so that none could see his face. None of Gilead's company ever would. But they could hear the bellowing Tilean oaths that the beast spat as he circled in towards Vintze with his jewelled broadsword clamped in one gauntlet and a cavalryman's axe in the other.

They were a blur, Reiklander and Tilean, swirling and circling and exchanging two, three blows each second. Broadsword and axe rained and jabbed at straightsword and buckler. Sparks flew. Maura's axe dug a chunk out of Vintze's thigh. In return, the thief's poignard punched a hole through Maura's shoulder.

From the speed of their blows, they sounded like mad tinkers working metal in a forge to fend off some curse.

The appearance of Maura himself had driven the Tileans back and allowed the remnants of the company to close. Gilead, Bruda, Harg and Fithvael hacked through the mob to reach the duel, and Dolph and Madoc stood over Cloden, watching in awe.

Thunder rolled above them. None saw the way Maltane's inner fastness blazed on the top of the mound.

Sword against axe, sword against buckler, sword against sword, axe against buckler, poignard to thigh, axe to buckler, sword against sword... shrieking down the length in a fizzle of sparks. Tilean broadsword into Reikland shoulder.

Reikland buckler into grilled Tilean helmet.

Reikland straightsword against Tilean shoulder plate.

Tilean broadsword into Reikland buckler again, and again.

Reikland straightsword clean through Tilean helmet plume.
A fluttering mass of blue and white feather-plume.
Tilean axe into Reikland swordarm.
A great spray of blood.
Reikland straightsword bouncing off the mud from nerveless fingers.
Tilean broadsword glancing off desperate Reikland buckler. The sliding sword blade caught between the blade and bulky tines of the Reikland poignard.
A twist of a Reikland wrist.
Fragments of broken Tilean broadsword shattering in every direction.
Tilean axe-head hard into Reikland chest.
Ninety seconds, barely as many heartbeats.
Vintze fell.

The company, even Gilead hacking through the foe, paused in dismay. Maura boomed a victory call from his hound's-skull helmet.

A second later, a far louder boom shook them all.

Dolph's set charges blew, lighting the sky with a flare brighter and more brilliant than the worst of the lightning. The powder threw a forty-yard chunk of earth into the air and set off a landslide of wet mud that rolled down over the Tilean camp. Dozens of Tileans were buried. Many more were maimed by splinters and flying rocks. An entire gun carriage with a two-ton cannon flew through the air and crushed down onto the Murderer's files as they fled and fell. The horse pens were smashed open and panicked steeds stampeded in all directions. Everyone else was thrown flat.

Eyes swimming, ears dull, they struggled up. The main force of the Tileans in the camp were fleeing, those that were still able. Upwards of forty Murderers lay broken, wailing or dismembered in the torn mud.

Bruda thought she was first back on her feet. When a blade cut across her back and felled her into the mud, she realised she wasn't. Then she passed out.

Madoc saw Bruda fall, and saw Maura standing over her, his golden armour blackened by soot, a massive blade in his hands, about to finish her.

Madoc sprang in, blocking the downward blow. The broadsword shattered.

Calmly, Maura looked around for a fresh weapon and found Cloden's greatsword lying in the mud. Effortlessly, he swung the massive blade of Carroburg. The Murderer smashed Madoc away, reopening his throat wound.

Dolph's mace crashed into the Murderer's side, denting the golden armour. It was like striking a boulder with a twig.

Maura roared and turned about, transfixing Dolph through the torso on the length of the greatsword. He lifted the Ostmarker clean off the ground. Then he shook him off the blade, like a cat suddenly bored of the dead vermin it had been playing with.

Dolph's armoured corpse slammed into Fithvael as he ran forward in horror, and the weight dropped him like a cannonball. Fithvael felt something in his left leg snap as he went down under the heavy, metal-shrouded mass.

Maura turned to meet Harg, who raged at him like an angered bear. Hargen Hardradasson, lord of the faraway fjords and ice lands, was berserk, frothing at the mouth, channelling his battle-madness into each swing of his axe.

He was a terror to behold, but Maura met that terror and smashed open the old face wound almost precisely along the jagged line that had been there for twenty summers. Harg fell, trying to hold his face together, yowling like a wounded wolf in a trap.

Maura hefted Cloden's smoking blade above Harg's bowed head and muttered something in Tilean.

The blow never fell.

Shadowfast, Gilead was there in an eye-blink, his blade, his dead brother's blue-steel blade, ripping into Maura.

Maura reeled and fell back, deep gouges across his ornate chest plate, some of which oozed blood. By the time he managed to throw a swing of his own, Gilead had slashed the Murderer's chest plate clean away with his blade.

The two of them, swords scything, battled across the camp clearing. The whirling greatsword nicked Gilead's precious sword again and again, and ripped away the elf's long shield.

Dragging himself clear of poor, dead Dolph, wincing as the broken bone-ends ground at every move, Fithvael watched them battle. Part of him was proud of Gilead, part of him deathly afraid. He wanted to see this as titans clashing, as was written in the myths, but all he could think of were monsters assailing each other. He saw Maura rip open Gilead's shoulder, saw Gilead thrust his longsword clean through Maura's thigh.

They were both washed with blood. Maura was driving Gilead back into the edges of the woods, where the land fell away sheer to the valley floor. Sword against sword, return, pass, parry, clash, steel of Tor Anrok against Carroburg power.

Then they were lost from view in the brambles and the trees. It was treacherous in the sheer woods. Cliffs of mud, loosened by the storm, poured cascades of dark water down into the clearings below. Plunge pools had formed in the dark crevices of the escarpment.

Neither would break. Maura, a powerhouse, swung the greatsword two-handed with all the deftness its master Cloden had ever shown. Gilead sliced and chopped, parried and stabbed, instinctively recalling every move and pass he had been taught.

By his father; by Fithvael te tuin, master-at-arms; by dead Nithrom, so many years ago.

Maura hit Gilead in the face, ripping open a wound that would leave a scar for the rest of his life. Blinking aside the blood, Gilead threw himself at

Maura. The pair lost their footing and went over the edge of a mud cliff, falling through a cascade of rain-flood into a basin below.

They hit the water in a spray, churning round to find each other. Maura was weighed down by his armour and his massive weapon, but still he came up first.

They were chest-deep in the water. Maura hacked at Gilead, but his greatsword's blade struck only the water.

Gilead pushed himself at Maura and the two of them fell again, down the next flash-flood cliff, through another cascade, into another churning pool.

Gilead surfaced first, but Maura had struck below the water. The greatsword stuck into Gilead through the left hip. The water swirling around them went darker still.

Maura surfaced, snorting and hacking inside his hound's-skull helm. He twisted the blade under the water.

Gilead screamed. And in his rage sliced the helmeted head clean off with the blue-steel blade forged in Tor Anrok so long ago, Galeth's blade.

Maura's head bobbed away in the current, washing over on another cascade, still encased and unseen in its helmet.

Gilead, the greatsword still through him, sank to his knees in the blood-stained water, and began to drown.

So, THERE IT is, just as I promised you. The tale of the Battle of Maltane, in all particulars. A better, more rousing, bloodier tale of heroism you'll never hear at my fireside.

What's that you say? Ah, but there's always one! Why can't you be content? Must I really tie up all the loose ends?

Very well. No, he did not drown. Bruda found him. She was weak from her wounds, but she had seen the battlers slide over the edge. She found Gilead and dragged him out of the pool and blew life back into his lungs with her own mouth.

The greatsword? They never found it. As he sank, Gilead must have pulled it out. It is rusting, even now, in a glade pool west of Maltane, I am sure. Cloden had to travel back to his homeland to get another and that, as I understand, was an adventure in itself.

Well, yes, of course Cloden lived. His shoulder was never quite the same, of course, but he went on to greater things. Had a warrior band of his own, so I am told. Never lost his touch with the greatsword, to the end of his days.

Harg? Well, he had the same scar as before, just fresher. I have no idea what eventually happened to him, but every winter I get sent another bearskin and a flask of foul Norse mead. I like to think he's probably a king again somewhere, somewhere frozen and uninviting.

And Vintze, it took him a while to mend, and the winters still make his chest ache. He rode with Cloden, so I heard. I saw him ten years or so back, in Vinsbrugge. He had a snowy beard by then, and further scars. We had a drink to the old times. But he's probably dead now.

Bruda? Like I said, she lived. She spent the winter in Maltane, healing up, then was gone by spring. I don't know how many years after that she survived. I always liked her tremendously, though. Well, yes, I am old, and thank you for mentioning it! But believe me, I can still recall how handsome a woman is!

Madoc? It took a long time with him. Bad wound. But you know he survived. The legends of the Silent Wolf are commonplace in this neck of the woods and beyond. Yes, that is him. The very one.

What more do you want? Oh yes, Brom and Drunn led the evacuees down the tunnel and out into the woods. Fifty villagers they saved that way. Drunn stayed on as headman, as you know, elected year after year after year for his bravery. Yes, I miss him too.

Master Brom, he was never the same after his twin was gone. He and Gilead had so much alike in that, but I don't think they ever spoke about it. Elves, heh? Too close. Brom… heh… I sometimes think about him and wonder where he ended up. Alone, truly alone, wherever it was.

Ah, what's that? Be patient. I was saving that part. Pour me another cup. Good.

Of course, the Tileans broke when Maura died. They never found his head, did I mention that? And actually, they broke long before that. Right after Dolph's explosion. The heart was out of them by then. They came at Maltane with a warhost maybe four hundred strong and left fully three-quarters on the fields and the slopes around the town. That's quite a thing, don't you think?

I'm getting tired and my cup is half-empty. What more do you want?

Oh, of course, of course.

When the Tileans had fled, the company went up to the inner mound, which was all ablaze by then. But they got the wounded and the infirm out of the scarcement all the same. Add those to the evacuees, and you'll see that Nithrom's band saved seventy-seven folk from Maltane. Not that there was a lot of Maltane left by then. It took us years to rebuild.

Oh, hush now. Very well, since you persist, they found young Erill in the courtyard, where Galvin had carried… him. Only the two of them had survived. No one knows what happened exactly, but they found the beast Hroncic's head in the temple, lying on Sigmar's altar.

The survivors burned Le Claux, Caerdrath, Nithrom, Gaude and Dolph on a great pyre, with full honours and much mourning. It was only fit.

The last I saw of the two elves was when they rode away one misty spring morning. They had wintered here to heal and left in the spring, just after Bruda. Both of them still limped when they walked.

No, I don't know where they were going. I don't think they knew either. I doubt Master Fithvael was going to stay with Gilead much longer. His companion had become so surly and withdrawn that winter.

Who am I to say? Maybe they're still travelling this sorry world together even now.

I liked Fithvael. He had a soul. His lord, well, I'm not too sure. I would doubt he'll ever find what he's looking for, but I know that losing the scent here, with Caerdrath's death, was one of the worst things that ever happened to him. The dark cloud that lived over him glowered over all of us that winter, and though I feel churlish to say it, it was almost a relief when that elven lord departed.

I think of them from time to time. I do wonder whatever happened to them. I suppose they just faded away and were forgotten. Like all myths, and, Sigmar help me, the land is full of them!

Me? I've been content to stay here in Maltane all these seasons, until now I am old and bent. Yes, my eye still hurts me, usually in winter when the wind bites and cuts into this old patch.

It often pleases me that I was part of a myth, given that this land is so full of them. I miss my father, though… if father he truly was to me. Certainly, I believe that to be so. And I never did learn what this glorious sword of his is called.

HAMMERS OF ULRIC

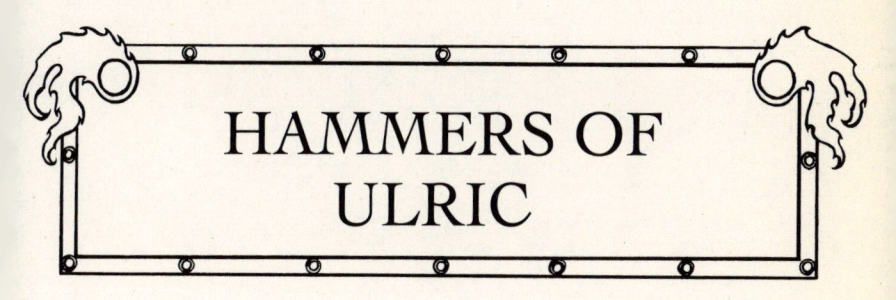

Hammers of Ulric had much the same genesis as *Gilead's Blood*, in that it derives from a few early short stories I wrote for *Inferno!* that later got worked up into the novel presented here. To borrow some terminology from my other job as a writer of superhero comic books, *Hammers* was the 'team book' to complement my 'solo character' book *Gilead*. Though it's dark and crunchy with some brutal action and daemonic nastiness, I think it's also quite a cheerful, high-spirited novel. I was playing here, exploring. Apart from the horses, the White Wolves are very much like proto-Space Marines, and there's a deliberate touch of Dumas's Musketeers about them too.

The other real star of the show here is the city of Middenheim, the focus of the action. It was nice to get a geographical landmark into the centre of the book, something really solid that everything else could hang upon. This was especially important because, as with *Gilead's Blood*, I was sharing the writing chores on *Hammers*, this time with Nik and with the redoubtable James Wallis. The knights were predominately my responsibility, with Nik principally handling the threads concerning the street boy Wheezer. James had created the wonderful Priest of Morr character whose adventures were set in Middenheim. And Marc Gascoigne had a barn, so we just got together and put the show on there... (Essentially, what I'm saying is it wasn't rocket science to plait these stories into a satisfying whole.)

It's hard to judge the lasting legacy *Hammers* has left, in as much as it has never provoked extremes of reaction. No one's ever told me it was their favourite Warhammer book and demanded I write more (at least, I don't remember that happening), but neither have I been bombarded with negative comments. It seems as if it's a novel that people were just very happy to enjoy. Looking at it now, I think it stands up very well, and if it's simply an early book that fell out of print before the Black Library buzz really began, here's your chance to ride with the White Wolves of Middenheim too.

JAHRDRUNG
A COMPANY OF WOLVES

IT WAS, TO no one's great surprise, raining in Middenheim that day.

Spring rain, fresh as ice needles, spattered down on that vast old city which sat brooding atop its granite crag, gazing down across the dismal forests around it. Another long winter season was slowly thawing, and the city, and everyone in it, was cold and wet and miserable to the bone.

In a puddled yard behind the Spread Eagle tavern, Morgenstern carefully adjusted a line of plump turnips he had arranged along the flagstones, each one sat on an upturned pail. Then he walked to the end of the yard, belched delicately with a hand to his mouth and little finger cocked, then spat on his meaty palms and hefted up the great warhammer leaning against the slimy bricks.

He began to spin it, crossing his grip deftly, looping the mighty head back and forth in a figure of eight around his shoulders. *Whoooff! Whoooff! Whoooff!* it hissed as it circled. But Morgenstern was standing a little too close to the back wall and, after another circuit, the hammerhead struck against the stonework. Several bricks shattered and dropped out, and the warhammer bounced to the ground.

Morgenstern swore colourfully, and wobbled slightly as he stooped to retrieve his weapon, rainwater dripping from his vast shaggy beard. Then he wobbled some more as he stooped to retrieve his tankard. He straightened up and supped from it. Then he tried unsuccessfully to replace the bits of brick, fussing as if somehow no one would notice the dent if he smoothed it over. Several more bricks fell out.

Giving up, Morgenstern turned back to his row of buckets and started to spin the hammer again, this time checking he had swinging room.

'Is this going to take much longer?' Aric asked from the tavern doorway. He stood leaning against the doorjamb: a tall, powerfully built young man not yet twenty-two, with a mane of black hair and bright blue eyes. He carried the gold-edged plate armour and the snowy pelt of the White Wolf Templars well.

'Hush!' said the older knight, concentrating on his swing and not looking round. Morgenstern adjusted the fall of his own wolf-pelt so it did not constrict the movement of his armoured limbs. 'Behold, my young friend, how a master of the warhammer displays his skill. See! Before me, the heads of my foes!'

'The turnips on the buckets?'

'Quite so. That is indeed what they represent.'

'These foes are what? Lying down? Buried up to the neck?'

Morgenstern smiled patiently. 'They are large and able-bodied warriors, Aric. I, however, am on a horse.'

'Of course you are.'

'For the purposes of this demonstration, imagine I am on a horse.'

Still spinning the hammer, Morgenstern began to prance back and forth on the spot like a hobbyhorse mummer in a mystery play. He made clip-clop noises with his tongue and occasionally admonished 'Steady there! Whoa, girl!'

Aric closed his eyes.

'Yah-hah!' Morgenstern barked suddenly and lurched forward, head back, as his imaginary horse bolted.

His great, thundering, armoured mass, with the hammer swooping about him in a vast circle, drummed down the yard, spraying up water and dislodging flagstones as he charged the buckets. His initial swing smashed the turnip on the first bucket, then, without breaking stride, he galloped in and out of the remaining buckets, decapitating each turnip in turn, slaloming between the rows, swooping and crossing the hammer with astonishing precision.

Aric by then had reopened his eyes. For all the pantomime idiocy, for all the drunkenness, for all the fact that Morgenstern was at the wrong end of his fifties and two hundred pounds too heavy, Aric was still impressed by the big man's weapon skill.

With a bellowing flourish, Morgenstern elegantly took out the last of his foes, bucket and all, crushing both with a blow that lofted them over the gable end. Then his boot slipped on the sheened cobbles, he stumbled at full pelt and went headfirst into the stables. Through a door he hadn't opened first.

Aric winced. He turned and went back inside. It was going to be a long day.

* * *

INSIDE THE Spread Eagle, he rejoined Anspach, Gruber and von Glick at the small table in the corner.

'Did he do it?' Gruber asked.

Aric nodded. 'All of them.'

Anspach chuckled his dirty, melodic chuckle. He was a handsome man in his late thirties, with devilish eyes and a smile that could charm chastity belts into spontaneous release. 'That's six shillings from each of you, I fancy.'

'By the Wolf, Anspach!' von Glick grunted. 'Is there nothing you won't wager on?'

Anspach accepted his winnings. 'Actually, no. In fact, that reminds me, I have a bag of gold riding on a certain goathead going the distance at the Bernabau this afternoon.'

Von Glick shook his head in dismay. A veteran Wolf of the old school, von Glick was a slender, angular man of sixty years. His grizzled hair was long and straggly, and his chin was shaven to pepper stubble. He was stiff and disapproving about all things. Aric wondered if there was anything von Glick couldn't complain about. He somehow doubted the prim old man had ever had the passion to be a noble warrior.

'So where's Morgenstern now?' Gruber asked, toying with his tankard.

'Having a lie down,' answered Aric. 'You know, I think... he drinks too much.'

The other three snorted.

'Brother Templar,' Anspach said, 'you're too recent an addition to this noble order to have witnessed it, but our Morgenstern is famous for the prodigious scale of his imbibing! Some of his greatest victories on the field of combat... like those orc-scum he took at the Battle of Kern's Gate... such feats have been fired by Ulric, and fuelled by ale!'

'Maybe,' Aric said doubtfully, 'but I think it's getting to him. His reflexes. His co-ordination...'

'He killed the turnips, didn't he?' von Glick asked.

'And the stable door,' Aric said darkly.

They fell silent.

'Still, our Morgenstern...' Anspach began, 'I'll wager he could–'

'Oh, shut up!' growled von Glick.

Aric sat back and gazed around the smoky tavern. He could see Ganz, their new, young company commander, sitting in a booth side, with the hot-blooded Vandam talking eagerly at him.

'What's that about?' he asked Gruber. The white-haired Gruber was deep in thought and snapped up with a start as Aric addressed him.

He looked almost scared just then, Aric thought. *That's not the first time I've caught him lost in thoughts he doesn't like.*

Gruber was the most respected of the Company's men, a veteran like Morgenstern and von Glick, who had served with old Jurgen from the beginning. His hair was thin, his eyes pale, his papery skin almost translucent with age, but Aric knew there was a power, a terrible force inside that warrior.

Except now... now, for the first time since he joined the Company eighteen months before, Aric sensed that Gruber's power was waning. Was it age? Was it... Jurgen? Was it something else?

Aric gestured again over at Vandam and Ganz. 'What's Vandam bending our commander's ear about?'

'I hear Vandam wants to transfer,' von Glick said quietly. 'He's a gloryhound. He wants promotion. Word is, he sees our company as a dead end. He wants to move to another mob. Red Company, maybe.'

The four of them grunted their disapproval and all took a drink.

'Don't think Ganz will let him. Ganz has barely had time to make his mark in command since the... since that business. He won't want to lose a man before he's had a chance to prove something.' Gruber looked thoughtful. 'If they ever let us prove anything again.'

'It's not long till Mitterfruhl,' Anspach said. 'Then the campaign season really starts. We'll get something... a good raid into the Drak. I bet you.'

Aric was silent. Something had to happen soon, or this particular brave company of White Wolves was going to lose its heart entirely.

The Great Temple of Ulric was almost empty. The air was still and cold and smelled of candle smoke.

Ganz walked in, and reverently placed his gloves and warhammer in the reliquary in the entrance hall.

The acoustics in the vast, vaulted chamber were superb, and Ganz could hear the precise intonations of four knights who were whispering prayers on the other side of the high altar, kneeling, heads down. He could also hear the faint squeak of lint as a Temple adept polished the brass finials of the lectern. The great statue of Ulric himself rose up like a thundercloud to block the light from the high windows.

Ganz bowed his head and made his observance, then crossed the chamber and knelt before the Sacred Flame.

He was kneeling there when he felt the hand on his shoulder. Ganz looked up into the face of Ar-Ulric, the High Priest himself, his craggy, bearded features catching the flame light.

'We should talk, Ganz. I'm glad you came by. Walk with me to the Regimental Chapel.'

Ganz got up and fell into step beside the venerable warrior. He saw the four knights were leaving, casting curious glances in his direction.

'I came to seek... guidance, High One,' Ganz began. 'This season will be my first as a commander of men, and already, I–'

'Do you lack confidence, Ganz?'

'No, lord. But I lack experience. And the men are... listless.'

They walked down a short flight of steps and reached an iron cage door where a Templar of Grey Company stood watch. He saluted the High Priest respectfully, and undid the padlock so that the cage door could swing open.

Ganz followed Ar-Ulric through and they entered the smaller, warmer interior of the temple's regimental chapel, decorated with standards, banners, trophies and the honour roll of memorial slabs.

Both men bowed briefly to the great wolfskin pelt on the wall, and to the snarling, silver-inlaid treasure on a raised plinth beneath it. The Jaws of the Wolf, the Temple's most precious icon.

The High Priest bent before it for a moment, murmured a blessing to Ulric and to Artur, then rose and turned to Ganz. His eyes twinkled like the first frost of a hard Jahrdrung. 'Your company is more than listless, Ganz. There was a time when White Company was the finest and best this Temple could field, performing deeds that the riders of other Wolf Companies like Red or Grey could only dream of. But now it is weak – it has lost its way. This whole winter they have idled here in the city, wasting their health and money and time. Several have become noted drunkards. Especially Morgenstern.'

'It is easy to exaggerate–'

'He relieved himself in the font in the Temple of Verena,' the High Priest said with great and sad certainty. 'During High Mass. And then he suggested to the priests that the Goddess herself was a "piece of all right" who could really do with a good… what was it again?'

Ganz sighed. 'Man in her life, High Priest.'

The High Priest nodded. It seemed to Ganz he was almost smiling but that could not be so and his tone confirmed it. 'Morgenstern is a disgrace. And Anspach. You know about his gambling? He owes a large amount to the stadium brokers and to various less-official wager-takers. And I have had audiences with that hotblood Vandam twice now to hear him petition me for a transfer to Red Company. Or Gold. Or anywhere.'

Ganz hung his head.

'There are others with problems too… each to his own. I don't pretend your job is easy, Ganz, taking command of a demoralised mob like this. And I know everything stems from that one incident last summer in the Drakwald. That beastpack got the better of you. They were strong. Sometimes, Ulric save us, the evil ones do win. It was a tragedy White Company lost so many good men. And to lose Jurgen. It can't be easy for you to take his place.'

'What can I do, High Priest? I don't command the respect Jurgen did. How can I rally White Company?'

The High Priest crossed to the far wall and lifted down the standard of Vess. It was old and tattered and stained with ancient, noble blood. It was one of the oldest and most revered battle standards of the Wolf Companies, carried at some of the Templars' greatest victories.

'You will take your company out, into the forests, beneath this old and venerable standard, and you will destroy the beastpack that broke your honour.'

Ganz took the shaft of the standard with amazement. He looked up and met the steely gaze of his old commander, Jurgen, the newest of the graven memorials on the wall. For a long while, Ganz stared into that marble face, remembering the long white beard, the hawkish look, the famous studded eye-patch. Ganz knew the High Priest was right. It was the only way.

IT WAS A cold dawn, and raining once again. The fourteen brothers of White Company assembled in the stable block behind the Temple, adjusting the harnesses of their warsteeds, grumbling in low voices, their breath steaming the air.

'A raiding party? Before Mitterfruhl?' Morgenstern complained, swigging from a flask in his saddlebags as he pretended to check them.

'A drink? Before breakfast?' von Glick sneered quietly.

Morgenstern laughed at this, booming and hard, but Aric knew it was sham good-humour. He could see the pale strain in Morgenstern's pallid face, see the way his great hands shook.

Aric looked about. Vandam was resplendent, his face flushed with determination. His white wolf pelt hung just so across the shoulders of his gold-chased plate armour. Gruber looked far away, distant and preoccupied as he fumbled with the harness straps of his stamping steed. Einholt, the old, bald warrior with the facial scar and the milky eye, looked tired, as if he hadn't slept well. Aric felt sure some old dream chased the veteran each and every night without fail.

Anspach laughed and joked with his fellows. Von Glick scowled at him. Ganz looked grim and quiet. The others began to mount up, exchanging jokes and slurs – haggard Krieber, stocky Schiffer, the blond giant Bruckner, red-maned Kaspen, the whipcord Schell, and Dorff, whistling another of his tuneless refrains.

'Aric!' Ganz called, and Aric crossed the yard. As the youngest of the company, it was his privilege to carry the standard. He was amazed when Ganz placed the precious Standard of Vess into his mailed hand. Everyone in the yard fell silent.

'By the decree of the High Priest himself, we ride under the banner of Vess, and we ride for revenge,' Ganz said simply and swung into the saddle.

He turned his steed about and the company fell into step behind him, riding out of the yard into the streets and the rain beyond.

THEY CAME DOWN the western viaduct out of the city, in the shadow of the great Fauschlag Rock. High above them, the craggy walls and towers of Middenheim pushed their way up into the cold, friendless skies, as they had done for two thousand years.

They left the smoke and stench and clamour of the city behind, moving past trains of laden handcarts bound for the Altmarkt markets: strings of cattle from Salzenmund, the piled wagons of textile merchants from Marienburg. All pulled themselves to the sides of the sixty-foot wide viaduct to let the Wolf Company pass. When a party of Ulric's best rode out, only a fool got in their way.

White Company left the viaduct and joined the Altdorf road, cantering into the damp woodlands, and followed the forest track for six hours before stopping to water their horses and eat at a village by the way. In the afternoon, the sun came up to glint off their grey and gold plate mail. The heat drew mist out of the wet trees, and they rode as if through smoke. In each village they passed, the locals came out to see a brave and feared band of Templars, singing a low battle hymn as they rode along.

They slept the night in a village longhall above a waterfall, and they rode at dawn into the darker paths, the long tracks of black mud that ran down into the oily darkness of the Drakwald Forest, a region that lay across the land like the fallen cloak of some black-hearted god.

It was noon, but a pale, weak noon, and chill rain pattered down through the naked branches of black elms and twisted maple. The ground beneath them was coated in a stinking, matted slime of dead leaves that had fallen the autumn before and now lay rotting back into the dark soil. Spring would be a long time coming here.

There seemed no sign of life except for the fourteen riders. Occasionally a woodpecker would hammer in the distance, or some loon or other bird would whoop. Aric saw cobwebs in low branches hung with rainwater like diamond chokers.

'Smoke!' von Glick called suddenly, and they reined up, sniffing the air.

'He's right!' Vandam said eagerly, sliding the long haft of his warhammer out of his saddle loop.

Ganz held up a hand. 'Steady, Vandam! If we move, we move as a company or not at all. Aric, raise the standard.'

Aric edged alongside the leader and pulled the old banner upright.

With a nod, Ganz led off and the column moved two abreast through the trees in the direction of the smoke, hooves splashing through the leaf slush and rot.

The clearing was wide and open – trees had been cleared for it and now the wood was being burnt on a stone slab set before a crude statue. Five shambling, hairy forms were worshipping at the fire.

'For Ulric! Wolves! Ride!' Ganz yelled and they broke into a gallop, tearing down the slope into the clearing itself, exploding water from the marshy ground with their heavy hooves.

The beastmen at the shrine looked round in horror, baying and breaking for cover.

At the back of the file, Morgenstern turned from the charge and looked to Gruber, who had reached a dead stop.

'What's the matter?' he bellowed. 'We're missing the fun!'

'I think my steed has thrown a shoe,' growled Gruber. 'Go on, you old fool! Ride on!'

Morgenstern turned again after the main charge and took a deep pull from his saddle bottle. Then with a huge cry he charged down the slope after the main party.

The low branch took him clean out of his saddle.

The rest thundered out across the clearing, Aric bellowing as he held the banner high. Three of the beastmen broke and fled. Two snatched up pikes and turned to face the charge, shrieking in a deep, inhuman way.

Vandam was by now leading the charge. His swinging mallet-head destroyed the skull of one of the defenders, smacking the goat-headed aberration back into the ground.

Ganz, just behind him, overshot the other and tried to wheel around. His horse lost its footing on the wet leaves and slid over, spilling him off.

The beast turned to capitalise on this but in a moment Aric and Krieber had run it down between their horses, smashing its bones.

Anspach galloped past the shrine after one of the escapees, whirling his hammer. Von Glick was close on his hind.

'Ten shillings says I make this kill!' laughed Anspach.

Von Glick cursed and tried to pull level, but Anspach hurled his hammer and it went spinning off after the fleeing creature. It decapitated a sapling and missed the beast by ten yards. Anspach swore and reined in his charge.

'Gods help you that you ever win a wager!' von Glick cried as he carried on and caught up with the beast at the tree line. He swung two blows which both missed, but the creature doubled back and was driven into the aim of Dorff, who crushed its brain.

The other two fled into the trees. Vandam, without breaking stride, galloped after them.

'Back! Vandam! Back here!' bellowed Ganz as he got up and righted his shaken horse.

Vandam paid no attention. They could hear his whoops echoing into the forest.

'Schell! Von Glick! Go and round that idiot up!' Ganz ordered and the two riders obeyed. Everyone else had galloped to a standstill around the shrine. Ganz looked back and saw that Gruber had dismounted at the edge of the clearing and was helping to prop Morgenstern against a tree. Morgenstern's horse was trotting around, with its reins trailing.

Ganz shook his head and spat an oath.

He strode up to the shrine and gazed for a moment at the crude statue. Then he swung his hammer and smashed it into splinters.

Ganz turned back and looked at his men. 'Now they know we're here. Now they will come looking for us and our job will be easier!'

* * *

'Vandam? Where are you, you idiot?' bawled von Glick as he rode slowly through the dark glades beyond the clearing. Dark meres stood stagnant between the filthy trees, and brackish water trickled down the slate outcrops. Through the trees and the mist, von Glick could make out Schell, riding a parallel course, yelling out 'Vandam! Come around the back or we'll leave you out here!'

Von Glick heard movement in the trees nearby and raised his hammer ready. Vandam rode out of the trees.

'Trust you to come looking for me, von Glick!' he snorted. 'You motherhen the whole company! You're so stiff you wouldn't know valour if it came knocking!'

Von Glick shook his head wearily. He knew too well his own reputation with the younger members of White Company: stiff, inflexible, an old bore who nagged and complained. Jurgen had once told him he was the backbone of the company, but von Glick had a suspicion the commander had been trying to make light of von Glick's attitudes. Von Glick hated himself for it, but he couldn't help himself. There was no discipline these days. The young Templars were reckless bravos, and Vandam the very worst of them.

'Ganz ordered me to find you,' von Glick said sharply, trying to hold his anger. 'What sense is it to ride off alone like that? There's no glory in it!'

'Isn't there now?' Vandam smirked. 'I ran one to ground, broke his back. The other slipped away though.'

That was the worst of it... Vandam's arrogance was matched only by his skill as a warrior. Damn his eyes! thought von Glick.

'We'll ride back. Now!' he instructed Vandam, who shrugged mildly and turned his horse around. 'Schell!' von Glick called. 'I found him! Schell!'

Von Glick could still make out the other rider, but the mist and trees were deadening his voice.

'Go on,' von Glick told Vandam. 'I'll fetch him.'

He spurred up along the edge of a mere in the direction of Schell who saw him at last and began to ride over. Von Glick turned his horse back.

The beastman came out of the bushes with a feral scream. Driven, hounded by Vandam, it had hidden, but von Glick had passed close by its hiding place and panic had galvanised it into fierce action. The iron barb of the spear took the old Wolf through the right hip. He bellowed in pain and the horse reared. The beastman clung on, shaking his weapon, which was wedged fast in the bone and meat and armour. Von Glick screamed, hooked like a fish, pushed back in the saddle by the spear so far he couldn't reach his warhammer.

Schell bellowed in dismay and galloped in.

Vandam, hearing the commotion, turned and looked in horror.

'Ulric's bloody fists!' he gasped. 'Oh lord, no!'

The spear broke. Freed, von Glick tumbled from the saddle and landed in the shallows of the mere. The beastman lunged forward.

Schell's horse leapt the mere at the narrowest point and the warrior swung the hammer spike down on the creature, killing it instantly.

He leaped off his horse and ran to von Glick, who lay on his side in the pool, his face pale with pain. It looked like his red and gold armour was leaking into the black water.

Vandam raced up.

Schell looked up at him with fierce, angry eyes that blazed from his lean face. 'He's alive,' he hissed.

GANZ STRODE ACROSS the shrine clearing to where Morgenstern was picking himself up.

'Let's talk,' he said. 'Away from the others. I'm sure you don't want them hearing what I'm going to say to you.'

Morgenstern, who had twenty years more service to the Temple than Ganz, looked sour, but he did not disobey. Talking low, they moved away across the clearing.

Aric joined Gruber, who sat to one side on a fallen log.

'You okay?' he asked.

'My horse was wrong-footed. Thrown a shoe, I thought.'

'Looks fine to me,' said Aric.

Gruber looked up at the young man, his lean, lined face hard but not angry. 'What's that supposed to mean?'

Aric shrugged. With his long dark hair and trimmed black goatee, he reminded Gruber of the young Jurgen himself. 'Anything you want it to mean,' he said.

Gruber steepled his hands and thought for a moment. Aric had something, a quality. One day he would be a leader, a lot more effortlessly than poor Ganz, who tried so hard and was liked so little. Aric had natural command. He would be a great warrior for the Temple in time.

'I...' Gruber began. 'I seem to lack the fire I once had. At Jurgen's side, courage was easy...'

Aric sat next to him. 'You're the most respected man in the troop, Gruber. Everyone acknowledges that, even bluff old warhorses like Morgenstern and von Glick. You were Jurgen's right-hand man. You know, after Jurgen's death, I'll never understand why you didn't take the command when it was offered you. Why did you hand it on to Ganz?'

'Ganz is a good man... solid, unimaginative, but a good man. He'd paid his dues. I'm just a veteran. I'd be a poor commander.'

'I don't think so,' Aric said with a shake of his head.

Gruber sighed. 'What if I said it was because Jurgen was dead? How could I take the place of that man, my sworn commander, my friend? The man I failed?'

'Failed?' Aric repeated in surprise.

'That dreadful day last summer, when the beastpack fell on us out of nowhere. We stood together as a company or we fell, each man watching the other's back.'

'It was hell, all right.'

'I was right by Jurgen, fighting at his right hand. I saw the bull-man swing in with the axe. I could have blocked it, taken the blow myself, but I froze.'

'You weren't to blame!'

'I was! I hesitated and Jurgen died. If it hadn't been for me, he'd be here today.'

'No,' Aric said firmly. 'It was bad luck and Ulric called him to his hall.'

Gruber looked into the younger man's face. 'My nerve's gone, Aric. I can't tell the others… I certainly can't tell Ganz… but as we rode in to the charge, I felt my courage melt. What if I freeze again? What if it's Ganz who pays the price this time? You? I'm a coward and no use to this company.'

'You are no such thing,' Aric said. He tried to compose an argument to snap the veteran out of his grim mindset, but they were interrupted by shouting. Morgenstern strode back into the clearing, bellowing, with a stern-faced Ganz in his wake. The big ox reached his horse, pulled three bottles from his saddle bags and hurled them at a nearby tree, smashing them one by one.

'Satisfied?' he bawled at Ganz.

'Not yet,' Ganz replied stoically.

'Ganz! Ganz!' the shout echoed round the clearing. Schell led von Glick's horse back to them, the old warrior slumped in the saddle with Vandam riding alongside to support him.

'Oh great God of the Wolf!' Gruber cried leaping up.

'Von Glick!' shouted Morgenstern, pushing past the dismayed Ganz.

They lowered the wounded man down and the company stood around as Kaspen, who had studied with a barber-surgeon and an apothecary, treated the ugly wound.

'He needs a proper surgeon,' said the thick-set, flame-haired man, wiping blood from his hands. 'Wound's deep and filthy and he's lost blood.'

Ganz looked up at the sky. Evening was slipping down on them. 'We'll return to Middenheim tomorrow. First light. The fastest will ride ahead to fetch a surgeon and a cart. We–'

'We will not,' von Glick said, his voice thin and bitter. 'We will not go back on my account. This mission, this undertaking, is a holy cause to refound the strength of this company and avenge our fallen leader. We will not abandon that task! I will not let you abandon this!'

'But–'

Von Glick pulled himself up to a sitting position, wincing. 'Promise me, Ganz! Promise me we'll go on!'

Ganz faltered. He did not know what to say. He wheeled on Vandam, who stood to one side. 'You bloody fool! This is your fault! If you hadn't been so impetuous, you'd never have led von Glick into that!'

'I–' Vandam began.

'Shut up! The company stands together or it falls! You betrayed the very foundation of this brotherhood!'

'He's not to blame,' von Glick said. His eyes were glittering with strength born out of pain. 'Oh, he shouldn't have broken from the pack and ridden off alone, but I did this to myself. I should have been wary, I should have been looking. I dropped my guard, like any old fool, and paid the price.'

Silence. Ganz looked from one man to another. Most looked uncomfortable, awkward, disconcerted. The company spirit had never seemed so deflated, not even after Jurgen's death. At least then there was anger. Now, there was just disillusion, a loss of faith and comradeship.

'We'll make camp here,' Ganz said finally. 'With luck, the beasts will come for us tonight – and we can finish this.'

DAWN CAME, COLD and pale. The last shift of watchmen – Schell, Aric and Bruckner – roused the others. Morgenstern poked the fire into life and Kaspen redressed von Glick's wound. The old warrior was as pale and cold as the morning, shivering with pain. 'Don't tell Ganz how bad I am!' he hissed to Kaspen. 'On your life, swear it!'

Anspach was going to water the horses when he found Krieber. At some time in the night, a black-fletched arrow had skewered his neck where he lay sleeping. The Templar was dead.

They stood around in silent mourning, more sombre than ever before. Ganz boiled with rage. He strode away from the group.

At the tree line, Gruber joined him. 'It is bad luck, Ganz. Bad luck on us, bad luck on poor Krieber, Ulric take his soul. We didn't deserve it, and he deserved a better end than this.'

Ganz wheeled round. 'What do I have to do, Gruber? For Ulric's sake! How can I lead this company to glory if we don't get a chance? I destroyed their shrine to bring them to us, to make them angry and drive them into a frontal attack. A pitched battle where we would shine! But no! They come back all right, and with typical beast cunning, they harry us and kill us as we sleep!'

'So we change our tactics,' Gruber said.

Ganz shrugged. 'I don't know how! I don't know what to suggest! I keep thinking about Jurgen, and how he kept command. I keep trying to think the way he did, to remember all the tricks and inspiration. And you know? *I can't remember a thing*! All those great victories we shared, and I can't recall the plan behind a single one of them!'

'Calm down and think, Ganz,' Gruber said, sighing. 'What about Kern's Gate? Remember? The winning stroke there was to swing around behind the orcs.'

'Yes, I remember it. Sound tactics.'

'Exactly!' Gruber said. 'But that was Morgenstern's idea, wasn't it? Not Jurgen's!'

'You're right,' Ganz said, his face brightening. 'And it was the same with the siege at Aldobard... there it was von Glick who suggested a two-pronged attack.'

'Yes,' Gruber agreed. 'Jurgen was a good leader all right. He knew a good idea when he heard it. He knew how to listen to his men. The company is strength, Ganz. We stand together or we fall. And if one of us has a good plan, a good leader knows not to be too proud to adopt it.'

* * *

'So?' Ganz said, trying to sound lighter than he felt. 'Any ideas?'

Late winter wind sighed through the elms. The company coughed and shuffled.

'I bet I know–' Anspach began.

There was a general groan.

'Let's hear him out,' Ganz said, hoping he was doing the right thing.

'Well, myself, I like a wager,' Anspach said as if this were news, getting up to address them. 'So do many folk – the chance to win something, something important and valuable, something more than you normally get a chance at. These beastmen are no different. They want revenge for the smashed shrine, but not so much they're going to risk their stinking hides in a frontal assault on armoured cavalry. Who would give them good odds on that? They'd rather live. But if we tempted them with something more – something they might feel was worth risking their necks for – we could lure them out. That's my plan, a tempting wager for them. And I'll bet it works.'

There was some nodding, a few sneers. Dorff whistled aimlessly. Morgenstern turned a belch into an approving chuckle.

Ganz smiled. For the first time there seemed to be a slight sense of union, of all their minds working as one.

'But what do we offer them?' Kaspen asked.

Anspach shrugged. 'I'm working on that. We carry gold and silver, between us probably quite a lot. Maybe a pot of coins...'

Vandam laughed. 'You think they'd care? The beasts don't value gold much.'

'Well, what else have we got?' asked Schell, scratching his sinewy cheek thoughtfully.

'We have this,' Aric said and lifted the standard of Vess.

'You're mad!' cried Einholt. A quiet, reserved warrior, he seldom said anything. This outburst startled them all. Aric wavered, looking into Einholt's scarred face, wishing he could read anything except scorn in the man's one good eye.

'Think! Think of the prestige, the glory they would achieve amidst their foul kind to capture this. Think of the victory it would represent,' Aric said at last.

'Think of the disgrace if we lose the bloody thing!' scoffed Vandam.

'We won't,' Aric said. 'That's the point. It's precious enough to lure them out en masse...'

'And precious enough to make damn sure we fight to the last to keep it,' von Glick finished for him. 'A good plan.'

Ganz nodded.

'So,' Dorff asked, 'do we just... leave it out in the open for them?'

'Too obvious,' Ganz said.

'And I won't leave it,' Aric said flatly. 'It's my duty. I cannot abandon the standard.'

Ganz paced the circle of men. 'So Aric stays with the standard. The rest of us lie in cover ready to strike.'

'Aric can't stand alone,' Gruber began.

'It'd still look too obvious,' Anspach added. 'Someone has to stay with him.'

'I'll do it,' Vandam said. There was ferocity in his eyes. Ganz knew the young warrior was eager to make amends for his earlier rashness.

He was about to nod when von Glick spoke up. 'A brave offer, Vandam. But you're too good in the charge to waste. Let me stay, Ganz. We'll stay with Krieber's corpse and it'll look like the standard bearer has been left to watch the dead and the dying.'

'That would be more convincing,' Anspach said.

'I'll stay too,' Gruber said. 'They'd expect at least two men. And my horse has thrown a shoe.'

Ganz looked around at them all. 'Agreed! Let's do it! For the glory of Ulric and the memory of Jurgen!'

The ten riders mounted up and thundered off across the clearing to disappear into the dark woods. Ganz paused before he rode. 'May the wolf run beside you,' he said to Aric, Gruber and von Glick.

Aric and Gruber made von Glick comfortable by the shrine. They covered Krieber with a saddle cloth, tied the horses off to the west, and lit a fire. Then Aric planted the standard in the clay soil.

'You needn't have stayed too,' he told Gruber.

'Yes, I did,' Gruber said simply. 'I need to do this very much.'

EVENING SLOPED DOWN on them, speckling the heavy sky with dark twists of cloud. Rain lanced down, slantwise, and a wind picked up, lifting the ragged hem of the old standard and swishing through the miserable forest.

The four remained by the fire – the two living warriors, the dead man and the man halfway between.

Von Glick's eyes were clouded as dark as the heavens. 'Ulric,' he murmured, gazing up at the cold sky. 'Let them come.'

Gruber reached out and pulled at Aric's arm. This message needed no words. Stiff from the cold, the two men lifted their warhammers and rose, standing by the guttering ashes of the fire, looking across the clearing.

'By the sacred flame, Aric my brother,' said Gruber, 'now we'll see a fight.'

The beastmen attacked.

There were perhaps four score of them, more than Aric remembered from the pitched battle the previous season when the beastmen had caught them by surprise and Jurgen fell. The misshapen monsters were clad in reeking pelts, their animalistic heads crowned by all manner of horns and tusks and antlers, their skins scaled and haired and furred, bald and muscular, diseased and slack. They bellowed as they charged in from the eastern tree-line, their foul collective breath gusting before them, eyes wild like insane cattle, wet, drooling mouths agape to expose ulcerated gums, black teeth and hooked fangs. The ground shook.

Aric and Gruber leapt onto their horses and galloped around to stand between the charge and the lonely standard.

'For Ulric!' yelled Aric, his hammer beginning its swing.

'By the hammers of the Wolf!' raged Gruber, holding his horse steady.

'For the Temple! *For the Temple!*' came a third voice. The riders glanced back. Hammer in hand, von Glick stood beside the standard, supporting his weight against the haft.

'For the Temple!' he screamed at them again.

Their battle roars as feral as the beasts, Aric and Gruber leapt their horses into the front of the pack as it came to them, giving themselves momentum and meeting the charge head on. The hammers swung and flew. Blood and spittle sprayed from cracked skulls. The hooves of the warhorses tore into flaccid flesh. Spears and blades thrust at them. The war cry of the two wolves echoed above all. Aric rejoiced. He had almost forgotten the ecstasy of combat, of the raging melee. Gruber laughed out loud. He had just remembered.

Von Glick stood his ground by the standard, despite the blood that leaked down his armour from the broken wound, and slew the first beast that charged him. The second fell, its skull cloven. The third rocked back, its ribs cracked. Now there were three, four around him, five. He was as deep in the fight as Aric and Gruber.

Aric struck left and right, blood painting across his grey armour, foam flecking back from the frenzied mouth of his steed. He saw Gruber laughing, striking...

Falling.

A lance thrust took down his mount. Gruber fell amongst the howling beasts, his hammer swinging in furious denial of the end.

They heard the thunder.

Above, in the sky as the storm broke.

Below, on the ground as the Company of Wolves charged in behind the beastpack.

Inside, in their hearts, as Ulric bayed the name of Jurgen.

THE KNIGHTS OF the White Company charged in line abreast, with Ganz at the centre, flanked by Vandam and Anspach.

'God's teeth, but I need a drink!' shouted Morgenstern as they swept in.

'No, you don't! You need this kind of courage instead!' rallied Ganz.

They hit the beastpack as it turned in confusion to meet them, ploughing over ranks of the fierce creatures, toppling and trampling, warhammers raining down as furiously as the downpour from above. Lightning flashed on the grotesque mayhem. Blood and rainwater sprayed into the air. The baying creatures turned from their original targets and swept into the fight with the cavalry force. Aric rode forward across the corpse-strewn ground and helped Gruber to his feet. The older warrior was speckled with blood, but alive.

'See to von Glick and watch the standard. Give me your horse,' Gruber said to Aric. Aric dismounted and returned to the banner of Vess as Gruber galloped back into the brutal fray.

Von Glick lay by the standard, which was still stuck upright in the earth. The bodies of almost a dozen beastmen lay around him.

'L-let me see...' von Glick breathed. Aric knelt beside him, and raised his head. 'So, Anspach's bold plan worked...' breathed the veteran warrior. 'He's pleased, I'll wager.'

Aric started to laugh but stopped. The old man was dead.

IN THE THICK of the combat, Morgenstern wielded his warhammer and drove his horse through the press of bodies, swinging left and right, destroying the enemy as easily as if they had been a row of turnips on upturned pails. He laughed his raucous laugh and set about himself. Nearby, Anspach saw his display and joined the laughter, smashing down with his own hammer.

At the heart of the fight, Vandam, the fiercest of all, glory singing in his veins, destroyed beast after beast, three times the number of any of them. He was still slaughtering the monsters as their spears cut him down.

In the tumult, Ganz saw the great bull-man, the pack leader, the beast that had slain Jurgen. He charged forward, but his hammer was dragged down by the weight of creatures on him. The bull-man swung to strike at him.

The haft of Gruber's hammer blocked the axe. Gruber, yelling the war cry, rode in on his commander's right hand, guarding his flank. Ganz pulled his weapon clear and, before the massive bull-head could swing again, drove its snout back into its skull in an explosion of blood.

'In the name of Ulric!' Ganz screamed, rejoicing. The heavens thundered their applause.

SMOKE ROSE FROM the storm-swept field, smoke and the steam from the blood. The Wolf Templars dismounted one by one amidst the carnage and kneeled in the mud to offer thanks to the raging sky. Fierce rain washed the blood off their armour as prayer cleansed their spirits. Of the beastman horde, not one had survived.

Ganz walked quietly to view the fallen.

Von Glick, at Aric's feet. Ganz was sure Aric was guarding the old man's body more than he was guarding the fluttering banner.

Vandam, skewered four times with crude lances, twisted at the top of a mound of dead.

'He has found his glory,' Morgenstern said. 'He's transferred to that better company. Ulric's own.'

'May the wolves guard his brave soul,' said Ganz.

Across the bloody, torn-up field, Dorff began to whistle a tune that resembled a battle hymn. Anspach caught it up and began to sing, making a shape and melody out of Dorff's notes. Einholt joined him, soft and low. It was a mourning song, of victory and loss, one of old Jurgen's favourites. Within three bars of it, all the other voices had joined the song.

* * *

THEY CAME BACK into Middenheim three days later. It was raining then too.

Mitterfruhl was almost on them all, but the High Priest came away from the preparations at the Temple, drawn by the excited whispers. He and his entourage were waiting for them in the Temple Square as White Company rode in, eleven riders, proud behind the fluttering banner of Vess, three noble dead lashed to their steeds.

Ranked in honour behind the motionless priest, Red, Grey, Gold and Silver Companies, the fighting packs who, with White, made up the Templar force, raised their voices in a throaty cheer.

Ganz, tall on his horse, gazed down at the High Priest.

'White Company has returned to the Temple, lord,' he said, 'and the heart has returned to White Company.'

THE DEAD AMONG US

THE GOD OF DEATH stared down on me as I prepared the corpse for burial. His hooded eyes were not visible but I could feel his gaze on my hands as they moved over the cold body before me, and he saw that the work was good. The atmosphere in the vaulted room beneath the temple was quiet and damp, smelling faintly of mildew, ashes and of the thousands of the dead of Middenheim who had passed through here on their last journey.

I chanted the words of the ritual under my breath, my mind aware of nothing but their rhythm and the power they held, my hands moving in the sacred patterns of the ceremony. I had done this many times before. The body before me was nothing but a carcass, its soul already blessed and freed and fled to the afterlife. My job now was to seal the corpse, to make sure that no other entity could move in and take possession of this empty shell.

A footfall on the stone steps intruded upon my concentration and broke the spell. Morr was no longer watching; the carving of the patron deity above the altar was just a carving again. The footsteps stopped for a moment, then came on down into the Factorum. The tall, well-aged frame of Brother Gilbertus blocked out the faint light for a moment as he passed through the doorway. I knew it would be him.

'I'm not disturbing you, am I?' he asked.

'Yes,' I said plainly. 'You are. That's the third Funeral Rite incantation you've interrupted this month, brother, and as penance you will take my place to perform it. This body goes out to be buried in the forest at noon today, so I suggest you start the ritual as soon as you've finished telling me why you're here.'

He didn't protest. Instead he said, 'They've found a body.'

'If you hadn't noticed, brother, this is the temple of Morr, who is the God of Death. We are priests of Morr. Bodies are what we deal with. One more corpse is hardly a reason to barge into the Factorum while another priest is performing a ceremony. Clearly your apprenticeship in Talabheim has taught you little. I may have to give you more lessons.'

He stared at me blankly, my sarcastic tone unnoticed or not understood. I stared back at his greying forelock and the furrows of age around his eyes, and thought for a moment how old he was to be a new priest. But then I had joined the temple late in life as well. Many did.

'It's a woman,' he said. 'Murdered. I thought you'd want to know.'

I blinked. 'Where?'

'Through the heart. With a knife.'

'Where in the city, dolt?'

'Oh. The alleyway behind the Drowned Rat, in the Ostwald.'

'I'm going out.' I pulled off my ritual robes and flung them into the corner of the room. 'Start that Funeral Rite now and you will be finished by the time I get back.'

A COLD JAHRDRUNG wind whistled over the slated rooftops and between the bleak stone buildings of Middenheim. If there had been any leaves on the few trees that grew on the heights of this rock, the pinnacle in the air that men called the City of the White Wolf, they would have been ripped off and hurled into the sky. But it was the last days of winter, the festival of Mitterfruhl was not passed, and the spring buds were not yet beginning to show. There would be no new life here for some time.

The wind cut through my thin robe as I strode up across Morrspark, the frosted grass crunching under my feet, and out into the streets, which grew narrower and less well-kept as they led south-west into the Ostwald district, crowded with early morning bustle. It was bitterly cold. I cursed myself for not putting on a cloak before leaving the temple, but haste was more important than my comfort. Rumours and falsehoods spread fast in a city as compact and tight-knit as Middenheim, and where an unexplained death was concerned, anybody speaking ill of the dead would only hinder my work.

The alley behind the Drowned Rat was narrow and sloping, stinking and crowded. A couple of members of the city watch were trying to keep onlookers away and not doing a good job of it, but the gawpers drew back slightly as I approached. The dark robes of a priest of Morr will do that, and it's not out of respect. Nobody likes being reminded of their own mortality.

As the crowd moved apart to let me pass, I saw the bald pate of Watch Captain Schtutt standing beside the corpse. He looked up, saw me and smiled in recognition, his face creased by middle-age and good living. We'd known each other for years, but I didn't smile back. He started to say something by way of a greeting, but I had already crouched down by the body.

It was a woman – or it had been. Probably turned twenty; probably beautiful. Dark brown hair with a wave to it. Something about her face said she had Norse blood, although with one eye and most of a cheek missing it was hard to tell for sure. She had the most delicate ears. Her clothes, gaudy but cheap, had been slashed all ways with a blade of some kind – a hunting knife or dagger, I guessed – before the fatal blow had slipped between her ribs and into her heart. This had been a competent murder, and someone had tried hard to make it look like something less polished. Her left arm was missing, and someone had thrown a rough brown blanket over an object a couple of feet from her. Blood from the cobbles had begun to seep into its fabric.

She wasn't Filomena. Filomena had been blonde.

I REMEMBERED WHERE I was, and looked up at Schtutt. 'What's under the blanket?'

He muttered, 'Don't lift it,' and there was something nervous in his voice. Then he turned to the pack of vultures and gossip-seekers and spoke loudly: 'All right, bugger off, the lot of you. Nothing more to see. Constable, get them out of here. Give the priest of Morr room to do his magic.'

I wasn't planning any magic but the suggestion of it, together with the taint of death in this narrow place, was enough to clear most of the crowd away quickly. Good old Schtutt.

He looked down at me for a second, his expression filled with some stress I couldn't identify, then bent down and raised one corner of the blanket. Underneath was something not human: a limb, maybe four feet long. It had no hand or bones, but large cup-like suckers along the underside. It smelled of decay and something bitter and sharp, like wormwood and stale wine.

It startled me. I felt Schtutt's gaze on my back, and that of the other watchmen too. Were they looking at the thing under the blanket, or watching to see how I'd react to it? I realised I was breathing fast, and steadied myself. Deep breath. Priests of Morr don't panic. They must not. They cannot be seen to.

'Right,' I said, and stood up. Be firm. Decisive. 'We need a cart to get all this back to the temple. High-sided if possible.'

'I saw a soil-collector's wagon on the way here,' one of the watch suggested.

'That'll suit. Go and fetch it.' I waited until he had gone, then gestured down at the blanket. 'How many saw this?'

'Two or three.'

'Make sure they don't talk about it. Harass them, put the fear of Ulric in them, anything short of cutting out their tongues. The last thing we need is a panic about a mutant in the city.'

'Mutant,' Schtutt said. His voice was flat, like an echo. It was as if he hadn't dared to use the word until I'd spoken it out loud, confirming his worst fears. A tentacled limb? Well, it hadn't been hacked from a bog-octopus or a kraken from the Sea of Claws, not in an alley in the Ostwald. But now he'd said the word, I had to stop him saying it again where people might hear him.

'There'll need to be a full investigation. A dissection. If it is a... well, we'll burn it quietly. For the sake of Ulric, don't go talking about mutants around the city. Even among the watch. Keep it to yourselves. But circulate the girl's description: age, height, dress, everything except the arm.' I rubbed my hands; they were freezing. 'We've got to get the body back to the temple so I can start. Where's that bloody wagon?'

It arrived, and the body was loaded unceremoniously into the cart, the soil-collectors not too happy about having their work interrupted. Nobody wanted to touch the thing under the blanket. Eventually I bundled it up in its covering and dropped it beside the corpse, in the back of the stinking wagon, then stood back so I could wipe my hands on my thin robe where Schtutt wouldn't see me do it.

The drayman flicked his whip, the elderly horse strained at the traces and the cart rumbled slowly down the filthy cobbles of the slum-streets towards the open space of Morrspark and the temple at its centre. Schtutt and I walked behind it.

'Any idea who she was?' I said.

'Apart from being–' Schtutt caught my glare. 'No, we don't. She was dressed like a tavern wench or maybe a night-girl, but she couldn't have got work with an arm like that. Although maybe she disguised it with magic. She could have lured someone into the alley, dropped the disguise, and then he killed her out of horror.

'Or maybe it was a cult killing. They say there's powerful cults of Chaos-worshippers in the city. We do find sacrifices. Cats, mostly.' He shivered. 'If I thought there was going to be trouble with Chaos, I'd take my family and leave Middenheim. Go north. My brother has an estate about thirty miles away. Would thirty miles be far enough, you think? To escape the Dark?'

I didn't reply. I was following my own thoughts. Schtutt seemed happy to continue talking without a reply.

'We shouldn't have to wait for them to act. We should track them down and burn them. Burn their homes too. To the ground,' he said, and there was a certain relish in his voice. 'Get some witch hunters to come and investigate. Remember those two who came up from Altdorf? Seventeen Chaos-worshippers found and burnt in three days. That's the sort of men we need. Eh? Dieter?'

That broke my concentration. Nobody called me Dieter these days – not in eight years, not since I'd entered the Temple. I looked across at him, meeting his gaze in silence. After a moment he looked away.

'Ulric's beard,' he muttered. 'You're not the man you were. What have they done to you in that temple of ghouls?'

I could think of a hundred replies but none of them fitted the moment, so I said nothing. Silence is the first thing a priest of Morr learns. I had learnt that lesson well. A wordless void stretched between us, until Schtutt filled it.

'Why do you do it?' he asked. 'That's what I don't understand. I remember when you were one of the best merchants in Middenheim. Everyone came to you for everything. You weren't just rich, you were–'

'I was loved.' Schtutt went silent. I continued, 'Loved by my wife and son, who vanished. You know that. Everyone knows. They were never found. I spent hundreds of crowns, thousands, looking for them. And I neglected my trading, and my business failed so I gave it away, and I joined the Temple of Morr and became a priest.'

'But why, Dieter?' That name again. Not mine, not now. 'You can't find them there.'

'I will,' I said. 'Sooner or later their souls will come to Morr, and be received by his hands, and I will know it. It's the only certainty I have any more. It was the not knowing that was killing me.'

'Is that why you do it?' he asked. 'Investigating the unexplained deaths? In case it's them?'

'No,' I said. 'No, it just passes the time.'

But I knew I was lying.

THE CART TRUNDLED across the hard earth of Morrspark, still too solid for burials, and stopped outside the temple. The dark stone of the building and the bare branches of the high trees around it were silhouetted against a sky that was grey and heavy with snow yet to come, like outstretched hands offering a closed box to an unseen god.

Schtutt and his deputy carried the body down the stone steps into the vaulted gloom of the Factorum while I followed, the blanket and its unpleasant contents in my arms. There was no sign of Gilbertus, or the corpse he had been preparing for burial. Good.

The girl's body was laid on one of the grey granite slabs, and I placed the tentacle next to it, still wrapped in its blanket. The stench of the soil-wagon clung to the corpse's clothes, but there was another odour, bitter and unpleasant.

In the quiet and the semi-darkness she could almost have been any beautiful woman lying asleep. I stared at her still form. Who was she? Why had she been killed so deliberately, so coldly, and the deed disguised to look like something else? Did she have a powerful enemy, or was she dead for another reason? Was she more important dead than alive? The arm...

Schtutt shuffled his feet and coughed. I could sense his uneasiness. The bodies on the other slabs could have had something to do with it.

'We'd best be going,' he said.

'Yes,' I said abruptly. I wanted to be alone with the body, to try to get some feel for who or what had killed her. It's not that I like dead people. I don't. I just prefer them to the living.

'We'll need an official report,' he said. 'If it's mutant business the Graf will have to be told. You'll dissect her today?'

'No,' I said. 'First we do the rituals to rest her soul.'

No, not 'we'. I would do the rituals personally.

'Then we do the dissection – for the records, and for the Graf's precious paperwork. Then, if we can't find a next of kin, she gets a pauper's funeral.'

'Off the Cliff of Sighs?' Schtutt asked, shock in his voice. 'But surely mutants must be burnt? To cleanse them?'

'Did I say she was a mutant?' I asked.

'What?'

I grasped the section of tentacle that had lain beside the corpse, and shoved it at him. It felt cold and rubbery in my hand, and damp. Schtutt recoiled like a slapped dog.

'Smell it,' I said.

'What!'

'Smell it.' He sniffed at it, cautiously, then looked at me.

'Well?' I asked.

'It's... sour. Bitter. Like something stale.'

'Vinegar.' I put down the unclean flesh. 'I don't know where that came from, but I do know it wasn't attached to anyone who was alive this morning. The damn thing's been pickled.'

SCHTUTT AND HIS man went eventually, promising that they'd try to find out who the girl had been. I almost asked them not to. The last way you're going to learn anything about a death in the Ostwald, with its twisting alleys and shadowy deals, is to have heavy-booted watchmen asking questions with all the subtlety of an unwashed ogre. Even if they got an answer it wouldn't do any good. I still wanted to find out who the girl was, but the more I thought about this, the more I suspected that it was her death, not herself, that was important. Someone had wanted to convince people that there were mutants in the city, and they would have managed it if the investigation had been left to the likes of Schtutt.

He wasn't a bad man, I reflected as I prepared the ritual. We'd known each other quite well in the days before I joined the temple: he'd been a young merchant trying to muscle in on trade franchises held by families much older and more powerful than his. He hadn't done well, but he hadn't given up, I'll say that for him. Then the Sparsam family had framed him for evading taxes, and part of his punishment had been a month with the city watch. And that was that: he found his niche in life there, and he was a much better watch captain than he'd been a merchant. Which didn't mean he was much of a watch captain.

I lit the last of the candles around the body, sprinkled some blessed water over the body with the appropriate ritual gestures, breathed deeply, and began the deep, slow chant of the Nameless Rite. Inside, I was waiting. The spirit of Morr moved over me and through me, within the patterns I had created with my hands and my mind, and flowed out from me to encompass the body of the woman before me, to bless it and protect it from evil.

And stopped. Something was resisting.

The energy of the Lord of Death hovered in me, waiting for me to use it. But I felt as if I was trying to force two lodestones together: the harder I pushed, the closer I came to the body, the greater was the repulsion. I kept chanting, drawing more of Morr's energy to me, trying to spread it out over the corpse, but it slipped away like rain off oiled leather. Something was wrong, very wrong. But I wasn't going to give up. I chanted on, summoning all my force, pushing Morr's power out over the corpse. The nameless resistance pushed back. I couldn't break it. Impasse.

One of the candles guttered and snuffed out, burnt down to its stub. It had been three, maybe four inches long when I'd started the ritual. Hours must have passed. I let my chanting cease and the divine power slipped away, taking the last of my energy with it. My knees felt like green twigs, and I felt myself swaying with exhaustion. Alone in the shadows, I stared at the body. The Factorum was absolutely quiet except for my own faint panting, absolutely still – but not tranquil. It was tense, as if waiting for something. The chill of the spring and the cold stones stuck needles through my robe and I shivered. For an instant I felt what the normal people must feel in here: the terror of being surrounded by the dead. The terror of not understanding.

I snuffed out the remaining candles between my fingers and hurried away, upstairs, to the comparative warmth of the main body of the temple, and felt my momentary fear fade as I did. For a moment I considered visiting the main hall and praying for a while, but instead I slipped in through the side entrance that led to the priests' private chambers, headed down the narrow stone corridor, and knocked on the door to Father Zimmerman's room. I felt uneasy about having to do this, but sometimes the only way to deal with a problem is to kick it upstairs.

There was a shuffling from within the room, a muffled voice, and then the door opened part-way from the other side and Brother Gilbertus squeezed out. I was reminded of a cat moving through a small space, or a snake. He smiled his bland smile at me and disappeared off towards the refectory. I pushed the door fully open and entered. Father Zimmerman was sitting at his writing desk. It looked as if he had been drafting a letter. Ink stained his fingers, and there were broken quills on the floor. He turned around and I saw there was ink on his white beard too.

'What is it?' he said. There was irritation in his voice: not, I guessed, from having his meeting interrupted. It probably had more to do with the fact that he didn't like me. That was fine by me. I didn't like him either.

'There's a new body in the Factorum, father.'

'Bodies are our stock in trade, brother. You may have observed that in the years you have been working here.' I thought of my words to

Gilbertus earlier that day, and cursed the Talabheimer. He'd been here, telling tales of my disrespect for the dead, no doubt.

'I've been trying to bless it for burial,' I said. 'The blessing won't... won't take. It's as if something is resisting it.'

'This would be the mutant girl?'

Bugger the Talabheimer, and bugger him again. 'Yes, but she's not–'

'You waste too much time with street-scum and the dregs of life, brother. It's not a good attitude for a temple such as ours, with a certain standing in the community. You should think of other things, and spend more of your time on the good works that I have suggested you pursue.'

'I don't work for you. I work for Morr.'

'Perhaps you would be happier working for him with a solo ministry? We have been asked to establish a shrine in one of the Wasteland towns to deal with their plague victims, you know. I could recommend you for the post.'

He gestured to the writing desk. Obviously matters of transfer and administration were on his mind, but then he'd always been a petty status-minded pen-pusher, more concerned with appearances than with the real business of Morr's work. I hated him, but I realised that I wasn't going to get what I needed without an apology, so I gritted my teeth and backtracked.

'I'm sorry.' A breath. 'But we have a corpse down in the Factorum which I can't cleanse and prepare for burial. I don't know if it's enchanted or what else, but I thought you might know, and I thought you'd want to be told about it.'

'And you thought that I, being an older, more experienced and more powerful priest, might perform a Purification Rite on it for you? You did.'

I did, so I nodded – and saw his expression change, and instantly knew I'd made a mistake. It was the answer he'd wanted. He glowered at me. I could feel his dislike now, and I'd given him an excuse to vent it.

'You thought,' he hissed, 'that the senior priest of the temple of Morr in Middenheim has time to sully his hands blessing the corpse of some street tart?'

'I didn't–'

'You presume to ask me to waste my time with one of your low-lifes, and a mutant to boot? You dare to come in here and insult...'

I lowered my head and let the words wash over me. It was nothing I hadn't heard before. The antipathy between Father Albrecht Zimmerman and me was the main reason I was still only a second-tier priest after eight years in the temple, and was unlikely to rise higher. I'd accepted that. The father might be close to retirement but I knew his place would go to someone who acted like he did, thought like he did and disliked me as much as he did. Probably Gilbertus, who might be new but who seemed to be doing a lot of wheel-greasing recently. Ambitious, that Gilbertus. That letter on the father's desk was probably about him.

Eventually the words slowed and stopped. A new paragraph was about to begin, so I started paying attention again.

'As penance, I want you to go to the Cliff of Sighs, where you will find Brother Ralf, who is due to officiate at a funeral. You will take over for him. Then come back here and pray to Saint Heinrich that your good intentions do not overcome your common sense. Pray hard, brother. Pray until the tenth bell. That is all.'

I left.

IT WAS NIGHT. I lay awake on my hard, narrow bed and stared at the pattern of the moonlight as it fell on the stone wall of the tiny window of my tiny cell, the harsh brightness of Morrslieb's aura slowly eclipsing the warmer glow of Mannslieb. My body was completely exhausted, drained from the energy of the ritual I had performed that day, but I knew I would get no sleep tonight. It was too cold for a start, spring or no spring, and my single blanket did a bad job of keeping me warm enough to get comfortable. Besides, my mind was filled with the dead girl.

Who had she been? Where had she come from, to die so ignominiously on the streets of Middenheim? Had her death got anything to do with who she was, or had she simply been in the wrong tavern, with a kind word for the wrong man, who had led her into a dark back alley as dawn approached and stuck her over and over again with a short knife, carefully angling his blades to make the attack look frenzied. And then cut off her arm, to replace it with something inhuman, hiding her real one – he must have had a bag with him, probably a big one, watertight perhaps – and sneak away.

I could visualise the sort of man he must be, but right now I wasn't interested in him. I wanted to picture her.

She had been beautiful once. Perhaps she had been beautiful last night: what was left of her complexion hadn't had the blowsy gin-blossoms of an old street-walker. Laugh lines had creased the fresh skin around her mouth and eyes, and she wore no cosmetics. This was not a woman who had relied on her physical charms to earn a living. Not for long, anyway.

What had brought her, this Norse beauty, to Middenheim? The Norse were too pragmatic and down-to-earth to believe the old stories of the clifftop city with its streets paved with the gold dug from the mountain below. Something other than dreams of foreign places and easy fortunes brought her here. It was probably the arm of a merchant or traveller – possibly Norse but probably not: they were loyal to their own, particularly abroad – who had abandoned her when she made eyes at another man or got pregnant, or any of the thousand other reasons that men break their promises to women.

How long had it been since the stability and love she had thought were hers had been revealed as a hollow joke? Her clothes had seemed quite new and probably too expensive for the sort of woman who drank in the Drowned Rat, so she probably hadn't been on the streets too long. Unless she had robbed someone recently. No; people can disguise themselves in life, but a dead face reveals the true character behind it, and I had seen nothing of the petty criminal in what remained of her features. There was nothing of the ground-down, hardened street-walker there either. She'd been new to the idea of having to rely on her charms and a low-cut dress to earn a living. Or new enough that she didn't yet know how to spot the sort who would be good to her, and the sort who hated her kind and wanted nothing but ill for them.

Someone in the city had to know who she was, and I wanted to bless her with her real name when I buried her. Someone knew. It might be the person who had killed her, and that meant I had to find him. Nobody at the Drowned Rat would admit to remembering a thing about last night – it was that kind of a place, and not even the fear of Morr would persuade them to talk.

There was a faint sound, a sudden vibration that seemed to run through the temple building. It came again a few seconds later. Then a pause, and a third. From somewhere further down the corridor came a scrape of wood, and the thud of a thrown-open door. Running footsteps. I thought briefly about getting up to investigate, decided that I was still too tired from the failed ritual, and rolled over. Let Zimmerman sort it out. If he was so protective of his status as head of the temple, let him take some of the responsibility that came with the position. I went back to my thoughts.

That arm – the arm that wasn't hers. It all came down to that. There are easier ways to spread the fear of Chaos and mutation around a city like Middenheim than faking the murder of a mutant in an alley. So why? The only other reason I could think of was that a dead mutant would spark an official enquiry. Lots of paperwork. Probably a promotion for someone in the Watch. Maybe a witch-hunt, and a couple of old women burnt. And the temple would be involved, because we'd have to dissect the body and make the official report. Which meant that the first place the corpse would be brought was here. But why? And why the corpse of a tall, fair-skinned Norse beauty, as nameless as me, instead of some local good-time girl?

There was a scream, and I jolted to full consciousness. – I must have dozed off. Someone pelted down the corridor outside my room, shouting something. There was a distant crash.

Trouble. I dashed outside, tugging on my robe as I went. It was dark and I couldn't see anyone in the faint moonlight, but there was a lot of noise coming from the main hall of the temple so I headed that way. Unsteady light and shouting told me I was going in the right direction. The connecting door was open – no, it was ripped off its hinges and lying on the floor. I jumped over it and arrived in the main hall.

It was mayhem. A tempest had been here. Everything was smashed. The Flames Eternal had gone out again, but in the faint light from the night-lamps on the pillars I could see three priests, two with makeshift weapons – a broom, a rod of office – circling but keeping well back from someone. It was her.

* * *

IT WAS HER. The face I'd been imagining as I lay in bed smiled dully, deadly. She looked like hell, as you would if you had been murdered a day ago. Her movements were jerky, abrupt, and there seemed to be no sight in her eyes or expression on her face except a blank grin. With her one arm she clasped the torso of Brother Rickard. The rest of him lay a few yards away. As I watched, she dropped the body and began to cast her head from side to side, as if trying to feel for something with some strange inhuman sense. It was like... I didn't know what it was like.

'Stay back!' It was Father Zimmerman. I doubted that any of us had any intention of getting any closer. He struck a stance and began to chant. From the sound of his syllables it was a ritual, but not one I recognised. The dead woman's head snapped upright, as if she had found what she was searching for. Then she took a slow, stiff step towards him.

'Father! Move!' I yelled as I looked desperately for a weapon to defend myself. The cult of Morr has never been big on armaments, and its temples aren't exactly prepared for battle. The corpse took another step towards the father. He kept chanting, faster now, and there was panic on his face. I could have run in to pull him to safety but I didn't; instead I ran away, up towards the high altar. The flattened disc of the great bowl lay there, its gold plate and the heavy liquid in it gleaming slickly in the low light. Behind me there was a scream, high like an old woman.

I reached around the rim of the bowl and lifted it with both hands. It was heavy with the liquid, which sloshed between the shallow rims. As I turned with it, I heard the snap, and an instant too late saw Father Zimmerman die, his spine broken like an autumn twig. The dead woman dropped his body and it hit the floor, twitching.

I took measured paces across the marbled tiles. The liquid slopped in the great bowl, a little spilling out with each step. The puppet-corpse was casting its head around, looking for a target as I drew closer to it. The other two priests backed away from us both. She was fifteen feet away. Ten. Her head turned in my direction, and her slashed face bared its teeth at me in a dead smile.

I flung the great bowl at her, its contents flying outwards in a wild shower. Not holy water but oil, blessed for the anointing of mourners. It covered her, soaking the remains of her once-fancy clothes. The bowl hit the floor edge-on with a clang and spun away. I leapt backwards, grabbed a night-lamp from its niche on the nearest pillar and flung it at the sodden abomination.

It was like a flower blossoming, or the sun breaking through clouds. The temple was filled with the light from the burning woman. She blazed. Something in her must have sensed what was happening as she slowly began to flail against the flames. She fell over. Her body crackled. There was a smell of roasting.

The other two priests – Ralf, I could see now, and Pieter – stood in shock and watched as the body and the temple burned. I didn't have time for that; I headed for the main doors and outside into the fierce chill of the night, my mind working furiously as I went. Dead Norse women. Missing arms. Animated corpses. On the steps I saw Gilbertus coming up.

'Where are you going?' he said.

'To raise the alarm.'

'I've done that. What was it?'

'An animated corpse. Someone was controlling it. The father is dead.'

'Ah.' He didn't seem surprised. 'Are you coming back inside?'

'No,' I said. 'For one thing it's on fire, and for another I know who killed that girl.'

'Oh. Who?'

'A necromancer,' I said. 'A necromancer with a grudge.'

IF YOU WANT to know about grudges, you have to talk to a dwarf. I didn't relish the idea of having to go and see this particular dwarf at this time of night, not because he'd be in bed – I knew he wouldn't – but because of where he'd be. The Altquartier area was unpleasant enough during the day, but past midnight it was at its worst: the cheapest tarts, the pettiest criminals and the most desperate people. And at its heart lay the Bretonnian House.

Lit by harsh moonlight, the place looked just as tattered as I remembered it: an old, small tavern, its front black-painted, with cracked panes of glass in the windows and the stale smell of boiled cabbage seeping from the cheap eating room above. It looked closed but I knew it wasn't; places like this were never closed, if the patron or a regular owed you a favour. In years gone by I'd had some good evenings, some useful tip-offs and two fights in here. I hoped that the latter wouldn't be repeated tonight.

I knocked on the door, and after a few seconds it opened a crack. 'Who's there?'

'I'm looking for Alfric Half-nose,' I said.

'Who wants him?'

'Tell him…' I paused. 'Tell him it's the man who was Dieter Brossmann.'

The door closed. I could imagine the conversation that was happening on the other side. After a long minute it opened, to reveal a short, scrubby man with a pudding-bowl haircut. 'Enter,' he said.

I did. There's a trick with long robes and dresses that all high-born ladies know and all priests should learn: keep your steps light and short and silent, and if you do it right it looks like you're gliding, not walking. With the black robes of a Morr worshipper, it can look very eerie. The place had fallen silent as I came in, and the quiet lay over it like a blanket of cold dew as I moved across the small room. There were maybe ten people in, from cheap hoodlums drinking cheap beer to the less disreputable with glasses of wine or absinthe in front of them.

A man in a flat black Bretonnian hat, seated at the bar, nodded and raised a glass to me. His face was cracked with age and hard living like an old painting, and his eyes looked like bloodshot poached eggs. I recognised him from the old days, but couldn't remember his name. He probably had several.

There was a sound from one of the booths at the far end of the room. Nobody looked that way, so I knew it was what I was after and glided over to it. The great bulk of Alfric was squeezed in there, with one of his henchmen and a fat human in opulent robes sat opposite. The table was covered with empty tankards on the dwarfs' side, and gold coins. Alfric looked up. There was more grey in his beard than I remembered, and the scars around his ruined nose were a flaming red: a sure sign he'd been drinking heavily. But it would be unwise for me to assume he'd be drunk, or unobservant.

'Good evening, brother,' he said. 'Sit down. How may I be of service to the Temple of Morr this evening?'

I didn't sit. Instead I said, 'Alfric Half-nose, whose family name is Anvil-breaker, I am here to restore the balance of honour between our families.'

'Oh yes?' Alfric didn't look as if he was interested. The fat man was sweating, I noticed. He wasn't a merchant, or at least not a good one: he clearly didn't have the nerve for negotiating tricky deals. Idly I wondered who he was, and what had made him so desperate he'd come to see Alfric after the second bell of the night. He looked worried, but his problems were his own. I had mine to deal with.

'Five years ago,' I started. 'I... Oh sod it, I'll cut the formalities. You owe me a favour from the time I burnt the body of that storekeeper your grandson shot. I'm calling it in.'

'So I do, so you can.' Alfric took a swig from his tankard. 'You always were impatient. Always wanted things done your way. Your name and your taste in clothes, are they the only things you've changed since your family disappeared?' I said nothing. 'You haven't found them yet, then? Well, if you need some help, you know where to come.'

I knew he was trying to needle me, to show how displeased he was that I'd interrupted his business, so I didn't answer him. Instead I said, 'The temple was attacked this night. Someone animated a corpse against us. It looked like it was sent to kill people, not do damage, but it did a lot anyway. And Father Zimmerman is dead.' It was the second time I'd said that, but the first time I understood it. Suddenly I felt very tired. There was a spare place on the bench next to the merchant, and I sat down.

Alfric watched me, his dark eyes glinting like wet stones in the faint lamplight. 'Sounds like a necromancer's work.'

'I thought so.' A pause. 'Are there any of... such a calling in the city?'

'None that I know of. And that means probably not.' He paused for another swig. I trusted his word: Alfric's eyes and ears were everywhere in Middenheim. The dwarfs had built the place and their tunnels still pervaded it, like woodworm in a rotten cabinet. Alfric and his informants knew them all, and from listening at their secret entrances and watching at their spy-holes, he knew all the city's comings and goings. Best informant and biggest blackmailer in town, Alfric Half-nose.

'So who could have done this? Do you know of anyone with a grudge against the temple?' I asked.

Alfric swilled the beer around his mouth and swallowed. 'Shut up. I'm thinking about necromancers.' He took another slow mouthful and savoured it thoughtfully.

Necromancy, I thought. If it was a necromancer then asking about grudges was pointless. Necromancers hated priests of Morr as much as we hated them. Both sides dealt in death, but we saw it as a passing, a stage in a process. They saw it as a tool. We were interested in freeing souls; they wanted to enslave them with their dark, unholy magics. Of course they'd have a grudge against us. Of course any ambitious necromancer would want to destroy the power of the local Temple of Morr, and if that meant killing its priests – well, like us, bodies were their stock in trade. But there was something about the way the girl's corpse had moved, something about the way it had sought out Father Zimmerman... I grasped for the idea, but couldn't catch it.

Alfric's voice broke my thoughts. 'One of your own corpses, was it? Corpse in the temple?'

'Yes,' I said. 'And there was something–'

'I'll know how that's happened, brother,' and he leant on that last word. 'That new priest of yours, the one from Talabheim...'

'Gilbertus.'

'Gilbertus. He's sloppy. Doesn't do the blessings properly. In too much of a hurry, like you. You should watch him at the Cliff of Sighs sometime. Goes through the motions all right, enough to fool the mourners anyway. But mark my words, those bodies are going over the cliff unblessed. Careless.

Dangerous too, if there's a necromancer around: unblessed corpses, ready to be raised. Now if there is a necromancer in town – and I'm not saying there is, mind – then be careful. Nasty, necromancers. My grandsire tangled with one. They're fast. If they start to chant at you, count to five, he said. You'll never reach six. You'll be dead by then.'

Something, some idea about necromancers and the Temple, was forming itself in my mind, trying to push its way through the day's exhaustion. I stood up. The thoughts would take a while to clarify and it'd be morning before I'd know if I had heard the answer I needed, but the long cold walk back to the temple would help. 'Thanks, Alfric. The debt is cleared. I'll leave you to your business.'

He looked surprised for a moment, but it took more than that to ruffle his scarred composure. 'Good seeing you again, Dieter,' he said, and turned back to his sweating customer without another word.

I walked to the door and out into the cold night. It had started to snow, and I pulled my robe closely around myself. It was only as I turned the corner away from the Bretonnian House that I realised he'd called me Dieter, and that I had forgotten to ask him anything about the dead girl. A brief image of her burning face with its dead smile flickered in my mind. Somehow her identity didn't seem so important now.

* * *

THE CLIFF OF SIGHS is a place where contradictions meet. From its edge you can see the whole of the Middenland stretching away as far as the Middle Mountains: hills, tiny towns and the vast green carpet of the Drakwald Forest with the Talabheim road winding its way through it. In the days when I could still appreciate beauty, I thought it the most romantic and lovely place in the city. Step closer to the edge, look down and you see the shattered ruins of the coffins, the shrouded bodies spread across the rocks or hanging in the branches of the trees after being dropped, and sometimes the unconsecrated corpse of a suicide or murder victim as well.

Or you could have done if it wasn't snowing so damned hard. I wrapped my cloak more tightly around me, and watched the mid-morning funeral party. Gilbertus's voice was muffled by the snow but I knew the sombre incantation he was chanting so well that I would have noticed the slightest error. So far he hadn't put a syllable wrong. Around him, the mourners huddled to protect themselves against the cold, and against their mutual grief and the fear of death. The bare pine coffin sat on its bier at the edge of the cliff. This was not an opulent affair.

Gilbertus turned slightly and I pulled my head back out of sight around the corner of the building. It was bloody cold and the sharp wind was turning my feet and fingers numb, but to move too much would give away my presence. Instead I stood, a silent shivering statue, and listened to the chant.

There.

He'd missed something. Nothing as obvious as a dropped word or missing line: just a subtle change to the rhythm of the incantation. Two lines later: again, and quickly again. Then a whole section I didn't recognise.

This wasn't some misremembered lesson. He was changing things. I didn't understand the language of the sacred chants – almost nobody did, we just learned them by rote – but I could tell that there was something wrong here. Fear crawled slowly up my spine, and I would have sweated if it wasn't for the cold.

A final blessing was said, the bier was pushed to the edge of the rock and tipped, the coffin slid off it and into space, and the mourners were ushered away from the cliffside before the crash echoed up from below. They didn't hang around, the party dispersing quickly, eager to get away from this place of death, into the warm, to console each other and start on the funeral meats, I guessed. Gilbertus lingered a moment, and I stepped out to meet him.

'Well met, brother,' I said.

'Aye, brother. Cold.' He stamped his feet. 'Are you here for a funeral?'

'In a way,' I said. 'But I want to talk to you about the attack last night.'

'Yes,' he said. 'Unpleasant affair. You've been told there's a meeting after supper to discuss who's to be acting head of the temple?' Something in his tone, his whole stance, had changed. His voice wasn't the voice of an apprentice any more. Yesterday he had spoken to me with respect. Today it was arrogance. He paused and turned away, and I wondered if he didn't want me to see his face as he spoke again:

'Last night you said you thought you knew who was behind the attack. Do you still know?'

'I was wrong last night,' I said.

'Oh yes?'

'Yes,' I said. 'I thought it was a necromancer with a grudge. It's not: it's a necromancer with ambition. Do you feel ambitious, brother?'

'When it's cold, I feel cold,' he said. A new tone, halfway between fear and aggression, had entered his voice. 'Why don't we find somewhere warm to discuss this?'

'I'm happy here,' I said. 'This won't take long. I've only got four questions. First, if you'd gone to raise the alarm last night, why didn't I see your footprints across the frost in the park?'

'Because I went a different way to you, clearly. What's the second question?'

'How did you know the dead girl had been stabbed through the heart?'

'A watchman told me. Next?'

'Where did you get the tentacle?'

He whirled to face me and I thought he was about to cast a spell. I did nothing. For a moment he paused, then let his arms drop slowly to his side. He was frightened, I could tell. Frightened but still confident.

'What do you know?' he asked.

'That you're not going to leave this cliff without killing me.'

I stepped towards him, my hands slightly raised, palms and wrists exposed. Merchant's trick. Makes you look vulnerable, unthreatening. He didn't react, or at least he didn't try to move away, which was good.

Instead he said, 'Apart from that.'

'You arrived here six months ago, disguised as a junior priest from Talabheim,' I said. 'We were expecting a Brother Gilbertus to come from there, so I imagine you killed him and took his place. You've spent six months making sure that there are a lot of unblessed corpses buried around the city which you could use your magic to reanimate later.

'Yesterday morning you killed a girl behind the Drowned Rat, enchanted the corpse, and then made it look like a mutant so it would have to be brought back to the temple for an investigation, and so there wouldn't be too much surprise when I couldn't perform the ceremony of Nameless Rite on it. You also persuaded Father Zimmerman that I was wasting the temple's time, so the corpse would lie in the Factorum all night, unblessed, ready for you to reanimate. When I met you outside the temple, you'd been there all along, controlling the dead thing.'

'You know all that?' he said.

I moved closer to him. Only a few feet separated us. Behind him, the edge of the cliff dropped away into eternity.

'It's mostly guesswork,' I admitted.

'So much guessing... for a ruined merchant still obsessed by the loss of his family. I am impressed.' The disguise had dropped completely now: he wasn't Gilbertus any more. He'd never been Gilbertus at all, except in the minds of some too-trusting priests. If any of them had been around, they wouldn't have recognised this sarcastic arrogant who dared to taunt me with my grief.

But there was no one else: the Cliff of Sighs was deserted. Just us and the swirling snow: he with his plan and his magic, I with a new-kindled memory of Filomena, and the sadness and anger that it brought.

He smiled again. 'So, brother, why would a priest of Morr – or even a necromancer – do what you've described?'

'Because,' I said, and I didn't try to keep the bile out of my voice, 'because you're ambitious. Because there would be no more powerful position for a necromancer than leading a temple of Morr. All the corpses you need, brought to your doorstep by the good citizens of Middenheim. You probably have some scheme for taking over the city in a couple of years.'

'Perhaps.' He was close to me now, and he wasn't smiling any more. His face was set cold and hard against me. Snowflakes whirled in the space between us. 'And your last question?'

'I was going to ask who the girl was,' I said. 'But it's not important any more.'

'She was young. Strong. Susceptible to my magic. A potential tool. We're alike, you and I, brother. I had no interest in the girl when she was alive, and neither did you. All the suffering, all the pain in this city, and you only have use for them when they're dead. We could work together. We could learn a lot from each other. And I could use a man like you. What say you? Join me. Come back to the temple. I'll tell you about the girl there.'

'I said it wasn't important.' But his suggestion had thrown me off-guard. Were we similar? Had I the seed of necromancy in me? Then he started to chant: high-pitched and fast, and my fate suddenly became a lot more short-term.

Count to five, Alfric had said. Five seconds to survive.

One. I moved forward two paces.

Two, and I was in front of him, the dagger drawn out from under my cloak.

Three. I plunged it deep into his stomach. Blood gushed onto my hand, hot over my numbed fingers. I raised my face to his, and our gazes met. His eyes were full of horror.

Four. A long second passed. He didn't stop chanting.

Five. I twisted the knife hard, my fingers slipping against the blood. Gilbertus gave a pain cry. The chant was broken, his spell useless. He paused for an instant, then launched himself at me. The snow-covered ground slid under my feet and I went down.

He landed on top of me, grasping at my neck. I tried to roll away, but he pinned me to the ground. He was bleeding to death, but he was still larger and stronger than me: at the very least he could take me with him.

His fingers found my neck and squeezed, twisting my head to one side. Snow covered my face, filling my eyes and nose with gritty cold. I could feel the warmth of his blood on my stomach, and the hilt of the knife in his wound pressed itself hard against my kidneys. My mind fogged with pain and darkness.

I felt like a dying man. Images formed in my head: faces. Father Zimmerman, his face contorted in death-agony. Brother Rickard, torn in half. Schtutt. My wife, Filomena, and my son Karl, smiling, the last morning I had ever seen them. And the half-face of a dead Norse girl whose name and story I would never know.

No. My job here was not finished. I had Morr's work to do.

Something poured a last burst of strength into my tired limbs. My arms found his, breaking his grip around my neck and pushing him off from me, so he rolled away across the whiteness of the burial site.

I rolled over to follow him. He was crouching, trying to get to his feet, one hand groping to pull the knife out. I kept rolling, crashing into him. I felt him fall sideways and slip, and then he grabbed my cloak and hung on. For a moment I couldn't understand why, then I felt his weight pulling at me and I knew the truth: we were at the edge of the cliff, and he was part-way over.

I didn't know if he was trying to pull himself back or wanting to take me down with him, but it didn't matter. I was sliding across the snow, being pulled over the edge of the cliff. I flung out my arms and legs, trying to get any kind of grip. All I found was soft snow. I slid further towards death.

My left hand found a small crevice in the rock, and I held onto it for dear life. I could see over the edge now. Below me, Gilbertus – the man I'd called Gilbertus – dangled. One of his hands was wrapped in my cloak, the other grasped desperately at the sheer stone of the cliff. The wind caught his garments, whipping them around him. Below us, an infinity of snow whirled and blew, obscuring everything else.

Gilbertus raised his head and stared into my eyes. His were pools of glistening darkness, like gazing into an ancient well. Even at this moment I could read nothing there. His face was as white as ice. Below, blood still spurted from his wound, spiralling away to the blizzard below.

'Pull me up,' he said. There was weakness in his voice.

'No,' I said. I wanted to batter away at his hands, to make him let go, but I was afraid that the slightest movement would make me slip further over the edge.

'Pull me up,' he said again, 'and I will take you to your wife and child.'

'You're lying,' I said, and at that moment there was a tearing, rending sound as my cloak ripped across. The necromancer swung sideways across the cliff face, held suspended in the air for a moment by the thicker fabric of the hem, and then it also parted and he dropped.

His body plunged down, fading, blown away among the blizzard, and disappeared into the whiteness. There was no scream or sound of impact. Possibly it was muffled by the snow.

I lay there for a while. Blood hammered in my temples, and my hands reflexively gripped onto whatever they could find. The snow and the rock were cold against my face. It reminded me I was alive.

EVENTUALLY I PUSHED myself back a yard, slowly, and stood up. Blood stained the area, but flurries of snow were already covering the pools and strands of crimson, and the footprints and marks of the recent scuffle.

My ribs ached. I looked around. The area was still deserted. No signs, no evidence, no witnesses, no complications. I whispered thanks to Morr.

For an instant I saw Gilbertus's face again, felt the weight of him suspended from his fist in my cloak, and heard his last words. He hadn't known anything. He couldn't have known anything. He would have said anything to save himself. No. He had been lying. He must have been.

His spirit had gone to Morr now. Even necromancers had to make their peace with the god of death eventually. It occurred to me that although I still thought of him as Gilbertus, I didn't know his real name.

I turned away, to walk back to the temple. Now Gilbertus was dead his spell should be broken and I should be able to lay the dead girl's soul to rest. I'd say a blessing for his spirit as well, and if anyone asked me what I had done today, I would say that I had given peace to two unquiet souls.

I wondered if I would ever do the same for my own.

CATCH AS CATCH CAN

THE INVISIBLE BOY had been in the city for a whole year now, and he was celebrating that triumph. He still had no job, nor any prospect of one, and his meagre supply of ready cash was reaching its limits again. But by nightfall he would have a good meal and a few glasses of beer inside him, never the less.

He had been called Wheezer, back when there were people who spoke to him or knew him, back before the city. Now he was nobody. But he was happy.

The smell of the city had burned at his nostrils and throat for a while when he had first arrived, and the stench had made him feel ill, but gradually he had come to ignore it. He was especially happy because he hadn't sneezed or wheezed once during the entire time he had lived in the city.

Back in the old good country air, he had suffered all year round from a nose that ran constantly. Through the spring and summer, he never stopped sneezing and his eyes never stopped streaming. And during harvest, he wheezed. That was how he'd come by his name. He was Wheezer.

Now he saw the funny side of all those years spent breathing good, pure country air. Bless the city's filthy, smoggy atmosphere, where, summer or winter, he felt better and better! His old nickname was now a kind of private joke. If he ever found anyone to ask him his name of course. It had been a year and no one had spoken to him. No one noticed him. No one even seemed to see him.

* * *

THE WEATHER WAS cold, wet, dark and miserable. Never mind winter, the change to spring was by far the worst part of the year.

Kruza sneezed heavily into a beautiful linen handkerchief that he had, only minutes before, lifted out of the pocket of some local gentleman. He wouldn't be able to sell it now, but he needed a good nose-wipe at this time of the year, and with all his other work the loss of the fence's price of one handkerchief was a trifle.

Kruza didn't feel much like work. He begrudged going out in this awful slanting drizzle, and the wind was the kind that went through you instead of round you. But it was his day tomorrow and he still had the small matter of his quota to fill. He would have finished days ago if it hadn't been for the fact that he'd found a new and very accommodating fence, and had decided to sell one or two of his better items on the outside. Just so long as the master didn't get wind of it.

'Wind, damnable wind,' Kruza muttered to himself as he passed out of the Altquartier and made his way down the steps to the Great Park. Even on a day like today there would be people trading there, which meant there would be other people with full purses. And aside from sitting in a nice little tavern somewhere drinking a long glass of ale, or better yet a hot toddy, the market gave the best shelter of anywhere in Middenheim. The stalls' awnings almost touched in places, shielding the people as well as the produce from the worst of the wind and rain.

Kruza mooched around for a while, strolling between the stalls, taking his time to pick out a likely victim. A little care spent choosing his mark now cut down on the number of targets he needed, and in the long run would give him more time in that tavern later in the day.

WHEEZER FOLLOWED THE old cut-purse into the market in the big park. He loved the market. Mostly he stole what he needed, and of course that included money, but he took great delight in robbing the market stalls to fill his larder and make the derelict hovel he called home as pleasant as possible.

During his first year in the city, he had successfully filched enough cooking utensils, bed linens and other household items to furnish a warm and friendly nest, albeit one he enjoyed entirely alone. He'd stolen his entire wardrobe, and he'd even managed to pinch a series of small mirrors, including one in a gilt frame. He loved the mirrors and stood or hung them indiscriminately around the single room he lived in.

Today though, Wheezer needed cash. He had to eat and while his own larder (the outside sill of his single high window at this time of year) was all but full, he was celebrating his first anniversary in the city tonight and had decided to eat in style at one of the better taverns. He might even find himself a girl, he thought, and that would certainly mean hard cash.

Wheezer had his mark in sight. He usually chose the older cut-purses, although he knew, to his cost, of one or two who were still as quick of eye and fleet of foot as he was. This old coot with his one patched eye looked safe enough, though. Wheezer kept close to the old thief, feeling no need to slink or skulk about. He watched as the old man made his move.

Wheezer stood by as the old man lifted a tiny gold sundial from the pocket of an equally aged butler out doing the daily provisioning.

No good, thought Wheezer. *Who needs another timepiece? Next time.*

He followed the man on a little further, up a short cobbled slope, and round the side of a tiny handcart selling illicit liquor. Wheezer pocketed a bottle as he sidled past, just for good measure. After all, he was supposed to be celebrating today.

The old cut-purse's next target was a fat, bossy middle-aged woman. She had stopped to reprimand the man with her, surely her scolded and erstwhile cuckolded husband. Wheezer was mesmerised for a moment, the woman might well be as big as a barge and well past the prime of her life, but she was also very feminine.

Yes, a wench tonight, I think, Wheezer said to himself as he passed the woman and the cut-purse, doffing his cap to one or other of them, or perhaps to both. Neither one of them saw him, and he didn't expect them to. Putting his cap back on his head at an angle, Wheezer watched the old cut-purse snatch the little bag of money from the fat woman's waist. It was done in a moment, without anyone noticing, and the purse looked satisfyingly heavy to Wheezer. He loitered for a moment at a stall, picking up a couple of bars of rough soap and casually pocketing them while the owner's back was turned, before following the old thief onward.

KRUZA STOOD BY a stall, fingering a woman's silk shawl, when he saw Strauss. The old cut-purse had been the best in his time, and had earned himself the right to work solo in Middenheim. After twenty years of toiling for the likes of his Low King, not to mention training three generations of cut-purses, including Kruza, Strauss was in his retirement. He visited the market once a fortnight or so, just to keep his hand in, and always liked the dullest days and the oldest marks.

Kruza was not surprised to see him today and greeted him with as much cheer as he could muster, given the cold and his reddening nose.

'Well met, master,' he called as the near-blind old thief drew level with him.

'Is that you, Kruza, my boy?' the man returned, beaming his toothless grin from ear to ear. 'How goes it with you?'

'It's too cold and too damp and I have a quota to meet,' answered Kruza, trying to make it all sound like a joke and failing.

'You young pups of today,' Strauss remonstrated, 'never happy in your work. Still giving the master his pound of flesh then, are we? Only another fifteen years and a couple of hundred recruits and perhaps he'll let you off his hook.' He laughed.

'Only if he or I live that long,' Kruza said.

* * *

WHEEZER WATCHED as the old man, with his pocket full of another woman's money, stopped to speak with the tall, broad-shouldered fellow, who was apparently examining women's clothing. An odd occupation for such a strong, confident-looking man.

Now's your chance, Wheezer, old son, he thought to himself. He cleared his mind and moved in a little closer.

What is the old man blathering on about, he wondered as he slid two long, slender fingers into the side pocket of the old coat that hung from the blind old man's shoulders. He was walking away slowly and very calmly when he heard the words 'Stop! Thief!' begin to ring out – and then stop short very suddenly.

KRUZA, ASTONISHED AT the brazen outrage, wanted to cry out to stop the young chancer robbing his old friend. But since the purse had originally belonged to someone else, he realised it would do no good, and the words 'Stop! Thief!' came out strangled and barely loud enough to be heard by the old man standing next to him.

'I'll get him!' he said firmly, but very quietly to Strauss, and walked away purposefully toward the young man in the cap. He wondered why he couldn't remember what the boy looked like, except for the vaguest impression of a teenage kid with fair hair. Kruza prided himself that he never forgot a face, not the face of a mark, not the face of a fellow cut-purse and especially not the face of an enemy. There was something odd about this one. He realised at once that he would have to stay close to the boy; if he let him out of his sight, he would not know him again.

WHEEZER LEFT THE park by the north-east gate and worked his way up the winding steps and slopes towards the north part of the Altquartier. He had made his home in a derelict building in the far north of the quarter where life was rough, but not so bad as it was further south in the heart of the district. He had stumbled upon the place, back then little more than tile-patched rafters open to the sky with rotting attic boards, late one night only a few days after he had arrived in the city. It had been cold and wet then, as it was now, and he had needed to find shelter fast.

It had taken Wheezer only a matter of days in the city to get the lay of the land, even though some of Middenheim's native citizens knew only the streets and byways of their own local quarters despite a lifetime of city dwelling. It had taken him a little longer to find a permanent place to sleep, but not too long.

Wheezer's room was the only occupied part of the ramshackle old building and was towards the top, on the third floor. His one window looked down into a narrow courtyard and the windowless backs of other buildings, so no one overlooked him. The front of the building was barred and boarded, but there was a cellar window at the side that served as a convenient front door where Wheezer could not be seen entering. The room was as solitary and isolated as he was himself, but it suited him well, and he had no desire to spread himself out among the other rooms that must exist in the building, but which Wheezer had never explored.

THERE WAS HONOUR among thieves, even in Middenheim, and so if it took Kruza all afternoon to track down the brazen knave who had robbed venerable Strauss he would do it.

Discreetly Kruza followed the cocky young cut-purse out of the Great Park and watched him as he climbed in through the cellar window of the tall, narrow, crumbling building. Two minutes later, as the clatter of shod feet on old wooden stairs died away, Kruza slid his body, shoulder first, through the cellar window and looked around to get his bearings. In no time, he had found new scuff marks on the dusty floor and followed the ragged footprints up three flights of rickety, creaking stairs. He took his time, moving silently, as he didn't want to warn the young thug of his arrival.

Five minutes later, Kruza was leaning nonchalantly in the doorframe of a cluttered, low-lit room, watching the scrawny kid take off his cap and coat, utterly oblivious to the fact Kruza was there. Kruza gently ran his thumb down the length of his short-sword, reassuring himself of its cutting edge.

He looked on as the small, slender boy took soap and liquor from where he had secreted them in his pockets along with the heavy purse that Strauss had lifted. Then Kruza began to take in the room properly for the first time. It was extraordinary. The floor was thick with rugs and carpets, and there was a low couch covered in a colourful array of fabrics and cushions. Clean clothes and spare shoes were neatly arranged in one corner, half shielded from the room by an elegant, foreign-looking screen of pale wood. There was a deep bowl and ornate pitcher of eastern design gracing a low oval table and a large sheet of thick coarse material hung on a hook nearby. Then there were the mirrors. Kruza didn't believe he had ever encountered so many mirrors in one room, nor so much opulence in the room of a petty scoundrel. Yet despite the mirrors, the young thief was obviously used to being alone, since he had still not noticed his intruder.

Kruza had planned to surprise him. He had wanted the young thief to turn and catch him standing in the doorway, preferably running his thumb along the blade of his short-sword. But the boy just hadn't noticed him, though Kruza had held the relaxed menacing pose and repeated the gesture several times. Kruza began to feel rather silly repeating the theatrical threat.

Eventually, bored with looking into the remarkable room, Kruza was beginning to want to take a seat on that inviting couch. Then the tickle started and he knew that introductions were imminent. He had no choice in the matter, so he raised his short-sword in an aggressive stance. The sneeze came in a torrent of wet snot and doubled Kruza over with its force, his sword hand still pointing the gleaming weapon at the thief's back.

The young man, standing in the middle of the room with his back to the door, clutched his chest suddenly and fell to his knees.

Kruza thought for a moment that he'd killed his foe without even waving his sword, and cautiously entered the room to assess the situation. The lad was white, dark circles of fright ringing his wide grey eyes. Kruza realised that the thief was little more than a child and he almost felt sorry for him. Kruza didn't want to kill him like this; he didn't want the lad to die without knowing what he'd done. He tucked his sword in the back of his belt for easy access and knelt on one knee beside Wheezer, pulling him up.

'Don't faint on me, you little runt,' Kruza said. 'I don't plan to have to carry you over to that couch. I'd sooner kill you right here.'

'You already scared me half to death,' replied the pale-faced, quivering youth.

'It was just a sneeze,' Kruza said. 'Be thankful. At least it saved you from a full frontal short-sword attack.'

Wheezer flopped down on the couch. Kruza stood over him, his hands on his hips, leaning in so that he was looking down directly into Wheezer's face.

'Now listen to me,' he began, putting one hand squarely on the pommel of his sword, ready to draw it at any moment. 'What do you mean by stealing from old Strauss? There's honour amongst thieves in this city! Has your boss never told you the rules?'

'Strauss? Boss? I have no idea what you're talking about!'

'Strauss,' Kruza explained impatiently, 'is the name of the man you robbed this afternoon in the market.'

'But he was a thief,' Wheezer said, matter of fact. His voice had an unusual inflection, almost as if he was not used to talking. 'You can't steal from a thief, when what you're taking doesn't belong to him.'

'What about the stall holders on the market? You stole from them.'

'Hardly,' Wheezer said, 'When one man has more soap or liquor than he can use or sell, that's not stealing either. I never take from an empty stall or a busy one.'

Kruza looked down at him quizzically. 'Did your boss teach you nothing?'

'What boss?' Wheezer asked innocently.

'Ulric take me! You know,' Kruza was becoming impatient. 'The man you work for. The man you sell merchandise to.'

'I don't have a boss,' Wheezer answered.

'Then who do you sell your stolen goods to? Who's your fence?'

Wheezer shook his head, as if the street thief was suddenly speaking Bretonnian. 'Do you want a drink?' he asked suddenly.

'I– what?'

'A drink. I'm celebrating today. And you know, you're the first visitor I've had here, so it's only right.'

Kruza blinked. Had he missed something? The kid was… strange.

'Look, who do you sell your merchandise to?' he repeated, slowly and carefully.

'No one,' Wheezer said, beginning to catch on. 'I don't sell anything. I just take what I need or sometimes what I want. Why would I want to sell anything to anyone?'

Kruza didn't know whether to pity or laugh at this lost, lonely boy with such strange, innocent ways. There seemed to be nothing immoral about him, nothing memorable about him, almost nothing real about him at all. He did what he did and that was an end of it.

But then how, wondered Kruza, had he become so good at the stealthcraft, without a teacher. The kid must have the gift. The kid must be a natural. Kruza smiled suddenly. A thought had occurred to him.

'Perhaps I will have a drink with you after all,' he said at last, taking his hand off his sword hilt and sitting down again.

'Good, because as I said: I'm celebrating!' Wheezer announced, selecting two rather elegant, if mismatched, goblets and the bottle of pear brandy he had liberated that afternoon.

WHEEZER WAS SO excited to finally have an audience that he talked non-stop for a very long time. But Kruza didn't mind. He needed to put the lad at ease. Besides, the liquor was warming and the room was extremely comfortable. Wheezer got up, still talking, and lit a fire in the small grate just before dark. It burned gently, bringing warmth and light to the room, making it seem even more exotic than it had when Kruza had first beheld it.

'I arrived here a year ago to the day,' Wheezer was saying, 'come to collect my inheritance, or rather to be recognised by my illustrious parent.

'I turned twenty and left the forest for the city, my real home. You see, my mother lived here when I was born. She was the most beautiful artiste of her era, treading the boards of all the great theatres in all the great cities. She came to Middenheim once a year to perform, and it was on her last visit here that she met and fell in love with my father. He was young, of course, and impetuous and fell for my mother at first sight! Back then, who wouldn't have? Now, his great and noble family weren't too impressed with him, and had the gall to try and buy my mother off with cheap trinkets and idle promises, not to mention a great deal of money.

'Naturally, she declined and stayed in the city to have me, so that my father would have to recognise me. Great plan, but of course things never work out the way we expect and she died. A horrible death really. She died three days after I was born. She bled to death.

'So, off I went. Actually, I didn't go away, I was taken away by an old wetnurse who worked for my grandfather. She was paid to take me into the forest and well, you know, kill me. She didn't have the heart to do it, of course. Instead she stayed with me and then her sister came to live with us too. Wonderful women, we never wanted for anything. They're both dead now and I wonder if they were witches, 'cause though we never went without, neither of them did anything practical. We didn't raise pigs or keep a garden, but there was always meat and greens and good bread...'

Kruza let the story wash over him as it rattled on. He was beginning to feel that the story and the kid were just part of some elaborate fever-dream brought on by his infernal ague.

'So I became a man, and before she died, my "aunt", who must have been over seventy before she took to her deathbed, told me everything. After I buried her and her sister – they died right there in the same bed on the same day – I set out to the city from the forest that had been my home my whole life. And that's it, well most of it. I can't mention my father's name, of course, not before he recognises me, officially, so to speak, but I can tell you he runs a great city, lives in a great palace and doesn't live a million miles from here. In fact, on a clear night I can see the top of his palace roofs from my little window.'

Kruza's head was floating about the room with all the good strong liquor he had drunk, but he knew when he was listening to an outrageous fairytale, or several woven together. Still, it was no business of his. He wanted the boy to relax and trust him.

Kruza left late. Remembering he still had a quota to fill, he secreted a little gilt mirror as he left, sliding it beneath his jacket.

'It's all right,' Wheezer said, having noticed. 'You have it. I took it from a thief. It doesn't belong to anyone now, so take it by all means.'

Kruza felt guilty for the first time since he was a child. 'Look, what's your name?' he asked.

'Oh, I don't have one,' the lad replied cheerily, 'being a bastard and everything. And my mother didn't live long enough to give me a name. When I was big enough to need a name my aunts called me "Wheezer". You can call me that.'

'Okay,' said Kruza. 'My name's Kruza.'

'Funny,' said Wheezer, 'I thought your name must be "Sneezer",' and he laughed at his joke. 'Did you hear that?' he asked rhetorically, 'Wheezer and Sneezer!'

Kruza blinked again, forced a grin. 'I'll see you around,' he said, and left.

A natural, that's what the boy was. The gift in his fingers, his tread, in his sheer anonymity. It was rare. There were a lot of good thieves in Middenheim, Kruza amongst them, but there was only a handful of true naturals. If the boy proved to be what Kruza thought he was, then Kruza was duty bound to begin recruiting him for his Low King.

Or keeping him for myself, Kruza wondered. The thought kept coming back to him. How easy would it be to fill his quota then, to get the Low King off his back, to finally start getting ahead, getting somewhere on his own?

But recruiting the boy wasn't going to be that easy either way. Wheezer had all sorts of crazy rules about whom he would steal from and what he would take. He saw no reason to steal for the sake of selling goods on at less than their value. He stole only to live.

But he was so good at it, and Kruza hated to see such raw talent wasted.

He left it two days, and then the next morning shadowed the sleepy alley where Wheezer lived until he saw the boy emerge from his ruin. Kruza strode from the shadows, as if he was just passing, a chance encounter.

'Oh. You again,' he said.

The boy's face lit up. *He is so unaccustomed to being spoke to, Kruza thought with a touch of pity.* Just a touch; there wasn't room for much except business in Kruza's heart.

'Where are you going?'

'To work,' Kruza said, sniffing. It was another cold and wet day.

'Can I come?' Wheezer asked.

And that was how the games began. That simple.

The two of them strolled down to the Great Park, Kruza hunched over with the cold and sticking close under the awnings that would keep the wind and rain off. Wheezer almost strutted through the park, throwing out his puny chest and taking deep breaths of the freezing, damp air. He appeared to be in his element. Kruza led him to a stall crammed with all manner of household goods and they watched as a local gentlewoman, escorted by her houseman, fondled bolts of cloth on a stall nearby. Kruza almost gasped as Wheezer picked up a package of spills and half a dozen tallow candles from the stall, tucking them into his jacket. But no one else seemed to notice.

A natural, by Ulric. Kruza smiled. He nodded to his brazen companion. 'Bet you can't lift madam's money pouch,'

'Where?' Wheezer asked, looking about him.

'There,' Kruza answered, 'with the snooty-looking houseman in the short grey cloak.'

'No problem,' Wheezer said, a cock-eyed smile across his face. He walked off past the affluent woman with the heavy pouch at her waist and nipped it off without even touching her. Kruza watched, only feet away, amazed at the speed and skill with which Wheezer performed the dare. He had been ready to step in and cause a little confusion to cover Wheezer when he got caught, which had seemed inevitable with the houseman standing guard.

But it never happened. Wheezer walked around the next stall and came back behind Kruza.

'Good, good…' Kruza murmured as they walked on together. 'Where is it then?'

'Where's what?' Wheezer asked innocently.

'The pouch, you dolt,' Kruza replied. 'How much was in it?'

'No idea,' Wheezer said, 'but it was heavy enough. You can check it if you like. It's in your jerkin pocket.'

Kruza looked wide-eyed at Wheezer and slid two fingers into the pocket, drawing out the full pouch. His bottom jaw dropped so far, so fast, he almost dislocated it. He hadn't felt a thing and he was one of the best. The kid was amazing. Invisible.

Wheezer seemed to like the game, and would take any dare. As the day went on, Kruza became more and more intrigued by what the young, untrained cut-purse could do. Kruza didn't need to recruit Wheezer. The kid would give him anything and do anything for him so long as it was prefixed with 'I bet you can't…' Kruza was looking at a meal ticket.

Wheezer stole lunch for them from a stall-holder while having a conversation with him at the same time. They sat and ate the fresh sausage, a small earthenware jar of pickles and two small loaves of good bread, sitting on an empty, covered handcart behind one of the clothing stalls. Kruza's tall, athletic frame perched next to Wheezer's small compact one. Kruza was a grown man of twenty-four. Only a few years older than the other. But sitting next to him, Wheezer looked like a child from the slums.

Kruza's mood had improved dramatically. It was worth coming out in the cold and wet to watch Wheezer at work, especially when Wheezer was working for him.

During the afternoon the lad lifted two time-pieces from the inside pockets of gentlemen whose outerwear looked completely impenetrable, and completed the hat-trick by removing a barely visible necklace from a middle-aged gentlewoman whose cloak was buttoned high to her throat. Together, the conspirators then liberated a total of seven items from one young dandy who they tripped and then 'saved' from an undignified fall down a steeply stepped lane. While dusting the man down, Wheezer managed to empty three of his outer pockets and two that were concealed beneath. He had also taken the short dagger that the dandy kept in the top of one of his long boots. He was a marvel.

As EVENING FELL, Kruza and Wheezer retired to the Drowned Rat in the Ostwald district. Kruza opened the door from the grubby street with its lengthening shadows, and they all but fell into the tavern. Pockets full, a good day's work done, and coins to spend on beer and a good supper.

Several of Kruza's friends and colleagues were crowded into the small bar, and introductions were made all round, but no one could remember Wheezer's name and very soon they forgot he was there at all. Wheezer thought them all fine fellows, apart from that chap with the flat hair, Arkady, who seemed a little churlish. Idly he found himself wondering if he had been Kruza's last best friend.

Soon the drink was flowing and the food forgotten as Kruza exchanged stories and information with his colleagues. They talked constantly of the 'Boss', although sometimes they called him 'The Man' or 'The King', complaining about him, cursing him and generally displaying their hatred for him.

Some time later a fight started. Good-natured at first, just a few fists flying to prove a point, then someone pulled a dagger and chaos broke out. Wheezer had no idea what they were fighting over, and slid down off his stool and sheltered between the barrels that held up either end of the bar. He stayed there with his arms wrapped round his knees, watching the mayhem.

Kruza threw himself with gusto into the melee. There was nothing like a good brawl to end a good evening. Eventually, the fight broke up when the landlord began arbitrarily swinging a club around his bar, screaming that enough damage had been done and he would call the guard. Four men had sustained gashes and one had had his earlobe bitten off. The others had slashed clothes, and bruises were rising up on their faces and bodies from the blows of fists and hilt-pommels jabbed hard against flesh during the closer, hand-to-hand bouts where there was no room to use a blade.

Wheezer was astounded to see them all on good terms when they were kicked out of the tavern, united now in cursing the pot-man, as they had been in cursing the Low King.

A WEEK LATER Kruza and Wheezer were meandering back to Wheezer's room. The place was more comfortable and private than Kruza's, and he had begun to adopt it as his own. Wheezer could not have been more happy. He had company at last.

They turned east, and cut across the Wynd and up into the south side of the Altquartier. From there they turned north toward the crumbling old building where they now both lived. It had been a goodly walk and Kruza decided there was time for one more drink. The single pale light outside the Cocky Dame shone to him like a beacon and he was about to enter the sleazy one-room tavern with its cabbage smell when Wheezer stopped him by grasping his forearm.

'I've seen that before,' Wheezer began, pointing out a covered handcart steered down the sloping street by a sombre man in a long cloth cape. 'What is it?'

'The dead,' Kruza said plainly. 'No one's concern but the priests of Morr.'

'They carry them off the streets?' Wheezer asked, 'Where do they take them?'

'That one'll no doubt end up turning over and over in the air until it lands at the bottom of the Cliff of Sighs, more broken than it is already.'

'The old priest who tended people back in the forest always came to their homes. Bodies weren't moved, and if a homeless body was found in a field then that was where it was buried. Don't the people here bury their own people on their own land?' Wheezer asked.

'Huh!' Kruza snorted, raising his hands and turning his body in a gesture that encompassed the entire city. 'What land? The wealthy find a resting-place in Morrspark, but even they are buried one above the other, five or six deep. The rest tumble over the cliff. The priests seal the bodies and bless them and for all but the most destitute there are mourners. But this city has little sentiment. It goes about its business, and leaves the priests to go about their's.'

'What of their belongings?' Wheezer was full of questions tonight and Kruza was still only three parts full of good ale.

'They are priests – they have few belongings...'

Wheezer interrupted. 'Not the priests!' he exclaimed. 'The dead!'

Kruza pushed through the tavern door, dragging Wheezer behind him. 'You're far too ghoulish for my liking. Come and have a drink with me and let's have an end to this talk of corpses.'

But the talk of corpses did not end. It began again later that night, when Kruza was settled on the couch in Wheezer's room, and Wheezer himself was lying on a pile of cushions on the floor. Kruza was now full of ale and more tolerant of Wheezer's questions – up to a point.

'The dead people,' began Wheezer, 'where do their possessions go?'

'I don't know,' Kruza said. 'Some are robbed before they're cold. Those who die quietly among their families are relieved of their possessions by their loved ones.'

'And the rest?' the other asked, innocently.

'The rest?' Kruza replied. 'I suppose the priests of Morr collect their belongings and return them to their mourners. Perhaps if there is no one to pass the possessions on to then they go into the coffers of the Temple, or perhaps to the Graf himself.'

'Or should I say your "illustrious parent"?' he added, and laughed so much he had to stagger off his couch and take a leak out of the room's single window. When he returned to the couch, he was asleep and snoring a ragged drunken snore before Wheezer could form his next question.

In the morning, however, Kruza remembered enough of the previous night's conversation to give Wheezer a word of warning.

'If you are thinking of robbing the dead, think again!' he said firmly. 'The dead are respected by all but the lowest of the low-scum in this city, which has its share of grave-robbers. Friendless, perverted men.'

'Sure,' Wheezer said.

'Friendless, Wheezer,' Kruza reiterated. 'If I get wind that you have robbed a corpse, I shall cut you off and I'm sure you don't want that!'

Wheezer looked at his feet. 'It's just that a corpse can't own any–' he began, but was interrupted with a glare.

'Friendless, Wheezer!' Kruza said between gritted teeth, holding the much shorter man by the front of his jerkin and lifting him to his toe tips. 'Friendless!'

KRUZA CONTINUED HIS work, and his manipulation of Wheezer's talents continued to make him prosper. It had been a very good month. Two or three days out of every week the two would pair up and visit the markets and crowded areas of the city. By night they would eat and drink in various seedy taverns. One night Kruza took Wheezer to the Baiting Pit, but the youth didn't like it much and they left.

'I saw bears in the forest, where I lived with my aunts,' Wheezer explained. 'They were beasts of the wild and harmless enough if you respected them.'

Kruza shook his head. The kid was from another world.

* * *

WHEEZER HAD PROMISED Kruza that he would not rob the dead, even though he didn't understand how it could be called stealing at all, let alone the lowest of low crimes.

He wasn't going to rob the corpses, of that he was convinced, but he had become fascinated by the biers and carts that were wheeled around the streets with their dead cargo. Sometimes he would see an important-looking man in temple robes, calming the bereaved or asking questions or leaning over biers. Often the biers were steered through the streets wheeled by one man, or sometimes two, in long drab cloaks. Other times he saw corpses being tossed onto any available vehicle and being driven off by one of the city watch, and once he saw a body being removed by a White Wolf Templar, splendid in his plate armour.

Wheezer became quite fond of a good funeral, witnessing grand burials in Morrspark and simple ones at the Cliff of Sighs. No one seemed to mind him being there. In fact, no one ever noticed that he was there – except for one time.

He had climbed up to the Cliff about a fortnight after his conversation with Kruza and watched a lone priest performing a ceremony. The priest had stood over a rough plank coffin going through the necessary rituals and chanting the prayers that were almost familiar to Wheezer by now. Wheezer expected nothing, and was ready to turn away and make his way back into the city, when the strangest thing happened.

The priest stopped and spoke to him. Just briefly, pitying his loss, saying something about the corpse being at peace.

Wheezer didn't hear the actual words. This was only the second person to speak to him voluntarily since his arrival in the city more than a year before. Kruza had been the first.

'THE DEAD OF Middenheim,' Wheezer began out of nowhere, one night as they made their way to a tavern. 'They're not all taken away by priests, are they?'

'No, not all,' Kruza said. 'Since the Temple of Morr burnt down there aren't really enough of them to do all the burial work, without having to go out to collect every single body in the city.'

'I saw they were working on the temple,' Wheezer said. 'So, can anyone take a body away?'

'There are the men in long grey cloaks,' Kruza answered, 'I don't know who they are, but the priests use them a lot to carry bodies. They also ask the City Watch or anyone else who is considered more or less trustworthy.'

'Like the White Wolf I saw?' Wheezer asked rhetorically. 'You said before that the bodies were taken to the temple, Morrspark and the Cliff of Sighs, but what about the other place?'

'What other place?' Kruza asked. 'Where else would they take them?' He was becoming impatient now, Wheezer could tell, and he didn't want to make his mentor angry, so he said no more. But there was another place.

* * *

HUNGOVER AND GROANING on the couch the next morning, Kruza didn't notice Wheezer sneaking out, or if he did, he didn't care. Wheezer rose early and went into the city to watch for carts. He was almost obsessed by the bodies and their resting places now, and if Kruza couldn't tell him what the 'other place' was then he would find out for himself.

Wheezer quickly spotted his first body of the day, some old man who had died in the night – perhaps violently, since this was the Altquartier – but maybe just quietly in his bed. His body was carried the short distance between where he had died and the nearest place the vehicle could get to the corpse: across a courtyard and down a short alley. Then it was heaved onto one of the narrow handcarts and wheeled away by a guard who had recently been relieved from his night watch. The middle-aged, thickset man was disgruntled at having been given the task when he was due home for his breakfast, and he manhandled the body as though it were a sack of grain. Wheezer followed the guard and his cargo until he realised they were heading toward the Temple and not that 'other place'. He let them go and began to look around for the next body.

Leaving the Altquartier and following the Garten Ring round the eastern side of the park, Wheezer detected a commotion on the other side of the wall. A cut-purse had been careless and was being attacked by his mark. The cut-purse, a man who reminded Wheezer of Kruza, what with his height and square shoulders and casual style of dress, won the fight shortly after producing a dagger from his boot. And a woman was now lamenting the loss of the bold, stout man in his thirties who that day had decided not to be a victim of robbery and was now lying on the mossy slope, a victim of murder.

Wheezer stayed close as first the City Watch and then the priest of Morr appeared. It was half an hour before a pair of constables was dispatched with the body and it was soon apparent to Wheezer that they, too, were heading for the Temple of Morr.

It was almost noon and Wheezer was prepared to give up his corpse-chasing for the day when a tall man in a long, drab cloak crossed in front of him, hauling a long body-shaped barrow with two large wheels at its centre. A second man, similarly dressed, brought up the rear of the vehicle, clutching a pair of handles on the back of the makeshift bier and following his colleague. Wheezer decided he would try one last time to follow a corpse to the 'other place'.

Wheezer followed the cart without much expectation of success. He had already failed twice today. He was delighted when the cart's course turned west and then north. Wheezer had been in this part of the city before, with its wide streets and grand houses. He had dressed carefully that morning in clean, anonymous clothes so that he could walk about unmolested by the city watch, who never seemed happier than when they were ousting some wretch or urchin from the better parts of the city. Wheezer had thrown a tatty old cloak over his neat ensemble for his walk through the poorer regions but discarded it now, as the cloaked men with their cart turned left at the Temple of Shallya. Wheezer could hear the orphans inside chanting prayers by rote, accompanied by the sporadic coughs and pained cries of the patients in the infirmary next door. He had gone there once himself when he had torn his hand open, fortunate to have the money to pay for his treatment. The physician who had attended him there had neither looked at nor spoken to Wheezer while he cleaned and dressed the wound.

Now Wheezer was in the Nordgarten district, amongst the homes of merchants and gentlemen. He did not hide in the shadows or skulk in doorways. He thrust his shoulders back and marched down wide, cobbled streets within sight of his quarry. He passed errand boys and visiting shopkeepers in the street, but it was a damp day, and cold, and the local residents were happy enough to stay in the warmth and comfort of their opulent homes.

Wheezer began to get excited. He would find out something that Kruza did not know, perhaps something new about the dead and their belongings. The 'other place'.

Wheezer saw the house ahead. It was taller and narrower than those around, giving it an imposing air. He did not know what it might once have been, but it didn't look much like the other houses in the area. Perhaps it had been a minor temple once. It was a tall, slender tower with narrow windows and a strangely curvaceous spire, which rose up in soft waves to a tiny dome at its crown. Under the base of the spire was a deep gallery of arrow slits. A second circular tower was fixed to the side of the main building, the breadth of perhaps two men passing, but with its own tiny dome and more of the unusual slits for windows.

Wheezer drew level with the makeshift bier as the two men worked it between the pair of narrow doors on the alley side of the building. It was darker in the alley, and these doors could not be seen from the street. Standing to one side of the double doors, slightly in view of the cloaked men, if they had cared to see him, Wheezer casually slid a hand out and lifted the rough, ragged-edged tarpaulin that covered the wagon. He lifted it a little higher as the two men continued to struggle with the bier, which was almost as wide as the doors.

His first glimpse suggested to Wheezer that this was no body, and his second, longer look confirmed it. On the wagon were all manner of objects, most of which Wheezer did not recognise at all, although he suspected that some of the odd-shaped glass vessels had come from an alchemist's shop. There were other things which he did recognise and, since there was no corpse to be robbed, he thrust his hand at the nearest shiny, metallic object under the tarpaulin. He pulled it out and tucked it into his jerkin. Then he stepped out entirely from behind the doorpost, doffed his cap at the cloaked men, who still did not seem to see him, and walked out of the alleyway and back towards the Temple of Shallya where he had left his cloak.

Having retrieved it, Wheezer wanted to get back and confront the sceptical, dismissive Kruza with his findings. But there was something else he needed to do first.

Wheezer crossed back into the Great Park by its south-west gate and headed toward the herbalist and apothecary stands that huddled together in their own tiny enclave, shielded on one side by a bank and on the other by the east wall of the park itself. Trade in this part of the market was thin, but Wheezer had no problem picking up the bits and pieces he wanted and he was soon on his way home. In his pockets he now carried a small, scented beeswax candle; two bundles of herbs; and a couple of rough crystals hewn from different types of rock. He wasn't quite sure what all the things under the tarpaulin had been, but it couldn't hurt to take a few simple precautions.

'KRUZA!' HE CALLED, almost before he had reached the third flight of stairs, and ran up them stretching his legs to make them climb two stairs at a time. 'Kruza?'

He found the cut-purse sitting on the edge of the couch in only his shirt, which spilled to his knees. His head was in his hands and almost between his knees as he leant forward, the weight of his head almost unbearable with its attendant hangover.

'Shhh!' exclaimed Kruza and winced.

Wheezer wanted to laugh, but instead he crossed to the small, segmented wooden box that sat in a corner, where the gilt mirror had once lived. He lifted the lid and drew out a clutch of dried herbs. He took the ever-simmering kettle from its frame high over the fire, lest it dry up, and made a tea from the twigs and dry leaves. He handed it to Kruza, who balked at the smell of it, but downed it when pressed.

Wheezer left Kruza alone for half an hour, but the older cut-purse felt better surprisingly quickly and no sooner felt ravenously hungry than Wheezer had provided him with a plate of cold meat, pickles and bread.

'Now that you feel better,' Wheezer said, excited, 'I have something for you.' He lifted the object that he had stolen from under the tarpaulin, taking it out of his jerkin at the collar button and holding it out at arm's length in front of him. It swung in small circles before their eyes.

The thing Wheezer had stolen was quite beautiful and both of them gazed at it with equal hypnotic wonder. It was a chain made up of large, flat, square sections joined by fat gold links at the corners. Every square section was engraved like an elaborate belt buckle, each bearing a different motif or scene. In the centre of the chain, which was long enough to hang around a broad man's shoulders, was a larger ornament.

'Like the chain of office the Graf wears on feast-days,' murmured Kruza in a husky undertone.

'It's trying to eat itself,' Wheezer said, mesmerised.

The ornament consisted of a great dragon or snake forming an eternal circle by feasting on its own tail. Every scale of its armour-plated body was etched into the solid gold from which it was crafted. Its eyes were domed orbs of sightless ivory.

'It's beautiful!' breathed Kruza.

'Take it, then,' Wheezer said, thrusting it at arm's length, closer to Kruza's face. 'And when you get tired of it, perhaps it can help with your quota.'

'The quota!' Kruza cried, leaping off the couch as if a fire, lit long ago under the offending piece of furniture, had finally penetrated its solid base and was now biting at Kruza's backside.

'It's my day and I haven't filled my quota! Sigmar's blood!' He snatched up the heavy trinket and thrust it into his shirt. Then he pulled on breeches and boots and his short leather coat and hurried out of the room, snatching up the cloth sack holding his other acquisitions before slamming the door behind him without another word to the youth.

'CURSED THING!' KRUZA yelled, storming back into the room with no regard for disturbing Wheezer. He threw the trinket onto the couch. 'He wanted nothing to do with it. The Man, who will sell anything and deal in anything, wouldn't touch it... and so my quota was lacking.'

'Oh.'

'Do you know what my penalty is for being short of my quota?' Kruza yelled, his voice still hoarse from the previous night's revelries. 'Take your trinket and may it bring you good fortune!'

Wheezer thought Kruza would leave, but instead of turning for the door, the cut-purse slumped down on the couch. Wheezer had failed, as the month had gone on, to realise that Kruza needed him more and more with every day that passed. While the cut-purse used the skills of the young, invisible thief, his own stealth-craft had become dull with lack of use and too much good living. He slouched on the couch, fingering the flat square plates of the unacceptable ornament, trying to read the story etched and carved there.

'Where did you get this, anyway? It must be tainted or horribly important for the master to turn it down flat with such an odd expression on his face. Come to think of it, I don't think my quota was doubled for any reason other than the insult of offering him this particular piece of merchandise.'

'I got it from the "other place",' Wheezer said, disinterested now, trying to work out how he could repay Kruza for his faux pas.

'What other place?' Kruza asked. And then recognition dawned. 'Ulric damn you if you stole this from a corpse!'

'No! No!' Wheezer exclaimed, backing away. He didn't care to feel the tip of that short-sword at his throat again. 'That's just the point! There was no body on the bier that went to the other place.'

'Don't talk in riddles, boy,' Kruza returned. His mood was dark and furious, and he felt like lashing out.

'I followed a corpse barrow... well, more of a covered handcart really. Anyway, I followed it to the "other place", the place I told you about. The place where the cloaked men take the bodies when they don't take them to the Temple of Morr. Only they don't take bodies at all. I lifted the cover on the wagon. There were so many things there. I snatched that thing off it,' he said, pointing to the chain. 'But I swear I wasn't robbing a body. There was no body!'

'Smugglers,' Kruza said to himself.

'What?' Wheezer asked.

'It has to be smugglers. They dress like servants of the priests of Morr, so that they can move merchandise around Middenheim. The only people never stopped by citizens or the Watch in this city are the dead. And bearers of the dead.'

Realising at last what his companion had said, Kruza leapt off the couch and grabbed Wheezer by the arm.

'Take me there!' he said. 'Now!'

Wheezer managed to persuade Kruza to wash and shave and tidy up his dress before taking him into the Nordgarten, a district that Kruza seldom visited. The pickings might be rich, but the risks were high. The Watch would be on him quicker than Altquartier rats on a dog's corpse if they suspected the smallest misdemeanour.

Kruza had little confidence walking the broad, curving streets of the better districts of Middenheim, and he unconsciously copied Wheezer's upright stance and confident gait as they passed the Temple of Shallya. The orphans were still chanting.

Wheezer walked straight up to the strange tower-building and around into the adjoining alley. He was ready to enter, without a qualm, but Kruza was more cautious.

'Let's take a look about first,' he suggested. 'There may be people. The cloaked smugglers you saw before.'

But inside himself, Kruza was itching to get on. He could smell riches in there. Riches that his Low King would accept. One swift robbery, with his silent partner in tow, could shorten his working week by several days and lengthen his leisure time by the same.

They exited the alley, back out onto the main street, and followed the building round to the tall, slender, curved tower on its other side. The tower was sheathed in gloom and shadow and Kruza began to feel rather more at home. There was no effort involved in finding the squat door in the side of the tower below a line of glassless, slit windows. It was low and black and smelled oddly of pitch.

Wheezer opened the door and Kruza took a deep breath before ducking his head and shoulders to follow the lad in. They stood together on the small square landing that signalled the ground floor level and looked up and then down at the winding, spiral staircase. Looking directly up through the shaft of the stairs, they could see shafts of light coming in through the west-facing windows. Looking directly down, they could see nothing.

'Down,' hissed Kruza, turning from the lit upper floors. Unlike Wheezer, he was only invisible in the dark. Wheezer trotted happily down the stairs, looking back to his comrade, who took every step slowly and carefully so as to make as little noise as possible. He realised for the first time that Wheezer could be as soundless as he was invisible. Kruza's own careful steps made a sloppy 'tak' sound, while Wheezer's footfalls were like a whisper.

'Keep looking down,' hissed Kruza, anxious that Wheezer might walk into something and have them both killed before they had even seen a foe. They continued down the stairs, one flight and then, just for good measure, a second. Wheezer looked to where they were going and the slow and nervous Kruza looked to where they had been.

At the second floor below ground, Wheezer stepped out onto a wider, arched landing that led to only two or three shallow, curved steps and then, as far as he could see, nothing. He had reached the bottom. Thirty seconds later Kruza joined him, almost knocking him down the last few steps as he continued to keep watch behind them.

There was still no light. There was a slight smell of spoiled milk, which Kruza didn't notice, but which Wheezer thought odd in a room two storeys below ground level. The air was very still and slightly chill and while the steps down had been damp, the floor of the cellar room was perfectly dry, even dusty underfoot.

Wheezer steadied Kruza, whose widening eyes shone out stark and white in the gloom. Then he reached into his pocket and took out the beeswax candle, which he lit, filling the air with the pungent scent of spices, casting a pool of light around himself and Kruza and making shadows in the underground place.

The cellar was a kind of circular lobby and Wheezer walked around it from one vaulted arch to the next. He stopped at each, examining the posts either side that made the doorways and then moved on, completing the circle and not crossing the centre of the floor. Kruza had stayed resolutely where he was, looking back up the steps every few seconds as if he had a nervous tick.

'This is just an entrance hall,' Wheezer said, 'but there are more rooms beyond those arches.'

He undid the top two buttons of his jerkin and pulled out a large pouch, tied around his neck with a cord. He took something from it that Kruza couldn't see.

'What are you doing?' Kruza asked, before jerking his gaze anxiously back up the stairwell.

'It's all right,' Wheezer answered, beginning to work his way back around the circle of arches, slowly. 'Someone's scrawled glyphs all over the doorways. But a little country magic will soon cancel them out.'

'Glyphs!' Kruza exclaimed as loudly as he dared, his voice still little more than a hoarse whisper. 'Magic! Right, this is all starting to spook me out! Bodies! Jewels that even a filthy fence won't buy – and now glyphs!'

What had seemed like such a good idea now was rapidly turning sour.

'What are you doing? What do you mean by "country magic"?' he hissed as Wheezer began to brush an arch support with a bundle of dry old leaves and twigs, holding his candle up to each glyph in turn and murmuring what sounded like old rhymes.

'You know the kind of thing: herbs, spider webs, rabbit droppings, all good fodder for simple country magic, just as good as your fancy town stuff any time. And these glyphs are pretty basic,' Wheezer said, moving to the next arch support.

Is there no end to this kid's weirdness, thought Kruza, *or was he really raised by witches?* Down here, the half-remembered details of that nonsense story seemed so much more believable.

It began to get lighter as Wheezer entered each side-room for just long enough to light a lamp and then on to the next.

Somehow it didn't seem quite so cold to Kruza now, or so menacing, so when Wheezer reached the fourth archway, Kruza crossed the floor to watch him weave his little bit of country magic, kicking up dust as he went.

Wheezer heard him and turned, seeing what Kruza had not.

The tall, athletic cut-purse ordinarily had a long stride, but now he was creeping and cautious. Any other time Kruza would have stepped over the thing on the floor. Now he shuffled through it.

'DDDDOOOOO...!' Wheezer started to scream out, but it was too late.

Kruza looked up at the scream, standing squarely in the confusion of sandy dust around his feet. He saw Wheezer's mouth, wide, in full scream and he felt the tension in the kid's body.

Ulric damn me, he thought very quietly to himself.

Wheezer's candle went out and the soft glow the oil lamps were giving out turned to a hard white light. More white light filled all the rooms around the lobby and for a moment Kruza thought he saw the glyphs on the arch supports whirling and dancing. Kruza could not move or speak and Wheezer's frozen face with its half-finished warning cry was locked in its strange and terrified expression. The moment seemed to last forever.

Don't let it end, Kruza thought, knowing that it must.

'...OOON'T!' Wheezer's cry finished as eight tall, grey-cloaked figures emerged from the eight archways. The man in the fourth arch from the left, standing right behind Wheezer, was lifting his arms. Kruza could see bone-pale, wasted forearms and gnarled, taloned hands emerging from the cloak. He could see nothing of the face beneath the hood. Wheezer stepped neatly to one side and stood against one of the tall columns that separated the arches, but the man kept coming. Straight for Kruza.

Kruza wanted to run. He wanted to run very badly. He could not.

He looked at Wheezer. The lad seemed to be shrugging.

He looked at his feet.

For the first time Kruza saw what he had stepped in to: the remains of an elaborate sand painting, criss-crossed with lines of black ash and swirls of cobalt and purple crystalline sand that Kruza did not recognise. He recognised only that this was a trap and he was caught in it.

Why are they taking so long? Kruza wondered, looking again at Wheezer. There was something flying through the air between them.

Kruza caught and snatched open the pouch Wheezer had thrown to him. Seeing what it was he dropped it onto the sand in disgust. An unlit scented beeswax candle, and a bunch of dried twigs and leaves, fell out of the pouch.

Kruza laid his right hand on the pommel of the short-sword which stuck out of his belt, under the back of his jacket. He took hold of the hilt and pulled it free, high over his head. His left hand came to join his right and he stood with his feet shoulder-width apart, knees slightly bent, four-square in front of the cloaked man who was still walking towards him.

I have all the time in the world, he thought as he bent his arms, bringing the short-sword up, at an angle, to shoulder height. Attack, his mind told him. He waited just a moment.

Kruza brought his sword down at the very moment the cloaked figure reached his hands out as if to strangle Kruza. The sound the sword made as it sliced into the side of the cloaked figure's neck was one of a blunt knife through a sheaf of dry paper. Nevertheless, there was blood. It gouted out of the wound in short, thick spurts, bright red in the white light, almost purple against the grey cloak.

Stunned, Kruza lifted his sword to strike again. Adjusting his stance, he realised that he had taken a step outside the sand trap. He was free of it. The bleeding man stood, his arms still in front of him, apparently unaware of the deep wide slash that had taken his head half off his body and ripped partway down into his torso. Then he sank slowly to his knees and his hands came down toward the sand.

'KKKRRRUUUZZZAAA!' Wheezer screamed.

Kruza looked up at the lad, who was pointing to the single foot that remained inside the edge of the sand painting. Kruza skipped to one side as the bleeding figure's taloned hands landed in the sand and it began to whirl with colour, coming to rest in its original pattern. The body of the cloaked figure was gone. So was the pouch and its spilled contents.

Seven remained.

The remaining cloaked men began to emerge from their archways in a kind of staggered formation. None of them saw Wheezer. They all saw Kruza.

He stepped forward again, looked once at Wheezer who remained pressed against the pillar, and once at his short-sword. The blood was gone, but the blade gleamed a promise to Kruza. The cut-purse didn't know if time had really slowed or whether it was the strange vitality in his body; whichever it was, it seemed to be working in his favour for the moment.

With the next two swings, one high and sloping, the second low and slicing, he took out two more of the grey men. He heard the paper sound again, but this time the blood remained on his sword. There was a path now between the men emerging from the right and left. Wheezer was standing right in front of him, flanked by two empty archways. Kruza looked once behind him, but the circle of men was too complete. They could not get out the way they had come. Facing front, he made a break for it, catching hold of Wheezer's arm as he went and spinning him into one of the antechambers.

Bathed for a moment in bright white light, the pair were confused. Then Wheezer saw another archway and they ran off through a series of underground chambers, which must have covered a large area beneath this part of the city.

'We need to get out of here!' Kruza managed to speak with confidence and at full volume for the first time since entering the cellar. 'We need to get back to the steps.' But Wheezer had already sprinted on, down a long, wide corridor with a high vaulted ceiling. It could almost have been a room if it wasn't for the fact that every few yards a wide archway or sometimes a door led in to other places that dwarfed the connecting corridor.

Wheezer stopped, eyes wide, looking into a great, circular room, isolated on one side of the corridor. There were no other doorways and no windows in the large open space, but there was much more. A series of small carts and stretcher-wagons littered the room, some covered in tarpaulins, some brimming over with their contents spilling and scattering randomly across the room. There was also a large pile of clothes, some ragged and worn, but others quite respectable and even elegant. If these people were smugglers they were smuggling a very strange array and variety of goods.

Kruza had not thought for a long time that they might be smugglers. Something much bigger was going on here. Kruza did not know what it was and Wheezer seemed completely oblivious.

The youth was working his way over the piles, picking out the things he could carry easily, mostly jewellery, of which there was a great deal, and smaller household items that he could tuck into various pockets in his clothes. Wheezer began to pull the tarpaulins off the carts, first one at a time and then, in a great flurry of activity, he went round the whole lot, tearing covers dramatically from carts to reveal all manner of riches beneath. Kruza stood and stared, impressed that the kid could be so single-minded, so confident or perhaps just terminally oblivious to his situation. Then Kruza remembered the cellar lobby and the cloaked men that had attacked him there and realised the fact that essentially Wheezer was invisible and that, consequently Wheezer was safe. He, on the other hand, was not.

'Wheezer! Come on! We have to get out of here!'

'Look at all this stuff!' The other exclaimed eagerly. 'There's weeks' worth of quota here and we may not get the chance to come back!'

Kruza thought he would never come back even if he ever did get the chance. This had turned into a dangerous fool's errand and one he swore he would never repeat.

'Come on, Kruza! It's there to be taken!'

Wheezer turned and lifted the last tarpaulin from the last pile of goods. The biggest pile, wider and higher than a man, closest to the doorway on the opposite side. Kruza, who only stood in the doorway and watched, could not see this corner. The tarpaulin slid off in a fluid motion like silk on highly polished wood. It had no right to do that. The tarpaulin almost rippled as it fell to the floor with a whisper. It had no right, Kruza thought afterwards.

Wheezer stood back from the smugglers' great pile of goods, so that Kruza could see the look on his face. It had never looked whiter. His eyes were great grey, vacant orbs. Kruza strode across, grasping Wheezer by the elbow for fear the lad would faint, and looked to the corner where the tarpaulin lay. On the floor was a pile of bodies, strewn into a corner, stacked as a farmer might stack hay with a pitchfork. To begin with Kruza did not know what he was looking at. Then he began to make out arms and legs and torsos and one or two swollen heads. The bodies had no natural angles; they were so broken that they had no form. The pile might have been old clothes filled with sawdust that had spilled out. No one was left in these bodies. No life. They were like scarecrows. But they had been alive once. Wheezer saw it, but Kruza felt it.

Some little thing caught Kruza's eye and he moved gingerly toward the mountain of human debris. Grasped in the hand of a dead arm that appeared not to be attached to any other dead thing in the heap, was a long, broad chain made up of flat sections joined together with links at the corners. Hanging from the chain, which was big enough to go around a broad man's shoulders, was a talisman. A great scaled snake or dragon, eating its own tail.

Kruza could not bear to look at it. He turned the mesmerised Wheezer around by the arm and began to march him away from this place. He would rather walk back the way they had come and confront the grey cloaked figures than stay for a moment longer in this place.

They strode back up the arterial tunnel, both taking firm steps, feigning the confidence that Kruza knew he for one, did not feel. If he felt his fear now he was dead for sure. He could not feel it and he could not show it.

There was nothing to hear, but the cool slightly damp air of below ground had given way to the spoiled milk smell that wafted freely from chamber to chamber, becoming stronger as they neared the entrance.

Kruza felt sure they must come upon some of the grey cloaked men, but they did not. They walked solemnly, half scared, back to the place where they had come in. Wheezer's sense of direction was unerring, just as it was when he was above ground in the city. They were soon back in the white-lit chamber that they had run from. Kruza had been waiting all the time for the grey cloaked figures to follow them, but they had not. Wheezer stepped out into the archway, which led back into the entrance cellar, Kruza close behind him.

Before them they saw eight grey cloaked figures all standing with their backs to the central sand-painting that was whirling and coalescing. The sand was spinning like a small typhoon, rising up in spirals of cobalt, purple and black among the yellowish grey of the dust. All eight figures had their hands raised in a similar gesture to that of the first grey man that Kruza had killed. They could see eight pairs of withered arms and gnarled hands, taloned but old and lifeless. These were not smugglers. Kruza believed now that these were not even men. He had thrust his short-sword into them, three of them, and killed each one. One had disappeared before his eyes. All three had now been replaced. Wheezer began to walk around the circle as the sand began to swirl more slowly, and losing height, but not shape, the whirlwind laid itself out in another intricate pattern on the floor.

As Kruza followed Wheezer, his mind whirling with panic and unanswerable questions, he saw the weapons. Each grey man was now armed with a pair of blades: a long, elegant sword with a narrow edge and heavily caged hilt and a shorter, slender dagger with a viciously curved hilt that would do serious damage to any blade it might encounter. Kruza's hand flew to the pommel of his own short-sword. He was never afraid of a brawl, but fighting off eight unknown entities with a total of sixteen blades was nothing short of madness. He would pull his own weapon only if attacked, otherwise he did not wish to provoke – only to leave.

Wheezer tried to shield Kruza from the cloaked men. He had become confident in his ability to remain so anonymous that he was virtually invisible. But Kruza was nervous, his adrenaline was pumping and he smelled of fear. Wheezer didn't know how long he could protect his friend and mentor, but he had got him into this.

The circle that was formed by the grey men began to change formation, always facing outward. The circle divided at the furthest point from Wheezer and Kruza and the figures at the two ends swung around, forming an arc that threatened to cut them off from their escape route.

Wheezer stood very still. Beads of sweat formed on Kruza's forehead, despite the chill that had fallen over the room, and he could feel his hair pasted to his head in sweat. It trickled down his back and dripped down his sides and the insides of his thighs. Kruza knew he had to wait for the attack, but felt panic rising with the gorge in his throat.

White light from the surrounding rooms glowed more strongly and the pattern at the centre of the room appeared to be giving off its own multicoloured light, like a rainbow, rising straight and vertical from the floor.

The grey men had completed their arc. They lifted their arms away from their sides, straight out, parallel to the floor. When their blade tips touched they took a small step backward, widening the arc. Then all sixteen blades came forward together, pointing straight at Kruza.

He knew they could not all attack at once, not without killing each other, although perhaps that did not matter to them. The room was silent except for the sound of Kruza's breathing and the cold swish of blades in the air.

He did not know whether his own body smell was worse, more acrid, than the smell of old, spoiled milk that was so intense now that it burned in his nostrils. His senses were heightened. He could feel every dink and dent in the pommel of his old short-sword. He moved his hand down and felt the cold hilt of the weapon. It was rough and beginning to flake, but it fit his hand now like nothing else could.

Wheezer stepped forward. They did not see him. He was not armed.

Kruza took one small sideways step, his back firmly against the wall. A grey-cloaked figure took a step toward him. Kruza had unsheathed his sword and swung it round, sending sparks from the wall behind him as the tip of the blade came into contact with stone. The sparks held in the air, vermilion for a moment, and then died. Swung hard, the short-sword disarmed the first assailant of his longer blade, leaving only the dagger. The grey cloaked figure chopped the air, hoping to catch the blade of the short-sword and twist it, break it off.

Kruza thought he had never moved so fast. The short-sword came swinging low, below the line of the dagger. Its superior reach sliced, superficially, across his bizarre attacker's midriff, baring the flesh under the cloak, which stood out pale and unreal against the blood which oozed from it. Startled, the grey man looked down as Kruza swept his blade up through the figure from navel to sternum and beyond. The dagger dropped and the figure crawled away, his place taken instantly by another.

Kruza killed three of the men in grey. They were like automata, cold-blooded, thoughtless of the risk, and they fought with one style. Kruza began to catch the rhythm of their attack and was more confident, dispatching the third villain with a single, shoulder-high side-swipe. It was the only blow in the bout and it was deadly. Kruza heard the torn-paper sound and turned to rebut a new onslaught.

Wheezer watched the battle, unarmed and unregarded. Kruza forgot he was there.

The next three grey men, seeing their colleagues fall at the hand of the intruder, attacked together. Six blades moved close, weaving between each other, thrusting, parrying and rallying to attack again. Kruza fought hard and fast, his short-sword in three places at once, but he knew he was defeated. First came the long slash down his arm, his blood pouring down his sleeve and onto his free hand. He held the arm across his body, lest it become a weak point, and thrust with renewed vigour. Then came the slash to his head, curving down in an arc over his face, missing his eye, which was soon filling with blood from the long gash.

Wheezer looked on. No longer silent, he was shouting instructions and warnings to his friend and stamping in the sand.

Kruza was blind on one side and still he hadn't harmed any of his current assailants. He thrashed harder and stronger, turning to his blind side and fighting on, but the grey men were advancing and were close to ending the fray. The blow came soon and was almost welcome. He was struck in the shoulder. A long blade, thrust high and straight, made its way into his body through his leather jerkin – and out again through the back. There was little blood. The sword was steaming hot and cauterised the wound as it was withdrawn.

Kruza fell to his knees, his short-sword still gripped in his hand. His grasp had locked around it when his shoulder was opened and he could not let it go. He dropped his head, waiting for the fatal blow.

Wheezer stamped and screamed, but the five remaining figures did not flinch or turn. The youth let out a huge roar, ready to launch himself at the nearest grey man. But something made him look round. They took no notice of Wheezer. They didn't see him. But there was something they would take notice of.

Wheezer took half a dozen fast strides, almost running, to the centre of the cellar. Then he slid down onto his knees through the multi-coloured dust ornament that adorned the floor and which, until Kruza had dropped to the ground had, been giving off its eerie light.

Dust and sand flew everywhere and Wheezer found himself in the middle of the sand-painting on both knees, unable to move. He held his hands together, high in front of him, like he was praying, and, filling his lungs, he let out a blood curdling cry the like of which Kruza had never heard and hoped never to hear again.

'KKKKKRRRRUUUUZZAAAA!'

The scream hung in the room, echoing in circles around the vaulted ceiling, as though it would never escape.

The grey figures were turning away from him as Kruza heard the second cry.

'RRRRRRRUUUUUUNNNNNN!'

He did not think. He should have been dead and he had no idea if he could even stand, but he had no choice. Wheezer's screams compelled him.

Kruza stood, his arms crossed over his body. He staggered slightly. The sword still in his grasp made him look like some iconic statue of a great warrior-thief. He looked once at the backs of the grey men as they descended on the sand-painting. He did not see Wheezer. He turned and ran.

He ran up the stairs, out through the pitch-covered door and into the alley beyond. He ran out of the Nordgarten and didn't stop running until he reached the tall derelict house in the north of the Altquartier. All the time he ran he believed that Wheezer was right behind him. The lad had played bait, given himself the job of decoy so that Kruza could escape.

But the lad was invisible and he would escape, more easily than I, Kruza thought. *Wouldn't he?*

KRUZA WAITED FOR Wheezer. He slumped onto the couch in the attic room, and waited. When he awoke it was fully daylight and Wheezer had not come.

When he awoke the second time it was dark. The blood of his open wounds had dried and was flaking off onto the couch below him and Wheezer had still not come.

When he awoke a third time he found the energy to wash in the cold water on the washstand. He ate from Wheezer's windowsill larder. The bread was stale. The youth had not come.

Kruza did not know how long he had been in that room, but his wounds were scabbed and the food on the windowsill was gone or spoiled. Wheezer had still not come.

When it came light again, Kruza pulled himself off the couch and straightened the cushions. He emptied the cold, bloody water out of the wash bowl.

After an hour or so, Kruza left Wheezer's room, closing the door firmly behind him. On the stairs down he noticed that there were no footsteps showing in the thick layer of fresh dust. He slid out of the window, wounded shoulder first and closed it firmly behind him.

Kruza walked away. He knew, as surely as he had known the lad was a natural thief, that Wheezer wasn't coming back.

MITTERFRUHL
A WOLF IN THE FOLD

It was the milk-girl who saw them first.

On a late spring evening, one month past Mitterfruhl, the sky was a dark marble blue and the stars were out. Thousands of them, polished and glinting in the heavens.

The Ganmark family had ruled the border town of Linz, a cattle-market hub at the edge of the Drakwald, for sixteen generations. Two hundred years before, the serving Margrave had established the manor at the edge of the long lake, three miles from the town. The manor house itself was a fine dwelling, with farmlands adjoining, a park and splendid prospects across to the dark stands of the Drakwald to the east.

Lenya, the milk-girl, liked working there. The work was as hard as it had been on her father's little farm, but to work at the manor house, to live in the manor house, it was almost like living at the Graf's palace in far Middenheim. It felt like she was advancing herself. Her father had always said it would be one of her many older brothers who made something of himself but here she was, the last child, the only daughter, working at the Margrave's hall, thank you very much.

She had a straw bed in the servants' wing, and the food was always plentiful. She was only seventeen, but they were good to her – cook, the chamberlain, all the senior staff. Even the Margrave had smiled at her once. Her duties were simple: in the morning, collect the eggs, at night, perform the evening milking. In the meantime, polish, clean, scrub, peel or chop anything you were told to.

She liked the evening milking, especially at this time of year. The spring sky was so clear, and the stars were, well, perfect. Her mother had always told her to count the stars when you had the chance. To make sure they were all there. If an old star went out, bad luck was sure to follow.

As she crossed the stable yard to the dairy, she noticed there seemed to be more stars out that night than usual. Like the speckles on an egg, or the twinkling bubbles on the lip of the milk pail. So many. And that beautiful blue one down by the horizon...

New stars. A good sign, surely?

Then she saw the other new stars, stars in the tree-line above the manor house. Burning, hot stars, like eyes, like–

Lenya dropped the pail.

She realised they were torches, flaming torches held aloft in the black, armoured fists of three dozen sinister horseback warriors.

Even as she realised this, the raiders broke into a charge, thundering down on the manor house. They seemed to move like part of the darkness, as if the night was blurring, as if they were made of smoke. There was a strong scent in the night air, sweet but dusty-dry.

She cried out a little, in surprise and confusion.

Then she saw the other, smaller stars... the fires that were burning behind the matt-black visors and in the sockets of the flaring, infernal horses.

Lenya Dunst cried out again. Fiercely, lustily, she cried out for her life.

'IN THE NAME of Ulric, now we'll see some fine sport!' Morgenstern announced, bellowing a laugh. Around him, in the stable block of the Temple compound, his fellow knights of White Company joined his laugh, and playful comments flew back and forth. Thirteen powerful steeds were saddled and near readiness for action. There was power in the straw-floored stone chamber, the bridled power of great horses and potent fighting men.

'Ten shillings, I'll wager you,' Anspach said with a chuckle, 'I'll have badged my armour with the blood of the enemy by the first night! Yes, I will!' he roared at the hearty gainsayers all around.

'I'll take that,' Gruber said quietly.

There was a stunned silence. Gruber was the oldest and most worthy of the company, and everyone knew how he disapproved of rakish Anspach's wagering habits. But there had been a new spring in his step, a new fire in his eyes, since their great victory in the Drakwald before Mitterfruhl. Jurgen, their dear, lost leader, had been avenged, and honour had been returned to them. Of them all, Gruber most personified the reanimation of their spirits.

'Well?' Gruber asked the dumbstruck Anspach, a wry grin on his old, lined face.

Anspach roared and stuck out a mailed fist. 'Done!' he cried.

'And done!' Gruber agreed with a more mirthful laugh.

'Now that's the spirit of the company I like to see!' howled the huge warrior Morgenstern and clapped his hands together.

Off to his right, the company's young standard bearer, Aric, smiled and made a final check of his mount's saddle. Straightening up amidst the hubbub, he caught the eye of youthful Drakken. Drakken was barely twenty, just a wolf cub really, transferred into their company to replace one of the brave souls they had lost in the Drakwald raid. He was a short, yet powerful, stocky young man, and Aric had seen his skill with the horse and hammer in practice, but he was completely inexperienced, and was certainly overawed by the boisterous, oathing company.

Aric crossed to him.

'All ready?' he asked, good-naturedly. Drakken quickly set to his saddle again, trying to look efficient.

'Relax,' said Aric. 'It was only yesterday I was like you: a virgin to war, and to the company of Wolves like these. Go with it, and you'll find your place.'

Drakken gave him a nervous grin. 'Thanks. I just feel like an outsider in this... this family.'

Aric smirked and nodded. 'Yes, this is a family. A family who lives and dies together. Trust us, and we'll trust you back.'

He cast a glance round the room, and picked out a few of the rowdy company for Drakken's benefit. Each of the warriors wore the gold-edged grey plate armour and white wolf pelt of the Temple. 'Morgenstern there. He's a prize-winning ox, and he'll drink you under any table anywhere. But he's got a good heart and heavy hammer. Gruber... stick close by him; no one has the experience or sheer courage of that man. Anspach... never trust his judgement or take his wagers, but trust his right arm. A fury on the field. Kaspen, the red-headed fellow there – he's our surgeon too. He'll see to any wounds you collect. Einholt and Schell, why they're the best trackers we have. Schiffer, Bruckner, Dorff – great horsemen all.'

He paused.

'And remember you're not alone in being new. Lowenhertz also transferred in, same time as you.'

Their eyes wandered across to the last knight, who was alone in the stable corner, checking his horse's shoeing.

Lowenhertz was a tall, regal-looking man, handsome and aquiline. It was said he had noble blood, though Morgenstern had sworn this was a bastard heritage. He was quiet and aloof, almost as quiet and reserved as Einholt, if that was possible. Ten years he'd served in the White Wolves, first in Red Company, then Grey. It seemed he had never found a place to suit him, or one that wanted him perhaps. No one knew why he had come to them, though Anspach wagered it was because he was biding his time until a command came up. Gruber thought so too, and that was enough for all of them.

'Lowenhertz?' murmured Drakken. 'He's not new blood like me. He's had time in the companies, and he... he has an air to him. He frightens me.'

Aric thought about this and nodded. 'Me too.'

Their conversation was shut off by the slamming open of the stable door. Ganz, the young company commander, resplendent in full plate and wolfskin, strode in.

'This is it...' Kaspen murmured.

'Moment of truth,' Schell agreed, his whipcord face tense with anticipation.

Dorff broke off from a wavering, tuneless whistle.

'Well, sir?' Anspach asked.

Ganz faced them. 'We ride for Linz at once–'

He had to wave down their cheering. 'Enough! Enough! Lads, it's not the glory we were hungry for. I've just had our orders conveyed by the High Priest himself.'

'And? What does the old fart have to say?' Morgenstern asked raucously.

'Respect, please, Morgenstern!' Gruber yelled.

'My apologies, old friend! I should have said what does *his highness* the old fart have to say?'

Ganz looked sad and tired. He sighed. 'Three companies of Knights Panther have been sent out to Linz to hunt down these raiders and make sure no harm befalls the town itself. We must go to provide... escort.'

'Escort?' Gruber said.

The silence which followed was total.

'The Margrave, his family and many of his household staff escaped the raid that burned his manor. As you know, Linz owes fealty to the Graf here in Middenheim, and his excellency the Graf is most concerned for his cousin the Margrave's safety. A long story cut short, we are to escort the Margrave's entourage back here to the city to keep him and his safe.'

There was an audible, collective groan.

'So the Panthers get the glory?' Anspach mused. 'They get to hunt down and battle these raiding jackals while we get nurse maid duty?'

Ganz could do nothing but shrug. 'Technically, it's an honour...' he began.

Morgenstern said something both uncomplimentary and physically challenging about 'honour'.

'All right, old friend,' Ganz said, unamused. 'Let's just do the job we've been asked to. Mount up. White Company rides with me.'

IT WAS TWO days' hard ride to Linz. Late spring rain, brisk and horizontal, washed across the meadows and trackways as they rode. Then the pale sun came out again.

They could see the ruins of the Ganmark manor from several miles away, and smell it even before that. Dark, almost oily smoke hung in the air like a sinuous raincloud against the spring afternoon and there was a curious smell, like sweetmeats and spices mixed with the ash from a funeral urn.

Riding beside Ganz, Gruber wrinkled his nose. The young commander looked over at him.

'Gruber? What is it?'

Gruber cleared his throat and spat sideways as if to rid his mouth of the smell on the breeze. 'No idea. Like nothing I've ever smelt.'

'Not in this part of the land,' said a voice from beside them. Ganz and Gruber looked over to see the chiselled profile of Lowenhertz. The tall knight rode in beside them, skilled and coolly measured.

'What do you mean, brother?' asked Gruber.

Lowenhertz smiled a not entirely friendly smile. 'My great grandfather was a Knight Panther. Went on two crusades into those hellish distant lands of heat and dust. When I was a child, he used to tell stories of the ancient tombs and mausoleums, the dry, deathless things that haunted the nights. He told me stories. I remember them clearly, stood in his old solar, where he kept his books and mementoes, the old armour, the banners and gonfalons. There was always a smell in that old room – mortuary dust, dry bones, and the sweet pungent stench of the grave spices. He always told me it was the smell of death from the far-off tombs of Araby.'

He shrugged. 'I can smell it once more. And so much stronger than I did in my great grandfather's solar in childhood.'

Ganz was silent as their horses jogged on through the open meadow. Small, green butterflies, early risers in the fresh spring, whirled in formation across their path. Ganz looked ahead, down the sweep of the valley, to the blackened timber skeleton which was all that remained of Ganmark manor. Smoke still curled up, like dark fingers clawing the air.

'I'd take it as a personal favour, Lowenhertz, if you didn't share such observations with the rest of the men.'

Lowenhertz nodded curtly. 'Of course, commander.' With that he spurred his mount forward and rode ahead of them down the winding track.

AT THE GATES of Linz, an honour-guard squadron of Panther Knights rode out to meet them, haughty and resplendent in their decorative, high-crested helms and armour. Their captain saluted Ganz stiffly and the White Wolf returned the greeting. There was little love lost between the Templars of Ulric and the regal warriors of the Graf's household bodyguard.

'Sigmar bring you safe! Captain von Volk, Knights Panther, Graf's First Royal Household.'

'Ulric look to you! Ganz, Commander, White Company.'

'Welcome to Linz, Commander, I stand relieved.'

The Panther captain fell in beside Ganz and his men rode around in a precision display until they were perfectly flanking the Wolf formation as an escort. The Panthers were in precise line, and even the light hoofbeats of their graceful steeds was in perfect time, compared to the powerful, tired syncopation of the straggled and dusty Wolves. Ganz felt someone was showing off.

'Glad you're finally here, Commander Ganz,' von Volk said curtly. 'We've been chafing to get off after these creatures, but of course we couldn't leave the Margrave and his entourage undefended.'

Ganz nodded. 'You've sent scouting parties out?'

'Of course. Four field groups. They've had no success, but I feel confident that once I field my entire force I'll have these raiding scum good and proper.'

From behind them, Gruber snorted with quiet derision.

Von Volk turned in his saddle. He was a tall, thin, fierce man with bright, flitting eyes. They lustred behind the golden grille of his ceremonial visor. 'What's that, soldier? Oh, I'm sorry, old man… were you just talking in your sleep?'

Gruber did not rise to it. 'Nothing, sir. Just clearing my throat.'

Von Volk turned away without a care. The silk draperies of his helmet's crest fluttered out behind him. 'Commander Ganz, the Margrave awaits you in the Guild Hall. I'd like you to have him and his party away by dusk.'

'And travel at night?' Ganz was all reason and charm. 'We'll leave at dawn, captain. Even a raw recruit knows that is the best time to embark on an escort drill.'

Von Volk scowled.

'Mobilise your men and get on your way,' Ganz added. 'We'll take it from here. Good hunting.'

'MY DEAR, DEAR fellow!' the Margrave of Linz said, pumping Ganz's hand. 'My dear, dear fellow! How we've waited for you!'

'Sir,' Ganz managed. The vast panelled chamber of the Guild Hall was full of baggage crates and rolled carpets. Around it hung the twenty or so servants and staff who had escaped the raid on the manor.

And presumably carried this stuff to safety, Ganz mused. *How in the name of Ulric do you roll a carpet during an attack?*

The Margrave, a portly, pale aristocrat in his late thirties, had put on his best robes to greet the Wolves, but sticking-out tufts of hair and an overwhelming scent of clove oil told that he hadn't seen decent sanitation since the attack.

'I asked for Wolves, most particularly,' said the Margrave. 'In my letter to my dearest cousin, the Graf, I requested Wolves above all, a company of Wolves. Oh, let the gaudy Panthers do the hunting work, but give me Wolves to see me and my family home.'

'The Panthers are fine warriors. They'll find your attackers,' Ganz said smoothly, not believing it for a moment. 'But, assuredly, we'll get you home. Now how many are you?'

The Margrave ushered him around. 'We fill three coaches and four baggage carts. Sixteen servants, the luggage, plus myself and my children, and their nurse…'

He pointed to a pair of ghastly, knickerbockered five year olds who were thumping each other ferociously on a pile of rugs. An elderly and emaciated black-robed nurse watched over them.

'Hanz and Hartz!' sighed the Margrave, clasping his palms together. 'Aren't they adorable?'

'Unbearably,' Ganz said.

'And then, of course, there's my wife…' the Margrave added.

Ganz looked round as indicated. Her ladyship was pouring drinks for the thirsty Wolves herself, from pitchers her servants carried.

She was tall, shapely and hypnotically beautiful. Her dark, ringletted, luxuriant hair ran all the way down to the extraordinary curve her hips made in her sheer silk gown. Her skin was pale, her eyes dark and deep like pools. Her lips were full and red and–

Ganz turned back to look at the ugly children very quickly.

'They're not hers, of course,' the Margrave continued. 'Their dear, dear mother died in childbirth. Gudrun and I married last year.'

Gudrun, thought Ganz. *Ulric! Heaven has a name!*

'WINE FOR YOU, brave knight?' she asked softly.

Gruber took the beaker and gazed at the vision before him. 'Thank you, lady,' he said. She was amazing. Quite the most beautiful woman he had ever seen; dark, exotic, mysterious… yet here she was serving all these dirty, stinking warriors wine. Serving them by hand herself.

'You are our salvation, sir,' she said to him, perhaps noticing his puzzled look. 'After our nights of terror and pain, this is the least I can do.'

'She's amazing…' Anspach breathed, clutching his untouched goblet as she moved on.

'If I was thirty years younger and a hundredweight lighter…' Morgenstern began.

'You'd still be a fat old wastrel with no chance!' Einholt finished.

'Lord Ulric above us,' Drakken murmured to Aric. 'She's quite lovely…'

Aric couldn't take his eyes off the Margrave's wife, and he nodded before realising Drakken wasn't looking at her at all.

'Drakken?'

'Her, Aric.' Drakken smiled and pointed to a young girl huddled amid the servants. She was barely eighteen by Aric's guess, short and trim, but dirty and soiled from the adventures that had overtaken her, and dressed in a milk-maid's smock. She was… pretty, he had to admit.

'Drakken!' Aric hissed. 'First rule of Wolfhood… if a goddess gives you wine, you don't drool after her cherubs.'

'What goddess?' asked Drakken, staring at the milk-girl.

Aric smiled and shook his head.

THEY LEFT LINZ at dawn. The carts and coaches rolled out in line, flanked by the thirteen Wolf Knights, into the rich dawn mist.

At the head of the column, Ganz called Gruber, Anspach and Lowenhertz to him.

'Ride ahead. Scout the woods,' he told them. They spurred away.

Aric, the standard of the company held aloft, moved up beside Ganz.

'Drakken needs some purpose to settle his nerve, sir,' Aric said.

Ganz thought for a moment. 'You're right,' he said at last and called back for the youngest knight. Drakken rode forward eagerly.

'Join the scouts,' Ganz said. 'They could use an extra hand.'

Smiling fit to split his face, Drakken charged forward at a gallop off into the smoky woodland.

ANSPACH REINED UP sharply. For a moment, he had almost lost his bearings in the mist. The sun was up, but there was barely any light amidst the swirling vapour and dark trees.

'What was that?' he said to Gruber, just a few yards away.

'Probably Lowenhertz,' said Gruber. 'He went off to the left.'

'No!' said Anspach sharply, heeling down his prick-spurs deep to turn his horse hard. 'With me, Gruber! Now!'

The two warriors plunged through the woodland, kicking up dirt and wafting the mist. They caught a sweet and dry smell of ash. Anspach freed his hammer from its clasp.

They found Drakken in a clearing. His horse was dead, and so was one of the black knights who had ambushed him. Drakken's grey plate armour was ripped open and his shoulder was gashed, but still he screamed fiercely, swirling his warhammer to crack another head as he had the skull of the man who brought him down.

He was surrounded.

There were four more dark warriors, each clad in strangely angular black plate armour with spike-pointed, almost bulbous helmets. They swung dark blue, serrated swords that hooked into fang-like curves, and a fine mesh of chainmails rattled around their waists. Their horses were huge and black, and, like the knights themselves, their eyes glowed with an internal fire. There was something almost insubstantial about the edges of them, about the hem of their swirling cloaks, as if they were solidifying out of the mist and darkness itself. The smell of sweet spice and ash was intense.

Drakken ducked a swing that severed a young tree behind him. Anspach and Gruber leapt their horses forward to avoid the crashing timbers and branches.

Gruber swung his hammer round and came about. The nearest of these almost ghostly raiders filled Gruber's nose with the dry, dead stink and swung forward with his sword.

Anspach and his horse exploded into the gap between them and he crushed the enemy's head with a downward blow of his warhammer. The matt-black spiked helmet shattered and dark fumes billowed out as the glowing eyes went dark.

Gruber found another two on him hard, slashing with their venomous hookswords, relentless.

'Ulric curse you!' he spat, battling for a break.

Lowenhertz blasted out of the mist and undergrowth, his horse at full leap.

His whizzing hammer smashed the first warrior out of his saddle, and then with a skilled and powerful reverse turn, Lowenhertz broke the chest of Gruber's second attacker.

The remaining dark warrior spurred forward with a raucous, unintelligible curse, his red eyes blazing from behind his visor slit, his vile horse wretched and stinking.

Anspach swung his hammer round sideways over his shoulder and destroyed the last warrior outright.

For a moment, the impact resounded around the deadened clearing.

Anspach leapt down and helped the shaken Drakken up.

'Well done, youth! You're a Wolf now, no mistake.'

Gruber turned to Lowenhertz.

'Thanks go to you. You saved my life,' he said.

'Think nothing of it,' said Lowenhertz. He gazed down at the bodies of the foes. Inside the rent-open armour of the nearest, nothing but powdery bones could be seen, flaking away like ash in the breeze.

There was a long, chill silence.

'In the name of Ulric!' Gruber hissed, fear clawing deep. 'Let's get back to the convoy!'

'THE DEAD DON'T lie still,' Gruber murmured to Ganz as they rejoined the halted train. Anspach was helping the injured Drakken to a cart, and Kaspen had dismounted to tend the young man's injury. Lowenhertz rode in silently, a way behind Gruber. A hush had fallen when the four warriors had returned, the bloody Drakken sharing Anspach's horse, all of them flecked with dark smudges of blood. Ganz was dreadfully aware of the way the Margrave's people stared at his men in fixed horror and silent alarm.

'Don't riddle, report!' he hissed.

Gruber shook his head, fear still shaking him, easing off his mailed gauntlets. 'We met a bevy of dark... things – Ulric save our souls! They were not... mortal! No doubt the very same abominations who took down the Ganmark Manor. Caught Drakken but by Ulric's teeth he gave them what for. We did the rest, Lowenhertz, the lion's share. But they're out there. Ulric help us, commander! These things are spectres!'

'You mean ghosts?' asked Ganz, in a tight whisper.

'I do not know what I mean! I have never met their like before!'

Ganz cursed. 'Hundreds of miles of forest and farmland, Knights Panther hunting for them, and they stumble on us! What are the chances?'

'What are the chances?' cut in Lowenhertz quietly but significantly. He seemed to appreciate the commander's urge to keep the talk out of civilian earshot. 'They raid the manor, then they find us...' He trailed off.

'What do you mean?' Aric asked, easing his grip on the lofty standard.

'I mean: maybe they're after something. Something that was in the manor, something that's here with us now!'

There was a long silence. Horses whinnied and shook off flies.

Ganz wiped his fist across his mouth. 'You seem to be remarkably well-informed, Master Lowenhertz,' he said finally.

'What do you mean?' answered the knight, his eyes hooded.

'You seem to know much of the ways of darkness,' said Ganz frankly.

Lowenhertz laughed out loud. There was little humour in it, but it shook the clearing and made everyone look.

'It is merely logic, commander... these creatures have wit. They are not brute beastfolk, not savage greenskins from the rockslopes. They move with a purpose; they have a meaning and a task to all they do. This is not a random chance.'

'Then we'll be careful,' said Ganz, simply.

'We should try to discern the nature of their purpose, sir. Perhaps by–'

Ganz cut Lowenhertz short. 'We will be careful,' he repeated more firmly. 'Aric, go check and see Drakken is comfortable and ready to move. We will ride on.'

He looked down as the Margrave hurried up on foot from his carriage. He was attended by two servants who scrambled after him and his face was not happy.

'Are we in danger, sir knight?' he asked breathlessly.

'You are in the company of Wolves, noble sir,' Ganz said gracefully. 'You requested us, I seem to recall, and knew we would see you safe...'

'Aye, indeed! I don't mean to doubt... But still... Are they still out there?'

'On my honour, Margrave, on the honour of my men and in the name of Ulric who guides us, we will be safe.'

By his side, Gruber sat back in the saddle. He was still shaking from the combat, his pulse thundering. *Too much, too hard for an old man*, he thought. His eyes scanned the carriage train as they made ready to move out.

In the door window of the Margrave's wagon, he caught sight of the nobleman's wife. She gazed out from the shadows, a wicked smile on her lips.

Gruber looked away. He wished to dear heaven he had not seen her look.

Aric rode back to the cart where Drakken was being minded. It carried several of the kitchen staff and the elderly nurse of the noble children. Drakken did not seem to notice. The milk-maid, Lenya, was vigorously helping Kaspen dress his wounds.

'Keep them clean and dry, and watch for infection,' Kaspen told her.

'I know what to do, Red-hair,' she nodded curtly, obediently.

Lenya stared aggressively down into Drakken's eyes as Kaspen got down off the wagon and balled up a cloth from the bowl of water to wring it out.

'I'll look after you, Wolf. Don't worry. I've tended to my brothers' wounds and scrapes often enough, many worse than this,' she said.

'I... I thank you,' said Drakken, a foolish smile on his face.

Aric watched them, chuckled and rode back to Ganz.

'Drakken's as happy as a cub,' he told the commander.

'Then we ride. Move on!' cried Ganz. 'Move on!'

AT NIGHTFALL, THEY camped on a rocky slope overlooking a bend in a nameless stream. The Wolves built watch-fires all around the perimeter and stood in guard shifts all through the night.

At midnight, Ganz did his round of the duty. He passed a few moments with Einholt and the hulking Bruckner at their posts as the rest of the party settled down for sleep.

Crossing to check on Aric, Ganz saw a dark shape out beyond the edge of the firelight.

He stiffened and crept out into the darkness, his hand sliding his hunting knife from its sheath.

'Lowenhertz!' he hissed.

The knight turned in surprise, lowering a beautiful brass astrolabe through which he had been sighting the heavens.

'Commander?'

'What in the name of the Wolf are you doing out here?'

'It is difficult to take accurate readings close to the firelight,' Lowenhertz began.

'Readings?'

'Of the stars, commander. To see if any strange patterns or manifestations could be discerned. My great-grandfather taught me that celestial signs and augurs accompanied the machinations of the deathless ones…'

Ganz cut him off, angry and snarling. 'I now see why you have never made command yourself! They don't trust you, do they? Our Temple elders don't trust you with the lives of men because you are too far gone, too close to the darkness itself!'

Lowenhertz paused and frowned. 'Oh!' he said at last. 'I see. Commander, you think it's me, don't you? You think I'm a part of this danger?'

'I–' began Ganz, wrong-footed.

Lowenhertz laughed as if at a truly rich joke. 'Forgive me, sir. I am just what I seem to be: a loyal servant of Ulric whose mind sometimes asks too many questions! My father was a Knight Panther. He died at Antler Hill, torn open by the hounds of Chaos. I have always sought to be one step ahead, to know more of my foe than they know of me, to serve the Temple as best as my body – and mind – are able. I would not have you distrust me! But if I can serve you and you can trust me…'

There was a long silence. Ganz extended his hand for the astrolabe. 'So have you found anything?' he said quietly.

DRAKKEN CURLED UP in the rolls of carpet behind the wagon and relaxed in the firelight. A shadow fell over him and he blinked up out of his half slumber. Lenya was there, her smile luminous in the shadows.

'Are you thirsty, knight?' she asked.

'My name is Drakken,' he said. 'Krieg Drakken. I wish you would call me that.'

'I will, Krieg. On two conditions. One, if you tell me you're thirsty and two if you call me Lenya.'

'I am thirsty, Lenya,' he said softly.

She snorted and turned away to fetch a drink.

Drakken settled back and closed his eyes. His shoulder ached, but all in all this was turning out to be a fine debut as a White Wolf.

A shadow fell across him again.

'I hope the water is cool…' he began, then tailed off when he realised it wasn't the returning Lenya. The old nurse crouched down by him.

'Calm now, my little pet,' she said warmly. 'Oh, but I know I'm not so handsome as yon milk-maid, but I care as much for the well-being of my guardians. And you have had a long day.'

Drakken relaxed and smiled. Her tone was so reassuring and calm. No wonder she made her life as the custodian of children.

'I only stopped by to bless you, my lamb,' she said and reached into the neck of her smock. 'I have a lucky charm, given me by my mother years ago. I would have you take it in your hand to speed you to health.'

The nurse held out a glittering amulet attached to a long cord around her neck. Its mount was pewter, but the thing itself was a curve of glass, shaped like a claw, a fragment perhaps of something else, something very old.

'Always brought me luck and health,' she said.

He smiled and took it in his hand. It felt warm.

'Now blessing be on you, my poor wounded knight. The blessing of all the gods.'

'Thank you, lady,' Drakken said. He felt warmer, safer, more whole.

'Now Lenya returns with a cup of water,' said the nurse, taking back the charm and getting up. 'You'll have no more time with an old fool like me. Be safe, knight.'

'Again, thank you,' said Drakken.

Then Lenya was at his side again, offering the cup to his lips.

'Old Maris fussing over you again?' she said with a grin. 'She's so kind. The children dote on her. The Margrave was lucky to find her last year when he needed a wetnurse.'

'She's a fine old lady, and very caring,' said Drakken between sips. 'But I know who I would wish to have care for me…'

'Do you make a habit of spying on women?' asked the Margrave's wife with a delicious curl to her lips.

Gruber stopped in his tracks and fumbled for the right words. 'I was patrolling the camp, my lady.'

'And that brought you back behind my carriage as I was dressing for bed?' she returned.

Gruber turned away, too conscious of the fact he was in the company of a woman who wore little more than a satin shroud.

'I apologise, lady. I–'

'Oh hush, knight!' she said with a chiming laugh. 'I'm flattered a man as worthy and distinguished as you would blush in my company. I appreciate your efforts. We are all in your care.'

Gruber shifted awkwardly and then turned to go.

'What is your name, knight?'

'Wilhelm Gruber,' he said, turning back. He felt suddenly bold. 'Who are you, lady?'

'The wife of the Margrave of Linz, unless that had passed you by,' she replied, laughing again.

'Is that all?' he asked sharply.

She said nothing in return. There was a long silence.

'You'd best return to your patrol, Gruber,' she said at last. 'I don't know what you think I am, but I'm not happy at the implications.'

'Neither am I, lady,' Gruber said as he strode away. 'We'll see.'

GANZ WATCHED THE stars through the polished lenses of Lowenhertz's astrolabe. He was about to ask the name of another constellation when Lowenhertz gripped his arm hard.

'What?'

'Quiet!' hissed Lowenhertz. 'You smell that?'

Ganz inhaled. The sweet, ashy flavour of death was unmistakable.

They ducked low, and saw the glowing eye slits of warriors moving down in the vale by the stream.

'I have nothing but my knife!' whispered Ganz.

Lowenhertz tossed him his warhammer and pulled a long war-axe from his saddlebag.

'Give the word, commander. They've come back for us.'

IT WAS A dark blur of night and firelight. Ganz thought he counted fifteen of the foe as they charged the camp from the east on foot. They were silent, the shades of the dead.

Ganz was not silent. He bellowed his warning as loud as his lungs could bear, and he and Lowenhertz leapt across the stream-side rocks to meet the silent charge.

The camp came to life. Hallowing answers came from the sentries, and roars from the sleeping men as they roused. Screams and cries rose from the terrified civilians.

Einholt met the first of the attackers, blocking and whirling his warhammer as he bayed out a call to his wolf brothers. In five seconds, Bruckner and Aric, the other two sentries on duty, were by his side, blocking the passage between the crackling watch fires against the red-eyed ghouls that swept out of the night.

Ganz and Lowenhertz were with them a few seconds later.

There were at least twenty of the attackers now, Ganz was certain, but it was so hard to disentangle their dank shapes from the night, or their flashing eyes from the blazing fires. It was as if they were made out of the night itself.

A gleaming jet blade whistled past his head and Ganz swung back to guard himself. In doing so, his feet slipped on the earth and he half stumbled. The dark one rose up over him, blade poised. Morgenstern, only half-armoured and bedraggled from slumber, burst through the darkness and laid the creature low with a two-handed hammerblow of huge force. Ganz leapt up and called his thanks to the man-mountain, who was already driving on into the press.

He saw Aric fall, gashed in the shoulder. Einholt and Lowenhertz leapt to block him, standing their ground as he pulled himself up again. Lowenhertz's axe whistled in the cold air.

With wolf-fire in his blood, Ganz spun his borrowed hammer, used the haft to block a hard sword swing, and then slew his attacker with a sideways smash of the hammerhead.

'For the Temple! For Ulric! White Company!' he bellowed.

Across in the camp: pandemonium. Hammer held tight, Gruber tried to marshal the chaos.

'Kaspen! Anspach! Get the Margrave and his people into cover by the wagons! The rest of you forward to fight!'

Screaming servants and crying children ran in every direction. Cook pots and fire hearths were upset and kicked over.

'Damn it!' Gruber cursed.

He saw Drakken limping into the centre of the camp as fast as he could manage. 'My weapon! Any weapon!' cried the young man hoarsely.

'You're more use to me here!' Gruber shouted. 'Get the children in a wagon. Keep their heads down!'

There was another scream, more piercing than before. Gruber wheeled and saw two dark warriors had burst into the encampment from the opposite direction to the main attack, a sneak pincer to get round the cordon. They charged in towards the wagons.

It was the Margrave's wife who had screamed. She was in the open, trying to catch hold of her two terrified children. The nurse was by her side, trying to scoop the boys into her arms. The warriors bore down on them, swords raised.

Gruber raced forward, lashing out a one-handed hammer swing that shattered armour and knocked one of them to the earth. The other he met and blocked, glancing his hammer haft against the slashing blade once, twice, three times to ward off the deadly swings. By then, the first dark warrior was back on his feet.

Gruber dented the helm of the second one and sent him sprawling in time to meet the renewed attack of the first. He stared into the red-lit slits and met the furious assault, swinging a blow that smashed its shield. Then he stabbed hard with the butt of the haft, connecting with jaw. The foe went down and this time a well-placed blow ensured it would not rise again.

The second one was upright again now, intent on the Margrave's wife once more.

With a roar, Gruber hurled his hammer. The great, spinning weapon swooshed across the clearing in flickering circles and broke the creature's back.

Gruber crossed to the Margrave's wife and helped her up. The nurse gathered up the children.

'Get to the wagons!' he hissed.

'Th-thank you...' she stammered.

'They were hell-bent on getting to you,' Gruber snarled, fixing her eyes with his. 'What is it about you? Are you the jinx who brings this darkness down?'

'No!' she implored, horrified, 'No!'

There was no time for debate. Gruber recovered his hammer and rejoined the fight.

'THEY'RE RETREATING!' ANSPACH announced at last.

'Thank the Wolf!' murmured Ganz. The fight had been intense, and too close for comfort. Several of his men were wounded, and there were seven dark warriors twisted, skeletal and dead on the ground. The others, like the wraiths of fairy tales, melted away into the trees.

'Regroup!' Ganz told his men, 'Let's get inside the camp and build up the firewall. There's a long time till dawn.'

'Commander!' Gruber was calling.

Ganz joined him. The warrior whose back Gruber had snapped was still alive, twitching and hissing like a reptile on the ground. The civilians stood round in a wide, fascinated horrified circle.

'Clear these people aside!' Ganz snapped to Dorff and Schiffer. He turned to Gruber. 'I'm beginning to think Lowenhertz is right. We have something or someone these creatures want – that's why they took the manor and now hound us.'

'I agree. This was not a raid, this was a mission to retrieve. They were too direct, putting themselves at risk to get into the camp rather than harry us from a distance.' Gruber took a deep breath. 'I believe it's part of the Margrave's household, and I think I know what...'

'You think it's me,' said a voice from behind them. It was the Margrave's wife, clutching one of the sobbing children. 'I don't know what I've done to earn your mistrust, Sir Gruber. I can only imagine that you are threatened by me. All my life, my dark looks and lively manner have made men imagine me some she-devil, some brazen thing to be feared. Can I help my looks, or my appetite for life? Can I help the way I was made? I am no daemon. On my life – on the lives of my children, sirs! – I am not the root of this!'

Ganz looked over at his second-in-command. The older, white-haired man dropped his gaze to the earth.

'Seems both of us have jumped to conclusions today, old man. Both of us wrong.'

'You too?' Gruber asked.

Ganz nodded. 'Milady, take the children to cover in the wagons. We will finish this. Lowenhertz!'

The noble knight arrived. His chest plate and shoulder armour had been badly damaged in the fight and so he was stripped to his woollen pourpoint now.

'Commander?'

'You have learning, Lowenhertz... or so you like to tell me. How do we get information from our guest here?'

Lowenhertz looked down at the crippled dark one and sank to his haunches. He listened for a moment and shuddered. 'I can make little out from its rasping... the language... perhaps it is the tongue of far Araby. There is one word it repeats...' Lowenhertz thickly repeated the word back to the creature with distaste. It stirred and hissed and yelped. The White Wolf then muttered the low, guttural word again.

Ganz turned. 'We're getting nowhere...'

Lowenhertz tried the sentence again until the creature replied at last with a guttural response of his own.

'I don't understand him. The words are too strange.' Lowenhertz tried harder, repeating the word. It was no good.

Then the creature reached out and with a bony hand drew a curved symbol in the dust.

'What is that?' asked Ganz.

'I wish I knew,' said Lowenhertz. 'I cannot understand him. That picture makes no sense. What is that? A harvest moon? A crescent?'

'It's a claw,' said Drakken suddenly, from behind them. 'And I know where it is.'

THE OLD NURSE, Maris, backed away against the wagon, terror in her eyes and her hands clutched tight to the throat of her dress.

'No!' she said. 'No! You shan't have it!'

Ganz looked round at Drakken and Lowenhertz at his side.

'She's just the wetnurse,' he said.

'She has the amulet, shaped like a claw. She blessed me with it,' Drakken said.

'If it is what these creatures of darkness seek, lady, you must give it up for all our sakes,' Lowenhertz firmly said.

'This trinket my old dam gave me?' stammered the old woman. 'It's always brought me luck.'

Gruber joined them. 'This makes sense of it. Those warriors I fought... I thought they were after the Lady and her children, but they were after the nurse.'

The Margrave and his wife approached.

'Please, sir!' the old woman cried. 'Make them stop this nonsense.'

'Dear Maris,' the lady pleaded, 'you have always been kind to my children, so I will defend you from harm, but this is too important. Let us prove this. Give me the charm.'

Wizened hands shaking, the old woman produced the claw talisman and handed it to the Margrave's wife. She turned and marched across to the stricken foe. Ganz made to stop her, but Gruber held him back.

'She knows what she's doing, that one,' he told his commander.

'Lenya told me the nurse had only been with them for a while. Her predecessor had fallen ill and she was brought in from far away,' said Drakken.

Lowenhertz nodded. 'If this malign charm has been in her family for some time they may have known nothing of its power. But it has brought them after her every step of the way. They have caught her scent – or the scent of the thing she owns.'

'But what is it?' asked Aric.

'The talon of some dark daemon they worship? The shed nail of a god?' Lowenhertz shrugged. 'Who knows? Who wants to know?'

'A man of learning like you?' Ganz asked.

Lowenhertz shook his head. 'There are some things better left unknown, commander.'

The Margrave's wife showed the charm to the broken creature and then jumped back as it reared up, snarling and mewling, clawing at her.

Gruber slew it with a quick, deft blow.

'There's our proof,' he stated.

Everyone froze as a keening sounded through the forest around them. The grave-smell of spice and dry bone wafted around them again.

'They have the scent again, fresher than ever,' said Lowenhertz. 'They're coming back.'

'To arms!' Gruber cried, rallying the men.

Ganz held up his hand. 'We'd never take them. They have superior numbers and the night on their side. We barely drove them back before. There is only one way.'

The White Company and their civilian charges drew into a huddle at the centre of the firelight. Beyond the ring of flame, they saw the dark riders approach and heard their hooves. Dozens of red eyes glowed against the blackness, like infernal stars.

Ganz counted the dark shapes out beyond the fire. Once again, there were twenty, despite the number the Wolves had killed. He swore softly. 'They will always return at full strength,' he whispered to Gruber. 'We will never wear them down. We cannot fight because they will overwhelm us. We cannot run because they will outstrip us. They are driven beings of the dark who will not stop until they have what they want.'

The foe stood beyond the flames, a ring of evil forms that circled the camp entirely. The sweet ashen smell was wretched.

'Then what do we do? Fight to the last? Die in the name of Ulric?' Gruber whispered.

'That… or deny them,' said Ganz. 'Perhaps this is the only chance for survival we have…'

He took the charm and stepped forward so that the dark riders could surely see him. Then, before they could react, he set it on a rock, and swung Lowenhertz's warhammer up and round in a powerful over-shoulder swing.

The riders screamed in horror with a single voice. The hammerhead crushed the talisman. There was a burst of light and a flash of green, eldritch flame. The blast knocked Ganz backwards and vaporised the head of the hammer.

The talisman was gone.

Red lightning, like electric blood, speared around the clearing horizontally, and there was a fierce hot wind. The wraith-like creatures shrieked as one, twisting, swirling in the air like flapping black rags until they were at last whisked up into the darkness of the night and were gone.

FOUR DAYS' GRUELLING drive brought them back to Middenheim. White Company escorted the Margrave's party right to the Graf's palace where they were to be cared for and tended. There were many partings now. As the Margrave effusively thanked Ganz time and again, Ganz found his eyes wandering the courtyard. He saw Drakken, sheepish and clumsy, kiss the feisty servant girl, Lenya, goodbye. Not for the last time, Ganz was sure. He saw Morgenstern and Anspach horseplaying with the children, and Aric consoling the frightened old woman Maris. And Gruber stood with the Lady Margrave.

'Forgive me, lady,' Gruber was saying softly. 'I mistrusted you, and that is my shame.'

'You saved my life, Sir Gruber. I'd say we're even.' She smiled and his heart winced again.

'If only you were younger and I was free,' she murmured, saying what he was thinking. Their eyes met, fierce for a second, then they both laughed aloud and said farewell.

IN THE GREAT darkness of the Temple, the Wolf Choirs were singing low, heartfelt hymns of thanks. The voices hung in the still, cool air.

Lowenhertz was knelt in prayer in front of the main altar. He looked up as he heard the footsteps come up behind him.

Ganz looked down at him. In his hands, he held an object wrapped in an old wolf pelt.

'The Panthers will be most aggrieved we stole their thunder,' Lowenhertz said as he rose.

Ganz nodded. 'They'll live. And to think we thought we were going to miss the action.'

There was a long pause. Ganz fixed him with a gaze. 'I suppose you'll be transferring again now.'

Lowenhertz shrugged. 'Not if you'll let me stay, commander. I have looked for my place for a long time. Perhaps it is here in this company of Wolves.'

'Then welcome to White Company, warrior,' Ganz said. 'I will be proud to have you in my command.'

'I must see the priest-armourers,' Lowenhertz said. 'I need a new hammer consecrated.'

Ganz held out the pelt bundle. 'No need. Ar-Ulric himself allowed me to take this from the Temple reliquary.'

The old warhammer in the pelt was magnificent and covered in a patina of age and use. 'It belonged to a Wolf called von Glick. One of the bravest, a fellow and a friend, sorely missed. It would please him for his hammer to be carried by a Wolf again, rather than tarnish in an old relic chest.'

Lowenhertz took the venerable weapon and tested its weight and balance. 'It will be an honour,' he said.

Around them, the song of the Wolf Choir rose up and soared, out of the great temple and beyond into the skies above Middenheim like smoke.

THE BRETONNIAN CONNECTION

IT WAS ONE of the workmen who told us, running over from the charred shell of the Temple of Morr where he had been working. The news must have been all over Middenheim by the time we heard it, retold from marketplace to coffee house, from inn to slum, shouted from window to window high above the twisted streets and steep alleys. It would be on everyone's lips by now. We stopped digging, rested on our spades and pickaxes, and stood in the half-finished grave as we contemplated what we had learned. It was the start of a spring day in the City of the White Wolf, and death was in the air.

Spring comes late to Middenheim. The ground in Morrspark stays frozen for months. Digging graves is hard and we welcomed the rest, although there would be more work soon. Countess Sophia of Altdorf, courtier and Imperial Plenipotentate to the Graf of Middenheim, former wife of the Dauphin of Bretonnia, beauty, socialite, diplomat, patroness of orphans and the diseased, had been murdered in her bed. We felt more than sorrow at the death. We were priests of Morr, God of Death. This would be a busy week for us.

We looked at each other, placed our tools on the ground and walked through the gravestones towards the Temple of Morr where it stood at the centre of the park, swathed in scaffolding as if wrapped in bandages and splints. There were people crossing the park, hundreds of them in ones and twos, heading towards it as well. Some of them were crying.

THE RECENT FIRE had burned the temple almost to the ground, but the underground Factorum and the catacombs, where the wealthy dead rested, were intact and in use. All of Morr's priests in Middenheim – four of us, plus one from the Temple of Shallya assisting while the priests who had died in the fire were replaced – gathered in the Factorum, the ritual room where the dead are prepared for burial, cremation or the long drop off the Cliff of Sighs to the rocks far below. Corpses lay on two of the granite slabs and the doorway to the burial vaults stood, black and forbidding, like the mouth of the underworld. The room was filled with the smells of death, embalming oils and tension.

Father Ralf came slowly down the steps into the Factorum, clearing his throat noisily. The High Priest's chain of office hung heavily around his neck, and he fingered it as he looked at us. Approaching sixty and with bad arthritis, he had never expected to rise as high as this job and didn't particularly welcome it, but there had been nobody else. All the other priests were too young, too inexperienced, or me. He didn't like me. That was fine: nobody liked me. Many days, I didn't like myself either.

'I'll keep this short,' he started. 'I'm sure we're all shocked by the death of Countess Sophia. But the job of the Temple is to provide moral and spiritual reassurance at a time like this. We must be strong, and be seen to be strong.' He broke off for a fit of coughing, then resumed: 'I myself will see to the late Countess's funeral arrangements. Pieter, Wolmar and Olaf, you stay in the temple. There will be many mourners, and they will need your presence and counsel. The rest of you will attend to normal business.'

'The rest of us,' I said, 'is two of us.' I gestured at myself and Brother Jakob. 'And the Countess's murder won't stop ordinary people from dying.'

Father Ralf glowered at me with his rheumy eyes. 'These are exceptional times, brother. If you had not burned down the temple, then perhaps your workload would be lighter.'

I thought about reminding him that I'd burnt it down partly to save his life, but it wasn't a good idea. Not today, not with this mood in the air. Ralf might be inexperienced at running things, but he was keen to make his authority felt, and prone to over-react. Best to let it go. 'So,' I asked, 'should Brother Jakob and I return to grave-digging, or is there more pressing business for us?'

'Jakob will finish the grave. As for you, a flophouse in the Altquartier, Sargant's, has sent word that a drunk beggar has died there. You seem to have a fondness for such people: deal with the body. And brother, don't make a mountain out of it. We have more important things to worry about.'

I waited while the others left, filing up the stairs into the daylight and the crowd of mourners outside. Jakob hung back as well. I felt sorry for him. He'd only been at the temple a few months, and the upheavals which had followed the death of Father Zimmerman had unnerved him. Now there was something really big happening, and instead of being allowed to help he had been sent to dig graves.

'Why us?' he asked, and there was bitterness in his voice.

'Because you're young and I'm not liked, and neither of us would do a good job of comforting the mourners,' I said. 'You'd best get on with that grave while the sun's thawing the ground.'

He looked at me with curiosity in his eyes. 'What did Father Ralf mean when he said you had a fondness for beggars?'

'Go and dig,' I said.

I THOUGHT ABOUT Jakob's question as I walked through the ancient city's winding streets to the Altquartier. Was it beggars I cared about? No. But anyone who died alone and unmourned, whose death nobody cared about: those were my people. Somebody should care for them, and if no one was willing to do it before they died, then I would do it afterwards. People often showed their best side in death, losing their unappealing habits, becoming calm and serene. It was much easier not to hate them in that state; and besides, it was my job. If that job sometimes brought me unexplained deaths, then I regarded it as my duty to find out what I could about them. Besides, as I told my few friends, it passed the time.

The town was awash with news and gossip about the death of the Countess. People saw my robes and stopped me in the street to pour out their grief, and it seemed that everyone had something to say: some testament to her goodness, some anecdote about her legendary love-affairs, or just sobs and moans. I noticed that it was only the humans who seemed to be so carried away. The elves, dwarfs and halflings seemed to be more reserved, but they have always been few in Middenheim. The marketplaces were still busy but the street-entertainers were absent: no jugglers, no dwarf wrestlers, no illusionists making bursts of pretty lights with their petty magics. The city was more alive than at any time since the last carnival, but its life was strangely subdued.

All the talk on the streets was of the killing: was it murder or assassination – and if the latter, who was to blame? Most of the people with theories seemed to believe the Bretonnians were behind it somehow. The Countess's death would not only allow the Dauphin to remarry, but she was still well-loved in her own country. Tensions had been high between the Empire and Bretonnia for the last few months, and there are few better ways to spur an invading army than the murder of a national treasure, particularly one in a foreign country who might be embarrassing if left alive. Other theories blamed beastmen, probably remembering a few months back to when the Templar's Arms was attacked by mutants, or mythical skaven creeping up from the long-abandoned tunnels under the city. I heard all these ideas and more, and I let them wash over me like spring rain over the city's granite walls. It was just a death, no more important to me than any other.

The twisting streets narrowed and became darker, lost in shadows from the high buildings, as I entered the Altquartier. Buildings come and go here but its slum-like feel never changes. Sargant's flophouse was a new name to me but looking at its exterior, a former merchant's warehouse off a typically steep Middenheim alley, I knew what it would be like inside: infested with lice, fleas and vermin, with straw mattresses on the bare floors of long dormitories, and the smell of boiled cabbage, dirt and desperation. Like every other flophouse in the city, it stank of wretchedness. Shapeless men in rags, some with crutches or terrible scars, stood outside and passed a skin of cheap wine between them. As I approached the door they moved aside, respectful of the robes of a Morr worshipper. Even those with nothing to live for are still afraid of death.

A big, bald man, muscle gone mostly to fat, was waiting just inside. His clothes were mock-opulent, cheap copies of the latest fashions, and he wore a short, business-like knife on his belt. I didn't expect him to be worried by my appearance, and I was right.

'You're Sargant,' I said.

He didn't move, but stared at me for a long moment.

'Didn't you used to be Dieter Brossmann?' he said, an edge to his voice. I met his gaze.

'That was my name a long time ago,' I said slowly. 'For eight years I have been a humble priest of Morr. Now, the body.'

'Aye. Follow me then.'

I accompanied him down dark corridors, hoping he would ask no further questions about the man I had once been, and waited as he unlocked a thin pine door. The room beyond was small and windowless, and Sargant didn't follow me in. I saw a bed with a body on it, and one chair nearby. A small oil lamp stood on it, illuminating the face of the corpse.

It was Reinhold. Morr take me, but it was Reinhold! He looked old and worn and tired and dirty, but he hadn't changed so much from ten years ago, when I ran the largest family firm in Middenheim and he was my eyes and ears. Little Reinhold, who knew every watchman and warehouse guard in the city, who could pick any lock in half a minute, and who even knew at least a part of the ancient dwarf tunnels under the city. Reinhold, who had taught me so much. What had brought him to this end, I wondered, and then thought, I did. Partly, at least, when I closed down the firm and became a priest.

But there would be time for such thoughts later. I had a job to do. Grateful that Sargant had left me alone, and guessing that he couldn't have known the link between Reinhold and my former self, I placed my fingers on the body's forehead – the skin felt greasy and cold – and began to chant the Blessing of Protection, to seal it against the influence of the dark forces that prey on corpses. Reinhold's soul was already with Morr and beyond my help. I'd light a candle for him when I returned to the Temple.

In the candlelight, Reinhold's face looked old and solid, as if carved from the pine-wood of the Drakwald. I moved my fingers slowly over his face and downwards as I intoned the ancient words of the prayer. I reached his throat – and stopped. There was a mark, an indentation about the size of a gold crown, pressed deep into the flesh around his Adam's apple.

I'd heard of this trick. You wrap a coin or a stone in a piece of cloth. Then you loop it around your victim's throat and pull hard. The coin cuts off the windpipe – or the main vein, I was never sure which – and death comes a little quieter and less obvious. Reinhold had been murdered.

His pockets. Sargant would almost certainly have been through them, but there might still be something there that could tell me a little. Reinhold's clothes had the hard, clammy feel of grease, dirt and sweat that comes from being worn day after day for months, and with a smell to match, and I felt unclean handling them. More than that, it felt like I was invading my dead friend's privacy. But that didn't stop me.

A handkerchief, filthy. A grubby copy of a small Sigmarite prayer-book. Five bent strands of wire, which I recognised as improvised lock-picks. Bits of gravel. No money. The right pocket was even clammier than the left one, and contained only a small clasp-knife, very blunt and rusty. I pulled out the blade, and was not too surprised to see it had reasonably fresh blood on it. That was the Reinhold I'd known.

I sat in the semi-darkness and thought for a moment, then resumed the Blessing of Protection. There was little I could do for Reinhold now. Part of me knew that Reinhold's last journey was destined to be the long drop off the Cliff of Sighs, the pauper's exit from life and the city, but that was inevitable. He had no family vault under the Temple, nor the money to pay for a grave-site in Morrspark where the more wealthy dead already lay four, sometimes five deep. The best I could do for him was to find out why he had died. I wasn't looking for revenge: that's not what being a priest of Morr is about. It would be enough to find out the reason.

As I finished the blessing the door opened and Sargant came in. 'Done?' he asked.

'Almost.' I stood up and moved to the door, heading back towards the street. No point in letting him know what I knew. 'I'll send a cart for the body. Did he die in that room?'

'Aye. Most nights he was in the dormitory wi' others, but last night he came up late with money and asked for a room for hisself. He smelled of drink and he had sausage and a skin of wine for his friend. They drank past eleven bells, then he went asleep. This morning, there he was, stiff as a board. "Eat, drink an' be merry," he said t'me yestiddy, "for tomorrer we die." An' he were right.'

I stared at him. Did Reinhold know he was going to die – that someone was planning to kill him? And if so, why did he go quietly to it instead of fighting? Had life on the street really ground him down so far that he wouldn't even defend himself against assassination? Or was there another reason? I needed to know more about Reinhold's recent life, and I knew I wouldn't get the information from Sargant.

'This friend of Reinhold's,' I asked. 'Can you give me a name?'

'Louise,' he said. 'Little Bretonnian rat, she is. Here most evenings. They were courtin'. Wanted to spend last night together, but I won't be havin' that kind o' behaviour, not in my house.'

No, of course not. You'd take money from people with nothing for a night's shelter in this squalor, but you'll forbid them anything that might give them a moment's comfort, even something as little as the warmth of another person's care. I knew too many men like Sargant: Middenheim was full of them. We were almost back at the flophouse's front door when I noticed something that surprised me. 'You're wearing a black armband,' I said. 'Are you in mourning?'

The big man looked down at his arm, as if momentarily surprised. 'Aye,' he said.

'For Reinhold?' I asked.

He stared back at me. 'Not that old drunk,' he sneered. 'The Countess.'

He turned and was gone, back into the sordid darkness of his domain. I watched him go, then looked over at the group of beggars who still stood around the door. One of them glanced up at me and I caught his eye. He twitched like a mouse trapped by an owl. 'Don't run away,' I said. 'I'm looking for Louise.'

IT TOOK A couple of coins and two hours of being guided through the city's many back-alleys to cheap inns and beggars' hideaways in old cisterns and abandoned cellars, but eventually we found her: a bag of rags and bones huddled near a brazier down near the watch-post beside the ruins of the South Gate. She looked up as we approached, recognising my guide. Her face was bloody and bruised. I crouched down in front of her.

'Who did this to you?' I asked.

'Men.' The word sounded thick and blurred, although whether it was from her Bretonnian accent or her torn lip was hard to say. I realised I had no idea how old she was – twenty, thirty, fifty even. Street people age fast, and rain, frost and cheap wine hadn't been kind to her.

'What men?'

'Men who hear my voice, who say I am spy, I kill the Countess. Stupid men, Lady take them!' she said. 'Who are you to ask such things?'

She gazed at me with grey eyes, and I remembered another woman. But she had been blonde, and her face had been filled with life and joy. Filomena had been her name and I had loved her... and not seen her for eight years. There was a silence. I remembered Louise had asked me a question.

'I was a friend of Reinhold,' I said and she turned away, her shoulders hunched. I didn't move to comfort her: she had so little left in her life, I felt I should let her keep her grief. At least I didn't have to tell her the news. After a long minute she turned back to me, tears streaking the filth on her face.

'You are priest, you bury him, yes?' she said.

'I will attend to him in death.' The reply seemed to satisfy her. 'Louise... was there anyone who hated Reinhold?'

'Hated?' She looked blank. I tried another tack.

'What did Reinhold do yesterday? Was he working?'

Louise wiped her face on a filthy sleeve. 'Didn't get work. He went looking but didn't get.'

'So what did he do?'

'Morning, Wendenbahn for begging.' I nodded: the street was popular with merchants, who gave charity to beggars for luck. 'Came back at two bells, scared.'

'Scared?'

'Saw a man. Reiner said man looked for him. No friend. Then he take his… he go out again and he…. He come back late,' she finished lamely. No, that wasn't it. She was hiding something from me, something important, because she was nervous of me. I knew how to deal with that: move to a safe subject, build up her confidence, and come back to the secret later.

'Louise,' I asked, 'do you know who this man was? Did Reinhold tell you anything about him?'

A long pause as she tried to remember. 'From the west. From Marienburg. From past days, Reiner said. Called him "Grubworm".'

Grubworm: Claus Grubheimer. I remembered. Strange, however much we try to escape our pasts, it's always there, waiting behind us to tap our shoulder or slip a blade into our back. Ten or eleven years ago, a fresh-faced merchant with an Empire name and a Bretonnian accent had arrived in Middenheim, bringing big ideas and a permit to trade herbs from Loren. While I shook his hand and talked to him of partnership and assistance, Reinhold had picked his locks, copied his paperwork and stolen his samples. Then we planted some Black Lotus on him and tipped off the Watch what he was trading. I'd had a five-crown bet with Reinhold that they'd have his head on a pole before he could flee the city. Reinhold had won, and that was the last time either of us had seen Grubheimer. Until yesterday.

But had Grubheimer killed Reinhold? And if he had, was he looking for me? And what about Yan the Norse and Three-Fingered Kaspar, who'd also worked for me then? I hadn't seen them in years. Perhaps they were dead too. Fingers of cold panic gripped my shoulders. Be calm, I told myself, be calm. And yet my old instincts, long buried under my life as a priest, were screaming that if Grubheimer was in town, it was for one reason: revenge. I needed time to think, but if Reinhold was already dead then time was the one thing I didn't have.

'I have to go back to the Temple,' I said and stood. Louise's eyes followed me.

'Money?' she asked, in her voice the only sound of hope I'd heard from her. I looked down at her pitiful form.

'Reinhold gave you nothing at all?' I asked. She said nothing, but her eyes broke away from mine. There was something she didn't want to tell me: that hidden detail again. It could wait. I turned away, to begin the walk back through the maze of cold streets filled with sorrowful people. Something in me was crystallising, hard and sharp. I knew I'd find out what it was in a moment.

'Wait! The Countess–' she said behind me.

'No. Don't talk to me about the Countess,' I said, and walked away.

The hard thing inside me was steely-cold with fear, and something else. I knew that if Grubheimer was back in the city, he was here to kill me: he might be a citizen of Marienburg but his blood was Bretonnian, and they were not a people to forgive their enemies. I had forgiven mine eight years ago, when I became a priest and tried to forget all of the many bad things I had done. I regretted none of those things, but when I joined the Temple of Morr I knew I would never do anything like that again. Now, eight years later, a priest would be an easy target for Grubheimer to kill.

Ever since my wife and child had disappeared, a part of me had wanted to die but it was a very small part, and as I passed through the narrow streets I could feel the hardness in me building, to fight against it. Grubheimer was a desperate man, a man who would garrotte a beggar in his bed for a ten year-old revenge. If the priest I now was was to survive this, then I would need to be hard. I would need to become once more the man I had left behind: to think about life in a way I had tried to forget for eight years. It was not an appealing prospect.

But even as I wondered about it, I felt the coldness in me swell and grow, filling me with dead emotions, covering the mind of the priest of Morr and replacing them with old thoughts, old behaviours. Was the life I had led for eight years really so easily overcome? Had the past I had fought so hard to bury really risen so close to the surface? And having let the wolf out from the cage, could I ever get it back in there again?

Part of me felt panicked and sick, but I looked down at my right hand. My fist was clenched; not in anger, I realised, but in resolution. And then I looked up at an alley I was passing, and I knew what needed to be done. I walked into the gloom I used to know well, knocked hard on the door of the Black Horse tavern, and entered.

Its decor had not improved. The noontime drinkers were fewer and more subdued than I remembered, and I didn't recognise the young man in the apron who moved towards me as I crossed the threshold. He opened his mouth.

'Stop,' I said. 'Is Grizzly Bruno here?'

He chewed his lip, which is what you'd do if you're new in your job and a priest comes into a hole like the Black Horse and asks for a man with a reputation like Grizzly Bruno's. But his eyes flicked to the ceiling. I thought they would; I'd been watching for it.

'He's upstairs,' I said.

'He's asleep.'

'No I'm not,' came a heavy voice and there was Bruno, as huge and bear-like as ever. We stood awkwardly, unsure of how to greet each other. Finally he said, 'Father,' and I, grateful to escape one of his hugs, said, 'Bruno.'

'Been a long time,' he said.

'It has.'

'I take it this isn't social.'

'It isn't.'

'Well, father,' and he put weight on the word. 'What business can I help you with on a day like today?'

'Bruno, do you remember a Bretonnian herb trader called Grubheimer? About ten years ago? Got himself chased out of town for smuggling Black Lotus?'

'Can't say I do, father. It's been a long time.' But he looked interested.

'Some associates of mine,' I said carefully, 'were not unacquainted with the bag of weed that the Watch found on him. Now he's back in town, and from what I hear he's not happy. *Very* not happy.'

'I thought you'd put things like that behind you. When your wife and boy went missing.'

There was a pause. It came from me. 'I did,' I said, 'but it looks like he didn't. And I do not care to be reminded of it.'

'So – what? You want him warned away? Out of the city? Dealt with?'

'I need to know where he's staying. That'll suffice for the time.'

'A shame,' Bruno said, 'but I'll get someone on it. Can I offer you a glass of brandy and the warmth of my hearth? I'd appreciate your advice on a piece of tricky business.'

'I'm sorry, Bruno,' I said. 'I don't do that any more.'

'But you still ask for favours from old friends. I understand.' I started to say something but he held up one slab-like hand. 'No. Today I forgive you. With such a big death in the city, Morr's people must have much to do.'

'All deaths are the same size,' I said. 'It's only the living who think different.'

He looked at me for a moment, then shrugged. 'Whatever you say. You're the priest. I'll send a messenger to the Temple if I hear of your Grubheimer.'

'Thanks, Bruno,' I said. 'And any time you or your boys need advice on death, you know where to find me.'

He chuckled. 'Maybe I'll do that. But when it comes to death we have more experience than you, I think.'

A recent memory filled my head: a man plunging down into blizzard-whipped snow from the Cliff of Sighs, his blood still warm on my hands. 'Oh,' I said, 'you might be surprised.'

THERE WAS NO need to bring Reinhold's body back to the Temple. A pauper's body should be flung from the Cliff of Sighs with the briefest of blessings. But however he might have died, Reinhold had lived as more than a pauper. Besides, with Father Ralf and the others occupied with the death of the Countess, nobody was going to notice, and preparing the body would give me time to think.

On my way back to the Temple, crossing from the hubbub of the streets into the relative solitude of the frozen Morrspark, I heard the sound of a spade ringing against the unyielding ground. Brother Jakob was still digging. He was standing in the grave, and the sight of him there sent an unexplained shiver down my back. I walked over, and he looked up, his face pale with cold.

'I don't suppose you're here to help,' he said bitterly.

'No, brother,' I said. 'I have other business.'

He put down the spade, rubbed his hands to get the blood back into them, and looked at me.

'You told me you're not liked around here, brother?' he asked.

'It's true enough,' I said.

'So why do you stay?'

I looked down at him. 'Why? Don't assume that "being hated" is the same as "hating", brother. I have devoted my life to Morr. I work in his temple, and I tolerate the pettiness of those whose dedication is less than my own.' I paused to stamp my feet; they were going numb. My words sounded hollow, even to me. 'But that's not what you meant to ask. You want to know why you should stay.'

He stared at me as if I had just told him his innermost secret. He paused. 'I hate it here.'

'I know.'

'I want to run away.'

'What do you want to do?'

'I want to be a knight, fight for the Empire, live and die a hero. But without my father's help I'd never get a rank or a command.'

Ah, his father, some minor noble with three sons in the army and the youngest sent into the priesthood to pray for them. 'Run away. Join a band of mercenaries,' I suggested.

He looked at me with disdain. 'There's no honour in that,' he said. 'And mostly they're Tilean too.' He spat on the cold earth.

'But it would be better than being a priest, eh?' I said. 'Life's what you make of it. If you do not make your own way, a way will be made for you. You must choose, brother, you must choose.'

He didn't reply. As I walked away I heard the ring of the shovel against the earth, striking out like a slowly tolling bell.

THE HALF-REBUILT TEMPLE was crowded with mourners, its normally quiet spaces filled with noise and jostling. Father Ralf's coffers would be doing well and he would be revelling in the attention which was being paid to him. The throng of people, normally obedient to one wearing the robes of Morr, seemed not to notice me and I had to shove my way between them as I made my way towards the entrance to the priests' quarters in the far wall, and my cell which lay beyond.

I didn't get there. A wailing woman tugged at my robe, begging for a blessing, and then a man in rich clothes wanted to know what the Countess's death augured for the spring rains, and I was trapped by the crowd, speaking words of comfort and saying short prayers for someone I didn't care for to people I hated. Then Father Ralf stood beside me, at my shoulder.

'Is the soul of our departed brother flying to Morr?' he asked, using the Temple's code to ask if I'd tipped the corpse from the Cliff of Sighs. I shook my head.

'Sadly, his passing was swift but not welcomed,' I said, meaning he was killed. Father Ralf looked exasperated.

'I sorrow. I must learn more of this. Be in the Factorum in five minutes.' He turned away to minister to the needs of some well-dressed goodwife. I left: I'd been heading to the Factorum anyway. The Watch would be bringing Reinhold's body there soon.

The Factorum was cold and smelled of death. I sat on one of the scrubbed marble slabs, thinking, waiting for the corpse, and trying to piece together what I knew. Reinhold had failed to find work yesterday, but he had come back with money all the same: money, and the news that Grubheimer was back in town. He returned late, got drunk, took a room alone, and there he was killed. Killed by an assassin, killed almost as if expecting it, almost as if he offered no resistance. Almost as if he felt he should die. That's a rare thought for Middenheimers, who cling as tenaciously to life as their ancient city clings to its rocky mountaintop.

Yet the more I thought about the way Reinhold had looked, the more I believed he had been prepared to die. He hadn't put up a fight. People reach that state for many reasons but desperation is not one of them: it may be a reason to take one's own life, but not to lie back quietly and let it be taken. Drugs, perhaps his wine was drugged? No; if they wanted Reinhold dead, they could have poisoned the wine. There was something more here. I'd seen it before: the sense of something completed, finished, over. A man who was determined to leave on a high note, so when people looked at his life they'd say, 'What did he accomplish? He accomplished this.'

But Reinhold had been a down-and-out, unable to find a day's work to pay for a night's lodging. The thought of imminent death can drive one to incredible ends, but only to escape it – not to welcome it. What had happened to him?

I knew I didn't have the secret of this yet but, looking at the facts, I thought I knew where it had to be hidden. I needed to find where Reinhold had got the money, and I needed to know whether he had got it before or after he saw Grubheimer in Wendenbahn. This wasn't some penny-pamphlet tale of intrigue: I was already certain that my friend had been killed by Grubheimer or someone hired by him. And I knew that meant Grubheimer would come after me. Possibly he wanted to kill my old associates first, working his way through what was left of my organisation, knowing that I'd know he was coming for me. That was good. It might give me some time.

There was a sharp knock at the door and Father Ralf entered without waiting for permission. He glared at me. I stood up, my knee-joints cracking.

'I told you to deal with this matter quickly,' he said, 'and you start a murder enquiry out of a flop-house stabbing.'

'It was more than that,' I said. 'I sense it. The dead man was a friend of mine.' My voice sounded false to me. It was my old self, Dieter, playing the role of a priest of Morr. It made me uneasy.

Father Ralf glared at me in exasperation. 'Friendship has no place in the life of a priest of Morr, brother. Besides, I did not think you cultivated friends.'

'He was a friend in my former life.'

No answer. Even Father Ralf knew of my past and my old reputation, and therefore what sort of man the deceased must have been. There was a long pause. Our breaths formed white mist, swirling in the cold lamp-lit air.

'Well,' he said, then stopped a moment. 'And another thing. I've learned you spent the afternoon walking around the city with beggars, refusing to listen to mourners who tried to speak to you. This is not behaviour becoming of a priest of our order, brother. It makes us look haughty at a time when we must be at our most open and approachable. Ar-Ulric himself mentioned the matter to me.'

I said nothing. I didn't remember ignoring anyone on the street but that didn't mean it hadn't happened. But I doubted that Ar-Ulric, the highest priest of Ulric in the whole Empire, had taken any interest in the matter. Father Ralf was trying to intimidate me and make himself look important at the same time. It might have worked if I cared about either him or Ar-Ulric. But I didn't.

'At six bells we are holding the mass ritual of mourning and remembrance for the Countess,' he continued, 'to be led by myself and Ar-Ulric. You will take part prominently because it is important that you are seen there. And you will be seen to weep for the Countess. Am I clear?'

'Yes, father,' I said plainly. Disagreeing would only have started an argument, and I needed to get rid of him so I could think. He seemed to want an argument anyway, but we were interrupted by another knock at the door. I opened it, and in a blast of cold air there was Schtutt.

'Help me get this dead bugger inside, father,' he said, gesturing to a lump lying on a cart behind him. 'I'd have brought one of the lads but everyone is over at the Nordgarten, minding the mourners at Countess Sophia's townhouse.' Then he noticed Father Ralf behind me and dropped into an embarrassed silence.

Ralf made for the door, turning back to me as he reached it. 'Six bells, brother. Do not be late,' he said, and left.

Together Schtutt and I lifted the body – the rigor mortis was wearing off and Reinhold felt like a sack of logs – and carried it down the steps, dumping it on one of the marble slabs. Schtutt was panting.

'I'm not as fit as I used to be in the old days, eh?' He wiped his brow. 'But none of us are. He certainly isn't.' He gestured at the body. He seemed to be in a mood to chat but I, aware of the passing of time and the presence of

Grubheimer somewhere in the city, wasn't. Still, a thought pricked me.

'Schtutt, do you remember a Marienburger named Grubheimer? Tall, greasy black hair, Bretonnian accent, got run out of the city for smuggling Black Lotus? About ten years back?'

'Can't say I do. But if he sounds Bretonnian he wants to watch out. The city's too hot for them at the moment, with the rumours about them killing the Countess and all. There've been two stabbed in brawls already, and another one fell from a high window and broke his neck.'

'Unfortunate,' I said nervously, feeling panicky and distracted. The notion struck me that if Grubheimer had learned which flop-house Reinhold was staying in, he must know by now that I had become a priest, and if I stayed around the Temple I would be an easy victim. I needed to move. 'But I should–'

'Though,' Schtutt said, warming to his theme, 'I've heard from the best authority that the Countess was not assassinated.'

'No?' I feigned interest.

'No. More like a robbery, they reckon. There's an old dwarf tunnel as comes out in the Countess's cellar. Nobody knew it was there, but the murderer got in that way. And a stack of her jewels was missing, including the Dauphin of Bretonnia's engagement ring. Money gone too. She must have come across the robber, and–'

So the dwarfs were likely to pick up the blame for the killing. They didn't do well in Middenheim. 'A tragedy, truly,' I said. 'We are all the poorer for her loss. Now, there is much I must do.'

'Aye. I'll be off.' He looked discomforted at having his chat cut short, but left anyway.

I sat on the cold slab next to Reinhold and stared down at the body of my friend. How did his death piece together? And why were my instincts telling me that it was important to work out why Reinhold had lain down to die, when there was a man in the city trying to kill me? When I had allowed myself to think like my old self once more, I had expected a surge of ruthlessness, of sudden thought and decisive action, but there had been none of that. Perhaps the thing I had feared, the part of me I had buried eight years ago when I joined Morr's temple, had lost its edge in time, as I had hoped. Perhaps I had succeeded in destroying my dark half. Perhaps that success would lead to my own destruction.

I still needed to know where Reinhold had got his money. If I was honest, other than running and hiding, I could think of nothing better to do. The old Dieter had never run or hidden, and I wasn't going to start now. I needed to talk to Louise again.

THE SUN HAD set by the time I left the Factorum and the wind had picked up. Down by South Gate it chilled my marrow and blew the embers of the guards' brazier into fierce redness. I gazed out over the long, twisting bridge, lit by torches, as it curved down from the cliff's edge to the ground hundreds of feet below. Workmen were still busy with ladders and ropes, lanterns and stone and mortar, toiling to repair the huge breach in the viaduct that the magics of the traitor-wizard Karl-Heinz Wasmeier had caused, as he fled from the city after the last carnival. It would take weeks more to finish the job.

Behind me, in the glow of the brazier, Louise finished the pie I had bought her with the appetite of a woman who has not eaten all day. Now she would be more inclined to talk. She knew I had been Reinhold's friend, but I would still be asking hard questions. Better to start with softer ones, to make it sound as if I cared.

'How did you come to Middenheim?' I asked. She glanced at me in that way that horses do if they're nervous and about to shy. I smiled at her, my face feeling odd at the unaccustomed gesture.

She said, 'Back home, in Bretonnia, I worked for a woman. She was with a noble, brought me here when that was... when she left him. She was wild, fierce, but much money. I serve for six years. Then she throw me in the street with nothing. For no reason.' She stopped. I had expected anger or rage, but she must have told this story so many times that its emotion had all drained away. Yet I could tell there was still deep, black pain, far below. But was there resentment? Hatred? I didn't know.

I looked at her for a moment while I groped for the right thing to say. Then it came to me, all of it, in a sudden rush like a spring flood, and I said, 'You're talking about the Countess! You said her name this afternoon. You were trying to tell me something.'

Louise didn't speak but her eyes said I was right.

'Louise, what are you afraid of?'

She said nothing.

'Did Reinhold give you something last night?'

She nodded, despite herself. Tears were beginning to streak her cheeks. With frightening speed, skeins of logic were weaving themselves together in my mind.

'Reinhold knew how much you hated the Countess, didn't he? And you're afraid that he had something to do with her death. You're scared, because you realise now that you don't really want her dead, and because you don't want to believe Reinhold could do something like that... and because if he did kill her, then people might think you're involved too.'

She shook her head. For a moment I was confused.

'Louise, do you mean that's not what you believe, or,' and the realisation hit me hard and sudden, 'or because it's what you know?'

She nodded, a little nod, her silent weeping unabated.

'Did he give you some jewellery last night?'

A tiny nod.

'And you recognised it.'

Another, tinier.

'Because it was the Countess's.'

She didn't need to nod. I already knew I had the truth. I took a deep breath. This wasn't going to be easy.

'Louise, you have to trust me. The jewellery was the Countess's, but Reinhold didn't get it from her. He stole it from the man who killed her – that Bretonnian he saw earlier that day.'

'The Grubworm,' she said in a small voice.

'Yes, Grubworm. And then Grubworm went to the flop-house and killed Reinhold to get it back, but he'd already given it to you.' I paused. She said nothing. I had no idea if she believed me. 'Louise, it is my duty as a priest of Morr to understand death. We commune with death, we speak to it. We live our lives surrounded by it, and we comprehend things about it that most people could never understand. We know who killed the Countess. He will be arrested soon. Reinhold had nothing to do with it.'

I paused to let my words sink in. She still said nothing, her head buried in her hands. The cold wind blew between us, the thin flames of the brazier warming nothing at all.

'But you must give me the jewellery,' I said.

At last she looked up and met my eye. A long moment passed, and then she scrabbled amongst her dirty rags, and I knew I had won. She held out a balled fist, and I reached out to receive what lay within. As I did, she grabbed my arm with her other hand, and held hard.

'I have your word for the truth?' she hissed.

'You have my solemn word as a priest of Morr,' I lied.

A jewelled ring fell into my hand: heavy, with the soft warmth that only solid gold has. I cradled it, thinking. I didn't know what I was going to do with it, but I knew that at least I now had the truth of yesterday evening in my grasp.

Because Reinhold *had* killed the Countess. He knew the old dwarf tunnels under the city better than anyone except a dwarf. He could pick the locks, there had been blood on his pocket-knife, and he'd given Louise that ring. More importantly, I'd known Reinhold for long enough to understand what he was capable of doing. He believed that the ends justified the means, and his means were ruthless. I'd never asked him to kill anyone, but he had killed while working for me, more than once.

So he'd seen Grubheimer in town. Maybe Grubheimer had spied him and threatened him. Or maybe Reinhold had simply heard that the man was back and asking dangerous questions. Anyway, he'd realised his days were numbered, and so he looked for a grand gesture, a last stab at posthumous fame, on which to die. And given that his lover had reason to hate her, what better than the murder of the beloved Countess Sophia?

He'd stolen some of her jewellery to make it look like a burglary, fenced most of it cheaply before the murder was discovered, drunk or gave away most of the money and used the rest to buy a squalid room for the night. He gave his girlfriend her ex-employer's famed engagement ring. Then he died. Maybe he died happy. I hoped there had been a tiny shred of contentment in his mind as Grubheimer's garrotte had throttled the life from him.

But Reinhold wasn't stupid. He knew – he must have known – that the jewellery he had stolen, fenced or given to Louise would be traced back to him, and his name would resound around the city: Reinhold the Knife, the man who killed Countess Sophia. A black legend, but for some people infamy is better than anonymity. Particularly if you're dead. I guessed – no, knew – that he had wanted that to be his epitaph.

Louise coughed, a long, racking cough, and I remembered where I was. There was still the business with Grubheimer to be concluded. The ring in my hand could come in useful, though at that moment I didn't know how.

'I must go,' I said, and turned away. Louise grabbed my arm again.

'One thing more,' she said. 'You say you Reinhold's friend, but he never mentioned priest. What friend were you, to let him live like this?'

I turned back slowly. 'When Reinhold knew me,' I said quietly, 'my name was Dieter Brossmann.'

Louise dropped my arm, staring wildly. She made a strange sound, half gasp, half scream.

'You!' she spat. 'You betrayed him! You let him sink in life, to the dregs! You – you are no friend! He should have killed you! You should die! You are evil! Evil! Give me my ring!' She made a lunge for me. *'Give me my ring!'*

Two Watchmen began to hurry towards us. A Bretonnian beggar-woman screaming at a priest – they would know who to arrest. I turned away, leaving them to it, and walked swiftly back up the steep streets towards Morrspark and the Temple.

HALF THE CITY must have been crowded into the park. It was full: nobles, knights and rich merchants jostled by shoemakers, peddlers and servants. They were all packed into the cold, dark expanse, lit by occasional torches on high poles. People were even standing on the graves to get a better view of the ceremony on the Temple's steps. And yet there was no sound from any of them. As I pushed my way through the silent masses I could hear Ar-Ulric's great voice booming out over the park, interspersed with the higher, weaker tones of Father Ralf. I didn't bother to listen to what they were saying. All that mattered was that I had missed the start. There would be trouble later. If I lived that long.

I shouldered my way between the gathered ranks, heading for the Temple and the small door at its rear. I needed to be alone, and to hide the Countess's ring, and my cell would be the best place for both. As Father Ralf and Ar-Ulric were on the steps at the front of the temple, the press was less great at the back and as I approached the door I could see it was ajar.

As I put my hand on the ornate handle, a voice behind me said, 'Dieter.'

I whirled around. There, a few paces away, was a figure I knew: medium height, greased hair greying at the temples, and a nose that spoke of aristocracy and brawling. He was larger these days, fatter or more heavily muscled. I didn't want to find out which. Instead I leapt through the door and slammed it behind me.

Grubheimer! Grubheimer was here. He had spoken to me. He had wanted me to see him. He hadn't tried to kill me. Which meant… which meant… he must have set a trap for me. And I had almost certainly jumped into it.

He had called me Dieter, and I had answered to that name for the first time in eight years. I did feel more like my old self now: calmer, more confident, more ruthless. And part of me, the priest, felt appalled and scared by that, but I ignored it. For now I had to be Dieter, or die.

I ran to my cell. It was pitifully obvious that someone had moved the thin mattress since I had been here. I lifted it, and underneath lay a small leather pouch. I pulled it open and stared at the fine grey dust inside. I didn't have to smell it to recognise it: Black Lotus powder. A foul substance. Fatal to its owners, in more ways than one. Grubheimer had put this here. He was framing me the way I'd framed him ten years ago.

Then I heard footsteps, fast and light, in the corridor. They stopped outside. I tucked the pouch in my robes, grabbed a chair as a weapon, and yanked the door open. In the corridor stood Brother Jakob.

'I saw you come in,' he said. 'Father Ralf is furious. I thought I'd better tell you.'

If he'd thought that might worry me, he was wrong. I moved forward, into the corridor, grasping him by the arm. 'There are bigger things in the air tonight. Come with me.' The implications of the Black Lotus were still flooding through my mind. Grubheimer must have known I'd find the drug. He must want me to be caught with it in person, and that meant he'd act as soon as he could. I had to dispose of the powder immediately. One hiding place came to mind and I acted without thinking of the consequences. Like Dieter.

'Take this for safekeeping,' I said, thrusting the pouch into Jakob's hands before he could protest.

'What is it?'

'Something many men would kill for. If you see trouble, stick close to me.'

I unbolted the door and we stepped outside. The massed mourners were singing the last verse of a funeral hymn, filling the world with the music of sorrow and regret. At any other time I would have been deeply moved by it, but right now it was a distraction. Almost dragging Jakob by the arm, I made my way around to the front of the Temple.

We didn't get far. A knot of Watch uniforms was moving roughly through the crowd towards us, carrying flaming torches to light their path. At their centre was Grubheimer. He pointed to me. 'This is the man,' he said. 'He is the one who offered to sell me Black Lotus this afternoon.'

'Officer, this man lies,' I said, not to Grubheimer but to the Watch Captain with him, a man I didn't know. 'I am nothing but a priest of Morr.' My voice sounded loud: the hymn had ended and from the front of the Temple Father Ralf was proclaiming a prayer. I knew its words well. The crowd around us were silent, their attention on us.

'Search him,' Grubheimer said, his voice gruff, his accent strong. 'A brown leather pouch.'

Jakob stared at me, suddenly trying to pull free of my grasp. I didn't let him go. And with a lurch I realised that I still had the Countess's ring in my closed hand. If they searched me, Grubheimer would have been more triumphant than he could possibly have dreamed.

'I have no such pouch,' I said. Jakob pulled harder. From the temple steps, I could hear Father Ralf nearing the end of the prayer to Morr.

'Maybe his catamite has it,' Grubheimer said. I drew myself up, aware of the aura my priestly robes would give me, and knowing how little they matched my terrified thoughts. And suddenly I remembered a cool, calm voice – not mine, not Dieter's, but Reinhold's – and I knew what to do.

'You accuse me of this crime,' I said slowly and with emphasis, 'because I know who you killed last night.' Grubheimer's face showed surprise, but not worry. I took a quick step forward. Before he could react I had dipped my hand into Grubheimer's waistcoat pocket and a moment later held up a heavy gold ring to the Watchmen's eyes. A simple sleight-of-hand. Reinhold had taught his friend Dieter how to do it, too many years ago.

'The Countess's engagement ring,' I said, measuring my voice carefully against the last words of Father Ralf's prayer. 'This is the assassin who killed her.'

The prayer ended. Silence spread across the park.

'This Bretonnian,' I proclaimed with a voice like the wrath of the gods, 'is the man who killed the Countess!'

Scared realisation broke across Grubheimer's face like a crack of thunder. There was a murmuring of voices. Hundreds of people had turned to look at us. How must it seem to them? Two priests, members of the Watch, and one accused man. Grubheimer knew he was caught: I saw it in his face. I grasped Brother Jakob's arm more tightly and watched as Grubheimer did what I'd expected: he panicked. But not the way I'd hoped. He didn't run. He pulled a knife and lunged at me.

Without thinking, I spun away, dragging Brother Jakob around in front of me as I went. His feet slipped on the cold, hard ground, and he screamed as he began to fall. Grubheimer's knife met his chest, slicing through the thin black robes. Blood sprayed across the crowd. I lost my balance and fell.

Someone shouted, 'Murderer!' and people began to run.

I hit the earth hard, smashing my nose against the frozen ground and knocking the wind out of myself. Grubheimer stood fixedly above me, staring down, knife in hand. He looked so startled. Something had emerged from his breast. It was six inches of sword-blade. Over the Bretonnian's shoulder, I could see the man who had stabbed him: tall, bearded, scarred. He seemed familiar. In an instant he had pulled out his sword and disappeared into the milling crowd. Grubheimer crumpled slowly to the ground like a puppet, and died there. He didn't take his eyes off me for a moment.

There was movement: people were milling about, and there were cries of terror and sorrow. A rush of noise, of whispered words, swept across the park. The solemnity of the service was broken and lost.

Beside me on the ground lay Jakob. With one hand he was trying to staunch the bleeding from the slash across his stomach, but he wasn't succeeding. The light in his eyes was fading but he stared at me as if to say: You did this.

I reached over to him and placed my hand on his breast, over his heart, and tried to think of some farewell that would make sense, to either of us. I felt his heartbeat flutter and cease, and I realised there was only one thing I could say. I knelt beside him, placed my other hand on his forehead, and began the Ritual of Final Parting, willing his soul into the arms of Morr.

That was the last touch. It was done. I was safe. Overwhelming relief and tiredness swept through me and I slumped, lying beside Jakob, my face level with his dead eyes. You, I thought: a life among the dead was no place for a man like you. You said you wanted to die a hero's death. Well, you did. The man who gave his life to stop the Countess's assassin from escaping. And perhaps you died happy.

I doubted it, but it didn't matter. What mattered was that I would be the person who attended to his corpse, and that would let me dispose of the Black Lotus.

I would need a story to explain how I had discovered Grubheimer's guilt and the ring, but that could wait. The people of Middenheim had their assassin. With the murderer revealed as a Bretonnian, the diplomatic crisis would get worse and there might even be a war, but if that happened it would be far away. Father Ralf would be furious I had spoiled his service of remembrance, but I would live with the consequences of that tomorrow.

And what of Louise? She had lost the man who made her grubby life worth living. And Reinhold: I had stolen his triumph, his posthumous glory, the infamy that would have kept his name alive long after his body had been devoured by worms, and I had given it to the man who killed him. But I had saved Louise from the knowledge that her lover had killed her mistress. Maybe that was a good thing. I didn't know, and I wasn't sure if I cared.

But it had worked. It had all come together. I had survived. Only one innocent had died. Reinhold was avenged. It felt good. I almost grinned.

A voice I recognised said, 'Father.' Above me, Grizzly Bruno offered me his hand, and I took it and climbed to my feet. Somehow I knew that his presence was no accident. People had gathered around us, pushing and shoving, trying to get a glimpse of the two bodies, and the Watch were attempting to keep order. The mood of mourning had been shattered; everyone was talking excitedly about the assassin. I could just hear Ar-Ulric's strident voice battling against the noise, but nobody was listening any more.

I turned to the man who had helped me. 'Thank you, Bruno.'

'More thanks than you know, father,' he said in a low voice. 'The man who stuck your Bretonnian? One of mine.'

'You had me followed?'

'And with good reason,' he smiled. 'You didn't notice?'

'No.' I forced a smile. 'The priestly life slows the instincts.'

'Not too much I hope, father. You owe me a favour, and I'd still appreciate your advice on that business I mentioned this afternoon. Right up your old street, it is.'

'My old street,' I repeated, a strange thoughtfulness in my voice. This afternoon I had wondered if I would be able to cage the wolf of my old memories and instincts once I had dealt with Grubworm. I had forgotten to ask myself if I would want to. I had forgotten how good victory tasted. I had forgotten so many things.

Bruno looked at me. 'How about it, father?'

I smiled and reached out to shake his hand.

'Call me Dieter,' I said.

MY BROTHER'S KEEPER

THEY COULD SMELL the city long before they could see it.

As that last day of their journey wore to a close, a pungent scent began to reach the caravan, carried on the cold, wet, spring air. A smell of industry: tanneries, blacksmithies, breweries, wood-fires, charcoal burners. A cloying combination of metal tang, ash, chimney-soot, and the sweetness of malting hops.

In the jolting confines of the staff carriage, Franckl oathed his distaste and emptied his insulted nostrils noisily into a lace kerchief. Curled in a corner seat, surrounded by piled strong boxes and chests that threatened to topple onto her, Lenya Dunst looked away in mild revulsion. Franckl was the Margrave's houseman, a fussy, prissy pustular wretch in his late forties, too in love with cross-gartered breeches and stiffly-laced doublets to realise they made him look like a bloated spatchcock ready for the griddle.

'That awful reek,' he moaned, wiping his pendulous nose on a corner of lace. 'What manner of place are these Wolves taking us to? Is this salvation? I think not!'

The other members of the Ganmark household crammed into the lurching carriage had no answer for him. The undercook was asleep and snoring wetly, the two chambermaids were pale and dumb with fear and fatigue, and the pot-boy had received too many claps to the back of his head from Franckl in his life to start conversing with him now. Maris, the old wetnurse, was lost in her own dreams. Or nightmares, perhaps. Since Commander Ganz had destroyed her trinket and saved them all, she had been distant and listless.

Lenya caught Franckl's eye.

'I thought a man as... worldly as you would have visited Middenheim before, Master Franckl,' she said sweetly.

Franckl harrumphed, and then realised that the lowly milkmaid was his only audience. He dabbed his nose. After all, she was a pretty little thing, almost comely in a wildcat sort of way.

'Oh, long ago, my pet, long ago... As a younger man, I journeyed far and wide, visiting many of the great cities in the Empire. Ah yes, the adventures I've had... Hmm. It's just that the sweet woodland airs of Linz had quite stolen the stench of Middenheim from my memories.'

'Indeed,' Lenya smiled.

Franckl leaned forward conspiratorially and smiled loathsomely into Lenya's face. He put a hand on her knee. It was still clutching the snorted-on kerchief.

'My dear young pet, I was quite forgetting that such a place would be new to one such as you, a lithe, healthy damsel reared in the free pastures of the country. Hmmm. It must be an overwhelming prospect.'

'I'm looking forward to it,' she said through a gritted smile.

'So young, so brave!'

So eager to get there! thought Lenya. Despite all she had been through, this was an opportunity she relished. To go to the city! To Middenheim! To move in high circles, to advance herself! As it was, she relished the stink Franckl made such a show of loathing. To Lenya, it smelled of nothing more wonderful than the future.

Franckl squeezed her knee.

'Now, you mustn't be afraid, my pet. Middenheim will be frightening to you. So many people, such a great wealth of experiences and... and odours. You must always remember, when it gets too much for you, that you have a stout and true friend to turn to. Are you afraid, Leanna?'

'That's Lenya, actually. No, I'm not.' She tensed her leg under his hand, so he could feel the tight, lean thigh muscles bulge and twist. 'Are you?'

He took his hand away sharply and looked for something else to do. He slapped the pot-boy's head for a start.

Lenya leaned over and pulled back the window drapes on the carriage to peer out. Rain fell outside. The distant perfume of Middenheim was stronger. The escorted caravan was just now clattering onto metalled cobbles from a dirt track. Lenya started back as a White Wolf cantered up alongside her carriage and glanced in at her. His smiling eyes found hers.

'Everything all right, milady?' the darkly handsome Wolf asked, majestic in his gold-edged plate mail and white pelt.

Lenya nodded. What was the Wolf's name? She hunted her memory. Anspach, that was it, Anspach.

'Everything is fine. Where are we?'

Anspach gestured ahead. 'We're just reaching the western viaduct into the city. Another half hour, and we'll be home.'

Lenya leaned out and looked down the cobbled pavement ahead. The long slow slope of the viaduct which led to Middenheim seemed to go on forever. The city itself was invisible in the drizzle.

The household carriage was one of the last in the now bedraggled caravan. The two smarter carriages ahead carried the Margrave and his family, followed by a series of four or five farm carts. A flatbed, carrying household essentials and covered in oilcloths, brought up the rear.

Franckl suddenly pushed past Lenya and stuck his head out to speak to the Wolf. Through the drizzle, he got his first glimpse of the city of Middenheim.

'By Sigmar!' he exclaimed as he caught sight of the vast rock for the first time. 'Look at it!' he cried. 'It's like a monster rising out of the ground!' Lenya and one of the chambermaids struggled to get a look too.

Lenya gasped despite herself. It was true. Middenheim was a huge, black monster. One she was dying to meet.

ON A CLEAR day, Middenheim could be seen from miles away, a great black monolith penetrating the sky. Now, in the thick wet of spring, they came upon it almost by surprise. The smell of the city grew stronger. The industrial odours mixed with those of people going about their business, thousands of people. Smells of food and clothes, house-dust and bodies came together in the air and drifted into every crevice of the wagon where Lenya sat with the houseman, the nurse and the rest of the staff.

As they advanced up the titanic western viaduct, the gloom melted away. With the clouds parting and a huge orange sun setting behind it, the Fauschlag stood stark and craggy against the gauzy sky. The jutting rock was indivisible from the great city that grew around its slopes and rose above it in a series of hard spikes and steeples.

As the convoy neared the city, traffic on the viaduct grew denser and the low rumble of the noisy city began to separate into a rich weave of individual voices. The caravan's progress was impeded by all manner of vehicles: hay-wains, wagons, trains of oxen, noble carriages, straggles of pilgrims, peddlers with handcarts, outrider messengers with miles to go, surly details of city militia. Motley clad people were leaving the city for their homes on the outskirts or entering it to ply their trade.

'Keep the caravan tight,' Ganz called to his men and they all moved a little closer in formation. He could see the increasing mass of people ahead. Some were no doubt trying to sneak in or out of the city, past the guards, for reasons of their own, and Ganz didn't want any trouble now. They edged round a milliner's heavily-laden wagon with a broken axle that was impeding the flow. Morgenstern and Aric rode smartly ahead to hold back the oncoming traffic so that the noble convoy could pass. Morgenstern cursed at a Sigmarite devotee who tried to interest him in a lead pilgrim's keepsake of his god. They pressed on, up the slow curve of the viaduct towards the snarling city above.

Lenya sat by the window of her carriage and gazed out in awe, breathing it all in. Even when they were forced to run close to the low wall of the viaduct to pass the broken cart, she did not flinch from the yawning drop below, the travertine supports of the ancient viaduct which reached away into the depths of the misty chasm. Franckl glimpsed the drop and fell back into his seat, looking green.

Lenya leaned out further to look ahead. Heavily-laden carts and oxen-rigs made slow progress cheek by jowl with grand vehicles and gilt landaus, urchins banging the wheels with sticks and running away, giggling at their own audacity.

The caravan managed to stay together as dusk fell and a heavy purple sky settled over Middenheim. There were no clouds, and the stars and the rising pair of moons made the forty foot high wood and stone keeps, either side of the city southgate, appear even grander than they would have by daylight.

'Well, we've arrived at last,' Franckl said. As he pointedly pulled closed the window curtain for the last time before entering the city, Lenya saw walls the height of four tall men and three times as thick as a guardsman's torso growing proudly out of the seamless rock face below. The rock had been hewn into a great city wall by hundreds of dwarf masons, but they had done more than tame the rock; they had given it hard lines and a form that only appeared to add strength and longevity to the stones.

Passing through the south gate, there was light once more, the light of thousands of braziers and lamps burning for the folk of Middenheim. A soft yellow glow to light their way and to keep them safe from the city's human parasites, who stalked the unwary to rob them of their possessions or their lives.

Lenya pulled the window drapes open again and pegged them up to let in the light. It let in noise too: the noise of thousands of people hawking their wares, screaming at each other or calling out at them from street corners. And all the smells that had collected and built during the last stage of the journey now came together in a wave that took Lenya's breath away and apparently scorched the hairs in the houseman's nostrils.

'Sigmar save me!' Franckl gasped. 'Too much, too, too much!'

Nothing like enough, thought Lenya.

She looked across at Maris. The wetnurse had almost stopped breathing altogether as she sat huddled in the corner of the wagon.

'I don't think I can bear the noise a minute longer,' she moaned.

'Or the stink,' Franckl added. 'Haven't these heathens heard of latrines?'

'You can't crap in a field when you live on a rock, so you'd better get used to it,' Lenya said, coarse and unsympathetic as she drank in the sights inside the city walls. The caravan was crawling now, thanks to the press of people around them. Lenya was stunned by the relentless grey stone of a myriad disparate buildings. 'This is what they've brought us to and there's no getting out of it now. But it must be nothing new to a travelled man like you, Master Franckl.'

Franckl fell glumly silent.

Others in the Ganmark convoy looked out in wonder. Most of White Company's charges were new to Middenheim. Some had never seen any city before, much less one so large or so grand. While the Wolves marched them steadily onwards and upwards past the Square of Martials and then the Konigsgarten on their way to the Middenplatz, the eyes of amazed passengers took in the awesome uniformity of barrack buildings and the Parade Square. This was the only truly flat land on the rock, used by the militia for drilling and military parades, but now it was empty, save for the central fountain spitting silvery water up from its heart.

Franckl was the first to catch sight of the Graf's palace itself, their destination.

'By all that's holy!' he exclaimed. 'Did you ever see such a place?'

'I thought you said you had?' Lenya snapped, pushing him aside to get a look.

Maris the wetnurse huddled tighter into her corner. Her hands over her abused ears and a wide kerchief folded and tied around the lower half of her face, she looked like a frightened bandit.

Lenya leaned out of her window to see a series of great stone buildings surrounded by tall, iron railings ending in spear tips, as much for security as for decoration. Beyond the railings, the private quarters were faced with beautiful carvings which softened their lines and bulk, while adding exquisite ornamentation. The tall, scrolled marble pillars made the Graf's home unique among the buildings of Middenheim. No dwarf hand had wrought such decoration. The pillars and facade of the inner palace were the work of legendary artisans, brought in from Tilea and Bretonnia, and sent away again richly rewarded for their efforts.

They passed in through the Great Gate and down the flags of the entrance drive into the yard of the Inner Palace. The caravan came to a halt. Lenya heard Ganz shouting out orders to dismount and stand attendance. She pushed open the carriage door and was down before the houseman could move. The palace yard was wide and cold. She gazed up at the buildings, quite the most beautiful structures she had ever seen, even in her dreams. Franckl almost fell out of the carriage behind her, slapping at the pot-boy's head and sending him after their luggage.

The undercook woke at last and climbed down. The chambermaids cowered together beside the horses. Maris took a long time to emerge.

Lenya saw the Wolf commander with the Margrave, shaking hands, her master effusive and excited. Nearby she saw handsome Anspach and the huge Wolf, Morgenstern, chasing the royal children in play around the yard, whooping and laughing. She saw the old warrior Gruber in quiet conversation with her lady. The tall young knight named Aric appeared behind her, taking Maris by the arm to look after her. Lenya turned again amid the activity, and found Drakken in front of her. He was smiling his sleepy, winning smile.

'I–' she began.

He kissed her.

'I'll look for you later, Krieg,' she finished.

He smiled again, then he was gone and the Wolves were departing under curt orders from their commander.

Pages and servants in pink silk livery were emerging from the palace to take in the Margrave's luggage. They were flanked by others who held torches and lamps. A tall, emaciated man in a regal, black, high-collared jacket and lace choker strode out to meet them all, pacing the ground with a silver-knobbed cane. He wore a white, ringletted and ribboned wig of the latest fashion and his skin was aristocratically powdered white.

'I am Breugal, chamberlain to the Graf,' he said in a strangled, haughty voice. 'Follow me and I will show you to your quarters.'

'Sir, I greet you!' Franckl started, striding forward, hand outstretched to take the chamberlain's. 'As one houseman to another, I rejoice in the welcome you–'

Breugal ignored the hand and turned aside. He jerked his silver-topped cane at his waiting pages. 'Get them inside! The night is chill and I have better things to do.'

The pages scurried forward, snatching up luggage. Franckl remained with his hand outstretched and untaken, amazed.

Lenya felt real sorrow for him then, sorrow and shame. Breugal strode away on clacking high heels, cane-end ticking rhythmically on the flags. Franckl and the undercook picked up their few personal belongings and followed a disdainful page into the palace.

'I shan't stay,' Lenya heard the wetnurse muttering to the Templar, Aric, as he escorted her inside.

Lenya followed them into an inner courtyard. She lifted her eyes to look at the buildings around the small cobbled space. They were shockingly spare, dank and plain compared to the great courtyard, but some of the windows were lit and Lenya could hear people moving around inside, looking out, invisible to her. As she got used to the sounds, she began to pick out voices.

'By Ulric, that old nursemaid won't last five minutes,' she heard a half-broken voice laugh. 'And the old houseman ain't fit for overmuch either,' it continued.

Lenya realised she was alone and began to walk across the courtyard to the open door.

'Look at the poor, lost, little milkmaid,' the voice came again, joined in laughter by another youthful cackle. 'We can share that one if you like… but I get first go!' Lenya picked up her ragged skirts and, scared now, hurried toward the safety of the archway and her travelling companions.

This was Middenheim. Palace life. Not what she had dreamed of. Not at all.

* * *

THE FIRST WEEK at the palace was tough enough, but Lenya knew it would get tougher. It was a friendless place. She seldom saw the other servants she had arrived with, and the palace staff treated her like horse flop. Less than horse flop. She found herself craving the company of Franckl or the pot-boy. At least they knew who she was. The palace staff, the haughty ladies, Chamberlain Breugal, even the lowliest of the low, like the grate sweepers and the spit-boy, treated her with utter contempt. And there was a particular page, a rat-arse called Spitz. Spitz was the page that she had heard slurring her when she arrived. She despised him, but he was not her only problem. Endlessly, she found herself lost in the bowels of the palace. No matter what, she still couldn't find her way around. For all its fancy stonework, the palace was a dark labyrinth.

The Margrave and his entourage had been invited, albeit briefly, into the staterooms the evening they arrived. Lenya had been impressed by how grand they were, but soon realised she was unlikely to see them again. The Margrave received little more than political charity from the Graf, and his entire household were second-class citizens taking up space. Their given rooms were damp, and many of them were dark and windowless. They were oddly shaped and unaccommodating and Lenya, who could scout her way successfully across any heavy woodland, still could not find her way from one dingy room to another without becoming hopelessly lost.

At the end of the first miserable week, Maris left. The wetnurse, who had spent the entire time locked away, refusing to eat or drink and virtually unable to perform her natural functions, just upped and left. With the house at Linz completely gone, the nurse still preferred to live in a barn rather than endure the horrors of city life a day longer. She wandered away out of the north gate one nightfall, her bag in her hand.

With the nurse gone, Lenya became the constant companion of Gudrun, the beautiful Lady Margrave, who plunged herself into self-imposed isolation in the palace and dragged Lenya with her. The lowliest servants of the palace saw fit to scold, abuse and beat Lenya for a week or two. But it wasn't long before she was fighting back.

It was mid-afternoon, although Lenya could hardly tell time in the windowless recesses of the palace. She had been sent on an errand to the main kitchen. Returning, cross and spiteful after a particularly prolonged tirade from the larder man, she felt a hand land squarely on her behind, causing her to drop the jug of warm water that she had been sent to beg. Loud laughter behind her made Lenya turn.

'You'll have to beg for another, now!' screeched the barely grown voice of the adolescent page who stood behind her. It was Spitz. He was short and wiry with thin hair, a pallid face and large teeth, and he'd been following Lenya around since he'd seen her standing alone in the courtyard on the night she had arrived. All he wanted from his wretched little life was to become the next Breugal. He was a loathsome creature, full of his own importance, and he took Lenya for an appealing, easy target. Most of the ladies of the house, even the serving women, were completely inaccessible to him, but this was one pretty girl who had no status and, better yet, no defences.

Leering at her, spittle spilling from the corners of his lips, Spitz pushed his hand hard against Lenya's thigh and squeezed.

'Take your filthy hand off me,' Lenya growled. 'Or take the beating of your life!'

Spitz laughed again. 'Who's going to defend your honour then, my little milking cow?' His other hand came to meet the front of her dress, low on her belly.

Lenya's arms came up and under the page's hands, thrusting them off her body. Then she took his greasy head between her hands and held it firmly, as he looked at her in shocked wonder.

'You want me?' Lenya asked sweetly and then pushed his head down as hard as she could. She folded the page in half, cupping her forearm under his neck and lifting him into a tight stranglehold. Then she thrust his head between her skirt knees, squeezing until his face went a greyish puce and he passed out. She let go, dropping him to the floor. She made a wiping motion with her hands and began to walk away.

She turned to the slumped body as the page began to come round, clutching his head.

'That's the last time *any* of you touches me,' she said.

THOSE FIRST WEEKS that Lenya spent at the palace felt like months. No, like an eternity. Lenya was not given to sentiment; she only knew that life in the country had been better than this, but she suspected that the city could be better than anything. Unfortunately, the Lady Margrave had decided that Middenheim was far too dangerous a place for any of her servants to explore unescorted, and with no friends in the palace and enough enemies among the staff to last her a lifetime, Lenya's opportunities for recreation were limited.

One afternoon, she stood with her elbows on the wall of a balcony, her hands under her chin, looking again at the view, as she remembered events of the last month and tried to put them behind her. From her vantage point Lenya could see clear across Middenheim. She could hear the buzz of a thousand voices, accented with the louder cries of a multitude of street traders. She could see down into the wider streets and avenues in the north of the city. South and east the streets became narrow in a tightly packed grey maze that she could never follow. In some places the roofs were so close together that all she could see was a narrow strip of darkness. She could only guess at what might happen in those dark, grimy, intimate places. She knew there were thieves and beggars and people of strange races, and she knew that her only hope of some kind of happiness was to escape into that city and become part of it.

Lenya had her back to the balcony door and did not hear the footsteps coming up behind her. She didn't know she had company until a pair of thick, solid hands came over her head to cover her eyes. With the shift in her light, Lenya swung round, one tight, hard fist jabbing into the silhouette of a face right behind her.

'Lenya! Ow!' Drakken cried. 'It's me.'

'Krieg! Gods, never surprise me!'

'Rest assured, I won't,' Drakken replied, wiping his bloodied nose against his sleeve. 'Jaws of Ulric, it was supposed to be a nice surprise.' He looked meekly down at the tiny, fearsome, tight little woman who sometimes cradled his heart and once or twice had bloodied his face.

'Call yourself a Wolf?' she snarled at him, watching his heart sink in his eyes. Then, hating herself for hurting him, she repented. 'I'm sorry, Krieg,' she said. 'It's just... I need to get out of here!'

'So let me take you for a walk in the Konigsgarten.'

The safety of the formal garden close to the palace was not quite what Lenya had in mind. She had taken numerous walks there with Drakken. He was a White Wolf, of course, and she had seen his bravery in battle. She wished he would be strong like that with her. Instead he was as strong as dishwater, as passionate as the well-laid, over-clipped, mossy pathways of the Konigsgarten. Oh yes, there were trees and grass and flowers, but they were forced to grow where few plants would choose to grow naturally. The rock yielded only lichens and tiny faded rock-plants. There was no soil. To Lenya, there was no nature in the garden, the plants were either forced or non-existent, and green was supplied by mosses rather than grass and twisted, stunted trees that could find nowhere to root and consequently grew only sparse dark leaves or brittle needles. There was as much spontaneity and liberty in those tight clumps of faded petals and blocks of spongy moss as there was in Lenya's life. And she hated it. She sighed.

'Not today,' she said. 'Go and wipe your nose – and stop being such a lap dog!'

Drakken turned away, hurt and puzzled.

Lenya listened to his footsteps retreating in the quiet. She looked out towards the uniform grey of the buildings of Middenheim, and then turned fast on her heels. Fearing he was gone, she called Drakken's name.

'Krieg? Krieg!' She could see him before she heard his footfall. 'You could take me out!' she said. The idea suddenly felt real to her and she smiled at him. 'Wolf Drakken,' she began again, 'would you do me the honour of escorting me into the city?'

Her smile made his heart tumble all over again. Nobody had ordered him not to take Lenya out of the palace and grounds, yet he knew that the Lady Margrave insisted Lenya be close at hand at all times.

'Lenya,' he began, hating himself for disappointing her. He could see it in her face now, a mixture of petulance and defiance and a kind of bravado. A face he could love, but feared he might never understand.

'Don't tell me,' she said. 'I know. The Lady Margrave *wouldn't approve.*'

That last she said in a haughty, crabby voice that, to herself at least, exactly mimicked her ladyship. 'Then I shall go alone!' she insisted, spinning on her heels and folding her arms. Lenya had developed the skill of flouncing by practising on her father. He had sired a series of strong, lively boys before producing his only, cherished daughter. She wondered if perhaps she'd gone too far with Drakken, given him the chance to see through her little tantrum. Drakken could at least get her out of the palace.

'All right,' Drakken said, quietly. Then, realising the opportunity to escort and protect and be alone with this wonderful girl, he brightened. 'Lenya, I'd be proud to escort you into the great city of Middenheim,' he said and her broad, bewitching smile quenched any last doubts he had as to the wisdom of the venture.

Drakken and Lenya left the palace grounds without incident. Those Panther guards who recognised the young Wolf of White Company acknowledged them with a nod; those who did not merely allowed the short, powerful man in uniform and his tiny companion to pass unmolested. Drakken was proud of Lenya and she of him, although their relationship caused constant comment amongst the staff at the palace and no small amount of envy in the unmarried women there.

Drakken decided he first wanted to show Lenya his spiritual home, the Temple of Ulric.

'I've had quite enough of grey rock buildings and cold, dead places,' Lenya complained. 'I want to see people! Life! Excitement! There must be somewhere in the city where people go for their leisure, away from the dark streets and grey houses. There must be life here somewhere.'

Drakken grabbed Lenya's hand in his great paw and hurried her away, south, down a steep avenue of grand houses. They were weaving in and out of the throngs of people that Lenya had been watching from above for the past month. This was more like it.

'So, where are you taking me?' Lenya asked.

'To the Black Pool, a famous landmark,' Drakken answered. 'And if we take this road, I can still show you the Temple.'

Lenya was not pleased. She did not want to see a temple at all and the Black Pool didn't sound very lively either, but Drakken had grasped her hand so tightly and seemed so excited that there was nothing left for her to say. As they hurried down the avenue, tripping up and down short flights of steps and around steep slopes, Lenya tried to look about her at the rich houses, and the merchants and gentlemen and women who were visiting them. For so long she had seen nothing of the city and now she was being whisked through it too fast for her to take any of it in.

They turned a corner. Ahead, she caught sight of a tall, slender building and wanted to ask what it was. Drakken said something she couldn't hear and bustled her onwards.

Enough, she thought. She picked up just enough speed to come level with Drakken and jabbed her foot in front of his, an old trick she'd developed for use on her brothers. The Wolf lunged forward, arms splaying, his feet feeling for the stone pavement. Two, three mid-air steps and he managed to level his head, which he felt sure would plunge into the slabs and knock him unconscious in an instant. He found his feet and straightened. Behind him, Lenya had her hand to her face, ready for horror or hilarity, depending on the outcome of her lover's trip. As he turned, red in the face, she giggled.

'Let's slow down before we have an accident, shall we?'

Grudgingly, Drakken began a slower guided tour. Lenya caught sight of a mass of people congregating behind the low wall across the street. She could hear snippets of conversation and the low buzz that signalled excitement.

'What's that?' she asked.

'The Great Park,' he replied.

'Can we get in there? I want to see.'

'There's no gate nearby. We'll follow the ring around.'

They went on, but Lenya glanced at the activity over the park wall at regular intervals. There were people here; maybe some of them would be her kind of people. She might even begin her search, the secret purpose she had kept from everyone. At the very least she could be herself. At the palace she was invisible to the gentry and despised by the servants.

Drakken led Lenya around the Garten Ring, towards the nearest park gate. He was happy enough to do this because the route naturally took them past the Temple of Ulric, his place of worship, and also, since it housed the barracks of the White Wolves, his home. He looked at the massive structure with proud eyes.

'What do you think?' he asked. She didn't answer. He looked round to find her striding on without him for an entrance to the park.

Drakken cursed. He was about to run after her when a voice called out from the Temple atrium. It was Ganz, his commander. Drakken was torn. He couldn't ignore his commander's summons, but Lenya was almost lost in the crowds of the Garten Ring already.

'Wait there!' he yelled to Lenya. 'I'll only be a moment! Wait!' He wasn't sure if she'd heard him. Ganz called him again.

LENYA WAS SO taken with the hubbub of the street-life, she didn't really concern herself with Drakken's absence He'd catch up, she thought. She hunted for an entrance to the park.

Following the Garten Ring, south, down more steep and winding paths, Lenya quickly found the west gate into the Great Park. The gate, swung open on its posts, was made of that same dark timber used everywhere in Middenheim, and the walls were cut from the same grey rock, but what beckoned from within seemed more alive than anything she'd ever seen.

Lenya raised her head slightly as she passed a soldier from the City Watch at the gate. Dressed, as she was, in borrowed finery, the lady-in-waiting's cast-offs that her mistress had insisted she wear, she had some vestige of confidence. But the country girl within her made Lenya certain she would have to endure some quizzing at the hands of this authority figure and she wanted to make herself look as important as possible. She had nothing to fear. The Watchman merely nodded a slight bow in her direction, before going about his business.

The Great Park wasn't a park at all. It was a labyrinth of paths which wound between a ragged collection of stalls; open carts with burners selling hot snacks, which smelled of rancid grease, and tall, narrow stands with racks of foodstuffs, old clothes and household goods. Loud men waved their arms, demonstrating wares that they sold suspiciously cheaply and in huge numbers.

Lenya was mesmerised. There were people everywhere: buyers, sellers, browsers, barterers, families, couples, household staff from noble homes on provisioning errands, urchins dashed between adult legs causing their own particular brand of chaos. Lenya forgot that she was alone and began to walk around, listening to snippets of conversation, examining the goods for sale and taking it all in. She had never seen so many people in one place, clad in so many styles of dress, nor heard so many different dialects. Ahead of her a noisy crowd was gathering around a narrow handcart. She could just see the top of the tousled straw-coloured head which belonged to the man standing on the cart.

'Miladies and gentlemen!' bawled the voice, sing-song. 'Don't just stand there gawping – put your hands in your pockets for this once-in-a-lifetime purchasing opportunity!' A pair of long arms flailed above the tousled head and Lenya saw a huge showman's grimace. The crowd laughed, heckled and some began to move away. Lenya smiled to herself, pushing in to get a better look.

She felt a movement behind her rather than heard it and was only mildly surprised when she felt the brush of a hand against the side of her waist. She'd been expecting lightfooted Drakken to catch up with her sooner or later, though she'd warned him not to surprise her. His mistake. She didn't think twice: she rammed her elbow hard behind her, following it with a straight forearm and balled fist. It wouldn't hurt Drakken, not a big tough Wolf in armour like him. But instead of connecting with the broad solid torso of the White Wolf, Lenya's elbow and then her fist connected with a soft, bony, unfamiliar target.

'Whhooff!' a small voice choked from behind her. Lenya heard a slight body fall heavily. The crowd around her fell silent and began to turn in the direction of the sound. Lenya felt a dozen pairs of eyes on her as she turned to look at what or whom she'd hit.

Sitting on the ground behind her, clutching at his stomach, legs splayed out to either side, was a gangly young man, tidily dressed with flat black hair and a wounded expression. He was all arms and legs and Lenya had to step over one protruding knee to take a good look at him.

'By all that's wise!' she exclaimed. 'What have I done?'

The crowd returned their gaze to the salesman, who'd begun his banter again, dismissing the sort of scene they saw every day in the city. The man on the ground looked quizzically at Lenya and then let out a huge, bellowing laugh.

'I'm terribly sorry, sir!' breathed a stunned Lenya, grasping the youth by the elbow and trying to help him to his feet. He laughed again.

'Don't worry,' he answered. 'Truth is, I was due a rousting anytime about now. Just caught me unawares that's all.' He clutched his stomach again as he tried to laugh through the ache that Lenya had planted there with her tight fist. His humour was infectious and Lenya began to laugh with him, not knowing what he was laughing at, but enjoying the freedom. She hadn't laughed properly out loud in weeks.

Back on his feet, the young man gently took Lenya's arm and led her to a narrow set of winding steps with tall walls either side. She felt no apprehension. When they were alone, he began to talk to her.

'So, what's a country girl like you doing walking around in city finery?'

'And what's a city boy like you doing grabbing at young ladies in public?'

'Touché,' the youth answered, bellowing his startling laugh once more.

The pair sat on the stone steps, aware only of each other and the hum of the crowd that spilled over the walls surrounding them. For the second time, an opportunistic young man had seen Lenya as an easy target. This time the man had been after her purse.

The gangly youth with the flat hair introduced himself as Arkady, petty villain, pick-pocket and general scammer. He had no reason not to be honest. He might not be quite what he seemed, but then neither was this milkmaid dressed in all the finery of court. He'd expected the rich purse of a dolt who wouldn't even notice it was missing until she tried to pay for something, and when she found her money gone would probably have a swooning fit. Instead he had got an elbow in the stomach and a fist in the solar plexus and serve him right.

Lenya found herself telling him about the farm near Linz where she'd been raised, about her brothers – and how she'd come to Middenheim. She spoke of the revolting page and the dark damp rooms she was forced to live in. She talked of the palace, but not how she had come to be at liberty in the Great Park. She was talking to a criminal after all and didn't want to confuse things by telling him about her White Wolf. She had another thing to talk about. Her secret.

'My brother came here,' she said, finally. 'It must have been a year ago now. Came to make his fortune. I never thought I'd reach Middenheim, but now I'm here, I want to find him.'

'In a city this size?' Arkady laughed again – then stopped abruptly, realising this wasn't funny to the naïve but feisty country girl. 'Look, if he came from the country,' he began, 'he's probably back in the country by now.'

'And if not?' Lenya asked.

Arkady looked at his scuffed shoes. He didn't want to hurt the girl, but she had to know the facts of life. 'If he's still here, he's probably joined one of the less... recognised guilds. One of the local lords of the underworld may have recruited him to "run errands".'

Lenya looked dismayed. 'He's honest! He'd find honest work first!'

Arkady snorted. 'There's no honest work in Middenheim for outsiders. The roads aren't paved with gold and the guilds have business tied up tighter than a houseman's codpiece. It's all nepotism and dead men's shoes. Why else do you think there's so much "free enterprise" in Middenheim? Yon market trader on his handcart – the mouthy sod with the straw hair – shunts carts in and out of the city every week. Most of them are hijacked somewhere on the other side of the wall...' Arkady's story tailed off.

'So my brother's a criminal?' asked an indignant Lenya.

Or *dead*, Arkady thought, but instead said, 'He's probably back in the country by now.'

Lenya thought for a moment, then took a deep breath. 'If he's here, I still want to find him,' she said, determined. 'Where do I find one of these "lords" to talk to? Someone has to know where he is.'

Arkady was doubtful. This girl hadn't been anywhere except the palace and this was her first visit to the streets. She knew nothing yet of the filth, squalor, and poverty, not to mention the ruthlessness of the people who populated the poorer quarters of the city. On the other hand, she had taken him out single-handed with her elbow and one puny fist when she shouldn't even have heard him.

'You're going to take me to one of these knowledgeable gentlemen!' she told him fiercely, seeing the reluctance in his open face.

'Whoa! No way! Look, there are better methods. I know someone, a rogue, but with a good heart. I'm small beans, girl... I don't have contact with any of the "Low Kings". Too dangerous for a sprat like me. But he does. He carries a little more weight. And you'll be safe with him. He'll look after you and he just might be able to find something out about that long-lost brother of yours.'

Arkady got ready to leave. 'Meet me here, day after tomorrow. Can you find this place again?'

'I think so,' Lenya answered. 'But can't you take me now?'

Arkady looked over the wall. The sky was darkening to its familiar purple hue and the Great Park was becoming quieter. He was safe enough, but Lenya wouldn't be safe for long in this place at this hour of the day.

'It's late. You might be missed. Go home, girl, straight home. Come and find me the day after tomorrow.' And with that he started to jog down the steps two at a time. In half a dozen steps he had turned a corner. Lenya watched the top of his head bobbing up and down above the height of the wall and in a few more seconds he was gone. She stood and looked around her. It was getting dark, but she could find her way back. Then she remembered Drakken.

'Sigmar! Krieg!' she exclaimed under her breath and hurried up the steps and around the wall. She'd just have to find her way back to his beloved temple and hope he was still there.

Night fell fast in Middenheim and by the time Lenya retraced her way to the great Temple of Ulric, it was dusk and the yellow evening lamps of the city were being lit. Cross at herself and at Drakken, she paced about outside the Temple for a few minutes and was ready to find her own way back to the palace when she realised just how difficult that might be.

Lenya was not known at the palace, not by anyone outside the Margrave's entourage or the domestic staff. If she tried to enter the palace grounds at any time, let alone at nightfall, she would receive short shrift from the guard. Her day's adventure was fast wearing thin. Now she realised she had to find Drakken if she was to return to the palace at all tonight. She had no very strong desire to go back to the foetid rooms she was required to call home, at least for now, but she also had no choice. Arkady had gone and she was alone in a city that, while it enthralled her, began to look sinister in the low meagre light. Silhouettes of buildings around her loomed black, hard and spiky against the sky. Pools of yellow light gave the grey stones a sickly colour. The stones seemed to absorb light, sucking it into their surfaces and draining it to small, murky pools. Shadows were long and forbidding and seemed to bear no relations to their owners. Darkness masked the uneven ground beneath Lenya's feet, making steps and slopes even more treacherous than they were by day.

Don't panic! Lenya told herself. *This is Drakken's home, he must be here. And if he isn't someone will be.*

Lenya was ready to knock on the great door of the Temple and even open it if needs be. She threw back her shoulders and lifted her fist. Putting what she hoped was a confident smile on her lips, she knocked on the door. There was no answer.

Lenya squared up to the door again and then jumped wholesale out of her skin when she heard the voice behind her.

'Can I help you, my lady?' asked the voice. A voice full of confidence and ease mixed with authority and power. Lenya turned slowly and stared at the man behind her, seeing only as high as his slender, powerful chest. She didn't need to answer.

'What are you doing out of the palace precinct?' Gruber asked as he recognised the brave farm girl from the Margrave's entourage. 'This won't do. I'll escort you back. If young Drakken knew you were missing, he'd be sending out a search party.'

Lenya lifted her eyes slowly to meet the concerned look of the veteran soldier. Drakken did know she was missing. He'd never take her out again. She wanted to cry with anger and frustration. She'd be locked up in the palace for good now.

* * *

BACK IN THE comparative safety of the palace, Lenya spent a day and night working out what to do. She thought about her next meeting with Arkady as she bathed in cold water from the dish on her bed-stand that grew mould overnight. She thought about it as she tended her pale, frightened mistress in the sloping, windowless room that she never left; and she thought about it as she ate the cold leftovers, congealed on grubby plates, that had become the chief part of her diet.

She was grateful that Drakken had decided to keep away. He wouldn't take her out again and she didn't want to hear about how worried he was and how concerned he had been for her safety. She could rely on herself and she wouldn't have anyone suggesting otherwise.

Gruber had treated her well and kindly. Returning her to the palace via one of the more discreet side-gates, he had stopped and spoken to men from the City Watch on duty there. He introduced her to them as a girl under the direct protection of the Temple. The sentries nodded solemnly. None of them wished to get on the wrong side of the White Wolves. Now there were several of the gate guards who would recognise her if she needed them to. If any of these men were on duty, she could get in or out of the palace grounds without any trouble. If not it was a short walk to the Temple and she guessed that if Gruber had recognised her so easily then others would too. She would never be short of a trusty escort back to the palace.

Two days later therefore, Lenya left the Graf's palace, walked south towards the Great Park and found again the entrance she had used before. It was around the same time of day and the place was thronged with people again. The rocky paths were slick with the light rain and when clumps of people diverted her path onto the mossy terraces, the dark, spongy surface was almost greasy underfoot. She kept her eye on the milling people, but they all had business of their own to attend to and ignored her. She was also wary of the rougher-looking element and even crossed one path and joined another to avoid a bawdily drunken clutch of youths ready to leer at anything in a skirt.

It took her two or three attempts to find the flight of narrow steps where she had sat with Arkady only days before, and when she did find them she stumbled upon them by accident. She sat three or four steps down from the top, out of sight. After half an hour or so, Lenya began to wonder if they were the right steps after all. Then, suddenly, she looked up sharply, without knowing why. She hadn't heard anything new above the hum of the crowd, but as she fixed her gaze she caught sight of a head with flat black hair and stood, sighing with relief, to greet Arkady.

He came within a few steps of her, keeping low so as not to be seen over the wall, and beckoned her to follow him. As the steps led downward, turning sharply left and right as they went, Lenya realised why they had not encountered anyone else on the staircase. As they dropped steeper and narrower, the walls rose higher around them, becoming a low arch that dripped slightly with the thick black liquid of rotting vegetation. The steps went from being damp to being dark and wet and covered in old, slippery moss. The hem of Lenya's dress became heavy with brackish water and her tall boots began to leak.

She stopped. 'Where are we going?' she asked, apprehensive for the first time. She was with a complete stranger. Trusting him with her life in a strange city and he seemed to be leading her underground into silence and darkness.

He caught the tone in her voice. 'Trust me,' he said, and laughed. 'Honestly, it's all right. See, no one uses the old stairs much anymore, but they're safe and they'll get us to where we want to be.'

She looked at him in the gloom. 'Soon,' he said. 'I promise.'

Within a matter of minutes, the steps came to an abrupt end and Lenya followed Arkady across a tiny closed courtyard where facing roofs almost touched overhead. From there, she entered the back room of what she thought must be a private home, but was, in fact, one of the many one-room drinking holes that littered the alleys of the south-east corner of Middenheim.

'Now!' Arkady exclaimed. 'What in all the gods' names are we going to do about that awful garb?'

Lenya looked down at her dress. She'd never liked it and she already knew she couldn't wear it and walk safely through this district of the city. She needed no more than her instincts to tell her that.

'Can you get me a pair of breeches and a knife?' she asked Arkady, tugging at her dress sleeves. He looked at her, puzzled, then handed her the short knife he kept in the back of his own breeches. She had not noticed it before.

'I'll be back with the other in a moment,' he said, turning and leaving the way they had come.

Lenya took the knife and cut the sleeves off her dress at the armhole, showing the plain sleeves of her shift underneath. Then she cut the bottom four inches from her skirt; they were sodden now and smelled of standing water. Tossing the cloth into the fire, along with her petticoats, Lenya had another idea. She poked the dwindling black log on the grate until it flared and spat ashes through the grill. She spread the ashes with a twisted shovel from the hearth and rubbed them into her hands. Then she massaged the soot into the bodice of her dress and began on the panels of her skirt. When Arkady returned she was well on her way to looking like a common woman. He held out the breeches to her.

Lenya turned her back and cut right through the front of her skirt, from a little below the waist right down to the hem. Then she cut several inches from the bottom of the breeches and put them on. She turned to Arkady and held her hands up in a dramatic gesture, waiting for his approval. He smiled and reached out to her hair, which he tousled mercilessly until it sat in a lopsided mass on her head, dripping down onto her brow and neck. He stepped back and bellowed his great laugh.

'Almost there,' he said. 'See, those milkmaid arms are a dead give away, but I think I've got just the thing.' Ducking out again, Arkady returned a moment later with a short, battered leather jerkin. It belonged to the pot-boy and Arkady had whipped it off the hook behind the door. He held it open for Lenya to shrug into. It fit well enough, and completed her reinvention. Lenya could pass anonymously through the darker streets of the city now, could pass for anyone or no one. She was ready to meet this rogue that Arkady was so proud of knowing.

KRUZA SAT HUNCHED over a pot of ale in the single public room of the seedy establishment that incongruously called itself a tavern. He was partial to a pot of ale, but this weak, rancid mixture was turning his stomach and he belched loudly as Arkady and Lenya entered through the pot-door behind the plank-and-barrel structure which served for a bar. Arkady laughed his trademark laugh and Kruza lifted his head without any movement in his sloping shoulders.

Seeing the small, comely girl in clothes that were coming apart along several promising seams, Kruza straightened up. He smartened the front of his jerkin self-consciously and smiled.

'I thought you were bringing some rough and tumble farm girl!' he murmured to Arkady. 'This creature doesn't look like she belongs anywhere near a cow.'

'Wait till she opens her mouth,' Arkady grinned and Lenya, gritting her teeth, kicked him hard in the shin. 'I guess I'll leave you to it then,' he said, winking at the girl before retreating out of the door behind him.

Lenya sat next to Kruza, searching his green eyes for anything that might help her understand why she felt so drawn to him. Something there made her a little afraid and then he smiled again and her body relaxed.

'Arkady tells me you're looking for someone,' Kruza began.

'My brother, Stefan. Older than me by two years. A little taller. Fair-haired. Eyes like mine. He left Linz for Middenheim a year ago. Arkady said he was probably working as an errand boy for one of the... what did he call them? Low Kings?'

'More likely dead,' said Kruza, looking down into the fuzzy ale that he was never going to drink. 'And if he isn't, there must be a thousand men in Middenheim who fit his description.'

'But there's only one Stefan!' Lenya exclaimed. 'If you won't help, then I'll find these Low Kings for myself.'

Kruza looked again at the girl. Arkady had told him how she had fought him off in the market, but she didn't look nearly as tough as she talked. And he was sure she didn't have the money to pay him for his services. He sighed.

'Very well,' he said, 'I'll help you. But we're not going to the Low Kings. The last thing you want to do is tangle with men like Bleyden. We begin with the priest.'

Lenya was ready to protest. What use was a priest to her? But Kruza had already taken her hand and before she knew where she was, they had left the tavern and begun to walk along the narrow, dim and filthy street. This, she guessed, was the Altquartier, the roughest, poorest, most depraved part of the city. Lenya had only seen it at a distance, from her balcony in the palace. The narrow, winding thoroughfares were full of bustling, dirty people. Women shrieked at barefoot urchins and threw their waste indiscriminately onto the streets. There was almost no light: the sky was a series of thin, grey, jagged stripes above her, largely blocked out by the low roofs of leaning buildings. Ragged dogs growled and barked and slunk away when kicked by the indolent men who sat on narrow steps on the street. There was no order here, only bad smells, bad light and too much noise. Lenya stayed close to Kruza, as they became invisible among the ragged people of the slums.

Lenya soon realised she couldn't remember where she had come from. Her sense of direction was utterly blind down here. This was the steepest part of Middenheim, with more twists and turns and more slopes and steps. Alleys seemed to end in front of her and then would shift in a new, unseen direction at the last minute. She felt like she was in a maze with no clear way out, yet she knew the palace lay only a few minutes' walk away.

They hurried through the rat-runs of the Old Quarter for several minutes before Kruza began to slow down. Then he came to a stop, leaning against a wall and putting his fingers to his lips, suggesting to Lenya that she follow suit, although she felt that this would only draw attention to them. The alleys and byways of this part of Middenheim were by no means deserted. Several seconds later and Lenya began to feel bored and fidgety, until she realised that there was something going on and began to listen to the voices beyond the wall.

'Hans, oh my poor Hans!' a woman wailed, obviously deeply distressed. A low voice, indistinct, some snuffles. Then, 'Don't touch him! Don't touch him!' The wail turned to a shriek.

The calm, low voice answered, seeming to cajole the fretful woman, but concentrate as she did, Lenya could not hear his words, only his soothing, monotone.

Kruza turned and beamed at Lenya. 'That's our man,' he said, satisfied, and Lenya began to peel her back off the mossy damp wall. But Kruza made no move, so she settled back impatiently against the wall. She watched for a sign from her guide. For the second time in one day, she was putting herself in the hands of a complete stranger.

Waiting, she looked about her, but the alleyway had drained of people. She watched fascinated as a rat worked its way through a miserable and spreading pile of detritus. Pickings were slim in these parts. They smashed bones for the marrow and then crushed the bones to thicken their soups. Here, people ate the whole fruit – pips, cores, skins and all – and the same with vegetables. And when people in this quarter ate meat, they ate the whole animal, saving blood for sausages and chewing the gristles and sinews until they were soft enough to swallow. The only waste here was human waste. The people here were ragged-looking creatures with missing hair and teeth. The scrawny, balding rat with only half its share of fangs reminded Lenya of the people. Feeling something between pathos and horror, she realised just how low the inhabitants of the Altquartier had been brought. Rats prospered everywhere – but here even the rats struggled to survive.

When the voices from the other side of the wall began to subside and people began to trickle back into the alleyway, Kruza made his move. Taking two steps he turned to look at Lenya and watched her for a moment watching the rat. Then he took her by the wrist and led her out into the tiny courtyard beyond the wall. A narrow handcart with an awkward wheel was being pulled out of the courtyard by two men dressed in drab, full-length cloth capes. A third man stood for a moment, as if in contemplation, and then followed. As the handcart swung hard round a corner Lenya saw its cargo roll and sway before a hand fell from beneath the old weatherproof skin that covered it. She tugged at Kruza's sleeve.

'There's a body on that cart!' she exclaimed in horror and surprise.

'We had to wait for it to leave,' Kruza explained 'before we could speak to the priest. He has work to do and a little respect for the dead is always welcome.' Lenya wanted to ask more questions. She did not understand what was going on and she didn't like it.

Kruza and Lenya followed the men for two or three more streets, by which time the cart with its gruesome cargo had pulled away from the man that Lenya had supposed to be the third member of the party. She was relieved to see the handcart disappear out of sight as Kruza stepped up to speak to the fellow.

The man turned, a benign, almost vacant look on his face. She didn't know what she had expected, but it was not the elderly, haggard gentleman that she now beheld.

'A word, sir, if we may,' Kruza started. 'My companion is looking for a relation in the city... We hope you won't be able to help us, but...'

'I hope so too,' the man answered in his calm tones. 'Come, we will sit and talk. If the news is bad it should not be given in the street.'

Lenya and Kruza followed the man, Lenya pulling Kruza a few steps behind.

'Who is he?' hissed Lenya. 'What bad news?'

'He is a priest of Morr,' Kruza answered. 'He deals with the dead of Middenheim and sometimes uncovers their secrets.'

'And if Stefan is not dead?' Lenya asked in a panicked whisper.

'If Stefan is not dead then the priest of Morr will not know him.' With that Kruza quickened his step to catch up with the priest as he entered a hostelry a few streets north of the courtyard where the man Hans had died.

Kruza had missed his afternoon pot of ale and gladly furnished himself and his companions with a rather better class of beverage than had been available so far that day.

'And what is your brother's name?' the priest asked as Kruza returned from the barrel.

'Stefan Dunst. He left the country over a year ago. I haven't heard of him since,' Lenya replied.

'I have attended no one of that name,' the priest answered. 'Describe him to me.'

'He was small for a man,' Lenya said, her voice shaking slightly. She cleared her throat. 'Short and slender, but strong. His skin and hair were very fair, his eyes were pale grey and large, like mine.'

'And perhaps they still are,' said the priest. 'I have not attended any soul of that description whose name I did not know.'

Lenya relaxed with relief. 'Are you sure?' she asked.

'Quite sure,' the priest said as he stood, and left without another word. His glass of ale stood untouched on the table.

'Well, that's that!' Kruza exclaimed, draining his glass of ale and smacking his lips. But Lenya was not going to be put off.

'Not quite,' she said. 'He's alive. Now all we have to do is find him. And I think you know what that means.'

Kruza knew exactly what it meant and he didn't like it. He was just like a great many petty thieves and con-men in the city, perhaps a little more successful than most, but really just the same. Kruza worked for someone. He took fewer orders than the bulk of the low-grade parasites that worked in the city, he wasn't quite the errand boy that most of them were. And he commanded at least some respect; after all, he was useful. But the bottom line was that Kruza had a boss. It went with the territory.

And that territory was his and not a safe place for a girl like Lenya.

'There's nothing more we can do today,' Kruza said as he looked at Lenya. 'It will be getting dark soon and you should get back to the palace.'

'But you said you'd help me!' Lenya yelped.

'I can help you again another day,' Kruza said, trying hard to put the girl off.

'No!' Lenya said, her tone urgent. 'Today!'

'Besides,' she changed her tack, 'I can't go back to the palace until I can find something decent to wear. You don't think I arrived in the Altquartier dressed like this, do you?'

Lenya found herself caught in a cleft stick again. The last time she had ventured into the city she had almost got herself locked out of the palace and this time the change in her appearance would exclude her for certain. Or, at the very least, someone would want to know why she looked so dreadful. What had happened to her? Who had attacked her? Questions that she was not ready to face today, or any other day for that matter. Ruining her clothes had seemed like a good idea at the time, the only sensible thing to do. Now Lenya was horrified at the prospect of returning to the palace in such a sorry state of dress.

'I'm perfectly attired for street life in this city, especially after dark,' she said. 'What better opportunity will I have to find my brother?'

Kruza wanted to laugh, partly because she was right, but more because she was standing with her feet apart and her hands on her hips, looking for all the world like a cross between a common tart and a female streetbrawler. Her tone was as demanding and petulant as a dissatisfied new bride's. Taken all in all, this particular picture of Lenya was too persuasive to deny. Kruza decided he would simply have to look after her.

'All right,' he said, 'we'll try. But, I make no promises and I know a fine seamstress, who will provide you with a new suit of clothes before the night is out. And when she does, you will return to the palace.'

Lenya grinned. 'Good!' she said. 'Let's get started.'

'Not yet,' Kruza said holding her arm and gently drawing her back into her seat. 'First we must eat and there are things you need to know about the people we will be meeting tonight.' Kruza waved at the woman who sat on a stool beside the barrel, smoking a clay pipe with a long stem. Lenya felt like she was being fobbed off, but she didn't mind. She suddenly realised how hungry she was.

The sullen woman, the pipe still hanging between her lips, brought them a meal of fatty, meatless chops, black bread and preserved cabbage. While they ate, Kruza talked about the Low Kings and, in particular, his own boss, although for now he remained nameless.

'The Low Kings are aptly named. The monarchs of the underworld, the absolute rulers of the streets. Some are the lowest of the low: users, parasites, loan sharks. They run all the organised crime in this city and almost all cut-purses, scammers and petty thieves owe some allegiance to the lords of the dark. And only a handful of these Low Kings run the city of Middenheim. The Graf thinks he runs the city, so do the guilds. But the men who run the real city, the men who control the streets, run the whores, traffic drugs, fund the gaming houses, are very few. They hide behind their thugs and streetwalkers, and use bumpkins and out of city runaways as cannon-fodder. They never get caught and anyone who works for them in any capacity is dispensable. Do you understand?'

Kruza looked at Lenya, noting her expression. *She's scared*, he thought. *Good!*

The Altquartier didn't look quite so awful in the semi-darkness that awaited Lenya and Kruza as they left the tavern. The pale yellow-grey light was incapable of picking up the worst details of street-life and the small braziers which stood on innumerable street corners dissipated some of the smells that gathered in the damp warmth of the daylight hours. The narrow alleys were still full of people, but they seemed less harried in the gloom. Or perhaps Lenya was simply getting used to the environment.

The two of them walked together, without hurry, down a series of streets and alleys, turning this way and that. Then Kruza stopped and turned to her.

'Do you know where you are?' he asked Lenya.

'No,' she said. 'This place is a worse labyrinth than the palace.'

Good, thought Kruza again. He didn't want her to be able to find her own way here if she should be dissatisfied with his efforts at finding her brother.

The dark was almost complete when Kruza led Lenya into the West Weg. Crowds of people were collecting and she could hear the beating of drums and raucous pipe music pounding through the air. Turning a corner, the crowds now gathering in force and laughing and screeching with anticipated pleasure, Lenya looked up for the first time, her mouth falling open in wonder.

The building in front of her stood out like a squat stone drum, squeezed between lopsided buildings, its belly spilling out into the street as though it were pushing outward from its jostling companions. Large braziers outside the building sent long, flickering shadows and tall bright flames up the sides of the building, giving the impression that it was throbbing. Above the cries of the crowds pushing to get into the building, Lenya could hear other sounds, like animals in cages being poked and tormented. Faint roars of frustration and fear rose to her ears.

Kruza was impatient to move on and drew Lenya away from the crowd as more people came up, pressing behind them.

'What is this place?' she asked, having to shout above the fast increasing volume of the crowds.

'This is the Baiting Pit,' Kruza said with a tone that sounded a little like disdain or maybe resignation.

'Why are we here?' Lenya asked.

'You wanted access to one of the Low Kings of Middenheim. The man who runs this place, and others like it, knows more about the criminal workings of Middenheim than any other man I know or have heard of. He should do: he's the greatest, most successful, perhaps I should say lowest of the Low Kings.'

The quality of Kruza's voice made Lenya anxious. She had been so sure that she wanted to meet this man, so sure that he could help her find Stefan. But Kruza was obviously afraid of him, and looked and sounded like he would rather be anywhere than here.

'I couldn't bring you here by daylight,' Kruza said carefully, 'Too dangerous with only the boss and his henchmen around. We're safer now with the crowds and noise. If anything happens to upset or disturb you, anything at all, get in among the crowd, sit out the show and then leave with them. And when you leave, find someone safe to stay near. A city guard even, if you have to.'

'If we have to go in there, why aren't we going in with the crowd?' Lenya asked.

'There's another way in. Bleyden runs this place, I know my way around.'

'Bleyden?' Lenya asked. 'How do you know him?

'I work for him,' Kruza answered, something like shame in his voice.

'The gods save us, Kruza, surely you couldn't work for such a man? You talk as if you despise him.'

'All who work for him despise him. All who owe him money despise him.

He is a man with a great deal of money and power and no friends.'

Lenya saw the narrowest of alleys between the Baiting Pit and its neighbour, closed off with a tall ironwork gate. Kruza looked around him and then, opening the gate a bare few inches he sidled in, taking Lenya with him. She almost tripped on a top step that she could not see in the gloom. She steadied herself by grabbing at the gate behind her, making it clang shut heavily. Kruza's head whipped round, his green eyes glaring at her through the dusty darkness, but no one seemed to have heard them.

'Come on!' he hissed.

TWO NIGHTS BEFORE, on the day of his walk into Middenheim with Lenya, Drakken had returned to his barrack dormitory very late. Morgenstern had laughed about the boy having a heavy date with his pretty country girlfriend.

'He's lost his virginity on the battlefield. Perhaps tonight's the night he'll lose it in a bed!' the veteran Wolf laughed, his voice thick with drink.

'Or against the wall of a palace courtyard,' Anspach cut in and they all laughed. Gruber sat on his cot, thinking about Lenya safely back in the castle and wondering just where young Drakken might actually be, when the man burst into the dormitory hot and cross.

Drakken threw off his pelt and the pieces of his armour, sat on his bed and put his head in his hands. Gruber crossed over to him, waving a discreet hand at the others to get on with their own business and leave Drakken alone.

As Gruber sat down next to Drakken the thickset young man dropped his hands to his lap and looked up.

'I lost her,' he said quietly. 'I lost Lenya in the city. I – I couldn't find her again. Ulric's teeth, Gruber; what will become of her alone in the city at night?'

'Don't take on, lad,' Gruber smiled a reassuring smile. 'I found her outside the temple hours ago, safe and sound. I took her back to the palace. She's probably been sleeping for hours by now.'

For one awful moment Gruber thought Drakken was going to hug him, the poor boy looked so relieved. But Drakken simply stood up and then abruptly sat again, anger and frustration showing clearly in his broad face.

After a good night's sleep, Drakken's anger had subsided and all he wanted was to make sure that Lenya was safe. He had almost decided to go to her, but he could already hear her telling him nothing was wrong and chiding him for wanting to control her. So he didn't visit his sweetheart.

Instead he watched her. Drakken spent the whole of that day monitoring Lenya's movements. To his relief, she didn't leave the palace at all. Perhaps she'd been frightened by her day in Middenheim and decided the palace was a much safer bet. Drakken doubted it.

On the afternoon of the next day, he followed Lenya when she slipped out into the city. He watched as she made her way around the Garten Ring and into the Great Park, and he stood back as she wove her way through the crowds there. He saw her disappear down the steps where she had arranged to meet Arkady for the second time.

Drakken was deeply puzzled that she should know about the steps – and very worried that she had used them. He didn't know that she had merely taken a seat and was waiting. Drakken hurried out of the Great Park. He would have to move fast if he was to get to the bottom of the steps and keep up with Lenya. They led directly to the Altquartier and his own route, on foot, was much more circuitous. Less than ten minutes later, Drakken was hiding, panting, in the shadows of a tiny courtyard at the bottom of the Great Park steps. He was sure he had missed Lenya, but he didn't know what else to do except wait.

Half an hour later, Drakken was trying to formulate a new plan when he heard footfalls on the steps and plunged himself silently back into the shadows. A stab of jealousy lurched through him as he saw Lenya with Arkady, crossing the courtyard in front of him. What was his girl doing with this young cut-purse?

Drakken was there too when Lenya met the priest of Morr. He spoke to the priest himself after he had left Lenya and a second unknown cut-purse in the tavern. Drakken couldn't fathom what was going on. There had been two strange men, the priest of Morr and, to top it all, Lenya had done something awful to her dress. What the priest of Morr told the young Wolf made no sense to him either. Lenya had never mentioned any lost brother.

Now Drakken stood outside the Baiting Pit of the West Weg, wondering why anyone would bring Lenya to such a place, when he heard the clang of the side gate closing. He watched, only feet away, as Lenya and the unknown man descended the steps into the bowels of the Pit. Drakken had a terrible feeling of foreboding. He knew at once that he would have to save Lenya. He just wasn't sure from what.

'YOU CAN'T COME in here!' a blunt voice came out of the shadows and noise as Lenya and Kruza crossed the threshold at the bottom of the steps. 'We're closed!'

Lenya didn't like the sound of the voice that seemed to force itself out past a mouthful of food. She didn't like the smell of frightened animals and adrenaline-choked sweat which filled the air.

'Kled?' Kruza called out as the dwarf appeared. Lenya had never seen his like before. He was as broad as he was tall and heavy, hard muscle stood out on his thick torso and short neck. He was naked above the waist and hairless. His short, solid hand made a fist around something that he was tearing lumps from with his sparse and irregular teeth.

'Kruza!' Kled the dwarf exclaimed. 'We're closed! It's not your day.' Then the short man, who oddly reminded Lenya of a cruel parody of Drakken, looked past Kruza and grinned broadly, showing the contents of his mouth.

'Been recruiting, Kruza? Give her one yourself, have you?' Kled leered shamelessly, walking round Lenya in a tight little circle, leaving a ring around her where he had disturbed the newly raked sawdust of the Baiting Pit.

'No!' The single word that Kruza uttered sounded like a threat. Kled laughed, throwing back his head before filling his mouth once more.

'I want some information,' Kruza continued. 'Information about a young man, a country boy.'

'Probably dead,' Kled said.

Lenya had had enough of this beast. He didn't scare her! At least, she told herself he didn't. Lenya stepped past Kruza.

'The priest of Morr says not,' she said and swallowed the hard lump in her throat that was making her voice sound cracked. 'Take me to Bleyden. I need to talk with him.'

'Take you to Bleyden?' repeated the dwarf, his face pressed so close to hers that Lenya wanted to step back. 'Speak not so freely of my master, trollop, or you will regret it.'

'I have to find Stefan Dunst,' Lenya said, barely able to hold her ground. 'Your master may know where he is.'

'And the price he will ask may be too great,' Kled said, his voice all threat.

Kruza stood behind Lenya in consternation. He'd promised himself he'd look after her, but she wasn't helping.

'Kled,' he began, 'I don't see any reason to disturb Master Bleyden. Perhaps you could find out if Stefan Dunst has worked for him?'

'Not a chance,' said Kled. Behind him some invisible beast lurched against the grille of its cage, roaring a hysterical sound and making the pit echo with the clang of a huge weight throwing itself against metal bars. Kled spun around, picking up a club and moving to scold the animal.

Lenya saw her opportunity. Taking Kruza's hand, she moved away from Kled toward a low door in the wall opposite. She could see light spilling from around the door's poor seal and guessed it might lead her to the Low King they called Bleyden.

FROM HIS VANTAGE point, crouched at the top of the narrow stairwell, Drakken listened intently. He was hunched sideways on the steps, unable to sit squarely in the space that was somewhat narrower than his body. Listening and concentrating hard, he managed to hear every word of Kled's welcome. He waited, hoping that would be the end of the encounter. But when the animal roared and tried to tear its cage apart, the White Wolf heard only danger and careered down the flight of steps, as fast, but as noiselessly as he could.

LENYA PULLED AT the door handle, but it wouldn't open. Behind her, Kruza, beginning to sweat, moved her aside. He saw that there was no going back from this now. He took hold of the door handle and pulled. Then, in his frustration and near panic, he pushed, putting the weight of his shoulder against the door.

It flew open and Kruza fell heavily inwards, taking Lenya with him. As the door opened the sound of hundreds of excited, expectant voices rose to greet the pair. This was followed by a sudden lull, which was broken by a slow, solitary handclap of dissatisfaction. Lenya pulled herself up and began to brush sawdust from her skirt. Kruza, still on the floor on his hands and knees, raised his head, looking for all the world like a dog sniffing the air. He was not ready for what he beheld.

KLED BEAT THE cage of the frightened creature with his club and turned back to oust Kruza and his feisty tart once and for all. But they were gone, and the pit door stood open. Kled heaved it shut before animals could get loose into the undercrofts.

Something was wrong. The audience above had gone quiet and then began to clap out a slow, strange rhythm that the dwarf had never heard in all his years at the Baiting Pit. Kled dropped his club, took his jacket from its hook and was shrugging his great shoulders into it as he raced up the winding staircase that would take him to the trainers' viewing stand.

DRAKKEN STOOD AT the bottom of the stairs, looking into the cellar beyond. He saw nothing, but heard the beating of a cage and the low murmur of the audience. Then clapping. And then a huge cheer.

KNEELING IN THE sawdust, Kruza looked into the snarling muzzle of a stocky, barrel-chested dog with a square head and tiny, glinting eyes. The spittle on the bull terrier's gleaming fangs dripped and the wound on its side leaked a yellowish liquid. In less time than it took to take one shallow, frightened breath, Kruza was on his feet, jumping over the dog. A huge cheer rose from the astounded audience.

As Kruza rose and leapt, Lenya got her first view of her surroundings. Behind Kruza, a tall thick pole stood in the centre of the packed arena. Chained to it was a massive, howling, dirty brown beast. From the huge, studded collar around its neck hung several feet of heavy link chain. The great paws that stamped the sawdust floor were manacled together, restricting its movement.

Around the massive rearing bear several more bull terriers lurched and snapped, their crazed eyes desperate for a piece of the action. Lenya turned to run. But the door they had come through was closed.

STANDING AT THE edge of the trainer's platform, Kled put his fingers in his mouth and whistled a high pitched sound that cut across the raucous noise of the arena and made the bull terriers turn their heads for an instant. But only an instant.

Kled waved a curt message at the four brawny men who had risen from their seats in the frenzied crowd at the sound of the whistle, and were making their way down the tight tiers of seats that made up the auditorium.

Planting their feet firmly on the bench seats, they worked their way effortlessly through the crowd. Soon four huge bodies, clad in leather armour and pulling on horned helmets, made their way to the tall wall which surrounded the arena stage and vaulted down.

'Get them out of there!' Kled yelled at them. 'Get them out!'

There was already chaos. The crowd were running mad with excitement. Kled's men moved in.

One of the four dropped down right behind Lenya and tried to lift her up. He hadn't reckoned on the small woman being quite so fast. She ducked under his arm and slid between his legs. As he turned to see where she had gone he felt a hot, sharp pain in his calf. The dog that Kruza had come face to face with had lost his first target and now homed in on the thug's leg as his next good meal.

The remaining thugs armed themselves with the spears that stood around the arena walls, in case of emergencies, and began to stab at the dogs. Their job was to control the situation and get the intruders out of the arena as fast as possible, before the whole show turned into a farce. Kled watched anxiously from his vantage point.

Kruza landed within feet of the bear. Crouching down on his haunches, he held out a calming hand to the frantic animal. It raged, great jaws frothing, pulling at its chains, desperate to get at its tormentors after months of repeated abuse. Dogs snarled and circled around it. In another moment, one of the thugs was closing in on Kruza, jabbing dogs ahead of him with his spear. He was a huge man with dark tattoos showing on the parts of him that were not covered in shiny, black leather armour. His nicked steel helmet with its horn ornaments and low forehead was imposing enough, but the massive, square jaw and wide red mouth with its gruesome harelip were positively terrifying.

Still looking up, Kruza lowered his hand to the floor and then lunged forward with his shoulders, grabbing the fearsome gladiator around his impressive calves. Black leather hit the sawdust amidst a spray of dust. Kruza sat on his torso and started tearing at his helmet, one hand grasping each of the bone horns and swinging from side to side, half-throttling the man inside with the tautly-twisted chin strap.

There was a roar of laughter from the crowd. Prize fights were one thing, but this comic-tragic battle was something else. They'd certainly got their money's worth.

Kled put his head in his hands. Things were going from bad to worse. He would be out of a job tomorrow for sure. He looked up as he heard the rabble rising to their feet, stamping and cheering and clapping their hands above their heads. He looked out into the arena.

IN THE ENTRANCE to the arena, in front of the bait door, stood a figure. Kled looked again. A huge, masked man filled the doorway. He was naked to the waist and already slick with sweat. He carried a huge mallet in one hand, with a long haft and a heavy iron head. In the other he carried a crude wooden cudgel, tipped with a series of sturdy iron spikes. Not weapons, but tools, the tools of Kled's trade, taken from the cellar by this awesome gladiator. The man stood for what seemed like an age, long enough for Kled and the audience to take in his leather breeches and knee boots, the bands wrapped tight around his wrists and his glistening torso. The man was shorter than average, but what he lacked in height he surely made up for in breadth. Over his head the man wore a crude mask, a small sack with holes cut for his eyes.

An instant later, the mallet was being swung above his head as the gladiator worked his hand down its haft. He had seen something that everyone else had missed. They had been watching him – but he had been watching the bear.

The noise of the crowd and the unfamiliarity of the number of human bodies cavorting around the arena had brought the bear to a point beyond panic. It threw itself against the post with all its weight and then lunged away from it, falling to all fours. The top of the post had splintered with the force and the chain came away. The bear was loose.

The dogs around it were too slow to react. It savaged one, mauling it with teeth and claws, and then ripped another up into the air, its back snapped, howling. The remaining dogs scurried back, fearful at this change in the odds. The bear, berserk now, sprayed dog-blood from its muzzle as it shook it and lumbered forward at the human targets around. The crowd were howling.

Standing his ground, the masked gladiator swung his mallet hard, the end of the haft now clasped firmly in his grip. He let go. Swinging high into the air, the mallet turned twice, echoing the spin that the gladiator had used, and landed with a crashing thud against the side of the bear's skull. It moaned once and collapsed to the floor, burying two of the terriers, whining, beneath its immense bulk.

The crowd roared again, and Kruza leapt off the torso of his half-choked opponent, looking to avoid the next confrontation when it came.

Lenya turned, distracted, to look at the gladiator, and someone picked her up from behind. She looked around: it was the thug with the chewed leg. He was bleeding, but still strong and upright. Lenya struggled and kicked and the audience laughed.

Their laughter ended in another great roar of approval as the mysterious gladiator swung his cudgel, two-handed, into the thug's armoured back, making him drop Lenya and stagger back. The man turned, pulling a long knife from his belt. A thrust, another slicing attempt to sink the blade into the masked gladiator's chest. The gladiator replied with a second swing of the cudgel, which left the thug lying face down on the floor, blood and gore mixing with sawdust to form a thick, dark stain.

Kled looked on in awe. Two of his best men had been taken out by Kruza the cut-purse and this mysterious fighter. Not to mention the bear, his trusted ally and performer for more than two years now, and not easily replaced. Then Kled heard the chant from the auditorium of Masked Man! Masked Man! He smiled to himself. Perhaps he had stumbled upon something after all. Perhaps this masked man could use a job.

The gladiator picked up Lenya and the crowd booed. She looked over at Kruza as he tried to drag her away and she protested, kicking and screaming and shouting.

'Kruza!' she called.

'This is no place for you, lady!' the gladiator said.

Beating the masked man's chest, she hurled abuse. 'You bastard! Let me go! I have to help Kruza!'

To her surprise, he let her go.

The remaining dogs in the arena had turned away from the action when they realised that the bear was down and a meal awaited. The last two thugs, who had been trying to keep the dogs under control with their long spears, now turned on Kruza. The audience waited with bated breath as the leather-clad fighting machines circled the cut-purse, their spears low to the ground and threatening.

Someone in the audience shouted 'Kill!' Other voices joined in until the whole auditorium was filled with the rhythm of hundreds of slowly stamping feet, measuring out each rising call of the word. 'Kill!' 'Kill!' 'Kill!' 'Kill!'

Kruza shuffled his feet in the sawdust of the arena floor, preparing himself. The first spear came in to tangle his legs, but Kruza leapt at just the right moment and it missed him. The second spear tip came in higher, shoulder height, and as soon as his leap was over, Kruza was forced into a low squat, letting the spear blade whistle close over the top of his head. The jabbing spears came in thick and fast, but Kruza was quick on his feet. The audience were almost silent, watching the three men go through this curious dance.

Lenya threw herself on the back of the thug nearest to her, the way she'd fearlessly tackle her brothers in pretend fights back home. She'd had to jump just to get her hands over his shoulders and haul herself up; Kruza's assailant was taller than Lenya by almost two heads. She put her arm around his neck, so that her elbow nestled against his throat. Then she locked her wrists together with opposite hands and threw the entire weight of her body back and down. Her feet dangled in mid-air for a moment, but she could feel him going. She lifted her knees into the small of his back and kicked out again, throwing herself clear as she brought him down on his back, retching and coughing from her choke-hold.

THE MASKED GLADIATOR sidled around the fight, one eye on the feeding dogs, and picked his mallet up from the floor. Then he went for the remaining thug. His first swing matched exactly with the low forward lunge of the leather-clad fighter. Both missed, but the masked man's balance never wavered, and he brought the mallet round in another long arc. This time it connected. The double horned helmet flew off the thug's head and sailed way up into the auditorium, grasping hands rising up to catch the souvenir. Long before his helmet was caught, the thug was lying on the ground, his legs twisted in an awkward direction with the momentum of the blow, his head bloody and gaping.

Kled stood stolidly in the stand, counting his losses. Two useful armed fighters, at least a couple of dogs (and the rest would be useless for at least a fortnight after their vast meal), and his favourite baiting bear. And his gains? Well the masked man would counter any losses if he could be persuaded to fight again.

The thugs Kruza and Lenya had disabled were getting back to their feet, but neither looked like they wanted a rematch. The crowd were making a noise fit to raise the dead.

The masked gladiator turned to Lenya and Kruza. 'We're leaving. Now,' he told them, shouting over the din.

'The bait door's closed – ' Lenya began.

The gladiator raised his mallet. 'Not for long.'

KLED SCRAMBLED BACK down the winding stairs to the cellar, desperate to catch up with his new find before he disappeared into the night. Wild applause still rang in his ears, soon to be followed by cries of 'More!' and 'Masked Man! Masked Man!'

ON THEIR WAY out of the cellar, the gladiator, the sackcloth mask still firmly over his head, lifted a bundle over his shoulder and led the dishevelled pair away from their unexpected adventure. Lenya noticed that the bundle appeared to be wrapped in some kind of skin or fur.

THE STRANGE TRIO hurried away from the deserted exterior of the Baiting Pit and down a series of empty alleys. They stopped in a tiny square between the backs of tall buildings. There was barely room for the three of them, but there were no windows and they could not be overlooked. The masked man knelt down to his furry bundle and began to untie it. Then, impatiently, the masked fighter tore off his sackcloth hood, leaving his hair glued firmly down with sweat to his glistening forehead.

'Krieg!' Lenya exclaimed in a tight, breathy squeak. 'Krieg... But how....? What...?' She was so surprised she couldn't catch her breath and her fingers began to tingle. She thought she was going to throw up.

'You know him?' Kruza asked. Then the cut-purse saw what the half-naked man was taking from his bundle. He thought for a moment about running, but there was a look in the other's eyes that told him not to chance it.

Once dressed again in his pelt and breastplate the White Wolf, Krieg Drakken, led Lenya and Kruza to a nearby hostelry. Kruza did not know what to say, so busied himself at the barrel, furnishing all three with tall pots of good ale. He didn't like mixing with such a powerful authority figure, not one bit. But he didn't feel like leaving Lenya after what they'd been through.

'I could have helped you find your brother,' Drakken was saying in a stern tone. 'Why didn't you trust me? I nearly brought disgrace to my Temple, having to go into the pit to rescue you! If any had recognised me…'

'I'm sorry,' she said. She wondered why she had not confided in him. Was it simply that she owed him so much already? She didn't want to think about it.

'No one's going to find him now!' she murmured in a hollow voice. 'After all this…'

Lenya had never felt such hopeless futility. All the leads had been false, all the trails cold, all the risks not worth the taking. She had fought against it as valiantly as she could, but at last the great bulk of Middenheim had overwhelmed her will and her strength

'Oh Stefan!' she exclaimed. 'Why did you have to come to this place! Brave little Wheezer, out to make his fortune!' Her hands came to her face and tears began to fall.

'What did you say?' Kruza asked sharply. 'You said his name was Stefan.'

'Yes,' she sniffed, 'but when we were children his nickname was Wheezer…'

'Wheezer…' Kruza repeated, barely audible over Lenya's sobs. 'Ulric damn me!' he exclaimed. He stood up in alarm, his chair crashing down behind him.

'Your brother was Wheezer?'

MITTHERBST
WOLF'S BANE

THE NIGHT WAS old and dry. The lemon-rinded moons of high summer hung sullenly in a sky of soft purple. Moths beat against lit windows and masked lanterns. In the dim precincts of the Great Temple of Ulric, a warm silence filled the long hallways and cloisters. It was past midnight, and still the heat of the day had not subsided. Cooler than the streets in daylight, the great stones of the Temple building now radiated the heat they had absorbed, sweating warmth out of the walls and pillars.

Aric, the White Company's standard bearer, crossed the shadowy atrium of the mighty shrine, by the light of two hundred smoking candles. Sweat beaded his broad, young brow. Custom and observance forced him to wear the grey-gold plate mail and white wolf pelt of the Templar uniform, but he dearly wished he could strip it all off.

Guard duty. White Company had the vigilia watch, patrolling the palace of Ulric until first light and the chime of matins. Aric longed for the fresh chill and mist which he hoped the pre-dawn would bring to signal the end of their duty.

By the arched door of a side chapel dedicated to fallen sons of Ar-Ulric, Aric saw Lowenhertz. The tall Wolf had leant his warhammer against the jamb, and was standing, peering out across the city from an unglazed lancet. At the sound of Aric's approach, he spun like lightning and raised the hammer.

'Stand down, brother,' Aric said with a smile.

'Aric...' Lowenhertz muttered, lowering his hammer.

'How goes the night?'

'Stifling. Smell the air.'

They stood together on the narrow parapet under the arch and breathed in. Sweat; woodsmoke; corrupting sanitation.

'Ah, Middenheim,' Aric murmured.

'Middenheim in high summer,' Lowenhertz returned. 'Damn its rocky heart.'

Somewhere down below in Altmarkt, hand bells were chiming furiously and there was a distant fuzz of orange. Another fire in the tinder-dry streets. There had been a dozen or more that week alone. And beyond the city, brush-blazes, sparked by summer lightning, had regularly lit portions of the forest at night. Wells were drying up, latrines were stinking, brawls were flaring, disease was rife, and clove oil sales were booming. A hot, smoky summer by any standards and for Middenheim an exceptional season.

'Hottest summer in eighty years,' said Lowenhertz, who knew such things.

'Hottest I've ever known,' Aric answered. He paused, significantly.

'What?' Lowenhertz asked, looking round.

Aric shrugged. 'I... Nothing.'

'What?'

'I half expected you to tell me why. With your learning and all. I half expected you to tell me that a summer season as stifling as this was a sure sign of some disaster.'

Lowenhertz looked faintly angry, as if mocked.

'I'm sorry,' Aric said. 'I should continue with my rounds.'

As he walked away, Lowenhertz called out. 'Brother Aric?'

'Lowenhertz?'

'You're right, you know. A summer like this... not from any learning of mine, or signs, or portents. But heat like this gets to men's minds. Bakes them, twists them. Before autumn, there will be trouble.'

Aric nodded solemnly and walked away. He liked Lowenhertz, but there was nothing the man couldn't see the bad side of.

'THEN TAKE IT off!' Morgenstern snapped. The sweltering night had done nothing for his demeanour and his huge bulk was rank with sweat. He had shed his wolf-pelt and his armour, and was sitting by the font in the main chapel, dressed in his undershirt, pressing his face and neck against the cool stone of the water-filled basin. Above him, the great statue of Ulric rose into the gloom, silent, immense.

And probably sweating too, Morgenstern decided.

'It's against the rules!' protested Drakken, the youngest of the Wolves and the newest recruit, who had drawn this duty to share with the great, ox-like veteran.

'Ulric eat the rules!' Morgenstern spat, with a sideways nod of respect to the vast statue. 'If you're as hot as me you'll ditch that armour and sweat it out! Name of the Wolf, you're hot blooded enough to be courting that fiery maid from the Margrave's court! You must be curdling in there!'

Drakken shook his head wearily and pulled his pelt around his powerful, stocky form as if to defy the heat.

Short, surly, thick-set, stubborn, Morgenstern thought. *Our boy Drakken undoubtedly has dwarf blood in his ancestry. His bastard forefathers surely dug this city out of the rock itself.*

He got to his feet, aware that Drakken was trying not to watch him. Morgenstern reached into the font.

'What are you doing?' Drakken hissed.

The old veteran pulled a corked bottle of ale out of the holy water. 'Cooling down,' he said. He unpopped the flask and poured the chilled liquid down his throat. He could almost hear Drakken choking on his own saliva and envy.

Drakken spun round and strode across to the big man. 'For Ulric's sake, give me some of that!'

'*Some of what?*'

Aric advanced down the centre file of the great chamber, the thousands of candle flames rippling at the sudden breeze of his billowing pelt.

Drakken froze. There was a fluid plop as the bottle dropped out of sight into the font from Morgenstern's chubby fingers.

'Morgenstern?'

The huge Wolf turned soberly and dipped his cupped hands into the font water, raising them to baptise his face in a cascading splash of dancing silver.

'Holy water, Brother Aric,' Morgenstern said, shaking out his sodden locks like a hound. He saw how Aric stared at his unarmoured bulk. 'At late hours like this, I like to chasten myself with the watery blessing of Ulric, so that I may be fresh for duty.'

'Is that so?'

'Oh yes,' said Morgenstern, splashing his face and torso again. 'Why, I'm surprised an earnest young devotee of the Wolf like you doesn't know the ritual. Why else would I have stripped off my armour? I'm absolving my sins, you see? Before Ulric. Absolving, oh yes. It's chastening. Very chastening.'

'Very chastening,' agreed Drakken.

Morgenstern knew the young Templar was a heartbeat away from laughing. He grabbed Drakken by the neck and plunged him face down into the water of the font.

'See? Young Drakken is willing! He thirsts for chastening! Can I oblige you with a nocturnal baptism too?'

Aric shook his head. 'Forgive me for intruding upon your observances, Brother Morgenstern. I had no idea you were so... devout.'

'I am a Brother of Wolves, Aric. It wounds me to think you would believe me to be tardy in such details. A lesson to you. You imagine us veterans to be a slack lot, more interested in wine and song and womanly comfort.' Morgenstern held Drakken's struggling head under. 'The likes of me shame you younger Wolves! Why, I have half a mind to go outside right now and beat my naked back with bitter withy twigs to scourge my soul for Ulric's sake! When was the last time you did that?'

'I forget. Again, forgive me,' Aric said, turning away to continue with his rounds. 'I stand humbled before your strict devotion.'

'Don't mention it.'

'You might want to let Drakken up before he drowns, though,' Aric added as he walked away, smirking.

'What? Oh, yes…'

'You bastard! I nearly drowned!' Drakken said as he came up. Or that's what he would have said, had he not been trying to vomit up a lung. He lay gasping and retching on the tiles by the font for a good two minutes after Aric had gone.

Morgenstern kicked him playfully in the ribs. 'See the trouble you'd get me into, boy?' Morgenstern asked. He dipped into the font and pulled a second cooled bottle out.

A MOTH KNOCKED repeatedly against the lamp. Anspach thought to swat it, but it was a good bet a warhammer didn't make for an effective moth-swatter. He was just considering what odds he'd take to swat a moth with a warhammer when Aric appeared.

'How goes the night, Brother Anspach?'

'Hot and lousy, Brother Aric.'

They stood together at the foot of the steps under the corbel-vaulted ceiling of the entrance to the regimental trophy chapel. Beyond the cage door, on the wall, bas-reliefs and frescoes showed Wulcan, the smiting of Blitzbeil, the commemoration of the Fauschlag Rock and a score of other images from the long history of Middenheim.

'The patrol?' Anspach asked, obviously bored.

'Nothing. Lowenhertz watches the Chapel of the Fallen. Drakken and Morgenstern are clowning in the main hall. Kaspen and Einholt are falling asleep in the weaponarium annexe. Gruber paces the high turret solemnly. A quiet night.'

Anspach nodded, and pulled out a flask from under his pelt. 'Something to cool you down?' he suggested.

Aric hesitated and then accepted the offering. 'Tastes good,' he began appreciatively.

He handed the flask back and turned away. His toe kicked against something on the flags, something that skittered away. Searching for it, Aric picked it up.

A padlock.

'How long has this been lying there?'

Anspach shrugged, coming over. 'I have no idea…'

They both turned to look at the portico of the trophy chapel. The iron cage door was ajar.

'Oh no! Oh, curse me, Ulric!' Anspach spat leaping forward. Aric was beside him. They shoved the loose cage door open and thundered inside. Aric held up a lamp, and moths battered and wove around him.

The plinth in the corner of the shrine, under the great wolf-skin, was empty. The Jaws of Ulric, a silver inlaid relic made from the fangs of a great forest wolf in olden times, the greatest of their treasures, was missing.

Aric and Anspach backed away in horror.

'I'm in trouble,' Anspach breathed.

'You're in trouble? Anspach, we're all in trouble.'

MATINS. DAWN CAME, hot, branding, intense. In a private annexe deep inside the oven heat of the Temple, Ganz listened attentively to Ar-Ulric, the High Priest. Every now and then he murmured 'Yes, High Priest,' or 'No, High Priest' or 'Obviously, High Priest'.

'The Teeth of Ulric,' the High Priest was saying, his breath exhausting itself in the hot air. 'Of all relics, our most prized!'

'Yes, High Priest,' Ganz said, obligingly.

'It must be returned.'

'Obviously, High Priest.'

Flies and beetles pattered against the window grills.

'If we were to admit we had lost the relic, Middenheim itself would lose heart. The city folk would round on us, and despair. An ill omen. The worst.'

'Yes, High Priest.'

'I can give you two days' grace.'

'Sir?'

'Two days to find and recover the relic before I have to go public and bring shame and torment on us all – especially the White Company who were on guard duty when it was stolen.'

'I see, High Priest.'

'Two days, Ganz. Do not fail the Temple.'

HE WOULD NOT. Not. *Not*.

But for the life of him, he didn't know where to begin. Stalking back from the High Priest's chambers, through chapter gardens where feeble mists baked off the beds, Ganz cursed himself over and again. He had no choice. He had to… to… enlist them all to his trust…

Even Morgenstern – and Anspach.

'Well, sir,' Anspach said, looking suitably solemn. 'I think our best bet–'

'Silence!' Ganz barked. The room held the silence for a second and then sound thundered again as Ganz slammed the door on his way out. The remaining members of the Wolf Company looked at each other. Aric sighed. Dorff began to whistle, nervously and tunelessly. Morgenstern slowly and belatedly lowered his legs from the table he had been resting them on. Gruber skulked darkly at the back of the room. The others shuffled.

'I only said–' Anspach began.

'Oh, shut up,' Aric muttered. 'We've disgraced him. Disgraced our order. Our Temple, our city.'

'Is it really that bad?' Drakken asked quietly and suddenly wished he hadn't.

'The Teeth of Ulric were cut from the muzzle of the great White Wolf of Holzbeck by Artur himself, bless his fine spirit. They are holy of all holies. And on our watch, we let them be stolen.' Lowenhertz moved into the centre of the room as he spoke, his voice low, like the intonation of a funeral bell in the Temple of Morr. 'Disgrace barely covers it.'

Anspach rose to his feet. 'I know what you're all thinking. It was me. I was watching the reliquary. I was the one who failed.'

'I was with you when we found the broken lock–' began Aric.

Anspach shushed him back. 'After the event, I'm sure. It was me, Aric. And you all think I must have been drunk or stupid or distracted…'

'Were you?' asked Gruber, a stiletto voice from the back of the room.

Anspach shook his head. 'No, Gruber, not that anyone would believe me. Fact is, I thought I was performing my duties with particular vigilance.'

'I was drunk,' Morgenstern said suddenly. They all looked at him. 'On the way, at least,' he qualified. 'Drakken was in no state to stand a good watch either, thanks to me. I'm as much to blame…'

'I was covering the vigilia watch. For Ganz. It was my duty,' Aric said quietly. 'I saw Morgenstern's clowning. I saw Anspach ready at the gate. I saw Einholt and Kaspen dozing in the weapon hall.'

Einholt and Kaspen looked down.

'I saw us all! Neglecting our duties or performing them, one and the same. It was a quiet night and nothing was wrong. I should have charged you all with the spirit of Ulric so that none shirked. I did not. This is down to me.'

'Well,' Gruber said, walking into the light and igniting his pipe with a soft kiss of flame from the spindle. 'Aric may be right. Maybe it is his fault…'

'I was drunk!' Morgenstern exclaimed.

'Sleeping!' cut across Einholt.

'Distracted!' Lowenhertz snapped.

'Unwary!' Anspach cried.

'Enough! Enough!' Gruber cried, holding up his hand. 'All of us to blame… None of us? That's the whole thing, isn't it? The company failed, not any individual. And let's think about this carefully. I've seen Morgenstern drunk as a lord and still notice a goblin sneak by. Anspach may gamble his life away, but still his nose is sharper than any in the company. He would not have missed a theft like that. Lowenhertz, the sternest of us all; he would not have passed over some clue or hint that treachery was in progress. Einholt, not he, not even sleeping, Kaspen likewise. Drakken, with his eager eyes and sense of duty… Do you not see?'

'See what?' asked Aric.

'Magic, Aric! Magic stole the Jaws of Ulric! Despite our failings, only magic could have snuck in and robbed us of the prize. If we'd all been sober and studious and alert... still it would be gone! Go and fetch Ganz back. We have work to do.'

IT FELT STRANGE... wrong, somehow, to be out in the streets of Middenheim without the familiar weight of the armour and wolf pelt. Aric scratched inside the chafing collar of a light linen cape that he hadn't worn since he had first been admitted into the Company as a petitioner.

But this was how Morgenstern and Anspach had said it should go, and for all their manifold failings, they knew such things. If White Company was going to scour the city of Middenheim for the Teeth of Ulric, shake down every tavern, question every fence, prise up and examine the underside of every cobble, they could not do so as Wolf Templars.

So here they were, as the sun rose to mid-morning above the raked roofs, here they were scrubbed and shaved and heavy-headed after the long night, wearing ill-assorted tunics, capes and robes, most of which had festered in long-boxes and chests in the cellars of the chapter house for months and years. Morgenstern, in fact, had been forced to send Drakken out for new clothes. Since he had last worn his civilian garb, he had added many pounds and many more inches. Morgenstern had also appropriated a large-brimmed hat which he imagined gave him a dashing, mysterious air. It in fact made him look like a bulbous forest toadstool on the wilt, but Aric said nothing.

They all looked so odd, so unlike themselves. Gruber in a faintly genteel, faded robe and tunic that seemed a decade or two old-fashioned; Schell in a surprisingly rich velvet cape that smelled of pomanders; Lowenhertz in rough breeches and a leather tunic, like a woodsman. Even the ones who looked normal seemed odd. Aric wasn't used to seeing any of them like this.

Except Anspach, in his tailored coat, polished boots and suavely draped cloak. Though they all spent off-duty hours in the city's stews and taverns, only Anspach habitually dressed out of armour or company colours. Where Morgenstern could carouse until dawn in full armour in the Man o'War, the gaming halls, arenas and dice parlours that were Anspach's particular vice demanded a more refined mode of dress.

They assembled in the street, new men to each other, not speaking for several minutes in the warming glare of the strengthening Mittherbst sun. The air was yet clear and cool, the sky porcelain blue.

Finally Ganz joined them, almost unrecognisable in a serge doublet and hooded woollen over-robe. He said nothing, for there was no need for words, not many at least. Gruber, Anspach and Morgenstern had convinced Ganz of the correct course of action left open to them, and the labour ahead of them had been divided. Now as Ganz came out, he gave a nod acknowledged by all his men, and the party broke into smaller groups, heading away from each other into different quarters of the ancient town.

* * *

'LET ME DO the talking,' Anspach told Ganz and Aric as they approached the south doors of the Baiting Pit off West Weg. At night, on those times he'd passed it, this squat stone drum of a theatre had seemed to Aric like a mouth of hell, with its flaming braziers, hooting pipe music, drums, the pounding and cheering and roaring. The roaring of men and animals.

In daylight, in the unforgiving brightness of the summer light, it was a miserable, flaking place: worn, soiled and stained by all manner of unwholesome deposits. Hand-bills fluttered and shredded along the travertine walls between the daubings of less than sober or less than literate citizens. The blackened metal braziers were extinguished and dead. Two men were sweeping the gateway, pushing all manner of trampled trash out of the steps into the gutter trench. Another was pumping water from the street spigot into a row of buckets. All looked sour and half awake.

'It would have been better if we'd come tonight,' hissed Anspach, 'when the place is open. There would be activity to cover our–'

'There's no time,' returned Ganz. 'Now, if you so want to do the talking, do it to someone other than me!'

They entered, passing through the suddenly freezing shadow of the gateway into the tall-sided, circular pit, where tiers of wooden galleries overlooked a deep stone well, at the bottom of which was dirty sand and a few deep-set posts with manacle points. Caged grills in the pit wall at arena level led off into the place's dingy undercrofts. Down in the pit, another man was scattering sand on dark brown stains. The air smelled of mingled sweat and smoke, an overwhelming odour.

'We're closed,' said a blunt voice from their left. The trio swung around. A hefty dwarf, stripped to the waist and hugely muscled, tipped forward and got up off the stool where he had been sitting, chewing on bread and sausage.

'Where's Bleyden?' Anspach asked.

'We're. Closed,' repeated the dwarf. He took an unfeasibly large bite off the sausage and chewed, staring at them.

'Kled,' said Anspach with a soothing cock of his head and a shrug. 'Kled, you know me.'

'I know nothing.'

'You know you're closed,' Anspach corrected.

The dwarf frowned. He put the sausage to his mouth to bite again, then the bread, and then the sausage, undecided. His eyes never left Anspach.

'What do you want?' he asked, adding, 'we're closed,' again in case any had missed it, and to show that by enquiring what was wanted, he was making a huge exception.

'You know I've had a run of… ill fortune. Bleyden's been good enough to extend me a line of credit, but he insisted on me making some interim repayments as soon as possible. Well, here I am!' Anspach beamed.

The dwarf, Kled, thought for a moment more, his cheeks and lips bulging unpleasantly as his tongue chased lumps of meat out of the sides of his gums. Then he beckoned with the gnawed end of his sausage.

Anspach nodded to Ganz and Aric to follow smartly. Ganz was glowering, his face as dark as Mondstille.

'I hope you both have money,' Anspach said in a hushed voice.

'If this is some con to get me to settle your gambling debts–' began Ganz, choking on the words.

They were passing into a sequence of smelly, stuffy wooden rooms under the seating. Boxes of junk lined the walls, rows of empty bottles, buckets, the occasional dirty billhook. The dwarf stomped ahead, passing neatly under every low doorway where each of the Templars had to duck.

'Bleyden owns this place, and four like it,' Anspach said. 'He runs all the girls in Altmarkt, and has a lot of other business… dealings. He knows a lot about the fate of, shall we say "purloined" goods? But he won't talk to us unless he's got a good reason. And my outstanding ninety crowns is a very good reason.'

'*Ninety?*' Ganz barked, the word almost becoming a squeak as they ducked under another low beam.

'My dear Anspach,' a soft voice said from the smoky gloom ahead of them. 'What a *delightful* surprise.'

'LOOK THERE,' MORGENSTERN whispered from under his preposterous floppy brim. 'Ah! Ah! Ah! Not so obviously, boy!'

Drakken adjusted his stare to look at something on the ground by Einholt's feet.

'You see them? By the fountain, pretending they're not watching?' continued Morgenstern, looking studiously the other way.

'No–' Drakken began.

'I do,' Einholt said. Jagbald Einholt was the quiet man of the company, tall and broad and bald with a jagged beard and a long scar across his eye, cheek and throat. With his milky eye, it was often hard to tell which way he was looking. Now, with a furtive measure as practised as Morgenstern, he was assessing the watchers by the fountain while apparently regarding the weather cock on the Merchant Chandlers.

'Big bruisers. Four of them. Been with us since the Cocky Dame.' Morgenstern stretched as if he hadn't a care in the world.

Drakken dropped to his knees to adjust the strapping of his boot and got a good look from behind the cover of Morgenstern's voluminous cape.

'You were asking a lot of questions,' he said, straightening up and whispering to Morgenstern. 'Five taverns we've been in now, and in each one you've bent the ear of the barman with vague questions about something lost.'

'We've got someone's interest and no mistake,' Einholt mused.

'Let them make the move,' Morgenstern said, heading off. 'We'll try the Tardy Ass next. It's past midday. We can take an ale there too.'

'This isn't an excuse for a tavern crawl,' Drakken began.

Morgenstern looked hurt. 'My boy, I'm taking this all too seriously. What other morning would I have gone through five taverns before noon and still not had a jar?'

They moved west down the rolling cobbles of Scrivener's Passage, dodging between the pack carts coming up from the markets. A hundred yards behind, the four men left the fountain and followed.

THE GUILDHALL OF the Apothecaries on Ostwald Hill had a noxious, yellow pallor to it. It was a rotting, half-timbered building of great age and veneration that sagged as if poison was in the wood and stones. Gruber and Lowenhertz entered into the close air of the audience hall through an unattended archway, and gazed around at the stained glass fronts of the many workshops and apothecums.

'You know this place?' Gruber asked, wrinkling his nose. The air was dry, with an oxidised reek.

'I come here from time to time,' replied Lowenhertz, as if such visits were as natural for a soldier like him as a trip to the armour smiths. The response made Gruber smile, a thin grin cracking his old, lined face. The tall and darkly handsome Lowenhertz had been an enigma since he transferred to White Company in the spring. It had taken a while for them to trust him past his overbearing intellect and strange, wide learning. But he had proved himself, proved himself loyal, proved himself in the field of combat. Now they looked at his odd, educated ways with gentle good humour, and none in the company denied he was an asset. A man with the learning to think his way around a thousand subjects and still fight like a pack-sire wolf when the blood was up.

'Stay here a moment,' Lowenhertz said, moving away into the dimmer reaches of the Guildhall, under a stained and alarmingly singed Guild banner. Gruber loosened his cloak, checked the dagger in his waistband and leant against a wall. He thought of the others, in twos and threes, scouting the city just now. Aric and their commander, Ganz, following Anspach's lucky-charm ways into the gaming places and the wager-pits; Schell, Kaspen and Schiffer in the markets; Bruckner and Dorff checking with their drinking friends in the Watch and the Militia; Morgenstern, Drakken and Einholt doing the rounds of the taverns. He didn't know what alarmed him most – that Anspach's cavalier attitude might provoke untold trouble from the criminal underclass, that Bruckner or Dorff might say too much to their cronies, that Schell and his party might get inveigled into the clutches of the merchant class, or that Morgenstern was visiting taverns. No, that was it. Morgenstern was visiting taverns. Gruber sighed. He prayed to Ulric that between them, steady old Einholt and earnest young Drakken would have the strength to keep Morgenstern's thirst reined in.

As for them: it had fallen for Gruber to go with Lowenhertz to pursue the latter's lead. Lowenhertz had suggested that the Teeth of Ulric might have been taken for some mystical purpose, and in these alchemical workplaces that answer might be found. It had been Gruber's suggestion, after all, that magic had played a part in the theft.

He felt uneasy. Science didn't agree with him, and he was disarmed by the notion of men who spent their days mixing vials and philtres and potions. It was a short step from that to sinister black what-not in Gruber's book.

Lowenhertz reappeared under the Guild awning and beckoned. Gruber went over.

'Ebn Al-Azir will see us.'

'Who?'

Lowenhertz frowned at him. 'The chief alchemist. I've known him for years. He is from foreign parts, far away, but his work is excellent. Be appropriately humble.'

'Very well,' Gruber said, 'but it may kill me.' Gruber had precious little time for the outland types with their strange skins, odd scents and bewildering ways.

'Remove your boots,' Lowenhertz said, stopping him on the threshold of a narrow doorway.

'My what?'

'A mark of respect. Do it.' Gruber saw that Lowenhertz's feet were now bare. He cursed quietly as he yanked off his kid-skin riders.

The narrow door let onto a narrower staircase that circled up into the gloomy reaches of the Guildhall. Above, they ducked through a lancet archway and into a long, high attic room. The air seemed golden here. Sunlight streamed down thickly, like honey, through angled skylights of pumice glass, and was caught and suspended in rich hangings of silk and net. The room was carpeted in a rug of elaborate design, the hues and weaving astonishing and vibrant. Intricately wrought lamps and jewelled censers of gold filigree smoked around the room illuminating, in addition to the slow sunlight, a cluttered space of books and scrolls, chests and wall-hangings, charts and articulated skeletons – birds, beasts, and things akin to men. Stove fires cooked blue-hot under sculptural glass vessels in which liquids of vivid colours hissed and steamed and gave off oily vapours. A bell was chiming. The air smelled of rich, cloying sweetnesses. Gruber tried to breathe, but the air was too close. Perfume clogged his senses for a moment, perfume and incense.

On a rounded foot-table nearby, on the ivory inlaid top, lay a puppet, a glaring man in clown's pantaloons with jewelled joints and a belled cap. The puppet lay discarded, strings loose, in a rictus of death, like so many figures Gruber had seen on the field of war. That's how we all look when our strings go slack, he thought. The snarling stare of the puppet glared up at him out of a white porcelain face. Gruber looked away. He laughed humourlessly to himself. A sixty year-old veteran like him, afraid of a puppet a foot high!

A figure rose in the gloom, parted hanging nets and stepped out to meet them. He was small, dressed in a high-throated blue gown with embroidery at the neck and wide cuffs. His face was waxy and sallow, and there was a look of great age in his hollow eyes. Age, or perhaps…

'My old friend Heart-of-a-Lion!' he said. His accent was melodious and heavy.

Lowenhertz bowed his head, 'Master Al-Azir! How go your stars?'

The little man put his hands together. Long-nailed and dark, they emerged from his cuffs like the recessed blades from some mechanical weapon. Gruber had never seen so many rings: spirals, signets, loops, circles.

'My stars travel with me and I follow them. For now, my house is benign and it smiles on me the gift of heaven.'

'For that I am happy,' Lowenhertz said. He glanced a look at Gruber.

'Huh? Oh… as am I, sir.'

'Your friend?' asked Al-Azir with a flash of white teeth, inclining his head and circling a hand towards Gruber.

He moves like a puppet, thought Gruber, like a damn puppet on strings, all grace and motion lent by the hand of a trained puppeteer.

'This is my worthy comrade, Gruber,' said Lowenhertz. 'What trust you give to me must also go to him. We are brothers of the Wolf.'

Al-Azir nodded. 'Refreshment?' he asked.

No, it wasn't a question. It was an obligation, Gruber decided. Al-Azir made a brief hissing sound through his teeth and a huge man came out from behind the nets; bald, monumentally muscled and naked except for a breech-clout. His eyes were shadowed and unforthcoming, and he carried an ornate tray on which sat three tiny silver cups, a silver spouted pot and a bowl of jagged brown crystals with a pair of clawed tongs resting in them.

The vast servant set the tray down on the foot-table and retreated, taking the puppet with him. Al-Azir ushered them to sit on bolsters and satin cushions around the foot-table. He poured steaming oil-black fluid from the pot into the three cups with attentive care, each move slow and graceful.

Gruber watched Lowenhertz for a cue. Lowenhertz lifted the cup nearest him – it looked like a silver thimble in his hands –and dropped a cluster of the crystals into it with the tongs, which he then used to stir the thick fluid. He muttered something and nodded before sipping.

Lowenhertz didn't die choking and frothing, which Gruber took to be a good sign. He mimicked the process, lifting the cup and stirring the crystals in with the clawed tongs. Then he murmured, 'Ulric preserve me' and nodded. But there was no way he was going to sip.

He suddenly became aware of Lowenhertz glaring at him fiercely.

Gruber took a sip, licked his lips and smiled. Keeping that sip down was the hardest battle he had ever fought. It tasted like tar; smoked tar; smoked, boiled tar. With a bitter taste of mildew and a syrupy flavour of corruption.

'Very good,' he said finally, when at last he was certain opening his mouth wouldn't result in the reproduction of his last meal.

'Something troubles you,' said Al-Azir.

'No, it's quite nice really–' began Gruber, and then shut up.

'Something is lost,' went on Al-Azir, melodious and soft. 'Something precious. Eh! Precious.'

'You know this, master?'

'The stars tell me, Heart-of-a-Lion. There is pain in the ruling house of Xerxes, and both Tiamut and Darios, Sons of the Morning, draw hooked blades against each other. Eh! It is seen and written in water.'

'Your learning astounds me as ever, master. The heavens convolute and you read the signs. Tell me what you know.'

'I know nothing and everything,' replied Al-Azir, sipping slowly, head bowed.

Then cut to the latter, Gruber cursed inwardly. *Enough with this stars stuff!*

'What has been taken, Heart-of-a-Lion?' asked Al-Azir gently.

Lowenhertz was about to speak when Gruber cut in.

'Why don't–' He saw Lowenhertz's angry snarl and held up a hand for calm.

'Forgive my bluntness, Master Al-Azir,' Gruber corrected himself, 'but this is a matter of delicacy. We would appreciate knowing what you know before we unburden ourselves fully.'

He glanced at Lowenhertz, who nodded cautious approval, his lips pursed.

'For such help,' Gruber went on, 'my Lord Ulric may surely shine his thanks upon you. I am sure his light lurks somewhere in your firmament.'

'I'm sure it does,' Al-Azir replied with an ivory-white smile. 'Somewhere.'

'My friend is in earnest, Master Al-Azir,' Lowenhertz said. 'Can you tell us what you know?'

Al-Azir set his cup down and folded his hands so they each disappeared up the opposite sleeve. He stared down at the intricate inlay of the tabletop. 'The Jaws of the Wolf, so the stars say.'

Gruber felt his guts clench. He leaned forward to catch every soft, curling word.

'Jaws of the Wolf, precious jaws, bone bright. They are precious and they have been taken.'

'By who? For what purpose?' Lowenhertz asked.

'By darkness, Heart-of-a-Lion. Foul darkness. They cannot be recovered. Eh! I have seen woe on this rock-city! Pain! Pestilence! Eh! I have seen misery and weeping and lamentation!'

'Cannot be recovered?' Lowenhertz's voice seemed suddenly frail. 'Why not, master? What is the darkness you speak of?'

'Night. But not a night of the stars to read and learn from. A night without stars. That is when the Jaws of the Wolf will bite the living heart from Middenheim rock-city. Eh!'

Gruber looked up. Lowenhertz seemed on the point of leaving, as if he'd heard enough.

'What can we do?' Gruber asked directly.

'That's it,' said Lowenhertz. 'Master Al-Azir has said his piece. We must go now!'

'I'm not going anywhere!' snapped Gruber, shaking off Lowenhertz's hand. 'Master Al-Azir, if you know this much, you must know more! I beg you, tell us! What can we do?'

'Enough, Gruber!'

'No! Sit down, Lowenhertz! Now!'

Al-Azir made gentle shushing motions with his hands and Lowenhertz sat again. 'It is as I said. They cannot be recovered. They are lost to you forever.'

Gruber leant across the table to face Al-Azir. 'Your pardon, sir. I am a White Wolf, of White Company, beloved of Ulric. I know when a battle is lost and when it is won, but I will still stay the course. The Jaws of Ulric may be gone from us and beyond recovery, but I will fight on... fight on, I say! A Wolf fights to the death even when the battle is lost! So tell me this at least: who is the enemy I am losing to? What are his signs?'

The huge servant emerged from behind the nets, flanking his master. His sword was splayed and curved and almost as tall as Gruber.

Gruber didn't back off. He had a hand on the pommel of the blade in his waistband and his nose right in the face of the tiny, old alchemist. 'Tell me! It may not do me any good in your eyes, but tell me anyway!'

Al-Azir waved a hand and the servant and his sword departed. 'Gruber of the Wolf, I pity you. But I admire your courage. Eh! Even though you will lose what is dear to you. Look for the Black Door. Look for the north of seven bells. Look for the lost smoke.'

Gruber sat back on his bolster. He felt stunned. 'Look for–'

'You heard him,' Lowenhertz said from the doorway.

Gruber looked up into the eyes of Al-Azir, which fixed upon him for the first time. Gruber was amazed at the clarity and humour of the brown eyes in those sallow hoods.

Without thinking, he took up his cup and drained it. Then he reached his hand forward and clasped Al-Azir's as it was extended. 'If you've helped me, my thanks,' he said.

Al-Azir smiled. A genuine smile. 'You cannot win, Gruber. But make a good job of losing. Eh! It has been interesting talking with you.'

Out in the courtyard, Gruber was smiling as he pulled on his boots. Lowenhertz growled, 'What do you think you were doing in there? There are ways, customs, protocols!'

'Aw, shut up. He liked me... Heart-of-a-Lion.'

'I thought you were going to attack him.'

'So did I,' Gruber said cheerfully, leading the way to the exit gate. 'But you know what? I think he liked me better than you. You've been round there so long with your yes master, no master, and here I am, an ignorant Wolf, and he tells me what's what.'

'Maybe... but what have we got?'

'A lead, Lowenhertz – or weren't you listening? We've got a lead.'
'But he said we'd lose any–'
'Who cares? Come on!'

BLEYDEN WAS A small, slight man, little taller than the dwarf Kled, but rake thin. He wore an immaculate silk doublet and curious gloves of black hide. He perched in an upholstered throne chair that was set up on boxes to give him commanding height. Aric thought it just drew attention to his diminutive stature. He couldn't help smiling at the way Bleyden's clerical desk was similarly raised on boxes so he could reach it from the chair.

The little man took the bag of coins that Ganz handed him. Aric saw ice in Ganz's look as he handed over the bag. *He may kill Anspach for this,* Aric decided.

Bleyden opened the draw-string of the bag and peeked inside like a child with a bag of sweets. A delighted look flashed across his small, drawn features. *He must be eighty, judging from his thin silver hair and tight waxy skin,* thought Aric, *and no bigger than a stable lad from the Wolf Barrack. And this man is the Low King who rules the crime syndicates of the eastern city?*

Bleyden began to count off coins from the bag onto his desk top. His nimble, gloved fingers made neat, ten-coin piles in a row, each pile meticulously straightened and flushed. It took all of three minutes, three silent minutes where the only sound was Kled chewing the last of the sausage and scribing marks in the old doorframe with a large, rusty knife he had suddenly produced.

'Forty-seven crowns,' beamed Bleyden, looking up from the neat stacks and handing the folded purse back to Ganz. The commander took it wordlessly.

'A down-payment on my debt. Satisfactory, I trust?' Anspach said.

'Quite satisfactory,' the tiny man replied. He slid a red-bound ledger from a shelf under the desk, opened it carefully and made a deliberate mark in ink with his quill. He looked up. 'I am impressed with the fraternal loyalty of the Knight Templars,' he said, his voice oozing like treacle. 'To stand payment for a colleague.'

'We Wolves stand together,' Ganz replied without a trace of irony. Or emotion.

We'll stand together all right, Aric thought, *and watch as Ganz beats Anspach to death in the stable block tonight.* There was a smile that was battling to get out and stretch on Aric's face. He bit his cheek hard.

'Was there anything else?' Bleyden asked. 'I am busy. And we are closed, as I'm quite sure Kled informed you.'

'Information,' Ganz said. The word was hard and solid, like a splinter of the Fauschlag Rock. 'Anspach tells me you know things. About the circulation of… goods in the city.'

Bleyden raised his eyebrows at Anspach. 'Does he? I'm surprised at you, Anspach. You know what loose tongues do.'

'Fall out,' Kled said ominously from behind them.

Bleyden chuckled. 'What is your name, friend of Anspach?'

'Ganz.'

'Commander of White Company! Well, I'm honoured!' Bleyden chuckled again. 'I had no idea I was in the presence of such greatness. Commander Ganz... well, well, well. A stranger to my establishments. Why is that?'

'Unlike Anspach, I find no need to take risks or see death when I'm off duty. My working life is amply full of such activities.'

'And the fact that you are standing before me alive implies that the death you speak of is the kind you deal out. My, my, Commander Ganz. That's about as close to a threat as anything I've heard in years.'

'You should get out more,' Ganz said.

Great Ulric, but he's pushing him! thought Aric. He suddenly wondered where the dwarf and his rusty knife were. Behind them still. Should he risk settling a hand on the haft of the dagger in his belt, or was that going to give Kled all the excuse he needed? Aric swallowed. *Careful, commander,* he willed.

Bleyden was still smiling. 'Information comes at a price, Commander Ganz. All you've done is diminish Anspach's tally. I've seen nothing today that suggests to me I should volunteer information.'

'What would?' Ganz asked.

'Settling Anspach's debt might make me reconsider. Settling it with interest.'

'But I've given you all my–'

Bleyden pursed his lips and shook his little head. 'Coins are coins. If you're out of them, there are other ways to pay. A favour, perhaps? I would value greatly the idea that I could call upon a commander of a Templar Company when I needed it. Consider it a down-payment of trust.'

Aric could see how Ganz's shoulders tightened. Anspach looked worried. Aric knew the last thing he had intended was for their commander to pollute his hands by making an honour-promise to a beast like Bleyden. This was not going well.

But there was the honour of the Temple too, of the Wolves as a whole. Aric suddenly realised in his heart that Ganz would be prepared to take the offer, to corrupt himself and leave himself honour-bound to this scum if that was what it took.

Ganz was about to speak when Aric pushed forward and dropped his own purse on the desk. Bleyden looked at it as if it was a bird-dropping.

'My own coins. Fifty-eight crowns. Count it. That, with my commander, pays Anspach's dues... with interest.'

Bleyden sucked at his teeth.

'As I said, I am impressed with the fraternal loyalty of the Knight Templars. Ask away.'

Anspach cleared his throat. 'Has anything of... singular value passed into the secret trade this morning? Something that might fetch an impossible price?'

Bleyden tapped his teeth with his gloved finger tips. 'Have you Wolves lost something?'

'Answer!' Ganz hissed.

'No. Nothing. On my honour, however you value it.'

There was a long silence. For all that effort, nothing! Aric felt like striking the grinning child-man. He certainly knew how to string along his dopes for extra revenue.

'Let me out of here!' Ganz barked and turned to go. Kled stood aside from the door and made an 'after you' gesture that any chamberlain in the Graf's palace would have been proud of.

'Don't go away angry, Commander Ganz,' Bleyden said suddenly. 'I am a vicious and conniving businessman, but I am still a businessman. I understand the mechanisms of trade and I know when a customer should feel he's got his money's worth. Listen to me now...'

Ganz turned back.

'I don't know what you've lost, Wolf, and I don't care. If it comes into my hands, I'll get the best price for it and you'll get first refusal. All I can offer now is this... you're not the only ones.'

'What do you mean?'

'Last night, many noble bodies in this city were deprived of valuable things. You're not the first to come here today asking questions. Not the last either, I'll warrant. Everyone knows of Bleyden's skill in disposal of valuables. There is a word on the street too.'

'And?' said Anspach.

'Your money's worth, if it will help. Last night, the Merchants' Guild was robbed of the stamped gold scales that stand in their Guildhall, the symbol of their trade. Last night, something of great symbolic worth was taken from the chapter house of the Knights Panther. Last night, the ceremonial pledging cup of the City Militia went missing. Last night, the Alembic of Crucifal was taken from its locked cabinet in the chancel of the Alchemists' Guildhall. Last night, the Temple of Shallya was robbed of the Unimpeachable Veil. Is this picture clear to you? Is it worth your down-payment? Those are all I know of, but you can wager there are others. Last night, someone systematically robbed all the great institutions of this town of their most hallowed icons.'

Ganz breathed a long sigh. It was worse than he had feared.

'I don't know what's going on in Middenheim,' Bleyden said. 'This isn't a crime spree. This is a conspiracy.'

Ganz motioned the others to follow him. He paused at the door. And turned. 'My thanks, Bleyden. However you value it.'

'Immeasurably, Commander Ganz. And I ask you a favour.'

Ganz paused. 'What?'

'When you find out what's going on, tell *me*. Frankly, it's all rather worrying.'

* * *

They left the Tardy Ass by the back door and stood in a shadowed alley while Morgenstern relieved himself against a wall.

'One ale, you said,' Drakken remarked.

'We kept him to three; be thankful,' Einholt said wearily.

'And yet something!' said Morgenstern triumphantly, rearranging his clothes. 'I told you nothing happens in this city without the innkeepers knowing it first!'

Drakken frowned and shot a look at Einholt. Had he been in a different tavern, listening to a different conversation?

'What something?' asked Einholt.

'Didn't you see how dreary and dull it was in there? Didn't you see what was missing?'

'I'm not quite the expert you are in the details of Middenheim's hostelries,' Einholt said sourly.

'Pretend we didn't notice and tell us before we die of old age,' Drakken added.

'The Cup of Cheer! *The Cup of Cheer*! It was obvious!'

They shot him wounding looks of incomprehension.

As if he was explaining it patiently to babies, Morgenstern began. 'The Cup of Cheer is the mascot icon of the Guild of Vittalers. Every year they compete for it and the winning tavern sets it in pride of place above the bar, the stamp that marks them as the best ale-house in town. The Tardy Ass won it last Mitterfruhl and where was it? Aha! Under the cloth draped over the alcove above the bar? I think not! It's gone too!'

'Let me get this straight,' Einholt said. 'You're suggesting we compare the loss of the Teeth of Ulric to the theft of some battered chalice that innkeepers hold dear?'

'We each have our own treasures,' Morgenstern said. He was probably going to explain further when the four long shadows passed across them.

The four men from the fountain. They approached down the alley, two from either end, faces fixed and grim.

'Time for some fun,' Morgenstern remarked. And charged them.

His huge bulk felled the pair advancing from the western end, smashing one aside into a stagnant pool of horse urine and slamming the other against the wall. The other two were on Drakken and Einholt in a second.

Drakken dropped and swung low, punching the ribs of his attacker and then throwing him over his head, propelled by his own charge. Einholt was locked with his man, grappling and thrashing, overturning crates of empty bottles and refuse.

Morgenstern was busy slamming the head of his assailant back into the mouldy alley wall. He seemed intent on finding a space between the bricks that it would fit. His other attacker was now back on his feet. A glimmer of steel lit in his hands.

Drakken cried out. Ducking the renewed assault of the man he had sent flying, he dodged two, three, four punches before planting one of his own, which laid the man out on the cobbles, his jaw lolling. Einholt broke his man's grip with a knee to his softer parts and smacked him to the ground with an open hand. The man's flailing legs came round and ripped Einholt's feet out from under him. They went down into the muck and sewage, clawing and biting.

Drakken sprang down the alley past Morgenstern and his sagging victim, and tackled the man with the knife. He looped his hand in low, catching the wrist, and threw the man against the wall. A slam of the wrist, then another, and at last the knife flew loose.

Down the alley, Einholt finally got the better of his opponent and left him stewing unconscious in the drain ditch.

Drakken was locked in fury with the last one, hands around his throat. Morgenstern suddenly leaned over them, holding the fallen knife by the blade.

'Drakken! Boy! See the hilt? See the markings? These men are Knights Panther. I think we should talk to them, don't you?'

A HOT, DULL caul of evening hung around the city, and surly strands of twilight filtered into the window spaces and archways of the Templars' barracks. In the long, suffocatingly hot Temple eating hall, ranged around in the fluttered candlelight, sat White Company in their motley garb, and four others – the rather battered individuals encountered by Morgenstern's party. Ganz leaned down into the face of their leader, who was dabbing a bloody lip with a fold of cloth.

'When you're ready, von Volk of the Panthers.'

'I'm ready, Ganz of the Wolves.' The man looked up at him. The last time they had exchanged such grim looks, they had been on horseback at the gates of Linz in the spring.

Von Volk patted his swollen lip again and cast an angry look across at Morgenstern, who smiled broadly. 'Last night, at the chime of compline, the regimental shrine of the Knights Panther at the palace was robbed.'

'What was taken?' Ganz asked.

'Does it matter? We were out to retrieve our loss when we came upon a group of rascals asking questions and seeking information. It... it seemed to us that they knew something about our loss, so we tracked them and intercepted them.'

'Oh, that's what it was! Interception!' Morgenstern chuckled. 'And I thought it was a sound trouncing!'

Two of the Panthers sprang to their feet, eyes blazing and fists clenched, but Ganz shouted them into place.

He looked at von Volk a minute more and then sank onto the bench beside him, their eyes fixed. 'Panther, we too were robbed. And, as far as we can be certain, so was every other great institution of the city.'

Von Volk seemed surprised at Ganz's candour. He turned away, thoughtful. 'A conspiracy, then?' he murmured.

'And one we have a lead on,' Gruber said, stepping forward.

Ganz and von Volk looked at him.

'Ah, not a good one,' Gruber was forced to admit, grilled by the stern looks of the company commanders. 'But a lead nonetheless...'

As VESPERS STRUCK and twilight dropped across Middenheim like a damask curtain in a theatre pit, they spread out again. Wolves and Panthers together, splitting into parties to search the city even more thoroughly than before. Von Volk had summoned ten more Panthers from the Royal Barracks and they had arrived, clad in plain clothing, to be apportioned off into the working groups.

Aric was with the third group: Lowenhertz, Gruber, Einholt, von Volk himself and two arrogant, silent Panther knights named by their commander as Machan and Hadrick. They passed out into the streets, under the gently swinging lamps. Sultry evening swaddled around them. Now they were all shrouded in heavy capes to disguise their weapons and partial armour.

Gruber paused to look up at the sullen sky with its haze of ruddy, cloudy light. 'A night without stars...' he murmured.

'The stars are there!' Lowenhertz snapped. 'It's early yet, and the twilight haze and cook-smoke of the city are obscuring the heavens. But it will be a clear night. Not a night without stars.'

'Maybe,' Gruber returned, unconvinced.

They were on Tannery Hill, pacing the steep cobbles up to the crest of the city. To either side of them, taverns shook with laughter, music and carousing.

Eight o'clock struck. The bells of the city chimed irregularly, and mismatched. Aric listened to them. Bells, he thought. Just as Gruber had spoken of in his cryptic clues. The first, a delicate plink-plinking note down in Altmarkt. The second a dull bong from Temple Square. The third a triple chime, emptied by distance and the wind, from Ostmark. Then the fourth, a tinny strike from the small church in Sudgarten.

A pause, then the fifth, sixth and seventh came together, overlapping. The last peals drifted away from the College Chapels on the upper slope of the Palast District.

Then a long break, and afterwards the slender tower of the Milliner's struck eight. To the north of them, by several hundred yards.

'Is it just me...?' Aric began. He looked round to see both Gruber and Lowenhertz, transfixed by the staggered sounds and positions of the chimes.

Gruber stroked his lean chin and glanced at Lowenhertz.

'Well, Heart-of-a-Lion?'

'Just... just a coincidence. What are the chances? We happen to be standing where we can hear seven peals to the south and then one to the north. Al-Azir couldn't have–'

Gruber turned to face Lowenhertz fully. His face was expressionless, but

Aric could hear real anger in his tone. The Panther Knights and Einholt looked on, uneasy.

'You bemuse me, Lowenhertz,' Gruber hissed. 'You seem to know more about the mystical and esoteric world than all of us, you bother to chase leads from strange foreigners who would bewilder us with their customs, you urge us to look for secrets in the fabric of the earth... and you deny this? Why? Ulric take me, I'm a blind old heathen next to you, but even I can imagine that your Al-Azir, if he has the skills and knowledge you reckon of him, would have given a portent-clue, particular to us!'

Lowenhertz sighed. 'You're right, old man. You don't understand the delicate ways of enlightened souls such as Al-Azir, Ulric! I don't even pretend to! There was more to his meaning than this! His intellect and understanding is refined far beyond our capacity! He–'

'Would have given us a clue we could understand if we were sharp enough?' cut in Aric smartly. 'How would you explain the complex tactics of a cavalry formation to one untutored in the arts of horse-war? Simply? In words a simpleton could understand? I think so!'

'Aric's right,' growled Einholt. 'I respect you as a battle-brother, Lowenhertz, and respect your learning, but I think you're thinking too hard.'

Gruber smiled. 'Well put, Jagbald, old friend. Lowenhertz, you know your foreign friend was trying to help me, not you. I was the one that asked – a dumb soldier, not a man of learning like you. Wouldn't he have couched his meaning in a way I could understand? And do you not doubt his powers, to know ahead of time we – I – would be in the right place to understand that meaning?'

Lowenhertz was a silent shadow in the gathering dark.

'North of seven bells, he said,' Gruber went on. 'Could it hurt to test that? Could it hurt to believe he has a vision beyond ours? Wasn't that why you took me to him in the first place? And made me take off my damn boots and drink that foul tar?'

Lowenhertz sighed and nodded. He turned and strode uphill, north towards the thin spike of the Milliner's clock tower.

They checked the streets and alleyways around the Milliner's Hall for the best part of an hour. As the clocks chimed again, true dark was settling over the Fauschlag. The hot clouds of sunset had wilted away. The dark bowl of heaven was black-purple and starless.

Von Volk took Aric's sleeve suddenly and gestured upwards. 'Look for lost smoke, Wolf. Wasn't that the damn riddle?'

Aric nodded. He looked where the Panthers' commander was indicating. The night air above the street was hazed by chimney smoke from the homes and taverns around them. The smoke was almost invisible, but it dimpled and blurred the cold solidity of the darkness.

'Then where's that coming from?' asked von Volk.

Aric looked, and realised the Panther's eyes were keen. One column of faint haze seemed to have no source, no obvious flue or chimney to emit it. It simply vented from a space between stacked roof-slopes, ghostly and slow.

'Ar-Ulric seal my lips!' Aric began. He turned and looked at von Volk fiercely.

'Lost smoke?' the Panther asked with a predatory grin.

Aric called the others in to join them and together, the seven men prowled down Chute Lane towards the complex clump of ancient dwellings that the smoke was exuding from.

'Gods!' Einholt spat. 'Where's its source?'

'Nowhere…' murmured the Panther Machan dangerously, his hand inside his cloak, clutching the hilt of his sword.

Gruber stopped them all with a wave of his hand. They were edging into a dark alley, having to stoop low because of the way the buildings on either side leaned in, making a tunnel of relaxed, sooty brick. The alley was full of refuse, mire and a trickle of water. Rats chittered and darted around their feet. Einholt, Hadrick and von Volk filled hand-lamps with oil from a flask and lit them from the same taper, holding the pottery dishes up above their stooped heads as they led the way in.

Fifteen yards down the gently turning alley, probing deeper than anyone but rats or fleeing cut-purses had been in years, they saw it.

'Ulric damn me!' Gruber said, almost voicelessly.

A door. Lower than a man, more of a hatch, built into the brick wall of the alleyway tunnel. Timber-built and strong. And black with pitch.

'Look for the black door,' Gruber said.

'The lost smoke, the north of seven bells…' added Aric.

'On a night without stars,' Lowenhertz finished.

Lowenhertz pulled out his warhammer from under his cape and smashed the black door in off its hinges.

Darkness beckoned them.

WITHIN, A NARROW stairway led down below street level. They had to stoop and hunch, knocking scalps and elbows against the confines.

'Dwarf-made?' Aric wondered.

'As old as the Fauschlag itself,' agreed Einholt, ominously.

From what little they could see around them, by the flickering lamp-flames, the steps were hewn from the rock and turned gently to the right. The walls were travertine brick for as long as the old foundations of the buildings over the alley descended, and then became smooth, tooled stone. They'd gone down at least thirty feet. Leading the way by his lamp, von Volk touched the rock wall and his fingers came away with sticky blackness on their tips.

'Caulked with pitch, like the door. Like a boat's keel.'

'And fresh too,' Lowenhertz muttered, also touching the walls. 'This place is well-tended and maintained.'

'But why the pitch?' Machan asked. 'To keep the damp out?'

'Or to keep something in,' Lowenhertz finished.

The steps levelled out and they found themselves in an underground tunnel tall enough for them to stand up in, but so narrow they could only move in single file.

'Which way?' Hadrick asked.

'North,' Gruber replied with great and awful certainty.

They moved north. After a hundred yards, they came upon another flight of steps down and they descended. The air began to smell of damp antiquity, the sweat of the old rock that now surrounded them and on which Middenheim was raised.

Von Volk's lamp sputtered out and Einholt refilled it from his oil-flask. Once the lamp was reignited, Einholt tossed the empty flask away. 'That's almost it for light,' he told them all. 'I have a little more oil left,' Aric said. 'But maybe we won't need it,' he added, sliding past von Volk, scraping his back on the tarry rock wall. He edged ahead, his feet silent on the smooth, cold, damp of the stone. 'Look. Am I imagining that?'

He wasn't. Light. Cold, fretful light, ahead and below them. With Aric in the lead, they followed it, extinguishing their lamps to save oil as the light grew.

After another hundred yards and another descending stairway, they came out into a wide tunnel of rough rock, like a mine. Threads of tiny silver lamps were looped on wire along each wall as far as they could see in each direction. The rough rock wall was rich with scintillating shards that caught the light and made it seem as if they were walking amongst stars.

'Glass specks… crystal…' murmured Gruber, stroking the rough wall with his fingers.

'Or gems, precious gems,' returned von Volk, looking more closely at the shards. 'This is the spur of an old dwarf mine, or I'm a Bretonnian! An old place, dug long before the city was raised.'

'I fear you're right,' Lowenhertz said. 'This is an ancient, forgotten place.'

'Not forgotten, Heart-of-a-Lion,' Gruber said quietly. 'Who lit the lamps?'

Aric and Einholt both paused to inspect the silver lamps. They were intricate metal trinkets with compact glass chimneys. Their wicks burned with an intense white light, sucking fuel from the reservoirs beneath them.

'They're not burning oil,' Einholt said.

'Indeed not. I've never seen anything like this!' Aric muttered, amazed. Lowenhertz joined him to look. He sucked in a short, startled breath as he studied the lamp.

'Alchemy!' he said, turning to the others. 'These lamps are fired by an alchemical mix, a contact reaction… Gods! The best I know, Al-Azir included, could perhaps have wrought one such lamp in a month of industry!'

'And there are hundreds of them… ranged as far as we can see.' Gruber's voice seemed deflated of strength at the wonder of it.

They paced on down the lit tunnel, two abreast now, gazing about themselves. Gruber and von Volk took the lead, with Hadrick and Einholt behind them, then Aric and Machan, and Lowenhertz bringing up the rear. By now, all had drawn weapons: warhammers in the hands of the Wolves, swords in the hands of the Panthers. Hadrick also carried a crossbow, which he had wound to tension and let swing around his shoulder on a leather strap.

A crossway now, as the mine tunnel they traced intersected with another. The one they followed was lit with lamps and the other dark. There seemed no doubt as to the route they should take. Aric felt beads of perspiration gather on his scalp, despite the musty chill of the rock around him. He had lost all sense of time since they had come down here.

The passage widened and let out into a long, low cavern similarly draped with alchemical lamps. The walls seemed to be made of solid quartz and glowed like ice in the lamp-light. They advanced across the uneven floor.

'I'd be careful, if I were you,' said a voice from nowhere.

The Panthers and Wolves froze, looking about themselves, mystified.

Three figures approached from a side chamber none had seen was there. The Wolves and Panthers swung their weapons up ready. 'Make yourselves known!' cried von Volk.

The three figures stepped into the light of the lamps: a tall man in a long green cloak flanked by two Tilean mercenaries in leather hauberks and quilted leggings, their longswords drawn and their faces dark and stern behind the grilles of basket-helms. The green-cloaked man, whose face was long and clean-shaven, smiled a chilling smile which creased his pale, smooth skin. His eyes were hooded and deeply shadowed by dark skin.

'I am Master Shorack. My full title is longer and more burdensome, so you may know me as that. This pair are Guldo and Lorcha. They have no longer or more burdensome titles than that. They are, however, experienced and terrifying killers. So let's know you without delay.'

Von Volk and Gruber were about to move forward aggressively, but Lowenhertz stayed them both and pushed between them to face the cloaked man. Instantly, the two Tileans swung the tips of their long, gleaming blades to the point at his throat.

'Master Shorack, well met,' Lowenhertz said calmly, as if the swords weren't there.

'Is that you, Lowenhertz of the Wolves?' the cloaked man asked, squinting into the light. He made a subtle gesture and the Tileans smartly withdrew their blades, falling back behind him. He stepped forward. 'My, my, Lowenhertz. Who is this with you?'

'A mixed pack of Wolves and Panthers, master. Seeking the same as you, if I'm any judge.'

'Really? I'm very impressed. Everyone in the city running hither and yon to find their lost treasures, and you... Wolves and Panthers... get as close as me.'

'Who in Ulric's name is this, Lowenhertz?' Gruber spat indignantly.

'Master Shorack, Master Magician Shorack, of the Magicians' Conclave,' Aric said from behind. He'd never met the man, but he recognised the name.

'In person,' smiled Shorack. 'Humour me, Temple-Knights... what led you here?'

'A hunch,' Aric said.

'Determination...' von Volk said.

'Lowenhertz,' said Gruber, stepping forward. 'Or rather, me. From devious clues left by another of your stripe, Ebn Al-Azir.'

Shorack scoffed loudly. 'That charlatan? My dear sir, he's an alchemist, a tinkerer with the world's elements, a child in the realms of creation! I, sir, am a magician. A master of my art! There is no comparison!'

'I happened to like old Al-Azir, as a matter of fact,' Gruber said reflectively, realising he was voicing his thoughts. He paused, then continued anyway, turning to look into Shorack's dark eyes. 'Which is rare for me. Ordinarily, I'd have no truck with such people. In my experience, there are men who walk bravely in the light of goodness, and there are creatures who haunt the darkness and play with magic. There... is no comparison.'

Shorack cleared his throat, looking at Gruber intently. 'Was that some kind of threat, old warrior? An insult?'

'Just a statement of fact.'

'Assuming we're here for the same purpose,' Aric said softly from behind Gruber, 'maybe we should skip the insults entirely and work together.'

'Unless Master Shorack here is behind the injustice we seek to rectify,' von Volk said coldly.

Gruber grunted in agreement. He had been the first to ascribe the thefts to magic, and nothing he had seen so far had disabused him of the notion. Now an actual magician crossed their path, damn his hide...

'Sir! If I was your enemy, you would not be alive to conduct this charming bar-room spat!' Shorack's teeth gleamed in the light. 'Indeed, did I not first cry out a warning?'

'Warning?' Lowenhertz asked, clearly uncomfortable at the confrontation.

'Take it as a gesture of good faith. The hallway you were about to venture down is warded.' The Wolves and Panthers turned to look down the rough-hewn, glowing quartz chamber.

'Magic awaits the unwary and the unprepared here. Guarding magic. Simple stuff, so very much beneath my powers, but it would surely have caught you had you advanced.'

'And done what?' von Volk asked the magician.

Shorack smiled. 'Have you ever been drunk, soldier?'

Von Volk shrugged. 'On occasions. At feast days. What of it?'

Shorack laughed gently. 'Think how it feels to be drunk – if you are a tankard of ale.'

He turned and strode down the uneven floor, raising his hands wide, muttering a few high-pitched words that made Aric think for a moment of fingernails on glass. The sound made him catch his breath slightly. There was a smell too, a distant odour of decomposition, like a drain had been cracked open somewhere nearby.

'It is safe now,' Shorack said, turning back. 'The ward of guarding has been dispelled. We may all continue safely.'

'I stand in awe of your work, Master Shorack,' Gruber said, apparently with great humility. 'You speak baby-talk, break wind and tell us your invisible magic has saved us from a sorcerous trap we couldn't see.'

Shorack paced right up to Gruber till they were face to face. The magician was smiling again. 'Your scorn delights me. It is so refreshing to be disrespected. What is your name?'

'Gruber, of the Wolves.'

Shorack leaned forward until he was nose to nose with the old Wolf. His smile disappeared and was replaced by an expression as cold and hard and threatening as a drawn dagger. Gruber didn't even blink. 'Be thankful, Gruber of the Wolves, that you do not see. Be thankful that the magical world is invisible to your dull eyes, or you would claw out those eyes and die screaming in terror.'

'I'll remember to mention you to Ulric in my prayers,' Gruber replied tonelessly.

'Enough!' barked Aric, losing patience. 'If we're going on together, let's go on! Why don't you tell us what you're here for, Master Shorack?'

'You know already,' Shorack said, turning courteously to Aric.

'We know the Magician's Conclave must have lost something precious, as we have, a treasure as you put it. What?'

'It cannot be named. A charm. Priceless. To describe its properties and purpose would rob you of sanity.'

They all turned as Einholt chuckled. 'Invisible this, unspeakable that! Gruber's right – isn't it funny that we've only got this fellow's word for everything, and that he keeps sparing our sensitive ears from the actual truth. You should work the theatres, Master Shorack! You're a fine melodramatist!'

Shorack looked at him. Aric saw a strange look cloud the magician's face. It seemed like recognition... and pity.

'Einholt,' Shorack said flatly, at last.

'You know me, sir?' Einholt asked.

'Your name just came to me. The invisible world you mock spoke it to me. Einholt. You are a brave man. Stay out of the shadows.'

'Stay – what?'

Shorack had looked away, as if he found the sight of Einholt's face uncomfortable. *No*, thought Aric, *not uncomfortable. Unendurable. As if it... terrified him.*

'Shall we continue, Wolves and Panthers?' asked the magician brightly. Too brightly, in Aric's opinion. Shorack led the party down the quartz hall, his bodyguards at his heels.

'What did he mean?' Einholt hissed at Lowenhertz. 'What was that about?'

Lowenhertz shrugged. 'I don't know, Brother Wolf. But I know this: do as he says. Stay out of the shadows.'

MORE STEPS, A lamp-lit stairwell descending from the rear end of the quartz hall. As far as Gruber could judge, the steps brought them another hundred feet down into the rock, along a wide, sweeping staircase. Three times, Shorack had them stop so he could perform more pantomime and save them from invisible traps.

Enough theatrics! Gruber heard himself think. But there was no denying the cold chill of the nonsense words Shorack used for those pantomimes. Gruber caught Aric watching carefully and with concern. He saw, too, the black worry on Einholt's tense face.

Gruber edged down the steps until he was descending beside Shorack.

'You're a man of esoteric learning, Master Shorack. Have you any explanation for the troubles we find ourselves in? Why the thefts? Why something from each of the city's great institutions?'

'Do you know how to place a charm on a person, Gruber? A love charm, a luck-knot, a curse?' Shorack answered.

'No. I'm a soldier, as you know.'

'Any charm, from the simplest to the most abstract, requires a signifier. Something belonging to the individual you wish to charm. For a love-potion, a hank of hair; for luck, some coins from his purse or a favourite ring; for a curse... well, a drop of blood is the most efficacious. The signifier becomes the basis for the charm, the heart of the ritual that sets it.'

The stairs turned to the left and descended again steeply. The air was getting colder, damper, and now there was a taste of smoke.

'Imagine now you wished to place a charm upon something larger than a man – a city, let's say. A hank of hair won't do. You need signifiers of a different kind.' Shorack glanced at Gruber, one eyebrow raised to enquire if he was making sense.

'The items we've lost, those are the signifiers?'

'Indeed. Oh, I cannot be sure. We may be on the trail of some deranged trophy collector. But I doubt it. I believe someone is setting out to place a conjuration upon the entire city of Middenheim.'

Gruber sucked in his breath. In fairness, he had already begun to imagine such a thing, before he'd even conversed with the prim magician. From the battlefields of his career, he had seen the way the unholy enemy treasured marks of their foe for their mystical potency. They would go to great lengths to take standards, weapons, scalps, skulls. Gruber said nothing more, and led them down the steps.

The stairs brought them out, at last, into a huge chamber that Aric would think of ever afterwards as the cellar. Paved with violet tiles, it was as vast as the drill field of the Wolves' Temple barracks, but broken into sections by rows of pillars that flared upwards into corbel vaults. Aric imagined that once this place had been a huge larder, a wine-storehouse, a provisionary, crammed with racked flasks of dwarf brew, shelves of jarred root vegetables, muslin-wrapped cheeses and pickled fruit, and hung with salted meats. Now it was empty, the walls and pillars pitched black, strung with white lights. A stronger light source emanated from the far end, two hundred feet away, the glow criss-crossed by the back-lit shadows of the pillars. There was a low, sucking, rasping sound, as if the stones around them were taking long, slow breaths. And there was a smell of spoiled milk.

And another sound: a chanting. A murmur of priestly voices intoning something very far away. The sound came from the direction of the distant glow, and was given its rhythm by the beat of a bass tambour. The party spread out low, silently, hugging the pillars for cover. Gruber edged left with Einholt, Machan and von Volk. Aric took the right, with Hadrick and the Tilean, Guldo. Centrally, Lowenhertz advanced with Shorack and the other mercenary, Lorcha. They fluttered from pillar cover to pillar cover, darting between shadows, weapons drawn, moving towards the glow.

Lowenhertz settled into hiding behind a pillar. That sound – not the chanting, the seismic panting – filled his mind with fear. Shorack scurried up next to him, dabbing at the edges of his mouth with a silk handkerchief. There was blood on the cloth.

'Master Shorack?' whispered Lowenhertz.

'Nothing, my old friend,' the magician coughed back. Lowenhertz could smell the metallic stink of blood on his breath. 'Nothing. There are spirits loose in the air here – dead, vile things. The scent of them burns my throat.'

From his position in cover, Aric looked over at the source of the light. A wood fire, kindled in the stone basin of an ancient stone salting bath. The flames licked up, blazing the bundles of fragrant wood spindles incandescently, spilling off the sour stench. The smoke rose, as if pulled, up and out through a flue in the cellar's roof. *Now, at last, the source of the lost smoke becomes clear*, he thought.

Around the fire, stone blocks had been set like shoeing anvils or stools. They had been ranged around the central furnace in a peculiar, apparently random manner. On each one sat a priceless trophy: a glittering pledging cup, a crystal bottle, a gauzy fold of linen, a gold chalice, a beaded and pearled bracelet of panther claws, a mayoral badge, a sceptre, a silver timepiece, a furled dagger, a small silken bag… other items he couldn't make out. And one final one he could: the Jaws of Ulric, gaping, glittering in the firelight.

Aric could also see the twenty hooded figures kneeling amongst the blocks, facing the fire. They were the source of the chanting. One of them struck upon a drum.

At the heart of it all, his back to the fire so he faced the worshippers, stood a thin figure. Emaciated, wrapped in dark wadding, the figure seemed to jerk and move stiffly, like a puppet. It twitched in time to the beat. Aric could not see any detail, but he knew it was the most loathsome thing he had ever seen. He wished to be anywhere else now; fighting beast-packs in the Drakwald would be a holiday next to this horror.

Crouched behind the pillar next to Shorack, Lowenhertz realised how pale and perspiring the man had become.

'Shorack?' Lowenhertz whispered in concern.

Shorack settled his back to the pillar for a moment, trying to slow his breathing. His face was damp and pasty. 'This is… bad, Lowenhertz,' he murmured. 'Crown of Stars! I spend my life flexing my powers in the invisible world, and the gods know sometimes I tinker with the darker excesses. Their lure is great. But this… this is ritual magic so dark, so foul I – I have never seen or felt its like. Lowenhertz, I never even dreamed such abomination existed! This place is Death's place now!'

Lowenhertz looked at the magician in the dim light. The sense of him as a haughty, capable figure was all gone now, all his confidence and theatrical airs wasted away. Lowenhertz knew Shorack was powerful for an urban magician, among the best of his kind in the city. His skills had been enough to get them this far. But he was just a man now; a frightened man, way out of his depth. Lowenhertz felt immeasurable pity for the magician. And immeasurable fear for them all. If the great Shorack was scared…

From his vantage point, Gruber laid low on his belly and took in the scene. There were the lost treasures, and he had no doubt that they were being used, as Shorack had described, as signifiers in some great charm. *No*, he reconsidered, *curse is probably a far more appropriate word*. His flesh crawled. That panting, breathing sound around them, as if the walls were sighing. That beat, that chanting. And worst of all, that jerking puppet shape by the fire. Gruber wished Ulric had been merciful and spared him from ever having to see such a thing.

Von Volk was beside him. Fear made von Volk's eyes black, unblinking pits. 'What do we do, Wolf?' he whispered.

'Is there a choice, Panther?' Gruber mouthed. 'A great and stifling darkness is being born here that will overwhelm the city we guard with our lives. We must do what we were trained to do and pray it is enough.'

Von Volk nodded, took a deep breath, readied his blade and then looked across the cellar to Aric's group on the far side. The Panther commander caught Hadrick's eye and made a curt, chopping motion with his fist. Hadrick raised his crossbow.

The beat slapped. The chanting continued. The stones panted around them, sucking for breath. The fire cracked. The reek of death and decay choked the air. The puppet figure twitched.

Hadrick fired.

The crossbow bolt hit the twitching puppet in the chest and smashed it backwards into the fire. It shrieked – a ghastly, not-human noise – and clawed at the barb impaling it, floundering in the flames that licked into its filthy swaddling.

The hooded worshippers stopped mid-chant, jumped up and began to turn. A second later, the Wolves, Panthers, and Shorack's mercenaries were on them.

Aric charged the firelight, hammer whirling in his hand. It all became a blur. Lorcha was beside him, his longsword hissing through the air.

The puppet thing, ablaze like a torch, was still shrieking and trying to pull itself out of the fire.

The hooded chanters spun to meet them, throwing aside black velvet capes to reveal fierce men in mail-armour, brandishing swords and war-axes. Their screaming faces and their armour were plastered with blood and daubed markings.

Aric's whirring hammer smashed through the face of the first enemy he came upon. The hammerhead tore out the lower jaw, sending the pink, glistening hunk away like a blood-tailed comet, winking with exposed white bone. The next one was on him, and he blocked with his hammer-haft, stopping the axe-blow. Kicking low and hard, Aric dropped the attacker and then rolled in to crush his head flat between hammer and violet tiles.

Gruber waded in, breaking a neck out of true with his hammer, then spinning to face the next sword that came at him. Einholt was beside him, cleaving a ribcage with a sidewards strike. Von Volk broke his sword on his first clash with an enemy blade, and then savagely ripped the life out of his aggressor with the broken length, before throwing him aside and snatching up his axe. In von Volk's practised hands, it dug deep into the skull of the next foe within arm-reach.

Lowenhertz smashed a chanter backwards off his feet with a deft underswing that splintered a snarling face.

Machan struck at them, his sword whispering. Blood sprayed from the wounds he cut. Then he was scissored by two enemy blades. He dropped, screaming, in two, blood-venting pieces.

Hadrick had, by then, enough time to reload, and he slammed his bolt into the forehead of one of Machan's killers. A second later, he was carried back, shrieking, and pinned to a pillar by a foe whose lance had impaled him. Guldo decapitated the foe and pulled the lance out, allowing Hadrick to fall. But he was already dead.

Aric was nearly at the sacred jaws, but then he took a rip across the shoulder and went down on one knee. Gruber and Lowenhertz were hemmed in by fierce hand-to-hand on all sides. The top of Guldo's head was axed off and he fell, stone dead. Von Volk swung his axe up between the legs of a foe-man and split him to the sternum. But his captured axe was wedged and he tried in vain to pull it free.

Shorack raised his hand and with a gesture, at once slight yet full of unknowable power, wilted one of the chanters into fatty, smoking residue. The sounds and stinks of burning metal and flesh choked the air. The sorcerer shook slightly and took one step back as if to steady himself. Then he spun and destroyed the cultist closing on Gruber with nothing more than the clenching of his hand in the air. For a moment, Lowenhertz noted through the ferocious melee, the old Shorack was back with them, imposing, confident, capable, chilling.

Aric broke an opponent's hip and a ribcage. He turned. He saw. The burning, shrieking thing in the fire was getting up again, blackened and smouldering and tarry.

It looked at them through cindered eye-slits. It fixed its gaze on Shorack. It spoke through a mouth thick with fat blisters and crackling flesh.

'Die,' it said, its voice that of a dead thing.

Shorack screamed as if his insides were boiling. Gruber reached for him, but the magician was wrenched into the air by things none of them could see but all could feel. Cold forces of air, eddies of icy wind. Einholt smashed an axe-man aside and reached out to grab Shorack's trailing cloak. He realised with fear that he was seeing the effects of Shorack's invisible world for real now.

The magician spun up, away, out of his reach, thrashing and bedevilled by the harsh grip of unseen things. His green cloak, his clothes, one boot, all shredded off him and fluttered away. Weals and bloody rips scourged his flesh. Almost stripped bare, drenched in blood, half-butchered, Shorack slammed up into the vaulted roof. Bones snapped. It looked as if he had fallen upwards and hit the ceiling as if it was the ground. An immense, invisible force pressed him there, spread-eagled on his back. Blood pooled across the roof around him instead of pouring to the actual floor.

His ruined face, a mask of blood, glared down at Gruber and Einholt looking up from below. It was all the other Wolves, the Panthers and the remaining Tilean, Lorcha, could do to keep their attentions and eyes on the battle at hand. There was something mesmerising about Shorack's gruesome, inexorable demise.

Shorack looked down into the frantic face of Gruber. A moment before his eyes burst and his skull collapsed against the roof, he spoke. Eight words, forced out of a blood-filled mouth, the last act of his life, a monumental act of will power.

'Break. The. Charm. Without. The. Signifiers. It. Cannot.'

Eight words. A ninth, maybe a tenth, would have completed the whole, but the meaning was enough for Gruber.

An invisible force exploded Shorack's carcass across the roof in a shower of blood and meat. It coated the ceiling for a moment and then rained down on them all, leaving a pungent mist of blood vapour in the air.

Gruber was already moving, his hammer raised. Coated in Shorack's blood, he found two of the enemy turning to block him, axes raised. Gruber swung the warhammer round in a complete, whickering circle, both hands gripping the leather loop at the end of the haft, twisting his bodyweight to counterbalance the swing. Two skulls broke like earthenware before the swing was done.

Then he was clear, amongst the stone blocks set around the fireplace, each one bearing its precious icon. He knew he was within the weave of a great dark sorcery now, something invisible that laced itself between the signifiers. His skin prickled with static, his hair stood on end, and there was a smell that clawed at his sinuses. A smell of sweet corruption, like a week-old corpse. Magic, he knew, and would never forget. Black magic. *Death magic.*

He thought of Ganz, on the dangerous ride back from Linz, how he had driven the wraith-things back by destroying their precious talon. He knew he had to do the same... again... now... here. A signifier must be destroyed to break the charm. And he knew, clearly and coldly at last, what Al-Azir had really meant.

They cannot be recovered. They are lost to you for ever. Gruber of the Wolf, I pity you. But I admire your courage. Eh! Even though you will lose what is dear to you.

There was no choice. It was set, Gruber was sure, in the intricate and unchangeable workings of the stars. He had time for one blow and he knew, as a Wolf of the Temple of Ulric, where, in fairness, that blow should fall.

The Jaws of the Wolf, so holy, so precious, cut by Artur himself, glittered on the block before him.

He raised his hammer.

Something ripped into his back and agony lanced through him. Gruber screamed. Talons raked down his back from shoulders to waist, shredding off cloak, hauberk and undershirt and slicing deep cuts in his flesh. He stumbled to his knees. The blackened puppet-thing rose up behind him, its curled, skeletal fingers like hooks, red with his blood. It twitched, deathless eyes glittering, and smashed Gruber to the floor with a sideswipe. Blood poured down the side of Gruber's head where the swipe had struck. For the rest of his life, his left ear would be a rag of flesh, like a flower with the petals torn off.

Gasping, Gruber looked up at the monster that lurched and jiggled over him. Its long, angular limbs twitched and spasmed like a badly-worked marionette. *Or no*, thought Gruber, his pain lending his mind frightening clarity. *Like something half-finished. Like a mockery of a man, a skeleton that remembers how to move but hasn't the flesh or the sinew or the practice to do it well.* Backlit by the firelight, that was all it seemed to be: a large human skeleton, clad in shreds of tomb-dry skin and scraps of burnt bandage, twitching and jerking as it tried to behave like a man again. Tried to be a man again.

Only the eyes were whole: coral-pink fires of livid fury. It gazed down at him. Its bare, sooty teeth clacked open, tearing the dry, blistered flesh of its long-withered mouth.

'Die,' it said.

'Die yourself!' snarled Einholt, storming in from the side and smashing the dreadful thing into the air with an expert swing of his hammer. Twisting, the puppet-thing tumbled away into the darkness beyond the fire.

Einholt glanced down at Gruber once, but he didn't hesitate. It seemed the veteran Wolf had wit enough to arrive at the same conclusions as Gruber. Einholt swung around, hammer lifted over the block, resembling for all who saw, the great god who first wrought the Fauschlag. Then the Jaws of the Wolf, the precious icon of the Wolf Order, disintegrated into a million flying fragments under his hammerhead.

And then… nothing.

There was no great explosion, no fiery flash, no sound, no fury. The cellar just went cold. The walls stopped breathing. The reek of magic vanished and the static charge in the air dissolved. The fire went out.

Blackness. Cold. Damp. The smell of blood, and of death.

Flints scraped together and a small light pierced the gloom. A lamp was lit. Carrying it, Lorcha moved into the circle of blocks, retrieved the small velvet pouch and put it in his jerkin.

'It is made right,' he said to the others in the darkness around him, his accent thick with Tilean vowels. 'I will inform the Conclave.'

A moment later, and he and his lamp were gone.

Aric lit a taper from his pack and raised its small yellow light aloft. Lowenhertz did the same, lighting the last of the lamp-oil he carried. Faint light filtered into the gore-soaked chamber. Urgently, they took kindling from a stack behind the fireplace and made torches. Einholt helped Gruber from the floor.

'Ulric love you, Brother Einholt,' Gruber said, embracing him.

'May Ulric forgive me too,' Einholt replied.

By the kindling light, they gathered the trophies into sacks, Aric reverently handing the panther claw bracelet to von Volk.

The Panther took it and nodded to Aric. 'Ulric watch over you for what you have done here. Your sacrifice will be known to all of my order.'

'And perhaps our orders may not be such rivals from this time,' Gruber suggested as he limped over. 'Panther blood has been spilled to achieve this too.'

He and von Volk clasped hands silently.

'We have everything,' Einholt said. He and Aric carried sacking full of the most precious things in the city. 'I suggest it's time to get out of here. Our light won't last long and there are citizens of Middenheim who will be relieved to get these trinkets back.'

Lowenhertz loomed behind them, a torch raised. His face was pale and determined in the half-light. 'There's… there's no sign of it. The thing Einholt struck. It's destroyed or–'

'Escaped,' Gruber finished.

CONFESSION

THE AIR ABOVE Middenheim was cold and still. Below, winds found their way in and out of every byway and alley, whining through gaps in the stones and sucking over damp cobbles. Autumn had come.

The street braziers were built higher, their flames licking against the stone walls, making their black surfaces matt with soot, their fires burning till dawn. Dusk came early now and for many the working day was foreshortened. Citizens were keeping shorter hours, preparing for the harshness of the winter to come, when many would die of the cold and the numerous winter ills and ailments that befell the towering city's population year in and year out.

But for some, the autumn season simply meant they began and ended their working days in darkness. One such was Kruza. He went about his work sleekly, picking his final mark of the day. The last of the merchants were leaving the city in torch-bearing gaggles, among them a rotund middle-aged man with a florid flare of red across his high, round cheeks and magnificent bulbous nose. His pockets looked heavy and, tucked half into the breast of a long, embroidered coat which would not fasten across the fatty mound of his chest, the strings and clasp of a pouch were clearly visible. Kruza spotted him coming out of one of the better alehouses at the edge of Freiburg and followed him into the north end of the Altquartier slums.

Kruza strode easily on past his mark, whose own rolling gait and small steps made slower progress down the steep cobbles. The cut-purse paused for a moment and then turned back the way he had come, checking the position of the purse in the merchant's coat as he passed him, very close. The mark took no heed.

Kruza had marked his target and was ready to make his move when he saw something ahead of him. He flicked his eyes up and away from his intended victim, just in time to see the hem of a long, grey cloak disappear into the doorway of a tavern on the opposite side of the narrow street.

Kruza paused, then took a few more hesitant steps. When he turned back to his mark, the man was disappearing down and round into a sloping sideway. Kruza began to follow the merchant again, trying to concentrate, reminding himself of his quota.

But he could feel the hunting eyes behind him now.

He turned sharply on his heels and this time the pair of cloaked figures, for there were two of them now, barely had time to duck out of sight.

In an instant, Kruza forgot his mark and ducked into the shadows himself. He held the cold palms of his hands flat together before his face, as if in prayer – to Ranald, maybe, the trickster thief-god. No, to any god who would listen. His hands were suddenly clammy with sweat. He felt a bead form on his forehead and find the groove of the long scar down the side of his face. It trickled down the scar to his jaw. It hung there for a moment, then it was joined by another droplet of sweat. The two fell as one from his chin.

He had watched for this moment for months, prepared for it over and over, but now it had finally come, he was not ready. He could never be ready for the return of the grey men who bore the gleaming tail-eating snake sigil. They had got Wheezer and now they would get him.

Kruza stepped out into the middle of the narrow street, looking about him, not for a place to hide, nor for support from others, but to get the lay of the land. He had a sick feeling that there was justice in them coming for him. They had taken Wheezer, and he had been an innocent. His soul wasn't soiled like Kruza's. Of course they would come for him, a hundred times as fierce.

There was only one way to deal with this. He had run before and Wheezer had paid the price. This time he would stand and fight. And if he died, then he would no longer have the boy's doom on his conscience. His hand on the pommel of his short-sword, Kruza stood with his feet braced on the cobble-ridges and his shoulders thrown back. He let out a huge shout – of challenge, of remorse, of warning. Those who heard it could not tell what it meant, only that they should stay away. Kruza heard doors bang and the shutters close on windows all around. Then silence.

The men in grey cloaks heard the cry too as they stood in the next alley, shielded from sight.

'A brave boy, this cut-purse of yours,' the taller, leaner figure said in a low, sardonic voice. 'He means to come to us!'

The shorter, heavily-built second figure turned lightly on his feet and stepped into the deserted street, pulling his companion after him. They stood, thirty paces from the braced figure of the cornered cut-purse, whose scream was still echoing around the close buildings and losing itself in the labyrinth of the Altquartier's streets and alleys.

The taller of the grey figures put a hand beneath his cloak, reaching for his weapon. His heavier companion raised his hands to the hood which cloaked his face in cloth and shadow, and opened his mouth to call out.

But Kruza flew across the thirty paces between himself and the grey men before any had a chance to speak. His short-sword was raised above him in a two-handed grip. He meant to bring it down hard, and fight to the death, even if it was his own. His bloodshot eyes, with their lids peeled well back, showed white all round the black holes of his massively dilated pupils. Another yell began to find its way past his gritted teeth.

Then came the impact.

Kruza barely held on to his short-sword as it bounced and twitched in his hands from the hammer blow which had swung from nowhere to knock it from his grasp.

He swung again in a crude, wobbling arc which was parried hard by a deft hammer-haft, sending tiny shards of steel and wood flying with the intensity of the blow.

Kruza's next swing came in low, but not deep enough. It tore a huge rent in the flowing grey of the taller figure's cloak.

The figure jerked away and threw his head back, freeing it from the shadowy cowl of the cloak's hood. Kruza saw a face with pink-flushed skin and dark eyes that gleamed back at him. There was no sign of the papery skin and pallid thinness of the other grey men. This man was flesh and blood – and ready to fight for all he was worth.

A hammer came in again, swung by the shorter grey man. Kruza blocked it ferociously and sliced in with his sword. The shorter man dodged it. He, too, had removed his hood and had shrugged off half of the cloak. Around his body, Kruza could see the pelt.

He had seen that skin before. His mind raced as he swung his sword again at the fur-wrapped torso. As he cut deeply through the hide, missing the man beneath, Kruza thought of that other man. Weeks back, at the Baiting Pit! The man with his parcel of armour wrapped in a hide, just like this one. The masked gladiator!

Kruza looked into Drakken's face, confused. *The White Wolf. Lenya's White Wolf! Was he one of the grey men?*

Kruza's nostrils flared wide as he sucked in air to control his panic. Spittle coated his lips and his teeth were clenched, allowing no more sounds to escape his body. There were two hammers whooshing through the air around him in a show of Wolf Temple strength. Or was it the strength of the grey men? He did not know.

His short-sword found only air with its next strike. Then, turning and striking again, he felt flesh rip at the end of his sword. Before he could savour it, he was on the ground, doubled over, shocked and winded by a solid blow to the centre of his chest.

Why... why was he not dead? Why had the blow not killed him? Why had he been allowed to live when he was prepared to die?

Kruza let out a soft moan as he lay on the ground.

ANSPACH RUBBED A fist against the flesh wound to his shoulder, as Drakken knelt down by Kruza's sprawled form, tentatively reaching out a hand to grab the broken thief.

Anspach was thoroughly enjoying himself. Drakken had spoken to him of a cut-purse whom he needed to find – some personal feud, so it seemed, one he wanted to keep quiet. The young Templar had enlisted Anspach's help to do it. It wasn't so difficult for a man with Anspach's knowledge of the city's underbelly, and the little battle in the quiet street of the Altquartier was a positive bonus. Something to warm the cockles on this cold autumn night. Drakken had not told him the young thief had so much spirit, or such a strong sword arm. No harm done. A light flesh wound to the shoulder that would heal in no time, and the indignity, for Drakken, of having his pelt rent into two pieces, neither of which would be big enough to cover the huge young Wolf's torso now.

Explain that to Ganz, Anspach thought to himself. He smirked down at the strange picture of a bedraggled Wolf, offering his hand to a young street thug. He felt almost nostalgic.

ON THE NORTH side of Middenheim, a giant, blond Wolf Templar strode down the wide avenues just south of the Palace. Alongside him was a tiny woman, her feet skittering in a half-run, half-skip to keep up with him.

'But why did Krieg send you? And where are you taking me?' Lenya gasped, breathing hard and trying to hold her skirts and cloak up out of the thin rime that was beginning to glisten across the even cobbles.

Bruckner stopped in his tracks. Lenya almost overtook him, and then passed and leaned forward, holding her side.

'I have a stitch. Can't we go a little slower?' she asked.

'A little, perhaps,' Bruckner said, not really looking at her. 'Drakken asked me to escort you, for your own safety. He will tell you himself why he needs to see you.' He still did not look at his companion, possibly because he would have to stoop a long way to look her in the face – or perhaps simply because he had a job to do, a favour to perform for a colleague, one that held no interest for him.

Bruckner strode on southward, checking himself after a few of his long strides and slowing down just enough for Lenya to keep up with him. If she ran every other step.

DRAKKEN AND ANSPACH half frog-marched and half carried Kruza out of the street and into an adjoining alley, where he could recover for a moment away from the people who had heard the fight and were now coming out to see what had happened.

The cut-purse sat, his back to a mossy wall. He coughed and spat onto the dark, earthy ground between his jutting knees. He seemed meek enough now as Anspach stood facing him, leaning against the opposite wall. There was only just room for the two of them. Drakken stood to one side, waiting for the cut-purse to recover so that he could continue the business of the evening. He had expected Kruza to come quietly, expected him to be a coward, like all street scum. He felt grudging admiration for the bravery Kruza had shown in fighting them, however ill-conceived it might have been.

Kruza looked up briefly at Anspach. In a single flicker of his eye, he took in the stature of the man: the slight injury he had suffered, the position of his warhammer, his elegant, relaxed stance. Kruza had the eyes of a thief and he used them now. He marked every detail. Then he leaned forward in another loud, convulsing coughing fit. His head bent, his hand darted out, the elbow still resting against his knee.

Drakken did not know what was happening. Suddenly Kruza was on his feet, the point of a short dagger pressed into Drakken's neck, with Anspach crying out and stumbling back, caught, off-guard and unsuspecting for one fleeting moment. But only for a moment.

Anspach brought his hammer round low at little more than half-tilt and took Kruza out at the knees. The cut-purse fell on his rump, hard on the earth floor of the alley, and dropped the knife that he had taken out of Anspach's boot during his dramatic coughing fit. Kruza raised his hands, knowing, at last, that he was beaten.

'It's over. Use me, as you will. Or kill me,' he said. And Anspach smiled again. This was turning into quite an evening of entertainment. That young cut-purse had taken his knife without him feeling it! *Ulric, but he was good!*

Anspach gave his hand to Kruza. The cut-purse thought he saw the Templar grin as he pulled Kruza to his feet. But their gaze had met for only the briefest moment, and Drakken was pushing in to take charge of the situation again.

'Behave! There's someone I want you to talk to,' Drakken said. 'Follow me. Anspach, watch our backs.'

LENYA AND BRUCKNER continued south at a slightly more leisurely pace, but try as she might, the serving girl could not draw the Wolf into any kind of conversation.

'You must at least be able to tell me where we are going?' she asked.

'You'll see,' was his only answer.

'How far is it?' she tried again.

'Not far,' he said curtly.

Down another sloping street, along the north wall of the Great Park, and then south again. He said nothing more and Lenya did not know what else to ask. She watched her feet traverse the cobbles, first smooth and broad and flat, then, in the poorer quarters, ragged, chipped, uneven. Here, the stones were smaller and arranged in swirls and mosaics that bore no resemblance to the even brickwork to the north. So... at least she knew that they were heading toward the Altquartier.

KRUZA FOLLOWED DRAKKEN, with his even stride, while listening to the relaxed, light tread of the one called Anspach behind him. They didn't have far to go. Turning north and west in the cold air, through almost empty lanes, they stopped outside the great double doors of the quarter's ostlers.

The ostler did a poor trade here. His stables were only full when the city was brimming with rich visitors. Sometimes the overspill from the more respectable handlers to the north would find its way here. But this establishment's richest customers were still only moderately comfortable merchants who left the city for their country dwellings by dusk and only needed somewhere to keep their horses during the hours of trade. It was not such a bad life for the ostler and his sons, and not a bad living. The stables were always empty at night, so the bedding straws were changed only with the turn of the moons, and the horses, who ate in their country stables at dawn and dusk, demanded little feed during daylight hours.

Drakken swung one of the doors open, just wide enough for the three to file in. There was the light of a single torch, resting in its rusty sconce against the courtyard wall. The yard opened into a series of narrow stalls, with stable half-doors. The place smelled of stale bedding-straw and age-old horse dung.

Kruza had never been near a horse. There were few in the Altquartier, and those he met with in other parts of the city he gave a wide berth to. But there was no noise here, no snort or trample, and the cut-purse relaxed slightly when he realised all the stalls were empty.

But he did not relax for long. Drakken rounded on him as soon as they were off the street, pushed him back against the coarse boarding of a stall panel. He stood with his face tilted up to meet Kruza's. Their noses were almost touching.

Drakken had a deep frown on his face and Kruza tensed all over again. His body felt like a series of taut cables and blocks of unyielding rock, like the pulleys and counterweights of the lifts that served the Fauschlag, yanking and stretching at themselves as they hoisted impossible burdens.

His chest felt so tight and hard he wondered how he would breathe. With Drakken right in his face, he wondered how much longer he would be allowed to breathe. Kruza looked slyly at Anspach, who stood guard by the great, black door, which hung on its hinges, just ajar. No ally there. Kruza knew the Wolves would stick together.

'She'll be here soon,' Drakken began.

She? thought Kruza and then realisation dawned. *Lenya! I must account to Lenya for Wheezer's death. That is why they have brought me here. And then this Drakken will kill me!*

'After the fight at the Baiting Pit, you took flight. I suppose I can't blame you. I scared you off, calling you a thief and a liar and a murderer. And mayhap that's what you are. But if you are, then Lenya deserves to hear it from your own mouth. She will not listen to me.'

'Lenya needs to know what happened to Wheezer. She sought him out. She talks of nothing but her brother, of the dead ends she followed. She talks of you knowing him. If you really know what happened to her brother, then you must tell it plainly and put her mind at ease once and for all. And if you killed him, then you will answer to the Watch,' Drakken finished grimly

What can I say to her, Kruza wondered? The moment when he could have told her everything was long gone. Gone with that last meeting, the night they were saved from the Baiting Pit by this same White Wolf. When he realised, with true shock, that her brother was the same boy he'd tried to forget. *I don't want to tell her any of it. I don't understand it. All these months I have tried not to think of it!*

But with this pair of White Wolves watching him, he knew that he would have to tell Lenya something. He decided in that moment that he would rather have paid with his life in the street where the three of them had done battle, than face Lenya with his story.

There was no more time for thought. Lenya was backing into the stable courtyard through the narrow door. She was talking to someone who must have been on the other side.

'Why would you bring me here? This can't be right!' she exclaimed and then, turning, saw them. Her eyes locked onto Kruza, who bowed his head and said nothing. Then she was running towards Drakken. She put her hands on his broad torso and he took her elbows gently, one in each hand.

'Lenya,' he said, 'I brought you here to talk to the cut-purse. Ask him what you like about your brother. He will answer your questions.' This last he said with his eyes locked on Kruza. It was a warning.

Lenya turned, Drakken still holding her gently,

'You knew Stefan?'

'No… I knew Wheezer…' Kruza realised they were repeating the last words they had spoken that night after the fight in the Baiting Pit.

'Leave us, Krieg,' she waved an arm at her Templar-lover, her intent gaze not leaving Kruza's face.

'What power the milk-maid has,' Anspach said wryly to Drakken as they stood together in the street with Bruckner, outside the ostlers. Drakken looked at him.

'Power over the Wolf and the cut-purse both,' Anspach finished, amused. Drakken glanced down, a deep flush of anger and embarrassment climbing up from his neck, over his face and deep into his brow. It was followed by a frown that furrowed into the flush on his crimson forehead, leaving purple and white lines.

* * *

'I KNEW WHEEZER,' Kruza began by repeating himself. 'I knew him by no other name. He said he had no name. The bastard child of a nobleman and a mother who died in childbirth. I couldn't know he was your brother.'

I called him "brother", but I never even knew that for sure. No one really knew him, Lenya thought. *Mostly we barely noticed him. But she said nothing.* Kruza was talking and she thought if she interrupted him, he would stop. She wanted to hear it, whatever it was he had to say.

'He didn't look like you.'

He didn't look like anyone, she thought.

'You said he was honest, do you remember?' Kruza asked, but he didn't wait for an answer. 'He was, in a strange way. I caught him stealing from an old cut-purse, a teacher of mine. But he only stole what didn't belong to anyone, or what was surplus or excess. I was his first visitor. His first friend in Middenheim. I hope I was his friend.'

If you were his friend, you were the only friend he ever had, thought Lenya, and the memory pained her. *People were cruel to him, if they saw him at all. In the end no one even seemed to see him.*

'I've never known anyone who could steal like he could. Silently, without being seen. I... I used him.' He hung his head. 'I'm not proud of it, but at least I didn't recruit him and let Bleyden get hold of him and use him worse. We were friends.' It was as if he was talking solely to himself.

You couldn't use Wheezer. He had his own kind of freedom, his own ways, thought Lenya, but said nothing. She knew truth when she heard it.

There was a long pause, and she realised that they were still standing in the middle of the stable courtyard. It was open to the stars and the night was turning purple and cold. Grey and black clouds the colour of the Fauschlag Rock were scudding across the sky, obliterating the twin moons, and she felt the deepening chill. Kruza stood stock-still in front of her, as he had been standing when she first entered the courtyard. Lenya put her hand out to Kruza, who shrugged it off before it even met his sleeve.

'Don't! You won't like me after you've heard this. I used him... he stole to help me fill my quota. I would dare him. It was a game,' he said, not looking at Lenya.

Just don't try playing hide and seek with him, Lenya thought.

'He stole for me and I listened to his tales. He had the most extraordinary room, full of beautiful things. We drank together and I would fall asleep on his couch, half-listening to his stories. I knew I was using him, using his skills as a thief, but I meant him no real harm. He liked to play the game and then go back to talk about the witches that brought him up. Nonsense like that. No one else saw him, you see.'

Mother's little foundling, she thought, *and now I'll never know why she called him that, and why we all laughed, my father, my brothers, even my mother, sadness in her eyes. Maybe he didn't belong to us at all. Maybe he never belonged to anyone.*

'I think he died, Lenya. I'm sorry. I think he's dead.' Kruza had thought it for a long time, but he'd never said it before.

Dead! Before I could find him or understand him. Why did he have to die? The moan that was in her heart never found its way to her lips. She felt slightly faint.

'He was invisible, he should have been safe... but he didn't come out. He never came out.' Kruza's voice was low and he was surprised by how calm he sounded. He knew what to tell her now. 'I thought it was just a trick, or luck, that no one ever saw him. But it wasn't.'

'He stumbled on a smuggling scam, a big one.' Kruza paused, looking at Lenya for the first time. She looked pale. The girl shivered.

Lenya was cold and afraid. She turned about in confusion, looking for somewhere to go, somewhere to feel safe and warm. There were only the empty stables around them, but surely they would yield some heat. She turned her back on Kruza and walked toward the half-door on the nearest stall. She placed her hand on the old blackened latch. It was well-greased and moved easily under her hand. She turned again to Kruza. He realised she was waiting for him and walked toward her. She turned into the dark stable, which smelled much like the stables back in Linz. It reminded her of the horses she sometimes tended and the cows she often milked there. Kruza remained standing, slumped a little against the half-door. He was tired and heart-sore. Even though he had survived the ordeal with the Wolves, he felt the worst was yet to come.

'There were smugglers. Wheezer knew. He followed the bodies, told me the story,' he began again once Lenya was settled in a pile of old hay.

No one ever saw Wheezer. That's how he could disappear for days at a time. 'Off with his folk!' mother would say. Now, I don't think she was being fanciful. We never knew where he was or what he was doing, but I was always happy to see him return from the woods. I loved him and I loved his stories. Lenya took a breath when she remembered again that Stefan was dead, her memories of him tumbling over and over in her head.

Kruza went on, halting. 'Only they weren't bodies. And the grey men weren't from Morr's Temple. They were smugglers, bringing all manner of things into the city. Ah, I don't even know why I'm talking to you. Wheezer's gone.'

There was a part of Lenya that wanted to ask about the smugglers, who they were, where Wheezer had followed them to. But she knew if she asked, Kruza might not want to talk to her at all. She felt a chill that she hadn't expected in the warm, close air of the old stable.

Kruza made small circles in the hay dust on the floor with the point of one of his boots.

'Wheezer took me to the smugglers' place. I didn't want to go in there at first,' Kruza said, looking at Lenya in a way that prevented her asking the question he dreaded: Where did Wheezer die?

She sat still and Kruza continued to make the small circles with his foot. His head was bowed and she could barely hear him. 'Wheezer was excited. There was so much there, he said. "It's there to be taken," I remember his words. It seemed... it seemed like an easy job.' His voice dropped yet further.

Lenya leaned up onto her knees, closer to him, wanting to hear it all, whatever was left of his reminiscences. Kruza lurched back from her unhappily, as if he didn't want to be any closer.

'The smugglers were there, dozens of them. They saw us. I tried...' he blurted, unconsciously running his hand down the narrow scar on the side of his face, almost hidden by his hair. Lenya had not seen it before.

He got that scar trying to save Wheezer. He was Wheezer's friend, she thought. *Why does he doubt it?*

'I got out and I waited. I waited in his room. I don't know how long. I waited until there was fresh dust on the stairs, but Wheezer didn't come back.'

Kruza paused for a moment, then suddenly turned on his heels and left the stall. He crossed towards the door that led out onto the street, which was open just a crack. A moment later, it swung wider out on its hinges and Drakken stepped in out of the shadows.

'Well?' he asked.

Lenya, emerging after Kruza, was about to answer when she realised that Drakken was talking to the cut-purse. Kruza looked like he had seen a ghost. He had that same look he had when Lenya had first said the name Wheezer all those months ago.

'It's okay,' Lenya told Drakken, on Kruza's behalf. She took the lad's arm. 'Thank you,' she said, not knowing what else she could say. This man had tried to save Wheezer's life. He had a scar. There was nothing left. She had mourned Wheezer for too long already.

'Now do what you will with me,' Kruza said as Drakken stood before him. 'I will die peacefully, if die I must.'

'No!' Lenya cried, firm and unafraid. 'Let him go, Drakken. He has done no wrong. He was Wheezer's friend and he did him no harm.'

Lenya allowed Drakken to take her in his arms.

'And thank you, Krieg,' she said. 'I can let Stefan rest now.'

THEY PARTED. KRUZA strode away from the place as fast as he could, trying to lose himself in the dark streets. He thought that he had put Lenya's mind at rest. Maybe...

He wondered if Wheezer was at rest. He wondered if his own mind would ever be at rest.

He had told the story. He had told what had happened to Wheezer. Well, so he had left some things out, things his mind had long since tried to blank. There were things in this city that you didn't speak of, that you forgot as quickly as you could. Like the grey-cloaked men and their hideous place.

Lenya knew quite enough. Now she could mourn and sleep easy. As for himself, he would forget. Forget it all. He would go to the Drowned Rat and wash it all out of his mind. Lenya, Wheezer, the damn Wolf… even the grey men.

LONE WOLF

THE MAGICIAN WAS *looking at him, intently, fiercely, as if he recognised him.*
'Einholt,' said Shorack flatly, at last.
'You know me, sir?' he asked, surprised.
'Your name just came to me. The invisible world you mock spoke it to me. Einholt. You are a brave man. Stay out of the shadows.'

Einholt sat up on his cot in the darkness. His mouth was dry and his skin was wet. The dream had changed. For the first time in twenty winters, the dream had changed, melted away, been replaced by another.

Perhaps he should be pleased, but he wasn't.

The dormitory around him was quiet and lit only by pre-dawn starlight shafting from the clerestory windows. His brothers in White Company snored or coughed under rumpled blankets on the rows of cots set against the white-lathe walls.

Naked except for his knee-length undershirt, Einholt swung out of his bed and put his bare feet flat on the cold stone floor. He murmured a hoarse daybreak prayer to Ulric, breathing deeply. Then he pulled his wolf-pelt around his shoulders and crept down the length of the dormitory, half-blind, his night vision still weak.

He pulled the heavy dormitory door closed behind him quietly and stepped out into the cloister yard. Hooded candles burned with pale light around the square, set on plinths next to the entrance of each of the Wolf Company dormitories. The sky was lightless yet, and the air was cold and grey with the dawn light. Not yet matins, Einholt thought. By the candle-plinth next to the entrance to White Company's sleeping hall, there was a jug of water and a pewter cup. Einholt took a long draft of the icy liquid, but his mouth remained dry.

'*Your name just came to me. The invisible world you mock spoke it to me. Einholt. You are a brave man. Stay out of the shadows.*'

He tried to shake the thought out of his head, but it was stuck as fast as a flint under a warsteed's shoe. Just theatrics, he chided himself. He'd said as much before, to the man's face, in fact. That haughty magician had been an actor, full of dramatic flourishes that meant nothing. He'd just been trying to scare him.

But Shorack had known his name. And there had been nothing theatrical about the way he'd died, crushed against that pitchy cellar roof.

Einholt paced his way through the sleeping precinct of the Temple, along cold halls and through vestries with rough matting floors.

Stay out of the shadows.

He murmured the prayer of protection they had all learned by rote on admission to the Order, over and over to himself. Torches that had burned through the night fluttered as they began to die in wall sconces. Dead smoke drifted through the cool air. Outside, far outside, early cockerels began to crow. Something rumbled. Distant, autumnal thunder, the cold sky rubbing icily against itself.

Einholt tried to remember his dream. Not the dream of the harsh night, not Master Shorack and his warnings. The original dream. The one that had lasted twenty winters. His scar twitched. Funny, it had been with him for so long, haunted him for so many years, and now it was hard to remember even a scrap of it. The new dream had usurped it completely.

Your name just came to me. The invisible world you mock spoke it to me.

He entered the Temple via the west porch, under the great barrel-vaults of the vestibule. Two Wolf Templars stood guard, warming their hands at a brazier set on a brass tripod. Fulgar and Voorms, of Grey Company.

'You rise early, Einholt of the White,' the latter said, with a smile, as he approached them.

'And dress informally,' Fulgar smirked.

'Ulric calls me, brothers,' Einholt said simply. 'Would you delay answering him by stopping to dress?'

'Ulric watch you,' they intoned reverently, almost as one voice, letting him pass.

The Temple opened to him. Ulric, a vast shadow in the dome, loomed over him.

Einholt knelt before the altar, the multitude of candles flickering around him. A long moment's contemplation, and he at last snagged the old dream, as one would catch the sleeve of an acquaintance passing on a busy street.

Hagen, twenty winters past. How could he have forgotten that? The Red, the Gold and the White Companies together, great Jurgen in overall command of the field. The phalanxes of green-pigs down in the vale at the edge of the brook, raucous and whooping. Four hundred of them, more besides, shambling, heavy-set, shaking spears and axes into the winter noon.

'Now we'll see glory,' von Glick had said with a gleeful laugh that they all joined. Von Glick. Younger then, firm and thick with muscled middle age, hair dark and wild.

Gruber too, the great unswaying oak of the company, at Jurgen's right hand. Morgenstern, a trimmer man then, the company rogue, throwing witty jibes down the slope at the greenskin beasts. That was a time long before drink had coarsened and slackened his bulk, before Anspach had joined them and taken Morgenstern's crown as company joker, before he had become nothing but company drunkard.

Kaspen was there, of course, a red-headed youth, his first time on the field. Reicher as well, bless his arm. And long-mourned Vigor, Lutz and the boy, Drago, the young pup Einholt had been given to personally train, recently and heroically baptised in action and now hungry for more. Vigor would see another three seasons, Lutz another decade in the service of Ulric. Drago would not see another daybreak.

Jurgen rose in the saddle and beheld the foe. Grave behind his studded eye-patch, he turned to the Temple companies. He told them battle was drawn.

That's wrong, Einholt told himself. Dreams do that, they play with the facts. Jurgen lost his eye at Holtzdale, years later. But this was the great Jurgen as he remembered him best, branded into his memory. And Reicher. Hadn't he fallen at Klostin, years before the fight at Hagen?

Twenty long winters turning the events of that day over in his sleep. No wonder the details weren't right anymore. Hadn't there been one awful night, years back, just after the battle, when he dreamed that he and only he, Jagbald Einholt, had sat on the rise, facing the green-pig horde alone?

Kneeling before the altar, Einholt sighed. He leaned forward, resting on his splayed hands now as well as his knees, as the memories, both true and false, swirled up around him like flames. As they had done, every night for twenty years. Until tonight.

The massed charge down the slope. That was true. Jurgen's booming order, the wailing cry of the Templars, the thunder of hooves.

Dawn thunder rolled outside the Temple, outside his dream. *Hooves*, he thought.

He could smell the mashed sap of the torn grasses, the roped spittle of chargers, the stinking adrenaline sweat of the men around him. He was moving, making his own thunder as he came down the slope outside Hagen, horse and Wolf fused into one fighting being.

They caught the enemy at the brook, riding them down despite their superior numbers. More of the foe died from trampling than hammer-blows that day.

His steed hit the water in a wall of spray, breaking two squealing pigs under its lashing hooves. Kaspen was next to him, rejoicing in the glory of battle, his youthful fears forgotten. How many times had Einholt seen that transformation since then? Aric, on his first venture... Drakken at Linz... a wonder to behold. A wonder in honour of the Temple. Wolf-cubs, thrown into the fire and coming through unburned and jubilant. Like Drago.

Had he ever been that young? Had he ever been baptised in battle that way? Surely, but so very long ago.

For the glory of Ulric now, in the brook-bed, water thrown up, blasting all around them, drenching them. Blood drenching them. Scything hammers cutting the spray, shattering fanged snouts. Broken, exploded green carcasses, floating in the water around their steeds. On the far side, chasing down the stragglers, Wolves urging their mounts up into the bulrushes. Thick stems snapping and whipping on either side. Screams from behind. His hammerhaft slick in his hand.

Young Drago, galloping past, yelling out, 'With me, Einholt!' Drago turning to the left into a spinney of willows. Full of the wolf-spirit, over-confident.

Not that way. Not that way. He was bolting after Drago now, bending low under the slashing fronds of the weeping trees. Not that way.

Cut right, no, *left*! Where in Ulric's name was Drago?

Every time. Every night. The same fierce effort to change the facts.

Not that way. Not into the willow stand. Not this time...

Drago was screaming suddenly. A scream choked in blood. Too late! Always too late! Drago, down in the rushes, his dead steed on its back nearby, hooves curled up towards the weeping branches overhead. Blood-steam in the air from its ripped belly. Pig things, crowding round Drago, hacking down at him again and again and–

Einholt's curse was white-hot. He ploughed into them, his hammer whirling. Bones snapped and things squealed. A greenskin reeled away, blood fountaining from its cloven skull. Drago! *Drago*!

Dismounting, running to him, blind to the danger.

You are a brave man. Stay out of the shadows.

Drago! There! Crumpled in the rushes, like a fledgling in a nest. Alive, praise Ulric please, alive! Struggling through the bulrushes to Drago, the shadows of the willows falling across him.

Stay out of the shadows.

Drago...

Dead. Unmistakably dead. Torn. Ruptured. Butchered. His splintered hammer still clutched in hacked-off fingers.

Rising, turning, raging.

You are a brave man.

A green thing right behind him. Foul breath. Snorting rage. A reek of animal sweat. An axe, flint-bladed, vast, already sweeping down.

Now, oh yes, now the point of the dream. The moment that always woke him, dry-mouthed and wet-skinned. Every night for twenty winters.

The impact.

Einholt swung back onto his haunches in front of the altar, realising he had cried out. His hand went to his face, an involuntary gesture, tracing the line of the livid scar with shaking fingers. From the brow, down through the eye, down the meat of the cheek to the line of the jaw. Einholt closed his good eye and let blackness wipe the world away.

'Ulric watch over me...' he murmured. A tear of pain trickled from his good eye. His bad eye hadn't wept for twenty years.

'He is always there to watch over you, brother. Ulric does not forget his chosen ones.'

Einholt switched round to see who had spoken. By the glow of the candles, he saw a hooded priest of the Temple standing behind him. He couldn't see the man's face under the fold of the hood, but the priest radiated kindness and calm.

'Father,' Einholt breathed, recovering his scattered wits. 'I'm sorry... a dream, a bad dream...'

'A waking dream, it looked to me.' The priest approached, holding out thin, pale hands in a gesture of calming. He seemed to limp, unsteady. *He is old*, Einholt thought. *One of the frail, ancient masters of the Temple. This is an honour.*

'I have been troubled by my dreams for a... a long time. Now I am troubled by the change in them.' Einholt breathed deeply to clear his mind. What he'd just said already seemed stupid to him.

The priest knelt beside him so they were both facing the high altar. His movements were slow and shaky, as if old, rheumatic bones might shatter if he moved too swiftly. The hooded cleric made the sign of Ulric and uttered a small blessing. Then, without looking round at the Templar, he spoke again.

'The way of the Temple Knight is never peaceful. You are raised and bred to take part in the bloodiest of wars. I have seen enough Templars come through this place to know none are ever untroubled. Violence perturbs the soul, even holy violence in the name of our beloved god. I can't count the nights I've listened to the complaints and fears of Wolves who come to this high altar for succour.'

'I have never shirked from battle, father. I know what it is. I have seen a share of it.'

'I'm not doubting your courage. But I understand your pain.' The priest shuffled his position, as if making his fragile old form more comfortable.

'Your dream of twenty years. It scars you?'

Einholt managed a thin laugh. 'I was too late to save a good friend's life, my pupil's life. And I paid the price. I wear my scars, father.'

'So you do.' The priest seemed not to look at him, but Einholt could not tell how the unseen head moved inside that cowl.

'This has troubled your dreams for years. I understand. But Ulric burns such things into our dreams for a purpose.'

'I know that, father.' Einholt wiped a hand across his sweat-drenched, bald scalp. 'The memory focuses my thoughts, reminds me of the duty and the dues we owe to the Great Wolf. I have never complained before. I have lived with it and it has lived with me. A badge of honour I wear when I sleep.'

The priest was silent for a moment. 'Yet tonight, for the first time in years, it brings you here, makes you cry out.'

'No,' said Einholt simply, then turned to look at the cowled shape beside him. 'I came because the dream has gone. For the first time, it didn't come to me.'

'And what did?'

'Another dream. The first new dream I've had since the Battle of Hagen.'

'And was it so terrible?'

'It was nothing. A memory.'

'Of something recent?'

'I was one of the brothers who destroyed the curse below the city just days ago. I smashed the Teeth of Ulric so that the magic would founder.'

The priest tried to rise, but faltered. Einholt reached out a brawny arm to support him, and felt how thin and skeletal the arms of the old man were beneath the robes. He helped the priest rise. Stiffly, unsteadily, the old priest nodded his thanks, the cowl barely moving, and shuffled round behind the kneeling Wolf.

'Einholt,' he said at last.

'You know me, sir?' Einholt asked, surprised. He felt a terrible sense of déjà vu. As if it was Shorack beneath the cowl, Shorack repeating the strange act of recognition he had made in the quartz tunnel under the Fauschlag.

'Ar-Ulric himself has praised your action,' the priest said. 'The commanders of the Knights Panther have sent letters of commendation. Other institutions in the city, on recovery of their trophies, have honoured your name. Of course I know you.'

'Will Ulric forgive me for my crime?'

'There was no crime.'

'I broke the Jaws of the Wolf of Holtzbeck. Our holiest of holies. With my Temple-blessed hammer, I smashed them apart.'

'And saved Middenheim, perhaps. You are a brave man.'

Stay out of the shadows.

'I–' Einholt began to rise.

'Ulric forgives you a thousandfold. You knew when to place valour above possession. When to put the city before the Temple. Your sacrifice makes you most beloved of Ulric. You have nothing to repent.'

'But the dream–'

'Your conscience belabours the act. It is understandable. You feel guilty for simply being part of such a momentous undertaking. But your soul is clean. Sleep well, Einholt. The memory will fade. The dreams will flicker and die.'

Einholt rose fully, turning to face the stick-thin figure in the cowled robe. 'That... that is not what I dream of, father. I know that breaking the Jaws was the right thing to do. If I hadn't done it, Gruber would have, Aric,

Lowenhertz. We all knew it must be done. I do not repent the act. I would do it again, if events were repeated.'

'I'm glad to hear it.'

'Father... I dream of a magician. He was part of our fight. He died. The invisible world where Ulric dwells, that realm alien to me... tore him and broke him. Magic, father. I don't know anything about that.'

'Go on.'

'Just before we fought, he spoke to me. He knew none of the others, but he knew me. He said–'

'Einholt,'

'You know me, sir?'

'Your name just came to me. The invisible world you mock spoke it to me. Einholt. You are a brave man. Stay out of the shadows.'

Einholt realised he had paused.

'What did he say?' prompted the old man.

'He said the invisible world knew me too. It had told him my name. He warned me to... to stay out of the shadows.'

'Magicians are fools,' the priest said, jerking as he shuffled around to turn away. 'All my life, and believe me it's been a long one, I've mistrusted their words. He meant to scare you. Magicians do that. It's part of their power, to be theatrical and play upon honest men's fears.'

As I thought, Einholt realised, relieved.

'Einholt... brother... there are shadows all around you,' the old priest said, holding up a palsied, frail hand to gesture at the many sidelong shadows that were cast by the altar, the candles, the lancet windows in the gathering dawn, the statue of Ulric himself.

'You cannot stay out of shadows. Don't try. Middenheim is full of them. Ignore the magician's foolish prattle. You can do that, can't you? You're a brave man.'

'I am. Thank you, father. I take your words with gratitude.'

Outside, matins struck. Behind it, came a rumble of... hooves. No, Einholt reassured himself. Dawn thunder. An early winter storm chasing the edges of the Drakwald. That was it.

He turned back to speak to the Temple father again, but the old priest was gone.

HE HAD BEEN in the Temple balneary for almost an hour when Kaspen found him.

'Einholt?' Kaspen's call broke the steamy quiet. There had been nothing louder than the slosh of water and the sound of Temple servants pumping fresh water into the heating barrels in the adjacent furnace chamber since he had first come into the bath-house.

Einholt pulled himself up to a sitting position in one of the great stone tubs, wiping water from his goatee and looking across at his red-haired Wolf brother.

'Kas?'

Kaspen was dressed in his Temple workshirt, breeches and boots. His thick mane of fire-red hair was pulled back in a leather clasp behind his skull.

'Your cot was empty when we rose, and when you didn't join us to break your fast, Ganz sent me to find you. Some of Grey Company said they'd seen you in the Temple at dawn.'

'I'm all right,' Einholt replied, answering his friend's unspoken question, but he felt stupid. The pads of his fingers were wrinkled like dried fruit. The water in the stone basin around him was tepid. *Ulric, it didn't take a man an hour to wash night-sweat from his body!*

But some things took more effort to wash away.

Einholt pulled himself out of the water and Kaspen threw him a scrub-cloth and his undershirt. Einholt stood dripping on the flags beside the basin, rubbing water and dead skin off his body vigorously with the rough cloth.

'So... you're all right.' Kaspen turned and helped himself to oat-cakes and watered honey from the bench table by the door. Einholt knew that tone. He and Kaspen had been particular friends since the younger man had joined the company. That was... *twenty years since*. Einholt had been in his prime then, twenty-five years old, and the teenaged Kaspen had been one of the pups given to his charge to train. A red-haired youth, still clumsy and long-limbed, joining the other young cub already in his charge.

Drago.

Einholt pulled on his undershirt, wrapping the scrub-cloth round the back of his neck. 'What's on your mind, Kas?'

'What's on yours? Is it the dream again?'

Einholt flinched. Kaspen was the only other member of the company he had confided his troubled sleep to.

'Yes. No.'

'Riddles? Which?'

'I slept badly. I can't remember why.'

Kaspen looked hard at him, as if waiting for more. When no more came, he shrugged. 'Rested enough for weapons drill?' he asked.

THE HOURS BETWEEN terce and sext were given to weapons drill each weekday for every Templar, no matter his level of experience. In the sparring yard, Gruber, Drakken, Lowenhertz and Bruckner were already at work, along with Wolves from Red Company. The other members of White Company were on a watch rotation at the Temple.

Einholt and Kaspen strode down the yard steps in full armour, pelts slung away from their hammer-arms ready for practice. The morning was damp and cool, though the dawn thunder had gone. The autumn light was glassy and sidelong, and threw long shadows off the canopies along the eastern side of the yard. Gruber and the other men of White were working at the row of pels in the shade, refining techniques against the wooden practice posts with double-weight weapons to develop their strength. The men of Red were wrestling on a straw mat, or putting stone shot to build their throwing power.

Einholt felt no inclination to join them. He stopped in the middle of the yard, in the clear light. Out of the shadows.

'Let's allow Ulric to guide us, Kas,' Einholt said, as he did from time to time in the yard.

Kaspen made no comment. He knew what that meant, had known it from the day Jagbald Einholt, his friend and one time mentor, first led him out into the practice square. He stopped beside him, facing the same way into the morning sun, placing himself carefully so that he was two hammer-and-arm lengths from his comrade.

Wordlessly, they began. Perfectly matched, perfectly synchronised, they raised their hammers and began to swing them. Round to the left, back to the right, high to the left, low to the right, two-handed holds, grips flexing expertly as they nursed the centrifugal pull of the heavy-headed hafts.

Then, smartly, full circles to the left ending in hard stops, hammers raised; a drop that allowed the hammer-heads to begin to fall before they used that descent to power into underswings to the right.

Round again, the other way, hammers hissing in the air. Faster now, switching to a one-handed grip on the haft-loop; up right, figure-eight, switch hands. Down left, figure-eight, switch back. Straight to the right and around, arresting the swing and switching hands again. Straight to the left and round, feet gently pivoting as they urged their weapons through the air, barely moving anything else but their arms from the shoulders.

Faster still, like a murderous, silent dance whose rhythm was struck out by the rush of their weapons, as only two master warriors who have practised together for years can manage.

Now the increasing force and speed with which they moved their weapon-weights around moved them too. Wide swings round to the rear in their right hands, causing them both to jump-step smartly to stop the hammers tearing away. A mirror repeat, reverse step.

Then back to twin-palm grips, this time with the right at the base of the haft, left at the head, spinning the hammers before them like staves, practising the use of the haft for blocking. With each return, a grunt and a stamp forward. Block right, hilt upright. Block forward, haft cross-ways. Block left, haft upright. Repeat. Repeat faster. Repeat, repeat, repeat.

In the far shadows, Bruckner stopped his work and nodded his companions over to look. They all stopped, even the Wolves from Red Company. Though the most novice Wolf was an expert with the warhammer, few Templars in any of the noble companies could put on an exhibition drill of such perfect matched-timing as Einholt and Kaspen. It was always a pleasure to watch.

'Ulric's name!' Drakken murmured in awe. He'd seen the two Wolves practise many times, but never like this. Never with such flawless grace, never with such speed.

Gruber frowned, though he had seen it on occasions before. *They're pushing themselves. Like they have something to get out of their systems. Or one of them has, at least.*

'Watch them closely, and learn,' he told Drakken, who needed no encouragement. 'I know you can handle a hammer well enough, but there's no end to the mastery. See the way they switch hands? There's barely any grip there. They're letting the hammers do the work, using the force of the spin to carry them where they want them.'

'Like a horse,' Lowenhertz said beside him, clearly impressed. 'You don't force it, you guide its strength and weight.'

'Well said, Heart-of-a-Lion,' Gruber remarked, knowing there was little any could teach the saturnine Wolf about hammer-use. 'There's more skill in the controlled use of a warhammer than in a dozen sword-masters with their feints and nimble wrists and fancy prancing.'

Drakken smiled. Then his expression ebbed. 'What are they doing?' he asked, nervously. 'They're moving closer to each other!'

'Krieg, my lad,' Bruckner chuckled, 'you'll love this bit...'

Einholt and Kaspen now moved well into hammer-reach of each other, head on, their circling weapons and arms just blurs. The pace of the practice was marked out by the whistling chop of the weapons as they punched through the air. Each side-swing precisely missed the swing of the other, so that Einholt and Kaspen were like a pair of hurricane-driven windmills face to face, the sails of one slicing deftly in between those of the other.

There were impressed murmurs from the Red Company men behind them. *Now the switch*, Gruber thought, waiting for it.

Breaking his rhythmic swing out from the cross-swirling hammers, Einholt went low and swung at Kaspen's legs, as the red-head leapt over it and swung high through the empty space where Einholt's head had been. Without breaking speed, they reversed and repeated, Einholt leaping and Kaspen ducking. Neither was stinting on strength. If either faltered, if either connected, the blows were full-force killing blows. Mirrors, they swung at each other, each side-stepping to dodge the other's circling weapon, Kaspen left, Einholt right, then back again, across and repeat.

'Madness!' Drakken gasped.

'Want to try it?' Bruckner joked to the stocky young Wolf.

Drakken didn't reply. He was all but hypnotised by the dancing warriors and their whirling, deadly hammers. He wanted to rush out there and then and tell Lenya all about the incredible show he'd seen, though for the life of him, he didn't know how he'd describe it or make her believe it.

Left. Right. Under. Above.

Whooff! Whooff! Whooff! Whooff!

Drakken looked to Gruber as if he was about to applaud.

Above. Left. Under. Right.

Whooff! Whooff! Whooff! Whooff!

The hammer-spinning fighters circled each other, moving around, advancing towards the watchers under the awning.

Right. Above. Left. Under.

Whooff! Whooff! Whooff! Whooff!

Their turning bodies edged into the shadow of the canopy.

Lowenhertz suddenly grabbed Gruber's arm. 'Something's–'

Under. Left. Right. Right–

The hurtling hammers crossed together and struck. The powerful crack resounded across the yard. Einholt and Kaspen were flung backwards from each other by the impact, Einholt's hammer-haft splintering.

Curses and oaths broke the suddenly still air as the Wolves of White Company ran forward to their two sprawled comrades, the men of Red close behind.

Einholt was sitting up, clutching his armoured right forearm. His right hand was bruised and swelling. Kaspen lay on his back, unmoving, his left temple torn open, blood leaking down onto the flags.

'Kas! Kaspen! *Aghh!*' Einholt struggled to rise, the pain of his sprained arm knocking him back down again.

'He's all right! He's all right!' barked Lowenhertz, stooping by Kaspen, pressing the end folds of his wolf pelt into the head wound to staunch the blood. Kaspen stirred and groaned.

'Just a graze,' Lowenhertz insisted. He flashed a reassuring look back across to Einholt, as Bruckner and Gruber got the bald Wolf onto his feet.

Nursing his arm, Einholt pushed past his comrades to reach Kaspen. His face was as dark as Mondstille.

'Ulric damn me,' he murmured.

Kaspen was sitting up now, grinning ruefully, dabbing at his head and wincing.

'I must be getting slack, Jag. You caught me a good one.'

'Get Kaspen to the infirmary!' Gruber snapped, as men of Red Company helped Bruckner and Drakken carry the bleeding Wolf out of the yard. Gruber glanced round. Einholt was looking down at his broken hammer. He chafed at his swelling, purple wrist and hand.

'You too, Einholt!' Gruber snarled.

'Just a sprain…' Einholt murmured.

'Now!'

Einholt wheeled on the veteran Wolf. 'It's just a sprain! Some cold dressing and a herbal balm and it'll be fine!'

Gruber stepped back involuntarily. Einholt, quiet, self-mastered Einholt, had never spoken to him or anyone else like that Not ever.

'Brother,' he said, forcing calmness into his voice. 'You're a brave man–'

'And I'll stay out of the shadows!' Einholt spat, and strode away across the yard.

* * *

LOWENHERTZ EDGED QUIETLY into the regimental chapel of the Wolves. The air was thick with incense, the rich perfume hanging heavy in the cold autumn air.

Einholt was kneeling before the empty plinth that for years had been the resting place of the Teeth of Ulric. His wounded forearm, stripped of its vambrace, the leather under-sleeve pulled back, was clutched to his chest, the flesh puffy and black.

'Einholt?' he breathed.

'You know me, sir?'

'Like a brother, I hope.' Lowenhertz was glad when Einholt looked up, the fury gone from his eyes.

'It was the shadow, wasn't it?'

'What?'

'The shadow of the canopy. It made you hesitate for a moment, made you mis-swing.'

'Maybe.'

'Maybe nothing. You know I was there. I heard what Shorack said to you.'

Einholt got to his feet and turned to face Lowenhertz. 'And I recall your advice. "Do as he says. Stay out of the shadows." Wasn't that it, Heart-of-a-Lion?'

Lowenhertz looked away. 'I know what I said. Ulric save me, I didn't know what else to say.'

'You're not like the others. Not like me. You take magicians and their kind seriously.'

Lowenhertz shrugged. 'Sometimes, maybe. I know they can often be right when they seem wrong. But Master Shorack was always a showman foremost in my experience. Full of cheap tricks. You shouldn't take his words so seriously.'

Einholt sighed. He looked away from Lowenhertz. 'I know what he said. I know what I dream.'

Lowenhertz was silent for a moment. 'You need help, brother Wolf. More help than I can offer. Stay here. Here, I say. I'll find Ar-Ulric. He will calm your mind.'

Lowenhertz turned to go.

'Kas is all right, isn't he?' Einholt asked, quietly.

'He'll not forget the lesson today, but yes. He'll be fine.'

'Been a long time since I taught him anything,' Einholt said sourly, looking back at the great Wolf Pelt on the wall. 'Twenty winters...' He coughed. 'Two pupils I've let down now.'

'Two?'

'Drago. Before your time with us.'

'Kaspen's no pupil any more,' said Lowenhertz. 'He knew what he was doing today. Practice accidents happen. I once broke a thumb in...'

Einholt wasn't hearing him.

Lowenhertz paused in the cage-door of the chapel. 'Brother, you're not alone, you know.'

'My hammer,' Einholt said quietly. 'I broke it. Funny, I've been wanting to ever since I used it to smash the Jaws. Didn't think it should be used for anything after that.'

'The weaponsmiths will bless you a new one.'

'Yes... that'd be good. The old one was... used up.'

'Stay here, Jagbald. I'll find the High Priest.'

Lowenhertz was gone and Einholt sank down in front of the Great Pelt again. His fingers twitched. His scar ached. His mind was flushed with images of Hagen Field over and over again.

The greenskins, their tusks so white and sharp... the willows... Drago screaming. The impact. The shadows of the trees.

Stay out of the shadows.

'You are still not at peace, Wolf.'

The old voice crackled through the air behind him.

Einholt looked up. It was the ancient, cowled priest from the dawn before. 'Father?'

Einholt supposed Lowenhertz must have sent the old man to sit with him while he sought out Ar-Ulric. The fragile figure stalked towards him, one claw hand out to steady itself against the chapel wall. The thin form cast a long, brittle shadow in the candle light.

'Einholt. You broke the spell. You smashed the Jaws. Ulric is pleased with you.'

Einholt paused, looking down at his knees. 'So you say... but there's something in your voice... as if you are not, father.'

'This world has taught man that he must make sacrifices. For those sacrifices to be truly potent, that which is sacrificed must be valuable too. Things, lives, men. The same for all. I believe the most valuable Temple Wolf of all now is the one that shattered the Jaws of Ulric and dismayed the darkness. That's you, isn't it, Einholt?'

Einholt got to his feet. The throbbing pain in his wrenched forearm was terrible.

'Yes, that's me, father. What of it? Do you mean that somehow I have become more than I was before? That my action has bestowed some particular significance upon me?' Einholt fought to keep fear from his voice, but true fear was what he felt. Nothing in the holy shrine reassured him. The old priest's words disquieted him in ways he could not even begin to explain. 'You talk as if I am now invested with some power...'

'The history of our Temple, our Empire – even the world itself – is full of men who have become more than men by their deeds. Champions, saviours, heroes. Few choose such roles. Fewer still are ready to deal with what it really means. Your actions have made you a hero. That is your destiny. The blood of heroes is more holy than that of mortal men. In the invisible world, such men are luminous.'

Einholt opened his mouth to speak, but his voice died. He shivered, his breath shallow and fast. 'I-invisible world? Just this dawn past, in the Temple, I told you what the magician had said to me, told you he said the invisible world knew me too. Said it had told him my name. You told me to forget it. To dismiss it as nonsense. Now you... echo his words.'

'You misunderstood me, Templar–'

'I don't think I did! What is this, father? What game are you playing?'

'Calm yourself. There is no game.'

'In the name of Ulric, father, what are you saying to me?'

'You simply need to understand your destiny. More than most men. Seek that, and your mind will find peace.'

'How?'

The old priest paused. 'Ulric always amazes me, brother. To some he gives the question, while to others he gives the answer.'

'What does that mean?' Einholt barked, yet louder and angrier than before.

The old man in his cowled gown held up his arms in a calming gesture. His limbs quaked and shook, so very frail. 'Ulric has given the question to you. He has left the answer to others.'

Einholt grabbed the priest by the front of his tunic and held him tight so that the old man gasped inside his cowl. His breath stank of age and putrescence. Einholt tried to look into the darkness of the cowl, but light seemed to refuse to enter.

'*Which others?*'

'You're hurting me, wolf brother! My old bones!'

'Which others!'

'Morgenstern. Morgenstern knows.'

Einholt cast the old priest aside and rushed out of the chapel. Those Panthers, Wolves and worshippers of Ulric present in the Temple were perplexed to see a Wolf Templar, rushing from the regimental chapel and out towards the door, evading each pool of shadow and following the lances of sunlight shining in through the western windows.

EINHOLT ALMOST COLLIDED with Aric on the steps of the temple.

'Morgenstern! Where is he?'

'Einholt?'

'Morgenstern, Aric! Where is he?'

'Off duty, old friend. You know what that means...'

Einholt spun away from Aric, almost throwing the younger knight to the floor as he raced away.

THERE WAS NO sign of him in the Split Veil, or the Coppershiners. The Swan in Sail had last seen him a week Tuesday, and he had a tab to pay. The surly staff in the Drowned Rat said he'd been in early, supped a few, and then heaved his bulk out, saying he was heading down to the stews in Altquartier.

Altquartier, with vespers approaching and the sun heaving sideways in the sky. Einholt descended the steep streets and curling, mossy steps of Middenheim, past late-goers chasing homewards or barwards as the sun set. It became increasingly difficult for him to dodge the shadows. He hugged the eastern side of every curving street and alley, hungrily keeping to the last shafts of sunlight shafting over the roofs opposite. He avoided three streets completely because evening shadow had blanketed them entirely. But he kept on.

You are a brave man. Stay out of the shadows.

The Cut Purse. Its beckoning lamps shining. Early yet, late sunlight splashing the edges of the street. He kept to the light, a fever in his brain now, bursting in through the bar-doors so sharply that all present looked round at him.

'Morgenstern?'

'Here an hour since, now off to the Cocky Dame,' said a bar-girl who knew her employer didn't want any trouble with the Temple.

Einholt was running now, running like a lone wolf hunted by a pack of hounds. The pain in his dangling arm was forgotten, or blanked at least. He eked out every thread of sunlight in his path, skirting round the rapidly growing shadows of the early autumn evening.

Thunder, in the distant sky. Like hooves.

He hurtled into the Cocky Dame, lower on the city slopes, deeper in Altquartier. Einholt smashed two drinkers off their bench as he slammed in through the curtain door. He picked them up, tossing coins from his purse into cursing, scabby faces which bit off their snarls in alarm when they saw who had unseated them.

'The Wolf Morgenstern. Is he here?'

The chief barmaid was a powdered, dissolute sow with several black teeth, a stained balloon cap and a scent of week-old sweat not even a whole bottle of perfume could mask, though that's how much she'd clearly applied. She grinned a lascivious domino grin and propped her low-cut bosom up under her arms and pushed it out at him. 'No, my fine wolf, but there are more interesting things in the – *ow!*'

He had pushed her and her pallid frontage aside. 'Where's Morgenstern?' he snarled into the face of the barman, grabbing the startled bruiser by the collar of his patched jerkin. Einholt yanked the man off his feet and over the bar-top towards him on his chest, scattering earthenware jugs and pewter cups.

'Gone! Not here!' The barman stammered, trying to wrestle free from this mad Wolf, gazing up in true fear. The tavern all around fell silent. Brawls were common, but to see a Temple Wolf, in full armour and pelt, blood-mad – that was a frightening novelty.

'Where?'

'Some n-new place down in the old quarter! Opened just a few days ago! I heard him say he wanted to try it out!'

'What new place?'

'I forget–'

'*Remember*, Ulric damn you!'

'The Destiny! That's what they call it! The Destiny! Used to be something else! Now it's the Destiny!'

Einholt threw himself out of the Cocky Dame, and skidded to a halt. He had grabbed at the barman with his wounded arm, unthinking. Now renewed pain coursed in his limb like fire. He should have been calmer, taken Gruber's advice, had it seen to. There would have been time enough for this madness on the morrow. Time – and safety. Now the sun was done. Vespers had just struck.

The shadows were everywhere. Long shadows of evening. Black smudges of twilight. Dark stains of night. Daylight was a vague, departing twinkle above the glowering, blind roofline, far out of his reach even if his arm had been sound.

Einholt turned, panting hard. He reached up to grab one of the lamps hanging outside the Cocky Dame, then winced and pulled back with a curse. Spitting to clear his mouth, he reached out again more gingerly, now with his good arm, folding his damaged limb against his breastplate. He lifted the lamp off its hook and held it above him. Light surrounded him. He cast just the smallest shadow, a little pool under his feet. Raising the lamp high, he hurried down the Altquartier street, pulse throbbing, arm aching, mind tumbling.

After a while, he yearned to change hands with the lantern, but his bruised forearm was worse than useless. Sweat pricked his skin as he maintained the effort of keeping the lamp aloft. It was brass and lead glass, as heavy as a hammer. Twice he had to set it down on the cobbles and crouch into its light, resting his over-stressed arm.

By the twitching light, round the next steep corner, he saw the newly-painted sign: the Destiny. One of the festering, one-room stews in the grimmest Altquartier slums, changing hands and identities almost from day to day. *Destiny*. He chuckled at the irony despite himself. He had found his destiny, all right.

Einholt pushed in through the drape doors.

'Morgenstern! Morgenstern of the Temple!' he barked, swinging the lamp around. In the flickering gloom, various drinkers slid away from him and removed themselves from the attention of his questing light.

He pushed further into the stink, half-stumbling over a discarded wooden board in the gloom. The old sign board of the inn, its previous identity, taken down when the new management took over.

He was at the bar now, a row of lacquered barrels with a teak plank on the top. He slammed the lamp down on the teak, smashing a bowl.

'Morgenstern?' he gasped, out of breath, into the faces of the staff.

'No Morgenstern here, Templar… but if your name is Einholt, there's a fellow yonder waiting for you.'

Waving the lamp like his own personal totem, Einholt glanced around. At the end of the bar he saw–

The old priest. How in the name of Ulric had the old, lame man got here ahead of him? How had he known?

'Father? What is this, father?'

'An end to things, Einholt.'

'What?'

'Want a drink?' asked the barman, convivially, moving close. Einholt pushed him away roughly.

'What do you mean, father?'

The old priest's voice rose out of his robes, pungent and sallow. 'You were the Wolf that destroyed the spell. Broke the Teeth of Ulric. Saved your city.'

'Yes, father.'

'Good. It can be only you. You are the most... *guilty*.'

'What?'

'You are my truest foe. I could not touch you in the Temple, but now I have chased you out into the shadows where you are vulnerable at last.'

The skeletal priest slowly turned towards Einholt. The cowl flopped back. Einholt was appalled by what was revealed beneath. He was a Wolf Templar and a servant of Ulric, who had fought beastmen and things of the Darkness – and still he had never seen anything so monstrous.

Einholt backed away.

'Look,' said the unliving thing that had masqueraded as the priest. It gestured with a claw at the discarded sign board Einholt had stumbled over.

He saw what it said.

You are a brave man. Stay out of the shadows.

Einholt started to cry out, but the rake-thin creature under the cowl suddenly moved so very fast. A blur. Einholt knew what was coming. It was like... the moment. Like the point of the old dream. The moment that had always woken him, dry-mouthed and wet-skinned. Every night for twenty winters.

The impact.

Einholt saw his own blood spray the dark, dirty bartop beside him. He heard thunder outside, hooves of the riders come to carry him away to the invisible world where lost souls like Drago and Shorack had found their miserable destinies.

Einholt, life spilling out of him like water from a shattered flask, fell across the old sign board. His blood, hero's blood, more holy than that of mortal men, gushed across the faded lettering he had read: 'Welcome to The Shadows Drinking House'.

Stay out of the shadows.

The thing stood over him, blood dripping from its ancient, soot-blackened, sharpened finger-bones. The figures in the dim bar around it, patrons and bar staff alike, collapsed as one, like puppets with their strings cut. They had all been dead for hours now anyway.

Its eyes glowed once, twice... *coral pink.*

MONDSTILLE
HAMMERS OF ULRIC

It seems to me now, looking back on that fiercely hard winter, that the evil which swarmed over us was a long, long time coming. A destiny, for Middenheim perhaps. Destiny can be that cruel. I have seen the hand-marks of Destiny on the poor frames of countless men and women who have come into my care. Angry stab wounds, mindless battery, jealous beatings. In the service of Morr, I have been witness to the manifold unkindnesses of Destiny.

It has dealt me poorly too, back when I was a merchant, before I took the way of the dead. Death is cruel, but life is crueller. Hard, cold, unforgiving, like a bleak Mondstille at its most savage.

There are those that fight against it. Ganz, worthy Ganz, and his valiant crew. The servant girl, Lenya. The street-thief Kruza. Morr look to them, Ulric too. Sigmar. Shallya. Hell, any of them. Any of those feeble gods, high up in their invisible world, who claim to watch over us but who simply watch us.

Watch us. Watch our pain. Watch our discomfort. Watch our ends. Like the crowd in the Bear Pit on West Weg, cheering us to our tormented doom.

I've had my fill of gods and the invisible world. I've had my fill of this life and any other. I am a man of death. I stand at the brink of it all, watching like the gods. And the daemons.

They all cheer, you know. Gods and daemons alike. They all cheer.

— *from the papers of Dieter Brossmann, priest of Morr*

* * *

WINTER ARMED THE city for war. Frost, as thick as a dagger's blade, coated every surface and icicles as sharp as swords hung from every eave and awning. Snow, like fleece under-armour, swaddled the rooftops tightly, under the plate-mail of ice.

War was coming. Far to the west, along the borders, the noble armies of Bretonnia were chafing for the spring, anxious to assault the Empire, the recent loss of Countess Sophia of Altdorf a perfect excuse. Though rounds of ambassadors shuttled back and forth, no one really doubted that come next spring, nations would be in conflict. News had also drifted in that beast-packs were rising in the ice forests of the Drakwald, making huge numbers, stinking the air with their scent, harrying settlements and townships. They'd never risen in Mondstille before. It was as if something, something huge and dark and redolent with the reek of evil, was drawing them out of their woodland haunts.

Armoured for war, shivering, nervous, Middenheim crouched on top of the aching cold of the Fauschlag Rock and waited for its suffering.

Only a very few, rare souls knew that the real war would be fought within.

WATCH CAPTAIN SCHTUTT was warming his numb hands at a feeble brazier in the guard post on Burgen Bahn when he heard distant wailing trickling down through the frosty Osstor district. It was past midnight.

'Sigmar spank me! Not now!' he hissed. Pfalz, Blegel and Fich, his companions on the late watch, looked round at him unenthusiastically.

'Pfalz, come with me. You two: stay in here,' he told them. Blegel and Fich looked relieved. Yes, like they wanted to go outside.

Schtutt pulled on his mittens, placed his leather cap on his bald scalp and took up his pole-arm and his lamp. He thought about adding his barbute, but the idea of the cold cheek-guards against his face was intolerable. 'Come on, Pfalz! What are you buggering about at?'

Pfalz got his gloves on and picked up his pike. 'Coming, captain.'

'We won't be but a moment,' Schtutt told Blegel and Fich.

Like they cared.

He opened the door. The fierce cold of Mondstille cut down into him like a glass portcullis. He gasped. He heard Pfalz groan beside him.

The night air was clear and crystal-hard. Schtutt pulled the watch post door closed behind them and they shuffled out to meet the winter darkness.

The captain stopped for a moment and listened to the cold, hoping desperately that whatever the trouble was, it had died down, or had been his imagination, or had at any rate frozen solid. But there it was once more, the wailing – the fear.

'Come on! Let's see to it!' Schtutt said to his lieutenant, and they clumped off over the frosty cobbles and crisp patches of lying snow, leaving the only sets of tracks. They followed the sounds to the next turn in the road, where the street to the left dropped away steeply down a stairway flanked by snow-flecked, overhanging houses. There, the shivering sounds ebbed away for a moment.

'Up there?' Pfalz suggested, gesturing with his pike to the right. He wiped his watering nose on the back of his glove.

Schtutt shook his head. 'No... down there... down towards the college.'

They hurried down the steps as best they could, going gingerly because of the rime-ice under the snow. Last thing Schtutt wanted was to brain himself going arse-over-end on the Ostweg stairs in the middle of the night.

Ahead, in the slit of sky visible between the steep townhouses on either side, they could begin to see the noble, grey dome of the Royal College of Music, iced with snow that reflected the moonlight, so that it glowed like a small half-moon itself. The shriek came again, from an alley hard to the left of the foot of the stairs. Needles of ice hung from the low-arched gate of the alleyway.

'That came from the Wolf-Hole,' Schtutt said. There was a small street-shrine dedicated to Ulric a little further in that direction. The alley brought them into a small crossroads square, where five alleys met. In the centre sat the Wolf-Hole shrine, a font-like bowl of black stone, with a small graven image of a wolf's head raised on a plinth in the middle. Traders and local householders would leave lit candles, coins or votive offerings of flowers and herbs on the lip of the shrine as they went about their daily lives.

Tonight, in the coldest hour of darkness, someone had left another kind of offering altogether. Blood, dark as wine, spattered the snow around the Wolf-Hole.

The first body, a middle-aged man in his night shirt, was draped over the font so that his head, arms and shoulders were under the water level inside the bowl. Whether he had drowned before the back of his torso had been ripped away was not clear.

The second, a woman in a torn brocade surcoat, lay at his feet. She was twisted into a posture even the contortionists in the Mummer's Company would have found impossible to mimic.

The third, another man in the black doublet and hose of a merchant, lay on his back a few yards from the Wolf-Hole. He had no face left to be known by.

The snow was speckled in all directions with blood, and with bloody scuff-marks where heavy feet had moved and churned.

Schtutt and Pfalz stood together, speechless, viewing the scene.

The captain shivered, but for the first time that night it wasn't from cold. He forced his mind to think, his body to move. He was City Watch, damn it, he had a job to do!

'Left! Left!' he hissed at Pfalz with a curt swing of the lantern, as he himself stalked around the right hand side of the Wolf-Hole, pole-arm held out straight and ready in his left hand.

This was recently done. Steam rose from the wounds. Schtutt saw that the blood had been... used. Markings had been daubed on the font-bowl and on the statue of Ulric. Letters. Words. Others had been marked on the walls surrounding the little cross-yard.

Murder. Desecration. Schtutt swallowed hard. He thought about sending Pfalz back to the guard post to rouse the others so that they could investigate in well-armed numbers. A good thought, but that would mean being left here alone, which was a truly bad one.

Pfalz pointed. A trail of blood led down one of the adjacent alleys. They followed it, boots crunching on the frost. Another moan, a half-shriek, from up ahead.

'Gods!' Schtutt snarled and plunged down the alley at a trot, Pfalz at his heels. The doors of a house to the right, a well-appointed respectable townhouse, had been kicked in and splintered. More bloody words daubed the walls and wood. Inside, firelight, loose and spreading, danced. Someone was shrieking.

They pushed inside. The hall had been ransacked and defaced. Two more bodies, hacked beyond the point of recognition, were piled inside the door, spreading a lake of cherry-bright blood across the floorboards. A lamp had been smashed, and flames were taking hold of the newlpost and lower risers of the staircase and the tapestries along one wall. The air was full of acrid ash-smoke, and the firelight flared and flickered in Schtutt's vision. He didn't even think to notice how nice the warmth was.

A woman, her clothing ripped and bloody, was cowering on the floor by a door beneath the stairs. She shuddered and moaned and, every now and then, rasped out a thin shriek of pain and fear.

Schtutt ran to her, bending low. She was bruised and had a cut to her arm, but he could make out no greater injury than that. As he leant by her, she glanced up in surprise, and flinched in terror, pulling back from his touch.

'Easy! Easy! You're safe now! I'm a captain of the Watch. Who did this? Is he still here?'

Her pale, bruised, tear-stained face regarded him almost blankly. Her lips quivered. 'Ergin. Where's Ergin?' she asked suddenly, tremulously.

'Ergin?'

'M-my husband... where is he? Ergin? Ergin?' Her voice began to rise into a panicked wail.

Schtutt tried to calm her. Her screams were piercing his nerves. He glanced around, saw where Pfalz had set aside his pike and was trying to beat down the flames with a length of the tapestry he had pulled down.

Schtutt was about to call to him, and tell him to send out for the firewatch, when he saw the figure on the stairs, creeping down towards them. A man, or at least a shape of a man, covered in darkness and crouched like a wild beast. There were only three bright things about him, three things which flashed in the flamelight. His wide, white, staring eyes, and the steel hand-axe in his grip.

'Pfalz!' Schtutt bawled as the figure pounced, throwing itself off the lower landing of the staircase, down onto the fire-beating watchman. The woman shrieked, louder and more hysterically than before, probably prompted as much by the volume of Schtutt's roar as anything she had seen.

Pfalz looked up in time enough to raise his arms in defence. The figure flew into him and they both smashed over onto the floor. The slicing axe skidded off the mail-shirt of the cursing, struggling watchman. Pfalz fought to get the daemon off him, but both were now wrestling in the lake of blood from the corpses that covered the floor, and they slipped and thrashed, unable to get purchase, spraying red droplets into the air.

Schtutt charged in, his boots also slipping on the gore. As he closed, he realised why the figure seemed so dark. It was drenched from head to toe in blood. It soaked the clothes, matted the hair, stained the skin. *Not his own*, Schtutt thought.

He didn't dare risk a thrust with his pole-arm for fear of striking Pfalz. Instead, Schtutt brought the haft of it down like a flail across the attacker's back. The pole broke loudly, and the bestial figure convulsed with an animal yelp and tumbled off Pfalz. But it still had the axe.

Pfalz had taken a gouge to his ribs, and was clutching it as he looked round and yelled, 'Kill it! Kill it, in the name of Sigmar, captain!'

Schtutt had two feet of pole with the blade-head still attached. He faced the creature, low and set. The figure had turned its entire malevolent attention onto him.

'Put it down… put the cleaver down,' Schtutt ordered, in a practised, bass tone that had ended a good few tavern brawls before the body-count could escalate into double figures. He could hear Pfalz's pain-inspired urgings, but he still felt he had to try. A hand-to-hand fight with a maniac was the last thing anyone needed at this hour of the night.

'Put it down. Now.'

If the blood-soaked thing had any intention of putting the axe down, it was down through Schtutt's head. It leapt right at him, axe raised, howling a noise Schtutt would never forget.

'You idiot!' he managed to spit, just before the figure cannoned into him and knocked his breath out. The flailing axe smacked into Schtutt's temple and spun his head round as they went over. Simultaneously, the blade-head of Schtutt's pole-arm punched right through the killer's torso, driven as much by the figure's momentum as by Schtutt's muscle-power.

Schtutt landed on his back, the impaled killer thrashing out its death throes on top of him, wild and frenzied, like someone suffering a brain-fit.

Schtutt felt the body go limp at last. He felt the blood from his pain-wrenched head pouring down into his eyes.

Fine night to go leaving your barbute in the guard post, he thought, and passed out.

KRUZA WAS HUDDLED in a corner of the Drowned Rat, wrapped in his velvet cloak. When frost actually began to form on his glass, he realised it was late enough. He tossed coins onto the table and shambled out into the painfully cold street.

The moons were up, winter moons, curled like claws. There was something about this winter that chilled him beyond the weather. Everywhere, talk was of bad omens and ill portents, of gathering war and rising darkness. The same talk as every day, every year, actually, but now it seemed different. It was no longer the doom-mongering of the gloomy drunks at the crowded bars, the nerve-jangled alarmists in the gaming-dens, or the crafty soothsayers working their business. It was... real. It was an ill time, and Kruza didn't like the feel of it at all.

There were stories doing the rounds, from the stews of Altquartier to the exclusive drinking halls of the Nordgarten. Spook stories: stories of vile murder, lunacy and strange phantoms in the snow. It was said a respectable butcher in the Altmarkt had run mad with a skinning knife the day before, killing two of his employees and three of his fellow traders before the Watch had cut him down. A novice sister at the Temple of Shallya had hanged herself from the hands of the water-clock in Sudgarten, stopping the mechanism forever at the hour of midnight. In the stables of the coach-runners on Neumarket, the animals had gone into frenzies the night before the first snows, and ripped and bitten at each other in the narrow barns; two had died and four more had been destroyed.

Moreover, luminous balls and arcs of green fire, like trapped lightning, had played around the towers of the Temple of Myrmidia for half an hour two sunsets past. People said shades had been seen to walk in Morrspark. A terrible smell of charnel corruption had invaded the Office of the City Clerics and driven the staff out, pale and bilious. Grotesque faces had been seen, for an instant, pressed to windows, or in household mirrors. In the Cut-Purse Tavern, a water-stain in the shape of a howling face had seeped into the plaster wall of the pot room, and no amount of scrubbing could wash it out. Three men known personally to Kruza had seen old relatives, long dead, standing over their beds when they woke, misty and screaming silently, before vanishing. Some even said there was plague in the Altquartier.

Certainly, winter-ague and influenza was rife. It was winter, after all. But plague? That bred in the hot seasons, in the stink and the flies. The cold was its enemy, surely? And death? Common currency in Middenheim. But even by the city's wretched standards, murder and violence was alarmingly common.

An ill time indeed. Kruza looked up into the darkness, at the twinkling, ominous stars. He wished sometimes he could read the wisdom others told him was indelibly written there. Even without such skills, he saw only threat in the faraway lights. Perhaps he should consult a star-reader. But did he really want to know what was coming?

He moved off, down the icy lane. Almost at once, although he had been sure he was alone in the side-street, he felt there was a presence beside him, a panting exuberance.

He looked round, his hand on his dagger-grip.

No one. His mind playing tricks. Too many scare-stories, too much imagination and far too little wine.

But… it was still there. Unmistakable. A breath. An invisibility that shadowed his movements, just unseen, always behind him.

It reminded him of–

Now that was just stupid. It was only because the boy had been on his mind of late.

But–

The breath again, just at his heels. He whipped around, suddenly very sober, his dagger drawn.

Wheezer?

'Come on, Kruza! It's there to be taken!'

Kruza started, but there really was no one there.

Just a winter wind, hissing through the arches and doorways around him.

He shuddered and headed for his bed.

AT THE GRAF'S Palace, high on the rock, ceremonial banners fluttered stiffly, weighed down with frost. Large black iron braziers burned at the Great Gate and lined the length of the entrance drive. Two horsemen on warsteeds rattled past the guards without breaking stride and flew down that line of fire.

Inside the palace, Lenya was kneeling in a passageway near the main hall, warming her hands illicitly on a back-grate of the main kitchen chimney flue. She was resting, secretly, for a moment. The chief domestics had forced the staff to work flat out all evening for some important, unnamed event.

She froze in the gloom as she heard a tik-tak tik-tak coming down the stone passage, and pulled herself into hiding behind a chilly suit of display armour. The chamberlain, Breugal, limped past her, not noticing the lowly servant girl far away from her business and area of the palace.

Breugal strode into the wide, cold space of the main entrance, his silver-headed cane chipping time in rhythm with his steps. He stopped. He thinks no one can see him, grinned Lenya from hiding. She had to stifle her laughter as she saw him adjust his ribboned wig and exhale onto a palm in front of his face to test his breath.

The riders drew up outside. One stayed with the horses; the other strode in, slamming open the great doors of the hallway.

Ganz, commander of White Company, paused for a moment on the threshold and kicked the ice off his sabatons, rowel spurs and grieves against the doorjamb.

Breugal observed this disdainfully, watching the ice-hunks skitter away from the Knight Templar's leg armour across the polished marble floor.

'Someone will have to clear that up,' he said snidely to Ganz as he paced forward, his cane-end clicking.

'I'm sure,' Ganz said, not really listening.

'The palace is honoured by a visit from the worthy Temple, but I'm afraid the Graf has retired for the night. He is expecting important guests early tomorrow and he needs his rest. You must return tomorrow… later tomorrow.' Breugal steepled his fingers together, his cane tucked under his armpit, bowing gravely.

'I'm not here to see His Highness. I was sent for. Find me von Volk.'

There was a pause. Breugal looked stiffly at the expectant Ganz.

'Find... you...'

Ganz stepped forward towards the chamberlain. 'Yes? Wasn't it clear enough? Find me von Volk.'

Breugal backed away from the huge knight. He looked like he was choking on something utterly distasteful.

'My dear... sir. You can't come in here at the dead of night and demand such things of the Royal Chamberlain. Even if you are a Knight of Ulric.'

Breugal smiled his most courtly smile, the smile that said he was the true master here. A smile that had broken courtly love matches, ruined careers and terrified three generations of household staff.

Ganz seemed stunned for a moment. He turned away. Then he snapped back, fixing the chamberlain with a stare as hot as the sun itself.

'I'll tell you what I can do. I am charged with the power of the exalted Ar-Ulric to serve the Temple and Ulric and the Graf. I'll come in here any time I damn well please and all the Royal Chamberlains will scurry hither and yon until my will is done!'

'Understand?' he added, for good measure.

Breugal's astonished mouth made several unsuccessful vowel sounds as he stepped back.

From her cover, Lenya grinned a triumphant smile. *I do believe Herr Breugal is going to wet his britches*, she thought. *This is priceless!*

'He understands all right, Wolf!' a voice rang out from the far side of the hall. Von Volk, flanked by two other Knights Panther, strode out across the marble to greet Ganz. Von Volk had his ornamental crested helm under his arm, his head bare, while the other two were regally adorned with full closehelms rising a foot above their scalps into gilded panther icons and crenelated fans.

Ganz and von Volk met in the middle of the hall, armour clashing as they smacked gauntlets. Their smiles were genuine.

'Von Volk! It is good to meet you again under better circumstances! Gruber has spoken well of you.'

'Ganz of the White! And I have spoken well of Gruber!'

They turned together and both looked darkly at the waiting Chamberlain.

'Was there something?' asked von Volk.

'N-no, sir Knight Panther,' Breugal began.

Von Volk leaned into his face and snarled like a big cat. 'Then go!'

Breugal went. *Tik-tak tik-tak*, as fast as his cane could pace.

'I apologise for that self-important arse,' von Volk said.

'None needed. I've known many of his type. Now, why the summons?'

Von Volk breezed his waiting men away with a flick of his hand. They backed off. Lenya craned to hear.

'The ambassadors from Bretonnia are arriving in the next few hours. His Highness the Graf wants their visit to be as secure as possible.'

'None of us wants war with Bretonnia,' Ganz noted dourly.

'There's the point of it. There's sickness in the Panther barracks. An ague, a phlegmy fever. I've seventeen men down, bed-ridden. How's your Temple?'

'Healthy as yet. What would you have us do?'

'Support us. When the ambassadors arrive, security will be our foremost need. I haven't the men. I'm hoping the Temple Wolves will reinforce us.'

'Ar-Ulric has told me to provide you with everything you need, Panther. Consider it a pledge of strength.'

Lenya almost spilled out of her hiding place as she leaned to hear the last of this. *This is terrible*, she thought. *This is truly terrible. Plague, disease, foreign invaders...*

'I'll go and marshal my men,' Ganz said to von Volk, and saluted as the three Panthers exited. Ganz stood alone in the middle of the hall for a moment, then looked directly at Lenya's hiding place.

'I can see you, milk-maid. Don't worry, Drakken will be amongst the troops I send. Try not to distract him.'

Ganz turned and left through the main doors to his waiting horse.

Lenya sighed. *How the hell does he do that?*

BY THE TORCHLIGHT, Gruber looked down at the Wolf-Hole shrine. Abruptly he knelt and, head bowed, uttered a prayer of blessing in its direction.

'I didn't know what to do, sir,' said the Watch captain with the bandaged head, from behind him. 'I didn't know if I should clean it off...'

Gruber stood and turned, his gold-edged grey armour gleaming in the torch light. 'You did right, captain. And valiantly.'

'Just did my job,' Schtutt said.

'In exemplary fashion,' Gruber smiled. But the smile was hollow, Schtutt noticed.

'Schell! Kaspen! Hold that crowd back!' Gruber called sharply to the Wolves who edged the small yard of the Wolf-Hole, facing the gathering, anxious crowds. Gruber followed the bald Watch captain down the alley to the invaded townhouse.

'This is where you killed it?' he asked mildly.

'With my broken pole, sir!' Schtutt replied, holding his gore-caked weapon up.

'Very nice.'

'There is a matter of–'

'Of what?' asked Gruber,

'Of... jurisdiction.'

'A shrine of Ulric has been abominably desecrated. Can there be a question?'

Schtutt thought about the words, and then about how big and armoured the Wolves were, and then about how he'd had quite enough of fighting this night.

'All yours,' he said to the wiry veteran Gruber, and took a pace back.

Gruber stepped into the townhouse. He cast a quick glance at the mashed corpses in their lake of blood. The fire had been put out, and neighbours were consoling the weeping woman. The murderer lay in the middle of the floor, the hole Schtutt's weapon had made horribly visible.

'Ergin, my Ergin...' murmured the woman, inconsolably.

'Your husband?' Gruber asked, moving forward.

'Y-yes...'

'Where is he?' Gruber asked.

The woman pointed to the ruined killer's corpse in the middle of the floor. 'There.'

Her husband... did this? Gruber was amazed and appalled. The rumours of madness in Middenheim had seeped back to the Temple quarters of late: rumours of killing and insanity and shades. He hadn't believed a word of them until now.

A robe-shrouded figure entered the room behind him. Gruber was about to cast a question when he recognised the man's office and simply bowed instead.

'Gruber, of Ulric.'

'Dieter Brossmann, of Morr. I was about to ask the circumstances of Morr's work here, but I see it plainly, Wolf.'

Gruber moved close to the hooded priest. 'Father, I want to know everything about this act, all the details you can learn before you bury the shreds.'

'I will supply them. Come to me before nones and I will have searched out the facts, such as they are.'

Gruber nodded. 'These markings, the words daubed here and on the Wolf-Hole basin. They mean nothing to me, but I sense their evil.'

'And I too,' said the priest of Morr. 'I don't know what they mean either, but words written in fresh blood can hardly be good, can they?'

JUST BEFORE DAWN, the snow began to fall again, coating the city with a powder two or three inches thick. Up on the Palast Rock, the entire household staff had been working through the small hours. Already ovens were lit and water-barrels heating. Housemen in pink silk liveries were out with shovels, clearing the main approach drive and laying rock salt. Amongst them, Franckl paused, cursing at the starchy high collar of his new livery. All of the Margrave's staff had been seconded to serve the Graf during this critical visit by the Bretonnian ambassador. Like the Royal Bodyguard, too many of the palace staff were sick with the wretched winter ague.

Throughout the palace, servants were at work, changing linen, scrubbing floors, polishing cutler-ware, laying fires and wiping frost off the insides of the guest apartment window panes.

The staff had all been wondering what was afoot since the moment Breugal set them to work suddenly in the late evening as if it was early morning. A visit, that much was certain. When Lenya overheard Ganz and von Volk talking in the main hall, she became the only member of the domestic staff of a rank lower than chamberlain to know the details. And she had no one to tell. Even now she was working as part of the house-staff, she was alone and friendless.

In the palace, that was. As she hurried down the west gallery with two buckets of warm water to replenish the girls working on the main staircase with hog-brushes, she saw the snow out of the windows, settling down in the light of the braziers down the drive, and wondered how Kruza was faring on a night like this.

Just before the chime of vigiliae, a detachment of Wolf Templars rode up Palast Hill and in through the Great Gate, whipped by flakes, their thunderous hooves muffled by the snow. Aric led them, the Bannerole of Ulric held high in his left hand. Behind him, Morgenstern, Drakken, Anspach, Bruckner and Dorff in a tight pack, and then a dozen more Templars, six each from Red and Grey Companies. A Panther knight at the Gatehouse hailed them, and directed them around the inner courtyard to the Royal Guardhouse.

They reined up in the stone square before the guardhouse, the breath of their chargers steaming the air. The horses trod uncomfortably on the unfamiliar depth of the snowcover. Uniformed pages, their cold faces as flushed pink as their silk coats, scurried out to grasp reins.

Aric dismounted smartly and, flanked by Bruckner, Olric from the Grey and Bertolf from the Red, marched across the doorway where a squad of Knights Panther in full armour, torches raised high, waited for them under the portico. Aric saluted the lead Panther.

'Aric, of the White, Bearer of the Standard. The Great Wolf watch you, brother. Ar-Ulric, bless his name, has given me command of this reinforcement detail.'

The lead Panther had raised his ornate gold visor. His face was stern and dark, and his flesh looked pasty and ill next to the rich gold and reds of his steepled crest.

'I am Vogel, Captain, Graf's Second Own Household. Sigmar bless you, Temple Knight. Herr Captain von Volk told me to expect you.'

Aric sensed tension. The man seemed ill, and unlike von Volk, he still seemed to harbour some of the stiff rivalry that had become tradition between the Templars and the Bodyguard. Relations between the Wolves and Panthers may have thawed in von Volk's eyes, mused Aric, but the old prejudices are deep rooted.

'We appreciate the assistance of the Temple in this fragile hour,' Vogel went on, sounding anything but appreciative. 'Border scouts report the ambassador's party is just a few hours away, despite the snows. And the brotherhood of Panthers is... unmanned. Many of us are bedridden with the fever.'

'We will say deliverance litanies for them. They are strong, robust men. They will survive.' Aric sounded confident, but Vogel seemed unsteady as he turned to lead them in. The Wolf leader could see dark tracks of sweat on the Panther's exposed, pallid cheek. And there was a smell. A smell of rank, sickly sweat, of illness, half-cloaked in the pomander scent of the courtly knights. Vogel was not the only Panther here who was sick.

Ulric protect us too, Aric thought. It smells the way the city air does when the plague visits. And hadn't Anspach reported some loose rumour about plague in the stews and slums?

The Panther honour guard fell in behind Aric and Vogel, and the Wolves followed en masse. They marched down a marble colonnade into the draughty main halls of the palace, where candles and – such luxury! – oil lamps burned in wall sconces, for mile after mile, it seemed to Aric, in every direction down the tapestry- and mirror-lined promenades.

'Just tell us what you'd have us do, and we'll get to it,' Aric said. 'What duties would you have us perform?'

'I don't expect you Wolves to have a working knowledge of this labyrinthine palace. The layout can be disconcerting to strangers.' Vogel seemed to enjoy the word 'strangers', as it emphasised the fact the noble Wolves were on Panther turf now. 'Don't stray, or you'll get lost. We need patrols to sweep the palace, so I'll draw them up from the Panther companies. You Templars would do us a service if you agreed to stand watch on the guest apartments.'

'It will be an honour to serve,' Aric said. 'Show us the area and the places to watch.'

Vogel nodded. He waved up two of his knights. Their visors were shut and they seemed like automatons to Aric. He had never realised before how much he appreciated the Wolf custom of going to battle helm-less, hair flying. Faces and expressions communicated a lot, particularly in the heat of war.

'Krass! Guingol! Show the Wolves the layout of the guest quarters.'

'Aye, sir!' said Guingol. Or Krass. *Who in Ulric's name could tell behind those golden grilles?*

Vogel turned to Aric. 'Stand firm, Wolf. All of you. The watch-word is "Northwind".'

'Northwind.'

'Repeat it only to your men. If any you meet can't provide it, detain them. Or slay them. No exceptions.'

'I understand,' Aric said.

Vogel saluted.

'May the day pass well,' he said. 'May none be found wanting.'

'As you say,' smiled Aric courteously.

Vogel and his men turned and clanked away down the gallery, armour jingling. Aric turned to Guingol and Krass. 'Let's get on, shall we?' he asked.

They nodded and strode forward. The Wolves followed.

'This place smells bad,' whispered Bertolf of the Red.

'Like sickness,' Bruckner agreed.

'Like plague,' Olric said dourly.

Behind them, in the ranks, Drakken glanced uneasily at Morgenstern. 'The Grey Wolf is right, isn't he? Plague?'

Morgenstern chuckled deeply, richly, stroking his vast, cuirassed belly as he stomped down the hallway. 'Boy, you're too much the pessimist. Plague? In this cold snap? Never!'

'Ague, maybe,' Dorff said sullenly from behind them, his directionless whistling drying up for once.

'Oh, ague! Yes, ague! Perhaps that!' Morgenstern chortled. 'Since when did anyone ever die of the sneezes?'

'Apart from the dozens who died last Jahrdrung?' Dorff asked.

'Oh, shut up and whistle something cheerful!' snapped Morgenstern. Sometimes morale was just too difficult to build.

'What's the betting,' said Anspach, who had been silent up until then, 'what's the betting that this is the worst mess we ever got into?'

The Wolf Templars slammed to a halt, the White Company men bottling the Red and Grey behind them. Aric, with his Panther escort, had gone on a few more paces before he realised they had all stopped behind him, squabbling and confrontational.

'I was only saying!' Anspach said.

'Keep it to yourself!' one of the Red Company snarled.

'He's right!' a Grey Templar snapped. 'Doom is coming to the Fauschlag!' Others murmured agreement.

'Plague... it's true...' Drakken said, wondering.

'I've heard that!' said another Red Wolf. 'Thick and rife in the Altquartier stews!'

More agreement.

'We're on the brink of disaster!' said Olric, shaking his head.

Bertolf was beginning to explain something about ghosts walking the streets when Aric pushed past the bemused Panther escort and rounded on the gaggle of Templars.

'Enough! Enough! This kind of talk defeats us all before we've even begun!'

Aric had thought his voice was fierce and commanding. This was his first duty as a commander, and he intended to prosecute it with all the firmness and vigour of Ganz. No, of Jurgen. He was going to prove himself a fine leader of men. But he found himself shouted down by the arguing Wolves, comments blasting back and forth quicker than he could counter them. A boiling hubbub of voices filled the passageway. Aric had anticipated some trouble from the men of the other companies put under his command, but he had expected the men of White to follow him. Now there was nothing but mayhem, fierce conversation, disruption. And no discipline.

'Enough!' said a deep voice next to the increasingly frantic standard bearer. Silence fell, hard as an executioner's axe.

All eyes turned to Morgenstern. Very softly, he said, 'There's no plague.

There's a touch of fever, but it will pass. And since when have we been afraid of rumours? Eh? Eh? This great rock-city has stood for two thousand years! Will such a place fall in one night? I think not! Doom on all our heads? Never! Not when we have armour on our backs, weapons in our hands and the spirit of Ulric to lift us!'

The silence was broken now as men of all Wolf Companies voiced their agreement with the great White Company ox.

'Let's do what we have to do and make the morrow safe for all good souls! And the morrow after that! For the Graf, for Ar-Ulric, for every man and woman in this beloved city!'

Morgenstern's throaty voice rose above the men's murmurings. Like the holler of a hero of old.

'Wolves of Ulric! Hammers of Ulric! Do we stand together, or do we waste the night with dispiriting rumour? Eh?'

They cheered. They all cheered. *Ulric take me*, Aric sighed. *I have a lot to learn.*

Guingol and Krass showed them the layout of the guest block. Aric appointed duties to all of the seventeen Templars in his command. He remembered, at a nudge from Morgenstern, to tell them the watchword.

He was left at the main doors of the guest apartments with the portly soldier.

'Thank you,' he hissed, a full three minutes after he was sure they were alone.

'Aric, Aric, never thank me.' Morgenstern turned to look at him, compassion in his huge, bearded face. 'I did as much for Jurgen when he was young.'

Aric looked at him.

'In panic, no one listens to a commander. They listen to those in the ranks beside them. They know the truth comes from the common man. It's a trick. I'm glad I could help.'

'I'll remember this.'

'Good. I remember when old Vulse used it, back when I was a pup. Who knows, in years to come, you'll be the old ranking veteran who can do the same for another generation of scared cubs.'

They both smiled. Morgenstern pulled a hip-flask out from under his pelt. 'Shall we bless the night?' he asked.

Aric paused, then took the filled cap Morgenstern offered. They drank a shot together, Aric from the cap and Morgenstern from the flask, clinking both together before sipping.

'Ulric love you, Morgenstern,' Aric whispered, wiping his mouth and handing the cap back to the big Wolf. 'I'll do a circuit of the men, make sure they're all in place.'

Morgenstern nodded. Aric slid away down the passageway.

As soon as the standard bearer was gone, Morgenstern sank back against the door jamb and knocked back a deep swallow from the flask.

His hands were trembling.

Plague, yes. Doom, yes, Death to them all, certainly. It had taken all his strength to speak out. To keep Aric's position as leader.

But in his great heart, he knew. He knew.

This was the end of everything.

KRUZA AWOKE IN the last hours of the night. His low, spare attic was cold as hell. His scar itched damnably.

He tried to remember what had woken him. A dream.

Wheezer.

He had been telling Kruza something. Wheezer had been standing next to the Graf and the Graf hadn't seen him.

Something about... the serpent, the self-biting monster. The world-eater.

Kruza shook so hard he had to crawl across the attic boards and pour a drink from the flask on the table. It was chilly, almost icy. Only the lead-weight of the liquor had kept it from freezing. He swilled it down, and the heat of the drink hit the back of his gullet.

Wheezer... what were you trying to tell me? What were you trying to tell me?

Nothing. Silence. Yet something was there.

The trinket? Was that it? The ceremonial necklace? Or something else?

Mist floated around him. His limbs felt hard and rigid with the cold. He took another drink. It warmed everything above his throat and everything else was rigid and dead.

Lenya. He remembered now. *Lenya. You want me to watch for your sister! She's in danger!*

That was no problem. Defending Lenya was something he didn't feel was an arduous task. Ranald take that Wolf of hers... Lenya...

Then he realised – or remembered, or simply imagined – what Wheezer had really been trying to tell him from the quiet world of phantoms. It wasn't just Lenya, though she was important.

It was everyone. It was Middenheim. It was the whole city.

He got up, pulling on his leather breeches and jerkin. His face was troubled, but he was not shaking any more.

FIRST LIGHT CAME, pale and clear, the sky a translucent blue. Snow lay a foot thick on the countryside and the city. Only the sheer black sides of the rock were free of it.

A train of gilt carriages and emblemed outriders churned up the southern viaduct, now just recently repaired, and flew in through the gate, puffing up sheets of snow. Holding the regal pennants of Bretonnia high, the vanguard of knights stormed up through the empty streets, leading the convoy of coaches towards the palace.

At the Great Gate, an honour guard of Panther Knights was mounted, and they turned to ride in with the speeding coaches. As the hurtling procession reached the entry yard, and pink-clad pages with torches ran out to form a fan of fire to greet the honoured visitors, housemen rolled out a velvet carpet to the foot-rest of the ambassador's carriage.

NONES WAS YET to strike as Gruber led Ganz in through the porch of the Temple of Morr. They looked up at the burned sections of the eerie temple, and the stretches that artisans were beginning to rebuild, many covered in tarpaulins against the weather. The day was clear and very cold, snow threatening again. Behind them, the escort detail of Schell, Schiffer, Kaspen and Lowenhertz.

Brother Olaf admitted them into the Factorum. The chamber was a cold, dank place, vaulted, smelling fiercely of astringent lavender-water and embalming fluids. Under the swinging ceiling lamps, Father Dieter looked up from the body on the cold slab as the Wolf Knights entered, rowel spurs clinking on the hard steps.

Gruber led them down the steps into the dark chamber. Even he was unnerved by the plinth slabs and the cold air. And the shrouded corpses laid out on those blocks. He had seen Father Dieter once before, in Osstor Street by the Wolf-Hole. Now Gruber saw him un-hooded. A tall, grim man, tonsure-headed, his eyes clear and cold, as if driven by some great, old regret.

Dieter looked up. 'Wolf Brother Gruber.'

'Father. This is Ganz, my commander.'

Ganz approached the priest of Morr and made a brief, respectful bow.

'What can you show us of this horror, father?' he asked simply.

Dieter led them across to the slab in the centre of the room where a male corpse lay, naked. The only distinguishing mark, as Ganz could see, was the wound through the white chest.

'The Wolf-Hole killer,' the priest said quietly, his hand flowing out to indicate the body. 'He was covered from head to foot in the blood of others when he came in. I have washed the corpse.'

'What has it told you?' Gruber asked.

'Look here.' The priest ushered Ganz and Gruber closer, indicating the sunken features of the dead man. 'When all the blood was gone, and despite the rigor, I saw a sallowness, a pale, sweaty pain.'

'Meaning?'

'This man was sick. Very sick. Out of his mind.'

'How can you be so sure?' asked Ganz.

'Because he's not the first like it I've had in here. Or the last. He was sick, brother Ganz, death-sick. Madness was in him.'

'And is that why he attacked and murdered?' Gruber asked.

'Most likely.'

'And the desecrations? On the Wolf-Hole and the house?' asked Gruber.

The priest of Morr opened a small chapbook. 'Like you, I didn't recognise them, but I took them down carefully. I have since compared them to writings in our Librarium.'

'And?'

'They are names. The script is antique, and thus curious to our eyes, but the names are... common. The names of people. Citizens. Amongst them, the name of our killer here, Ergin. Also the names of his brother, his brother's wife, his neighbour, and three others who lived in the quarter nearby.

'A roll-call of the dead,' breathed Lowenhertz quietly.

'Indeed,' the priest said, looking up sharply, as if surprised by the Wolf's insight. 'Or a roll of those that would be dead, if we assume they were written by the killer. A list then, almost a celebration of the sacred murder.'

Ganz frowned. 'Sacred? What was sacred about that act?'

The priest smiled slightly, though it reminded Ganz of the way a dog smiles before it bites. 'Not in our terms, commander. I meant no blasphemy. But can you not see how this was a ritual thing? A ritual crafted by madness. The setting, for instance. It was more than chance that the murders desecrated a shrine holy to the patron deity of this city.'

'Have you seen this before?' Ganz asked.

'Yes, twice now. Twice in the last two days. A butcher ran amok in the Altmarkt, exhibiting similar signs of fever-madness. He had gouged the names of his five victims and himself in a side of meat hanging from his awning. Also, a scrivener in Freiburg, at the start of the week, just before the snows. Three dead there, stabbed with a quill-knife before the man threw himself from a window. Again, the fever-madness. Again, the names... the killer and his three victims, entered into a ledger the scrivener was working on, in a delicate copperplate hand.'

'Again the ritual,' Lowenhertz said, uneasy.

'Quite so. However, the incident at the Wolf-Hole last night was a little different in one respect. There were more names on the walls than victims at the scene.'

'You checked this?'

'I made... enquiries.'

'A priest with the instincts of an inquisitor,' mused Gruber, almost smiling.

'I can't be sure,' Father Dieter said, apparently ignoring the remark, 'if it was simply that Ergin was stopped by the valiant watch before he could reach his... quota. Or if the madness is causing the afflicted to enscribe other names down.'

'Other names?' asked Lowenhertz.

'A roll-call of the dead, you called it yourself. Who can say when the killing might stop?'

Ganz was pacing now, his hand to his brow in thought. 'Slow down, father. Let me try and take this in. Something you just said fills me with great alarm.'

'Has anything I have just said not?' asked the priest mildly.

Ganz turned to face him, pointing a finger as he locked onto the specific thought. 'You said if the madness is causing the afflicted to do this. I am no doctor of physic, but I know enough to realise a disease, an ague, doesn't direct purpose! That there is a brain-fever in Middenheim, so dire it can drive men to bestial rages, I can accept – but one that guides them on a particular course? Sets their agenda, their ritual, as you call it? Makes them perform the same way, makes them use the same old script? It beggars belief! No ague does that!'

'Quite so, Brother Ganz. But I never said it was a natural ague.'

The Factorum was quiet for a moment as this sunk in. The priest and the Wolves were as silent and unmoving as the dead around them. Gruber broke the still air at last with a low curse. 'Ulric damn me! Magic!'

Father Dieter nodded, pulling a shroud over the body of Ergin.

'I've had my fill of that this year already,' Gruber added.

'Have you?' the priest asked, suddenly and sharply interested. 'You're not alone. A dark undertow of the foulest sorcery has pervaded this city since Jahrdrung last. I have experienced it personally. And that is one of the clues for me. Another of the names, daubed on the wall near the Ulric shrine: Gilbertus. In the early year, just before Mitterfruhl, I had... dealings with one who called himself that. He was trying to pervert this holy Temple in the service of the darkest magic of all.'

'Where is he now?' Schell asked, not really wanting to know.

'Dead. Appropriately, as his name appeared in Ergin's list.'

'And the others?' asked Lowenhertz.

The priest consulted his chap-book again. 'Common names, as I said: Beltzmann, Ruger, Aufgang, Farber – I know a Farber, and he still lives, but it may not be him – Vogel, Dunst, Gorhaff, and another, curious, as it was written twice. That name is Einholt.'

All the Wolves froze. Ganz felt a trickle of ice-sweat bead down his brow. Lowenhertz made a warding sign and looked away.

'Does that mean anything to you? I see it does.'

'Commander!' the agitated Kaspen gasped, his face shockingly pale under his mane of red. 'We–'

Ganz silenced him with a raised hand. 'What else?' Ganz asked, stepping towards the priest and trying to master his own nerves. He wanted to stay circumspect until he had got the measure of this dour funeral cleric.

'Two more besides. Another name, but not a local one – Barakos. Anything?'

The Wolves shook their heads.

'And a symbol, or an indication of a symbol at least. The word "Ouroboros", in the antique script again.'

'Ouroboros?' Ganz asked.

Gruber looked round at Lowenhertz, knowing in his stewing gut that he would know.

'The wyrm that eats itself,' said Lowenhertz darkly. 'Its tail in its mouth, the universe consuming all that it is and all that has come before.'

'My, my,' Father Dieter said. 'I had no idea the Templars were so learned.'

'We are what we are,' Ganz stated flatly. 'Is that what you think this symbol means, father?'

The priest of Morr shrugged, closing his chap-book and binding it shut with a black ribbon. 'I am no expert,' he said, self-deprecatingly and inaccurately. 'The Ouroboros is an ancient sign. It means destruction.'

'No, more than that,' Lowenhertz said, moving forward. 'It means death defied. Undeath. Life beyond the grave.'

'Yes, it does,' said the priest of death, his voice hard. 'It is the symbol of necromancy, and that was the self-same vile sin Gilbertus was guilty of. I thought that menace had vanished with Gilbertus when he pitched off the Cliff of Sighs. I was wrong. Gilbertus may have just been the start.'

'What do we do?' Ganz asked.

'Fleeing the city might be a good option,' the priest said phlegmatically.

'And those of us who can't? Those of us who are needed here? What do we do?'

'Fight,' said the priest of Morr, without hesitation.

IT WAS NEARLY midday, but the streets of the Altquartier were mournfully empty and thick with snow. No more had yet fallen and the air was glassy, but the sheer cold kept the population inside, around their hearths, desperate for warmth.

As he stalked down Low File Walk, wrapped in his cloak, Kruza wondered if other forces were keeping the streets quiet. Those rumours of plague. He couldn't believe them still, but there was a sickly smell in the cold, windless air. Of corruption, And of spoiled milk.

The thought hooked him, the memory. That smell, down in the pits of the tower house in the Nordgarten. The place he had last seen Wheezer alive.

It had been months since he'd last visited Wheezer's lonely home. In fact, Kruza thought, hadn't the final time been just after he'd last smelled that stink of spoiled milk?

He found his way up the dark stairs of the ruinous place, lighting a candle from his tinder box as much for the warmth it afforded his fingers as for light. Snow had blown in through empty window cases and drifted on the steps, and ice crusted the walls, like sheets of pearl.

He opened the door. It took a kick of his boot to free the ice around the jamb. Miraculously, almost painfully, the room was precisely as he had last seen it. No one had been here. Frost caked every surface, sheening the many mirrors and making the carpets and hangings crisp and rigid. It was as frozen as it was in his memory.

Kruza crunched across the rug, glancing around. He set the candle down on the low table, where the flame-heat melted the covering frost into great, wobbling beads. Kruza realised he had his short-sword drawn. Just like when he had burst in the first time, the very first time. His sword... drawn.

When had he done that? What instinct had made him unsheath his weapon?

He looked around. *Now, where would it be?* He closed his eyes, trying to remember. Wheezer was in his mind. Wheezer laughing. Wheezer pulling a sack of bread and cheeses from the gable window ledge where he left them to stay fresh. Wheezer sitting by the fire, making up his tortuous, fairy-tale autobiography.

Kruza opened his eyes and looked again. He remembered taking a gilt mirror from the corner by the door at the end of his first visit. To make up his quota for Bleyden. The segmented wooden box where Wheezer kept his herbs sat there now. Kruza crossed to it. He reached out to open the lid and paused.

Here?

There was a noise behind him. Kruza spun like a cornered fox, blade out. Wheezer was there, nodding, smiling. *That's the place, Kruza, that's the place.*

But it wasn't Wheezer. It wasn't anybody. The candle stub Kruza had put on the table had slid off onto the floor, carried by the thawing drips of frost.

Kruza stamped out the feeble flames which were licking into the carpet where the candle lay.

'Don't do that, Wheez–' he said to the empty room, and caught himself doing it. Like he still believed Wheezer was with him.

Kruza went back to the herb-box and pulled open the lid. The scents from within were frail and thin in the cold. He rummaged inside with his numb fingers until he found the trinket and pulled it out.

The segmented metal band, the world-eater ornament with its sightless, ivory eyes. It was – damn it all – warm.

Kruza tucked the thing inside his jerkin and headed for the door. Ice crunched under his boots. He took one last look back at the frozen room. As sure as he was of anything, that Wheezer was a natural, that Wheezer was dead, as sure as he was even of his own name, he knew he wasn't coming back here. Ever.

He reached the street and hurried up the hill through the snow, slipping occasionally on the ice under the powder-cover. There was no one around, but somehow Kruza felt more guilty than he'd ever done in his life before. He, master of ten thousand thefts, all of them guilt-free, now felt the sting of shame for stealing a dead boy's trinket. *Stealing from the dead, Kruza!*

Worst of it was, he was sure Wheezer would have wanted him to have it. Or was the guilt in his mind because he was sure Wheezer would have rather Kruza never touched the sinister ornament again?

Before he could consider, he heard sobbing from his left; a side-lane. A woman, crying hard. Involuntarily, he went that way, into a jumble of ruins where a long burned-out stew-house stood. Snow clung to the blackened beams, and icicles hung like infernal defences.

There was something written on the sooty stone wall nearby. Words that he couldn't read. They were fresh, written in a dark liquid. *Tar? What is this?* And then as quickly, he thought, *What am I doing here?*

He saw the woman, a slum-mother, curled in a crotch of fire-black beams, sobbing. She was covered with blood. Kruza stopped abruptly. He could see a pair of feet, a man's, poking out from behind a heap of snow. The snow around the feet was dark red.

Enough. Not your business. Time to go, he thought, just as the man with the sword came out of the ruins behind him, shrieking from a foam-flecked mouth, death in his hideous, blazing eyes.

A MIDDAY FEAST was underway at the palace. Having rested briefly through the early part of the morning and then bathed in more warm water than the palace would usually raise for a week, the foreign ambassadors were being entertained by the Graf in the main hall. The air was thick with cooking smells from the kitchen, and delicious aromas from the platters the page-boys paraded out into the hall in series under Breugal's watchful eyes. Music, made by a bass-viol, a crumhorn, a psaltery, a tambour and a sack-but in the hands of the Graf's court players, filled the air.

'Quickly! Quickly now!' Breugal hissed in the side passage giving into the main hall, scurrying the platter-laden pages along. He tapped time with his cane and his eyes were as bright as ice. He had put on his finest two-horned periwig and an embroidered, broken-sleeve doublet under his houseman's coat, and his chisel face was extra powdered, white as the snow, or as the faces of the dead.

He cuffed a passing page as the boy made slow progress, and then clapped his hands again. He had heard many tales of the opulence of the Bretonnian court, and he would not have his own house found wanting in the eyes of these visitors.

Breugal stopped another page and sampled the goose-liver stuffed hog-trotters to make sure the cook was performing his duties. Excellent. Too much salt, but excellent all the same. *Let the haughty Bretonnians put on a feast as fine as this!*

LENYA WAS SERVING in the kitchen, one of several house-maids helping the undercooks decant mead and wine into the table jugs. The great low-vaulted kitchens, with their steaming pots, roaring fires and bellowing men, were all but overwhelming. She thought she'd welcome the heat after the aching cold of the weather, but here it was too much. She was sweating, shaking, flushed, and her throat was burning and hoarse. Wiping her hands on her apron front, she looked round as she heard someone call her name.

'Lenya! Lenya, girl!'

In the shadows of the back-doorway of the kitchen block, she saw Franckl. He was beckoning to her, pale and sweaty, his doublet front pulled open to expose a waxy, sweaty chest. His pink-silk livery-coat was dark under the armpits, big half-moons of sweat.

Glancing round to make sure she wasn't being watched, she crossed to him.

'Franckl?' The hierarchy of the Graf's palace had long since made them equals in status.

The Margrave's old houseman was mopping his pale brow, He looked as if his heart would seize and burst in another minute.

'Damn Breugal's had me shovelling snow since midnight,' Franckl gasped.

'You don't look well, sir,' she admitted.

'A drink is all I ask. Something cool but warming, if you understand me.'

She nodded and slunk back into the kitchen, dodging scurrying pages with armfuls of serving dishes.

She sneaked a stopped bottle of ale from a cooling bucket by the winery door and hurried back.

'Here. Don't say I never did anything for you. And don't let anyone see.'

He nodded, too busy breaking the stopper and choking down the cold ale. His face went pink with relief and delight. His eyes watered.

'What is this?' came a voice.

They both looked around. Franckl coughed out his last mouthful of ale in a spray. Leaning on his cane, Breugal stood over them, utterly disdainful and menacing, utterly composed... except for the trickle of sweat oozing out from under his wig and blotting the powder on his brow. Even he wasn't immune to the baking heat and chaos of the kitchen.

Neither Lenya nor Franckl spoke or even moved.

Breugal raised his cane and pointed the silver tip at Franckl. 'You, I will have whipped for this. And you...' The cane point moved slowly across at Lenya. Breugal smiled suddenly; a little, repellent, rat-like grin as an idea occurred to him. 'You I will have whipped also.'

'Is there trouble here?' asked a voice.

They all glanced round. A Wolf Templar stood, framed in the outer doorway, his hulking armoured form black against the snow outside.

Breugal frowned. 'Just a household matter, good Sir Wolf. I am dealing with it.'

Drakken stepped out of the door shadow. 'When you've so much to do? Sir, you're the Master of Ceremonies, the fulcrum on which this entire feast depends. You haven't time to waste chastising the indolent.'

Breugal paused. He had just been flattered, he knew he had. But it was not like any flattery he had experienced before.

'Captain von Volk of the Panthers has commanded my Templars to patrol the palace. Discipline and security are our duties. Charming the ambassador from Bretonnia is yours.'

'Quite so, but–'

'No buts,' Drakken said sharply. His commanding presence reminded Lenya of a hooded gladiator she had once seen dominate the action of the Baiting Pit.

Drakken leaned down and casually took the ale-flask from the speechless Franckl. 'I will take this man into the yard and break this bottle across his wretched skull. The girl I will beat with my fist until she knows correction. Will that serve you?'

Breugal smiled, without much fun in his eyes. 'Yes, Sir Templar, but I assure you I can easily deal with this infraction of–'

'You have work to do,' Drakken said, stepping towards the chamberlain. His spur chinked on the kitchen step. 'And so have I. All interlopers and malingerers are the guards' duty to punish.'

'No, this isn't right at all!' said Breugal, suddenly. 'You have the watch, of course, but–'

'Captain von Volk was very clear. All interlopers are the business of the guard. The watchword is Northwind, as I'm sure you know. We Templars prosecute that duty with a force fiercer than any north wind.'

Breugal knew he was out-ranked. He backed away. 'I am in your hands. Sigmar invest you with radiance.'

The chamberlain tik-takked on his cane away across the kitchen, cuffing pages and ordering staff about viciously to make up for his disappointment,

'And Ulric bite your bony arse,' Drakken muttered as the bewigged man departed.

He pushed Franckl and Lenya out into the snowy yard and closed the door. Lenya was laughing out loud and even Franckl was smirking. Drakken held the ale-flask out to the houseman, who flinched briefly, expecting the worst, and then accepted it.

'Leave some for me,' Drakken smiled and Franckl nodded, taking it and hurrying away towards the shelter of the timber store.

Lenya grabbed her Templar gleefully, ignoring the cold, hard bulk of his plate mail under her hands and forearms.

'You found me, Krieg!' she cried, delightedly.

He smiled and kissed her mouth roughly.

'Of course,' he murmured as their lips parted.

'Ganz said you would be here.'

'My commander is right in all things.'

Lenya frowned, leaning away from him, her arms still about him. 'But how did you find me?'

'I sneaked away.'

'From?'

'From my patrol. They won't miss me.'

'Are you sure?' she asked curiously. She had a bad feeling Drakken was taking a big risk.

He kissed her again. And again. He knew he was sure.

THEY HAD BEEN interrupted by a convoy of biers which had arrived at the porch of Morr's Temple from the Wynd district. Father Dieter went down to assist the watchmen and the other initiates of Morr as they unloaded the miserable burden.

The Wolf Templars went outside and stood together by their tethered horses, waiting.

'Why don't you tell him, sir?' Kaspen asked.

'Tell him?'

'About Einholt! Ulric's breath! He said his name was writ in blood!'

'I heard him,' Ganz said, his voice low.

'I agree with Kaspen here,' said Lowenhertz, his voice slow with considered thought. He looked up at Ganz. 'This priest of Morr is an ally, I'm sure. Gods, he knows what he's talking about! Tell him about Einholt. Fit the pieces together... the puzzle pieces you and he hold separately!'

'Perhaps,' Ganz said.

Gruber took the commander to one side. 'Lowenhertz is right. I think we should trust this man.'

'Do you trust him, Wilhelm?'

Gruber looked away, then right back at Ganz, straight in the eyes. 'No. But I know when a risk's worth taking. And I know it's now. You weren't with us in the tunnels under the Fauschlag. You didn't see what I saw, what Aric and Lowenhertz saw. You didn't see what Einholt did.'

'You've told me. That's enough.'

'Is it? Ganz, there was an evil down there like nothing I have felt before, or hope to do again. There was a... thing. It escaped. Ulric take me if this isn't part of this curse falling on our city. And from what the priest there says, he knows about it too!'

Ganz spun away, silent. His thoughts were broken by the priest re-emerging from the Temple. The man was wiping blood from his hands with a scrap of winding sheet. Ganz crossed to him. They stood face to face in the snow at the foot of the Temple steps.

'It's happened again,' the father said. 'Freiburg now. A wealthy merchant disembowelled his entire family and staff and then hanged himself. Twelve dead. Two hundred and eighteen names on the wall.'

'What?'

'You heard,' Dieter growled. He plucked a scroll of parchment from his belt and opened it out. 'My friends in the Watch wrote the names down. I haven't begun to cross-check them yet. But you can see the way it's building, can't you? With each act of murder, the list becomes longer. How many more before it numbers everyone in the city. You, me, the Graf...' His voice trailed off.

'Einholt was a beloved member of White Company. Three months ago, he was singular in valour and... saved this city. There is no other way to describe it. He saved it from some skulking darkness in the tunnels below. Then, a week later, he vanished. We haven't seen him since.'

'He is dead.'

'So we suppose,' Ganz said – and then realised it wasn't a suggestion.

'I know it to be true. It was a simple thing to check the records of the city and find the missing Einholt.'

Ganz glared at the priest, who held up calming hands.

'Forgive me that I knew. I have no doubt Einholt was the bravest of you. My... sources told me what he did.'

'What kind of priest are you?'

The priest of Morr looked darkly at Ganz. 'The best kind: one who cares. And one who knows.'

'What do we do?' asked Ganz, sighing in admission.

'Let's consider the facts. A force of dark necromancy threatens this city...'

'Agreed.'

'We have seen its mark. As I can conjecture, it has been with us at least a year. It has had time to take a firm toe-hold. To plan. To scheme. To build.'

'Again, agreed.'

The priest paused for a moment, his breath wiping the air with steam. Ganz realised for the first time how frightened the priest was behind his confident bearing.

'We have seen its sign too, the tail-eating snake, as I said. It inflicts upon Middenheim a distemper, a magic-fever that corrupts minds and makes them do its bidding, for some fell cause we are yet ignorant of.'

'Are we?'

'Maybe. Its curse is on us now, though, wouldn't you say? Its ritual menace is all around us.'

'Yes.' Ganz was grim. 'Do you know why?'

Father Dieter was silent for a moment. He looked down at his feet, half-buried in the snow. 'The last act? The finale? It's making ritual lists of the dead. Unless I'm a fool, those lists will soon number every soul in Middenheim. Necromancy is death magic. The greater the death, the greater the magic. It works, as I understand it – and believe me, Temple commander, I have made no great study of its vile aberrations – by sacrifice. A single death allows it to work some unholiness. A multiple death will work greater magic. The blood-sacrifice of a city–'

'Ulric take me! Could it be that much?' gasped Ganz.

'That much? That little! Ten thousand souls sacrificed here is nothing to the hundreds of thousands rendered up to the Dark Ones if Bretonnia goes to war with the Empire. Isn't that the point? This city-state hangs upon the cusp of conflict. What greater sacrifice to the foul hells of necromancy could there be than the heaps of the slain, murdered in open war?'

Ganz turned away from the priest. He felt as if he wanted to be sick, but choked it back. That would be unseemly in front of his men, in front of outsiders.

'You said we should fight?' he said, his voice thin, glancing back at the priest. 'Where do you suggest we make our stand?'

'Where is Bretonnia? What place is most vulnerable? Where does the *power* live?'

'Mount up!' Ganz bellowed at his men, running forward through the snow. 'Make for the Palast Hill! Now!'

'I'm coming with you,' Father Brossmann said. Ganz wasn't listening.
'Ganz!'

On his charger, Ganz cantered around in the snowy yard and saw the priest of Morr racing up behind him.

He held out his hand and yanked the man up behind him.

'I hope you know how to ride!' he spat.

'In another life, yes,' said the priest grimly.

They galloped out of the temple yard, kicking up divots of snow, heading for the palace.

KRUZA DUCKED THE scything blade. The man was mad, that was clear enough from his eyes. It reminded Kruza of the intense determination behind a public executioner's hood. The sword whickered into a soot-flaking cross-beam and stuck. Kruza ripped round with his short-sword but missed his frenzied attacker.

The man was plague-sick, Kruza could see that. His skin was pallid and sweaty, cold and white with fever. He ripped his sword out from the beam and attacked again. The sword was a long, rusty broadsword, far longer in reach than Kruza's short blade. The sword whipped around again, trying to find Kruza's throat. He ducked and came up behind the swing, jabbing with his own blade.

The blade bit into ribs, through ribs, into organs and wetness.

The fever-driven man went down, screaming and convulsing.

'Kruza! Kruza! Kruza!' The man ranted as he died.

Kruza was already running for the palace hill.

THE SNOW THAT had choked the sky's gullet all day began to fall heavily as the daylight faded. It was only mid-afternoon, but the snow-clouds added their bulk to the sky and made it like early night. Thick snow, at first, then as the temperature dropped, sleet and freezing rain came, driving hard across the city, fusing into the laying snow as it fell. Wilting slush became rigid and unbroken snow-cover began to glow like glass as it transformed into ice.

Lenya had escaped the kitchen after her meeting with Drakken. Her lips still tingling, she found shelter in the timber store where Franckl and a dozen other housemen, pages and domestic girls had escaped out of the rain. Someone had lit a small fire and Franckl's bottle obviously wasn't the only one stolen that day. Lenya slipped into the musty gloom, the rain pattering off the tiles like slingshots, and found a place beside Franckl, accepting a swig from his bottle.

'That's a good man you've found there,' he said.

'It is.' Lenya wasn't comfortable in this throng. She wanted to get back inside, but she was sure she'd be frozen alive by the time she reached the kitchen arch across the yard. Winter thunder rolled, hard and heavy above the city rock, like the hooves of god-steeds.

She crawled up a stack of timber until she could see out of the window-slit towards the main gates, blurry through the hail. Distantly, she could see watchfires, steaming out, Panthers pulling the braziers into cover, sliding the gates closed. Their decorative plumes wilted and sagged on their helmets.

She jumped as something banged off the roof. Then again, and again. Like fists. Outside, she saw hail the size of cannon-lead smacking down into the snow, puffing it up and fracturing the ice crust with their weight. A murder storm. The most lethal a winter in the Empire could unleash. In a moment, the banging got louder and more hasty as the strikes overlapped. Hail was lobbing down now, and thunder barked again. Through the pelt, she saw a Panther at the gate struck squarely by a stone and go down, his comrades running to him. Another dropped immediately, hit, his helmet torn off.

Lenya gasped. She'd seen storms of all force out in Linz, on the farm. Never like this. Never this fury.

GANZ PULLED HIS riders in under the sloping side-roof of a coaching inn as the deadly hail fell. Riding on into this would be madness. Behind him, on the saddle-back, the priest whispered, 'Just the start...'

Ganz made no answer. The palace gates were only two streets away. In this elemental assault, an impossible distance.

KRUZA REACHED THE palace walls. He was cold through to the bones in the icy downpour and at least one hail-stone had smashed into his shoulder, leaving an aching bruise. Another ricocheted off the stones by his face, filling his eyes with ice-chips.

He ducked and sank down. The gates were shut. He had no idea how he was going to get inside.

IN THE PALACE, the guests were retiring. The feast had been a rousing success and now the ambassadors from Bretonnia asked for rest before the night's festivities. The Graf and his nobles were also returning to their quarters for a while. Hail drummed on the roof and thunder twisted the air.

Patrolling the guest apartments, Aric watched as Knights Panther and torch-bearing pages ushered the visiting dignitaries to their rooms. Already he could smell the kitchens as they stoked up the next round of entertainment. *Sleep well*, he thought. *You'll need all your strengths replenished come compline chime.*

He crossed into the corridor where Drakken was supposed to be on guard. Aric was standing by the doors into the guest rooms when the young, stocky knight appeared.

'Where have you been?' he asked.

'On duty–' Drakken began.

Aric's eyes quested into the young man's face. 'Indeed? Here?'

'I left for a moment...'

'How long a moment?'

Drakken paused. 'I suppose... half an hour...' he began.

'Ulric damn you!' Aric spat, and wheeled towards the doors. Thunder rolled outside, and a gust of wind breathed down the corridor, extinguishing all the lamps. 'How long did half an hour give them?'

'Who?'

'Whoever wanted to get inside!', Aric snarled, his hammer raised, kicking in the door.

Drakken ran after the Wolf, down a velvet-lined antechamber and into the first apartment. The carpet was on fire here from a spilled lantern. Two servants, in the tunics of Bretonnia, were dead on the floor. Words – names – had been daubed on the walls in their blood.

There was a scream from the adjoining room.

Aric burst through. A maid in waiting was pressed to the wall, on her haunches, shrieking. A hulking shape, almost a black shadow, backlit by the fireplace, had the Bretonnian ambassador held in the air by his throat. Blood dripped down. The ambassador was gasping out his last.

The hulking shape turned and looked at the sudden intrusion. It dropped the half-dead ambassador onto the ornamental rug.

Its one good eye glowed coral pink.

In a voice as low as the underworld, as dull as hoof-beats and as thick as tar, it said two clear words.

'Hello, Aric.'

THE BOMBARDMENT OF hail was even fiercer than before. Under the stable lip, the Temple warhorses skipped and shuddered.

'We cannot wait. Not now,' said the priest, a shadow behind Ganz.

'But–'

'Now, or all is lost.'

Ganz turned towards the dimly lit faces of his men.

'Ride! In the name of Ulric! Ride!' he shouted.

Exploding out of cover, ice-chips shattering around their hooves, the thunder breaking above them, they rode.

KRUZA WAS HALF-BURIED in a snow-drift, his hands still flat against the aching cold of the stone wall, when the firelight throbbed over him.

He blinked and glanced up at the three Knights Panther standing around him.

'No weather for lazing out here,' said one.

'Not when the Graf is waiting to hear the sound of your voice,' said another.

'W-what?' Kruza asked, numb in almost every way.

Lenya oozed in between two of the Panthers.

'I was telling them that the great minstrel singer was late, and the Graf would be most displeased if he didn't arrive in time for the feast,' she said.

'Of course...'

'Come on!' she pulled him up. 'I saw you at the gate,' she hissed into his ear. 'What are you doing here?'

'Protecting you,' he murmured. He was sure there were icicles on the underside of his tongue.

'Great job you're doing!' she said.

The Panthers helped her into the gates with him as hail belted down around them.

There was a sound of thunder outside, like hooves.

'HE THWARTED ME, so I chose him. He made me weaker than ever, so it was right I should take his form as my own.'

The thing with the pink eye was speaking, though Aric wasn't really listening.

'A thousand years, alone and buried within the Fauschlag. Can you imagine that, Aric? A thousand years. No, of course you can't, you're too far gone with fear.'

The impossible hulking shape paced around the candle and firelit chamber, circling the Templar.

'I took the form anyway. A good strong form. There was justice in it.'

'What are you?' asked Aric. 'You look like–'

'Einholt?' the thing sneered at him. 'I do, don't I? I borrowed his corpse. It was so full of zest and vigour.'

Einholt looked back at Aric with a blazing pink eye. The other was milky and dead, bisected by the scar, just as Aric remembered it. Einholt, pale, armoured, speaking, moving, alive. But not Einholt. No, that look. That penetrating, burning look…

'I am Einholt. He is me. It's amazing how his memories are preserved in this brain. Like inlay work on a good sword. My, these memories are mother-of-pearl! So bright! So hard! That's how I know you, Aric wolf-son. I know what you did. Not so great a crime as this Einholt, but party to it.'

'You have the face of my friend, but I know you are evil,' Aric said, raising his hammer hesitantly.

'Then go on! Crush this!' Einholt said, grinning and pointing at his own face. 'I dare you! Kill your long-lost comrade forever!'

Aric lowered his hammer. He sank to his knees.

'I wanted life again. Form, volume, bulk. You cheated me of that, just as the priest cheated me last Jahrdrung. But now, I am returned, renewed! Eager! Salivating for life!'

Einholt smiled down at the kneeling, weeping Aric. A warhammer was in his left hand, and he brought it up.

Drakken's flying hammer slammed him back across the room.

Einholt, or the thing that had once been Einholt, crashed into a side-table and shattered it under its falling bulk. It let out a raging snarl of anger that was entirely inhuman as it pulled itself upright. Drakken's fierce blow had dented its upper left breast-plating and torn the shoulder pauldron clean off.

Its one good eye throbbed like pink fire in time to its roar. Einholt's hammer was still in its hand.

Drakken pulled Aric up. The young Wolf yanked his dagger from his belt, his hammer too far away to retrieve.

'Come on!' he yelled.

'The pup has more spirit than you, Aric. Young Drakken has fewer qualms about striking his old comrade Einholt.'

Or a terrible guilt of dereliction to make up for, thought Drakken. We wouldn't be here... the ambassador wouldn't be vomiting blood on the floor, if it hadn't been for me...

Aric rose. It was as if Drakken's abrupt intervention had galvanised him anew, given him confidence. He looped his hammer through the air, circling the pink-eyed shade.

'Go!' he said to Drakken.

'But–'

'Go!' Aric repeated, his eyes never leaving the enemy before him. 'Get the ambassador out of this place. Sound the alarm! Go! Go!'

Covered by Aric and his looping weapon, Drakken dragged the gasping, semi-alive Bretonnian dignitary onto his shoulder and stumbled to the door. As soon as he was outside in the hall, he began to bellow at the top of his voice. By then, the maid had already run screaming from the suite. Cries and alarms filled the palace halls.

Aric and the thing circled.

'Shall we try it, Aric wolf-son?' asked Einholt-that-was, his hammer slowly whickering the air as it made lazy figure of eights.

'Try what?' Aric replied stiffly, his hammer held in a more defensive guard.

'Man to man, you and me...'

'You're no man.'

The thing laughed. The bottom edge of Einholt's laugh was stained with the inhuman rumble. Like thunder.

'Maybe. But I am still Einholt. One of the best hammer-arms in the Temple. Remember the displays I used to put on, me and Kaspen? What was it Jurgen said? "The art of the hammer lives in its best form as long as Jagbald Einholt is alive"? Guess what, little pup Aric –little starched-front, duty-bound Aric – Jagbald Einholt lives, and more immeasurably now than you could ever imagine!'

'No!'

'Oh yes, boy!' the thing hissed, its pink eye pulsing as it circled again, the hammer loops increasing in speed. 'Did you never think how it would be to face one of your own? Did you never idly suppose who in White Company could master who? Could you beat Drakken? Possibly, but the pup has fury. Gruber? Maybe with your youthful power. Ganz? Not him. Lowenhertz? Not him either. And... Einholt?'

It paused. It winked its dead, milky eye, slow and chilling.

'You don't stand a chance.'

Einholt's hammer snapped out deftly, hard, breaking the steady flow of Aric's returns, knocking the standard bearer's weapon out of true. Aric cried sharply as the snagged haft-loop tore into his fingers as he tried to arrest the knock. The pink-eyed thing smacked him in the chest with the butt of his hammer-head a second later.

Aric recoiled. His breastplate was dented and his breath was gone. He struggled to bring his own hammer round to deflect the next blow, but once-Einholt was already there, leering, circling round with a blow that shattered the upper vambrace of Aric's left arm and broke the bone.

Pain sparked like white stars, like snowflakes, across his vision. Aric kept the grip on the hammer with his remaining hand, pushing backwards, crashing into furniture.

'You're not Einholt!' he bellowed.

'I am!'

'No! What are you? What are you? The thing from the cellar?'

The shade's next blow took Aric in the right hip and spun him to his knees on the fire hearth.

Aric gagged. His vision already failing, his left arm dangling broken at his side, grinding agonisingly with every move. He struggled to stay conscious.

'The thing from the cellar?' said the monstrosity, the lowest register of its so-familiar voice twisted again by the thick, thunderous undernotes. 'I am all this city fears and more. I am the power that will blot Middenheim from the map and bleed the stars dry. I am Barakos.'

'Well met!' Aric snapped, smashing his hammer upwards in his one good hand.

The blow knocked the thing several yards back across the room, blood spraying from its broken jaw. It destroyed a lampstand and writing desk as it fell.

'Jagbald Einholt trained me well,' Aric gasped, and collapsed onto the rug, consciousness fleeing his pain-assaulted mind.

DRAKKEN SLID THE ambassador off his shoulder at a turn in the hallway, laying him down on an ornamental chaise. He couldn't get his bearings. There was shouting and confusion in the palace all around. He cupped his hands to his mouth and yelled 'Here! Here! To me! Send a surgeon!'

Two page boys appeared, side by side, took a look at the blood-flecked, comatose Bretonnian on the couch and fled, screaming.

'Drakken?' The young Templar look around. It was Olric of the Grey, racing up, sweaty and pale.

'What in the name of Ulric is going on?' he stammered.

'Murder! Evil! Magic! Here in the palace! Quick, Wolf brother! We must get him to a surgeon!'

Olric looked down at the crumpled man in his regal robes.

'Faraway gods! That's one of the foreign nobles! Come on, grab his feet. No, the end of the chaise, as a stretcher.'

They took the ambassador up, on the chaise, each gripping the stunted legs of the piece of furniture. Olric, his hammer slung over his back, led the way, backing down the hall under the twitching lamp light.

'Panthers! *Panthers!*' he cried. 'Show yourselves! Show us to the infirmary!'

Struggling with the other end of the chaise, Drakken wanted to explain, wanted to tell Olric what he had seen back in the royal apartments. But the words choked in his mouth. How could he begin to tell this fellow Templar that Einholt, one of the White, was the assassin?

He was struggling with his words when six Panther Knights appeared, hurrying down the hall to them. Vogel, his visor raised, led them. The others, hidden behind their gilt face-plates, could all be Krass and Guingol, over and again, for all Drakken could tell.

Olric turned, fighting with the weight of the chaise. 'Vogel! Good! Look to us, man! Foul murder has been done!'

The Panthers paused, and Vogel slammed down his visor. He paced forward, and punched his broadsword through Olric's torso. Olric bellowed, his mouth bubbling blood as he went down, his end of the chaise smashing to the marble floor. The Bretonnian noble slumped off the makeshift stretcher and rolled limply across the floor.

Vogel pulled his sword out of Olric, ripping the backplate of the Wolf's armour away. Olric dropped on his face hard, falling into a lake of his own blood. The Panthers, Vogel at the lead, moved in on Drakken.

The young Wolf could smell the sickness smell again, riper and fuller than before. Spoiled milk. The smell of madness and the magic of the dead.

Vogel flew at him but Drakken was ready. He ducked under the sword arm and deflected the swinging blow with a lash of his armoured left arm. At the same time, he pulled out his dagger and slammed the blade deep into Vogel's neck, punching it up through the throat armour and through the madman's spine. Blood jetted out through the multiple joints of the Panther's gleaming, segmented helm. Vogel fell, pulling Drakken's buried knife away with him.

Unarmed now, as five more closed, swords ready.

A shockwave of stone on metal rang down the hall as Morgenstern and Anspach came in on the Panthers from the rear. Anspach sent his first foe face-down, the back of the ornate Panther armour splintered and bloody. Morgenstern decapitated another as easily as hoisting a turnip off a buckettop. The helmeted head thukked off the ceiling and went clattering away.

The three remaining Panthers turned to face the onslaught.

Drakken could hear Morgenstern and Anspach yelling out the battle cry of White Company, and repeating the war-chant, 'Hammers of Ulric! Hammers of Ulric!'

Drakken snatched up Vogel's fallen sword and waded in, swinging the unfamiliar weapon like a hammer. A Panther was in his face, slicing hard with expertise.

Drakken blocked the strike as he would have done with a hammer haft, and sparks flew from the blades. He came around again, circling the sword around his head two-handed, as a hammer-man would turn his weapon, and cut the Panther through the shoulder, down to the belly. The sharp sword cut armour plate like a hot-iron through ice.

Morgenstern slammed a Panther into the hallway wall with his bulk, and killed him with repeated blows from his circling hammer. Anspach clove in the plumed helm of the last. They grouped, back to back, defending the fallen body of the ambassador, as dozens of other Knights Panther charged down at them from both sides.

THE HAIL CEASED. An oppressive stillness settled over the city and the night. The sky was an ice-haze of cold, smoky fumes, making the stars glint pink and bloodshot. Thunder moaned in the stillness, like distant packs of cavalry, turning far away for the next assault.

The palace gates were locked shut.

'Open!' Ganz bellowed, his steed bucking. The priest clung tight to the armoured warrior to remain seated.

'The palace is closed!' yelled a Panther Knight back from the gateway, behind the bars. 'Alarm has been sounded! No one may enter!'

Steadying his horse, Ganz looked further, and saw the lamps flashing in the windows of the great palace, heard the cries and bells and screams.

'Let us in!' he repeated, his voice a thunder all of its own.

'Go back!' returned the gate-guards.

Gruber slung his horse in around Ganz, and came up to the gates sidelong, hammer whirling. With celebrated precision, he smashed the padlock off the gate-bolt. Then he reared his horse and the front hooves crashed the gates open as they came down.

The six Wolves bolted down the main entrance yard through the gates as the Panthers rushed out to waylay them. The hurtling fury of Ulric's Temple Men at full charge. What could they do against that? Better they tried to stop a storm, a north wind, a thunderbolt. It was over in seconds.

Ganz's Wolves threw themselves off their steeds at the palace entrance, letting their chargers run free. With Gruber and the priest of Morr at their head, they crashed into the main hall, and had to stand aside as a gaggle of court musicians and domestics fled past them out into the night. Kaspen caught one by the throat, a lute player who clutched his instrument to his belly to protect it.

'Murder! Madness! Murder!' the man gagged, trying to tear free.

'Go!' snapped Kaspen, throwing the man out of the door. The six knights and the priest advanced across the great space off the hallway. The vast building beyond rang with screams and yells and incessant hand-bell alarms.

'We're too late,' said Ganz.

'We're never too late,' snapped Dieter of Morr. 'This way.'

'Where are we going?'

'The guest apartments.'

'And how do you know where they are?' Ganz asked.

'Research,' the priest of Morr smiled back at him. It was the coldest smile Ganz had ever seen in his entire life.

BACKED INTO A corner, sweeping at anything that came in range, the three great White Templars stood in a line, side by side: Morgenstern, Anspach, Drakken. Two hammers and one novice sword against twenty fever-maddened Knights Panther who bottled them in a back end of the corridor. Already, four more Panthers lay dead or dying. It was all the three Wolves could do to fend off the attacks now, to keep the weapons away.

Through the press, Drakken could see von Volk and a dozen more Panthers charging down from the end of the hall. This is it, he thought. *This is where the sheer weight of numbers–*

Von Volk cut a Panther knight down with a swing of his sword. Then another. He and his men hacked into the back of the insane press that had cornered the Wolves.

That first blow had been historic, unprecedented. The first time a holy Panther Knight had slain another of his kind. It didn't remain unprecedented for long. Drakken knew what he was witnessing was extraordinary. Panther against Panther. He thought of Einholt. *Had a Wolf ever killed a Wolf?*

He thought of Aric. The thought was too painful to keep in his head.

Morgenstern bellowed, and urged Anspach and Drakken up with him to crush the mad Panthers against von Volk and his relieving force.

Three fierce minutes, and nearly twenty-five noble Knights Panther lay dead or broken on the hallway floor. Von Volk pulled off his helmet and sank to his knees in horror, his helm crashing out of his loose grip and rolling away across the ground. His other, loyal knights also sank down, or turned away, horrified at what they had done. What they had been forced to do.

'In the Graf's name…' gasped von Volk, tears in his eyes. 'What in all of creation have we had to do here tonight? My men… my…'

Morgenstern knelt down in front of von Volk and grabbed the knight's clenched hands between his mighty paws. 'You have done your duty and may Ulric – and Sigmar – thank you. There is rank insanity in the Palace of Middenheim tonight, and you have kept your duty well and seen it off. Mourn these poor souls, yes. I will join you in that. But they were turned, von Volk. They were not the men you knew. Evil had taken them. You did what was right.'

Von Volk looked up into the face of the obese White Wolf. 'You say. They were not your own.'

'Still enough, you did right. Our loyalty is to our kind, but when evil strikes, our truest loyalty is to the Crown.'

Morgenstern pulled out his flask and von Volk slugged greedily from the offered bottle.

'It's only the start of the horrors we may have to face now,' Anspach advised, helping von Volk up.

The Knights Panther captain nodded, wiped his mouth and took another slug of the fire-water.

'Sigmar look to all those who have done this here tonight. For I will show them no mercy.'

THEY FOUND ARIC face down in front of the guest room fireplace, blood matting his hair and seeping out of his armour joints. Dorff and Kaspen lifted him up and laid him on the bed, stripping off his armour. There was no surgeon to call, as the palace doctor was attending to the Bretonnian ambassador. The priest of Morr pushed in.

'I usually tend the dead, but I know about medicine, a thing or two at least.' With the help of Kaspen, who had been trained as White Company's bone-setter and wound-binder for the battlefield, Dieter began to dress the young knight's injuries.

'A madness befell my men,' von Volk was saying.

'A madness befalls this city,' Lowenhertz returned. 'We have learned that foul necromancy permeates this place, seeking its own ends. The fever is part of it. It is not a true plague, it is magic-born, bred to infect us all with insanity and killing glee. Is that not so, priest?'

Father Dieter looked up from his work splinting Aric's shattered left arm.

'Quite so, Lowenhertz. The sickness that afflicts Middenheim is magical in nature. A madness. You've seen the signs, von Volk. You've read the words on the walls.'

'A madness that makes those touched kill and kill again for the glory of blood-letting,' Ganz said, without life or spark in his voice. 'At any time, it could afflict us. It is spreading, pestilential, all around us.'

Drakken stepped forward. 'I know the evil,' he said.

'What'

'The thing you said you fought in the cellar,' Drakken said to Gruber. 'The thing with the pink eyes. It was here. But it wasn't a stick-form, a flimsy thing, it was...'

He couldn't say the name.

'What?' Lowenhertz snarled impatiently.

Gruber held him back from the pale young Wolf, who was still about to speak.

But it was the priest of Morr who finished the sentence. 'Einholt.'

They all looked around and then back at Drakken.

'Was it?' asked Ganz.

Drakken nodded. 'It said it was him, but it wasn't. It had borrowed his body like you might borrow a cloak. It wore him. It wasn't Einholt, but it looked like him.'

'And... fought like him.' Aric eased up onto his good elbow and looked at them all. 'It was Einholt's flesh, Einholt's blood, Einholt's skill and memories. But it was a hollow, evil thing inside. The thing said it had taken Einholt for revenge, because Einholt had somehow stopped it... in the cellar, I suppose. It wanted a body. It chose Einholt.'

Father Dieter had finished dressing Aric's injuries. He pulled Ganz to one side.

'I fear,' he said reluctantly, 'that we are not simply dealing with a necromancer here.'

Ganz looked round at him, feeling the ice-sweat trickle down his back.

'To possess a form, as your man Aric relates... this is something more.'

'It said its name was Barakos,' Aric said, leaning forward, listening to them from the bed.

'Barakos?' Dieter mused, his eyes lifted. 'Why, then, it's true.'

Ganz grabbed the priest of Morr by the front of his robes and slammed him into the hardwood panels of the stateroom. The Wolves and Panthers looked on in shock.

'You know? You knew?'

'Let me go, Ganz.'

'YOU KNEW!?'

'Let me go!'

Ganz released his grip and Father Dieter slid down so his feet were on the floor. He rubbed his throat.

'Barakos. The name appeared on the walls at Wolf-hole. I asked you all if you knew it – you did not. I cast it aside myself, hoping that it was just a coincidence. The name of some Araby merchant now in town who would fall victim to the plague-murders.'

'And what is it really?'

'Nothing. Everything,' the priest said. 'In the old books, it is written "Babrakkos", an ancient name even when Middenheim was founded. A dark power, deathless, necromantic. Also known as Brabaka, and in the nursery rhyme: Ba ba Barak, come see thee tarry! You know it?'

'I know it.'

'All those references refer to a pestilential liche-thing that threatened Middenheim in the earliest of days. Babrakkos. Barakos now, perhaps. I think it's back. I think it's living again. I think it wants the city of Middenheim dead so as to conjure enough death-magic force to make it a god. An unclean god, but a god never the less, as we would understand it, Ganz of the White.'

'A liche...' Even Ganz's voice was pale. 'How do we fight such a thing?'

Father Dieter shrugged. 'It has clearly already begun upon its work. Tonight is its hour. We have the men, but not the time. If we could find the foe, we might be able to thwart it, but–'

'I know where it is,' a voice from the door said.

The Wolves and the Panthers looked round. Lenya smiled at them as Drakken, humbly, led her in.

'Not me, actually. My friend here.' Lenya dragged the shabby figure of Kruza into the light behind her and Drakken. She held up the ornament, the world-eater, the biting snake. Lamp-light flickered off it.

'This is Kruza. My friend. My brother's friend. He knows where the monster dwells.'

SNOW, IN ICY pellets, had begun to fall out of the frosty pink night again. It was like riding down into Hell.

The dark cityscape was dotted with dozens of fires; numerous buildings blazed from Ostwald to the Wynd. Screaming and wailing and clamour rolled down the streets all around, where fever-maddened citizens brawled or fought in packs like wild beasts. Bodies littered the cold streets, the falling snow forming crusty shrouds over those that had lain longest. Names, written in blood, wax, ink and ice covered the street walls and the sides of buildings. The cold air smelled of spoiled milk.

The company rode out through the broken gates of the palace and down the steep Gafsmund streets into Nordgarten. Ganz led them, with Gruber at his side, carrying the standard. Kruza and the priest rode on stubborn palfreys taken from the palace stables, close at the lead knights' heels. Kruza had never been on a horse before in his life. But then again, every single thing that had happened to him tonight was new – and none of it was welcome.

Behind the lead four, Morgenstern, Kaspen, Anspach, Bruckner and Dorff, then Lowenhertz, Schell, Schiffer and Drakken. Next, in a close formation, the vengeful von Volk and six of his best Panthers, all men who had yet shown no signs of the fever. Bertolf, of Red Company, had ridden hard for the Temple, to raise the companies there in support. Aric, by necessity of his wounds, had been left at the palace, where von Volk's trusted Lieutenant Ulgrind was trying to re-establish calm.

Packs of feral citizens howled at them as they passed, some hurling stones, some even running out to dare the Templars in their insanity.

At the top of one of the sloping residential avenues, Ganz stopped them and looked round at the shivering cut-purse. The company leader mused for a moment that the fate of them all, the fate of the city itself, depended upon the sort of street-filth who would normally be invisible to him. The young man didn't seem much, rangy and lean in ragged clothes, his expression clearly showing he wished to be elsewhere. Any elsewhere. But he had come to them, so Drakken's girl had said. Come to the palace, braving the deadly storm, fired by some need to serve even he couldn't explain. Somehow, Ganz thought, in a moment of wonderful clarity, it seemed just. The foulness threatened them all. It was only right that the city stood to face it together, from the highest to the lowliest.

'Well, Kruza?' Ganz asked, making sure he remembered and used the ruffian's name. He wanted the young man to know he was an important part of the enterprise.

Kruza thought and then pointed down the hill. 'Down, and then the second turn to the left.'

'Are you sure, Kruza?'

'Sure as I can be,' the cut-purse replied. Why did the big warrior keep using his name like that? He was scared enough – by the night, and the evil, and the simple fact of being here amongst this company of Wolves. Somehow, hearing his name on the lips of a warrior of Ulric was most terrible of all. He shouldn't be here. It was wrong.

'Come on, Kruza! It's there to be taken!' the priest muttered encouragingly, beside him.

Kruza looked round. 'What? What did you say?'

'I said, come on. Show us the place,' replied the priest, frowning. He could see the fear in Kruza's eyes. 'What is it?'

'Just ghosts, father, voices of the dead – but I guess you know all about that.'

'Too much, lad, too much.'

Ganz led them on, at a canter now. Kruza was having trouble staying in his saddle, but the big, elderly Wolf – Morgenschell, was it? – spurred forward and came alongside him, taking the palfrey's reins.

'Just hold on. I'll lead you,' he said, his voice rich and deep and encouraging.

The big Wolf winked at him and it made Kruza smile. It made the armoured giant seem human somehow, like the sort of man he would happily sit and sup with at the Drowned Rat. More than anything else, that wink steadied his nerve. But for it, he might have fled, leaving them all to their heroic doom. It was the wink that made him stay with them. Kruza grasped the saddle-front and clung on as the great Wolf dragged his steed down the slope into a gallop.

Rocks and abuse rained on them from a group of shadows at the street bend as they tore by. A house had been sacked and was ablaze. Bodies curled in the stained snow. One had been nailed upside down to a wall, and bowls set under it to collect the blood for more inscriptions.

'So,' Anspach considered out loud to those around him. 'What are the odds tonight, you reckon? I have a bag of gold pieces says we can take this monster down, even if it does look like one of our own! I'll give three to one! That's better than the Low Kings would give you!'

'And who'll be around to collect if you lose?' Bruckner asked sourly.

'He's right,' Kruza cried, turning to look back. 'You sell the wager sweetly, but those odds are just the sort of deal Bleyden would offer!'

The Wolves around laughed loudly. Ganz heard it and it cheered him that they could keep their spirits so.

'You know Bleyden?' Anspach asked, spurring forward, genuinely interested.

'Doesn't everyone?' the priest asked dryly.

'This is not for your ears,' Anspach said. He looked at Kruza. 'You know him?'

'He's like a father to me,' Kruza said, and even above the noise of the hooves, the Wolves could hear the acid irony in his tone. They laughed again.

'There's a matter of a tally,' Anspach went on, ignoring the jibes. 'If you could have a word...'

'You mean, if we live through this night?' Kruza asked, mildly, jolted by his steed.

'Oh, I'll make sure you live through this night,' Anspach told him seriously.

'There, lad!' said Morgenstern. 'You've Anspach as your guardian angel! You shouldn't have a fear in the world now!'

More laughter; more jibes and taunts. Ganz let them have their jokes. He wanted them ready when the time came. Full of jubilation, confidence, full of the strength of Ulric.

They turned into the next street. It was deserted, and the falling snow clung to every horizontal like a pelt. Ganz slowed his horse to a walk, and the others made double file behind.

'Kruza?'

Kruza looked around, though he knew exactly where it was. The tall, narrow, peculiar townhouse was just as he remembered it. It was fixed in his mind. The lean, slender tower with narrow windows and that strangely curvaceous spire, which rose up in soft waves to a tiny dome at its crown. The gallery of arrow slits under the base of the spire. The second circular tower fixed to the side of the main building, the breadth of perhaps two men passing, but with its own tiny dome and more of the strange slits for windows.

A place branded on his mind. A place of horror and foul magic and death.

He raised his hand. He pointed.

'*There*, Wolf,' he said.

HE WOKE, HEARING distant fighting. Pain washed back into his body, like a tide. But it was softer now, as if he was floating.

Aric looked up from the bed. His broken arm throbbed. *Like the single pink eye had throbbed.*

In the flickering grate-light of the guest chamber, he saw the girl, Lenya, taking a glass of hot, brown liquid from a silver tray carried by a cadaverous old man in brocade, periwig and powder.

'Will there be anything else? The knight looks pale.'

'That will do, Breugal,' Lenya said, and the chamberlain nodded and left the room.

'You have no idea how much fun this is!' she laughed. 'The palace staff, even stuffed-rump Breugal, are falling all over themselves to help me as I tend the poor, brave knight who saved the ambassador's life!'

'S-so he's alive?'

Lenya started, almost dropping the glass. 'You're awake?'

Aric crawled up into a sitting position on the satin bolsters. 'Yes. Why, who were you talking to?'

'Um. Myself.'

'He's alive, the Bretonnian?'

'Yes… here, drink this.' She held out the glass and helped him sip. It was pungent and full of spices.

'What is it?'

'A tonic. From a recipe my brother taught me. The High Chamberlain prepared it by hand himself, if you don't mind!'

Aric smiled at her infectious good humour. The warmth of the balm was seeping into him. He felt better already.

'Your brother knows a good recipe.'

'Knew,' she corrected.

'He was this Wheezer, the boy the cut-purse was talking about?'

'His name was Stefan. But yes, he was Wheezer.'

'I will thank him when I see him.'

'But–'

'I know, I know. The cut-purse says he's dead. But for his courage, Ulric has surely taken him to his hall. I will thank him there, when I arrive.'

She thought about this for a moment, and then nodded. Her smile returned.

Aric was glad of it. He could see why Drakken loved the girl. She was so full of spirit and energy, it sometimes obscured her beauty. But that beauty was there. Her vivid, ice-light eyes, her hair so very dark.

'I heard fighting,' he said.

'The Panther, Ulgrind, is driving out the last of the fever-mad. It's got to the staff now. The chef attacked some pages, and a matron-lady stabbed a houseman with her embroidery needles.'

'Is the Graf safe? His family?'

'Sequestered by Ulgrind in the east wing.' Lenya looked down at him, holding out the glass for him to drink again. 'They say the city is running mad. Wild creatures, murdering in the streets. I never wanted to come here, and now I wish I never had.'

'You liked it back in Linz?'

'I miss the open country. The pastures and the woods. I miss my father and my mother. I visited their farm every week when I was serving at the Margrave's hall. I write to them each month, and put the missel on the Linz coach.'

'Has your father written back?'

'Of course not. He can't write.'

She paused. 'But he sent me this.' She showed him a cheap, tarnished silver locket that held a twist of hair, hair as dark as hers.

'It was his mother's. The clip is from my own mother's locks. He got the local priest to write my name and place on the wrapper. It was enough to let me know he had received my letters.'

'You're a long way from home, Lenya.'

'And you?'

'My home is down the hill, at the Temple of Ulric,' Aric replied quietly, sipping the warm tonic.

'Before that, I mean.' Lenya sat on a high-backed chair by the posted bed.

'There was no before that. I was a foundling, left at on the steps of the Temple just hours after my birth. The Temple life is all I've ever known.'

She thought about this. 'Do all Wolves join the Temple that way?'

He pulled up straighter, laughing, minding his splinted arm. 'No, of course not. Some are proposed as children, the sons of good families, or soldier lines. Your Drakken, he joined at eighteen, after serving in the Watch. So did Bruckner, though a little younger, I think. Lowenhertz was the son of a Panther. He came to White Company late in life. It took him a time to find his right place. Anspach was a cut-purse, a street boy, without connections, when Jurgen himself recruited him. There's a story there that Jurgen never told and Anspach refuses to relate. Dorff, Schell, Schiffer – they were all soldiers in the Empire's ranks and were sent to us on the vouchsafe of their commanders. Others, men like Gruber and Ganz, they are the sons of Wolves, following their fathers.'

'Are you the son of a Wolf?'

'I often think so. I like to think so. I believe that's why I was left on the Temple steps.'

Lenya was silent for a while. Then she said. 'What about the big one, Morgenstern?'

'Son of a merchant, who proposed him for admission when his father saw how strong he was. He's been with us since his teenage years.'

'So you are all different? From different places?'

'Levelled as one by Ulric, in his holy service.'

She paused. 'What about Einholt?'

He was silent for a while, as if wrestling with thoughts. 'He was the son of a Wolf, serving in the Temple since childhood. Old Guard… like Jurgen. He recruited and trained; Kaspen, for one. Myself, when the time came. There were others.'

'Others?'

'The fallen, the slain. Brotherhood has its price, Lenya of Linz.'

She smiled and held up a finger to silence him. 'Hush now, you make me sound like some high lady.'

'In Drakken's eyes you are. You should cherish that.'

'I fear for him,' she said suddenly. 'There was something in his face when he left. Like he had wronged and wanted to make amends.'

'Krieg has nothing to prove.'

She stood, looking away from Aric into the fire-glow. 'It was because he was with me, wasn't it? He came to me, did me a service, in fact. He left his post, didn't he? That's why you're hurt.'

Aric swung his legs off the bed and paused for a moment, fighting the pain in his arm. 'No!' he spat. 'No – he was true. True to the company over and again. Whatever he thinks he did, whatever wrong, I absolve him of it. He saved me.'

'Will he save the city too?' Lenya asked, gazing into the embers of the fireplace.

'I trust him to.'

She looked round at him suddenly, horrified. 'What are you doing? Lie down again, Aric! Your arm–'

'Hurts a lot, but it's splinted. Find me my armour.'

'Your armour?'

Aric smiled up at her, trying to keep the pain from his face. 'I can't let them have all the glory, can I?'

'Then I'm coming too!'

'No.'

'Yes!'

'Lenya–'

She grabbed him by the shoulders so hard he winced and then shrunk back, apologising. 'I need to be with Drakken. I need to find him. If you're going – and you shouldn't with your wounds – if you're going, I'm coming with you!'

'I don't think–'

'You want your armour? That's the deal!'

Aric stood up, swayed, and found his balance. 'Yes, I want my armour. Get it and we'll go.'

THEY WAITED OUTSIDE for a moment, their horses in a wide semicircle in the street facing the main arched doors. The moment was long enough for snow to begin to settle on their shoulders and scalps. Around them, the howls of the city rolled. Above them, snow-thunder, like the grinding of mountains on the move, shook the air.

'There was a small door to the rear,' said Kruza out of nowhere. 'That was where Wheezer and I got in…'

'It's long past time for sneaking, my friend,' Ganz said, looking round at him. He pulled his hammer from the saddle-loop and turned it once, loosening his arm.

'Hammers of Ulric! Knights of the Panther! Are you with me?'

The rousing 'Aye!' was half-drowned by the thunder of his hooves. Ganz crashed his horse forward and took the doors in with a massive up-swing of his hammer. Wood splintered and caved. Checking his steed's step for a second, Ganz ducked and rode right in through the front arch of the townhouse.

His horse stamped into a paved hall tall enough for him to rise upright again. Lamps in the wall brackets guttered in the sudden wash of air. Snow fluttered in around him. The chamber was bathed in yellowish light, and the stink of spoiled milk was unmistakable here. Gruber and Schell ducked in on their horses behind him. Ganz had dismounted, looking around.

'Kruza!' he yelled.

The thief appeared in the door, on foot, rubbing his sore rump, his short-sword in his hand.

Ganz gestured around. An arch led off the hall onto the stair-tower. Two other doors were next to each other in the left wall.

'The stairs,' Kruza gestured with his sword-point. 'We went down, two flights.'

Gruber had checked the other doors in turn by then, kicking them in. Empty rooms, cold and dark and layered with dust.

Ganz moved towards the stair-tower. The other Wolves and Panthers had entered on foot now.

'No welcoming party?' von Volk asked dryly, his blade glinting in the lamp-light.

'I don't think they were expecting us,' Morgenstern said.

'I don't think they were expecting anyone,' Lowenhertz corrected.

'Let's go and tell them we're here,' Ganz said, but a voice halted him.

The priest of Morr, cowled and stern, stood in the centre of the hallway, his hand raised.

'A moment more, Ganz of the White. If I can do anything tonight, any little thing, perhaps it is to bless those bound for war.'

The warriors all turned to face him, eyes averted from his gaze. He made a sign in the air with one elegant hand. His other, by his side, clutched the symbol of his god.

'Your own gods will look to you, the gods of the city you come to fight for. Ulric will be in your hearts to inspire you to courage and strength. Sigmar will burn in your minds with the righteousness of this undertaking.' He paused a moment and made another sign.

'My own lord is a dark shadow next to such awesome forces of the invisible world. He does not smite, he does not punish, nor even judge. He just is. An inevitable fact. We come to find glory, but we each may find death. It is Morr who will find you then. So in his name above all, I bless you. Ulric for the heart, Sigmar for the mind – and Morr for the soul. The God of Death is with you tonight, with you as you destroy that thing which perverts death.'

'For Ulric! Sigmar! And Morr!' Ganz growled, and the others caught it and repeated fiercely.

Anspach saw how Kruza stood back, saying nothing, his eyes dark with fear.

'And for Ranald, Lord of Thieves!' the Wolf said aloud. 'He has no Temple in Middenheim, no high priest, but he is worshipped well enough and he'll miss the place if it goes. Besides, he's played his part tonight too.'

Kruza blinked as eleven Templars of Ulric, seven Knights Panther and a priest of Morr volleyed the name of the thieves' dark trickster-spirit into the close air.

Then Ganz and von Volk led the party off down the stairwell, brisk and determined.

'Ranald was my lord for a long while, brother,' Anspach hissed to Kruza as he swept past, pulling him on. 'I know he relishes every little bit of worship he can get.'

The stairs swept down. Weapons ready, the pack descended. Intricate lamps shedding a white alchemical glow were looped down the walls.

Gruber pointed them out to Ganz. 'Just as in the cellar where we bested it last.'

'He's right,' put in von Volk. 'It was the same.'

The lower basement, circular, arched and dust-floored, was lit with the same white light from dozens of lamps. The walls were blank. Kruza looked around in confusion.

'This... this is not as it was. There were doorways, lots of them, and... it's changed. How can it have changed? It's only been... three seasons!'

Kruza crossed to the walls as the warriors fanned out. His trembling fingers traced the seamless stone. 'There were doors!' he repeated, as if angry with himself. 'All around! They can't have been bricked up – there would be some sign!'

'It's uniform and smooth,' Drakken noted, checking the far side. 'Are you sure this is the same place, thief?'

Kruza whirled angrily, but the steady haft of Anspach's hammer kept his short-sword from coming up.

'Kruza knows what he's talking about,' Anspach said calmly.

'We know magic is at work,' said Father Dieter from behind. 'Magic has done things here. You can smell it. Like rancid milk.'

Lowenhertz nodded to himself. Or like grave spices, sweetmeats, ash, bone-dust and death all wrapped up together. Just as he had smelled at the Margrave's hall in Linz, and in his great grandfather's solar, all those years ago. Had the wraiths they had fought this spring in the woodlands above Linz been part of this too? The priest had said the evil was old and great and had been planning for a while. And it was after power, strength, that much was also clear from everything he had heard. The old wetnurse's amulet, the one Ganz had destroyed. Had that been a piece of this puzzle as well? A trophy, a powerful talisman their fell enemy had been trying to recover? Had they already thwarted it once before this year, without knowing it?

The irony made him smile. 'We've beaten you at every turn, even when we didn't realise it,' he murmured. 'We'll beat you now.'

'What did you say?' asked Ganz.

'Thinking out loud, commander,' said Lowenhertz, hurriedly. He glanced at the priest of Morr. The father had said something about defeating a necromancer called Gilbertus in the youngest part of the year; another part of it. Lowenhertz knew he would enjoy discussing this with the priest when all was done, putting the scraps together into a patchwork of sense.

Sharply, Lowenhertz realised he was imagining a time when it was over and they were all alive. *That was good*, he decided.

Kruza was busy searching the walls, fingertip by fingertip. His hair was dripping with sweat and melting snow. He would find it, he would. They had believed in him. He would not fail now.

Simply, unbelievably, the answer was there. Square ahead of the door from the stairs. Kruza didn't know where the other doors had gone, and he believed the priest when he spoke of magic. But here it was. Not magic at all.

'Ganz!' he called, in his eagerness, not caring about respect or rank. The Wolf commander crossed to him, apparently past caring either.

Kruza pointed to the wall, to the solid stones that matched the walls around, and pulled them aside.

Ganz started despite himself.

A drape of canvas, like a tapestry, painted perfectly to match the stones around, completely masking the archway beyond.

'We go to war, but the skills of a cut-purse show us where the war is,' chuckled Morgenstern.

Beyond the painted drape, a dark passageway, unlit and thick with warmth and smoke, led off into the unknown. Ganz marched through as confidently as he would through the doors of the Temple. The others followed.

Drakken was at the rear of the file. Kruza, holding the drape, caught him by the arm and glared into his face.

'You wanted me to look a fool in the eyes of your mighty comrades, Wolf?' he hissed.

Drakken shrugged off the arm. 'I didn't need to. You were doing well enough on your own.'

'She doesn't love you, Templar,' Kruza blurted suddenly.

Drakken turned back. 'And you'd know?'

'I know how she looks at me.'

Drakken shrugged.

'And I know you don't love her,' added Kruza, pushing his luck.

'We're here to save the city, and you think of her?'

Kruza grinned, almost triumphantly. 'You don't. That's why I know you don't love her.'

'There will be time for this later,' Drakken said, disconcerted, and passed under the arch.

Kruza let the drape drop back behind Drakken. Alone, he walked to the centre of the room and knelt in the dust, running the fingers of his left hand through the soft soil. This was the place. The place he'd last seen Wheezer. The place where Wheezer had–

Come on, Kruza! It's there to be taken!

Kruza started. There was no one there. Of course not. Wheezer wasn't outside him, he never had been. Kruza knew the ghost haunted secret spaces inside his mind.

'I'm coming,' he said, raising his sword and pushing in through the drape.

* * *

IN THE DRIVING snow, Aric's horse reared on the steps of the Temple of Ulric, and the Templar felt the girl behind him on the saddle hold tight as he fought the reins with his one good arm.

'What are we doing?' she gasped into his ear as the horse righted itself. 'Nordgarten, Kruza said! The place was in Nordgarten! You're as bad as Drakken, wanting to show me the Temple of the Wolf all the damn time!'

Aric dismounted. 'This is important. Come with me. I need your help.'

They strode in through the great atrium. Commotion filled the air. Bertolf had raised the alarm, and the stationed companies, Red, Grey, Gold and Silver, were martialling to support their White Company brothers.

With Lenya supporting him, Aric limped down the main aisle towards the great statue of Ulric. The cold air was rank with incense. The Wolf-choir was singing a hymn of deliverance into the night. Thousands of candle-flames shuddered as they passed.

Lenya was silent, looking around. She had never been in this great, pious place, and now realised why Drakken had wanted to show it to her. In a way beyond words, she understood what the Temple meant, what the Wolves meant. She was struck dumb, and surprised to find herself truly humbled.

They approached the great shrine of the Eternal Flame. Aric pulled off his wolf-pelt and began to wrap it around his hammer-head. With his one functioning hand, he made poor work of it. He glanced round. 'Give me strips off your skirt.'

'What?'

'Tear them off! Now!'

Lenya sat on the cold floor and began to shred strips of cloth from her skirt hem.

Aric had found a relic-bag and shocked Lenya by emptying out the dusty contents so he could pull free the leather thong. With the thong and the strips she gave him, the Wolf tied the pelt tightly around the head of his warhammer, using his teeth to brace against his one useable hand. She moved in, helping him to tie the bindings.

'What are we doing, Aric?' she asked.

Aric dipped the pelt-wrapped hammer into the Eternal Flame. The pale fire licked into it and Aric raised a torch of incandescent flame.

'Now? Now we're going to find the others,' he told her.

KRUZA JOINED GANZ and von Volk in the vanguard as the party pressed down the dark passageway. There was a dim light ahead, like a promise of dawn.

'This is not as it was before,' he told Ganz. 'It's utterly changed. I guess magic does that.'

'I guess it does,' said Ganz.

They reached the light and the passage opened out.

The chamber they looked out on was vast. Impossible. Immeasurable. The cold, craggy black rock of the Fauschlag arched up over them, lit by a thousand naked fires.

'Ulric's name! It's bigger than the stadium!' Anspach gasped.

'How could this be down here and we not know it?' breathed Bruckner.

'Magic,' said the priest of Morr. It seemed to be his answer to everything.

Ganz gazed down into the vast black bowl of the chamber, where flames flickered from hundreds of braziers, the firelight mingling with the white gleam of the thousands upon thousands of alchemical lamps roped along the rugged walls. There were hundreds of worshippers down there, robed, kneeling, wailing out a turgid prayer, the words of which punctured his soul in a dozen, evil places. The air was rich with the smell of decay and death.

At the far end, before the assembled worshippers, a raised dais, an altar. On it, a throne of rock, carved from the Fauschlag itself. On that, a cowled figure, soaking up the adoration.

Volcanic fire-mud belched and spurted in a pit behind the dais, and sulphur-smoke gathered in the upper spaces of the cavern. To the left of the chamber stood a great cage or box, as large as a Nordgarten mansion, shrouded in tar-treated canvas. It rocked and trembled.

'What... do we do?' Kruza stammered, knowing he wasn't going to like the answer.

'We kill as many as we can,' growled von Volk.

Ganz stayed his hand. 'A good plan, but I'd like to polish up the details.' He pointed his warhammer at the figure on the throne, far away.

'He is our enemy. Kill as many as necessary to reach him. Then kill him.'

Von Volk nodded.

Kruza shook his head. 'Your plan sounds no better than the Panther's! I thought you warriors were clever! Tactical!'

'This is war,' von Volk snarled back at him. 'If you've no stomach for it, go! Your job is done!'

'Aye,' sneered Drakken from behind. 'We'll call on you when we've done the work.'

'Ulric eat you whole!' Kruza spat back into Drakken's face. 'I finish what I start!'

'Then we're agreed,' Ganz said. 'The liche-thing is the target. Cut your way to it, by whatever means you can. Kill it. The rest is inconsequential.'

Ganz raised his hammer.

'Now!' he yelled.

But Kruza was already leading the charge, short-sword raised, bellowing a battle-cry from the seat of his lungs. The Wolves and Panthers followed him, bellowing too, weapons swinging.

The priest of Morr caught Lowenhertz by the arm.

'Father?'

'Could I trouble you for a weapon?'

Lowenhertz blinked and pulled his dagger out, handing it handle first to the priest. 'I didn't think you–'

'Neither did I,' said Dieter Brossmann and turned to follow the charge.

* * *

THEY FELL UPON the worshippers of undeath from behind, slaughtering many before they could rise from prayer. Blood sprayed the dusty floor of the rock-chamber.

Three prongs: Ganz with Drakken, Gruber, Lowenhertz, Dorff, and Kaspen; von Volk with his Knights Panther, and Schell and Schiffer; Kruza with Anspach, the priest, Morgenstern and Bruckner. They trampled the unholy congregation, chopping and hacking with their hammers and blades. The multitude rose and turned on them. Men and women and other, bestial things, throwing off their cloaks and hoods, raising weapons and raucous howls against the attackers. Kruza saw that each one wore a world-eater talisman round its neck, each identical to the one Wheezer had taken, the one now in his belt-pouch.

Von Volk's assault foundered as the enemy rose up around them, thickly, fiercely. A Panther fell, decapitated. Another spun back, gutted. Von Volk took a wound to his left arm and continued to hack away through the bodies that rose to meet him.

The thing on the throne stood up. It looked down in quiet wonder at the carnage below.

It tipped its head back up and rejoiced. Its unholy laugh thundered.

Death! More Death! Death unnumbered!

Kruza's party meshed into heavy fighting on the right side of the cavern. Cultists were all around them. Kruza stabbed out with his sword, ripping and turning. He had never known anything like this. The turmoil, the heat, the blood mist in the air, the noise. This was warfare, something he had never thought he'd experience, in his wildest dreams. A cut-purse, like him... waging war! At his side, Anspach, Bruckner and Morgenstern belted into the frenzied mob with their hammers.

A bestial, robed thing with ashen hide, glassy eyes and the snout of a goat, reared up at him. Kruza, his blade stuck solid in his last foe, flinched. A dagger tore out the thing's neck.

The priest of Morr looked down at the bloody blade in his hand. 'Morr is with me,' he repeated softly to himself. 'Morr is with me.'

Kruza spun and impaled a rabid woman with an axe who was about to shorten the priest by a head-span.

Morgenstern crunched a face nearby, chuckling. 'This reminds me of the fight at Kern's Gate.'

'Everything reminds you of the fight at Kern's Gate!' snarled the huge blond warrior, Bruckner, as he swung his hammer in the tight, stinking press.

'That's because he's senile!' Anspach barked, whistling his hammer down and over into a skull that flattened obligingly.

'I am not!' Morgenstern grumbled, rattling his hammer left and right, destroying bodies.

'No, he's–' Bruckner faltered. His mouth moved to finish the sentence, but only blood came out. A lance-head as long as a sword blade had impaled him from behind. He looked down at the steel jutting from his breastplate, blood jetting out around it. More blood found its way out of his mouth, foaming. He fell.

'Bruckner!' Morgenstern raged. Bruckner seemed to fall slowly in Morgenstern's mind, the long blond hair lank with gore as he struck the ground. White anger seared Morgenstern's brain. Like a bear, he shrugged off the cultists clawing at him, throwing them aside. One actually flew six or seven feet up into the air from the force of the Wolf's arms. Screaming as if insane, the Wolf flew into the thickets of the enemy. He was berserk. The dense enemy numbers recoiled and broke under his assault, smashed apart as they failed to get clear of him. Blood, meat and bone-shards flew out around his reckless frenzy.

Kruza looked down at the slain Bruckner in horror. He realised he had believed these Wolves to be invulnerable, man-gods who strode the battlefields of the world, denying danger. Despite everything, he had felt safe with them, as if the immortality was catching.

But Bruckner was dead. Just a dead man, not a wolf-god at all. They could all die. They were all only men. A very few men, surrounded by feral foe who outnumbered them five to one or more.

A hand grabbed him from behind, pushing him to the floor. Anspach blocked and killed two more cultists that Kruza, in his shocked daze, had been wide open to.

'Get up! Fight!' Anspach bawled. Kruza was shaking as he got to his feet. Robed creatures, stinking and yowling, were all around them. Kruza raised his sword and covered Anspach's back.

'I– I was lost there for a minute,' Kruza said, clashing blades with a cultist.

'Shock, fear, hesitation – they'll kill you quicker than any blade! Bruckner's dead! Dead! Hate them for it! Use the hate!' screamed Anspach. He said something else, but he was incoherent now. Tears of rage boiled down his blood-splashed face.

Kruza saw it, then, and the world turned upside down. Commotion and panic had pulled the canvas shrouds off the trembling cage close to them. The frenzied creature revealed inside the cage was an impossibility to Kruza. His mind refused to accept it.

A cultist pulled the cage open and the great snaking dragon streamed out to devour them all, and then the world, and then itself.

VON VOLK'S BLADE splintered in a cracking chest and he dropped it. Three of his Panthers were dead, crushed under the frenzy. Schell, the Wolf, howled out and threw him a captured sword. It spun end over end above the press. Von Volk caught it cleanly and laid in again.

Behind him, in a mob of bellowing and thrashing bodies, Schiffer was brought down, stabbed and pummelled into the dust by dozens of the enemy. His last act was to howl the name of his god up into the faces of the beasts that hacked and jabbed at him. A spear-point thrust directly into his screaming mouth silenced his oaths for all time.

Von Volk saw the lean Templar, Schell, turn back to drive the whooping carrion from Schiffer's smashed corpse.

He grabbed him. 'No! No, Schell! He's gone! We must fight onwards, to the throne! We must!'

'Hammers of Ulric!' Schell cried with fury as he turned back with the Panther leader to fight on. 'Drown them in blood! Drown them in blood!'

They fought on together, the other Panther Knights at their flank, cutting a swathe through the hectic mass.

GANZ BROKE FROM the mass first and charged the dais. Lowenhertz was behind him, with Drakken and Gruber. Kaspen was still caught in the vicious melee.

Dorff was dead. Kaspen had seen him fall a moment before, cut apart by frenzied cultists. His tuneless whistling would never haunt White Company again. Kaspen stood his ground, red mane drenched in blood, howling like a forest wolf, hammer whirling. He held ground and faced the rushing mob, partly to give his commander and the others time to reach the throne, and partly to make the bastards pay for Dorff's life, one by one.

Ganz reached the stone steps of the dais. Above him the hooded figure threw off its robes and laughed down at him. Volcanic flame-light from behind made the Templar armour it wore glow as if it were red hot. One pink eye gleamed.

'Einholt!' gasped Ganz. He had known what he was going to face, but still it fazed him. *Einholt, Einholt... Ulric spare my soul...*

'Oh, we're all friends here,' wheezed the one-eyed thing, beckoning to Ganz.

The commander of White Company saw how the Wolf armour it wore was rusting and beginning to moulder. The flesh of Einholt's grinning face was greenish and starting to stretch. It stank of decay, of the grave. It held out its hand to him. 'Call me by my real name, Ganz. Call me Barakos.'

Ganz didn't reply. He flew at the monstrosity, hammer swinging in a wide, sidelong arc. But the decaying thing was faster – terrifyingly fast. It smashed Ganz aside with a fierce blow of Einholt's warhammer. Ganz fell hard, clutching at his dented breastplate and the cracked ribs beneath. He tried to rise but he had no breath. His lungs refused to draw. His vision went bright and hazy, and there was a coppery taste in his mouth.

Barakos took a step towards him.

Lowenhertz and Drakken leapt up the last few steps and ploughed in to attack the liche.

Lowenhertz was first and fastest, but the undead thing somehow dodged his first strike, blocked the return and then sent Lowenhertz flying clean off the dais with a hammerblow that took him in the belly.

Sweeping around, not even looking, as if it knew precisely where everything and everyone was, it reversed the swing and snapped Drakken's collarbone as the young Wolf came at him. Drakken shrieked out and dropped to the stone.

Barakos stood over the writhing Templar, as if wondering how best to finish him. It chuckled dreamily, its voice like syrup. Then it looked up.

At the top of the steps, Gruber stood facing him.

'You again, old knight.' said the thing with the face of his old friend.

'I should have killed you in the cellar.'

'You can't kill what has no life.' The liche's voice was hoarse and dry, but there was a depth to it, an inhuman grumble that curled the edges of the words, like age-mould curling the edges of old parchment.

Hammers whirled. Gruber met the liche's attack with unbridled fury. Two smacks, three, hafts and head spinning and counter-striking.

Gruber feinted left and landed a glancing blow at the thing's hip, but it seemed not even to flinch. It blocked Gruber's next swing with the centre of its haft, then kicked at the Wolf under the locked weapons. Gruber staggered backwards and the liche rattled round with a wide, devastating blow that slammed the warrior away down the steps. The old knight bounced once off the stone, his armour denting and rattling, and crumpled at the base of the flight.

The thing was laughing down at Gruber when Ganz's blow smashed it back across the dais. Rotting straps tore and the left cuisse flopped away. The mail beneath was rusty and oozing with oily black decay from the corpse beneath.

Ganz sallied in again, before the creature could right itself. It managed to raise an arm to ward off the next strike, but Ganz's weapon smashed into the hand, tearing off the tarnished gauntlet. Several fingers came off in a spray of stagnant fluid and shattered mail-rings.

Ganz roared, like a pack-sire wolf, bringing his weapon around. He could taste victory now, taste it like–

The thing recovered, unsteady but ferocious, lashing out with a poorly executed, frantic blow.

The flat-side of the hammer-head struck Ganz across the neck and ear. He felt his cheek crack. His head snapped round with the blow and he lurched away, taking two steps before falling onto his hands and knees. Blood drooled out of his mouth onto the stone between his hands. The world spun upside down, voices and fighting booming in his rushing head as if heard from underwater.

His face white with pain, Drakken pulled at Ganz with his one working arm, shrieking aloud as the effort ground his shattered collar-bone.

'Move! Move!' he gasped. Ganz was a dead weight, barely supporting himself on his hands. The liche moved towards them. It was not laughing now. Pink fury throbbed in the one seeing eye. It opened its mouth and pus-yellow fluid dribbled out around shrivelled gums and blackened teeth. It flexed its two-handed grip on the hammer, ignoring the missing fingers.

Lowenhertz was suddenly between it and the two wounded Templars. He was breathing hard, raggedly, and the armour on his belly was badly buckled. Blood ran down the armour on his legs at the front.

'You... will... be... denied...' Lowenhertz said, dragging the words out one by one.

'I will destroy you all,' the thing returned, thunder back in the edges of its voice. As it spoke the words, two maggots fell from its mouth and adhered to the front of its cuirass.

'Make... sure you... do,' Lowenhertz gasped. 'For... as long as... only one of us... survives... . you will be... denied.'

Lowenhertz swung at the thing, which dodged deftly, but the knight reversed the swing abruptly with a display of arm-strength that one in his state should not have been capable of. The reverse hit the liche in the side. Rusty armour broke and straps snapped. Ribs cracked like twigs, and brown, viscous matter spurted out, more maggots amongst it.

It faltered, setting the head of Einholt's hammer down and leaning on the weapon to support itself. Lowenhertz almost gagged at the stink coming out of it. It was the old smell, the death smell, rich with spices and decay, from his great grandfather's solar, from the hideous tombs of the far southlands. But a hundred, a thousand times worse.

Lowenhertz took a step forward to swing the hammer again, but the creature knocked him away with a backward smack of its free hand.

Kaspen screamed as he charged in, reaching the top of the dais at last, a trail of slaughtered cultists in his wake. His red hair streamed out behind him. He was drenched from head to foot in blood, as red as his mane.

'Einholt!' he bawled, wanting to bring his hammer down, wanting to slay the foul thing. But it was Einholt still, his old friend, 'For the love of all we have shared, comrades of the Wolf, sons of Ulric, please, Jagbald, pl–'

Kaspen's old friend killed him with a single blow.

THE DRAGON, THE great serpent, the Ouroboros, slashed out into the cavern below, death incarnate. Its long neck, as thick as a warhorse's girth and armoured in livid scales each the size of a knight's shield, curling back in a swan-throated S-shape as it coiled to strike. Its beaked, wedge-shaped skull with back-flared horns, was the size of a hay-cart. Its eyes were fathomless dark pearls, a mirror only of unknowable terror. Where it had come from could not be divined; all that was true was that it lived, writhing in its foul undeath. And it raged, screeching its eternal anger at all life.

Kruza stumbled backwards and fell over one of the countless corpses that littered the floor. 'No, no... impossible...' he stammered.

Hooked talons, each as big as a man's thigh, dug into the rock as the vast thing found purchase. Its tail, so very long and slender, sliced around, throwing screaming cultists high into the air or breaking them like corn stalks. The wyrm made a noise, deep in its vast throat, high and keening, like a blizzard wind. Its scaled flesh was gold-green, like tarnished coins, but its vast head was white as bone.

The neck moved in a snap, the great curve suddenly straightening like a whip, driving the head forward and down hard as a lightning strike. The beak clashed, rending and butchering cultists. It raised its head, gnashing at the shreds of bodies and limbs in its huge maw, then slithered forward and struck again. It was wild, uncontrollable, killing everything it saw.

'How can we fight that?' Kruza gasped as Anspach grabbed him.

'We can't! We don't! Run!' replied the Templar, white-faced with fear.

Morgenstern appeared from the milling confusion and panic. He said something, but it was drowned out by another blizzard keening from the wyrm. There was a further clack of jaws, and more screaming, as it struck again.

'I! Said! Run!' Morgenstern repeated, emphatically.

'My plan exactly,' Anspach said. The trio headed for cover amid the milling enemy, heading for the rocky alcoves and depressions along the great cavern wall.

Then the world disappeared. There was no ground. Kruza was flying, looking up at the sulphur smoke gathering in the roof of the cavern.

Abruptly, the ground came back, hard under him, and pain jolted through him. He rolled over, looking around. The wyrm's great tail had scourged through the crowd, sending him and the two Templars flying. There were broken corpses and wounded cult-beasts all around. Kruza couldn't see Anspach or Morgenstern now.

The keening cry of the wyrm came again.

Kruza could smell the vast monster now, a dry, clean smell like hide-oil or grain alcohol.

He got up into a crouch, preparing to run – and realised the wyrm was upon him.

Kruza looked up into the dark, pearl eyes of the world-eater, the Ouroboros. There was nothing there, no spark of intelligence or reason or life. It seemed to fix on him, though. The swan-neck coiled backwards, ready to strike, ready to bring the huge arrow-head skull down at him, beak wide open.

In the last second left of his life, Kruza thought of Wheezer, Wheezer who had innocently brought him to this place and time and doom. *I'm going to be killed by a dragon, Wheezer! How do you like that, eh? Who'd have thought it? It's so unlikely, it's almost funny.*

It seemed right, though. He had failed Wheezer and Wheezer had died, died saving him. It was time to pay for that.

I just wish, Kruza thought, *I just wish that I could be as invisible as you. I never did figure out how you did that. Except that you were a natural. Invisible, like you, yeah, that's what I'd like to be.*

The wyrm keened its rage at the whole sorry world. Its neck flexed and whipped. It struck.

As if knowing its end was upon it, the ancient city of Middenheim shook. The sky stretched and broke as the storm exploded down from the ghastly magenta sky. Snow and hail bombarded the roofs, shattering some, smashed windows and tore away chimneys and weather cocks. Lightning lanced the streets, exploding houses, destroying towers. Lurid green energies, writhing like serpents, coiled around the Fauschlag. The northern viaduct buckled and collapsed into the deeps, a half-mile stretch torn clean away.

The Temple of Morr, still only half-rebuilt, burst into flames spontaneously. The fire was pink, unearthly. It made a sound like laughter as it burned.

Lightning struck the Temple of Sigmar and brought the top of the tower down through the nave roof.

The chaos and killing in the streets was now overwhelming. Fever-madness and storm-panic drove the population into frenzied rioting. The Companies of the Wolf, heading from the Temple of Ulric to assist Ganz's men, were caught in a mass riot, and found themselves fighting for their lives as lightning skewered the night, hail hurtled down, and death burned out the heart of Ulric's citadel.

Shades and spirits were everywhere. It was as if the doors of death were opened, as if the invisible world had been permitted to get loose and roam the city. Phantoms, pale, gaunt and shrieking, billowed around the streets, dozens, hundreds of them. Some spewed out of the ground in Morrspark, like venting steam. Many came crawling and shimmering, stalking back up from the depths below the Cliff of Sighs. The dead were walking, free; the living would soon be dead.

Lenya thought she would surely go mad. She clung to Aric as they rode as fast as possible through the chaos. Skeletal, emaciated things made of smoke circled them, laughing and beckoning. It was all Aric could do to keep the horse from shying. Thunder, so loud, and lightning, so bright, broke the sky into pieces.

'Lenya? Lenya!'

She realised they had stopped. Lenya slipped down onto the slushy street, soaked and bruised by the hail that still fell. She helped Aric dismount. He held the hammer-torch aloft. It blazed. Was that what was keeping the shades from touching us? Lenya wondered. She could see them all around still, flickering, darting ghosts, transparent white like ice on a window's glass.

'Where are we?' she asked over a crash of storm.

Aric gestured with the torch. There was a townhouse ahead, curious and towered. Warhorses, Temple warhorses, roamed the street around, trailing their reins, rearing at thunderflashes.

'Nordgarten,' he said. 'I can't say what we'll find in there. It may be–'

'Worse than this?' she asked, pulling him forward. 'I doubt it. Come on!'

The smoky things in the air around them were gathering, growing in numbers, lighting the street with their ghastly luminosity. Lenya tried not to look at them. She tried not to hear the whispering they made.

They reached the splintered doorway and Lenya helped Aric to limp inside.

* * *

FUNNY THING, THOUGHT Kruza. *I'm still alive.*

He felt his body and made sure it was still in one piece. The vast wyrm was slithering right past him now. It had struck, dismembering more squealing cultists just a few feet from him.

With this luck, I should go straight to the wager-pits right now, he thought stupidly. He turned and gazed at the huge, sinuous creature as it moved past, chomping and killing.

I'm invisible, he thought. *Ulric smile on me, I'm invisible! It can't see me!*

He stooped and picked up a sword. Not his own; that was long lost in the confusion. It was a long-bladed, basket-hilted weapon one of the beast-things had dropped.

He could see Anspach and Morgenstern, raising their hammers to confront the wyrm as the cultists scattered around them. *Brave, doomed*, he thought. *What can they hope to do against this?*

What can I do?

The thought dug into his mind. Kruza didn't know how, but he was sure he had been spared thanks to Wheezer. The dead were walking free again tonight, and somehow Wheezer had come to him, and generously shared his talent for invisibility.

No, that's not it. He's been with me all along. In my head. He was waiting to be called upon.

He tried the sword for balance and then calmly walked towards the slithering beast. Blood and body parts were strewn, steaming, in its gory wake. It showed no sign of noticing him. He got right up close to its scaled flank, close enough to hear its rasping breath, close enough to smell its rich, clean scent. It was keening again, killing. Morgenstern and Anspach would be next.

Kruza lifted his hand and placed it flat against the scaled hide of the wyrm's flank. The armoured flank was warm and dry. His fingers found a space between the scales and directed the point of the sword there. All the while the cut-purse was almost calm, as if safe within some sphere of protection, or the eye of the storm.

He put his full weight behind the pommel and drove it in.

The wyrm shrieked. The braying sound it made echoed around the room, louder even than its keening. Hot, syrupy blood gouted from the wound, smashing into Kruza. The liquid pressure knocked him over.

He was flat on his back and soaked with sticky wyrm gore when the monstrosity went into convulsions. Its vast, serpentine form spasmed and lashed, crushing cultists under it or pulping them with its jerking tail. Morgenstern and Anspach leapt into cover.

Shaking the chamber and vibrating wildly, the wyrm keened again, three times, each one louder and more shrill than the last. Its claws ripped into the rocky ground, striking sparks and sending shards of stone in all directions. Its death throes killed more of the foe than the Templars' brave assault had done. But they were death-throes. One last, bitter wail, and the wyrm collapsed. The ground shook. The tail lashed round one more time and fell dead and heavy.

I've killed a bloody dragon, thought Kruza, as he blacked out.

DRAKKEN STRUGGLED WITH Ganz, who was half-conscious and far gone. Lowenhertz lay still on the rock of the dais, next to Kaspen's corpse. The liche, panting and ragged, slowly swung around to look at the youngest Wolf.

'I'll give you credit, boy…' Barakos sneered through his borrowed mouth. 'You Wolves did more than I thought you capable of. You hurt me. I'll need another body now.'

It limped towards them. Drakken tried to scramble back, tried to bring Ganz with him, but his smashed bones knotted and meshed and he passed out for a second with pain.

When he came to, Barakos was right in his face, leaning down and leering. The grave-stink of his breath was horrific.

'But it's all too late. Far too late. It's over and I have already won.' The dead thing smiled, and the expression ripped the decaying skin around its mouth. Its voice was low, resonating with that undertow of inhuman power. 'Middenheim is dead. Sacrificed upon my altar. All those lives, thousands of them, spent and spilled, feeding the great power that will grant me a measure of godhood. Not much – just enough to turn this world into a festering cinder. A thousand ages it has taken me, but I have triumphed. Death has given me eternal life. The last few moments pass now, as the city rises to murder itself. Then it will be done. I'll need a new form to inhabit.'

Barakos looked at the terrified Drakken. 'You're young, firm. With my power, I can heal that injury in a second. You'll do. A handsome boy – I've always longed for good looks.'

'N-no! In the n-name of Ulric!' Drakken gasped, reaching for a weapon that wasn't there.

'Ulric is dead, boy. It's high time you got used to your new lord.'

'Barakos,' said a voice from behind them.

The priest of Morr stood at the top of the steps. Gore soaked his robes, and he had taken a head wound that drizzled blood down his lined face. He opened his hand and the bloody dagger Lowenhertz had lent him clattered to the floor.

'Dieter. Dieter Brossmann,' Barakos said, rising and turning to face the priest. 'Father, in many ways you have been my fiercest foe. But for you, the stalwart Wolves would never have recognised my threat. And when you defeated Gilbertus, my! How I cursed your soul and name!'

'I'm flattered.'

'Don't be. You'll be dead in a few more moments. Heh! Only you saw – only you knew – dogged, relentless, hiding in your books and manuscripts, hunting out the clues.'

'An evil as old as yours is easy to find,' the priest stated dourly, stepping forward.

'And why did you hide in your books, I wonder?'

'What?' the priest paused for a second.

'Dieter Brossmann, the worthy merchant – if a little ruthless. Why did you turn to the way of Morr and forsake your life in Middenheim?'

The priest stiffened. 'This is no time for games.'

'But of course: your beloved wife and child,' the liche hissed, backnoted by the burr of distant thunder.

'They're dead.'

'No, they're not, are they? They merely left you, left you and ran away from you, because you were brutal and unscrupulous and harsh. You drove them away. They're not dead, are they? They're alive, hiding away in Altdorf, hoping never to see you again.'

'No, that's not–'

'It is the truth. In your mind, you made them dead, sent them to Morr! To avoid the bleak truth that you destroyed your own family with your cruelty and your greed. It was conscience and denial that made you pretend they were dead, made you take the path of Morr.'

Dieter Brossmann's face was as hard as the Fauschlag Rock. 'I will pay for my crimes in another life, Morr watch me. When will you pay for yours?'

The priest of Morr moved forward again, raising his hands. 'You're dead, aren't you, Barakos?' he said simply. 'Undead, passed beyond. That form you inhabit – poor Einholt of the White – he's dead too. You may be about to embrace god-like powers, but right now you're a corpse. And so you should be taken to Morr.'

Another step and the priest began to intone the funeral litany, the Nameless Rite. Dieter Brossmann began to bless the corpse that stood before him, bless it and protect it from evil and send the lost soul to Morr, the Lord of Death.

'No!' gasped the undead thing, quivering with rage. 'No! No, you shall not! You will not!'

The priest of Morr continued to chant, driving all his will and the full holiness of his duty back into the foul being before him.

Ritual, ritual as old as Middenheim, dug into the liche, slowly dislodging its being from the body it dwelt in. It convulsed, coughing, spewing brackish fluid. 'No, you bastard priest! No!' It began cursing in a babble of a thousand tongues.

It was a brave try. Looking on, clutching Ganz, Drakken believed for a moment it would succeed. But then the staggering liche reached Dieter Brossmann and, flinching, smashed him back off the dais with a vicious blow of his deathless hand.

THE STORM SUDDENLY ceased. The last few pebbles of hail clattered across the streets. The pink night buckled and went dark.

A moment had come. The moment when a foul thing became a fouler god.

Every flame and candle and lamp and torch in the city went out.
Except one.

ONE STEP AT a time, Lenya supporting his weight, Aric mounted the dais. At the top, he faced the cadaverous relic that had been Einholt. A glance showed him the fallen Lowenhertz and Kaspen, Drakken clutching Ganz.

So much, so hard fought...

'You – again?' rumbled Barakos. 'Aric, dear boy, you're far too late.'

Aric, using his good arm, began to swing his hammer, turning it in great whooshing circles. The flame-head traced the circles with fire. The Endless Flame, the flame of the wolf-god. The hammer whistled round, the pelt lashed to it burning with unearthly radiance.

Aric let it fly, a perfect hammer release, just as Jagbald Einholt had taught him.

The burning hammer head struck the creature in the chest, knocking it onto its back.

Aric slumped, his strength gone out.

Lenya looked at the fallen liche, saw the tiny fingers of Eternal Flame crackling over its dented, decayed chest as it struggled to rise again. The burning hammer lay on its side, guttering out as if it were their last hope fading.

The one pink eye locked onto hers, as the Barakos rose like it was lifting itself out of the grave.

'I really don't think so...' it rasped, and it was too much to be endured.

Lenya rushed forward. It took all her strength to lift Aric's pelt-wrapped hammer. It took strength she didn't know she had to swing it up and bring it down on the liche-thing.

'For Stefan!' she snarled as the burning hammer smashed the dead monstrosity back into the rock of the dais.

The thing shook and ignited, blazing from head to foot with the Eternal Flame of Ulric. It jiggled and quivered, a living torch, issuing a keening shriek even louder than the great deathless dragon-thing, the world-eater, Ouroboros. The heat of the blaze was so great Lenya fell back. Barakos was incandescent, like a twitching firework, white hot and molten.

Undeath died. A clawing shade, frosty and steaming, tried to climb out of the torching body, tried to find a new home. But the sacred flames were too intense. The spirit folded back into the fire and was gone, shrieking out its last. Barakos, the endless, had finally found his end.

CAUTIOUS, TENTATIVE DAYLIGHT filtered down across the city as prime struck.

A week had passed since the night of horror. Middenheim was rebuilding, burying its numerous dead, and getting on with life.

In a canopy tent erected in Morrspark, and duly consecrated to Morr himself, Dieter Brossmann conducted a funeral rite for five Templars of Ulric. Their names were Bruckner, Schiffer, Kaspen, Dorff and Einholt. It was unusual. Usually the High Priest Ar-Ulric would consecrate the fallen Temple men. But Ganz had insisted.

The priest spoke softly, as if he was recovering from some injury. In truth he was – the dressing on his brow showed that, but it wasn't the physical wounds that really hurt him. Dieter Brossmann would have scars inside him for a long while yet.

In the palace, healers attended Captain von Volk, the only Panther to survive the battle in Nordgarten. Bedridden, he asked the priests of Sigmar who treated him if, may they forgive him, a priest of Ulric might also attend.

In the Spread Eagle Tavern, after the solemn service in Morrspark, Morgenstern, Schell, Anspach, Gruber and Lowenhertz raised and clashed their tankards. It felt as it always did after a great battle. Victory and defeat mingled, bittersweet. They did their best to carouse and celebrate the victory and forget what had been lost. More worthy names for the walls of the Regimental Chapel. More souls gone to run with the Great Pack.

'To the fallen! May Ulric bless them all!' Morgenstern cried, chasing the tang of victory in their hearts.

'And to the new blood!' Anspach added dryly.

They clashed again.

'New blood!' they choroused.

'What new blood?' Aric asked, limping in, his arm bound.

'Haven't you heard?' asked Gruber, as if some great irony was at work. 'Anspach here has proposed a new cub for the Temple...'

SHE KISSED his lips and then turned from his bed.

'Lenya – I love you,' Drakken said. It sounded stupid, and he felt stupid, trussed up in bandages and splints to set his collar wound.

'I know you do.' She looked away. 'I have to get back. Breugal needs the maids to draw water for the feast. I'm dead if I stay.'

'You fear Breugal still? After all that has happened!'

'No,' she said. 'But I have a job to keep.'

He shrugged, then winced, wishing dearly he hadn't. 'Ow... I know, I know... but answer – do you love me?' Drakken looked up out of the infirmary bed.

'I love... a Wolf Templar, of White Company,' she declared emphatically, and left the room to get on with her chores.

THE GREAT STATUE of Ulric lowered over him.

Ar-Ulric, great Ar-Ulric, finished his intonation, scent-smoke from the altar burners swirling around him, and handed the newly forged hammer to Ganz, who took it carefully, mindful of his injuries.

'In the name of Ulric, I admit you to the Temple, bring you in to White Company,' Ganz pronounced soberly, 'where you may find comradeship and glory. You have proved your bravery. May you endure the long years of training keenly, and find a purpose and meaning to your life in the service of the Temple.'

'I take this as a blessing, as I take this hammer,' came the reply.

'Ulric look to you. You are a Wolf now.'

'I know it.'

The initiate lowered the hammer. The heavy pelt and the grey and gilt plate were unfamiliar and burdensome.

'How do you move in this stuff?' he whispered to his new master.

'You'll get used to it... beast-slayer,' Ganz smiled.

Kruza flexed his armoured limbs and laughed.

IN THE ALTQUARTIER, down a filthy back-alleyway between stews, slum children were playing with a tight bound ball of cloth. They threw the ball back and forth against the narrow, greasy, dingy walls.

And chanted.

Ba ba Barak, come see thee tarry!
Slow not, wait not, come and harry.
Ba ba Barak come and sup,
And eat the world and sky right up!

And at the end, they all flopped down, shamming death. This time.

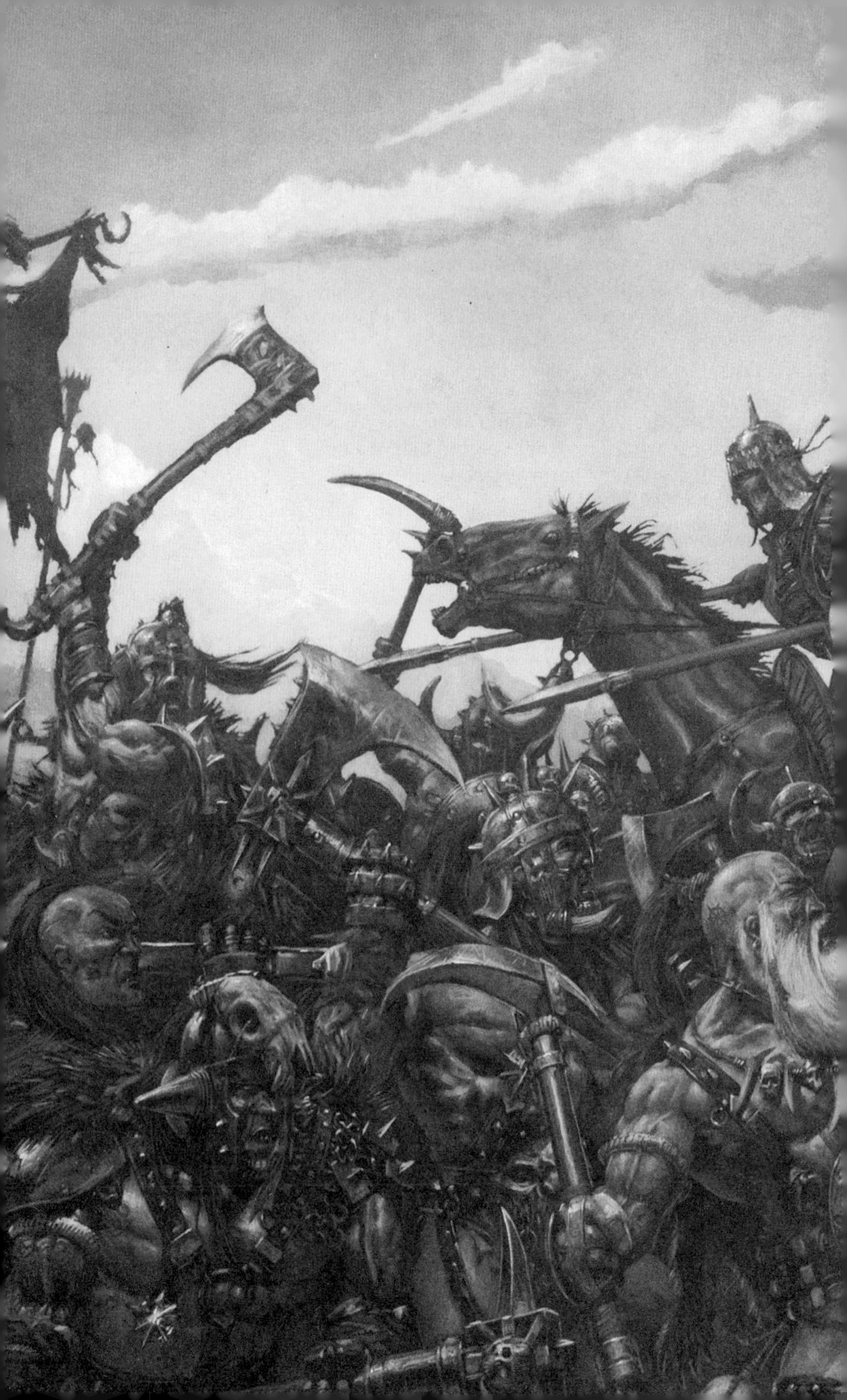

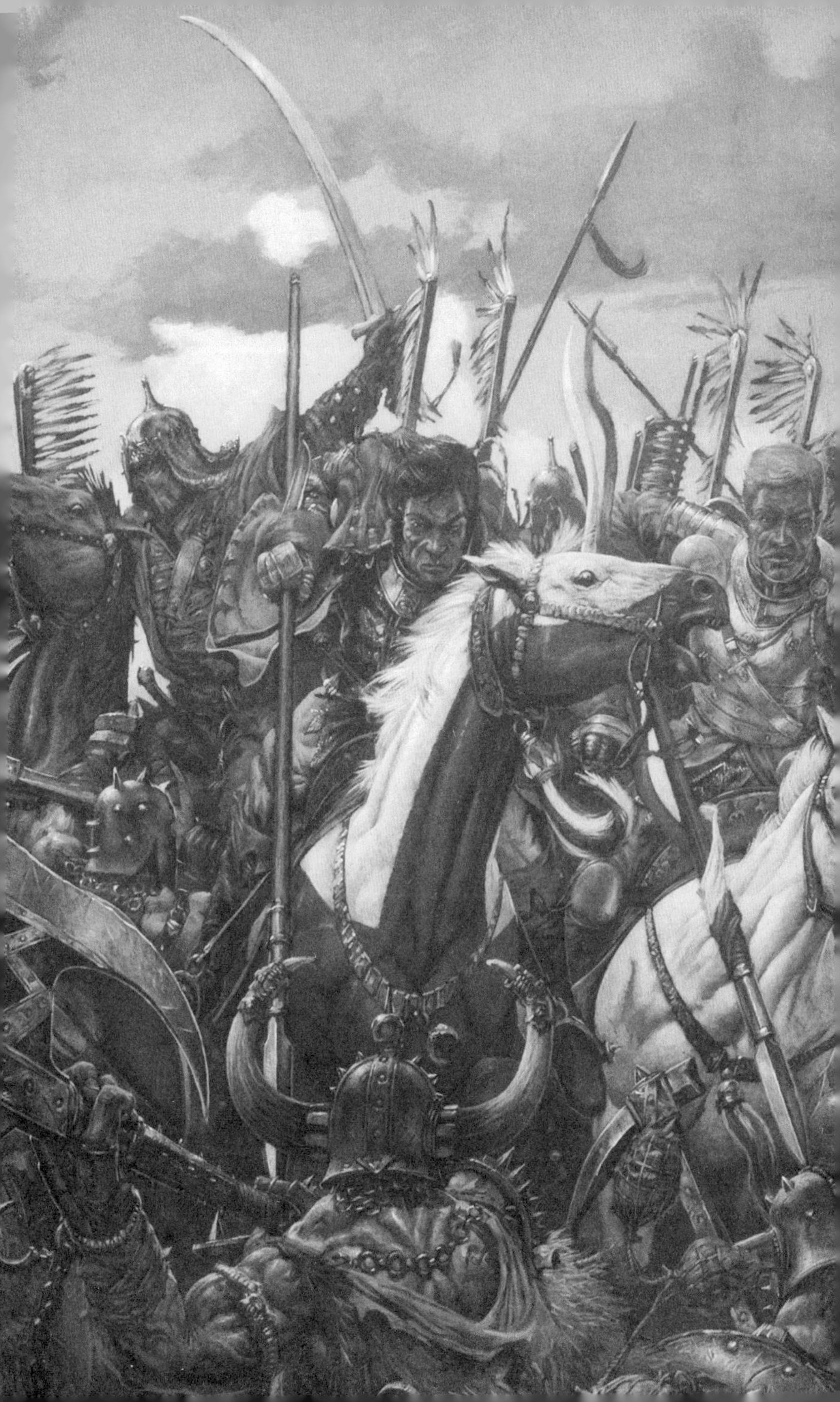

RIDERS OF THE DEAD

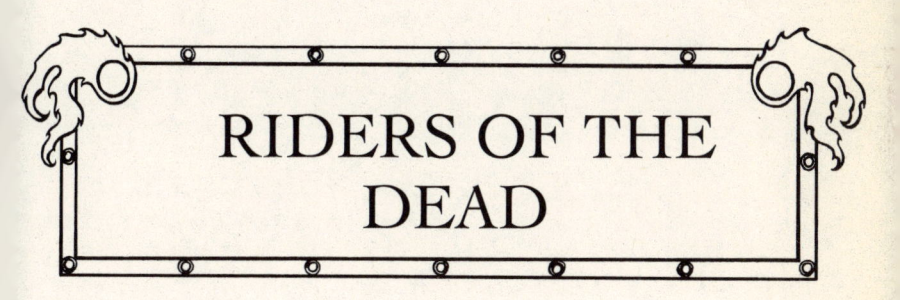

I'll make no bones about it, this book is a real favourite of mine. I'm very proud of it, I think it's one of my very best, and I have a very emotional attachment to it.

Riders marked a particular development in my thinking about the way I should write fantasy that I haven't been able to exploit much since. I believe fantasy works best if it is played in the most realistic way possible, so I set out to identify the closest real-world historical analogue to my subject matter, research that and then shift it sideways into a fantasy context. In other words, much more deliberately than ever before, I tried to write Warhammer the way one might write a historical adventure novel.

Obviously, there's magic and monsters, and all sorts of made-up stuff, but I was trying to build all of that upon a core that felt as authentic as I could manage.

It's also got an intensely tight plot-driving symbology (matched only in complexity by my Gaunt's Ghost novel *Honour Guard* and my recent Horus Heresy book *Prospero Burns*). It's also got an ending that was entirely deliberate.

I don't mean the end of the *plot*, I mean the end of the writing. A writer knows when the story of a book is over, but usually takes a few pages, or a chapter, an epilogue to wind down, tidy up and cool off, primarily for the reader's benefit. In *Riders*, although I was doing exactly that, I knew what the last few paragraphs would say, word for word, as I approached them. This, I believe, is unusual, as that kind of 'fade out' is usually a matter of finding the most graceful way of summing-up, switching off the lights and closing the door. *Riders of the Dead* is one of the few books I can actually picture myself finishing: in the old workroom that is now my daughter's bedroom, mid-afternoon on a sunny weekday, writing words that seemed astonishing to me, because they were just coming out of my fingers rather than being composed in my head.

As for the ending of the plot... well, I want to say a word about that, but if you haven't read the book, look away now because there follows something of a spoiler. A few people have, at conventions and Games Days, complained that *Riders* ends rather abruptly. During the epic final battle, they're waiting for the big confrontation that has been building up throughout the book to play out. When the clash comes, it's decided in a moment. This was completely deliberate. Dragging it out would have undermined the whole point of the book and the story. It is the lightning twist of fate, echoing the start of the story. The character who 'wins' only does so because of that split-second of chance. The abruptness of the finale is the very point of the entire interwoven scheme.

Anyway, that's my story, and I'm sticking to it.

Okay, everyone else can look back and unplug their ears now. Turn the page and read on...

DEMILANCE

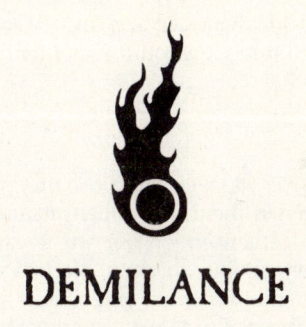

I

VATZL TO DURBERG, Durberg to Harnstadt, Harnstadt to Brodny, in one furious week, in one laborious gallop, a double line of helmet cockades and lance banners bobbing and fluttering.

A rest stop at Brodny, then out, into the edges of the oblast itself. After Brodny, all the place names began to change, for there the Empire slipped away behind them like a flying cloak cut loose.

The sparse haunches of Kislev lay before them.

To the west, the dogtooth line of the Middle Mountains, receding into violet haze. The sky, light and clear like glass. Endless acres of green crops, hissing in the wind. Grasslands riven with gorse and thistle. Larks singing, so high up they were invisible.

Brodny to Emsk, Emsk to Gorovny, Gorovny to Choika, through numerous oblast villages that no one had time to name, tiny hamlets where rough wooden izbas clustered around lonely shrines.

On the track, the massed columns of infantry under standards, each trailing behind itself a long baggage train like the tail of a comet. Ox-teams, kitchen wagons, tinkers with barrows, victuallers with heavy drays of kegs and barrels, muleteers, war carts piled with pike-shafts, stakes, firewood and unfletched arrows, all plodding north. The convoys of engineers, hauling the great gun carriages and the pannier trucks of shot and powder with oxen and draft horse, struggling with block and tackle where iron wheels fouled in the mud. Halberdiers and pikemen, in file, looking from a distance like winter forests on the move. Marching songs. A thousand voices, making the oblast ring. A hundred thousand.

The Empire was lowering its head and squaring up for war.

For that was the spring of the Year That No One Forgets. The dreadful year of waste and plight and hardship, when the North rose as never before and plunged its several hordes like lances into the flanks of the world. It was the two thousand five hundred and twenty-first year marked on the Imperial calendar since the Heldenhammer and the Twelve Tribes founded the Empire with sinew and steel. It was the age of Karl Franz, the Conclave of Light – and Archaon.

II

AT CHOIKA, WHERE the river was wide and slow, they rested their horses a day. The people there regarded them in a sullen manner, unimpressed by the sight of fifty Imperial demilancers jogging two abreast into the town square. Every horse was a heavy gelding, chestnut, black or grey; every man dressed in gleaming half-plate and lobster-tail burgonet. A light lance stood vertical in every right hand. A brace of pistols or a petronel bounced at every saddle.

The clarion gave double notes with his horn, long and short, and the troop flourished lances and dismounted with a clatter of metal plate. Girths were loosened, withers patted and rubbed.

The company officer was a thirty-two year old captain-of-horse called Meinhart Stouer. He removed his burgonet and held it by the chinstraps as he knocked grass burrs out of its comb of feathers.

Thus occupied, he barked sidelong at the clarion. 'Karl! Find out what this town is called!'

'It's Choika, captain,' the young man replied, buckling his gleaming silver bugle back into its saddle holster.

'You know these things of course,' smiled Stouer. 'And the river?'

'The Lynsk, captain.'

The captain raised his gloved hands wide like a supplicant and the lancers around him laughed. 'May Sigmar save me from educated men!'

The clarion's name was Karl Reiner Vollen. He was twenty years old, and took the teasing with a shrug. Stouer wouldn't have asked if he hadn't expected Vollen to know.

The company's supply wagons, with their escort of six lances, rattled belatedly into the square and drew up behind the lines of horse. Stouer acknowledged their arrival and limped over to the well fountain. He was stiff-legged and sore from the saddle. He tucked off a leather riding glove, cupped it in his hand, and splashed water from the low stone basin over his face. Then he rinsed his mouth and spat brown liquid onto the ground. Beads of water twinkled in his thick, pointed beard.

'Sebold! Odamar! Negotiate some feed for the mounts. Don't let them rob you. Gerlach! Negotiate some feed for us. The same applies. Take Karl with you. He probably speaks the damn language too! If he does, buy him beer. Blowing that horn and thinking hard is thirsty work.'

Gerlach Heileman carried the company's standard, a role that earned him pay-and-a-half and the title of vexillary. The standard was a stout ash pole three spans long. The haft was worked in gilt and wrapped in leather bands. On its tip was a screaming dragon head made of brass, from the back of which depended two swallowtails of cloth. These symbolised the Star With the Pair of Tails. Under this astrological omen, the great epochs of the Empire had been baptised. Some said it had been seen again, in these last few seasons.

Beneath the brass draco was a cross-spar supporting the painted banner of the company, a heavy linen square edged in a passementerie of gold brocade. A leopard's pelt hung down behind the banner and parchment extracts from the Sigmarite gospel were pinned by rosette seals around its hem. The banner's fields were the red and white of Talabheim, and it showed, in gold and green, the motifs of that great city-state: the wood-axe and the trifoil leaf, either side of the Imperial hammer. A great winged wyrm coiled around the hammer's grip.

Gerlach kissed the haft of the standard and passed it to the demilancer holding his horse. Removing his helmet and gloves, he nodded over at the clarion.

The pair walked together across the square, their half-armour clinking. Long boots of buff leather encased the legs of every demilancer to the thigh. From there to the neck, they wore polished silver suits of articulated plate over a coat of felt-lined ringmail. The horse company was a prestigious troop, recruited from the landed nobility, unlike the levies or the standing armies of the state, and so each demilancer was required to provide for his own arming. Their armour reflected this, and the subtle nuances of each rider's status. Gerlach Heileman was the second son of Sigbrecht Heileman, a sworn and spurred knight of the Order of the Red Shield, the bodyguard of Talabheim's elector count. Once he had served his probation in the demilance company, Gerlach could expect to join his father and elder brother in that noble order. His half-armour matched those rich expectations. The panels were etched and worked to mimic the puffed and slashed cut of courtly velvet and damask, and his cuirass was in an elegant waistcoat style that fastened down the front.

Though outwardly similar, Karl Reiner Vollen's half-armour was much plainer and more traditional. He could trace his lineage back to the nobility of Solland, but that heritage had been reduced to ashes in the war of 1707. Since then, dispossessed and penniless, his family had served as retainers to the household of their cousins – the Heilemans. Gerlach was two years Karl's senior, but they had grown up within the same walls, schooled by the same tutors, trained by the same men-at-arms.

Yet a world of difference existed between them, and it was about to get much wider.

* * *

III

THE PINE DWELLINGS of Choika-on-the-Lynsk bore roofs of grey aspen shingles that overlapped to give the appearance of scales. There had been a town here for a thousand years. This incarnation had stood for two centuries, since the razing of the previous version in the time of Magnus the Pious. Dry and old and dark, it would burn quickly when the hour came.

Vollen and Heileman walked under low gables into the gloomy hall that served as the town's inn. Ingots of malachite were inlaid around the door posts, and the lintel was hung with charms, sprigs of herbs, and aged, wooden-soled ice skates.

Under its roof of smoke-blacked tie-beams, the hall was dark. The compressed earth floor was strewn with dirty rushes, and there was an ill-matched variety of benches, stools and trestles placed about. Wood smoke fouled the close air, and twisted in the light cast by the window slits. Vollen could smell spices and spit-meat, vinegar and hops. Heileman couldn't smell anything that didn't offend his nose.

Three long-bearded old men, grouped around a painted table, looked up from the thimble cups of samogon they were warming in arthritic hands. Their hooded eyes were deep-set in their crinkled faces, and utterly non-committal.

'Hail and met, fathers,' said Heileman, perfunctorily. 'Where is the inn host?'

The eyes continued to twinkle without blinking.

'I said, fathers, the inn host? Where is the inn host?'

There was no reply, nor any sense that they had even heard his words.

Heileman mimed supping a drink and rubbing his belly.

Karl Reiner Vollen turned away. He had little time for Gerlach Heileman's arrogance, or his condescending pantomimes. He saw a huge broadsword hanging on the wall and looked at that instead. Its blade was mottled with rust. It was a Kislev weapon, a double-edged longsword of the Gospodar, deep-fullered and heavy-quilloned. A shashka, he believed they were called.

'What is you here?' asked a deep voice. Vollen turned back, expecting a man, but saw instead a heavy, sallow woman who had emerged from the back room, hugging a round-tipped serving knife to her streaked apron. Her eyes were permanently narrowed to slits by the ample flesh of her face. She stared at Gerlach.

'Food? Drink?' Gerlach said.

'Is no of food, is no of drink,' she told him.

'I can smell it,' he insisted.

She shrugged, humping up the slopes of her thick shoulders under her shawl.

'Is wood burns.'

'You miserable old mare!' snapped Gerlach. He tore a kid-skin pouch from his belt and emptied it onto the floor. Silver Empire coins bounced and skittered in the dirty rushes. 'I've sixty-two hungry, thirsty men out there! Sixty-two! And there's not a wretch in this ditch-town fit to clean the boots of any of them!'

'Gerlach...' Vollen said.

'Get off, Karl!' A blush was rising in Heileman's neck, the sign of his ugly temper. He closed on the flabby woman, then suddenly stooped and snatched up a coin. Holding it between finger and thumb, he pushed it at her face.

'See there? His Holy Majesty Karl Franz! On his orders we've come here, to take up arms and save this bloody backwater! You'd think you'd be grateful! You'd think you'd be happy to feed us and keep us warm so we might be fit and ready to guard your souls! I don't know why we didn't just leave you to burn!'

The woman surprised Gerlach. She didn't recoil. She lunged at him, slapping the coin out of his hand so hard it pinged away across the inn. She shouted a stream of curses into his face; a torrential proclamation in the harsh language of Kislev.

As she did so, she waved the serving knife expressively.

Gerlach Heileman backed away a step. He reached for his dagger.

Vollen interposed himself between them. 'Enough!' he snapped at Gerlach, pushing him backwards with one hand. 'Enough, mother!' he added, waving at her to calm down.

Gerlach walked away with a dismissive oath, and Vollen turned squarely to face the woman. He kept his hands raised and open to reassure her.

'We need food and drink, and we will pay for both,' he told her slowly.

'Is no of food, is no of drink!' she repeated.

'No?'

'Is gone all! Taked!'

She beckoned him with a rapid, snapping gesture and led him into a little side room where sacks of rye were piled up. There was a wooden coffer perched on the sacks. She lifted the lid and showed Vollen what was inside.

It was full to the brim with Empire coins. Enough to make the chests of most company paymasters look meagre.

She raked her fat fingers through the silver. 'Taked!' she repeated firmly.

'Tell me how,' he said.

IV

IN THE COURSE of the previous week, seven Imperial units had passed through Choika. The first had been another company of demilancers, and from her description, they were the Jagers of Altdorf. The folk of Choika had welcomed them and seen to all their needs: meat, sup, bedding, fodder. They had welcomed all seventy of them like brothers.

Two days later, an infantry column of nine hundred men from Wissenland arrived – pikemen mostly, but a fair number of arquebusiers. On their heels, two hundred more pikes from Nordland, and a train of cannon from Nuln. That night, the population of Choika had almost doubled.

Barely had these gone when another infantry mass marched in. Archers, arquebusiers and halberdiers, wearing yellow and black, she said, so that probably meant Averland.

Then sixty great fellows from Carroburg, shouldering their massive hand-and-a-half swords like polearms. After them, nigh on fifteen hundred Imperial levies, who drank so much they almost rioted.

A day behind the levies, thirty Knights Panther. These were the most impressive, she admitted, tall and armoured like princes. They were courteous and deserved much respect but, by then, the novelty had worn off.

Choika had been wrung dry.

'There's barely enough food left to see the town until harvest,' Vollen said. 'Wave as much damn money as you like, there's nothing to buy.'

They were standing out under the gables of the inn. Heileman turned slowly to face Vollen.

'I smelt cooking. It was rank, but it was food.'

Vollen shook his head. 'They're cooking for the town. Pooling what they have left. Our advance has even taken most of their firewood. What you could smell was supper for the entire place, roasting over the one fire they can afford.'

'We'll take that, then,' said Gerlach simply.

'You want them to starve?'

'If we starve, they'll be dead. Burned and split and raped when the Northers come in, with us too empty-bellied to stop it.'

Vollen shrugged.

'I'm not going to say anything to the captain, not this time,' said Heileman.

'What?'

'In respect of our association. I won't say anything.'

'About what?' Vollen asked.

Heileman's eyes narrowed. 'Damn you, Vollen! You showed me disrespect in there! I am vexillary! Second officer! No junior horse shows me up like that! You forget yourself, sometimes, and I'm man enough to appreciate why.'

Vollen reined himself in. He knew better than to push it. 'I am honoured by your kinship, vexillary. I will mind my place.'

Heileman bit his lip and nodded, shifting away. 'Good, Karl, that's good. I'd hate for you to forget you're only here because of me.'

Karl Reiner Vollen felt himself tense. It took considerable will to fight back the desire to swing for Gerlach Heileman. The conceited bastard...

Captain Stouer hallooed them from across the square. They walked together, over the cobbles, to rejoin him.

* * *

V

Handing over the reins of his gelding to one of the troop, Stouer watched as Heileman and Vollen approached him from the inn.

Stouer knew his vexillary looked forward to great things in his future. Heileman had the blood for it, after all, and the connections. Another summer or two and he would be a Knight of the Red Shield, or spurred to some other great order at least, part of an elector's life company. He looked the part. Heavy set and over two spans tall, with fair hair shaved short and a trimmed beard that grew white-blond. Noble of bearing and hazel-eyed, he had exactly the frame you expected to see filling a full suit of silver-steel plate, exactly the face you hoped to find behind the close-helm's visor.

The clarion, though. Ahh, Vollen. Like Heileman, a gifted horseman, and just as tenacious. But his future was not so bright. It was all down to blood. Vollen didn't have the lineage, or the connections. He might make captain of a state troop eventually, but that was about it. But for the recommendation of Herr Sigbrecht Heileman, Vollen wouldn't even have got a position in the demilancer company.

Vollen was a head shorter than Gerlach Heileman, and as dark as Heileman was fair. He was clean-shaven, like a boy, and his jaw jutted forward pugnaciously. His eyes were as blue as a summer sky. He was the most learned soldier Stouer had ever had the pleasure of commanding. Even the most noble-born sons riding in the horse troop were only partially literate, and Stouer had never had much of letters himself. Vollen had studied hard under his tutors and it showed. It was probably an effort to compensate for his lack of status.

'Say it as it is,' he instructed as they came up.

'There's no victuals here, captain,' Heileman replied. 'The town's been picked bare by the companies that have preceded us. They have some food cooking, but it's the last dredgings of their larders. We should look to our own supplies rather than deprive these people.'

Stouer nodded.

'Karl was all for taking the food by force, but I think we owe it to these kind folk to be respectful.'

Stouer glanced at Vollen.

'That true?'

The clarion stiffened, and looked like he wanted to spit. He said simply, 'My appetite got the better of me, captain. The vexillary is right.'

Stouer scratched an ear. He knew full well there was more to it than that, but he wasn't really interested. There was never any sense pampering soldiers. If what he'd been told at the Vatzl garrison was true, there were hard times ahead for all of them. Stouer had seen service in the oblast before, five summers previously. It was a hard country, more brutal in climate than any part of the Empire, and it seemed to go on forever. The people were by turns dour and hearty, though he'd never had much time for any of them. Their great, harsh territory, only partly conquered by civilisation, formed a natural buffer between the Empire and the Northern Wastes. He'd heard Kislev men state emphatically that they were the true protectors of the North, keeping the Empire's border secure. That was nonsense, of course. The Empire had the greatest army in the world, and when it moved north in times of invasion-threat, as now, it usually ended up saving the skins of the Kislevites too. But for the grace of Sigmar they held this land, and but for the army of the Emperor they would lose it.

And now the Northern tribes were rising again. Rising as never before. Thick and dark, like ants upon the tundra, spilling south. There had been omens, prophecies, signs. Even if the threat was exaggerated, it was going to be a hard year. Stouer had certainly never known the Imperial army to dispose a force of this size into the north, nor bind itself to so many allies. Bretonnian heavy horse, trained bands from Tilea, and from the damnable Old Races too. Everyone was taking this seriously.

The captain walked over to his saddlebags and took out a scroll-case. 'Karl! Your eye, please!' he said. Gerlach and the clarion were still regarding each other poisonously, and Stouer knew they needed a distraction or two. Like siblings, the pair of them. Constantly locking horns.

Stouer opened the case and unrolled a small chart. 'This is Choika, yes?'

Vollen examined the map and nodded. 'Yes, sir.'

'Here, the river. The crossing, here.' Stouer traced lines with his fingertip in a general way. It was all inky scratches to him, but he didn't want to betray his lack of learning.

'This is the Lynsk,' Vollen said, pointing. He was well aware of the captain's lack of letters, and knew that Stouer often used him as a clerk. 'Here's the crossing. About a league upstream.'

The captain studied the map and nodded sagely as if it made perfect sense. 'Our orders are to join up with Marshal Neiber and the Wissenland pike north of the crossing by noon tomorrow. At a place called Zhedevka. Now then, Zhedevka... Zhedevka...'

'There, sir,' Vollen pointed.

Stouer straightened up and took a deep, thoughtful breath. 'Still a few hours of light left. Gerlach, take three horse and scout the crossing. See what you can see. And be back by nightfall.'

'Yes, sir,' Heileman said. He pulled on his rein-worn gloves. 'Sebold? Johann? You too, Karl.'

Stouer bristled slightly. His intention had been to keep Gerlach and the boy apart and occupied. What the hell! If they were busy, they couldn't fight each other.

VI

FIELDS OF UNRIPE barley and rye stretched out from the trackway east of the town, and to the north, jumbled marshes and thickets of bulrushes clustered in the sodden flood plain of the river. The sky had clouded over and turned a peculiar, flat shade of white, though it was still bright. Where the track ran beside the river, damsel flies darted through the air, bright and exquisite as living jewellery.

Their lances slung secure in saddle-boots, the four demilancers hacked up the river trail and broke into a gallop where the track widened. All had their stirrups cinched short, as per regulations, so that when they rose, heads lowered for the chase, there was a good hand's breadth between them and their saddles. Gerlach led the way on his big grey, a seventeen hand three-year old called Saksen. The companies favoured young horses for their spirit and energy, though they could be skittish and difficult, and Saksen was unruly at the best of times.

Vollen came behind, alongside Sebold Truchs, a long-faced man who, at twenty-nine, was about the oldest trooper in the company besides the captain himself. Truchs was considered something of a veteran, and the younger men looked to him because of his experience. He rode a big chestnut gelding with a star on its brow. Vollen's mount, Gan, was a black of sixteen hands with a ferocious spirit, but more even tempered than Gerlach's grey.

Johann Friedel rode at the back of the group. He was nineteen years old, the third son of a merchant baronet, and as boisterous as his young black troop horse. For all of them except Truchs, this was their first experience of war. Real war. Their careers thus far had been spent in training and cavalry schooling, manoeuvres and ceremonial duties. They were all eager and scared in equal measure, but they showed only their eagerness.

Truchs had seen action four times: two border disputes and two scourge campaigns against the bestial filth in the Drakwald Forest. His colourful stories were numerous and, to be fair, contradictory. For though he had seen action, as the phrase went, he hadn't actually seen much action. A shield wall, at a distance, through the rain. A border town shelled by Imperial cannon, from the vantage of a windy hill three leagues away. An aborted charge and rally into what turned out to be an empty wood. And four dead bodies in a dry field outside Wurschen, terribly split and twisted by sword cuts. That was an image that still woke him some nights.

But still, his stories were good, all the better for the constant embroidery. And whatever he had done or had not done, it was more than any trooper in the company – except the captain, who had been in a real war once. Sebold Truchs would have been quite content not to have ridden north that summer, preferring to linger in the spartan enclosure of the Cavalry School at Talabheim, training and drilling and practising.

For there was one thing he knew for certain about this deployment to the bitter north: there was a real war waiting there for all of them, and their days of monotonous practice were gone forever.

The river was fast and high from the spring melt. Its headlong rush sounded like jingling coins. The track following it bent north in a long, slow curve. They came to the crossing: a broad timber bridge raised out of the water on five stone piers. Gerlach didn't break stride. He just nosed his grey on, and pounded across the boards, spitting sideways from the saddle to avert the ill fortune of iron hooves on wood.

The other three did the same, though Vollen merely did it out of custom. Gerlach's spittle, flying back in the slipstream, spattered across Vollen's cuirass. The vexillary could have aimed his mouth aside, but he hadn't bothered. Vollen said nothing and wiped it off.

They came off the bridge into the reeded banks of the north side, standing upright in the stirrups to urge their steeds up the sodden slope. Open grassland lay before them, wide and flat, vaster than any landscape Vollen had ever seen. Under the flat, white sky, it looked like a grey sea, the stalks rippling in the wind like waves. To the north-west, several leagues away, the horizon swelled up in a great mound, a curve rising proud of the grass like a pregnant bulge.

Gerlach reined in, and paced his excited, snorting mount. The others drew up behind him.

'Zhedevka? Over there?' he asked.

'It lies on the grasslands near a mound of the Old People,' Vollen said. 'So... yes, I'd say.'

'Old People?' Johann Friedel called out. 'You mean... the Slight Ones?'

He meant elves. Just say it, Karl Reiner Vollen thought. In this modern age, it was preposterous for a man to be coy about saying a simple word. Mentioning them by name was said to bring bad luck. And men still believed that, damn them for fools.

'Not elves,' Vollen said, and Johann jumped in his saddle at the word. 'The Scythians, the horse warriors of old. The Gospodars – and therefore the Kislevites – trace their ancestry back to them. They ruled here once, before Sainted Sigmar came. These lands were theirs. They built the towns whose ruins are said to haunt the Steppes. They raised the kurgans.'

'The kurgans?' Truchs said with alarm.

'That's a kurgan,' Vollen said mildly, pointing to the distant mound.

'Where? Where, damn it?' Truchs turned his horse in an agitated circle.

'Be still!' Gerlach snapped. 'Karl's playing with you. Using his damned education again, eh, Karl?'

The clarion sat back against his saddle rest and shrugged.

Even the most poorly schooled son of the Empire knew the word kurgan. It was the name of the bogeyman, the term for the dark tribes who lurked in the north under the Shadow. Kurgans were the very monsters they had come there to fight.

'A kurgan,' said Vollen, 'is a man-made hill, a burial mound from the early times. The vile tribes of the North are known by the term. Presumably...' he smiled, 'presumably because they want to hide the bones of all of us in the south under similar hills.'

Truchs touched the iron of his sword-hilt to ward against evil charms, and spat again. There was too much loose talk and bad luck in the air for his liking.

They rode north-west at a hard lick, Friedel just in the lead now. The cold wind was fierce in their faces and made them breathless.

As they got nearer to the mound – and realised just how huge it truly was – Johann Friedel pulled up sharply and called out a warning.

There were riders on the track ahead of them. A dozen horsemen emerged from the long grasses, silent and slow. Their horses were small, rangy mares, brown and bay, little more than ponies, with full, heavy tails and shaggy manes. The men were swaddled in cloaks, furs and blankets. Barbarian riders, there could be no doubt.

Gerlach slowed to a trot and moved to the fore. The shabby riders halted their horses and watched them approach, unmoving. Gerlach Heileman suddenly felt vital and proud of his gleaming armour and his sleek charger with its braided mane and docked, bound-up tail.

He stood in the stirrups again as Saksen pulled slow, glancing back past his shoulders at his outriders.

'What do we do? What do we do?' gabbled Johann.

'Hail them, vexillary,' advised Vollen.

'Hail them? Look at them, Karl! They're Northers! Raiders! Why should I hail them?' Gerlach unclasped the pistol holsters on his saddle-bow, and quickly cocked the firelocks of the ready-primed pieces. Then he drew his cavalry sword. It was a basket-hilted weapon with a straight, double-edged blade a span long. It had two deep fuller grooves down the length of the blade, and its tip was pointed like a spear. It was made for thrusting, as outlined by regulations.

'No,' said Vollen quickly, in disbelief. 'Oh no... vexillary...'

'Rise in the saddle to address!' Gerlach called out. Truchs and Friedel fell into step with him, and walked their horses forward, their sword blades resting upright against their right arms. Ahead of them, the riders remained motionless.

Vollen lagged behind, his sword still in its scabbard. Gerlach, Truchs and Friedel increased their pace to a brisk trot, their sword-hands now steadied on their right thighs with the sword points inclined slightly forward.

'Gerlach!' Vollen shouted.

'Get into line, clarion!' Heileman yelled back. 'Damn you! Get into formation or the captain will hear about this!'

The brisk trot was turning into a gallop. They were less than eighty lengths from the stationary horsemen.

'Present and charge!' Heileman howled. Three sword arms lifted, the swords pointed towards the enemy and carried crosswise to each rider's head.

The shabby horsemen stirred. Their horses wheeled around and there was a dull flash in the flat light as sabres were uncased and flourished.

Vollen tore his bugle out of its case and blew hard. A quadrille. Short-long-long-short. He did it again.

The three demilancers broke their gallop, swords waving, confused. The enemy horsemen spread wide, to either side of Gerlach's abortive charge. One of them raised a bone horn and returned Vollen's hoot.

Vollen spurred Gan forward and rode up to position himself face to face with the heathen men. Gerlach, Friedel and Truchs were riding out in a wide turn to come around.

The warriors were caked in mud and dirt, and Vollen could smell the sweat and soil of both horses and riders without trying. They sheathed their thin, curved blades and closed around him, curious. Raw, mustachioed faces glared at him from the folds of furs and grease-heavy cloaks.

'Imperial?' asked one. He was a big man whose bulk seemed to be crushing his ragged pony. His front teeth were missing.

'Yes,' nodded Vollen. 'The Second Company Hipparchia Demilance, ridden out of Talabheim. Hail and met.'

'You? You is leader of men?' pressed the toothless giant.

'No,' said Vollen. 'I'm clarion.'

'Klaaryen?'

Vollen gestured with his bugle.

Gerlach and the other demilancers galloped up and reined hard to stop. The cluster of filthy steppe riders broke to let them through.

'What the devil are you doing, Vollen?' Gerlach roared.

'Vexillary Heileman, may I present...' Vollen looked expectantly at the gap-toothed brute on the shaggy pony.

The big Kislevite pursed his lips and then said, 'Beledni, rotamaster, of rota of Yetchitch krug, of Blindt voisko, of Sanyza pulk, of Gospodarinyi, syet Kislevi.'

'They're on our side,' Vollen said to the vexillary, as if it wasn't clear enough. 'They're Kislevite lancers. Allies.'

'El-ays, yha!' the Kislevite leader of horse cried, and bowed low in his worn saddle to Gerlach, doffing his fur hat. His head was entirely shaved except for a long, braided top-knot and his drooping moustache. His men called out, and rattled the staves of their lances together. Each one had three spears slung in long canvas boots against the fore of their saddles: two short, slim javelins with long, sharp tips and one long pole, thicker and tipped with a narrow blade and a crossbar.

'These heathens?' asked Gerlach, incredulously.

'Heeth-eyns?' Beledni echoed, looking at Vollen for clarification.

'We show only respect,' said Vollen, slowly and carefully. Beledni thought about this and then nodded heavily.

Gerlach spat contemptuously. 'They don't even talk our tongue,' he said.

'Yurr tung?' said Beledni.

'They speak our tongue better than you speak theirs,' Vollen ventured.

Gerlach glared at him. 'Apologise,' he said.

'Apologise?' Vollen repeated.

'Yes, dammit! For our mistaken attack.'

Vollen paused. Unblinking, he returned Gerlach's gaze for a moment. 'You ask a lot of me, sometimes.'

'Are you refusing?' the vexillary asked. His face was flushed.

'Of course not,' Vollen replied. He took a breath and looked across at Beledni. The big man and his riders had been trying to follow the exchange between Vollen and Gerlach.

'Rotamaster, we are most sorry for our mistaken challenge, and uh...'

Beledni used the tassels of his riding crop to chase away a marsh fly that was buzzing around his face and made an odd little gesture with his other hand. It was a dismissive slight turn of the wrist as if he was spilling out a handful of corn. 'Is of no matter,' he added with a careless, almost theatrical frown.

'We meant no disrespect, sir...'

The gesture again, the down-turned corners of the mouth. 'Is of no matter,' Beledni said once more, and walked his shabby little horse ahead a few steps so that he drew level with Vollen. Beledni patted him on the arm, an informal, avuncular action. 'We will all live,' he said sagely. Then he leaned forward, his lips to Vollen's ear, so close Vollen was assailed by the smell of body sweat and rank breath. 'Vebla?' he said, and indicated Gerlach with his crop.

'Vebla, yha?'

Some of the Kislevite riders heard this, and snorted out chuckles.

'What did he say?' asked Gerlach sharply.

'I don't know, vexillary. I don't know the word.'

Heileman sat back against his saddle rest. He was annoyed. They were laughing at him, these heathens. Making him the butt of some crude joke.

He'd heard many stories of Kislev lancers, stories that described them as triumphant, spectacular, armoured in finery and feathers, masters of horse, as magnificent as Imperial knights. Someone had once told him that the lancers often scared their enemies from the field by the sheer splendour of their wargear, which attested to their prowess by all the riches they had won.

Not these dogs. It seemed that every story about the North was a lie. There was no magnificence in its landscape or its people, and their famous lancers were positively squalid.

'Zhedevka,' he said to Vollen. 'Just ask him where Zhedevka is.'

VII

WITHOUT COMMENT OR ceremony, Beledni's little troop of lancers led them another league north until the great kurgan was behind them. Zhedevka lay on the plains behind it, looking out across undulating grasslands and the distant shadow of a forest. Small patches of woodland dotted the landscape around the town.

It had ceased to be much of a town at all, now the Imperial army had arrived. Acres of tents and pot fires, great assemblies of pikes and halberds, musters of horse. In the fields north of the town, cannons had been drawn up behind sod-built palisades and wicker gabions, and stakes had been driven into the earth, facing the forest.

A fine drizzle came down from the east, pattering against their armour. The Kislevites drew their matted furs tighter. They rode into the town.

Gerlach tried to estimate the numbers there. He counted at least fifteen standards, all Imperial, as well as artillery banneroles, and colours flown by two sections of Tilean foot. That meant, even at a conservative estimate, six thousand men-at-arms.

This was what an army should look like, Gerlach thought. This was Imperial might. Combined with other forces that were now assembling along the Lynsk, they would scour the North and turn the rising darkness back.

As they rode down the muddy, tracked-up thoroughfare, he felt unashamedly proud. Here were marching halberdiers in clean, brightly coloured tunics: blue, red, gold and white. There, pikemen with spotless surcoats and glittering steel sallets. A cantering file of demilancers from another unit, cockades and banners rippling as they came past. Fork-bearded men in gaudy velvet puff-breeches and polished hauberks, sweeping whetstones along the white-steel blades of great swords. Pipers, fifers, drummers and horn blowers, the daylight gleaming off kettledrums and the long trumpets of field clarions. Archers in leather caps and long shirts, drilling with yew longbows against straw targets.

At a crossroads, they reined up as six Knights Panther rode by, followed by their squires and lance carriers. Huge destrier chargers, with shaggy feathering on their mighty hooves, were dressed in embroidered caparisons of purple, lilac and gold, their riders giants in full plate, leopard skins draped over their shoulders. Now that was glory and splendour.

Gerlach was annoyed to see Beledni and his men didn't seem at all impressed. Some of them even sneered at the gigantic knights. The only thing that seemed to take their interest was a crude wooden standard, a shield on the top of a ragged pole, hung with a red and white snake of banner cloth. The severed wing of an eagle was nailed, spread out on the shield front. This standard marked a field where the levies of the Kislev confederates were camped. More filthy men in furs, their dirty ponies wandering loose between their stretched hide tents. No discipline, no order, no sign of any pride.

Beledni gave a half-hearted wave, more to Vollen than the other demilancers, and turned his riders away towards the Kislev muster.

Glad to be rid of them, Gerlach rode on to the town hall, or the zal as it was called. It had a shingled roof shaped like an onion, and was the tallest structure in Zhedevka.

Marshal Neiber had made his quarters here.

Gerlach left Friedel and Truchs outside with the horses, and brought Vollen in with him as his escort. Neiber's trabanten of six swordsmen, two drummers and two fifers sat listlessly in the outer atrium of the zal, passing a bottle between them. They were all richly dressed in extravagant silk pludderhosen, broad hats puffed with heron feathers, doublets artfully slashed to reveal the conspicuous damask linings. None of them gave the two marching demilancers more than a passing look as they went by.

Neiber, field marshal of the entire host, was a heavy, sagging man with a bulging face that had been scored in early life by a duelling scar. His beard was square-cut and fierce. The field marshal's well-fed weight seemed to bow him down, and it was helped by the wine he had been drinking. A large fire had been banked up in an open grate, and the demilancers could smell poultry fat and onions.

Neiber was sipping wine out of a tiny thimble glass that he refilled regularly. The glass was from an expensive gentleman's travelling case that lay open on a side table, its leather straps draped open to reveal the satin-lined caskets that held the glasses. The case had a drawer for silver cutlery that was engraved with his heraldic crest. It was etched on the glasses too.

'Who the shit are you?' Neiber asked bluntly as they came up and saluted, their helmets tucked under their left arms.

'Second Company Hipparchia Demilance, ridden out of Talabheim, sir,' said Gerlach.

'Schott! Schott? Where are you, you noxious little leper?'

A short, balding man appeared, with an attitude that reminded Vollen of a mule that had been beaten once too often. He was wearing the doublet and surcoat of a staff aide.

'Here I am, my marshal.'

'Where the shit were you hiding?'

'I was supervising your dinner. As instructed.'

'Shut the shit up.' Neiber sat down on a low-backed chair by the grate and aimed the soles of his feet alternately at the fire. He was wrapped in a fur coat and damp hose clung to his feet and legs. The baton of his rank lay across his lap.

'Are my boots dry?' he rasped, swigging his drink and holding it out for a refill. Schott hurried to oblige.

'I'm working on that, my marshal,' the man answered as he poured.

'Second Company Hippos... demilancers... what the shit was it again?'

'Second Company Hipparchia Demilance, sir,' Gerlach repeated.

'That's it. Who's their commander, Schott?'

Schott crossed over to the mass of log books, patents of muster and orders of battle laid out on a nearby bench.

'Are you the commander?' Neiber asked, squinting at Gerlach and pointing the baton at him.

'No, sir. I'm vexillary, sir.'

'Well, where the bloody shit is your commander?'

'Stouer, my marshal,' Schott called out.

'Where's Stouer? Where the bloody shit is Stouer?'

'With the company, at Choika, sir.'

Neiber belched and got up. His baton fell on the floor and rolled under his chair. 'Not here?'

'No, sir.'

'What the hell's the point of them being at Choika? I mean, what the shitting hell is the point of that? There's no war down there!'

'We... we were ordered to report here to you by noon tomorrow, sir. The captain sent me ahead to make contact.'

'Did he? Did he indeed? Stupid arse. Refill!' Neiber waved his glass. Schott was still busy with records and patents.

'Refill! You, boy!' Neiber looked at Vollen. 'Get the bloody bottle!'

Vollen started forward, took the bottle from the side table, and refilled Neiber's glass.

Neiber emptied it. 'And another, while you're still hanging around like a spent fart.'

Vollen did as he was told.

Neiber looked at Gerlach. 'There's all kinds of shit in the forest out there, did you know that?' he remarked suddenly.

'No, sir.'

'All kinds of shit. I know that from the scouts I sent out.' Neiber tapped the side of his nose with his finger. It took a moment, as he missed the first time. 'Not all of them, mind. I sent out fifty and got five back. Five! Shit me out Sigmar, five! The foe is right on us. A day's ride from here, there's a horde of the heathen scum mustering in the woodland. And they'll be coming. Soon, mind you. Coming for us all. Boy!'

Vollen was already there with the bottle. Neiber drank, licked his lips, and sat down again. He looked tired and his voice dropped. 'All kinds of shit's coming. Bigger and harder and wilder than any of the idiots back south realise. They're meant to be over a fortnight away, but no. Oh no, no, no.' Neiber snorted hard and spat phlegm into the fire. He glanced at Gerlach. 'So having your company sat on their arses in Choika is no use to me. This Stouer must be a particularly stupid shit. Get back on your horse and go and tell him I said so. And tell him he better be here by dawn, or I'll ram a cannon up his arse and light the powder-touch myself.'

'Sir.'

'Where are my boots, Schott?' Neiber roared.

'Still drying out, my marshal.'

'You useless shit! I ought to have you shot. Hah! Ha ha! Shot! Have Schott shot! Ha ha ha!'

'Your wit is truly formidable, my marshal,' said Schott.

'Yeah, well shit on you too!' Neiber spat and threw his glass at the aide.

'You can go now,' Schott told Gerlach and Vollen, shooing them on out.

'Refill! Schott! Get me a refill! And... and another bloody glass!'

'Yes, my marshal.'

* * *

VIII

Outside it was getting dark, earlier and faster than they had anticipated. Braziers had been lit all across the camp, flickering like earthbound stars in the twilight. As they rejoined Friedel and Truchs, Gerlach and Karl could hear camp songs being sung.

'Vexillary!'

Schott called them back to the porch of the zal. He held out a wax-sealed parchment to Gerlach.

'Tell your captain to advance and join us with all speed. Your company is to take order in the right wing. I've marked the place on this plan. The water meadows east of the town, to ride in support of the Sanyza pulk.'

'The who?'

'The marshal wants strong demilance companies interlaced with the local regiments.'

'The Kislevites? Very well,' said Gerlach, not liking it at all.

'Move up and take position. With all haste as you can. Then have your captain report to the marshal here. We're not expecting a fight for at least three days, but get yourselves up and ready.'

'We'll ride directly,' said Gerlach. He paused. 'The marshal... is he all right?'

'He's drunk,' said Schott, matter-of-factly.

'Is that... usual?'

'No,' said the aide. 'He's drunk because he's scared. He has a good idea what's coming.'

'It can't be that bad–'

'Can't it? Have you fought a border war before, vexillary?'

'No.'

'Then, to be frank, you don't know what the shit you're talking about.'

IX

They rode south in the gathering darkness, the Imperial drums beating behind them in the camp at Zhedevka. Night was falling, sheathed in heavy rain. Over the receding tattoo of the Imperial drums, Karl Reiner Vollen thought he heard another drumming.

Darker, deeper, slower, throbbing from the forest.

ZHEDEVKA

I

CHOIKA TO ZHEDEVKA took ninety minutes of hard riding.

Captain Stouer got the company up and ready at midnight, in cold, driving rain. The four riders who had gone to Zhedevka and back had only been in their beds – bales of foetid straw in the barns – for three hours. Karl felt his joints aching with damp, and Friedel complained loudly, his eyes red from too little slumber.

The town square was bleak and deserted. It was so black they could see nothing much except what was illuminated in the flickering glow of their wagons' lanterns. No one, none of the townsfolk of Choika, came out to see them off or hold torches to light them as they prepared. The troops fumbled in the dark, struggling with chill armour, heavy tack and nervous horses.

Stouer's face was set grim, partly from lack of sleep and partly from his vexillary's gloomy report of Neiber's humour. He had listened intently as Gerlach recalled the field marshal's remarks about the gathering enemy.

He mounted up, leaning forward over his mount's neck to whisper reassurance in its ear, then called out to Gerlach. The vexillary walked his horse forward, and raised the standard.

'Company order?' asked Stouer.

'Company ordered and presented for travel, captain.'

At a nod from Stouer, Vollen blew the note for advance, and they moved out, splashing up the trackway in the pitch dark. He knew Captain Stouer was keen to get them in place by dawn. Stouer wanted to make a clean fist of things with the marshal.

It was surprisingly decent going. The rains ebbed and a watery moon came out. It seemed to be bouncing off the apex of the great kurgan. Mists rose and draggled the landscape.

Dawn should have been an easy mark to make, but the rain had mired the roads, and the company supply wagons were lagging behind and becoming bedded in. The horse troop turned back and dismounted to work them free.

By the time they had cleared the worst of it, a grey stain of light was spreading across the sky from the east. Dawn was less than an hour away.

Stouer dropped back and fell in beside Gerlach Heileman. 'We're going to be pushed to make it. Take them forward, vexillary,' he said.

'Captain?'

'Take them forward and get them into place. You know the plan. I'll ride on to Zhedevka and make report. It'll save time.'

Surprised by the prospect of locum command, Gerlach tried to hide his enthusiasm. 'Are you sure, captain?'

'The last thing I want to do is piss Neiber off.'

'I honestly doubt he'll be awake this early…'

'Whatever. Dawn, he said. Can you manage it?'

'It'll be an honour, sir,' replied Gerlach, hoisting the standard.

'I'll take outriders. See you in a few hours.'

Stouer broke west, following the track. He took Friedel, Anmayer and the clarion with him as flank riders. Regulations said that the clarion should accompany a field commander in his duties anyway, but Karl knew he was there because the captain anticipated having to look at charts and patents.

The vexillary led the main force away into the eastern part of the line.

II

THE CHRONICLES OF the Year That No One Forgets are extensive and thorough. It was a time, as Anspracht of Nuln memorably wrote, of 'living history', by which he meant that the daily turn of events was so significant that the future survival of the Empire might depend upon the details of a few hours. History was being shaped at such a rate it could be witnessed. This was not the long, placid drip of time that transmuted destinies so slowly that its progress was imperceptible to those living through it. This was a moment struck out hard and hot on the anvil of fate.

Every detail and particular is recorded somewhere, by Anspracht, Gottimer, the Abbess of Vries, Ocveld the Elder, Teladin of Bretonn and innumerable others, including the scribes and chroniclers of the Old Races.

Yet the Battle of Zhedevka warrants little mention in the compended histories of the time. It is a footnote in Anspracht, a passing reference in Ocveld. For it was just a small part of a much wider process called the Spring Driving. This mendaciously mild, general term encompasses a decisive horror – an onslaught from which the Empire barely recovered. It is notable that though the place name Zhedevka features infrequently in the general texts, it is woefully commonplace on tombs, memorial stones, chapel plaques and family lineages throughout the Empire.

For lives ended at Zhedevka. A great many of them.

It began in the pre-light of dawn, that peculiar time when bodies are cold and slow. The chaplains were still preparing for daybreak prayers, and the cooks had yet to start heating the breakfast pots. There was rain from the east, washing away all trace of the setting moons. The land was dark and streaked with mist.

There was virtually no warning.

III

AT THE CANNON-SET, along the north face of the town, a junior artillery observer from Nuln, sitting on picket duty by the earthwork, noticed that the faraway shadows of the forest seemed to be moving and flowing. He hurried to the tent of the master gunner, but the officer was looking for a mislaid love-token that his wife had given him, and made the junior wait.

In the interim, a sentry pike to the east of the gun-set saw the same signs, and immediately rang a handbell. Two more sentries picked up the alarum, and rang their own bells too, drawing the men of their company up out of sleep. In the tented field beyond them, a section of archers were similarly roused. The master of the watch came running at the sound of the bells, and a report was made to him. Runners were sent to the marshal's quarters, to the field commander of horse, and to the horn blowers camped near the town granaries.

Inver Schott, the marshal's aide, informed the runners that came knocking that the marshal was indisposed. When made aware of the urgency of the alert, he went to the horn blowers himself. They flatly refused to take orders without a command from the field marshal in person. The field commander of horse, also uncertain, sent his own runners to the marshal's quarters for confirmation, confident that the horns would sound if danger really was imminent.

No one, it is apparent from the records, believed a surprise attack was coming. Though raids and skirmishes might be staged without warning, battle and surprise were two concepts that simply did not go together, not when large armies were being fielded. Wars were just not fought that way.

Even when fighting the brute savages of the North, there was a protocol, a custom of battle. It was crude, but it was understood by both sides. Armies assembled on the field, faced each other, dug in, bellowed and taunted – sometimes for hours or even days – until a clash became inevitable. Indeed, it was often the case that the taunting and bellowing itself was the very matter of the battle. If an army was bellicose or large enough, the other would withdraw without any actual physical clash.

The root of this custom was the simple truth that armed forces of more than a few hundred men required huge motivation to attack one another. An individual unit might be rallied up to strike suddenly, but a mass of men needed firm coaxing. An army had to be worked up to a frenzy with phlegmatic speeches, insistent drumming and generous drink. It needed to be brought from the simmer to the boil. Then, and only then, would thousands of individuals attack as one mass.

And even if that impossibility could somehow be achieved without long notice, there seemed little advantage in charging, unannounced, out of the tree-line in the cold, grey wet of a spring dawn. Troops would be exhausted by the effort of such a charge, their push wasted, their strength depleted by the exertion.

It simply wasn't how battles were fought.

IV

THE FIRST WAVE of Northers hit the outer line nine minutes after the junior observer had first seen movement in the forest. They came sprinting, though they had already covered a league of rough ground from the forest line. And they were not simply fore-runners or berserks roaming madly ahead of their force. They were the front of it, the crest of a solid wave of horned shadows that flooded out of the woodland. Drum beats ruptured the daybreak air, their hammers pulsating through the raw din of the charging foe. It was, survivors said, the most awful sight, the most awful sound.

A nightmare, brought to life. An impossibility.

The cannon-sets were overrun before any of the great mortars and bombards of the Nuln Schools could be primed, let alone fired. The wicker breastworks were crushed flat by sheer weight of numbers. The observer who had first seen the rising was also amongst the first to die, hewn into pieces by war-axes and double-edged swords. The master gunner never lived to find his wife's love-token. Tents and wagons were set on fire.

At that time, the Wissenland pike, with their supporting cousins in the archery company, were the only Imperials on the field to have mobilised to any real effect. They staged a desperate defence of the north town line, raising a bristling pike wall. The tide of the enemy broke around them as waves broke around the prow of a galley, and washed in from the sides. Men were systematically beheaded. Their dripping skulls were spiked on the ends of their own pikes and carried forward by the horde as grisly trophies, like flotsam borne along by breakers. The archers, having felled several score with their first volleys, were overrun and maimed, left to die on the mud with their hands purposefully severed.

By then, the horde had swept into Zhedevka itself, and the massacre was under way.

At the west end of the Imperial order, around the cluster of granaries, the master of the watch managed to rally two companies of Nordland pike and halberd, and a fahnlein of arquebusiers clad in the yellow and black surcoats of Averland. They had been awoken by the tumult, but were milling around, confused and disjointed. Many were only partially dressed. The conscripted levies and the recruited patents had already fled in terror, leaving clothing and possessions scattered in their wake.

The master of the watch, along with a dazed sergeant major, quickly marshalled the Nordland pole-troops into pike blocks along the northern face of the granaries. The shorter, axe-headed halberds were laced between the much longer shafts of the pikes. The arquebusiers were lined up a little to the south. Smoke and mist billowed across the skirts of the town, filling the cold dawn air.

The pole-troops stiffened, tense, clammy hands clenching the hafts of their weapons, as a hellish noise rolled in through the smoke and became a solid line of charging figures. This was the first sight the Imperials had got of the foe. Ragged, hairy men with painted faces, draped in furs, black chainmail and leather armour. Teeth and bones and other trophies were strung in their tallow-stiffened hair, and their bare arms were wrapped in iron trophy rings beaten from the weapons of victims. Most wore horned or spiked helmets, and carried war-axes or thick swords. They came running. All of them were howling. They were terrifying.

Part of the Nordland block broke and scattered. The remainder held around their ensign and took the brunt. Northmen, in row after charging row, died against the pike block, but the weight of the dead bore the long hafts down, shattering many. The arquebusiers fired a crackling series of dull blasts, then reloaded and fired again. Their two volleys accounted for three dozen victims and created a wall of dense, white smoke.

They were reloading for the second time when they were consumed by the ravening force. Some fell back, drawing their S-hilted katzbalger swords and fighting a rearguard towards the edge of the pike block.

The field commander of horse had raised up sixty men, most of them demilancers. This troop, at full charge, came west across the main town highway and drove into the enemy's right hand flank with horse lances, for none had had time to prime their handguns. It was a bravura action that gave the Nordland pike's block a moment's renewed confidence. They pushed forward, pole-shafts dressed and lowered the way the drill repetitions had taught them. Chanting and pushing, they ground the enemy back about twenty paces.

But there was a roaring from the west now. An entirely separate flood of Northers spilled from the lowland mist, axe-heads whirling. They crushed in to meet their comrades like the jaws of a farrier's pincer. The master of the watch managed to sustain his block long enough to form them into a pike square, but they had been eroded by then, and their desperate resistance lasted about four minutes before the square shattered. They were butchered to a man.

The field commander of horse turned his demilance troop in a wide circuit around the stables behind the granaries and ordered them out with sabres raised, for many had lost or broken their lances in the first sortie. Several of the men pleaded with the commander to quit the field, but he kept on with the turn and charged the enemy mass, standing in the stirrups, sword raised crosswise to his face. His men followed, every one. They killed upwards of forty before their charge ran out of momentum and space.

Then they were wrestled over and dragged down, man and horse alike, and hacked to death with sharpened iron blades.

V

'WHAT'S THAT SOUND?' Truchs asked, suddenly.

Gerlach pulled up, and listened. The company was still a quarter league shy of the east line where they had been instructed to report. He could see little in the early gloom, but Truchs was right.

There was a distant rumble. A vibration in the air and earth. A ghostly din of voices and drums.

An instinct took over in Heileman's mind. 'Rise in the saddle to address!' he yelled. The men around him scoffed and laughed.

'Do it!' he bellowed. One by one, they demurred as the sound of screams carried to them through the distant murmur.

Stouer's orders had been to link with the Kislev pulk at the east line. Gerlach would be damned if he failed in that. With a brisk wave of his fist, he ran his demilancers out in a line formation, and bawled at those who were slow drawing their swords.

They moved ahead, in line, blades against their right shoulders.

'Steady to the front, and make do to fire in!' Gerlach shouted. He wished he could draw his own sword or prime his pistols, but his job was to hold the standard proud. The horse troop gained speed. A trot, a canter, now a gallop, riding into the mist, into the invisible world. Part of the company line was straggling, and Gerlach impugned their horse-skills. 'Tight! Keep it tight!' He was at such a speed now that the wind was beginning to swoop through the brass throat of the standard's draco, making a basso, bull-horn noise. The swallowtails of the standard were flowing out behind him.

Suddenly, horsemen were coming against them, riding out of the mist. Gerlach thought they were the enemy for a moment. Then he recognised them as ragged Kislev riders, belting away from the front, running scared on frightened ponies. 'Cowards!' he shrieked at them as they fled past, cutting holes in his company's already imperfect line.

The Second Company Hipparchia Demilance pressed on. Their hooves were so loud now he could no longer hear the ominous rumble, nor discern if it was drums or hooves or feet.

The demilancers drove down into the watermeadow basin, drawn by his hooting draco, and there met the enemy head on.

Enemy horses. Horned raiders, dark as twilight, mounted on heavy steeds with feathered hooves, none of them less than seventeen hands. They were already racing to drive out the Imperial order before them, and now they lashed their horses and rose into the charge.

Fifty horse lengths, thirty, head to head in a wide line. The Northers were wailing out an ululating roar that drowned the wet percussion of the hooves, but Gerlach couldn't hear it above the deep whooping drone of his draco.

At ten horse lengths and full stretch, the company behaved exactly as per drill and fired in. Some demilancers had paired wheel-lock pistols, one in each hand. Others fired petronels, the butts braced against the centre of their breastplates. The volley of shots was merciless. Enemy horse and enemy rider alike stumbled and sprawled, screaming. The demilancers went through them, over them, trampling many.

'Sword and lance!' Gerlach yelled, fighting to keep the heavy standard raised. Odamar and Truchs were either side of him, forming his vanguard, their war lances now drawn and lowered.

They were into the second wave. A series of bruising impacts and heavy thwacks, men tumbling from saddles. Odamar speared a Norther right off his steed with his lowered lance and the spray of blood fanned back to spatter Gerlach.

Then Odamar disappeared. There was a blur and a crunching yelp, and Odamar's gelding ran on, riderless.

Gerlach glanced sideways frantically and saw a tall, brass-helmed barbarian riding across his left flank, blood drizzling from his rising axe blade. Gerlach dropped his reins, drew one of his pistols and shot the brute through the forehead. The man's heavy, beringed arms flapped up as if in praise as his head snapped back. He fell sideways, and his horse staggered, unbalanced, then shed its dead rider and galloped on.

The body lay on the wet mud at Gerlach's feet, back arched and one arm bent clumsily under the torso. There was a scorched crater in the white flesh of the brow, a sooty dent with blood at the centre.

I have killed a man, thought Gerlach. The idea seemed preposterous to him. His entire mind concentrated into that glittering bloody spot in the middle of the sooty dent. I have killed a man. I have taken a life in battle.

Saksen bucked and turned loose now the reins were dragging. The sudden movement startled Gerlach out of his strange reverie. He fought to regain control, struggling to keep the standard upright and visible. He came to a stop.

'Regroup the line! Regroup!' he yelled into the uproar and the smoke. Another enemy rider broke towards him, riding downfield with his sword circling. The iron blade made a whooping noise as it swept around.

Calmly, Gerlach slid his spent pistol back into its holster and drew its twin. It banged out a little cloud of hot smoke as he fired it and unhorsed the Norther.

His charge had run out of steam. Around him he saw the demilancers fighting with sabres, saddle to saddle with the enemy riders. He saw friends and comrades torn down, gutted, thrown by wounded horses.

Gerlach drew his sabre and spurred Saksen forward, blade and standard raised as high as he could lift them, steering his trotting horse with his knees.

'For the company! For the company! For the Emperor!' he yelled.

Two Northers came for the vexillary, riding hard, standing in their saddles, heads and swords low. Gerlach turned Saksen in time to slash one across the back, and then reeled as a sword-edge smashed into his right arm's plating.

The company standard tumbled from his hand and stuck base-first in the ground, tilted at an angle. Cursing, Gerlach wheeled his gelding around and exchanged sword strikes with the Norther. Steel on iron, a furious ring.

Gerlach sliced a line down the enemy's cheek and, as he cried out, he speared him through the chest with his sword tip.

The enemy's corpse slumped out of its saddle, and Gerlach had to fight to break the suction and rip his sword loose before he lost it. Saksen whinnied and kicked back, terrified, and by the time Gerlach had fought for and regained control of his horse, he was some paces from the leaning standard.

Truchs galloped in and plucked it out of the ground, shaking it high for all the demilancers to see.

Gerlach made a quick mental note that Stouer should rightly honour Truchs for this moment of courage and virtuous display.

Then Truchs began writhing and screaming. It was a terrible sound, a distortion of a human voice. A barbed lance was projecting out of the man's belly, squirting scarlet blood in all directions. Truchs clawed at it, shrieking, and fell sideways off his horse.

And the standard fell too.

VI

STOUER AND HIS flank riders rode into Zhedevka just as horns started to sound. The southern part of the town seemed oddly empty and there was a strange murmur in the air, a throb.

'Drums,' said the captain, with great certainty. Karl nodded. He was still trying to make sense of the horn signals they'd just heard. Rushed, frantic, badly mouthed and poorly phrased.

A riderless horse came galloping towards them down the main roadway, eyes wild. It was an Imperial troop horse, and its reins were dragging. They had to draw their own horses over to avoid it. It kept running past them, and went on south out of the town gate.

The demilancers cantered forward behind Stouer, alert. They could smell smoke now and the throbbing was louder. Anmayer drew his sabre.

'Put that away!' Stouer snapped.

'Where is everyone, captain?' Friedel asked.

'Firearms,' Stouer growled. He pulled one of his wheel-lock pistols from its saddle holster. Anmayer and Friedel did the same. All three of them carried a pair, one on each side of the pommel. Instead of such a brace, Vollen carried a single petronel in a kidskin boot against the right block flap of his saddle, allowing him space for his bugle holster on the left. The four men checked their weapons were primed, and wound the wheels with their turnkeys to tighten the mainspring.

'Lay your dogs,' said Stouer. They all lowered into place the dog arm cock that held the lump of pyrites, from which the wheel would draw sparks.

A man suddenly appeared, running their way. His arms were held out wide and he was making an odd, mewing sound. By his garb, he was a handgunner or arquebusier from Averland. His surcoat was yellow and black. He was missing a shoe. One of his feet was clad in a wide-toed cut-out shoe, but the other was bare and the grey hose torn. His steps were oddly short and quick, so he tottered like a child that had just begun walking.

He came straight for Stouer, mewling, hands outstretched.

'Sigmar!' Anmayer suddenly said. There was a dark shape under the man's chin that they had all taken to be a goatee. It was not. It was the fletching of a black-feathered arrow. As the man turned to Stouer, they could see the rest of it – an arm's length of shaft – sticking out of the back of his neck.

The Averlander clawed at Stouer, who recoiled and shied him away, his horse jumping in distress. Then the man vomited blood in a great torrent down the shoulder of the captain's horse and fell against it, sliding down against the slippery flank.

He ended up on the ground, face turned to one side, his heels drumming and bubbles forming in the blood around his mouth.

Stouer made the sign of Shallya, and Anmayer spat and touched iron to ward off ill fortune. Vollen and Friedel stared at the man.

'Ride!' Stouer yelled. 'Karl, lead off! Take us to the marshal!'

Karl spurred Gan forward and they ran down the roadway towards the zal. The onion dome rose above the line of the other roofs.

Clearing the nearby buildings, with the zal in sight, they suddenly saw the battle raging at a distance through the northern edge of the town. What they saw mostly, in fact, was billowing smoke, but there was absolutely no doubting what it was they were looking at, even for men who had never seen battle before.

To Karl Reiner Vollen who, like Gerlach Heileman, had spent most of his life wishing to be a soldier in war, it seemed bizarre. It was messy and disjointed, difficult to track what was happening, with only odd details becoming evident. A horse turning in circles without a rider. A man kneeling, covering his head with his arms, sobbing. Dark horses with dark, horned riders moving past, so fast they caused weird eddies and curls in the drifting smoke. A seated corpse, legs out straight, torso lolling forward as far as the spear fixed through it would allow. A man on fire, walking slowly away from the edge of the turmoil.

It looked nothing like the tapestries in the Heileman house, nor did it resemble the woodcuts in the military histories he had pored over in his youth. It was, he realised, utterly real. The smoke, the confusion, the deranged behaviour of men caught up in a living nightmare, their minds lost to terror or pain or both.

'Forward!' Stouer bellowed. Horned riders were sweeping in and assaulting the zal, some of them dismounting and hacking at the doors with long handled axes.

'Give fire!' Stouer yelled as they rode down on the tails of the raiders. Some turned, howling. One thumped backwards out of his saddle, his throat blown open. Karl felt a dull tingle in his breastbone, the echo of an impact, and realised he had fired his petronel. He had killed the man. His lead ball had blown out that throat.

There was no time to reload. He pushed the petronel back into its boot, and rode down another raider, breaking the man under Gan's hooves. By then, Karl had his sabre loose.

Stouer and Anmayer had both fired and killed with their pistols in puffs of cracking white vapour, and were now engaged with sword. Friedel had missed. Two of the enemy riders slewed round and galloped for him, and he screamed in fear, losing his grip on the reins. His horse threw him and he landed hard.

Karl wheeled Gan about, leapt him over the dazed Friedel, and met the riders head on. The clarion's sabre was extended, tip forward, and it sliced through the reins and cheek-flesh of one of the men, almost by accident.

The man clutched his face and fell off his horse. The other sailed a longsword at Karl, and the clarion felt his head twisted brutally by the impact against the side of his burgonet.

He tried to turn, sweeping his sword, all blade-schooling forgotten. Gan was frenzied and ready to buck or flee. The air was thick with the smell of powder smoke, blood and dung.

Karl managed to get Gan around, though in the process he took another glancing blow across his helmet and Gan was gashed in the flank. His adversary was a massive man, his torso and shoulders rippled with muscle, a bearskin tied around his ribs flapping out behind him. Warrior rings, dozens of them, were coiled around his arms and he wore a horned helmet wrought from black brass with a full face visor shaped like the snout of a wolf. His horse was nineteen hands high, black as charcoal, with a billowing mane.

Karl jabbed with his sabre, his thrust rebounding off the warrior rings on the man's left arm. The longsword, a span and a half of razored iron blade three fingers wide, sliced around and Karl ducked. He felt a wrench at the nape of his neck and suddenly the air was full of fluttering feather scraps. The longsword had sliced off his cockade.

Desperate now, Karl hauled on his reins, wrenching Gan back a pace, and cutting out with his sabre. The horned Norther, howling through his wolf-face visor, deflected the chop with his sword and hacked in, leaving a bruising dent across Karl's right vambrace. Pain shuddered up his arm and he nearly dropped his sabre.

Instead, he tucked down and spurred forward, taking another whack across his backplate. The Norther's blow actually cut through the steel and was only stopped by Karl's mail undershirt. He felt broken rings of mail slithering down his back into his hose.

He turned and thrust again. The sharp tip of his sabre sank into the wolf-face's bare shoulder to the depth of a palm. Blood spurted out with the blade as he pulled it free. The huge Norther cried out and lost control of his massive horse. It galloped away, the wounded rider jerking in the saddle as he tried to cling on.

Karl tried to straighten up. His back and his right forearm both felt like they were broken.

Then Gan toppled sideways, hurling him off onto the ground.

Karl rose. Gan was on his side, his legs kicking wildly. Blood was splashing in every direction. The gash the wolf-face had given his horse was far more serious than Karl had realised.

There was nothing he could do. Gan kicked and kicked, head back and teeth bared, blood gushing out of him. In less than a minute, Karl's beloved gelding was dead.

Aware that tears of rage were streaming down his face, Karl ran over to Friedel and dragged him towards the porch of the zal. Friedel was moaning and sobbing. His bowels had loosened.

'Get out your sword! Your sword!' Karl shouted.

'I've fouled myself! I am so ashamed, Karl! I have fouled myself!'

'Shut up, Johann!' Karl yelled, trying not to gag on the stink of shit. 'Get your sword out and up!'

Anmayer was dead. He lay face down in the mud, his forearms, shoulders and scalp sliced in a dozen places from the relentless sword blows that had killed him as he shielded himself with his arms. Stouer had dismounted, a sabre in one hand and a spent pistol in the other. He was surrounded by enemy warriors, fighting like fury, bleeding from a dozen wounds. His left pauldron was hanging off by its straps.

The last time Karl had stood on that porch, just a day earlier – though it seemed like months before – he had been with Gerlach and they had been called back by the field marshal's aide Schott.

Schott, by some eerie coincidence, was there again, in precisely the same place. But this time he was dead, his body split to the backbone by a blade-blow.

The gaudy warriors of Neiber's trabanten were fighting a rearguard around the doorway of the hall. Two of the ten men had already fallen, but the others were battling hard with their swords.

As befitted a field marshal's life company, the men of the trabanten were elite fighters. The distinctive blades they were wielding were called katzbalgers: wide, round-tipped short-swords with double-curved quillons. The opulent finery of their clothing reflected their high status. They had slain upwards of a dozen raiders already.

Karl fell in with them. He'd utterly lost contact with the whining Friedel, though he kept calling out his name. Karl found himself beside one of the trabanten, an older man in rich wargear and multicoloured hose. They chopped at the enemy press. Karl felt his sabre cut through something soft and realised he had just killed another man.

One of the trabanten squealed as he was dragged under a mass of pushing enemy warriors and run through.

'What's your name?' the swordsman next to Karl shouted.

'Karl Reiner Vollen!'

'Get in there, Karl! Get inside! Find the marshal and watch over him!'

'But–'

'For the love of Sigmar, we can't let him die! I've sent a man to draw horses to the western door. Get him there! Get him clear! We'll hold the door!'

Karl faltered. The man was covered in blood, and his katzbalger was just a hacking blur.

'Please…' pleaded the struggling swordsman.

Karl broke and ran into the zal.

It was suddenly quiet. The din from outside was just a dull roar. He walked across the outer hall, past a lute that had been shattered when it was dropped. He heard a plink plink plink and saw it was the blood dripping off the fuller of his blade onto the paving.

He tore off his burgonet and tossed it aside.

'Marshal? Marshal Neiber? Sir?'

In the main hall, the fire had died back. It was cool and still. Every now and then the beams shook from a crash outside. The gentleman's travelling case lay open, with two glasses missing now from the satin rests.

Karl put his sabre down on the table, took out one of the engraved thimble glasses that remained and filled it from an open bottle of musket. He swigged it down and felt better. The beams shook again.

He set the thimble glass down and retrieved his sabre.

'Marshal Neiber?'

Karl pushed back a velvet door hanging with his sword tip and looked inside.

Empty.

He moved on, using his sword to poke open a scullery door. The kitchen was empty, and smoke floated out from the dying hearth.

He went forward into the state bedroom, and there was Neiber.

The field marshal was dead. Naked except for his hose, he lay on his back on the bed. He had been choked with his own field baton. His face was swollen and black.

Karl walked towards the bed. He laughed out loud at the idiocy of it. The trabanten band was fighting to the last outside to keep this man alive, and here he was, already dead.

Karl stiffened suddenly. This death wasn't self inflicted. Neiber had been killed.

He whipped around, his sabre rising, in time to smash aside the attack of the warrior who was pouncing at him from the shadows. A lithe, naked shape clad in leather swathes, its head covered in a brass bull-mask, with three twisted horns rising asymmetrically from the helm cap.

Caught across the snout of his helmet, the Norther tumbled away, and then sprang up again, a stabbing knife in each fist. He seemed at once ridiculous and terrifying to Karl. His head was armoured in the horned, brass mask, and he was draped in leather strips, and strings of shell-beads and bone-shards. But his feet, chest, arms and groin were exposed. All the vulnerable parts a man would usually armour with metal and modesty were bared, yet the head was locked in a metal cover. The Norther lunged at Karl, his bare feet padding on the tiles, his beads jingling.

Karl gripped his sabre and put both shoulders into the cut. His sweeping sabre hit the side of the Norther's helm and knocked him over into the shadows, the knives clattering out of his hands. A string of shells and bones broke and scattered their little, hard particles across the floor.

Karl ran. He ran towards the western door. The trabanten swordsman had said that horses would be there.

Karl wrenched open the door.

The Norther warrior with the wolf-face helm stood there, framed in firelight, blood running from his shoulder. He had an axe now. He lunged in through the doorway, smashing Karl off his feet and down on to his back. Then he swung the axe straight down to split Karl's head.

VII

THE DAWN SKY was as black as a funeral swathe. Palls of dark smoke swirled out across the oblast, driven sideways like fog banks by the wind. Zhedevka was burning.

From the eastern fields, Gerlach Heileman could see the bright flames leaping and lashing along wall posts and roof beams. The fire consuming the aspen shingles of the zal's onion dome was almost blue-white.

This image of the burning town came and went as the tide of smoke draped itself to and fro across the fields at the whim of the winds. The smoke smelled of timber, rusted iron and spoiled meat. It tasted of salt.

Gerlach realised it didn't taste of salt at all. He was tasting his own tears. He had been weeping for some minutes without knowing it.

Saksen was stamping and shuddering, foaming at the bit. Gerlach pulled the big horse round and cantered through the waves of black smoke. Bodies littered the trampled grass. Men, horses, broken wargear, splintered lances. Horses without mounts fled past like phantoms in the coiling darkness. Gerlach had tried to fight his way back to the standard, but all he had found was Truch's skewered corpse.

In the distance, he could hear the sporadic bang of firearms.

Linser and Demieter suddenly appeared, riding hard. Linser had lost his helmet and Demieter was bloodstained and lolling awkwardly in his saddle. They pulled up when they saw him.

'Vexillary!' Linser cried.

'Where stands the line?' Gerlach demanded.

Linser shrugged his narrow shoulders and wiped a glove across his face. His hand left a smudge of blood where it had touched.

'Line?' he asked, as if the word was new to him.

'We have to rally the troops and reform–' Gerlach began.

'There is no troop,' said Demieter softly. He was clutching his arms to his belly and his face, framed in the steel of his burgonet, was ash-white with pain. 'Sigmar, you bloody fool! There is no troop! It's broken!'

Kaus Demieter was one of the quietest and most respectful men in the demilance company. To hear this new, contemptuous tone in his voice took Gerlach by surprise.

'Kaus, we have to rally. Remember our oath? We–'

'Damn you, Heileman. Gods damn you, you pompous little prig.'

'Kaus–'

Demieter spat blood and glared at the vexillary. 'If we're lucky, really lucky, we might be able to make it back to the crossing. Back to Choika. If we do, we might live until tomorrow. But if we stay here, shitting away our chances because you have some fond notion of the rules of war, we'll be dead inside an hour.'

'He's right, Gerlach,' said Linser. 'This is bloody madness.'

Shouts and screams rang from the veils of smoke. They all stiffened as horned riders pelted past, half visible in the grey haze.

'Shit!' Gerlach said. He looked at the other two.

'Can you get me out of here?' asked Kaus Demieter. 'Me and Linser? Can you get us to the crossing? I want to live, Gerlach. I want to see my girl again.'

Gerlach smacked Saksen's rump and yanked the reins. 'Ride with me!' he cried.

They rose into a gallop, passing over the jumbled bodies in the grass, veering to avoid loose horses. The wind picked up and the smoke thinned, driven clear for a moment. Gerlach saw a group of Norther horsemen turning on the flame-strewn field, riding down towards them.

'Pick it up!' he shouted. They had the edge of a lead, over thirty horse lengths. They could outrun the foe. Another demilancer appeared, riding hard on a parallel course to link with them. It was Hermen Volks.

'This way!' Gerlach hollered.

South of them, dead ahead, the smoke banks drew back sharply. A line of horsemen sat there, silent and still, blades and axe-hafts resting across their saddle bows. They were clad in black armour, ring-scale, brass, full visored helmets with long horns, all of it caked with pitch.

The enemy had the field. Now they were scouring it, systematically driving out the survivors to annihilate them. Gerlach had hunted many times in the elector's parks. He knew how to run the quarry, how to beat it up into the rise, how to block it with outriders, how to corner it for the kill.

Now he knew what it felt like to be the stag.

'Turn wide!' he yelled, and the four demilancers switched left, churning across the peaty grasses, kicking up mud and spray. The line of Northers remained still, patiently forming a barrier to their right. When Gerlach looked back, he saw that the rear end of the barrier line was now peeling away, one by one, to join up with the pack of riders at their heels. There were twenty, thirty, more.

This wasn't war at all. It had ceased to be any kind of combat Gerlach had been trained to face. It was more like some preposterous, cruel joke. The whimsy of the god Ranald perhaps, who was nothing less than a trickster and delights in the misery of man.

Captain Stouer had once told Gerlach about a nightmare he kept having. He would come to the field of war, only to find he was alone, in the wrong place. Worse still, he was naked and without his weapons. Then the enemy swooped. Death resulted, of course, the terrifying death of a man alone against overwhelming odds, but it was the ignominy that made the nightmare so awful. The fact that Stouer was as vulnerable as a man could be and couldn't even fight back. Humiliation was the demilancer's deepest dread.

This seemed to Gerlach like just such a dream. It had an unreal quality. To be trapped, outnumbered, on a field of death where the grasses smouldered and burned and to every side lay the torn and brutalised bodies of friends and comrades. And to be quarry of a hunt, stalked down and ridden to the kill by faceless creatures in horned masks.

The hunting riders forced them north again, into the meadows, away from the escape route they had sought. The four demilancers were riding headlong in a tight group, though Demieter was lagging. Gerlach felt an uncomfortable rhythm tense through Saksen's stride, as if the gelding was tiring or, worse, had run lame or thrown a shoe.

There was a stand of trees ahead, overlapping another along the lowest part of the meadow. The trees ran east and thickened until they met the edge of the forest itself.

Gerlach turned them that way, towards the trees. Behind them, closing fast, warhorns blew and blades beat upon shields.

Three Northmen on black steeds broke out of the trees and thundered down to cut them off. There was no going wide. Gerlach wrenched out his lance and charged the first of them. There was a dull crump and the Norther he had been going for wailed out and tumbled from his saddle. His foot got hooked in the stirrup and his horse dragged him through the wet meadow weed.

Volks had found the time to reload his petronel, Sigmar bless him. But now he was fumbling with it as the other two enemy riders cut in across them.

Gerlach slewed Saksen hard to the right to return the favour and protect Volks. Lance down, and running at full stretch, he caught one of the intercepting riders side on and drove his shaft against the man's ribs. The speartip missed, but their horses rammed together. The impact smashed the Norther from the saddle and wrenched the lance from Gerlach's grip. As he came clear, he found he was barely hanging on.

They reached the stand of trees, crashing through the bare branches and the saplings, showering dew and bark splinters around them. Gerlach saw Volks to his left and Demieter to his right.

Linser was no longer with them.

Gerlach looked back. The third rider had cut Linser down, killing his gelding and spilling him onto the ground. A fair number of the hunters had stopped, drawing into a circle around the unhorsed lancer. Gerlach could see Linser on his feet, arms raised, screaming as he dodged and scurried back and forth, trying to escape the tightening thicket of stabbing swords and slashing axes. The Northers were laughing and goading, playing with their prey like huntsmen toying with a wounded boar. Gerlach saw Linser struck with a sword and lose part of his hand. His welling scream rose up like sharp ice into the smoky fog.

Oh, Sigmar! Oh, Sigmar, spare him!

'Heileman!'

Gerlach looked round. Volks was calling to him, urging him to spur on into the trees. Demieter was slumped against his horse's neck now, and Volks had taken Demieter's reins to trail him.

'Come on, Gerlach! For Sigmar's sake!'

The remainder of the chasers – those that hadn't stopped to torment Linser – had reached the tree stand and were crashing through after them. Gerlach pointed, and Volks followed him left into a maze of leafless ash and dark pine, guiding Demieter behind him.

There was a thick stench of leaf mulch and wood husk amongst the trees, and the ground was spongy and thick with a raft of rotten leaves. They were forced to ride more slowly now. Gerlach could hear the crack and splash of their pursuers in the woodland clearings behind them.

Riding slower, he had time to reload his pistols. He drove Saksen with his knees, fiddling with each wheel-lock in turn. Such work was meant to be done at a standstill. With the horse jolting, it was hard to manage. Gerlach lost a lot of powder and three shot-balls as he tried to finish the job. But by the time they had cleared the trees, both his pistols were primed and loaded, their wheels wound tight and their dogs laid down. Volks had accomplished the same feat with his petronel.

The space beyond the trees was still and grey. The stand had masked the area from the worst of the smoke fuming off the murdered town. Mist foamed the wet grasses and haunted the edge of the forest to their right.

Volks was steering his tired troop horse that way, tugging Demieter after him. He looked back at the vexillary.

'Gerlach? Come on, man! The woods!'

Gerlach wasn't listening. He was looking west, back into the burning, smoke-wrapped field of death beyond the trees. He'd as good as forgotten about the Norther riders smashing through the stand on their tail.

'Gerlach! For pity's sake!'

Half a league away west, a mass of enemy riders and foot troops was assembling around their chieftain. Many of them carried severed heads on the ends of their blades, brandishing them to celebrate his victory. Some had captured Imperial field banners and ensigns. Others were stabbing or whipping prisoners forward, ragged, bloodied figures in the rag-remnants of Imperial uniform. Gerlach could see William Weitz, Gunther Stoelm, Kurt Vohmberg…

A flash of gold. Five riders were galloping in from the north end of the field with another trophy to place at the feet of their chieftain lord.

The standard of the Second Company Hipparchia Demilance. His standard.

'Gerlach?' Volks called. 'Come on, man!'

'That's ours,' Gerlach said.

'Yes, but–'

'That's ours, Hermen.'

Volks looked at him. There were tears in his eyes.

'I know, but…'

Gerlach drew out his sabre. The enemy in the woods were scant seconds away.

'Don't be a bloody fool!' said Volks.

'Yes,' said Demieter, sitting up in the saddle suddenly. 'Be a bloody fool. There's nothing left for us now except glory.'

Gerlach stared at him. Demieter raised his arms briefly. His lower breastplate was cracked and his innards, pink and frothed with blood, were poking out. 'I'm never going to see my girl again, am I?' he said.

Gerlach shook his head.

'Let's do it,' said Demieter, carefully pulling his lance from its boot, one arm still wrapped tight to keep his guts inside him.

'Volks?'

Hermen Volks drew out his petronel. 'Come on then. Before I decide you're both mad.'

They spurred hard and charged west. They came out around the long stand of trees, out of the mist, two of them with firearms raised, one with lance extended. The hunting Northers came from cover behind them, turning to pursue.

Gerlach stood in the stirrups as Saksen gained speed, one hand to the reins, the other aiming his dexter wheel-lock. The Northers carrying their standard heard their hooves drumming the wet earth and turned.

There were cries of alarm and surprise. Sword blades flashed as they came out of scabbards.

At full charge, Gerlach fired and smacked a rider off his horse. He holstered the pistol and drew its sinister partner as Volks fired his petronel. One of the Northers recoiled and clutched at his arm, his horse suddenly bucking.

Gerlach fired his second pistol. The shot went low, killing a Northman's horse stone dead. The beast collapsed under him and threw him off. He tried to scramble clear, but the lifeless horse rolled and crushed his leg, pinning him.

Then they were engaged in a melee. Gerlach had to throw his last pistol away so he could draw his sabre. He hacked at the man carrying the standard and probably blinded him, but Saksen was driving ahead, and he overshot. A swirl of figures around him, men shouting and horses braying. Something struck him a dull blow side on, and Saksen staggered. Mud splashed up. Nearby, a wooden stave or a shaft snapped. A man screamed. Horse spittle splattered around in stringy droplets.

Gerlach manhandled his gelding round, running clear for a second, and then turned as a yelling Norther ran at him on foot, brandishing a long berdish axe. The tribesman had a red-dyed horse tail fluttering from his helmet spike and his wild eyes were black with white rims like a hound's. Gerlach wrenched forward and ran the man through the chest with his sabre – a perfect downward thrust that the sergeant majors at the Cavalry School had taught them all.

Gerlach yanked his sword out as the man collapsed. Close by, in the frantic struggle, an enemy rider crashed over, without reason as far as Gerlach could tell. A boar-spear jabbed at him, the stab too short. He sank his spurs and drove Saksen back into the press, thrusting left and right. Something made an inhuman squeal.

He saw Volks through the chaos. The demilancer had the standard by its shaft and was fighting to ride clear, dragging it behind him. A broadsword swung at Gerlach's face, and he blocked it with his sabre, grunting with effort. He could feel the sheer panic rising in the horse between his knees. The broadsworder, astride a heavy black stallion, tried to slash again, forcing his mount in against Saksen's flanks. The stallion was biting and kicking out. Gerlach struck once, twice, with his sabre, hacking with the blade edge because the melee was too close-packed to draw back for a clean thrust. He had no idea if he'd hit anything, but the barbarian with the broadsword was suddenly no longer in his field of view.

'Volks!' he yelled. 'Ride clear! Ride clear!'

He couldn't see the demilancer any more, but above the thrashing mass of bodies, the standard head appeared briefly, waving wildly, the banner flapping.

More Northers were gathering in, riding hard from their chieftain's side to join the skirmish. Gerlach hadn't seen Demieter since they'd engaged. Something hit him across the left shoulder blade, and almost simultaneously he felt a sharp pain in his right hip. The stinking, howling enemy were all around him, close and lethal, like a pack of wolves. His sabre was slick and sticky with gore.

The sun suddenly came out. It was the most peculiar thing. Perhaps the weather had turned. Or perhaps the gods had intervened for a second, commanding the elements to respond to the extraordinary moment of battle that now took place. Afterwards, that's what Gerlach felt sure it was. Ulric, fierce god of courage, pleased by the carnage he saw, or Myrmidia, goddess of war, saluting valour, or even trickster Ranald again, taking delight in spoiling the darkness of a scene that should have belonged to his dour cousin, Morr, deity of the grave.

The sun came out, bright as the armour of Sigmar. Cold spring sunlight, like bars of smoking silver, shafted down across the field through an aperture in the black smoke and the grey-cast clouds. Everything glittered: blades, sweat beads, blood, breastplates. Everything was touched by that light and the black armour of the massing foe turned blacker still, like night shadows, contracted by daybreak.

Out of the western slopes, riders were coming. They were close, almost into the fight, by the time Gerlach spotted them through the mayhem or had heard the sound of their hooves above the clatter of skirmish. There were forty of them at least, riding fast, riding hard, caught in the shafts of sunlight and lit up like angelic beings. Gerlach felt terror the moment he saw them, a more awe-filled dread than anything he had felt in the face of the Northers. The feeling hardly waned when he realised they were not the enemy at all.

They were lancers. Kislevite lancers.

Each one wore silver mail and sleeved coats of segmented lamellar plate inscribed with gold that glittered in the sun like a breaking summer sea. Their round-topped steel helms had hard peaks, long neck-guards of mail and heart-shaped visors lowered across their noses. The cloth of their clothes was crimson and blue and many were draped in the white-and-black pelts of snow leopards. Breathtaking eagle wings, each one two spans high, rose vertically from their backs, the long feathers fluttering in the slipstream of their rush. Their long lances were lowered to the horizontal and couched.

The stories Gerlach had been told of the noble, terrifying splendour of the winged lancers were true after all.

The lancers swept into the milling thicket of barbarians with such force Gerlach felt the earth shake. Couched expertly under the arm by men well braced in saddle and stirrups, the lances conducted not only the strength of the rider's arm but also the force of his charging steed. They punched through shields, through bodies, through horses, demolishing everything in their path. Northers and loose horses fled madly out of the way.

The main mass of enemy riders was riding face on to the Kislev charge when they met. Armed with hooked axes and billed swords, the Northers had no reach at all, and the first rank were dead and unhorsed by the long, relentless cavalry spears in a second.

Gerlach heard a huge voice bellowing commands, and a bone horn blew. The charge line broke with disciplined skill, the riders barely restraining their gallop, and they began to skirmish in twos and threes. Most left their long horse lances behind them, thrust tip-down and quivering in the soil as they switched to curved swords or dragged javelins from their saddle boots. The javelins, short and slim and light, flurried out like arrows, taking Northers to whatever afterworld had been prepared for them. Each lancer carried two javelins, and Gerlach gawped at the astonishing horsemanship they displayed. The lancers loosed the javelins overarm, then leant as they passed to pluck the missiles back out of the dead targets to throw again.

The melee around Gerlach had broken and the ground was covered in jumbled bodies. He looked around for Volks or Demieter – for anyone – but saw only the broken waste of slaughter that lay in the wake of the charge. A dazed Norther lumbered nearby, and Gerlach despatched him quickly. The vexillary's hands were shaking. He was dazed and breathless as he came down off the pitch of blind rage that had driven him into the fight.

The bone horn sounded again. The sun was folding back into the cloud cover and the light was failing, as if the gods had decided their display was over. The winged lancers were disengaging and turning. They had driven a deep wedge into the ranks of the enemy, but if they remained, without the pressure of the charge to their advantage, they would be overwhelmed by the sheer number of barbarians.

The lancers were sweeping back towards him now, standing in their stirrups and hallooing victory shouts. Each rider bent low to recover one of the lances they had left spiked in the earth. One of the front horsemen was brandishing a standard high for them to follow. It was the eagle wing on the shield, the long red and white stripe of banner snapping out behind it.

Gerlach saw Volks now, and Demieter, riding clear with them. Volks had the demilance standard, and was struggling to raise it up as he rode hard.

Gerlach started Saksen forward, coming across the front of the retreat, gaining speed to reach Volks. The enemy, shaken and mauled, was charging in pursuit, horse archers leading the reply, firing barbs from the saddle.

Gerlach turned hard until he was in with the lancers, riding with them. He lost sight of Volks and Demieter again, but he was close to the Kislevite leader and the man with the eagle wing standard. It was all he could do to keep his tired gelding up with the smaller, sprightly Kislev mounts. He began to lag a little.

The lead lancer, his face hidden by the heart-shaped visor that jutted down from the peak of his helm, turned, shouted something, and waved him up urgently. Black-feathered arrows hissed into the grassy mud around him. One hit a lancer to his left between the shoulder blades, and he rolled from his saddle soundlessly, hands raised.

'Go on! Go on!' Gerlach sang out to Saksen, leaning forward, straining. They were onto the eastern slopes of the meadow now, powering towards the forest line.

An arrow glanced off his right pauldron with a painful crack that jerked his whole torso round. Gerlach fought to steady himself, but his balance had been thrown. There was a strange moment of weightless confusion and then a hideous, jarring impact. He was out of the saddle, on the ground, dazed and bruised and not quite aware of where he was.

He got up. The enemy wave was just twenty lengths behind him, down the slope. Arrows chopped the air. He looked east. Two more lancers had been brought down by the horse archers. One was the standard bearer. He had an arrow through his throat and another through his torso. His horse had come over with him, but now it was struggling up, shaking its head, rattling its silver war harness and plated bridle.

Gerlach ran towards it, hands raised to calm it. But it was oblivious to him and took off towards the trees before he could grab its trailing reins.

'Yha! Yha!' a deep voice cried. The leader of the lancers was closing on him from the right hand at a spirited lick. He had turned back, sweeping right around, and was leading Saksen by his bridle.

'Come you! Yha!' the lancer cried.

Gerlach paused for a split second and then bent down and grasped the shaft of the fallen Kislev banner. He raised the eagle wing up and ran towards the approaching lancer.

'Take it! Take the damn thing!' he shouted, thrusting the banner into the man's gloved hands. Then he threw himself into Saksen's saddle and they turned to follow the main Kislev mass into the trees.

Screaming darkness followed them.

VIII

THEY RODE INTO the trees, into the gloom. The Kislevites had all but vanished. Gerlach caught glimpses of silver, red and gold as lancers wove in and out of the shadows and the moss-green trunks. The sounds of hooves and voices and jingling armour echoed around him under the roof of leaves. Gerlach forced Saksen on, over ragged earth, peat-black soil, clusters and outcrops of rock and root mass. Branches whipped and brushed at his face. A loop of thorn drew blood from his cheek. The hollow acoustics of the forest carried the dull, raucous sounds of the pursuit.

He caught up with two lancers. One of them was the leader, clutching the banner tight to stop it fouling in the branches. Together, they leaped a stream and turned to the right, following the leaf litter in the bed of the winding ditch. Gerlach simply stayed with them. He had no idea where he was going, except that it was vaguely east.

Over the space of an hour, they began to slow, allowing for their horses' fatigue. The sounds of the Northers fell away behind them.

Then they broke from the forest into a crow-haunted marshland skirted by dark trees. The winged lancers were gathering there, watering their horses while sentinel riders watched.

Gerlach reined up, and leant wearily across his saddle bow. His hands were still shaking. The Kislevite leader stopped beside him, and raised the heart-shaped visor, opened the cheek-guards and pulled his steel helm off. He tugged off the leather cawl after it. His head was shaved but for a long top-knot, and his moustaches were long and drooping. When he grinned, he exposed the gap where his front teeth were lacking.

It was Beledni.

'Quite a day, yha? Yha, Vebla? Quite a day!'

IX

THUNDER ROLLED ACROSS the marsh and the forest line, and lightning underscored the thickening blanket of granite-grey cloud. Some of the winged lancers touched the iron guard-bows of their swords to ward off storm magic, others boldly shouted oaths and prayers up into the sky to the Kislev thunder god.

Gerlach Heileman watched Beledni use the cuff of his glove to wipe sweat and greasy dirt from his face and shaved scalp.

'I didn't recognise you,' Gerlach said.

'Shto?' Beledni pouted and narrowed his eyes.

'I didn't recognise you... I didn't know who you were. In your armour.' Gerlach pointed to the Kislevite's intricately wrought hauberk of silver lamellae, the gold-chased pauldrons and gorget, the great, black-tipped feathers of his wings. Last time they had met, Beledni and his men had seemed like beggars in rags and furs.

Beledni smiled. 'For bittle, we dress. Dress in scale and szyszak and wings. We make our fine show when it time to fight. Dress... and shave, of course.'

'Shave? What does that matter?'

'Shto?'

'I me... never mind. Where did you come from?'

Again, Beledni frowned.

'In the battle. The battle. Where did you come from?'

Beledni thought about this. 'In bittle, we start come from to the east, with pulk.'

'What?'

'East... chast... chast... aah, word is "part", yha? East part of meadowland. Where pulk githers.'

'What? What is this word "pulk"?'

Beledni smiled and waved his arms wide. 'Pulk is... bittle...' he groped for the term, '...host. Bittle host. Rota of Yetchitch krug part of Sanyza pulk. Many rota make together pulk, many rota... one, two, more many!'

'Rota,' Gerlach murmured. He'd heard that word before too. He looked away, trying to spy Volks or Demieter amongst the gathered riders.

'Yha! Rota! Word is for it you have… "banner". Yha? Ban-ner? You much save Yetchitch banner, Vebla. Pick it up from ground when Mikael Roussa fell down to death. This honour you do for us.'

Beledni suddenly looked very serious. He held out his hand. Gerlach offered his own hand in puzzlement and got it almost crushed by the big rotamaster's emphatic paw.

A lancer – tall and slender, with a scar along his left cheek bone – cantered up and leaned to whisper into Beledni's ear. The rotamaster's face darkened.

'You come, Vebla. You come,' he said.

X

DEMIETER LAY BESIDE his horse on the black clay of the marsh bank. Winged lancers had dismounted and stood around him. Two knelt by him. Gerlach jumped down from Saksen and crouched at his side.

'Kaus?'

'Heileman? Is that you? I can't see so well. It's dark.'

'There's a storm coming in…'

'No, you're all shadows.' Demieter's belly wound was a terrible mess. The skirts of his armour were coated in blood.

'Where's Volks?' Gerlach asked.

Demieter licked his lips and swallowed before answering. 'Didn't you see him? I saw him, Gerlach. He came so close. They shot him down at the tree-line. Just as we got to the forest. Such a lot of arrows in his back.'

'And the standard? Kaus, the standard?'

A dry rattle wheezed out of Demieter's lungs. He was dead.

Gerlach got to his feet and pulled off his riding gloves. Somehow they'd managed to rescue the Kislevite's worthless banner and lose their own a second time during the fight. He felt sick to his stomach. Of the Second Hipparchia Demilance, only he remained. Not even their beloved standard had survived the field. He was alone and, as vexillary, disgraced by the loss of their colours. Better he had died on the meadow. Better the Kislev dogs had left him to die in glory.

Thunder grumbled again, twigs of light danced along the northern skyline under the black watermark of glowering cloud. Beledni and his lancers were all staring at him.

He had to salvage something. Some scrap of honour.

'We ride,' he said to Beledni. 'To Choika, or one of the towns on the Lynsk. We must ride there. Carry a warning–'

Beledni crinkled his chin and shrugged.

'We must ride there!' Gerlach said. 'The Northers just obliterated everything at Zhedevka! They'll go south, to the river! Beyond that! Sigmar has spared us from the day's slaughter. That's a gift we must use!'

'No,' said Beledni. 'East.'

'Damn it! Armies of the Empire are still coming north to the frontier! To the river! They'll be marching straight into destruction unless we warn them!'

'No, Vebla. Is best we can go east. Run clear. Turn bick later.'

'No—'

'Is only way, yha? We take horse west or south, we die many times death. Here is death, here is death, here is death also again. Is little much we can do. But east, yha? Little and much, much by little. Like tale of man who has pebble and wants castle. With little he—'

'Shut up! Where the hell is your loyalty? Where the hell is your honour?'

Beledni frowned, then pointed to the eagle wing banner.

'To rota,' he said, as if it was obvious.

A bone horn blew. The enemy, fanning through the forests, was in sight. The lancers scattered to their horses. Beledni looked at Gerlach.

'Little and much, Vebla, much by little,' he said, and turned to mount up. He pointed to Gerlach's troop horse. Dry sweat caked Saksen's flanks.

'You ride, Vebla. Ride to live. When you can live, then you can choose how to die.'

KURGAN

I

THE WHOLE OF creation had become an unpleasant place.

It had gone dark, and compressed itself into a single, slender, vertical line of immense density that was pressing against the bridge of his nose and his forehead.

All darkness, all creation, all the composite parts of the world, all 'matter' as he had read the great scholars of the Empire were calling it these days, had channelled itself into that line, making it a thousand times harder than rock, a hundred thousand times harder than iron. Even darkness was soaked up into it. The pressure it exerted would surely cave his skull in very soon.

The only part of the whole of creation that wasn't contained in that line was a smell. And that smell was the wafting reek of shit.

Karl Reiner Vollen coughed and realised he was alive. In an instant he knew that the hard line of pain pressing down his head was the great split the wolf-head's axe had made in his skull. He didn't want to move in case his face hinged open like a book.

He clawed around with a gloveless hand. He was sprawled on his belly on a very uneven surface, and his head was tilted back because his face was jammed up against something. A rung. A bar.

He felt his face. It wasn't split, though it was agony to touch his left cheek. The slender vertical line was the bar his face was jammed against.

He opened his eyes. Flamelight, blurry. The smell of ordure remained strong, but mixed now with smoke and sweat and blood. His mouth had lolled open during his unconsciousness, and his tongue and gullet were as dry as tar paper.

He tried to move. He groaned at the effort and other voices groaned and protested too. He realised he was sprawled across a pile of bodies. Karl slithered round and sat up. His head pounded.

He was in a cage. A cage of sorts. It had been made from pikes and pole arms, each long shaft stabbed blade-down into the earth, each a hand's breadth from the next. They staked out a circle five spans across. Brass chains had been lashed around the raised shafts midway and at the top to keep them true. The cage roof was open to the swirling storm clouds.

The pole arms, the pikes... were all captured Imperial weapons, the arms of fallen men.

Outside the makeshift cage, there was nothing to see except churned mud, smoke and fire. Soot and sparks billowed up from burning buildings. Screams and drumming rolled out of the dark. Karl had no idea where he was, but he presumed he was still in Zhedevka.

Inside the cage, the floor space was packed with a mound of bodies. Men of the Empire all of them: bloody, filthy, most of them unconscious, some of them undoubtedly dead. They lay in a jumble where they had been flung. Karl realised he was lucky to have been one of the last thrown in. He'd ended up on the top of the heap. Those at the bottom had surely suffocated. Limbs curled and flopped, some of them protruding through the spaces between the bars.

A man from Carroburg lay next to him, his slashed doublet was drenched with blood, his jaw broken. Beneath him was a Wissenland pikeman with an ear hanging off and swollen blue lips. An archer, beside and under him, was either dead or unconscious. Others were too filthy or bloodstained or stripped of their wargear to identify.

Karl's own clothing and half-armour were tattered and shredded. He felt his face again and winced. That axe! Why wasn't he dead?

'What will they do with us?' asked a low, scared voice.

Karl looked around. Another Wissenland piker sat on a slope of bodies with his back pressed to the bars, staring at him. The pikeman was young, his surcoat ripped, a long gash down his chest. His hair was lank with sweat or blood.

'Demilancer? What will they do?'

Karl shook his head.

'What's your name?' asked the young pikeman.

'Karl R–' Karl began. Then 'Karl.'

'That's my name too!' the pikeman said, bright for a moment. His face fell. 'Karl Fedrik, of Wissenland. They'll kill us, won't they?'

'They haven't done yet,' said Vollen. No one built a cage, however crude, for men they were going to kill anyway. He didn't want to say it, but he had a hunch death was the least alarming of their prospects.

'What then? What?' the young pikeman stammered.

'Shut up, boy! Shut the hell up, for Sigmar's sake!'

Karl glanced around and saw a grizzled veteran from Averland curled up against the bars on the other side of the cage. He too was clumsily perched on the pile of bodies.

'Just shut up,' the man said. He had a sword wound in his arm, which made him clutch the limb stiffly against his chest. His beard had been hacked off, recently, and crudely, it seemed, from the bloody grazes on his stubbled jaw.

Karl tried to move around, but the shapes under him groaned and cried out. He was sure it was just breath being squeezed out of dead lungs. The smell of decay was stifling. Flies billowed around them all.

Two Norther riders suddenly galloped past them outside the bars, and the boy pikeman shrank down. The riders disappeared again into the choking curtain of smoke.

'It's all right,' Vollen assured the boy. 'It's all right, Karl.' He didn't believe his own words at all. This was nothing like all right.

He looked across at the Averland veteran again, in time to see the older man sliding a dirk out of his bloodstained sleeve. The man grasped the little dagger, pressed the tip to his throat and closed his eyes.

'No!' Karl lunged, oblivious to the shrieks and moans that issued from the bodies under foot. He crashed into the veteran and wrenched the dirk back from his neck. Its tip had drawn a dark spot of blood. The veteran cried out and punched at Vollen, but the clarion kept his hand clamped to the wrist of the knife hand and slapped the man hard across the face with his free palm.

The man sagged, and Vollen took the dirk away from him.

'What the hell are you doing?'

'Give it back! Give it back!' the older man whined.

'No! What were you thinking?'

The Averlander shoved Karl backwards and spat at him. 'Damn you! We're dead! We're dead here! Give me back my blade so I can slit my own throat and have done! Spare me the pain that they will inflict on us!'

'No. Shut up!' Karl growled.

'Please! You bastard!'

Karl pushed the struggling man back against the bars so hard the brass chains jingled.

'We are men of the Empire... sworn to the service of Karl Franz! When death claims us, it claims us! Not sooner – not by our own hands! There is always hope!'

The man sagged back, breathing hard. The light of the flames reflected in his eyes. 'There is no hope. Not now, demilancer,' he said softly. 'You have no idea. The heathens have penned us here simply so they might have fodder for their death games.'

'No.' said Karl. 'We'll be stood hostage t–'

The man laughed in his face. He laughed so hard, blood flew in his spittle. 'Have you fought the North before, boy?'

'No?'

'What do you know of the Northers? The brute tribes? The Kurgan?'

'I have read a little–'

'Then you know nothing!' The man's head dropped. He sighed. 'Two seasons before I have fought the Kurgan. I've seen things that... I cannot say. Acts of barbarism. They are not human, you know. They are daemons. They make piles of skulls, and stretch the hides of their enemies. And their rituals. Oh, may Sigmar spare me. Their rituals. Blood sacrifices to their infernal gods. Why do you think we're still alive?'

'I–'

'Hostages? Ha ha ha! You idiot! They want us alive so that our hearts will be beating when they offer us up to their gods!'

The young pikeman on the far side of the ghastly cage moaned aloud at the thought of this.

'Shut up!' snapped Karl, and slapped the man again. 'You're scaring the boy!'

'He should be scared...' the veteran hissed.

'Shut up, you fool!' Karl replied and delivered another slap. 'We can get out of here. We–'

'No, demilancer. We can't. We're livestock now. Livestock. If you care for a fellow's life, really care, you'll give him back his dirk. Then, when he's done, you'll use it on the boy and yourself too. That is Sigmar's mercy.'

Karl shook his head.

The man reached out his hand. 'Please? The dirk?'

'What's your name?' asked Karl.

'Drogo Hance, from Averland.'

'Drogo Hance, we will get out of here. I swear it on the honour of my company. Death is not the only escape.'

The Averlander chuckled coldly and turned away.

There was a noise from outside the cage. Three horned warriors appeared out of the smoke, dragging a man in full plate armour. One had him by the ankles, the others scooped under the armpits. The man was unconscious or dead. From his armour, it was clear he was one of the majestic Imperial Knights Panther. His wargear rattled and clattered as they drew him across the turf.

The Kurgan warriors threw him down and began to strip the polished steel plate off his limp body. They cast it aside, breaking the mail and cutting the leather straps. Pauldrons, vambraces, breastplate, leopard pelt. They pulled off his mail coat and tore away his undershift and leggings.

The man was face down now, naked. He still hadn't woken up.

Karl crawled across to the bars to watch.

One of the Kurgan warriors moved away into the smoke and returned with a wooden keg. He set it down and the other two draped the naked man across it, so that it supported his chest and his head hung down over the rim.

Another of the trio, his arms thick with muscles, drew his pallasz, a long, straight, double-edged sword.

'Hold him, seh,' he instructed. The other two did so. The knight was beginning to stir. The Kurgan with the pallasz raised his arms up to strike.

'Wait! You wait!' a voice boomed.

The horned warrior dropped his arms slackly. Three tall figures were striding into the firelight out of the smoke. One was a Kurgan bodyguard in a scale-linked mantle, a berdish axe clasped across his chest. The other two were hetmen. A slender, but inhumanly tall figure in head-to-toe black plate armour... and the massive warrior with the wolf's head helmet.

His shoulder was now wrapped in blood-soaked bindings.

'What do you do here?' the tall, plated figure demanded of the men. His ornate armour had a coating of black pitch that had been scratched and inscribed with a sharp tool, leaving an intricate etching of spirals, loops and stars in bare metal. His helmet was a barbute, similarly decorated, with a horizontal gash as an eye-slit.

'Prizing of a skull, Zar Blayda,' answered one of the Kurgan, putting his hand flat across his heart.

'This skull?'

The warrior with the pallasz put aside his blade so that he could put his hand over his heart too. 'Zar Herfil craves two more to make his trophy heap...'

'Not this one. I want him for my own sport.' The tall hetman tugged a small leather flask from his sword belt. It was stoppered with wax, through which a long, iron pin had been spiked. The hetman slid the pin out, lifted the knight's slack head by the hair, and quickly pricked the skin of the right cheekbone three times. Then he let the head drop. 'There. I have made my mark upon him now. '

'But Zar Herfil–'

The tall, black-armoured figure swung round sharply and struck the swordbearer around the face. He yelped and stumbled back.

'Don't raise a question to my word, dog-boy. Herfil may have his skulls.' The tall black shape turned and gestured to the cage. 'Take them from there instead.'

The Kurgan hurried forward, leaving the naked, unconscious Knight Panther to roll slackly sideways off the keg. One of the warriors pushed up an axe head to loose the brass chains around the makeshift cage, and the other yanked the freed poles out of the soil and tossed them aside.

'They're all dead!' one of the Kurgan warriors announced, peering in.

'There's one,' said Zar Blayda, pointing.

The Kurgan warriors manhandled Karl Fedrik of Wissenland out of the cage. He was screaming.

'Leave him alone!' Vollen yelled, clawing at them. The Northers kicked him back hard.

Karl Fedrik of Wissenland, now so terrified and so absolutely sure of what was happening to him he had soiled himself, was thrown face down over the keg. The Kurgan with the pallasz flourished it twice and then chopped down, striking off the boy's head. Blood gouted in rhythmic spurts from the neck stump.

'Him too?' Zar Blayda said, pointing at Vollen.

'No. Leave him.' The words, deep and dark, came muffled out of the wolf-mask helmet. 'I have marked him.'

'Very well, then. That one.'

The men grabbed Drogo Hance and pulled him out of the cage. Looking back at Vollen as he was dragged out backwards, Hance screamed, 'I told you! I told you, you bastard! I told you! You could have spared me this! You could have made it quick! You bastard!'

The Kurgan warriors made it quick anyway. The pallasz swept down and Hance's head rolled.

Zar Blayda picked up the two heads by their hair. Hance and Fedrik, mouths open, eyes rolled back.

'Herfil will be pleased,' he said.

The wolf-mask glowered through the bars at Vollen as the men threw the naked body of the Panther Knight into the cage and reformed it.

'You will keep for me,' said the wolf-face. Then he turned and walked away through the wide lakes of blood emptying out of the two corpses.

II

LEFT ALONE, KARL vomited. Revulsion and terror, terror and revulsion, the two things throbbed and circled in his head. He was close to panic. The iron tang of warm blood was so strong he vomited again until his retching was dry. He tried to spare the others in the cage his indignity, but there was no space. 'I'm sorry! I'm sorry!' he gasped between retches, trying to wipe his spew off the men beneath him.

It seemed though, that everyone else in the cage was dead.

Shuddering with cold and the dry spasms of his gullet, Karl curled up against the bars. Outside, in the fiery dark, a crude horn blew out a long, deep atonal note, and others joined it, some close, some far away. The horns wailed and sang for minutes and then finally died away.

Karl realised he was curled in the very space his name's sake, poor Karl Fedrik of Wissenland, had occupied. The thought... the comparison... was too much to bear. He couldn't even bring himself to look at the headless bodies slumped outside the cage. He scrambled round until he found another place to sit. His movement ushered cries and groans from the body pile.

When he settled again, he realised there was something in his left hand. Something small and cold and hard.

It was Hance's dirk.

Karl raised it up to his face, slowly. A fine little piece, tempered in the blade-forges of Averland, the palm-long blade curved and waisted like a tulip. It had a simple brass hilt, and a grip that was wound in matt-black wire. A boot-knife, a belt-knife, a typical pole-armer's piece. Made for stabbing in through visor slits and armour joints once the halberd or pike had done its work and brought an armoured foe down. Pikemen called such dirks their 'true killers'. They were famed for the use of their long-shafted weapons, but their little dirks and daggers most often did the actual killing.

Karl stared at the dirk. The true killer. He realised Hance had probably been right. A little quick blade for a little quick death. Merciful, sparing. For the pain and horror that waited for him outside the rude cage was beyond imagining.

This was simple, this was honest.

Karl Reiner Vollen closed his eyes and said a prayer to Sigmar. He asked Emperor Karl Franz for forgiveness. The gods would understand, surely?

He pressed the flat of the dirk to his throat with one hand, and felt around with the fingers of the other for his neck vein. It was fat and pulsing. His heart was racing.

He turned the dagger so the edge was against his flesh. Another prayer, to remember his sisters, and his father and mother, and Guldin who had trained him to horse and–

He bit his lip.

His hand wouldn't move.

'Sigmar, please...' he moaned.

He couldn't do it. Some desperate will for life blocked him and stayed his hand. If nothing else, there was something so unseemly about an Imperial weapon being used to end an Imperial life.

'Gods damn you, Drogo Hance!' Karl sputtered, and dropped the dirk. Then, with tears welling in his eyes, he murmured, 'Gods spare you too...'

'Hello...?' a voice called.

Karl looked round. The Knight Panther, stripped bare and tossed onto the body heap, was struggling up, gazing around blankly.

'Is anyone there? Anyone? Hello... anyone...' The man's voice, rich and strong, was cracking weakly.

'You're fine. You're all right,' Karl reassured him, clambering forward across the mattress of limbs and torsos.

'Who is that? I can't see. I don't know where I am.'

'My name is Karl Vollen, sir. Second Company Hipparchia Demilance. I'm clarion. You're all right... just now, you're all right.'

The knight rolled over, vulnerable and exposed, and reached out towards the sound of Karl's voice. 'Karl Vollen? Where are you?'

'Here, sir.' Karl reached out a hand and the knight clasped it.

'I'm blind,' the knight said. There was a dark contusion on the man's temple and his eyes were rolled blankly, like loose kernels inside a husk-case.

He gripped Karl's hand tightly. 'Where are we?'

'We're in a bad place, sir, I can't lie. Captured and caged by the Northers.'

'Ahhh,' the knight nodded and sighed. 'I feared as much. They took my horse down. Poor Schalda. Then something hit me across the face. Across the head. A lance, I think. Maybe an axe. I'm cold.'

'They took all your armour and your clothes,' Karl said, wanting to add that they'd nearly taken his head too, but thought better of it.

'This is a pretty end for me,' said the knight.

Karl pushed down into the mass of bodies and found a man who was clearly dead. Dragging and straining, he managed to pull the corpse's jerkin and woollen undershirt off.

'Sir?' he said. 'Take these, and put them on. You'll be warmer.'

His eyes almost crossed in their blindness, the knight felt his way into the dirty clothes Karl had provided.

'Better,' he said. 'For this simple kindness, I am in your debt, clarion Vollen. Your demilance is from Talabheim, yes?'

'Yes, sir.'

'Are you sworn up? Are you ready for your spurs?'

The knight was asking if Karl was preparing for entry into a knightly order.

'I... my birth is not adequate, sir. I am not.'

The knight wriggled round so he was looking at Karl, even though he couldn't see him. His blank eyes glared at a point far above Karl's left shoulder.

'If we get out of this, Karl, your birth won't be an issue. It's in my power to reward you for your help.'

'I didn't do it because–'

'Of course you didn't! I meant no offence.'

'What is your name, sir?' Karl asked.

'Von Margur,' the knight replied, cradling his arms around his body.

'Von Margur? Like the great hero of Altdorf?'

Blind, looking the wrong way, the knight smiled.

'Gods!' Karl started. 'You are von Margur of Altdorf!'

'I am. Unless there is another I know not of.'

'I'm truly honoured, sir,' Karl began, and then his voice trailed off. He realised how ridiculous it was. They were penned in an enemy cage, awaiting barbarous death, and here he was hero-worshipping.

The blunt truth was that his hero was as helpless as he was. They were going to die.

'Karl? Where did you go?' von Margur called hoarsely.

'I'm here, sir,' Karl answered. He was groping into the pile of bodies to recover the dirk. His hand closed around it and he pulled it up.

And held it close to his heart.

III

AFTER A WHILE, the knight fell asleep, the deep, sick sleep of the wounded. Karl sat back against the bars, and slid the dirk into his undershirt.

He turned his head and looked out at the headless corpses for the first time. They were thick with flies.

A figure emerged from the smoke. A bull mask visor wrought from brass, three asymmetrical horns. Leather straps. Jingling strings of shell beads and polished bone. An otherwise naked body.

It was the barbarian warrior Karl had faced in Marshal Neiber's bedchamber.

The man plodded forward, his bare feet slapping the wet mud. He was short and squat of body, with a thick neck. In each of his hands dangled a long stabbing dagger.

He reached the bars of the makeshift cage and stared in at Karl. There was no doubt in Karl's mind that the horned devil recognised him. In fact, he had the distinct feeling the Norther had come to find him. There was a deep, sharp gash down the side of the Norther's helmet visor where Karl's sabre had sent him tumbling.

The man sheathed one of his daggers and reached his empty hand up to the gouge in his helmet. He slid the fingerpads back down the ragged score and cut them open on the bare metal.

With a whip of his wrist, he flicked his hand to Karl and spattered him with blood.

'I am Ons Olker, flesh,' he said, in halting but competent Imperial. 'I have blood-tied thee. For thy offence, I will take thy soul.'

Then he walked away into the smoke, shaking the blood off his hand.

IV

KARL WAS WOKEN by rain, pelting and cold. He wasn't sure when or how he'd fallen asleep. The rain – the heaviest that had fallen since they'd left Brodny – was icy. It roused many of the other penned men, including von Margur and several that Karl had supposed to be dead. With so many awake, there was no longer any space to crouch or sprawl. The prisoners were forced to stand, shivering, some moaning, on the bodies of those that would likely never rise again.

Someone was sobbing. Another was yelling out disjointed nonsense. Several joined together to recite Sigmarite prayers of deliverance and fortitude.

Karl found himself mouthing the old, rote-learned words. He was so wet and bone-cold, he could barely control his shaking. Beyond the cage wall, he could see less than four spans, so heavy was the rain. He wondered if anyone was watching them. It would not be impossible to pull up one or more of the pikes that formed the bars and make a run for it.

A run to where? An attempt to escape would surely provoke savage reprisal from the barbarians.

But still, how could anything be worse than the miserable plight they were in?

Karl took a good grip on the pole arm facing him.

'What are you doing?' hissed a man next to him. Karl didn't reply.

'Stop it!' the man added. 'They'll kill us all for sure if–'

Karl looked at him. He was a heavy-set man in early middle-age, wearing the ragged leather coat and apron of a smith or a gunner.

'They'll kill us all anyway,' said Karl.

'Karl? Is that you?' von Margur called, reaching out.

'Lad's trying to escape!' the heavy man said.

'Stop it, Karl,' von Margur said softly.

'There's no one out there, sir...' Karl began, rocking the pole shaft to work the buried head out.

'Yes, there is,' said von Margur.

'How could you know that? You can't... I mean...'

'I can feel them. I can feel them watching,' the blind knight said. He said it with such conviction Karl pulled his hands off the pole shaft guiltily.

After a few minutes, the rain ceased suddenly. The downpour had washed the smoke out of the air. What it revealed was a world in grey half-light, a kind of twilight without colour. Devastation lay all around: acres of mud, mangled fields, and the steaming black ruins of Zhedevka. Their cage of captured pikes was just one amongst twenty standing in a waterlogged pasture beside the dead city's west wall. Each cage was as full of filthy, forlorn bodies as theirs. Upwards of a thousand prisoners, penned like swine.

In the distance, great fires burned, so big even the torrential rain hadn't doused them. Mounds of timber higher than a barn, casting up huge flames into the desolate sky. Watch fires, funeral pyres, victory blazes... Karl couldn't decide what they were. He could see dark figures – just specks at that distance – ringing around the huge bonfires like worshippers. He could hear drums and chanting. Carrion crows, hundreds of them, circled the field, fluttering in the air like autumnal leaves.

One other thing, closer at hand, had been revealed by the deluge. Norther warriors with axes and boar-spears lurked around the edges of the cage pasture, watching over them all. Some had large hounds lying by them, kept on chain leashes.

'You see?' hissed the heavy man beside Karl.

'You were right, sir,' said Karl to the knight.

No one spoke after that. Even the man who had been yelling nonsense shut up. The vista before them was too bleak, too dismal, too apocalyptic for words.

Night fell, black and cold and clear. The freezing, glassy darkness of a spring night in the oblast.

They remained standing, shivering, aching from the chill. A moon rose, fuzzy and glittering like a white lamp. Stars came out, but they seemed dim and cold, and they resembled no pattern Karl could recall from his studies. He was sure that was just his imagination.

The second moon rose late, but it could not match the bright, frosty glare of the first. In the darkness of the distance, the drumming and chanting stopped and, one by one, the great fires were snuffed out.

V

KARL WOKE AGAIN at dawn, cold through to his marrow. He was shaken awake, and was still upright. He blinked round in the thin light and found that the heavy man had been propping him up so that he could sleep without falling. Karl was astonished by the man's kind effort.

'You're all right there, lad,' the man said with a nod. 'I couldn't let you fall. You'd like have been crushed.'

Karl could see from the man's drawn face and red eyes that he had been weeping. There was a tremor of cold and fear in his large, powder-stained hands.

'What's your name?' Karl asked.

'Ludhor Brezzin, of Nuln.'

'An engineer?'

'No, lad. Nothing so grand. I am a powderman and tamper, from the cannon crews. I... I was a powderman.' He shrugged his powerful arms as much as the tight pack of bodies would permit. Then he looked away and snuffled, rubbing his nose and eyes with his thick wrists.

'He has a son,' a voice whispered in Karl's ear. It was the blind knight.

'A son?'

'A boy about your age. All night he has wept for grief that he would not see the boy again.'

'He told you this, sir?' Karl whispered.

Von Margur shook his head.

Karl wanted to ask the knight how he could know such things, but the nobleman looked ashen and weak. The bruise across his temple had grown and become more discoloured. His eyes still rolled like a broken doll's, and now the left, nearest the bruise, was bloodshot. Though the blow that had felled him had not opened his head, it had done massive concussive damage, Karl was sure. Shaking the eyes loose and useless, and undoubtedly harming the brain. When von Margur opened his mouth to speak, his white teeth were outlined with blood.

'My adversary struck me hard,' von Margur said suddenly, conversationally, as if hearing what Karl was thinking. He turned his face towards the clarion, though his eyes did not look that way. 'It was the fiend in black armour, the one with the etched patterns...'

'The Kurgan called him Zar Blayda,' said Karl.

'He is a daemon,' said the blind knight. 'His thoughts are like molten iron. He fancies himself High Zar, and plots to murder Surtha Lenk.'

'Who?'

'I don't know. The words are just in my mouth.' Von Margur stopped talking abruptly, and held out a hand to Karl. The clarion took it. Von Margur's touch was like ice. Karl could see Zar Blayda's mark on the knight's right cheek. Three dark pinpricks of dried blood. The flesh around them was discoloured green.

There had been dye or ink on that pin. What had the wolf-face meant when he said he'd marked Karl too? The clarion gently felt his own face with his free hand. The left side was still a tender, swollen mass of bruise. There were numerous nicks and grazes. He felt a soreness on his own right cheek. A tiny, painful dot. A pinprick.

What did the mark mean?

'Karl,' von Margur said. 'I am afraid.'

'We're all afraid, sir.'

'I am afraid of myself. Things have got into my head. They're trying to get out. They make me see things and tell me the words for the things I have seen. I–' He stopped again, shook his head. And then he collapsed.

Von Margur began convulsing, his spine and limbs as rigid as spear hafts. A horrible drooling rattle was issuing from his throat, and pink froth was dribbling from his clenched teeth out over his grimacing lips.

Karl grabbed him and tried to support his thrashing weight. The fearful prisoners all around attempted to back off, not wanting to touch the man.

'Help me with him!' Karl yelled.

'Let him be, boy! He's touched by the curse!' one of them warned.

'He's possessed! Got the evil of the North in him!' another squealed.

'You bastards! You ignorant fools!' Karl shouted. 'It's just a seizure! Caused by his wound! Gods, we're men of the Empire! We're supposed to be civilised! Help me, you superstitious fools!'

Only Brezzin moved to help him. 'Make sure he doesn't bite his tongue,' the bulky gunner said, cradling von Margur securely in his powerful arms.

After a minute, the knight's body went limp and he stopped spasming. Brezzin released him gently, and von Margur abruptly sat up, bent over and spewed noxious black bile onto the bodies that formed the floor of the cage. Then he fell into a slumber.

'I thank Sigmar you didn't share the opinion of this ignorant rabble,' Karl said to the gunner.

'What, that he was possessed?'

Karl nodded.

'I do,' said Brezzin. 'But you needed help.'

VI

AN HOUR AFTER von Margur's seizure, the Kurgans came en masse to the cages. There was great excitement. Horns blew, drums thundered, dogs barked, and men laughed and shouted in the coarse dialects of the North.

The prisoners waited in apprehensive silence inside the cage rings.

A thicket of Northers closed around the cage Karl was in. They peered in, shouting taunts and poking with the tips of boar-spears. The prisoners pressed tightly together, watching the black visored faces that circled outside. Karl saw the brute he knew as Ons Olker amongst them, his asymmetrical horns distinct in the crowd.

Hooves thundered, and the Kurgan parted to let a rider through. It was Karl's nemesis, the great warrior with the wolf-face helm.

He dismounted and strode towards the cage. He still wore the bearskin and black leggings and boots, but his skin was clean and oiled to a sheen. He slapped his forearms together, making the warrior rings wrapped around them chime. This provoked a throaty shout from the Kurgan all around. Then he raised his hands and lifted the black wolf-helm off his head by the jutting horns.

His face was nothing like Karl had imagined. It was shaved clean of beard, head hair and even eyebrows. Ancient ritual scars ran in wide furrows diagonally down his cheeks, five on one side and two on the other. His eyes were bright and hard like diamonds. He was astonishingly beautiful in a feral way – handsome like a sire wolf is handsome.

He tossed the wolf-helm to one of the Kurgan and wiped his palms over his smooth, oiled scalp. 'Bring them out,' he ordered.

The Kurgan moved forward and shook the pike shafts out of the earth, pulling the linking chains down. Then with sticks and boar-spears, they herded the prisoners out of the open cage. A miserable, jumbled raft of bodies was left behind them.

Brezzin and Karl were supporting von Margur between them. Several of their fellow prisoners were sobbing and pleading. The Kurgan jostled round them, pushing in to slap and cuff the captives, pawing at them and toying with them, laughing out loud. One man fell on his knees at the feet of the wolf-face and began begging for mercy.

The wolf-face kicked him in the mouth.

'Tri-horn!' von Margur said suddenly, waking up with a start. Brezzin and Karl both looked at him in confusion. A hand grabbed at Karl's arm and he turned to look straight into the three horned bull-mask of Ons Olker. The squat, naked brute had pushed right into the press to reach him. He had one of his daggers out.

The wolf-face moved, knocking prisoners out of his way, and punched Ons Olker in the chest before he could stab Karl. Ons Olker fell, whining. Captives and Kurgan alike spread back to give them room.

The wolf-face slapped down another blow, connecting across Ons Olker's helmet with the mass of warrior rings around his forearm. The blow bent one of the horns that was already twisted.

Ons Olker whimpered like a dog. His beads rattled.

'What do you, Olker? What games do you play?' the huge wolf-face demanded.

'He owes me, zar! I have blood-tied him for he did me offence! I claim his soul!'

'Your blood-tie is meaningless. He already wears my mark, Olker. You must claim him from me, not strike behind my back.'

'I claim his soul!' the smaller man wailed.

The wolf-face kicked at him. 'Be off, dung-eater! Zar Blayda may prize you for your sight, but I do not. You are a runt and a dung-eater. Be off until your eyes peel back far enough for you to see something useful!'

Ons Olker hissed at the massive warrior, and made some warding sign with twisted fingers. He shook his bone beads.

'Damn thy charms! My shaman has already blessed me!' the wolf-face bellowed after him.

Ons Olker hooked his fingers under the rim of his bull-mask and lifted it back far enough to expose a ragged whiskered mouth of broken, brown teeth. He spat at the wolf-face.

'Curse thee, Zar Uldin! Thou owest me a soul!'

The wolf-face – Uldin – looked aside at one of his men. 'Fetch my pallasz here to me,' he said.

At that, Ons Olker turned and fled.

Zar Uldin slowly turned back and stared at Karl. His eyes were as bright and frosty as the moon that had glared at them the night before. 'You have cost me, little Southlander. This–' he touched the still-raw gash on his shoulder that Karl's sabre had dug during the fight at the zal. 'And now the curses of a war shaman. I think you may be too dangerous to keep alive.'

'You cost me my horse,' Karl said bluntly.

Zar Uldin's eyes narrowed. Then he laughed. 'You won't be needing a horse now.'

He walked away, dishing out orders to the Kurgan.

The prisoners were led up from the pasture onto the wide meadow where the battle had raged. The Kurgan herded them over to one of the great bonfires that had been burning the previous night. It was a steep stack of charred timber and ash – dry-white and smoking in the cold dawn. Karl could see that the prisoners from other cage pens were being led up to the other bonfire heaps. There was an odd smell in the air – it was smoke, but with a hanging odour like cooked meat.

Goading with boar-spears, the Kurgan forced the captives to dig in the ashes. The fire heap was still baking hot and searing to touch, and as they scooped ash-powder away with their bare hands they exposed pockets of furnace heat. In a few moments, their hands were scorched and blistered from glowing charcoal logs and glowing coals.

'What the hell are we doing?' one of the prisoners asked.

Karl scraped away at the hot ash with raw fingers and then discovered the answer. Several others made the same discovery simultaneously and cried out in horror.

They were digging up skulls. Skulls that had been burned clean. Skulls that had had the flesh roasted off them. Skulls that were chalky-white with ash and throbbed with internal heat. When they pulled them out, hot dregs of fluid dribbled out of them.

That was what the great fires had been for, to prepare the skulls of the vanquished for Kurgan victory heaps. The task of digging them out was another humiliating indignity for the captives to suffer.

VII

LAUGHING AND SHOUTING, the Kurgan made the prisoners dig up the skulls and stack them beside the fire. They made a loose heap of dusty white bone that clacked and knocked together. Some of the captives retched as they were forced to work, and one man refused. The Kurgan beat him and then stabbed him with their spears, and left him for the crows.

Zar Uldin reappeared, and some of the Kurgan began to carry the recovered skulls from the heap over to him. Patiently, like a child with building blocks, he began to stack them. His shaman was with him: a little, stunted man, wizened and as naked as Ons Olker. He wore an iron barbute with a snake inscribed around the crown, and chanted as he capered round the zar, shaking bead rattles and strings of shells and finger bones. He had marked symbols on his naked flesh with white ash from the bonfire.

Zar Uldin followed the barking instructions of his shaman carefully. He placed the first skulls in a square, thirteen to each side, all looking out, and the shaman made sure the square was aligned with one corner pointing north. Karl wasn't quite sure how he did this, though the shaman seemed to have a lightning stone and an iron needle.

Then Uldin began to stack the skulls the Kurgan brought to him inside the square, raising a pyramid. He chanted words Karl couldn't hear as he did so. The shaman hopped around him, rattling and singing all the while, and never letting his left foot touch the ground.

By then, all the captives were gut-sick and caked up to their elbows in chalk-white ash. Many were crying.

The pyramid rose. The shaman hopped and jangled his rattles and strings.

Karl pawed free another skull from the ash and dared to look about him. At every bonfire around the battlefield, the scene was repeated. Under guard from Northers, the captives were exhuming skulls from the char of each fire, and zars were building heaps with them as their shaman danced. A hundred paces away, at the nearest bonfire, Karl could see Zar Blayda in his etched black armour building a pyramid of death while Ons Olker capered around him.

Uldin's pyramid was almost complete. It was clear that the stack was built on mathematical principles. A specific number of skulls was needed to complete it.

'Three more!' Uldin demanded.

The captives had broken down the whole bonfire pile, sweating in the steam and smoulder. They dredged up two more skulls. Kurgan hurried the discoveries over to Uldin.

'Another!' he cried.

A man in the ragged uniform vestiges of a Nordland arquebusier uniform dug out the final skull. He seemed pathetically delighted to have pleased the zar so much. Uldin walked over to him, took the hot skull out of his grip, and led him by the hand over to the skull stack.

Uldin placed the final skull onto the pinnacle of the heap. Uldin's shaman whooped and yelled. The bone-white slopes of the pyramid seemed to gleam in the dank light. The eye sockets were like windows in the slopes.

All the captives stood, sombrely, and watched as the last skull clinked into place. A cold wind rose from the west and gusted white dust across the wet field.

Zar Uldin looked down at the shivering arquebusier from Nordland who had dug up the last skull and smiled in an almost friendly, reassuring way, as if the man had done him some great service.

Then Uldin took a flint knife from his shaman, grabbed the Nordlander and slit his throat.

The man was still wailing and choking and gagging as Uldin held him up over the skull heap and washed it with his hot blood.

Disgusted, Karl looked away. Some of the captives sank to their knees in woe.

Uldin threw the corpse aside and turned to his dancing shaman. He handed back the blood-wet flint knife.

Uttering some barbaric enchantment, the shaman took the knife and cut a slash down Uldin's cheek. Now he had five on one side, and three on the other. Uldin raised his massive arms and howled up into the sky.

Thunder rolled. The gods, Karl thought alarmingly, were listening. Vile gods he didn't have a name for.

The Kurgan led the captives back to the stinking pasture and caged them up again. Karl hadn't been able to count the skull heaps on the field.

VIII

IN THE NIGHT that followed, von Margur suffered another fit. When he woke up, clamped in the arms of Brezzin and Karl, he said something that sounded like 'kill me'.

'I cannot kill you, sir. I will not,' said Karl.

Von Margur shook his head. His eyes rolled slack and he smiled through the froth covering his mouth.

'No, Karl. I said... you will kill me. And you will kill Uldin. But not before you have marked the fifth scratch on his cheek.'

Then he fell asleep.

Karl Vollen hoped he would not wake up.

NORSCYA

I

FOR TWO FULL days following the slaughter at Zhedevka, the rota of Kislevite lancers rode east, and Gerlach Heileman went with them.

The oblast east of Zhedevka was an uninhabited hinterland of tangled forest and mud-flats where the great open steppes of Kislev slumped down to meet the natural barrier of the River Lynsk. The forest tracts were deep-shadowed wilds of maple, yew and elderly poplar where spring growth was beginning to bud. Tiny, smoke-blue flowers grew in profusion through the ground cover, forming drifts like blue snow. Songbirds haunted the glades, and there was a scent of rain and balsam in the air. Every few leagues, the forest would break open and reveal stretches of black clay that glistened in the pale spring light. Here, the spring melt-waters had driven the Lynsk up into its flood plains. The rota crossed the mud flats in single file, a line of blurry reflections spreading out away from them on the waterlogged clay.

The lancers rode in silence, following their lank banner. They did not stop, not even once.

By day, they moved at a steady trot, by night a slow plod. Some of the men slept upright in their saddles, heads nodding, but their horses moved on, following the group.

The nights were cold and fathomlessly black. The lancers lit no lamps or tapers. Between flurries of rain, the twin moons glared at them, fuming with radiant white light. Screech-owls mocked them. Thunder occasionally grumbled.

The days seemed even harsher. Rain fell frequently and hard, raising thin mists and streaming down through the dark boughs of the forest. In the open, on the mud flats, the rain came raw, and the ground clay, covered as it was with standing water, became indistinct in the splashing of the torrent. There was seldom any sun, just a white haze of backlit vapour. Very occasionally, something pale yellow and luminous tried to swirl out of the overcast cloud, but it never succeeded. They saw herons and waders, and once, from a great distance, a brown wolf trotting down the foreshore.

Three or four lancers lagged back behind the main group permanently, watching for pursuit. Every few hours, riders from the column would swing back and relieve them. Late on the first day, the outriders bolted forward, and the rota picked up its speed for a few leagues, racing wide across a clay floodplain and into another reach of forest. But no enemy appeared.

On the third day, Beledni turned them north.

II

DEMIETER CAME WITH them. The Kislevites had wound his body in a ground sheet and lashed it over the saddle of his troop horse. Gerlach insisted on leading it, tying Demieter's reins to his cantle.

No one spoke to the vexillary, and he spoke to no one. He had nothing in him left to say. He rode, hunched and exhausted, limp in the saddle, vaguely aware of the growing lameness in Saksen's gait. Hunger gnawed at him and his bruised body ached.

When the rota turned north on the third day, it raised its pace. Gerlach realised he was slowly being left behind. He decided he didn't really care. The change of route and pace seemed to alter the demeanour of the lancers. He could hear them now chatting to each other, laughing occasionally. He wanted them to go on and leave him. He didn't want to be around them any more.

Two lancers rode back down the file to join him. They fell in either side of him, and made smiles and gestures that indicated they wanted him to catch up.

'Go on. Leave me,' he said.

The riders looked at each other, not sure what he meant.

'Go on!' Gerlach gestured wearily.

'We go on but you go on,' said one. He was a tall man with a greying top knot and deep-set eyes. His mouth was wide and full of small, evenly-spaced teeth. The tall, curved wooden frames of the wings rising from his hauberk's back were thick with hawk feathers.

'Just go,' snapped Gerlach.

'Rotamaster sayt with you come. With you come. With...' the lancer faltered. 'How it you sayt?'

Gerlach sighed.

'Is you of come to now with his!' prompted the other suddenly. He was a smaller man, just a youth really, with a wispy moustache and very blue eyes.

The bright feathers of a jay interlaced between the heron quills on his wing frame.

He looked eagerly at his comrade, apparently proud of his linguistic skill. 'Eyh? Eyh?'

'Is you of come to now with his!' repeated the tall man with an enthusiastic nod. 'Is you of come to now with his!'

'Eyh?' said the boy again, pleased with himself. He looked at Gerlach. 'I tongue good you!'

'I don't think so,' Gerlach murmured.

'Eyh?'

'I said... never mind.'

'Shto?'

The older lancer looked solemn. He indicated the boy. When he spoke, a great deal of deliberation went into the choice of every word. 'Vaja is boy who... ummm... speaking most... ummmm... good word for his mouth. Is in your... ummm... ear for good also?'

The boy – Vaja – quickly hissed across at his comrade, correcting him. 'Ah!' said the older man. 'Vaja, his tongue is in your ear.'

'Eyh?' urged the boy.

Gerlach looked at him. 'It's very good. Good word.'

'You understand! Is good thing!' Vaja looked delighted, and the older man beamed like a proud parent. 'Is many time I read book. Same book. Many reads time. Is book. Oh! Is book again. So I learn.'

'Very good,' said Gerlach. He was so weary. He wondered what Vaja's book-learning would understand of the words 'get lost'.

The boy leaned over towards Gerlach. 'Vitali him. Vitali no good learn.'

Vitali looked hurt. 'Vitali speak little good,' he insisted plaintively.

The boy began to scold Vitali good-naturedly in Kislevite. They bantered back and forth. The main column had almost disappeared ahead, lost in the trees. Gerlach wished he could get them to leave him alone.

They shut up suddenly, simultaneously, and both looked over their shoulders. Behind them, the forest trail went quiet.

'Norscya,' hissed Vitali, and Gerlach needed no gloss to understand that word.

Vitali gave the boy instructions quickly and turned his horse round. He slid a javelin from his saddle boot and rested it on his shoulder, tip down.

'Yatsha!' he snarled and galloped away back down the track.

Vaja leaned forward and tried to grab Gerlach's reins. Gerlach waved him off.

'We have go! Ride!' Vaja gabbled.

Gerlach looked back. Vitali had vanished.

'We have go!' Vaja repeated.

'Oh, all right!' Gerlach replied, spurring Saksen up after the boy's cantering mare. Demieter's troop horse trailed heavily behind Gerlach.

They continued up the wet trail for a minute or so. Vaja kept looking backwards. He was agitated. There was still no sign of the company's tail-end ahead of them.

'Have you got a bugle?' Gerlach whispered.

'Shto?'

'A bugle? A horn?'

'Hawn?'

Gerlach mimed putting a bugle to his lips and blowing. Vaja nodded, and dutifully offered Gerlach his water skin.

'Sigmar spare me, no. We should warn the company. Warn the rota.'

'Rota…?'

'Warn them!' Gerlach barked. He untied the reins of Demieter's horse, and handed them to the boy. Then he pointed up the trail.

'Go tell rota. Tell Beledni.'

Vaja looked doubtful, so Gerlach smacked the rump of his mare and made him start forward. The young lancer slowly rode away up the narrow track, looking back.

Gerlach drew his sabre, and wheeled Saksen around.

III

HE RETRACED HIS route, looking for signs of Vitali. The forest had become ominously quiet. Mist drifted like campfire smoke through the bracken, and rainwater shone like diamonds on the bark of yew and larch trees. Gerlach jumped at a sound, but it was only a woodpecker drumming in the timbers nearby.

He followed the trail down into a dell where a wide pool had formed between exposed tree roots. The water was black and still, and avalanches of ivy cascaded down the clay banks and sagging trees.

Then he heard the noise. Shouting voices. Metal impacts.

Ducking under the low boughs, he spurred Saksen on, along the edge of the pool, into the sunken glade beyond.

Vitali had found the Norscya.

There were eight of them. Six ugly men on foot and two on black horses. All of them were wearing iron scale armour and horned barbutes darkened with pitch. They had surrounded Vitali, who was in the middle of a shallow stream, turning his mare in a circle and kicking up water.

There had been nine. One lay on a bank, half in the water, a javelin embedded in his chest.

The Norscya were tightening their circle around the lancer, jabbing with boar-spears and spade-tipped foot lances. One had a morning star that he was whirling in vicious, expert arcs.

Vitali had his second javelin out and raised overarm, shouting defiantly at the enemy, turning to face each aggressor that took his chance to lunge closer.

One of the riders was a partially armoured, bare-chested Kurgan with a sword. His helmet spikes rose high and straight, like a southerland buffalo. The other was altogether more impressive. He wore a long coat of blackened scale mail, and every single scale plate was finished with a thorny spike. His cloak was made of wolf pelts, half sewn together so they straggled around him, grey and white. His head was encased in a close-helm with a hinged visor that must have been made in an Empire smithy and taken as a trophy. It had been daubed black, and curling horns had been forged onto it. They were coiled around each other like snakes, the ends of each an open wyrm mouth. He was the leader, Gerlach knew that at once.

The snake-horned leader couched a long horse lance under his arm. It was three spans long and its black shaft was wrapped with strips of gold foil. He clearly intended to take this kill, once his men had corralled Vitali tight.

Gerlach sheathed his sabre and drew his one remaining pistol. He'd primed and loaded it the day before, and now he laid its dog and drove Saksen into the charge.

'Karl Franz!' he bellowed.

The Kurgan turned in surprise, seeing the tattered demilancer bearing down on them along the stream bed, sheeting spray up from his hooves.

The leader first, Gerlach thought. He aimed and fired.

The wheel-lock cracked, and smoke hissed out of it.

There was a distinct *thtang!* as the ball struck the snake-horned leader. He cried out, and was knocked out of his saddle so hard his horse came down with him. The horse lance in his hand splintered under the writhing steed.

Gerlach was two horse lengths from the nearest Kurgan foot soldier, the brute with the ball-and-chain mace. He slammed home his spent pistol and scythed out his sabre, chopping down hard with the edge and ramming the Kurgan into the overhanging ivy.

The others rushed him. Gerlach reared Saksen up, and drove its milling fore hooves at the first of them. Then, as his gelding dropped level again, he stabbed down, straight, with the point, and cut through the shoulder of another.

Vitali cried out, exuberantly galvanised by the sudden change in fortunes. He unleashed his javelin, and brought down one of the Norscya holding a boar-spear. Then he drew his Kislevite sabre, a curved sword with a beautiful slender blade and simple cross guard, and laid about himself.

They had now reached an impasse. Gerlach and Vitali had the edge of surprise and horse power between them, and were pushing the enemy group back. But the Kurgan had the reach of boar-spears and were growling and barking as they kept the horses at bay.

The remaining Norscya rider came up, broadsword swinging, and Vitali turned to meet him. The lancer's slender sabre would surely break at once under the weight of the Kurgan's heavy, straight blade.

Vitali was nimble. It was pleasing to watch. He ducked under the striking sword, came back up, and struck to the rear. The edge of his curved sword sliced into the back of the rider's neck, under the lip of his barbute. The Norther's horse carried him away into the misty woods, the man's body lolling from side to side in the saddle.

A horn blew, close and sharp in the forest confines.

Eight winged lancers, led by Vaja and Beledni, came cantering into the glade, kicking water in all directions. They had javelins in their hands as they drew up in a line beside Vitali and Gerlach. The remaining Kurgan, all on foot, backed away around the bole of an ancient oak, threatening with their boar-spears.

'Yhta!' Beledni ordered from behind his heart-shaped visor.

The lancers threw their weapons.

The cornered Norscya died, most of them pinned to the tree bole and roots by the narrow lances.

'I warn rota!' Vaja announced proudly to Gerlach.

Gerlach acknowledged this with a grunt. Vitali splashed his mare up alongside Gerlach and held out his hand. Gerlach took it. The lancer smiled and nodded. He said nothing, because he knew he didn't have the vocabulary, but the meaning was clear.

'Rotamaster!' one of the lancers cried out.

Gerlach turned.

The snake-horned leader was rising to his feet. He was spattered in clay, and his scale armour coat showed a dent where Gerlach's firearm had struck it. Gerlach wheeled his gelding round.

'Nyeh!' Beledni called out, holding off a hand sideways to block Gerlach. He looked round at the demilancer and shook his head.

'Nyeh. Savat nyor Norscya gylyve,' he said, but Gerlach had no clue as to his meaning.

Beledni dismounted.

The lancers drew back, leading Beledni's scraggy mare with them.

The Kurgan leader had produced a long, double-edged pallasz, and stood his ground on the far bank, defiantly.

Beledni took off the slim Kislevite sabre he wore around his waist and handed it to Vaja. Patting his horse around, he reached to the saddle and slipped out the long, straight length of a shashka. Gerlach saw now that most of the lancers carried a slim, curved sabre at their belt, and a long, straight sword in a scabbard about their saddles. A saddle weapon for use when horse warfare was done; a weapon to draw on foot. Beledni's shashka was every bit as long as the Kurgan's pallasz. It had a wide, straight pair of quillons, and a looped iron bar that curled back to the pommel to surround the owner's hand. The pallasz was triple-fullered right down its length, and had an ornate cage of curled bars guarding the user's fist.

Rotamaster Beledni splashed across the stream bed, dark mud spattering up around the shins of his knee boots. He held his shashka upright with his right hand, his left around the pommel.

The Kurgan warlord was waiting for him on the far bank, sword down.

Beledni was big and squat, but his enemy was wider and far taller. Gerlach sensed that a much larger, fitter man than the rotamaster lurked inside the thorny black plate. He tensed. There was clearly some ritual honour thing going on. Leader to leader. Maybe even something that he had provoked himself by failing to kill the Kurgan lord cleanly, or simply by dint of him just being there. Beledni seemed to think he owed Gerlach for salvaging the rota's banner. Maybe this unwise single combat was Beledni's way of making things even.

The lancers seemed content to watch. Gerlach began re-priming his pistol. He would not have the rotamaster's death on his conscience too.

There was a resounding clang. Gerlach looked up from his wheel-lock. Beledni and the snake-horned leader had begun. Straight sword against straight sword. They circled, exchanging cuts, causing sparks.

It was over very fast.

The Kurgan hammered a good slice at Beledni, and the Kislevite parried, tossing the cut aside and opening his adversary's guard. Beledni put both arms into the next swing.

Gerlach knew it was going to be a deathblow. What he hadn't counted on was the force that old Beledni could muster. The shashka tore through the neck of the close helm, popping out rivets as the plates deformed. He sliced the entire skull away. Like a cannonball, the skull, encased in articulated metal capped by the twined snake horns, flew off into the bracken.

The headless Kurgan collapsed like a felled tree and made a sound like a dozen dropped cymbals.

'Gospodarinyi! Gospodarinyi!' Beledni shouted, raising both arms and shaking his bloodied shashka. He turned to face his cheering men.

'Gospodarinyi!'

IV

WHEN THE MEN had stopped whooping and slapping him on the back, Beledni issued a curt order for them to return to the rota. The lancers recovered their javelins, washing the sticky tips and hafts in the stream, but made no effort to touch or move the enemy dead. They seemed to shun them, in fact. There was no searching the bodies for trophies or coins or rings. Men of the Empire would have at least thrown the dead into a ditch or gully or, if circumstance permitted, burned them. But the Kislevites just left them to bloat and wither and decay in the glade.

But then, just before they rode away, Beledni and Vitali went to the corpses one by one and put out their eyes with their dagger tips. Beledni had to search in the bracken to find the head he had taken off to do the same to it.

It occurred to Gerlach Heileman this was a strangely bestial thing to do.

They rode up the file to find the body of the rota. Gerlach rode behind Beledni, who was chatting in a low voice to the tall, thin lancer with the scar on his high cheekbone. This man's name, Gerlach gathered, was Maksim, and he was one of Beledni's most senior, trusted men.

They were discussing the Northers – Gerlach overheard the word 'Norscya' several times.

'There are more around?' he asked interrupting.

'Shto?' They glanced back at him.

'More Northeranders? Norscya?'

Maksim seemed amused by Gerlach's badly accented use of the Kislevite word.

'Nyeh,' Beledni said with a shake of his head. 'Not so much, I think.'

'What about those we faced back there? They must have been following us for days.'

'Nyeh, Vebla, nyeh,' Beledni assured him. 'For day, maybe, not long more. Norscya pulk go on horse, many men, south. Rich lands there.'

Indeed. The more civilised provinces of Kislev. The Empire. Beledni seemed to suppose that the Kurgan were so intent on the south that they wouldn't waste men or time pursuing a small company like the rota east.

'But what about the ones back there?' Gerlach insisted.

'Kyazak,' said Maksim.

'What?'

'Raiders,' said Maksim, turning his attention back to the trail ahead as if his word explained everything.

The rest of the rota was waiting for them on the saddle of a grassy hill above the forest line. One lancer had Demieter's horse in tow.

The daylight was beginning to fade. When they crested the hill, Gerlach saw a great plain stretching out before them. An unbroken territory of grass, gorse and thistle that rolled away towards a far-off line of dim hills. The steppe grasslands of the mighty oblast.

Beledni circled his hand. They would rest here for the night before starting off across the steppe.

Gerlach dismounted and sat down in the grass. He knew he should see to Saksen, ease the gelding's saddle, rub him down. But he felt very weak suddenly. In less than a minute, he was asleep.

V

WHEN HE WOKE, it was dark and warm. Night had fallen, glass-clear, and in the sky above the hillside, a multitude of stars glittered. Someone shook his shoulder gently, and he realised that was what had woken him.

He sat up. He was lying precisely where he had sat down. Someone had thrown a cloak over him. A large fire was crackling not too far away, and it threw out a pleasant heat. Around its jumping glow, Gerlach could see the figures of men, and what seemed to be small tents.

Vitali was crouched down next to him. He had removed his helmet, hauberk and wings, and was wearing a shabby velvet coat with cut-out sleeves that he'd thrown back over his shoulders to expose arms clad in a wool undershirt. He was offering a little wooden bowl to the vexillary. Steam rose from it. The smell of hot food made Gerlach's mouth flood with saliva and his belly ache and churn.

He took the bowl. In it were some lumps of meat mixed with stewed grains in an oily wet hash. It smelled amazingly good.

Vitali beckoned him to join the figures at the fire.

'You come, Vebla. You come to krug.'

Gerlach carried the bowl over to the ring of figures round the fire. The heat was quite intense on his face, and the smoke from the wood and spitted meat was thick. He sat down, with Vitali on his right. To his left was a thickset man in his thirties, who was already eating from a bowl with his bare fingers.

Gerlach started to scoop and eat. He had no idea what meat it was, but it was delicious. He realised he had been days without food. He was quickly wiping the empty bowl with his oily fingertips. His lips shone with grease.

There was a low conversation going on round the fire. All the men had removed their armour and put on coats and furs, so that they once more resembled the ragged barbarians he had first seen. All of them were eating. Cook pots and spitted haunches of meat were standing around the edges of the fire.

The man on his left, who had also emptied his bowl, took Gerlach over to the fireside and showed him how they could fill their bowls for more.

The meat was fresh. Hare or perhaps some small buck. Some of the men had evidently been busy as they rode through the forest, taking game and gathering wood. Near the fire, one of the Kislevites was splitting boughs with a small hand-axe. He took wood from the heap piled up to feed the flames.

Gerlach resumed his place in the circle and gobbled down his second bowlful. As he ate, he watched the sparks fly up. Invisible heat rippled in the cold air above the camp, distorting some of the stars.

By the time he had finished the second bowl, he felt tired. He sat back, uncomfortable and hot, and so stripped off his half-armour piece by piece, piling it up behind his back. He settled against it, feeling every ache and bruise and cut and graze on his weary body soothed by the heat and the warmth of food in his gut.

Drinking skins were passing around the krug circle. The men were swigging and handing them on to the man on their right. The heavy man took a deep drink, smacked his lips and pushed the skin to Gerlach.

'Starovye!' he said.

Gerlach thought for a moment that it was the man's name, but realised it was a toast or hail. He took the skin, raised it to the man and said, 'Health to you!'

'Starovye!' the man repeated.

'Starovye,' Gerlach agreed, and took a drink.

It was sweet and thick, with a sour taste of old, tepid milk, but it was strong and he felt its burn immediately.

'It's good,' Gerlach nodded.

'Yha. Koumiss,' the man replied. 'Koumiss, good for soul.'

Gerlach handed the skin to Vitali.

'Health to–' he began, then corrected himself. 'Starovye.'

'Starovye, Vebla!' Vitali returned with a broad smile full of his small, even teeth. He added something more in Kislevite, but Gerlach didn't understand.

'Vitali,' Vitali said, more slowly, pointing to himself. 'Vebla,' he pointed to Gerlach. 'Do war good together. Do war on kyazak.' He took a drink and passed the koumiss on.

'My name is Gerlach Heileman,' Gerlach said.

'Shto?'

Gerlach patted his own chest. 'Gerlach.'

'Shto? Nyeh Vebla?'

'No. Nyeh. Gerlach.'

Vitali pouted thoughtfully as he considered this, then shrugged.

'What does "kyazak" mean?' Gerlach asked.

'Kyazak, yha!' Vitali said, waiting for more.

'What does it mean?'

'Shto?'

'What does "kyazak" mean?'

Vitali looked helpless.

'Uh… shto kyazak?' Gerlach tried.

'Ah! Is… is… ummm…' Vitali screwed up his face. He looked past Gerlach at the thickset man.

'Mitri!' he called, then asked something in Kislevite. Gerlach caught the words 'kyazak' and 'impyrinyi'.

Mitri thought about it. 'Means… raider,' he said, his voice gruff and deep.

'They're all raiders,' Gerlach said. 'All Norscya… raiders.'

'Nyeh,' said Mitri. 'Raiders… kyazak… small numbers. Hunt for own. Not part of Norscya pulk.'

He explained some more. Gerlach realised that 'kyazak' had a specific meaning that 'raiders' did not convey. The kyazak were reavers, freebooting bands who moved at the edges of the main host, raiding for spoils. He'd never thought about it before, even though men of the Empire talked of the Northern tribes. The North wasn't one unified place, and the Northers were not a single race. They migrated south en masse, but only because they shared a common hunger for land and loot. They had no formal military organisation like the Empire. This made it all the more extraordinary that they could operate as a unified host, as they had at Zhedevka.

What alloyed them into one mass, Gerlach wondered, what dread force?

Muzzy now, and half asleep, he reclined by the fire and watched the activity around the ring. Some men were repairing helms or hauberks, using the pommels of their daggers as hammers. Others were adjusting and dressing the feathers that attached to their wood-frame wings. Two men were singing a long, slow song of strange, entwined harmonies. The skins of koumiss circled the ring.

Gerlach suddenly remembered his horse and sprang up. He was unsteady on his feet for a moment. The drink had either been stronger than he had thought, or it had taken a firm hold on his weak, empty system.

'Vebla?' Vitali called after him.

Gerlach walked away from the fire. It was dark, and much colder away from the flames. He'd stripped off his armour and mail shirt, and now his linen undershirt and felt coat clung cold and wet to his clammy body.

The lancers had pitched tents around the fire. As he walked amongst them, he saw they were simple structures. Each man had made a tripod out of his lance and two javelins, and artfully hooked his cloak or saddle blanket over it. He could hear the horses, and smell them, but the cold clear darkness was absolute.

'Vebla?' Vitali approached, carrying a bough that he'd lit from the fire.

'My horse,' Gerlach said. 'I didn't see to it. And it was running lame…'

Vitali shrugged.

'My horse?'

Vitali took him by the sleeve and led him down a slope. The horses had been corralled in a ring of gorse, though only Saksen and Demieter's mount had been tied up. The steppe horses grazed together obediently.

There was a light amongst the horses. As they came closer, they saw it was a little tallow lamp.

Gerlach could see two lancers from the company, stripped to the waist and sweating from their exertions, rubbing down the horses with handfuls of grass. An older man, in a long beshmet tunic, stooped in the lamp light, fixing a mare's shoe with deft taps of a small steel hammer.

'Borodyn!' Vitali hissed.

The man finished the job and carried his weak lamp over. It was a little pottery dish with a wick.

Vitali explained something to the man in Kislevite.

He raised his lamp to study Gerlach. Borodyn's own face was old and weather-beaten.

He took Gerlach to Saksen. The gelding, and Demieter's troop horse, had been unharnessed and rubbed down. Borodyn lifted Saksen's forefoot and showed Gerlach where he had reshod the lame foot, and applied salve to the sore hoof.

While Gerlach had slept, his horse had been cared for like one of the Kislevites' own.

'Borodyn, he master horse,' Vitali said.

'My comrade Vitali means "horse master",' said Borodyn. 'It is my honour to hold that noble post, and be master of metal also for the rota.'

His accent was thick, but he spoke Gerlach's native tongue very well.

Both Vitali and Borodyn saw the look of surprise on Gerlach's face. Vitali laughed.

'Borodyn has learning much!' he chuckled.

'Go back to the krug, man of the Empire,' said Borodyn softly. 'You need as much rest as Saksen.'

Gerlach nodded, and allowed himself to be drawn back up the slope by Vitali.

He stopped suddenly, and looked back.

'How did you know my horse's name?' he called out.

But Borodyn had gone back to his work and did not reply.

VI

BY THE TIME they had returned to the heat of the fire, the lancers had become more lively. Drink was still circulating, and the songs were faster and more robust. Several men were singing now, and one was accompanying them on a small wooden instrument like a shrunken lute. His fingers flashed as they plucked a rapid melody, and the instrument's strings gave out a hard, brittle chime. Two men were beating time on upturned cook pots. A few were dancing around the fire in circles and clapping.

Gerlach and Vitali sat back down, and Vaja joined them, with another young lancer called Kvetlai. They drank some more koumiss as it came by. Gerlach was feeling profoundly warm and sleepy.

'What are they singing?' he asked.

Between themselves, hoping to make the maximum amount of sense through a joint effort, Vitali and Vaja endeavoured to explain. They took a few words each, back and forth, comically repeating each other and overlapping. Vitali's command of Gerlach's language was far better than he realised. Young Vaja's, who kept correcting Vitali, was far, far worse than he believed. Kvetlai, who knew no Reikspiel at all, sat and watched.

The men, they explained, were giving thanks to the gods. To Ursun, the Bear Father, for protection. To Dazh, for the fire. To Tor, for victory.

Gerlach began to doze. Breathing deeply, he asked another question. 'The kyazaks. Why did you take their eyes?'

It took Vitali and Vaja a while to make sense of this. Then Vitali replied.

'Is to blind them, yha?'

'But they were dead.'

'Nyeh. Not spirits of men. Spirits will come. Angry. Looking here, looking there, looking everywhere to find men who kill them. Vitali want it to be hard thing for spirits to find him, yha?'

Gerlach laughed, and despite the heat of the flames, he shivered and touched the iron of his belt buckle as a charm.

* * *

VII

THE SPIRITS CAME for him late in the night. They came out of the forest like smoke, oozing between the black trunks, hissing the leaves. They boiled as vapour up the slope of the hill, and their passing distressed the horses in the corral.

The camp was asleep, but the fire still blazed high. Gerlach stood and watched the ghosts foam through the darkness towards him. They left frost on the grass in their tracks. They were moaning like a distant wind, groping with filmy white hands to find him, their eyes bloody holes in their white, drawn faces.

Gerlach wondered how he could fight them. His sword would not cut what was not there.

They loomed around him, a silver mist in the form of lean figures. They chided him, in sibilant whispers, for leaving them dead on the bloodstained ground.

He looked at their faces: the open mouths, the voided eye sockets, the sunken cheeks.

He knew them.

Meinhart Stouer, Sebold Truchs, Johann Friedel, Herman Volks, Hans Odamar, Karl Reiner Vollen...

VIII

HE WOKE WITH a start, cold with sweat. He was on the grass of the hill slope. The fire had died off to a meagre flicker. Men slumbered all around.

It was deathly cold. In the east, the first glimmer of dawn was stretching over the sky.

Gerlach tugged his cloak around him and tried to find sleep again.

IX

A BONE HORN was blowing a long, hard note. Gerlach stirred, and hearing it a second time, staggered to his feet. It was daylight. The fire was out and kicked over. Even the charred bones of the night's supper had gone. The tents had disappeared. He was alone by the circle of ash.

The horn wailed again. Presuming an attack, he gathered up his armour and stumbled towards the brow of the hill.

The rota had assembled on the steppe below. They stood by their horses, dressed in their furs and rags, their armour packed in bundles on the backs of their wooden saddles. The horn blower was astride his mare, head tilted back, blowing long notes into the early morning air. The eagle wing banner fluttered in the light wind off the steppes.

Beyond the rota, the sun was rising above the grassland. The sky was a diluted red, like blood in water, and the swaying grasses had turned russet and pink in the new light. Everything was still except the twitch of horse tails, the flutter of the banner and the waving motion of the endless grass. On the horizon, the distant hills were a jagged purple stripe.

Gerlach ran down the slope, stopping frequently to gather up the pieces of armour he dropped. Beledni saw him, and turned to beckon him close.

'What is this?' Gerlach asked.

'Is sunrise. Is time for goings,' said the rotamaster.

'Why didn't you wake me?' Gerlach asked, angry. Beledni shrugged. The bone horn blew again, saluting the low sun.

'We say farewell,' Beledni said.

'What? Why? Where are you going?'

Beledni shook his head and then smiled sadly and pointed. At the front of the assembled rota, Demieter's shroud-wrapped body lay over his horse's saddle.

'You say farewell, Vebla?' Beledni asked.

'What do you mean? I don't understand…'

'What his name?' Beledni asked, pointing to Demieter's corpse again.

'Kaus Demieter… but…'

Beledni raised his head and shouted out a brief but heartfelt declaration in Kislevite. The name 'Kaus Demieter' appeared amongst the alien words.

Beledni finished. The horn blew once more. Maksim smacked his hand across the rump of Demieter's gelding, and the horse took off, galloping into the grassland, the swathed body over its saddle bouncing and jerking with the motion.

'No!' Gerlach cried. 'No, what are you doing?' He threw down his armour pieces in a clatter and ran down after the departing horse, scrambling through the long grasses.

He would never catch it now.

He fell to his knees.

'It is good. A great honour,' said Borodyn, walking up behind him. 'A steppe funeral. The rota does great respect to your friend.'

Gerlach looked up at him. 'This is a joke!' he blurted. 'Kaus should have been buried with full rights from a cleric of Morr! What the hell is this? You cut his horse loose and forget about him?'

Borodyn shrugged. 'He was a horseman, yes?'

'An Imperial demilancer!' Gerlach snarled.

'Then he would want to ride. Ride forever, chasing Dazh's sky fire. Why would you wish him trapped in the clay where he is not free?'

Gerlach took a last look at the receding horse. It had almost vanished into the unbroken flatness of the grassland.

'You're heathen barbarians,' he told Borodyn. 'Heathen bloody barbarians!'

He strode back up the hillside through the rota. Borodyn patiently followed him.

Beledni was about to get on his horse.

'Rotamaster!' Gerlach shouted. 'I insist we ride for Choika or another Lynsk crossing!'

Beledni removed his raised foot from its stirrup and turned to face the vexillary.

'Nyeh,' he said.

'Don't "nyeh" me, you barbarian! I'm a demilancer! An Imperial demilancer vexillary! Sworn to the service of his Holiness Karl Franz! I will not ignore that oath and gallop blithely into the north or the east! The enemy is moving south! The enemy! The Norscya!'

Beledni shrugged. 'And what we do, Vebla?'

'Stop calling me that! You will address me as Sire Heileman! We have a duty… to… to Kislev and to the Empire! This is the hour of need! Why are we running?'

It took a long moment for Beledni to translate the gist of this in his head. 'Rota rides,' he said finally, pointing out eastwards across the steppe. 'You come.'

'You are an auxiliary unit of the Empire's defence and your duty is to–'

Beledni cut him off with an impatient wave of his gloved hand. He looked at Borodyn, who translated quickly in Kislevite.

Beledni nodded. 'Duty. Is funny thing,' he said.

'Is simple thing, you dullard! What are you, a coward?'

Borodyn, grim in his long beshmet, began to translate, but Beledni shushed him.

The rotamaster had a reproachful look in his eyes as he squinted at Gerlach. 'Coward?'

'What?'

'You call me "coward", Vebla?'

'If you ride into the east… yes.'

There was a murmur from the rota around them, delayed in places as men translated for their comrades.

Beledni tutted and took off his right glove. He handed it, and his riding crop, to Borodyn.

Then he punched Gerlach in the face.

Gerlach fell on his arse, blood weeping from his nose. He rolled and cursed.

'You not insult Beledni rotamaster,' Beledni said, taking back his glove and putting it on again.

Gerlach got up, and threw himself at the stout Kislevite.

They went over together on the grassy slope. Gerlach had a grip on Beledni's top knot, and the rotamaster was clawing at Gerlach's face. He had a finger in Gerlach's mouth, dragging his head aside. Gerlach bit down, and as Beledni yelped and yanked his hand back, he threw a punch that smacked Beledni's cheek. Struggling together, they began to roll down the slope. Beledni kneed Gerlach in the ribs, but the demilancer punched him in the eye.

At the foot of the slope, amid the long swishing grass of the oblast, they separated and sprang up. The men of the rota were following them down, clapping and chanting Beledni's name.

Face to face now, on foot. Punch answered by punch. They circled, jabbing and heaving at one another. Blood and spittle flew from every solid hit. Beledni was formidable, strong as a bear with a low centre of gravity. But Gerlach had huge upper body strength. He was a vexillary. He had been trained to hold the heavy standard aloft for hours.

Gerlach punched Beledni in the mouth and then the ribs. Beledni recovered and snapped Gerlach's head round with a savage hook. The men formed a circle around them in the bent and trampled grass, clapping.

Gerlach took a punch to his shoulder and then to his ear. He jabbed Beledni hard in the throat, and then dealt a massive blow that knocked the older man onto his back. Gerlach threw himself onto Beledni's sprawled frame, his right hand pressed flat across Beledni's face. He rammed his head back into the flinty ground.

Beledni's hand closed on Gerlach's throat. It wasn't a tight grip, but Gerlach instinctively knew that if Beledni chose so, a simple flick would crush his windpipe. He sat back, astride Beledni.

His face bruised and bloody, Beledni glared up at Gerlach. Both were fighting for breath.

'Is man with spear,' Beledni rasped. 'Is other man with spear. They fight. One spear breaks.'

'What?' panted Gerlach.

'Is story, Vebla. One spear breaks. One man has only point of spear left. Other man still has whole spear. So…'

'So what?'

'So… does man with spear tip attack man with whole spear from front, or from back?'

Gerlach got off the sprawled rotamaster, unsteady on his feet. He staggered aside in the grass and spat blood and phlegm. His face was throbbing. It felt twice its normal size. He sunk over, his hands braced on his thighs.

Some of the rota helped Beledni upright. His face was puffy. A dark shadow circled his left eye and his mouth was seeping blood.

'Well? Answer?' Beledni coughed.

Gerlach shook his head and spat more thick blood.

'Point of spear only. Front or back?'

Gerlach rose and turned to face the gasping, battered rotamaster.

'Back,' he said.

Beledni smiled a bloody, gap-toothed smile and nodded. 'Rota will ride east,' he announced.

Beledni shambled over to Gerlach, smiling still.

'Vebla strong man,' he admitted.

Wheezing and hoarse, Gerlach shrugged.

Beledni swung a huge punch that laid Gerlach out in the grass and made him see only flashing, revolving stars.

'Vebla never call Beledni rotamaster coward again.'

* * *

X

VAJA AND VITALI gathered Gerlach up and shouldered him over to where Saksen was saddled and waiting. Gerlach retched blood, and spat out a piece of tooth.

They tried to dress him in his armour, but he shook them off and sat down, so they wrapped his wargear up in a cloak and lashed it securely to the back of Saksen's saddle in the Kislev manner.

Vaja took off his shabby beshmet and handed it to Gerlach.

'That's yours,' Gerlach said, refusing the dirty velvet coat.

'Vaja has another,' Vaja said.

Gerlach pulled the smelly coat around his shoulders.

Borodyn appeared and crouched down to face Gerlach.

Without words, he grasped Gerlach's head and turned his face to examine it. He pulled open Gerlach's mouth and looked inside, fingering the bloody teeth like he was a horse at market. Then he pulled Gerlach's eyes open wide and stared into them.

'You will live, Vebla,' he announced.

Gerlach snorted. Even snorting hurt.

Borodyn produced a small clay pot of greasy goo from the folds of his cherchesska. 'Smear on bruises. It will help.'

Gerlach took the pot and got up.

'Beledni is impressed,' said the horse master.

'Good,' said Gerlach. 'But we're still heading east.'

'North-east,' corrected the old man. 'To Dushyka. Maybe there.'

'Maybe there what?' Gerlach asked.

Borodyn shrugged.

The horn blew again, and the men of the rota climbed into their saddles. Putting on Vaja's beshmet, Gerlach mounted Saksen.

The rota advanced, at a rising canter, down the slope and into the nodding grass ocean of the oblast, following their banner.

XI

THEY WERE SOON galloping, scything a trampled line through the whispering grass behind them. The further they rode, the more distant the hills ahead of them seemed to become. Gerlach had never known a flat space so vast.

'Where is this Dushyka?' he shouted to Borodyn as the horse master drew level with him, standing in the stirrups over his black mare.

'Three days!' Borodyn shouted back.

'But where?'

'Out there!' Borodyn pointed. 'The oblast!'

For the first time, Gerlach realised that the Kislev idea of territory and distance was utterly different from the Empire approach. They thought nothing of distances so vast that you couldn't see the destination. They simply trusted their noses and rode into infinity.

Saksen was galloping true and hard, without a hint of lameness. Ahead, the horn blew for the sheer joy of being blown, loud and into the wind. The men of the rota sent up a cry.

'What did they say?' Gerlach shouted over at Borodyn.

'They make the war cry of the rota,' Borodyn shouted to him.

'Which is what?'

'It is... Riders of the Dead!'

'What does that mean?'

'It means me and Beledni and all of us. And you,' Borodyn yelled. 'We are Yetchitch krug. We are the Riders of the Dead!'

TCHAR

I

His name was Skarkeetah. The stress fell upon the first syllable of his name when it was spoken. *Skar*keetah. The Kurgan held him in awe. He was above the common rabble and filth. A man of consequence. He was the slave broker.

He appeared first out of the lingering smoke that toiled around the ruins of Zhedevka. Drums announced his approach, then cymbals. Out of the waft, thirteen horse warriors from the bitter north, their plated armour silver with a wash of pink. They held their long-bladed lances high and straight. They had whips and wound lariats hooked on their saddles.

Then the children – none of them into their second decade – danced and capered. They were painted blue from head to foot, and clanged wide bronze cymbals.

Then came a curtained litter of massive construction, painted maroon, with gold leaf and buttons of pearl hammered on its hafts, and black silk drapes floating around its frame. Twenty shaved and sweating men in skirts of fur and mail carried it along. On either side of it rode a drummer on a white ass, slowly thumping on the broad kettle drum that was slung over his saddle.

Behind the litter rode Hinn.

Hinn was the slave broker's bodyguard and companion. He was quite the biggest man Karl Vollen had ever seen. His shoulders were like oak stumps and his biceps were as thick around as most men's thighs. He wore leggings of grey wolfskin, belted by a heavy leather band with a large gold boss. Waist upwards, he was naked, his extravagant muscles oiled and scraped. A mantle of feathers lay around his neck. The feathers were turquoise with black tips and each was the length of a man's forearm. Hinn wore a close-helm of gold, worked to resemble the head of a gigantic stork or heron. The crown of the helm seemed outlandishly tall and pointed. Huge iron ram's horns sprouted from the helm and curled over so far that the tips pointed at his shoulders. Hinn had a brace of pallaszs, one on each side of his saddle.

The captives had been driven out of their pike pens into the open, and stood in a loose huddle. In the distance, across the fields, they could see the mounds of trophy skulls they had been forced to erect.

At a word from Hinn, the slaves set the litter down.

Skarkeetah dragged back the black silk curtain of his litter and stepped out. He was a plump man with watery eyes and a straw-coloured beard. The crown of his head was entirely shaved, except for a patch behind his right ear from which grew a heavy, tight plait of blond hair. He wore a long, plain shift of astonishingly clean, white linen over white trews. His only decoration was a heavy gold amulet that hung around his neck on a wide chain and it thumped against his chest as he moved. The amulet was the size of a man's palm. There was probably more gold in that one piece than in the state crown of any elector count. It was shaped like a single staring eye that emerged from an interwoven circle of snakes. The pupil of the eye was set with a twinkling blue stone.

It made Karl queasy to look at it. Many of the captives around him uttered low moans of dread when Skarkeetah appeared.

It was the fifth day after the Zhedevka slaughter, but the pall of smoke that clung to the countryside was so insidious and thick that little daylight had been seen in that time. None of the captives had eaten, and the only water they had taken had been rain. More had died, especially in the last day or so. The cage pasture stank of putrefaction.

Skarkeetah faced the wretched, shivering mass of prisoners, and raised his plump hands into the air. When he splayed the fat fingers, he revealed a staring eye tattooed in blue on each palm.

'Tchar!' he cried out. The word made Karl shudder, and a general ripple of apprehension and revulsion passed around the prisoners. At the sound of the word, the Kurgan warriors waiting all around howled in approval and clattered their blades and shafts against their shields.

'Tchar!' Skarkeetah yelled again, his hands still raised. Rooks and carrion birds had been circling the field since the battle, and now – chillingly – they stopped clacking and cawing and flocked down, settling all over the litter, and on the puddled clay, and all about the slave broker's feet. One perched on the left horn of Hinn's golden helmet. Half a dozen came down to roost on Skarkeetah's outspread arms. They fluttered and bobbed. Skarkeetah turned his head from one side to the other, smiling and cooing soft, inhuman words at them.

'Sigmar bless us all,' Brezzin whispered to Karl. 'We are in the presence of a daemon.'

Skarkeetah lowered his arms, and the birds hopped down onto the ground – except one, an old, ragged raven with one clouded eye, which remained on his left shoulder, chattering its dagger-like beak.

The slave lord called out instructions to his bodyguard. The plate-armoured warriors dismounted, and trudged into the prisoner mass, jostling and cracking their whips. There was a method to their work. The guards took each prisoner in turn, grabbing him by the chin, and examining his face. Then, depending on what they saw, they pushed the prisoners away either to the left or to the right.

Most men went to the left, to the Kurgan warriors waiting to corral them with ropes and spears. One in every ten was shoved to the right, where Skarkeetah waited. These few were marshaled at spear-point into a line by Hinn and a handful of Kurgans.

The drummers had dismounted. They came over to the slave lord carrying bundles of wooden staves wound together in animal hides. The litter bearers, having set down their heavy burden, busied themselves setting up a small iron brazier and an anvil, both of which they produced from a casket-box mounted at the front of the litter frame. They dragged great lengths of black iron chain and fetters from the casket too, and brought them over by the armful to the brazier. The blue-stained children tossed down their cymbals and began to play around the litter.

The drummers rolled out the hides on the ground and laid the staves out along them in neat rows. Each stave was a rod of dark wood the length of a man's arm with one side planed flat. Every one had a distinguishing knot of tassels and feathers at its top end. The drummers drew fat-bladed dirks and sharpened them on whetstones from their pockets.

By now, the brazier was flaming brightly.

The bodyguard moved roughly through the crowd of prisoners, checking each one and determining their fate. They came closer to the huddle where Karl stood with von Margur and Brezzin. Karl could smell them. Cloves, oil and a deeper reek of corruption. The pink tinge to their silver plate armour was the stain of human blood.

Whips cracked and men shrieked.

One of the bodyguard reached von Margur. He gripped the blind knight's jaw so hard that von Margur cried out in surprise. The warrior twisted the knight's face to one side, then the other, and then pushed him, stumbling, towards Skarkeetah.

The bodyguard checked two more, thrusting them away to the left and the waiting Kurgan mob. He came to Karl.

Karl's spine jolted as the brute took hold of his chin and yanked his head left and right. The vice of the mailed hand was cold and unyielding.

The bodyguard grumbled something behind his silver visor and cuffed Karl in the direction of the slave lord.

Karl looked back. Brezzin had just been examined. The bodyguard was pushing the hefty powderman away to the left. Brezzin was protesting. He looked imploringly at Karl, utterly lost.

'Lad!' he called. 'Lad!' Cursing, the bodyguard drove Brezzin back.
'Brezzin!' Karl called after him.
'Sigmar watches over you, lad!' Brezzin shouted as he was dragged away. 'Remember that! Sigmar will watch over you!'

The bodyguard's whip snapped out like a pistol shot and Brezzin yelped. Then he disappeared in the jostling throng.

Karl felt shockingly alone then. The iron tongues of spears menaced him and drove him into the line.

Von Margur was two places in front of him, standing unsteady and confused. Karl realised that every man in the queue had a pin mark on his cheek. Some had three green dots like von Margur. Others had two black dots or three red ones in a line or three blue ones in a triangle. They had all been marked by zars.

Skarkeetah was moving down the line, studying each captive's mark. With each one, he called out something to the drummers, and one or the other used his dirk to scrape a notch on one of the staves.

'Zar Blayda!'
A notch.
'Zar Herfil!'
A notch.
'Zar Skolt!'
A notch.
'Zar Herfil!'
Another notch.

Sometimes, the plump slave lord would pause longer with a prisoner and converse with him in soft tones that did not carry. When he was done with each one, the prisoners were herded over to the braziers where the litter bearers were busy. Karl could hear the *tink-tink-tink* of metal worked on an anvil, and he could smell hot iron and the steam of a plunge-pail.

Skarkeetah had come to von Margur.

'Zar Blayda!' he declared, and this was scored on the appropriate rod by the drummers. Skarkeetah turned his head on one side and studied the shivering knight, who was gazing off into nothingness.

'You're a fine one,' Skarkeetah told von Margur. 'Tchar has you already. Bending you to shape.'

'I am a spurred and sworn knight of Karl Franz, may his majesty shine for ever, great is his radiance,' von Margur recited, his voice wavering. 'You will have no hold over me, daemon. Yea, though I walk beneath the Shadow of Chaos I shall fear no–'

'Be silent,' said the slave lord. 'You have no idea where you are or what you are about to become. Tchar will show you real radiance. Tchar will untwist your fibres and allow you to see. You are blessed, and you do not yet know it.'

'I am a spurred and sworn knight of Karl Franz...' von Margur began to repeat, faltering.

'No, sir,' said Skarkeetah. 'You are a possession of Zar Blayda, and a vessel for the cyclops lord of serpents. Wonders beyond your feeble imagining await you.'

'You lie,' von Margur said, his voice a tiny, quiet thing.

'Alas,' said the slave lord, 'that is the one thing I never do. Move him on.'

The Kurgan bundled von Margur towards the brazier.

'Zar Kreyya!' Skarkeetah said, looking over the next man in line. 'Zar Logar!' he instructed at the next.

He came to Karl.

Skarkeetah took hold of Karl's face in his pudgy fingers and then suddenly snapped back.

'Oohhh!' he murmured, gazing at Karl. The bedraggled, one-eyed raven on his shoulder danced and chattered. 'Oohhh, but aren't you a fine thing?' Skarkeetah said in admiration. 'I thought that blind knight would be the pick of the bunch for this haul, but you... you excel even him.'

Karl said nothing.

'Zar Uldin!' Skarkeetah shouted over his shoulder. He looked back at Karl.

'Blue eyes. A perfect sign. Tchar flows in your blood.'

Karl remained resolutely silent, his lips clamped shut.

'What's your name, chosen one?'

Karl closed his eyes. Skarkeetah laughed, a long, throaty chuckle.

'Blue. Like the sky. Blue, like the mutable truth of Tchar.'

Karl opened his eyes and saw Skarkeetah's amulet. The slave lord was holding it up in front of Karl's face. Light glanced off its twisted loop of entwined gold snakes and glimmered in the heart of the blue stone set in the eye.

It was very blue. Deep blue. Deep as an ocean. Deep as a chasm.

Karl spat on the amulet. The Kurgan around hissed in dismay.

Skarkeetah lifted the heavy god amulet and deliberately licked Karl's spittle off it. Then he let go of it and allowed it to thud back against his pure white shift.

The one-eyed raven bounced and clacked.

Skarkeetah slid his hands up behind Karl's head and folded them together. Slowly, he bent Karl's head down. The slave lord kissed him on the cheek. Holding him close, brow to brow, Skarkeetah whispered, 'Tchar has a special place for you. You'll resist at first, but you will come to adore it. I envy you that closeness.'

He let go. Karl yanked his head back, revolted.

Skarkeetah smiled. 'Move him on!' he cried.

The Kurgan jostled Karl up to the brazier. One of the litter bearers was taking white-hot iron pegs from the flames with a set of pincers. They forced Karl's left leg up onto the anvil and clamped a fetter around it. Another swarthy litter bearer hammered the brass cuff closed with one of the hot pegs. Karl was now shackled to the man in front by a two-span length of chain. A similar length of iron links trailed back, waiting to connect with the next captive.

'Zar Skolt!' Skarkeetah called. Another notch. Another beat of the hammer on hot iron.

II

A PACK OF Kurgan marched the marked and chosen away from Zhedevka. The captives had to fall into step because their ankles were linked by the clinking chains. Walking out of step caused them to trip and fall. Karl was forced to adopt a halting, shambling gait, the cuff of the fetter heavy around his ankle.

The sky was smeared with smoke, and for a while Karl believed the Kurgan were leading them east.

But then they came to a river, and a broad timber bridge raised out of the water on five stone piers. They trudged across it, their feet thumping the timber boards. Some of the captives spat to avert misfortune.

It was the crossing above Choika. Karl recognised it. The last time he had crossed it, the vexillary's spit had splashed his cuirass.

He wondered, briefly, what might have become of arrogant young Gerlach Heileman. Dead, no doubt, on the smouldering fields around Zhedevka.

They tramped on. Once in a while, they had to get off the track to allow a Norther brigade to pass. Horned, black warriors at full gallop.

They came to an ashy, smoky place where the vague ruins of buildings sat in the wash of smoke and soft rain.

Karl saw a stone basin he recognised. They were in Choika, the burnt remains of Choika.

The Kurgan herded them out along the southern road. Bullrushes on either side of the track bent in the wind coming off the oblast.

All along the southern road, to either side, the folk of Choika had been crucified. The Kurgan host had passed this way, without compromise.

Karl stared at the mud in front of him. The mud and the chain. Taut, slack. Taut, slack. Taut, slack.

III

THEY WERE MARCHED for three days, pausing for a few hours every night. They followed the trail through broadleaf forest and wet woods, where the only sign of life was the movement of the Northern forces. Disorderly hosts of Norther spearmen overtook them, flocking down the track with no formal file or rank. They strode to drum beats, holding aloft wretched and often obscene banners. Some brought along warhounds or hunting dogs with them in great numbers. Others rode in carts and wagons with stretched hide covers and solid wooden wheels. These were pulled by strings of oxen or mules.

Occasionally, enemy horsemen rode by, always heading south. Sometimes the horsemen could be seen riding through the forest itself, scorning the mire of the road. Once they were passed by a squadron of two-wheeled chariots, drawn by fast teams of four ponies each. Beside each whipping driver stood a bearded archer with a hooked, compound bow.

The days were grey and overcast, and often interrupted by periods of heavy rain. The nights were moonless and still.

There were about three-score prisoners in the marching group, all marked men from the Zhedevka battle. They were chained in six lines. About twenty Kurgan spearmen guarded them, along with three horsemen. A fourth horseman, one of the silver-armoured men from the slave lord's bodyguard, had command.

When darkness fell, the Kurgan gathered them off the track in woodland clearings and staked their chains to the ground with iron spikes. The Northers built fires for themselves, and ate and drank through the night. Only two wooden bowls were brought to each of the six chains. One was filled with rainwater, the other with ladled dredgings of meat stew from the Kurgan's cook pots. The captives in each chain quickly learned the importance of sharing.

Some supplemented their diet with stuff they could forage from the forest floor near where they were staked down: beetles, earthworms, even leaves and grass stalks. A few chewed for hours on bark or twigs, or pieces of leather from whatever belts or boots they had. The hunger was inhuman. It was a misery beyond anything Karl had ever known or could imagine. It eclipsed all the other miseries: the cold, the fatigue, their wounds, the chaffing of the iron fetters, even their predicament as vanquished captives, slaves of an enemy that treated them like animals.

Karl shook most of the time, and there was a pain in his gut like a blade wound. His fingernails had become cracked and lined, and his skin was slack and had lost its usual elasticity. His gums bled. He had been deprived of everything, including his basic dignity as a human being. But he would gladly have let it all go if he could now just have a bowl of broth or a hunk of bread.

He could see the other men were in the same state. He realised they were all reaching a strange phase. Sheer desperation. It was looming. Up until then they had borne every horror and every privation, hoping that some sort of end or deliverance might come if they were patient.

Now, it was clear, it would not. Sooner or later, someone would decide that the danger of resisting or escaping no longer outweighed the terrible hunger.

On the third night, staked down in a grove of poplars, two things happened that brought them all closer to breaking point. The night was pitch black, and the Kurgan were drinking and laughing around their fires. They were late bringing the meagre offerings to the captives, and some of the prisoners had collapsed in a weak faint. Karl sat with his knees pulled up and his arms wrapped around them, trying to preserve body warmth as the temperature dropped.

All through the latter part of that afternoon, the track had been busy with massing Northers, flooding south. Word had spread that a battle was coming, and the captives discussed which burg or crossing might be its site. There were various suggestions, but none of the captives had much sense of the geography of the region, let alone where they were.

After dark, a ruddy glow underlit the sky south of them. They could see it, vaguely, through the trees. The Kurgan guards were excited by it. The promised battle. A town ablaze.

One of the captives in the middle of a chain staked out close to Karl suddenly fell sick. He convulsed and vomited violently, and wailed out. It seemed he had found some berries or forest mushrooms which, in desperation, he had foolishly ingested.

A few of the Kurgan came to look at him, but did nothing. He was most likely going to die a wracking, agonised death by poison, and they didn't care. They offered him no aid or physic. They didn't even put him out of his misery.

After about an hour, the man fell silent. Karl couldn't tell if he was sleeping or dead.

Karl began to plot how he might escape. Most likely all the captives still awake were doing the same. Karl still had Drogo Hance's true killer concealed in his mud-stiff clothes. He knew he couldn't break the fetter – and certainly not cut off a foot – but if he could get the whole of his chain to act together, they could drag out the spikes and rush the slumbering Kurgan. Karl's dirk gave them one chance. They could grab other weapons. They could–

He gave up the idea. They would be hacked to death. As far as he could tell at least two of the men on his fetter chain were too weak to fight now, and three others too scared. Then there was von Margur. Even if he was willing, his blindness was a profound handicap that would undermine them.

Karl then actually considered cutting off his own foot. Ludicrously, what dissuaded him was neither the potential pain, nor the danger of dying from blood loss, nor even the futility of trying to flee by hopping. No, it was the fact that the little dirk didn't seem to him to have enough blade to shear through something as solid as an ankle.

There was movement out on the track. Chariots and horsemen were riding past at full stretch by torch light. Hurrying, no doubt to the battle south of them.

And then another sound. Karl thought it was the wind in the treetops at first. Many of the captives looked up, curious.

A swishing, whooping noise of air. Karl had once been to the great port of Marienburg, and it sounded to him like the brisk wind of the estuary cracking and flapping the vast canvas sheets of the merchantmen and privateers in the harbour.

The Kurgan heard it too. They jumped up and immediately kicked over their fires and stamped them out until their embers were extinct. They were scared. They spoke only in whispers, and came over to insist that the captives remained silent. The insistence was reinforced by hissed threats of bodily damage and a show of drawn blades.

The flapping, swishing sounds continued, moving overhead from the north into the south. In petrified silence, they all crouched in the dark, looking up.

Karl hoped – prayed to Sigmar – that the sound did not belong to what his imagination told him was up there.

Wings. The huge, leathery wings of unnameable things flying over the forest, invisibly black against the starless sky. Feral abominations of the most distant North, swooping down to join the battle at the summons of the Kurgan sorcerers.

The captive who had eaten poison berries woke up, yelling.

He writhed and screamed out twice before the astonished Kurgan managed to react.

They fell on him and speared him to the forest floor to shut him up.

Silence returned, except for the beat of vast batwings.

IV

IN THE MORNING, at first light, the Kurgan roused them up and marched them on. It was raining again, and dismally cold and grey. The sick man they had murdered for the sake of silence was hacked out of his fetter and left in pieces under the sighing poplars.

As they shambled south, his vacant loop of iron dragged and rattled in the middle of the file.

V

KARL VOWED TO himself he would not die that way. He would not allow these barbarians to end his life so shamefully, just because they felt they owned it.

He could not escape. Not unless some miracle occurred. But he had the true killer. A small Empire-forged blade, enough for one kill. When the chance came, he would go down fighting, and he would take at least one filthy-souled man of the North with him.

As he struggled along, he absently rubbed at the sore place on his right cheek. Zar Uldin's mark. He wished he could abrade the skin away and no longer be marked as property.

The rains fell harder, torrential, turning the track to slop. The stands of woodland off the road became indistinct, so heavy was the blurring veil of the deluge. Captives, Karl included, walked with their heads turned up and their mouths open, relishing the drink the sky provided. Karl said a benediction to Taal, the hoary god of the wilds and elements, who dwelt up there and showed his children this simple mercy.

The silver-clad bodyguard, riding alongside them, was now truly silver-clad. The heavy rains had washed away the ritual bloodstains that had made his armour seem pink. That made him weaker, Karl thought, because he was deprived of the magical protection the blood afforded him.

Karl decided the bodyguard of Skarkeetah would be the one. As far as Karl could make it so, the brute slaver in the glossy silver plate would be the soul Karl took to the other world with him. That ornate, studded silver armour would be red again.

With Kurgan lifeblood.

VI

IN THE LATE morning of the fourth day, they reached a town. The rain had ebbed, and a washed-out sun tried to brighten the day.

The town was raised in a wide clearing of the forest. A clutch of izbas huddled around a fine but decayed granite temple within a wall of stone and timber.

They never learned its name.

The Kurgan host had come like wolves, burning out most of the old, frail izbas and putting the population to the sword. Then they had occupied it, to use its wells, and plunder its larders and granaries. It had become an encampment, a supply base for their armies as they drove south through the fringes of Kislev and into Karl's homeland.

The place reeked of stale smoke and dung. It was teeming with Kurgan. They had pitched their round felt gers and canvas pavilions in the pastures outside, and some in the streets of the town itself. A mighty head of horse was penned in chain corrals at the edges of the temporary town, and there were strange, new forests of stored spears, their bases stuck down in the loam.

The Kurgan whipped the captives down the track through the pastures, through the field of gers and in under the town gates. Kurgan archers manned the ramparts, their composite bows tautly strung. Sentinels with long, ox-horn trumpets stood watch over the gateway.

Inside, there had been looting and destruction. The puddles in the muddy streets were dark and cloudy. Kislevite dead had been tossed into heaps against the inner wall. Flies were everywhere.

They tracked up the main street, across a paved marketplace where singed stakes and jumbled ashes told of ceremonial burnings, and into a temple.

The great granite building, dedicated to some Kislevite deity, had been ransacked and its altars desecrated. Its heavy doors and windows had been boarded up, save the main porch. Raised in stone, the temple was the closest thing the Kurgan had to a prison.

Inside, it was dry and gloomy. Rushlights flickered. The inner space, wide and long, had been cleared, and blankets spread out on the floor. The temple smelled of aged timber, dust and sour wine.

Their guards forced them down on the lice-ridden blankets. Iron braziers were lit. After a while, they could smell food, and their drawn bellies winced.

Karl curled up in the blankets. By the firelight, he could see the main altar. Things – probably very holy things – had been cast down and smashed. On the wide basalt plinth stood an iron coffer. It had four feet in the shape of bird-claws, and stretcher handles so that it could be carried on the shoulders of strong men. On the side facing them, looking into the temple, was a single eye wrought in iron, its lids formed by wreathing snakes. A fire inside the coffer flickered in amber through the spaces cast into the eye. It seemed as if the staring eye was blinking.

They were left alone for an hour or two. Then Hinn entered the temple. His footfalls on the stone flags were loud and heavy. Nine of the sturdy litter bearers followed him. They brought the anvil with them.

Hinn bowed to the coffer, and then stood up again to remove his beaked helmet. He raised it up off his head and set it down at the foot of the altar block.

His head was hideous.

His face was small and fleshy, like a baby's. He had no beard, but he had not shaved. No hair had ever broken that soft flesh. His skull was oiled smooth, it was tall and rose in a grotesque, rounded point of distorted bone. The height of his golden close-helm had been necessary to contain its abhuman shape.

Hinn's skull had been bound from an early age. Karl had once heard about this practice amongst the most savage Northern tribes. Tight bindings had forced his soft head into this elongated shape as it grew. His skull was almost twice the height from crown to jaw as that of a normal man, and when he turned side on, it was half the depth behind the ears from brow to nape. Bare, his skull resembled an egg-like cone, high and slender, with his infant face hanging from the front.

Hinn turned to face them all. His expression was blank, almost idiotic.

'Tchar blesses you, marked ones,' he said, in a voice that was pitched high and far too frail to be the product of such a massive body.

At a clap of his hands, Kurgan with spears herded the captives to the anvil, one by one. The litter bearers used a chisel and hammer to free them. They gouged several calves and broke at least one toe before the captives were all released.

It seemed a small price to pay.

Then the Kurgan brought food.

VII

THE FOOD CAME in a series of beaten copper pots, each one so full it had to be carried crosswise on bending poles by pairs of straining men. A steaming stew of oily fish, poached in grease and mare's milk. A hot brown broth, thick with chunks of root vegetable and fatty gobs of mutton. Beans and pulses, cooked in boiled mutton stock. Accompanying these, wooden trenchers were piled with farls of fresh, warm unleavened bread.

The litter bearers set the food down in the middle of the huddle of captives. All of the prisoners stared at the feast. Some were sobbing, others were openly drooling like dogs. No one dared to move.

Hinn smiled. It was a nasty sight. 'Eat,' he said.

That... that was the kindest thing Karl ever saw a Northerner do.

The captives fell on the pots, gobbling and craving. They tore bread and used their hands, ignoring the scalds and blisters they got from dipping fingers into hot food. They ate like famished wolves, tearing into the food in a pack, burning their lips, tongues and fingertips. Some consumed so much, so fast, that they fell in faints and stupors. Others gagged and coughed.

It was the best meal Karl Reiner Vollen had ever tasted.

The litter bearers reappeared and tossed drinking skins into the scrum of feeding bodies. The skins were full of a sappy alcoholic drink like wine, and they drained them, holding the heavy hide bags for each other, pouring the sweet, strong drink into each other's mouths.

They were laughing, their faces gleaming with grease, drops of broth in their beards. Karl found von Margur and helped the blind knight to one of the pots.

As the marked men consumed the food and drink, Hinn and the litter bearers moved around the temple, sowing seedcases into the braziers. Very soon the air was full of dry, spicy smoke. Breathing it in, the feasting captives began to howl and cry with laughter. They danced around, eyes streaming with tears, mouths wide with delight. One man laughed so hard he began to choke.

The hot rasp of the opiate smoke became overwhelming. Hinn and the Kurgan withdrew. Coughing and stumbling, the prisoners milled around in an intoxicated daze. Some of them crawled on the floor, still laughing. Others lay back on the blankets and fell asleep, snoring loudly, their bellies over-full. Two men threw up violently, and collapsed. The copper pots rolled on their sides on the blankets, scraped empty.

Von Margur slumped down in a bundle and began to sigh and weep. Karl, his head spinning, sat down heavily. His eyes were welling with tears, but he was still laughing hysterically. One of the marked men, a swordsman from Carroburg, staggered up to the altar and put on Hinn's golden bird-helm. He jigged around in it, and all those still conscious laughed so hard they were in danger of rupturing themselves.

Karl got to his feet, swaying and laughing. He had the true killer in his hand, clenched inside the folds of his dirty clothes.

He started towards the door, but he wasn't very good at walking any more. He felt so good.

'No!' von Margur growled, reaching out a hand to grab at Karl's boot.

'Get off! Get off, sir!' Karl giggled.

'No!' von Margur said, and then snorted with laughter at the pomposity of his tone.

'Let me go, sir…' Karl said.

'No… no, Karl,' von Margur said, still sniggering. His hand was clamped around Karl's shin. 'Please don't. What will I do without you?'

Karl stopped. He didn't have an answer to that. He sank down onto his knees.

'Sir? Sir? Take the knife and hold it so I can fall onto it and escape this. Please, sir. Please.'

Von Margur was asleep, semi-digested food leaking out of his half-turned mouth.

Karl got to his feet. It was difficult, and took a while. Once he was upright, he was quivering. He held the true killer out in front of him like a trowel.

Something very cold and very solid suddenly rested on his left shoulder. Karl peered down and fought to adjust his field of focus. The solid thing was shiny. A steel something.

The blade of a pallasz.

Hinn stood before him, one of his huge broadswords lowered horizontally across Karl's torso.

Karl wavered, hot and uncomfortable.

'I don't know how you came to have that pin-stick,' Hinn said, his voice ridiculously high. 'Here are your choices. Hand it to me and live. Keep it and die.'

Karl thought hard. He wanted to hack at Hinn. But he was fairly sure he would be dead if he tried to move.

Hinn kept the broadsword where it was and held out his other hand.

'Give it to me, Empire.'

Karl blinked. 'Your voice is funny,' he found himself saying.

'Funny?'

'Yes, funny. Like it's squeaky.'

Incensed, Hinn took the pallasz blade off Karl's shoulder bone and raised it up.

'There is another choice,' said a soft voice.

Skarkeetah loomed beside his bodyguard. He smiled at Karl.

'It was clever of you to have kept that dirk hidden. Put it away now and I'll let you keep it.'

That seemed very fair.

'All right,' said Karl, and tucked the dirk away in his ragged undershirt.

Then he sat down and fell asleep.

VIII

KARL WOKE UP in the early hours when the braziers had gone out, and the temple had gone cold again. Just the after-scent of the opiate smoke and the food hung in the chilly air. All of the captives were asleep.

The true killer had been taken from him.

Karl cursed, but he was too tired to care.

* * *

IX

THEY ALL SLEPT through most of the next day. At vespers, as the day was closing, the litter bearers came in with another meal and more wine skins.

The prisoners were slower to consume this offering. They were tired and muzzy.

Outside, there was an uproar: drums beating and fires glowing.

Hinn stalked back into the temple, a broadsword drawn in each hand. At some point in the night, he had recovered his close-helm. Now it shone on his head. The bird beak. The ram's horns.

He looked around for a while, and then pointed the long blade in his right hand at a well-built pikeman from Stirland who had the three green cheek dots of Zar Blayda's mark on his cheek.

'Tchar chooses you,' he said.

Then he raised the sword in his left hand and pointed its tip at Karl.

'And you.'

X

THE STIRLANDER'S NAME was Wernoff. Karl had established this as they were bundled out of the temple into the evening.

'What in Sigmar's name do they want from us?' Wernoff asked.

'I don't know.'

'Are we to be sacrifices, Vollen? Blood sacrifices?' Wernoff wondered in dismay.

'Sigmar, great be his blessings, will protect us,' Karl assured the pikeman.

As soon as they were out of the temple's doorway, they found themselves in a thick crowd of drunken, chanting Kurgan. Hinn's men dragged Wernoff away and Karl lost sight of him.

Hinn led Karl down through the crush of chanting bodies into the market square. The acre of paving stones was clear and empty, but rang with the sound of thousands of yelling Northers. Fires blazed around the edges of the square, casting a long, yellow glare over the paving.

Hinn jostled Karl to the edge of the baying crowd.

The pitch-armoured figure of Zar Blayda emerged from the far side of the multitude and walked out in the centre of the firelit market place. He stood there, drew his sword and held it up. As he brandished it, the crowd cheered and yelled.

Then Zar Uldin, in his black furs and wolf-mask, strode out to face him. Uldin ripped out his own pallasz, and waved it aloft, to more howls and roars.

The zars faced each other in the centre of the square, Blayda with his sword raised across his body, diagonal, Uldin with his vertical.

Now Karl understood, to a certain extent. Single combat, an honour match, zar against zar. He watched expectantly.

Blayda swung his massive sword. Uldin blocked it. Sparks flew from the clash. The crowd howled.

Then they stopped. The zars bowed to each other and went back into the mob on either side of the market square.

Karl blinked as Hinn shoved a pallasz into his hands. Then the brute handed him Drogo Hance's true killer.

'You might need this,' said the thin, high voice from behind the beaked helm.

Karl still didn't understand. The crowd was baying fit to break the sky. He tucked the true killer into his belt and hefted the huge pallasz.

Hinn suddenly shoved him out into the open. Sword in hand, he stumbled out into the empty square. The firelight danced. The Kurgan host yelled the moment they saw him.

Wernoff emerged from the crowd at the opposite side of the square. He staggered as if he had been pushed. He had a Kurgan broadsword in his hands.

Karl felt his soul sink. It was single combat all right. Zar Blayda versus Zar Uldin. But a duel fought by proxy, as sport. By their marked men.

DUSHYKA

I

THREE DAYS ON the empty steppe and they came in sight of Dushyka.

At least, Gerlach believed it had been three days. It seemed there were no dimensions his Imperial mind could grasp in the open oblast. The land was a flat, featureless prospect to all compass points, the sky an immeasurable arch beneath which he felt no more significant than a pin stick. There was no direction except *forward*.

If the men of the rota had told him it had been four days, or even five, he would not have been surprised. He moved in emptiness. In it, he became a nothing.

As time followed the rhythmic lurch of the horse, hour after hour, he came to a sobering revelation. The oblast had not diminished him; it had simply showed him how he truly was. Against the busy landscape of the Imperial principalities, he was a young man of repute, vexillary of a demilance, no less, with ambitions to match: to win glory for Karl Franz, to achieve great deeds in battle, to be the sort of man who made real things happen. That was why the fires of Zhedevka had left him so hollow. The sense of failure had been so great. Why had he not turned back the armies of the North single-handed?

Out on the steppe, he saw himself as fate saw him. A tiny thing, like a single blade of grass.

He was one small man, and here the scale of the universe was revealed... well, just a part of it. His mind might reel, giddy at the thought of the whole.

There was nothing he could have done. Nothing any man could have done. The North was a primordial torrent, in the form of flesh. He could have no more stopped it than raise up his hands and halt the giant clouds that sailed, sedate as galleons, across the oblast heaven.

The fatalism shown by Beledni, and by many of his men, seemed apt now. The slight, dismissive frown, the odd little turn of the wrist as if he were spilling out a handful of corn, 'Is of no matter'. So typically careless, so typically Kislevite. They had been raised in this emptiness, and it bred in them a dismissive philosophy.

Is of no matter. For nothing mattered. For nothing was big enough to matter in the long run, except the passing centuries and the empty steppe. All the rest was just dust, spilling from a tilting hand into the oblast wind.

Dushyka stanitsa. Dushyka town. A trading post on the route from nothing to nowhere.

A long, beamed hall with a handful of izbas packed around it inside a timber stockade. It was so old the elements had worn the wood pale as snow.

It appeared up suddenly, amid the limitless grass, under a sky that was just the blue side of colourless. It surprised Gerlach to come upon it so unexpectedly. Nothing but grass, then a township. The line of hills to the north-east still seemed as far away as when the journey began.

The men of the rota had somehow been aware of Dushyka before it came into view. The pace slowed, and conversations were exchanged between the front riders.

There was no sign of life in the town, except goats and short-necked ponies that grazed outside the stockade fence. The rota reined up in a line half a league short of the town and, at Beledni's gesture, Yevni the horn blower sounded his horn.

The sound rolled away across the open steppe and was eaten by the distance. They waited, horses twitching ears and tails.

An answering note came from the stockade, strong and clear. Gerlach saw movement as the town gates opened.

'Yha!' Beledni cried, and the rota broke towards the town.

II

STEPPE LIFE, GERLACH decided, was like an islander's way of life. The grass was the sea, and the scattered stanitsas the little island communities.

The greeting at Dushyka was very different from the one the demilancers had received at Choika. The townsfolk – what few of them there were – came out onto the packed earth of their yards and rattled busy welcomes with empty pots and pans. Hellos were called out, and men strode forward to clasp the hands of each rider in turn as the rota dismounted. Gerlach found his hand shaken by a dozen people he didn't know. They greeted him with cheerful informality as if he was a cousin or a brother returning home after a short time away.

The men of the rota seemed to know the townsfolk and vice versa, but it was hard to be sure. Maybe they simply knew each other as fellow sons of Kislev. Maybe that was enough.

The ataman emerged from the log hall. He was a bearded man with a wind-scoured face. He wore an old, spiked helmet with a wide fur brim on his head, a long cherchesska tunic with rows of charges down the chest, and a fleece draped over one shoulder. His deputy, the esaul, followed him, carrying a small mace. This – the bulava – was the ataman's symbol of power.

The ataman took the bulava from his deputy and handed it to Beledni. Simultaneously, the rotamaster handed the staff of the rota's eagle wing banner to the ataman. They each touched the totem they had been given against their foreheads and gravely uttered some oath or ritual remark. Then banner and bulava were taken back and returned to the hands of the deputies. Beledni and the ataman spread their arms wide and embraced each other, laughing and smiling. After that, Beledni, Maksim and Borodyn followed the ataman and his esaul into the hall.

Outside, the men of the rota sat around in the little yard, or saw to their mounts. Womenfolk brought bowls of pickled fish and sour cream, pitchers of chalky water, cups of koumiss and baskets of small seed cakes.

Gerlach accepted some from a little woman in a headscarf. They hadn't eaten much on the journey: just strips of dry salt-meat and biscuit handed out from saddlebags. Gerlach tried to show how grateful he was. Vaja and Vitali joined him, chuckling and tutting, to teach him how to say thank you like a Kislevite. There was a ritual to be observed, though they didn't explain it well. As usual, they were contradicting each other's use of Reikspiel.

You took the water first of all. Sip, rinse the mouth of the journey's dust and spit, then drink some more. Then a modest fingerful of the fish, to be eaten with relish. Then a seed cake, torn so that some of it could be handed back to the giver. The idea was, Gerlach worked out, that the folk of the stanitsa were selflessly offering their precious supplies to the visitors, and the ritual vouched for the visitor's willingness to share. Once this had been established, the words for thanks were spoken, and the koumiss drunk.

There seemed to be no warriors resident in the stanitsa, and no sign of armour, but a row of round, hardwood shields hung on the inner wall of the stockade and most of the men carried short, recurved bows, unstrung, in eastern-style bowcases on their belts. Several spare bowstrings were looped around the cases.

His spirits lifted by the food, Gerlach followed the lead of the other riders and worked on his horse and armour. He stripped the harness and rubbed Saksen with handfuls of straw. Then he walked him to a water trough that the local boys were filling from a pump. Women were shaking out armfuls of hay.

The younger boys took great interest in the Imperial troop horse. Gerlach realised how odd Saksen looked amongst the Kislevites' hairy, squat mares. Saksen was the biggest horse by far, with a longer neck and a much more powerful build. His fine grey colouring and tightly docked tail made him look an alien in their midst.

'Byeli!' the boys said, apparently impressed. 'Byeli!'

They turned their attention to the rider of the strange horse. It seemed Gerlach's own colouring and fair hair was just as intriguing. They followed the vexillary, cautiously, as he walked back to his harness and started to lay his kit and armour out on the hardpan.

Dented and battered in places though it was, his fine half-armour was still in reasonable shape. He hadn't worn it or his burgonet since the night they had camped on the hillside. His fabric clothing was in much worse shape, all of it dirty and torn. He'd almost forgotten that the beshmet he was wearing as a coat had belonged to Vaja.

His sabre was notched, and he couldn't remember where he'd lost his lance. His dagger was still intact. One pistol remained in his possession, but with precious little powder or shot.

He went through his saddlebags, finding there wasn't much in them. The company's supply wagons had been carrying most of their personal effects. Aside from his water flask and bedroll, there was a little comb of tortoiseshell, a folding razor, a tinderbox, a whetstone, a shoe-awl, a small bottle of polishing oil, a rag, a candle, and some beeswax in a pot. There was also a curry-comb. Gerlach looked at this particular item with a frown. He'd always been so scrupulous in his grooming of the gelding, yet he'd just brushed Saksen down with straw, in the brisk manner of a Kislevite outrider, without even thinking of this comb.

At the bottom of one bag were a few scraps of twisted silver and enamel chips.

It was all that remained of a symbol of Sigmar his father had presented him with the night before he set out. He wore a smaller, gold version on a chain round his neck that his mother had given him on his tenth birthday.

His father's gift had been altogether too large to wear except for ceremonial occasions. He carried it in his pack as a trophy. It had been entirely shattered. A brief examination revealed a blackened hole the size of his middle finger in the side of the buff saddlebag. A ball of shot had passed through it. He hadn't seen any of the enemy using firing pieces, though anything was possible. This was more likely a miserable stray shot from his own side during the chaos at Zhedevka. The holy symbol had stopped the shot and been destroyed as a result. Nothing else in the bag had been touched. But for that, Gerlach would have had Saksen killed or crippled under him on the field.

It was curious. It made him feel strangely grateful and humble.

III

GERLACH SET TO work oiling his armour and edging his sword. The boys gathered round with interest. They pointed to various details – the design of

Gerlach's sabre and the style of his armour – that were foreign to them, discussed them amongst themselves with almost professional concern.

Then he began to clean his wheel-lock, and they fell silent in awe.

One of them finally dared to address him. Gerlach looked up. The boy, no older than eight or nine, with fierce dark eyes and a mess of black hair, repeated his question quickly. None of them had any Reikspiel at all, and Gerlach had a passing knowledge of only a half-dozen Kislevite words.

'I don't understand you, boy,' he said at last. The boy frowned. 'I...' Gerlach pointed to himself, '...don't understand you.' He pointed at the boy.

'Douko,' said the boy.

'Dowkoe?'

'Douko,' the boy repeated, tapping his chest.

'You're Douko? Your name is Douko?' Gerlach asked, trying to do better with the name's pronunciation. This seemed to please the boy and his friends.

'Heileman,' said Gerlach, indicating himself. There had been a time, not all that long before, when vexillary Heileman would have considered chatting idly with peasant children to be beneath him. But some inner tension had relaxed, like a clock spring uncoiling, and he could think of nothing finer than wasting time under a wide blue sky.

The boy made a few struggling attempts to repeat Gerlach's name, but it was beyond him. The children urged Gerlach to repeat it so they might try again.

He did. They failed and laughed at themselves in a way that made Gerlach smile. He tried something else.

'Vebla,' he said, patting his chest.

They laughed so hard they were helpless with mirth. They repeated the word and then ran away across the yard, calling it out.

Shaking his head, Gerlach returned to his work. His pistol was clean, his sword whetted. He went back to his armour and tried to beat out the deep dent on his right vambrace. The damage had been done by the sword blow that had knocked the draco standard from his hand.

For a moment, the tension coiled in him again, as he recalled the proud anger that had propelled him through the battle. The old, arrogant Gerlach Heileman, who had ridden to war believing he could drive out the enemy was reinstated. A flush rose in his neck.

He hammered bitterly with his dagger pommel, as he had seen the Kislevites doing, but he was no armourer. Such repairs were the job of the smith who rode with the supply wagons.

Had been the job.

'Let me see to that.'

Gerlach glanced up. Borodyn, the horse master and master of metals, stood behind him. He had re-emerged from the ataman's zal, and now was going round the compound with his farrier's hammer, pliers and little anvil, making field repairs to the armour and harnesses of the riders.

Borodyn held out his hand. 'Please. I can get the dent out and stop it rubbing your arm.'

Gerlach gave him the vambrace and Borodyn put it over the anvil's nose and began to work out the twist with little, expert taps.

'They seemed to welcome us here.'

'It is the way,' replied Borodyn.

'What happens now?'

'What do you mean?' Borodyn asked, looking up at him.

'We spent three days getting here. What do we do now?'

'Rest, water our horses. Join the ataman at the Dushyka krug tonight.'

'What is a "krug"?'

'Literally? A circle. Any close circle. The circle of warriors around a fireside. The folk of a village like this gathered for a feast. And so, they refer to the band of warriors themselves, as well as the village community as a body. Tonight, the Dushyka krug – these people – welcomes the Yetchitch krug – that's us – to join them *for* a krug.'

'It's complicated. Your language is complicated. One word with so many meanings.'

'Just one meaning. The circle. It's simple. It is the world. Every journey comes back to where it starts, for the world goes round and if you ride forever you come back upon your own tracks. Every strong people is a circle. Every rota is a circle. The circle holds us in and holds us together. True circles are strong.'

Borodyn held up the vambrace and showed it end-on to Gerlach. He had beaten the dent out and, looking down into it, it now formed a perfect circle.

Gerlach smiled and took it. 'Like armour? A good illustration for your point.'

Borodyn frowned and thought about this. 'Oh, I see. I hadn't intended that symbolism.'

Gerlach shrugged. He was quite sure Borodyn had. There was something of the teacher in the armourer, even something of a priest. Implying simple things without drawing attention to them.

Gerlach slipped the vambrace on and rotated his clenched fist. 'It's good. Thank you.'

'Is of no matter,' Borodyn said, the true Kislevite.

'Where did you learn my language, horse master Borodyn?' he asked.

'In your country,' Borodyn replied, as if this was a strange question.

'You have been to the Empire?'

Borodyn nodded. 'Years ago, when I was a young man and hungry for journeys. Before Yetchitch called me home to the steppe.'

'Yetchitch. That's your home village?'

'Yes. It is where all the men of the rota come from. It is north and east of here. In the highlands of the open steppe.'

'Isn't this the open steppe?'

Borodyn chuckled. 'Of course not.'

'So I ride in the company of the *rota* of *Yetchitch krug*?'

'Yes,' Borodyn smiled.

'Because – like *krug* – *rota* means more than one thing? A banner, and the men who follow the banner? Who might also be called a *krug*?'

'Exactly. I told you it was simple.'

IV

AS EVENING FELL, a slow, languid process in the open vista of the oblast, they congregated in the long, beamed zal, where fires had been burning for an hour or more to heat the place. An extensive meal was being cooked; heavy, rich smells wafted out.

The men of the rota had put on their armour again, including szyszak helmets, snow leopard pelts and the tall wing crests, so as to look dignified and noble for the krug. They had spent some time out in the yard in the fading light, buffing up their gold and silver wargear, helping to set and straighten crests and details of each other's trappings.

They looked impressive, Gerlach had to admit, far more splendid than anything in this meagre stanitsa.

Dutifully, he dressed in his own half-armour and plumed burgonet. The warriors applauded him loudly when they saw him so accoutred.

Before casting off their ragged travel clothes and donning their fine wargear, the men of the rota had performed an odd rite. They had unfixed the long tips of their main horse lances, sharpened them, and then shaved. Heads, cheeks, chins, everything, with painstaking care – except for their topknots and drooping moustaches. Beledni had inspected each man's face for signs of stubble. Then they wound their top knots on their bald heads, slipped their leather cauls over them to form a cushion, before putting on their helms.

Beledni had mentioned shaving before, as if it was significant. It seemed to be the only piece of grooming these habitually grubby men worried about.

The winged lancers secured their lance tips back onto the hafts, and then left the lances and their swords at the door of the zal.

Gerlach, with his full beard in the Empire fashion, simply trimmed the proud point with his knife and longed for a bowl of hot water. He walked to the doorway of the hall, and placed his demilance sabre with the other weapons in the porch.

Inside, it was dim and smoky. The zal was full. Everyone from the village was there, even the children. Bolsters and rugs and quilted blankets covered the open floor, and the guests, ducking so their huge wing crests would not strike the low beams, took their seats on the ground to the clapping welcome of the villagers. A Dushyka man was banging a tambor, and another was playing a lively tune on a horse-head fiddle.

The music and clapping died away so that the old ataman, regal in furs and a striped dolmen, could pronounce words of welcome. Beledni rose stiffly to his feet and made a formal answer. Everyone clapped.

The younger women then went around with circular trays on which heavy stemmed glasses sat cup-down beside small bowls of salt. Gerlach was surprised to see such a delicate commodity as drinking glasses in this remote place. Clearly, the ataman was entertaining his guests with his finest chattels.

The lancers each took a glass, as did the ataman. When Gerlach was offered one, he picked it up and examined it. It was old and heavy and shaped like a handbell. The stem had no base. The only way to put it down was to empty it and overturn it. A toasting glass.

'Other of you hand!' Vaja hissed at Gerlach.

He was holding the glass in his right hand and saw all the lancers had theirs in their left. He corrected the mistake.

'Now… sol!' Vaja added. Each lancer had taken a pinch of salt between the fingertips of his right hand.

The esaul went round the circle of guests, filling each man's glass with clear liquid from a tall flask. This, according to Vaja, was kvass.

With a full glass that he couldn't put down in his left hand, and a pinch of salt in his right, Gerlach waited and watched the others to see what to do.

The ataman made a toast. It was loud and furious. He raised his kvass.

The lancers – and Gerlach – raised theirs. 'Starovye!'

Now that word, at least, he knew.

As the cry went up, the lancers licked the salt from their right hands and then downed the drink. The whole glass in one swallow.

Not wishing to offend, Gerlach did the same.

Someone had filled his glass with molten lead. It burned like flaming pitch as it poured down his throat. He wasn't even sure it had gone down his throat. It felt like it had simply burned its own way down into his gullet. He coughed and spluttered, eyes streaming.

Everyone in the room cheered.

Gerlach swayed slightly. Heat washed through his limbs and blood rushed unpleasantly through his head. He gasped for air and wished it wasn't quite so hard to stand up.

The esaul returned and refilled the glasses, and the young women went round with the salt again.

'I'm fine,' Gerlach said to the esaul as he tried to pour.

The village deputy balked in horror.

'Shto?'

'Vebla!' Vaja urged. 'Rotamaster not has make answer!'

Gerlach sighed and allowed his glass to be refilled. He took another pinch of salt.

Now they raised their cups as Beledni made the answering toast. Another cry of 'starovye!' another painful moment of liquid torture.

Flush-faced, Gerlach tried to master a way of standing that didn't require support. It was a tall order.

Vaja nudged him. 'Now is esaul's turn,' he grinned.

V

BY THE TIME protocol permitted him to sit down, many toasts later, Gerlach was giggling and in no state to stand anyway. The music resumed, and the lancers removed their szyszaks, gloves and wing crests. Food circulated. Rye bread, more pickled fish and sour cream, stews of pulses and salt-meat, cured basturma spiced with peppers, slices of kolbasi sausage, and parcels of barley and goat meat wrapped in cabbage leaves. A stuffed lamb shashlik was carved off the spit over the fire and portioned out. There was koumiss and – thankfully – water.

Gerlach ate well, his belly still burning from the kvass. As the food soaked the sting of the liquor away, he looked around him. The zal was a meeting house, as well as a temple. A rectangular box of ornately worked silver sat at the head end in a sacred alcove. In other places, cured meat and herbs hung to dry on the beams. Along the flat timbers of the wall were the sooty shapes of old murals. Stylised men with wings mounted on horse shapes that were too small for them.

'Were there lancers here once?' Gerlach asked Vitali.

'They not now here, Vebla.'

'What happened to them?'

Vitali shrugged. 'They in pulk,' he said.

Gerlach pressed the point. As usual, it took a long while to make decent sense of Vitali's answers. At least Vaja, deep in conversation with Yevni the horn blower, was not butting in and complicating matters further.

As far as Gerlach could establish, every single stanitsa on the steppe put all its efforts into raising and maintaining a rota of lancers. The size of the rota depended on the size of the village and the manpower available. Yetchitch must be a place of some size to have produced a rota as strong as Beledni's, Gerlach suggested. Vitali nodded. Yetchitch was a fine and wonderful place, and the thought of it made his eyes mist over. Dushyka's rota was barely half the size.

All the wealth of the village went into the rota too. The Kislevites wanted their warriors to be the best looking of any fighting men in the world. Every scrap of gold and precious metal went into their armour, every spare coin went into buying them the best cloth, silks from Cathay, satins and linens. A stanitsa would go without to provide for its warriors, because to send shabby men out meant dishonour for ataman and krug alike.

Now Gerlach understood why the lancers only wore their beautiful lamellar armour and finest outfits for battle – they were too precious for everyday use.

In normal times, the job of a stanitsa's rota was to defend the village.

Sometimes that meant joining with the rotas of other stanitsas to see off khazak or other troubles. But in times of large scale war, like now, the villages would send out their rotas to form pulks – army groups of significant size and hierarchies of loyalty too complex for Gerlach to make sense of from Vitali's enthusiastic doggerel.

All this suggested a system, a culture, of considerable size and complexity, one that Gerlach had not suspected of the oblast peoples. What he, with his southern eyes, saw as an empty region of thinly scattered villages was actually an intricate network of trade and cooperation. Once again, he chastised himself for prejudging the Kislevites as simple barbarian cousins. He reminded himself that Kislev operated on a completely different scale to his beloved Empire. These were not isolated communities, no matter how much they felt like it. After all, they were burning wood and eating fish that night. How close was the nearest forest? The nearest lake?

Vitali said that Dushyka rota had ridden for five weeks to join the pulk down by the Lynsk, ready to stand firm with the armies of the Empire. He and the men of Beledni's rota had left Yetchitch ten weeks earlier to do the same, leaving their home in the dead of winter. So far, the lancers of Dushyka rota had not yet returned home.

Gerlach took a swig of koumiss and wished them decent fortune. He had an unhappy feeling why they had not been seen again.

Vitali made his 'is of no matter' face. 'Is way of things, for riders of dead.'

'Riders of dead? That's what the horse master called us.'

'Yha! All rota lancers are riders of dead.'

Gerlach longed to know what that meant, but Vitali could not explain.

VI

THE NIGHT WAS clear like crystal, and there were more stars in the sky than Gerlach had a number for. The stars were swollen and fierce, as if they had been unleashed by the space the oblast sky provided. Back home, the stars were just fine pinpricks in the dark.

Gerlach wandered out into the yard where the horses were resting. He breathed in the sweet, cold air of the steppe. Behind him, the zal was heady with heat and life and music and singing.

He leaned back against a beam and sighed. He had overeaten, and had been forced to drink far too much.

In the course of the night, by accident, he had discovered that koumiss was made from fermented mare's milk. That had not stopped him drinking his fill.

He was amazed at himself. He was no longer the starchy vexillary who had ridden out of Vatzl barracks with a shit-eating grin on his face.

The stockade gates were still open, a trusting symbol of embrace to the empty steppe. Gerlach saw a shadow standing under the gate. He approached.

It was Beledni. He had a skin of koumiss in his chunky fist.

'Vebla,' he said when he saw Gerlach. 'You not about hitting Beledni rotamaster again? Is not time for.'

'No,' said Gerlach. 'In fact, I'm sorry about that. About the "coward" thing. I apologise.'

'Well, that very good. Beledni rotamaster very happy. Take drink with me.'

Gerlach took the proffered skin and swigged.

'You are good man, Vebla. Strong… fighter. I saw you ride to take back standard. Take back from many Norscya. More many Norscya.'

'It was my standard, rotamaster.'

'Yha. I would do same. For rota. I see you do this thing and I…' Beledni trailed off. He didn't know the words. 'I want. Nyah! I think I do it to. Whatever. That is why Beledni rotamaster gave charge.'

'You charged the rota to save me?'

Beledni shook his head. 'Nyeh, not save. Word is… "help". I saw Vebla's spirit. Brave. Alone. I want and wish men did same if Beledni rotamaster ride like that.'

So Beledni had led his horse lancers into the fight because he had been impressed by Gerlach's effort. He'd come to his aid because that's what he hoped other men would do if they saw Beledni taking the same huge risk.

'It didn't work,' Gerlach said.

'Shto?'

'I lost the standard. My standard.'

'But you save mine. Pick it up from ground when Mikael Roussa fell down to death. This honour you did for us.'

'Maybe. I'm glad that… mattered.'

They said nothing to one another for a good few minutes. Beledni passed the skin to Gerlach a few times.

'Can I ask a favour, rotamaster?' Gerlach said at last.

'Ask it. I owe to you.'

'Let me carry the rota. I am a vexillary. A standard bearer. It's my job. I lost mine, but I saved yours, and you lost Mikael Roussa. If I'm going to ride with you, let me do the job I'm trained for.'

'Is not right,' Beledni said. Gerlach sighed. 'Is order to things,' Beledni went on. 'Rota bearer is great honour. Man must be veteran to do job. Beledni rotamaster not want and wish to insult men of rota like Maksim, like Mitri, like Sorca, like Ifan. All wait in line for honour of to be rota bearer.'

'I understand.'

'But is special case. Is right thing. Vebla should carry banner. Men of rota will understand this. Or Beledni rotamaster will strike them on head.'

'Thank you, rotamaster. I will not fail in this duty, on my honour as a…'

Gerlach had been about to say 'demilancer of Karl Franz'.

Instead he said, 'A soldier.'

'Beledni rotamaster know this, Vebla. Beledni rotamaster not a stupid man.'

'Of course.'

'Or coward.'

'Absolutely.'

Gerlach took the skin and sucked a dreg of koumiss from the slack shape. 'Where do we go tomorrow?'

'Nowhere.'

'And the next day?'

'Nowhere too.'

'And after that?'

'If Dushyka rota not return in two day times, we ride to north and west, to Leblya stanitsa, where pulk was ordered to fall back if enemy too strong.'

Both moons were up now, brilliant in the dark sky. The moonlight cast shadows back from the two men under the stockade gate.

'May I ask another question, rotamaster?'

'Yha. Was that it?'

'No...' Gerlach smiled. 'What does "vebla" mean?'

'Aha! You ask Borodyn. Horse master Borodyn, master of metals, he has right words! Now you come, Vebla. Back to zal. We drink toast to you for being rota bearer.'

Gerlach sighed and followed the heavyset shadow back towards the zal.

VII

DAWN SPREAD OVER the eastern horizon like sour cream spilled into dark water. Light rose to the surface and curdled out across the blankness.

'I'm sorry about your horse,' Borodyn said to Gerlach soon after he woke. 'The children here were over-enthusiastic.'

Gerlach wandered out into the dawn and studied Saksen. The horse seemed very lively and fit. It had been made chalk-white above the belly line and blood-red beneath, and at the junction of the two colours was a carefully painted straight line. The red went up Saksen's throat.

'Your horse was a spirit thing to them. They had never seen its like,' Borodyn said. 'You should count yourself lucky. Only the great champions of Kislev get to have their horses dyed like that.'

'They called it Byeli. The children, I mean,' said Gerlach.

'Byeli. White. Without colour. I know Saksen is grey, but to them it seemed like a pale, white horse. Well, it is certainly a white horse now.'

'Not entirely white.'

'White above and blood-coloured below. A hero's horse, dyed like in the old days. The scriptures of Ursun say that death rides on a pale horse, his destruction to unfold.'

Gerlach smiled. His head was throbbing from the night's drinking. 'I like that. I feel like that.'

'Good,' said Borodyn.

The horse master stalked back to the zal.

'Horse master!' Gerlach called, hurrying after him.

'What?'

'I have a question.'

Borodyn stopped. 'Ask it.'

'Why is the rota called "the riders of the dead"?'

Borodyn shrugged. 'Once a man leaves his home village for war, he is already dead. He will die someday, so it is better to depart for war each year mourned as if already lost. That was not the question I was expecting.'

'What where you expecting?'

'I was expecting, "what does vebla mean?"'

'So? What does it mean?' Gerlach yelled after him.

'You will find out, Vebla.'

VIII

THE ATAMAN AND his esaul performed a blessing for them on the third day of their stay. They all huddled into the zal as the ataman went to the sacred alcove and took out the silver box.

It was an oclet: a silver-wrapped box with hinged doors. An icon. The face of Ursun looked out, painted in egg tempera on the seasoned fig wood, surrounded by silver. It was a piece of heaven, wrapped in precious metal.

They all bowed their heads as it was opened before them.

IX

ON THE THIRD morning, Beledni's rota rode away into the west. Gerlach hoisted the eagle wing banner high overhead, and rode, shouting from the saddle of his painted horse, into the oblast wind.

AZYTZEEN

I

WERNOFF WAS FAST on his feet but, as a lifelong pikeman, he wasn't used to sword play. Karl had been trained to fence. It was part of a demilancer's instruction. Hinn's loaned pallasz was bigger, straighter and longer than any blade Karl was accustomed to, and needed two hands to control, but he had the edge.

He didn't want the edge. He didn't want to be trading blows with a fellow warrior of the Reik.

Karl had expected the Stirlander to be restrained, and throw out a few obvious strokes for show. But Wernoff came at him with full-blooded effort, sweeping the heavy Kurgan sword from side to side. Wernoff had been drilled to handle five span-lengths of shivering pike haft. The sword felt short and light by comparison, even if he didn't know quite what to do with it.

Karl circled, his sword upright and firm compared to the other's wobbling, improvised sweeps.

Around the flame-lit square, the mobs of Northers yelled and stamped.

There was an art to using a broadsword. It is a clumsy object, and overheavy, but it did one thing superbly well. It cut. It lacked all the finesse of a rapier or sabre, which was why its use was no longer taught in the Imperial schools. The broadsword was an archaic weapon, current wisdom believed, a weapon for savages and barbarians. With a broadsword, there was no possibility of executing the deft moves of fencing. There was no riposte, or feint, or parry, or thrust to be had. There were just three basic moves: the block, the slash, and the remaining-on-your-feet.

A pallasz was so huge and heavy that if you committed to any blow, you were forced to follow it through. If you swung it, your torso went with it. If you blocked with it, you had better have set your feet braced square, or the impact would fell you. A broadsword duel was not a delicate thing. There was no space for fancy darts or quick footwork. It was a slow, slogging effort.

Karl was weary within seconds. The pallasz was such a leaden weight. He cut at Wernoff's swings, and finally deflected one so that the Stirlander's sword tip glanced off the paving.

'Stop trying so hard!' he hissed at the pikeman.

'They said I would be free!' Wernoff retorted.

'What?'

'They told me that if I killed you, they would set me free!'

Karl ducked the next stroke.

'You believe that?'

'It's all I have, demilancer!'

Wernoff was really trying to kill him. The idea jolted Karl harder than any broadsword blow.

'They won't!' he snarled. 'You believe them? You believe what they tell you?'

'I have to believe something!' Wernoff rasped, and thrust forward, lopping a chunk of flesh out of Karl's right shoulder.

Karl yelled out and felt hot blood coursing down his arm. The crowd went berserk, chanting and bawling.

He backed away as Wernoff, eager from the first sniff of blood, closed in.

Let him kill you, something inside Karl Vollen said. Just let him do it. It's what you want and, Sigmar knows, it's the closest thing to escape you're going to manage. Let him kill you.

Karl staggered back, his pallasz trailing over the paving slabs. Wernoff's blade whooped through the air, trying to find him.

But Karl couldn't let go. He didn't want to die. Not like this, performing in the market yard of a murdered town for entertainment. Not like anything, in fact.

He wanted to live. His life mattered.

It made sense. Why else had he been unable to take his own life in the pike pen? If he was going to give his life away, it would be for a damn good reason. And he certainly wasn't going to give these roaring bastards the pleasure of his death.

'Wernoff...' he said. 'I'm sorry. May Sigmar forgive me.'

'For what?' Wernoff asked, cutting in again.

Karl brought his pallasz up and blocked the Stirlander's blow. Then he swung hard, so Wernoff was forced to back away, out of balance thanks to the heavy counterweight of his thick sword.

With a broadsword, the damage was inflicted with the long edge. The demilancers had been taught to use the tip of a sword to thrust.

Karl did the latter. He performed an inappropriate stroke with his pallasz. The tip punched through Wernoff's unguarded sternum, and the rest of the blade followed it.

Wernoff jerked, stricken, like a butterfly on a pin. A great volume of blood squirted out around Karl's hands, under pressure.

'I'm sorry,' said Karl. Wernoff gagged, and then fell down so heavily his weight plucked the pallasz from Karl's hands.

Karl turned around slowly, gazing defiantly at the Kurgan host who were howling and cheering at him. Life was the only thing Karl had left, and keeping hold of it despite everything the Northers tried to do to him was the one way he could deny them.

Zar Uldin walked out from the crowd onto the square. His wolf-mask seemed to grin in the firelight. He crouched beside Wernoff's twitching body, wetted his hands with the blood, and marked an eye symbol on his bare chest.

He rose and faced Karl. It was hard to hear him over the noise of the rampant crowd.

'You do Tchar's work, little Southlander,' he said.

'No,' Karl answered, emphatically.

'Oh, but you do. Tchar rejoices in change, and the second holiest change in the world is the change from life to death. That is what you have done for him.'

'No,' Karl repeated.

Hinn came forward and retrieved his pallasz. They led Karl back through the crowd and into the temple. Uldin's shaman danced around them, shaking his bone-beads and sistrum. Behind them, another ritual bout was getting underway.

In the temple entranceway, Uldin pulled Karl round to face him.

'By what name are you called?' he demanded.

'Karl Reiner Vollen,' the clarion replied, involuntarily.

Uldin reached up and clutched at the air, as if snatching a fly. 'I pluck the name for Tchar and give it back changed.' He opened the hand again, and shook it at Karl as if brushing a cobweb off it.

'Now you are called Azytzeen. By that name you will be known to the Kurgan. Azytzeen!'

'Keep your damn words and names–' Karl spat, touching the iron handle of the true killer in his pocket to ward against the foul charm. He had never been a superstitious man, and had prided himself on scorning such customs. But he touched the iron without hesitation. It seemed to him some magic was very real, and the Kurgan tribes oozed it. It felt as if Uldin's words were actually stripping his name away from him and replacing it with something heavy and venomous.

'Azytzeen!' Uldin repeated, and his shaman started to sing the name, over and again, as he pranced and capered around them.

* * *

II

THE MARKED MEN remained in the temple for the next eight days. They were fed, well and regularly, and had to endure the squealing attentions of shamans who came in and performed rites at them.

All the zars sent their shamans to the temple to conduct rituals over their marked property. Ons Olker visited five times. Though he was busy with Blayda's marked souls, such as von Margur, his eyes constantly searched for Karl. Whenever he was around, Karl kept a firm hand on his true killer.

Uldin's shaman, whose name was Subotai, visited frequently, singling out Karl and other men with Uldin's mark, and daubing them with ash and body paints as he chanted and rattled. When he removed his snake-etched barbute, Subotai revealed a strange face. It was broad and flat, and his eyes were narrow. Karl had once seen a traveller's drawing of the men who lived in the farthest east, in the realm of Cathay. They had these facial characteristics.

'He is of the Man-Chu, who dwell far around the Circle, nigh on the territories of the Dreaded Wo,' von Margur said to Karl. Of course, the knight had not even seen Subotai's face. 'He was taken by Uldin as a war trophy years ago, but marked and spared because he has the sight.'

Only then did Karl notice that the shaman had three blue dots on his right cheek, a very old mark faded by time. Zar Uldin's mark. Karl knew he had the same thing on his own face.

Word of what Karl had done to Wernoff that first night spread amongst the captives the next day, and many men chose to avoid him. Though it was not the place or time for real friendships, Karl suddenly found himself short of comrades. But von Margur didn't seem bothered. Neither did a laconic crossbowman from Nordland called Etzel, who also wore Uldin's mark, and a Carroburger called Vinnes, who sported the red dots of Zar Herfil. Both of the latter had been forced to fight – and kill – in bouts after Karl's. The four kept themselves together. They understood.

During those eight days, other men were drawn out, and some failed to return. Gradually, the number of captives halved, and all those that remained had killed in a bout. Karl and his comrades were no longer shunned, but the mood had hardened. For most of each day, the marked men sat in bleak silence, consumed by their own thoughts.

Karl was called out twice more, into the firelit square and the blood-lusting crowd. He killed once, in a fight with another Stirlander, who seemed to give up and welcome the swift death Karl granted him.

In the other bout, Karl was drawn against a young man from Middenheim who, at the last moment, broke down and refused to do battle. The Middenheimer threw away his blade and tried to run, weeping and begging. Hinn executed him, and Karl was dragged back to the temple.

By the seventh day, only von Margur had not been called. Vinnes and Etzel couldn't understand why the Northerners were even bothering to persevere with the blind knight.

But Karl knew. He knew every time von Margur opened his mouth and said things that he had no right to know.

Von Margur had the sight. Possibly as a result of the grievous damage to his brain, he was special, and the Kurgan prized him.

III

ON THE SEVENTH night, Hinn and the Kurgan came for von Margur. A gale had come up in the darkness outside, and it moaned and whistled around the temple's stone bulk. The place was suddenly full of strange, cold drafts, and all the torches sputtered and danced.

'Help me, Karl!' von Margur cried out as he was led away. He was turning his head to and fro, eyes cast upwards, desperate to see. 'I am afraid! I am sore afraid!'

'Sigmar will save you!' Karl called out, a blasphemy that got him a hard slap from Hinn.

Etzel and Vinnes were called too, and a Reiklander called Brandt.

The captives waited for half an hour, hearing the distant Kurgan cheers above the howl of the wind. Karl went to the temple altar and knelt to pray for von Margur's soul. He dismissed the desecration that the Kurgan had heaped upon the altar, and steadfastly ignored their iron coffer and its flickering eye. He also cared little that the altar and temple had originally been dedicated to a Kislevite god whose worship and tenets he didn't know. All that mattered was that it was a sacred place, all the better for Sigmar to hear him.

The iron coffer gazed at him, nevertheless, as he did his devotions.

Then the Kurgan brought von Margur back. He was walking unassisted, as if he knew the way. He didn't knock into anything but simply shambled confidently back through the main hall of the temple and took a seat on the floor next to Karl. His hands were bloody.

'It isn't easy,' he said, 'is it?'

'No,' said Karl. He had no idea how the blind knight had survived for one moment.

Von Margur gazed blankly into space.

'I suppose it will get easier,' he said at last, and curled over on the rugs and matting like a child.

'What did they make you do, sir?' Karl asked.

But von Margur had fallen asleep.

Then Vinnes returned. He had been cut on the leg and the hip, and he was shaking and sobbing. The Kurgan washed his wounds with vinegar and left him. Vinnes refused to come anywhere near von Margur.

Karl went over to him.

'What happened?' he asked, offering the Carroburger a waterskin.

'They made me kill Brandt,' Vinnes sniffed. 'Gods alive, they made me gut him! He was no swordsman. He didn't stand a chance against me, but he fought like a bastard and gave me these.' Vinnes ruefully indicated his wounds.

'They're flesh cuts. You'll heal,' said Karl.

'I don't want to heal,' muttered Vinnes plaintively.

'What about von Margur? Did you see?'

Vinnes nodded.

'Dammit! And?'

'He slew Etzel.'

'No!'

'I watched it, Vollen. They were head to head, with a pair of daggers, each of them. In the square out there. Von Margur didn't even know which way to point. He kept calling out for you to help him. The bastards were jeering. Etzel – Sigmar! He didn't want to fight with him. Not a blind man. Not a bloody blind man…'

Vinnes looked round at Karl. He had managed to smear blood from his leg wound across his face. His eyes were terrible to behold. In them, fear, despair, humiliation, disgust, all in equal measures.

'I killed Brandt!' he cried out hoarsely.

'I know, I know… My friend, tell me what von Margur did.'

Vinnes swallowed and his voice dropped to a whisper. 'He fought. Suddenly, like a seeing man. Blocking every blow Etzel threw at him. Knife to knife. A sighted man who has been trained in daggerwork could not have bettered him. He seemed to know everything Etzel was going to do and parry it. All the while… all the damn while… his eyes were slack and looking the wrong way! Sigmar spare me, it was terrifying. Even the bloody Kurgan shut up in wonder at it.'

'Go on, Vinnes.'

'The daggers were flying so fast. Chink chink chink! Etzel was suddenly fighting for real, crying out in horror. Then… then, von Margur, he… he drove both his blades home at once. Both through Etzel's heart. And it was done.'

Karl gasped and sat back.

'I will not go near him, Vollen,' Vinnes announced.

'What? Why? He only did what we all have had to do.'

'I know that! But he's blind! Blind! How could he have done that if dark magic hadn't guided him?'

'I–'

'And look at him, Vollen! Look at him!'

Karl glanced across the temple at the slumbering von Margur.

Like a contented dog, the blind knight was grinning in his sleep.

IV

AT DAWN ON the ninth day, the zars came to the temple and divided the captives up according to their marks. Zar Uldin, escorted by his shaman

Subotai, drew off Karl and the seven others with the blue mark, and led them away into the square.

The town was now quiet and deserted. The Kurgan host had moved on. Only trampled mud lay where their gers and pavillions had once been pitched.

Uldin's eight marked men were roped together at the throat. Across the square, Karl could see other groups of captives being led away by their respective zars. He caught a glimpse of von Margur with Blayda and Ons Olker.

Subotai led Uldin's marked men out of the town under guard into a marshy paddock west of the main gate. More than five score Kurgan were gathered there, preparing their big, black horses.

This was Zar Uldin's warband. They were all clad in scale, plate and chainmail darkened with pitch, and their round shields were painted blue with the snakes-and-eye motif. One of the largest riders, a Kurgan called Yuskel, carried the warband's standard. It was a tall pole, the upper half of which was sheathed in clattering human jawbones. The cross spar had three skulls fixed to it: two human skulls on either side of a horse's. All three were gilded. Below the spar fluttered a leathery banner, the irregular shape of which betrayed its human source. On it was painted a wolf's head with a single, centred eye.

Yuskel was mounted on a curious beast: a stout horse with skin striped with thin, vertical black and white stripes. The stripes even extended into its thick mane. It was an angry, snorting creature.

Zar Uldin rode up on his big stallion, and his men shouted a welcome.

Uldin walked his mount between his men, clasping hands and slapping backs. A wineskin was tossed around. Then, with a clap of his massive hands, Uldin ordered them forward. A Kurgan with a huge carnyx that coiled around his torso like a serpent sounded the ugly blare of command.

The warband galloped away into the wind and the trees. Five solid-wheeled wagons pulled by oxen followed the riders, and the marked captives, strung together, were whipped along after the wagons. Subotai and six Kurgan horsemen flanked them.

Turning his neck as far as the rope around it would allow, Karl looked back at the nameless, dead town where he had been forced to cast his humanity away. He thought of Wernoff and the other Stirlander. He hoped they knew, wherever they were, that Azytzeen had killed them.

Not Karl Reiner Vollen.

V

FOR TEN DAYS, they toiled south and west. Uldin's warband roamed far ahead of the trundling wagons and the captives, but each night they caught them up at the camp-fire.

The world they passed through was desolate. Burnt forests and devastated villages. Miles of arable land churned up by hooves. Pastures full of slaughtered livestock. On the track, there were bodies: the executed inhabitants of overrun towns, fleeing refugees who had been overtaken and murdered.

The cool spring air was busy with flies and circling crows.

Apart from one day of heavy rain, the weather was improving. Spring was maturing and casting out the dregs of winter. Somehow, the calm breeze and the pale blue sky made the devastation more affecting. In other years, this time would have been sweet, a growing season for the populations living on the southern edges of the oblast and the northern borders of the Empire.

Not this year. This year that no one would forget.

Spring flowers, white and blue and yellow, grew up from fields of cinders and ruined woodlands. The early green crops sprouted through the brown bones of the recently dead, scattered across the fields. The warm, fresh breezes of springtime were tainted with the scents of rot and the gas of bloated bodies.

Karl had no idea where he was, but he guessed he was not far off the territories of his homeland. If they weren't in Ostermark yet, they would be soon.

And the captives were trailing the Northers' main advance. How deep had that cut now? What part of the Empire still remained free?

Karl was plodding home, but he was very much afraid nothing of it would remain when he got there.

VI

THEY WERE TRUDGING through a thin wood of scorched poplars. It was the tenth day since they had quit the nameless town. The poplars had heat-stripped trunks, and a few feeble burned branches protruding from them. It looked for all the world as if a great fire had burned them from above. From out of the sky.

They were walking behind the wagons, flanked by Subotai on his milk-white ass and the six Kurgan riders.

And there the enemy found them. Afterwards, Karl was astonished at himself for regarding them as the enemy.

There was a rumble of hooves, shaking the fire-dried earth. The Kurgan reacted in alarm and started shouting.

Eight knights templar of the Reiksguard plunged majestically out of the gloom, with maces and swords raised in their gauntleted fists. Their leader was swinging a warhammer strung with white ribbons. They were tremendous to behold. Laurel garlands decorated the gold symbols of their illustrious order. They were clad in full suits of silver-white plate. Their thundering steeds were thoroughbred destriers: massive horses clad with shaffrons, crinits and complete bardings of articulated steel, and caparisons of rich cloth.

The lead knight ploughed into the side of the convoy first, whirling his hammer. He smashed a Kurgan warrior off his dark horse and then dug in with his long, roweled spurs – elongated things designed to reach his steed's flanks under the deep, segmented apron of the armour bard. He surged about, his hammer turning. The air was cold enough for his breath to be visible as snorted plumes escaping the slits in his polished bascinet. He lunged at Subotai. The shaman was kicking the flanks of his white ass with his bare heels, and yelling curses at the magnificent knight.

The blunt face of the hammer hit Subotai square in the forehead of his barbute. The slip-on iron helmet buckled and flattened. A bloody vapour squeezed out of the eyeslits on impact.

Subotai fell backwards off his mount, his blood speckling the ass's white coat.

Karl wanted to run, but the thong attaching him to his fellow captives snapped taut and yanked him back. All around them, Reiksguard templars were fighting Kurgan horsemen from their saddles.

And the Kurgan were losing.

'Come on!' Karl yelled at Maddeus, the man behind him.

'We can escape now! They don't care about us any more! Come on!'

Maddeus tried to run, but fell down, strangled by the rope. The man behind him had just been trampled by a side-staggering destrier.

Karl snatched out his true killer and slashed through the rope tying him to Maddeus.

He was free. Really free.

'For Sigmar's sake, Karl!' Maddeus screamed, clutching at his throat noose. 'Me too!'

Karl ran forward and cut the rope behind Maddeus's nape with the dirk.

They started to run, heads down, into the trees. Karl tripped over a cinder root, and Maddeus dragged him to his feet.

Behind them, the templars were winning the horse to horse fight. One of the wagons had caught fire.

'This way!' Karl urged, as he and Maddeus slogged through the ash-dust. In their desperation, they barged against tree trunks that looked solid but disintegrated at a touch like powder.

They heard hooves behind them. It was the leader of the knightly detachment. He saw them and spurred towards them.

'Sir! Sir, stay your hand! We are men of the Empire, sadly imprisoned!' Maddeus called out, turning back with raised hands. 'Free us, we beg you!'

Karl had no doubt the knight heard Maddeus's frantic plea. He threw himself down as the knight charged on. Maddeus hurled himself the other way.

The templar passed between them, his destrier kicking up clods of black ash. He circled round and came back for another pass.

Maddeus squealed as the warhammer broke his back.

'You bastard!' Karl howled in outrage. 'We are not the enemy!'

The templar turned his horse and began to run Karl down.

'In the name of Sigmar!' Karl yelled, trying to escape the knight by doubling back around a tree. 'In the name of Sigmar, we are loyal to the Imperial throne! Loyal, I say!'

The knight suddenly sat upright in his saddle. A black-fletched arrow had just impaled his chest.

Zar Uldin galloped in, with many of the warband racing beside him. He was letting arrows fly from his composite bow. Uldin was riding without a hand on the reins. He drew the bowstring back past his ear and charged his arrows with such force that no bascinet, cuirass or mail could stop them. Each arrow made a spitting noise as it loosed a grinding crack and punctured its target.

Transfixed with arrows, the knight clattered off his horse.

Karl cowered against a tree stump as the Kurgan stormed past. They were whooping and yelling and their heavy arrows spat through the air. Each man had a clutch of six or seven arrows gripped between the fingers of the hand that held the bow itself, so as soon as they had fired one, their drawing hand could nock another as it went to pull the bowstring back. Their fire rate was astonishingly rapid, like some mechanical device designed by the Engineers of Nuln. The Kurgan horses, smart and hard-trained, seemed to need no rein control. This allowed the Northers great independence; they could turn in the saddle and shoot arrows in passing to the side, or even to the rear. Karl gazed as a Kurgan – Barlas – put an arrow into the chest of one templar as he charged him, and then two more between his shoulderblades as he galloped past.

The proud templars, the military elite of the Empire, were overwhelmed in under a minute. One, armed with a sword and cornered, fought on against the Kurgan riders closing around him and goading him with spears. Another, unhorsed, found himself facing Zar Uldin, who dismounted to meet him, drawing his pallasz.

Karl hurried over to where Maddeus lay face down, but the man was miserably done to death. Karl made the sign of Sigmar over him, and then began to run, as fast as his legs could take him, into the shadows of the extinct forest.

VII

HE RAN THROUGH the blackened poplars and the dried rags of burnt ivy. He ran towards the light and what he hoped was the south.

When he came out of the dead woodland, he found himself at the top of a low hill. In the wide valley below, and down on the plain of a distant river, a battle was raging. Ten thousand men and horses, twenty thousand even, resembled dark shapes seething like ants from a spaded hillock. Smoke and dust rose, swabbing out the low sun. It was impossible to tell who was who, or even who was winning.

But Karl Reiner Vollen had a feeling in the pit of his stomach that this was another day the Empire would mourn for years to come.

He stopped dead. He could run all he liked, but he could never outrun this tide of death. He leaned against an old, gnarled tree, and hugged his arms around his body.

After a while, he heard horses coming up behind him and looked round. Three of Uldin's warband walked their mounts out of the woods towards him. Their leader, a hairy man in a houndskull helm, was playing out the loops of his lariat. When he saw the look on Karl's face, he simply hung the rope back on his saddle without comment, and casually beckoned to the demilancer.

The three Kurgan turned their horses back the way they had come, and Karl walked after them, head bowed.

VIII

THE KURGAN WERE laying out their dead and stripping the templar corpses of their armour. The beautiful silver-steel pieces were being collected in a handcart. They were of such fine workmanship, they would be reused, altered, or used for barter.

Seven Kurgan were dead, including the shaman Subotai, as well as three of the marked men.

Zar Uldin saw Karl, and rose to his feet. He had been squatting beside Subotai's crumpled body. He had removed his wolf-helm, and his fine, shaved head was exposed.

'Azytzeen. You tried to escape.'

Karl shook his head. He looked up at the taller man's scarred, murderously handsome face.

'No. I fled for my life.'

Uldin narrowed his eyes.

'They were killing everybody. They killed Maddeus. I decided to run.'

The zar thought about this, and then shrugged lightly. He believed Karl.

'But escape was in my thoughts too,' Karl said anyway.

Uldin stiffened. 'And?'

'I changed my mind.'

The zar smiled. 'Change. There, you see? Tchar is in you.'

'No,' said Karl firmly. 'He is not.'

No longer interested, Uldin walked back over to the shaman's body. The hairy man in the houndskull tied Karl back up with the four surviving marked captives.

The gathering warband looked morose. It seemed the death of a shaman was a bad omen, and that a warband without a shaman was weak.

'Why are the bastards so grim?' whispered the captive beside Karl.

'The shaman's dead. That is misfortune for them all.'

'How do you know that, Karl?'

'I overheard what they were saying.'

The man looked at Karl nervously. 'You can understand their words?'

'Can't you?' Karl asked.

'Of course not,' the man replied, and the other three captives, listening in to the exchange, shook their heads too.

'But–' said Karl. Then he shut up because he was far too scared to think about what it meant.

Yuskel, the banner bearer, walked up to Uldin and put his hand on his heart. He said something about preparations. Uldin nodded, and gathered up the small, limp body of Subotai in his arms.

The warband felled the cinder trunks around the clearing, and raised a small wooden stockade. The work took most of the day. Some of the warriors had to ride away to locate and cut decent wood from groves that had not been scorched by the fire. The Kurgan dead were carried inside the stockade, and their weapons laid out beside them. Then the horses of the fallen men were slaughtered and gutted, Subotai's white ass along with them. The carcasses were bled, and then set upright around the paling wall. They were raised on sharpened stakes that propped them up through their slit bellies. Fresh staves were cut to support their lolling heads so they looked like they were alive and galloping.

The stripped bodies of the templars and the corpses of the three marked captives were left where they had fallen, to rot.

The warband gathered around the stockade as night fell. The drummers beat out a slow, pulsing rhythm, and the horn blower pealed long, atonal blasts into the closing dark with his serpent-coil carnyx.

Uldin, helmless, went around the stockade, whispering to each staked horse-corpse in turn and kissing its muzzle. He finished with Subotai's white ass.

Then he took a flaming tree branch from Berlas, the master archer, and set it to the stockade.

The Kurgan warband howled like wolves into the sky as the flames rose and engulfed the stockade and the bodies inside it. The horn blew, over and over, pulsing above the throbbing howls. Then the staked-up horse-corpses began to catch fire too.

Crosswinds drove the pungent smoke through the dead grove. Coughing, the captives turned away.

Karl was transfixed.

IX

AT DAWN, THE warband roused and rode away into the valley, trailing the wagons and the guarded captives behind it. The stockade pyre was still burning: a grim, black ring guarded by the smouldering skeletons of eight propped steeds.

Below, the battle had ended. The cold morning air was filled with the miserable perfumes of mass warfare: blood, faeces, charred wood, heated iron, powdered bone. There was no relief from it.

Those that had lost the battle had been crucified naked, alive or dead. The foul sentinels watched over the smouldering, debris-littered landscape. They were staked apart every few dozen spans, on frames of spear-shafts or wagon spokes. Black carrion birds fluttered and hopped all over the wide, wounded vista, like autumn leaves stirred by the breeze.

They marched until noon, when they reached a town. An Imperial burg. From the smoke trails wisping from the stone structures inside its high walls, it seemed clear that the Northers had taken it.

Someone told Karl it was Brunmarl. The news made him shiver. If it was Brunmarl, then they were in the Marches of Ostermark, inside the Empire. Brunmarl had a famous cathedral, he knew that much. There was no sign of a spire, though there was a large burning building that looked as if it might once have owned one.

Uldin led them through the great gates. Many more zars were massing their warbands inside the city walls. Standard bearers challenged one another loudly as they came in sight of rival banners. Yuskel was especially good at spitting out muscular torrents of abuse at other banner bearers.

Karl glimpsed Zar Blayda's banner – a bloody swordblade on a red field – down one side street, and Zar Herfil's boar's skull standard in a market yard. The horde had come here to roost.

Uldin's band were sent to billet in an old, sandstone building that turned out to be the town's library. Karl expected to see Kurgan defecating on the pages of the precious books, but he was surprised by the truth.

Warriors were carrying the heaps of ancient tomes out of the shattered building on wooden boards, and the shamans were working their way through the pages, arguing between them about the things they found.

Just as they came to acquire land and loot and blood for their bloody gods, the Northers had come to steal knowledge and learning.

He was nudged at spearpoint into the vacant halls of the library building. Karl stooped and picked up a slim volume that had been cast aside into the brick dust. It was a treatise on fortification, written in old Tilean, the ancient language.

'Those leaves there?' asked a shaman who looked up from nearby. 'Can you read them?'

'Of course,' replied Karl, and tossed the book away. The shaman, a tall, gangly youth with antlers rising from his cap of fur, leaped up and ran to Karl.

'You can read it?' he repeated. Ropes of shell beads tinkled around his long, thin neck. Both of his middle fingers were absent, so his hands were like curious claws as they pawed the old book.

'What is this word?' he demanded.

'That... "strong"?' Karl said.

'And this one?'

'Ahhh... "gabion"...a defence term.'

The shaman looked up at Karl. His eyes were wiped with kohl, and a black line had been painted around his mouth, making it wider. The flesh of his face, neck and shoulders was dusted with white chalk. The shaman rattled his sistrum at Karl, and hopped from foot to foot.

Yuskel dragged Karl into the building.

The marked captives were thrown into an undercroft and the hatch boarded up behind them. They waited in the dark for several hours.

Then the hatch opened again, and Zar Uldin stomped down the raw wooden stairs. He looked around and pointed directly at Karl. The warriors behind him surged forward to grab the demilancer.

Outside, it was dark, and torches had been lit in the beckets.

'Another fight?' Karl said sullenly.

'Yes, Azytzeen.'

Karl sighed.

'This is important!' Uldin snapped, turning to face him. 'You must prove my warband is still strong. The other zars know I have lost my shaman. I must win tonight, to prove that ill fortune does not follow me and those who ride with me.'

'And if I lose?'

'My warband will be broken up and shared between the other zars,' Uldin replied.

Karl smiled. The temptation was almost too great. 'And if I win?'

'The act might be favorable, and entice a new shaman.'

'So what I do tonight makes – or breaks – your warband?'

'Yes.'

'Then at last, I have power over you,' Karl said, and walked away.

'Azytzeen! Azytzeen!' Uldin called out, running after Karl.

'What is my name, zar? What is it?'

'I forget...'

'What is my name?'

'Uhh... Kerl?'

'Karl.'

'Seh! Karl!'

'Call me that and I might fight for you. Call me that bastard name and I will do nothing but seek a quick death. Who am I supposed to fight?'

'Some dog of Zar Kreyya's mark. Then, if you triumph, one of Zar Herfil's slaves.'

'What's my name?'

'Karl is your name.'

X

THE KURGAN OF Uldin's band took him with ceremony to the pit. Yuskel carried the standard with its gilded skulls before him, and Hzaer the carnyx blower came behind, booming out threatening notes that echoed down the firelit streets. Six warriors flanked Karl, their swords drawn. One was Berlas, the archer. Another was Efgul, the hairy warrior in the houndskull. The other four were Fegul One-Hand, Diormac, Lyr and Sakondor.

Karl knew their names because they told them to him. One by one, before their march to the pit, they presented themselves to him, bowed their heads, placed their hands on their hearts, and uttered their names.

It was not, Karl recognised, an honour as such. To them he was still marked scum. But it acknowledged his importance and the vital part he was about to play in the future of the warband. They told him their true names, and he knew there was magick in that. They were giving him power over them, by speaking their names with their hands placed as heart-truth. They were giving him power.

They led him to a derelict building that had once been a farrier's workshop or an ironworker's forge. The long, stone bath had been filled with water and oil, and heated slightly. There was steam in the air, and the strong scents of balsam and ginger.

Yuskel and Efgul made him strip and climb into the hot water. They dunked him several times and held him under. When he came up at last, coughing, he was cleaner than he'd been in weeks, and his skin was soft and slippery with oil.

Karl stood naked, dripping and tense, as Berlas combed back his hair and tied it in a tail behind his neck. Lyr shaved his face with the edge of a frighteningly sharp knife. Then Hzaer dusted blue powder over him, so that his head, neck and chest were all stained.

'Close your eyes,' Hzaer warned, and blew black ink through a straw into each of Karl's eye sockets. Now he was blue-skinned, and his eyes glinted out of jet-black circles.

They brought him brown leather trews and heavy black boots, and fastened on iron thigh plates. Then a chainmail breech-clout was added, supported by a wide leather belt with a fat brass boss-buckle inscribed with a snake. Hzaer and Berlas bound Karl's arms with leather windings that crossed around the base of his thumbs and tied off around his palms.

Yuskel brought a single pauldron of black metal and strapped it around Karl's left shoulder.

Then they stepped back. Skarkeetah and Uldin emerged from the shadows. The slave lord seemed luminous in his white-bear pelt. The gold and blue-stone eye glinted around his thick neck and the one-eyed raven was perched on his raised left wrist. Uldin carried a black iron barbute with short, twisted horns.

With Subotai dead, and fearing ill omen, the zar had called upon the sorcerous slave lord for help. Uldin had undoubtedly paid him, for Skarkeetah was not affiliated to any one warband.

Skarkeetah made no shamanic prancing or prattling. He waved no sistrum or beads. He looked Karl in the eyes and muttered some low, dark prayer of blessing that Karl did not understand. He didn't need to. Every syllable made his flesh crawl. The raven nodded and bobbed, clacking its thick, hooked beak. Then Skarkeetah held his amulet up and Karl was forced to gaze into the blazing blue stones in the pupil of the snake-wreathed eye. Light from the candles made the blue stones twinkle and spark.

'Tchar governs you now, more than you care to admit, more than you even know. Let him guide your hand tonight.'

Karl said nothing.

'Will you fight?' Uldin asked.

'I will fight,' Karl said, dismissively.

'Make it heart-truth or not at all,' Uldin replied.

Karl hesitated. Then he raised his right hand – his sword hand – and placed it over his heart. 'I will fight.'

Satisfied, Uldin placed a leather caul on Karl's crown and lowered the heavy barbute over his head. It was stifling and he could see very little.

'No,' he said, and took it off.

'You'll need it,' warned Skarkeetah.

'Not if Tchar is with me,' Karl mocked, but the reply seemed to delight the slave lord. Skarkeetah reached out and placed his plump fingers across Karl's left cheek and rested the pad of his thumb on Karl's lips.

'Tchar is most certainly with you.'

Horns, bone and metal, blew loudly in the city outside, and Karl realised there was a dull, distant roar that could only be cheering.

His Kurgan guard led him to the door. In the doorway, Yuskel paused and handed Karl his true killer. It had been taken from him with the rags he'd stripped off. Karl slid it into his belt.

Two hundred paces from the farrier's barn was a huge round drum of a building that Karl realised had once been the playhouse. Open to the sky, its wooden structure resembled a miniature amphitheatre. The stands and galleries were torchlit and groaned with stamping, cheering Northers.

They went in under the low eaves of the players' entrance. Under the seating, through the darkness of timber beams and rib supports, and into the flickering yellow light.

The bowl of the playhouse was a circle of dirt floor surrounded by high wooden panels. Tonight, the playhouse had its biggest ever audience.

Yuskel held a round shield so that Karl could slide his left arm into place. The shield was blue, with the snakes-and-eye emblem, and a black horse tail strung from the boss. Karl hefted it, and tested his arm for flexibility. Then Uldin handed Karl his own pallasz, hilt first.

Another carnyx sounded, and Uldin took a broadsword from Lyr and strode out into the dirt bowl. Zar Kreyya, a giant in spiked gold, emerged to meet him and they exchanged the ritual sword strokes.

The zars withdrew, and Karl edged out into the arena.

The host was screaming and wailing. Fists beat time on the playhouse's wooden rails.

A figure appeared on the far side of the pit. He was similarly dressed in iron and leather half-mail and armed with a sword and shield. His lean frame was painted green. Karl raised his pallasz and charged him.

Only when he was a few paces off did Karl recognise his opponent.

It was Johann Friedel.

XI

WHITE DYE HAD been rubbed into Friedel's eye sockets and into the hollows of his cheeks, and short lines had been wiped vertically on his upper and lower lips. He looked like a cadaver, like a death's head, the green pigment daubing him the colour of putrid flesh. His hair was caked to his scalp with lime wash.

'Johann?'

The figure growled.

'Johann? It's me. It's Karl.'

Friedel's deep-fullered sword came at Karl. He got the shield up and the blade crashed off it, jarring Karl's arm.

'Johann!'

Another blow to the shield. Another. Chips of blue painted wood scattered off.

'Sigmar's name, Johann! It's Karl!'

Friedel swung a cut at Karl with enough force to smack Karl's shield aside. Karl barely managed to get his pallasz up in time to fend away the follow-through.

It was Johann Friedel's body, right enough. But Johann Friedel no longer inhabited it. His eyes, framed by the white dye, were... blank. During his boyhood, Karl had owned a dog, a good game hound, that had been bitten by a rat and fallen prey to the frothing sickness. His father had been forced to kill the dog with a mattock to stop its suffering.

The look in Friedel's eyes was the same one Karl had seen in his dog's gaze just before the end. Vacant, wild, feral, deranged by pain and fear and sickness.

They circled, trading blows, sword to shield. Friedel stormed closer, and Karl put his shoulder behind his shield and barged him away. They crashed again, shield to shield now. There was a brute strength in Friedel that Karl had never suspected. He doubted it had been there the last time he'd seen the boy.

Outside the zal, just before Zhedevka fell, Johann Friedel had yelled Karl's name and begged him not to go away.

Karl was surprised by how much that fleeting memory hurt him. Surprised – and annoyed. Since his near escape in the ash wood, Karl had become hardened and composed. He had worn out his capacity to feel grief, or to feel much at all for any of the things or people he had lost at Zhedevka. It seemed the only way he could deal with the terrible events that had transformed his life was to grit his teeth and block them out. He'd already mourned Johann Friedel in his mind, convinced he was dead like everyone else.

But Friedel wasn't. He was worse than dead. He was a rotting echo of himself, lumbering out of the dark to remind Karl of his loss and rekindle his grief. To start Karl hurting all over again. And Friedel was suffering. Suffering like a dog.

It would not do. Karl would not have it so. This mocking atrocity had to end. End. End.

The crowd was screaming and booming. The noise was so great that Karl was physically shaken by it. For a moment, he forgot where he was.

He swept around, searching for his foe, and raised his sword. Blood ran slickly down the fuller groove and over his hand.

Friedel was lying on the dirt floor of the playhouse bowl in pieces. He was so rent and disfigured, Karl could not bear to look at him.

Uldin strode out into the pit, and raised his heavy arms, thick with trophy rings, to accept the adulation. Efgul hurried out after the zar, and ran to steady Karl.

'Spirit of Khar!' Efgul rasped. 'You brought him death like a daemon, Azytzeen!'

'Enough! I can't... I can't...' Karl panted. He was trembling hard. Efgul shook him.

'Stay true! You're halfwise there!'

'I can't...'

'Stay true!'

'You don't understand! He was my friend!'

'Then you gave him Tchar's gift! The gift of change! Life into death! Captivity into freedom!'

'Gods help me...'

'Listen to me, Azytzeen. Krayya's warband are of the Mark of Decay! Noork'hl, the Unclean! If that flesh-body was truly your friend, then you spared him the Great Corruption That Consumes!'

Efgul spoke urgently and earnestly, as if he was telling some grim truth. It was nonsense to Karl.

'I don't understand,' Karl said, looking at Efgul's shaggy face.

'You will, if you live.'

Horns sounded, and Efgul dragged Karl around. Uldin was making the formal challenge to the pitched-black figure of Blayda. Scrabbling Northers had dragged the bloody scraps of Freidel from the ring.

They all departed. Efgul too left, taking Friedel's sword to make a new trophy ring for Uldin's arms. Karl turned to face Blayda's ritual champion.

He was a tall man, stripped down to a chainmail clout and plated armour on his limbs. His skin was painted red. He had no shield. With both hands, he gripped the long handle of a Carroburg greatsword.

For a moment, Karl thought it was Vinnes, for he was of Blayda's mark.

It wasn't.

Yet even if it had been, Karl wouldn't have held back. Not any more. There was nothing he could face now that he was too afraid to kill.

KUL

I

THEY RODE INTO the north-west for twenty days and twenty nights. Gerlach Heileman thought his mind had become reconciled to the infinite openness of the steppe during the ride to Dushyka, but this journey dwarfed it. Twenty days' riding-worth of nothingness in all directions. Gerlach began to welcome the moonrise, or the occasional buzzards that hung in the daylight air. They were brief, precious breaks in the monotony of grass and sky.

Until he started to notice the clouds. This was some five or six days into the trek. He wondered why he had not seen them before. No two were the same. Their shapes and forms, their textures and colours, even their speeds. Some resembled objects – a castle tower, a grazing horse, an eagle's wing. Gerlach had already noticed that, from time to time, the lancers would point up at the sky and make some remark that was usually greeted by chuckles or nods. Now he understood. They saw it too.

'A ram!' someone would declare as they rode along.

Others would agree, or offer suggestions of their own.

On occasions, it was more abstract. A lancer would point and laugh, 'Mitri!' The cloud, a dark lump, looked nothing like the heavy lancer... except that its solidity and gloom somehow conveyed Mitri's demeanour. Some clouds just seemed to suggest things, as if they had inherent character.

It was strange. Once Gerlach had begun to observe the clouds, the open steppe didn't seem empty at all. It was changing all the time. There was always something to see, some pattern to identify. It had just taken a while for his southern-bred mind, accustomed to complex landscapes, to be re-educated. Now, he supposed, he saw the world as the Kislevites saw it. What he had taken to be a vacant blankness had a subtle complexity all of its own, if you knew how to appreciate it.

When Gerlach pointed at a cloud and said, 'A ewe suckling lambs!' the riders seemed delighted with him.

They stopped for a few hours each night. There was no wood, but the riders had brought kindling with them. Most of it was animal bones carefully salvaged from previous meals. In a world where there was little of anything, everything had a use.

Huddled round the weak, yellow flames of the fire, the men would talk idly and reminisce. Sometimes they would even talk about the things they had seen pass by in the clouds that day. This efficient frugality governed their way of life. Every resource in this hard, pared-down existence was used and reused until it was exhausted. The bones of one meal fuelled the next. The shapes of passing clouds stopped them going crazy with boredom during the day, and the memory of them entertained them at night. It was as ingenious as it was thrifty.

At the fireside, Borodyn told Gerlach something of the lore of the sky. It had, as Gerlach guessed, a lot to do with circles. No two clouds were precisely the same, and they went on forever, making long, repeated journeys around the krug of the sky. If a man saw a cloud that he had seen earlier in his life, he knew the sky had gone full circle, and that his time was over. Sometimes, Borodyn said, a man who had seen a cloud for a second time got on his horse and rode away from his stanitsa or his rota and into the embrace of fate, never to be seen again.

Each dawn, in the cold, almost green light of the oblast daybreak, Gerlach and the men of the rota rose and rode away into the grass. Gerlach wondered if any of them would ever be seen again either.

II

IT WAS EVIDENTLY possible to derive extraordinary amounts of information from the steppe, more than Gerlach would ever have believed. When the world was this monotonous – open grass, empty sky – then any variation, no matter how miniscule, was strikingly obvious.

Born to this life, the Kislevites were quick to read the signs and clues the steppe gave them. And once he'd begun to read the cloud-forms, Gerlach found himself noticing other details too. The grasses, for example, were not all the same, no matter how uniform they seemed at first. Old growth and new, different types of grass, brakes of thistle and hardy fern. One glance at the steppe grass around him told a rider how recent the last rains had been, how far he'd have to dig to find pockets of moisture, which way the wind was blowing, and what time of day it was. An experienced rider didn't even have to look. The sound his horse's hooves made was enough. Firm and dry, soft and damp, flat and hollow.

From the air temperature and the humidity, it was possible to predict the weather. The riders could tell if rain was coming, and from which compass point. They could tell if a gale was about to rise, long before there was any darkening of the sky. The pattern and motion of the grass betrayed wind direction, and the fluctuation of light across the horizon foretold the changing climate.

By the time they neared Leblya stanitsa, Gerlach had learned enough to understand how the rota knew they were approaching a stanitsa before it had come into view. They had smelled smoke, and other odours like animal dung and vinegar. There was nothing to see, of course, but after days in the open air of the steppe, the merest whiff of smoke from a distance was enough.

Maksim raised his hand and the rota slowed out in a long line either side of him. 'Leblya,' he said. Several men agreed. Ahead of them was some swaying grass, bleached almost white in the afternoon sunlight.

Gerlach was about to scoff, and then he smelt it too. A remote scent of charcoal and animal sweat.

'Many of men,' Beledni muttered. Gerlach wasn't sure if that was supposed to be good or bad. With a brisk 'Yatsha!', Beledni spurred forward and led them onwards.

From what he had been told, Gerlach knew that this stanitsa – Leblya – had been nominated as a suitable restaging post for the Kislevite pulk in the event of retreat or rout. Any rota or warband that had escaped Zhedevka was under oath to regroup here. Gerlach's spirits rose. If there were 'many of men' here, then perhaps the pulk could regain its strength and prepare to return into the war zone. They could assemble at Leblya, and return south to begin the counter-fight.

After another quarter of an hour's ride, Beledni pulled up again, and halted the rota. He conferred with Maksim and the hornblower Yevni.

'What is it?' Gerlach asked Vitali.

Vitali pulled a sour face. 'Blood,' he said.

'You smell it?'

'Yha. Vebla does not?'

Gerlach couldn't. Just smoke, a little stronger now.

Beledni turned to the men and shouted a curt order. At once, the men dismounted, and dressed themselves in their wargear as quickly as possible. Gerlach did the same. It was a peculiar sight. Almost sixty half-naked men standing beside waiting horses in the middle of nothing, pulling surcoats over their heads and buckling on corselets of lamellar plate.

As soon as their wing crests, leopard pelts and szyszak helmets were in place, the men bundled their cast-off everyday rags into ground sheets and tied them fast behind their cantles. Gerlach hurried to keep up with them.

Once a rider was ready, he gave a shout – his name – and then leapt into the saddle from a standing pose. Now that was simply showing off, Gerlach thought, a circus trick. But the brash display of horsemanship raised the confidence of the rota. Gerlach thought about trying it, but knew he'd make an utter fool of himself. Saksen was rather bigger than the rota's ponies, and he was nothing like as fit and nimble as the lancers. By the time anyone looked his way, he was already astride his horse, buckling on his burgonet and adjusting the fit of his riding gloves.

Gerlach realised he needed to be close to the front rank. He picked up the banner, and steered Saksen forward until he was between Maksim and Beledni. The rotamaster looked over at him, his deep set eyes twinkling behind the heart-shaped face guard of his szyszak.

'This matter now, Vebla,' he said. 'This time now here. It matter you carry banner.'

Gerlach nodded. Saksen pawed uneasily, he held one ear back and the other forward with uncertainty.

Gerlach patted his neck. 'Glory awaits us, byeli-Saksen, my old friend,' he soothed. His gelding was still stark and splendid with his white and red body paint.

Gerlach hoisted the banner, and the long red and white snake of cloth fluttered out behind the wing-shield in the steppe wind.

They advanced on Leblya.

III

LEBLYA WAS MUCH larger than Dushyka. There was an inner mound – an old Scythian earthwork – on which a sturdy zal stood inside a heavy stone stockade. The town clung around the skirts of the mound, a muddle of white-painted izbas and barns. About them, a second broader and lower stockade, with a wooden gatehouse.

The wide sky had gone a dusky grey-blue, and for now there were no clouds except a thin bar in the south, just above the horizon. The grasslands had turned a pale, washed-out lime colour.

Dark dots – racing horsemen – dashed around the outer stockade in considerable numbers. There were perhaps a hundred or more. Gerlach knew what they were even as Maksim said the word.

'Kyazak!'

Leblya was under assault from the horse raiders. Under siege, in fact. As they drew closer, Gerlach could see the attackers in greater detail. Men in black rags and pitch-treated iron harnesses. Their black helmets were capped with bull horns and antlers. They were using slings to pelt the stockade with flaming missiles. Wisps of white smoke rose from the outer stockade.

Beledni slowed the rota and spread them out in a line, two hundred horse lengths from the town. By now, the kyazak had spotted them. They were breaking off from their hectic circuits and massing to face Beledni's company. It was not an aggressive response, more an act of curiosity. They easily outnumbered Yetchitch krug. They seemed puzzled that this huddle of riders had not simply turned tail and run.

'Kul!' Vaja said and spat.

'Kul?'

Kul was a tribal determination, one of the most southerly – and most feared – of the Kurgan from the Eastern Steppes. According to Vitali and Vaja, they were particular brutes, seldom allied to any main Kurgan force. They were content to prowl the oblast for scraps the host left behind. They were famous for an especially unlovely method of execution they reserved for those beaten in war. Vaja tried to explain what it was. It had something to do with a man's ribcage. Language, perhaps thankfully, defeated him.

The Kul gathered to meet them. They were dismounting, and slapping their ponies away. Slowly, they assembled a wall of shields. Many of the Kul had long, berdish axes or clubs.

'Why don't they fight us on horse?' Gerlach asked. He knew for a fact that all the Kurgan tribes were bred to the saddle.

'They know us,' Beledni said. 'They see lancer wings. They fear rota charge and rota lances.'

'So they make a shield wall?'

'Yha, Vebla. They decide Leblya is theirs. Will not give it up. Will dig down, stand ground and hold land.'

'And?'

'Land belong to no one,' Maksim said. 'Land belong to holy Urzun, and Gospodarinyi live off land by his allowance. Kul will learn this. Land is not to be theirs.'

'We're going to fight them, then?' Gerlach asked.

'Yha,' said Beledni.

'We're… going to charge a shield wall?'

'Yha, Vebla,' Beledni said.

The idea alarmed Gerlach. The notion of a battle did not – but charging a shield wall? That was madness. One of the most basic rules of cavalry warfare, as his tutors had emphasised, was that horses – no matter how well trained – would not charge into an obstacle like a shield wall. It was simply against their nature. No matter how hard you drove them, they would break eventually, rather than launch into an impediment. That was why the shield wall, though ancient in terms of military ideas, was still sound in practice. Indeed, the pike companies of the Empire relied on the principle. If they stood firm and kept their pole arms squared and disciplined, they would turn aside even the most insane of horse charges.

'Not look so worried, Vebla,' Beledni said with a chuckle. 'Shield wall looks strong, but Beledni know Kul. Beledni know how Kul think.' He rapped the brow of his szyszak with a stiff finger.

'You've fought them before?'

'Yha!' replied the rotamaster, and briefly cocked his head to one side to show and tap an old scar on his neck. Maksim pulled up his left sleeve and revealed another deep, fading scar.

'We have fought Kul many times. Sometimes, we have won.'

That wasn't terribly reassuring, although Beledni was at least alive to make the claim.

'Is time,' Beledni decided. He sat up in his saddle and looked left and right, contemplating the ranks of his lancers. They all waited, poised.

He gave a cry, and they couched their long horse lances. Horses whinnied nervously. Beledni's open hand hovered for a long moment.

He dropped it.

Yevni blew a long note on his bone horn.

And the rota charged.

IV

THEY MADE THE best pace they could across the nodding gorse and saltgrass, hooves pounding the dry earth. Gerlach rode in the lead, holding the banner upright and away from his thigh. Beledni posted Vaja and Vitali to flank the banner.

One hundred horse lengths ahead, the shield wall drew tight and waited. Kul warriors behind the front line of interlocked shields cried out and waved latecomers into the mass.

A thick, strong mass. An unmovable mass.

Shield bosses glinted in the spring light. Axe blades rose. A Kul carnyx blew a long, sharp note. The Kul standard – a set of massive antlers transfixing a wolf-skull – was hefted up at the centre of the wall line. The sockets of the wolf's skull seemed to glare at them balefully as they rode in.

Ten horse lengths. Five. Mounts at full stretch, manes flying, teeth bared.

The Kul weren't just holding their ground. They were now surging towards the charge. Towards the charge! As if they welcomed it. As if they welcomed death. The discipline of their shield wall was forgotten in the eagerness to join the fight.

This was what Beledni had been anticipating.

One length. Kul voices rose in a united shriek, barring the horsemen's way with a shield of noise. Iron-shod hooves and iron-tipped lances tore the sound shield down. And then, with cataclysmic impact, they did the same to the wall of flesh and bone behind it.

The rota slammed into the dissolving shield wall, shattering it. Lances juddered as they tore into wood and bodies. Gerlach found himself churning Saksen forward through a mass of screaming, milling men. On either side of him, riders of the krug had released their lances and were cutting in with their sabres. Vitali and Vaja kept tight, protecting Gerlach's sides, but as they fought through a particularly heavy scrum, Vaja disappeared entirely.

Gerlach's right flank was exposed. A wide-bladed axe threatened him, and he dropped his reins and pulled his loaded wheel-lock out with his right hand. The point-blank shot punched off the axe man's jaw and threw him back into the scrambling bodies around him.

Gerlach recased his pistol and brought out his sword, hacking and stabbing at anything that came near him. With his left hand, he kept the banner aloft. It felt like a dead weight now, much heavier than the more considerable demilance standard had ever seemed. Vitali stayed with him, hacking and thrusting at the kyazak.

Through the frenzy of the melee, Gerlach saw Beledni cutting through bull-helms with his gleaming shashka. He saw Maksim sweeping with his curved sabre, splashing blood up into the air. He saw Mitri plunge his lance through two of the Kul at once. Borodyn, hurling a lance. Sorca, stabbing his sabre tip into the eye slit of a Kul barbute. Kvetlai, drenched in gore, cleansing his silver blade by rushing it through the air.

Vaja suddenly reappeared, fighting clear of the pack that had delayed him, howling with brutal triumph as a tribesman went under his horse's juddering hooves.

Gerlach cleaved through head armour and iron plate, and then turned hard to take off a hand clutching a knife. Jostling bodies were packing in around him, and the stench of blood, ordure and sweat was making him gag.

A Kul warrior came at him, and he used the butt of the banner shaft to bludgeon him away.

The melee was a jarring maelstrom of noise and motion and impact. Gerlach was no longer sure which way he was pointing. He was showered with droplets of blood and spit, and tiny shards of metal.

Gigantic spectral antlers rose up above the turmoil around him. For a moment, Gerlach imagined that some great steppe beast or death devil had come on them out of the dust and smoke.

But it was the Kul standard.

Yelling, Gerlach drove Saksen into the press, smacking his sabre to and fro all the while, slicing scalps and shoulders and cutting the tips off helm-horns. Vitali shouted out, trying to stay with the demilancer.

The Kul banner bearer was a short, thickset man in a mail shirt wound from heavy wire. His brass helmet was long-chinned and mounted with a single antler, pointing forward from the forehead. A witch-priest danced around him, jangling beads, strings of bones and a rattle of tin bells. The witch-priest was painted with bright crimson stripes to imitate his bones.

Gerlach hurled himself at them through the battle's chaos. The witch-priest saw him coming at the last moment, and turned to raise his rattle.

Gerlach put cross-wise power into his sword blow. He decapitated the witch-priest, and took off the gnarled hand holding the rattle as well. Screaming, the banner bearer tried to engage Gerlach, thrusting the antlers of the Kul standard at him. One of the antler tines gouged across his left shoulder plate and left a deep streak that later rusted badly.

Gerlach spurred on under the standard and hacked down both the desperate bearer and two swordsmen who ran in to defend him. Vitali and Vaja came up on Gerlach's heels and began to defend him against further attacks.

The Kul banner crashed to the ground.

He had expected the Kul spirit to be diminished by such an event. Gerlach stiffened in shock as they roared and fought on with renewed frenzy.

Then he heard the drumming of hooves. The Kul were drawing in reinforcements. For all their efforts, the rota of Yetchitch krug was about to be slaughtered.

A second force struck into the straggling line of the battle from the direction of the town itself. But they weren't another wave of Kul at all. They were horse archers, pouring out through the stockade gatehouse, thirty-five or forty strong.

Their brown, long-maned steppe ponies swept them in amongst the hindquarters of the Kul's loose battle-gang. They rained long, red-feathered arrows into the Northers' backs from short but sturdy recurve bows. The rear line of the Kul formation began to topple and fall like a row of cornstalks under a scythe.

The horse archers had great turning speed and a prolific rate of fire. Some of the lancers – Gerlach, Vaja, Vitali and a half dozen more – had swept so deeply into the Kul ranks they had almost broken out through the back. They were now surrounded by the closing enemy host. So it was that Gerlach was one of the first to see the horse archers curling past, their onslaught causing the rear files of the Kul to turn in panic to try to protect themselves.

The archers were Kislevites, wearing grubby but embroidered beshmets or sleeveless sheepskin coats over hauberks of hardened red leather. They had long aventails of mesh dangling back around their shoulders. Their helmets were simple, spiked 'tops', with wide brims of fur around the rims. They rode with short stirrups, giving themselves a forward seat that put each rider's weight over his horse's shoulders. This favoured an animal better than placing the weight in the centre of its back.

Gerlach was impressed by the power of the small, tasselled, double-curved bows. The 'self' bows of the Empire, expertly shaped from single staves of wood, had tremendous penetrative power, but were so long they could not be shot from the saddle, especially a moving one. But these recurve bows easily drove shafts clean through iron pot-helms and brass corselets.

Harried now from front and back, the Kul began to waver and break. As men turned to run, they were brought over by arrows or javelins. Lancers broke through melees to ride them down. A few masses of resistance remained, where defiant Kul warriors had closed in tight, but Beledni and Yevni regrouped a good number of the rota and split these mobs with lance and sword.

The Kul began to flee en masse now, ditching shields and even weapons as they ran for their scattered ponies. Only a very few made it. This handful galloped away into the steppe in all directions, disappearing into the grass and leaving only the sound of their racing hooves and jingling bits behind them.

Beledni raised his sword in triumph, and Yevni sounded his bone horn again and again. Shouting and roaring, the lancers dismounted, and the horse archers cantered, whooping, in wide circles around the battle site. The general mayhem had raised a vast cloud of fine dust that the steppe wind was only now beginning to disperse.

As that dust billowed around him, Gerlach hoisted the rota banner high into the air, as high as his tired arms could manage. The dismounted lancers greeted it with cheers as they set about blinding the corpses of the enemy.

V

THE LEADER OF the horse archers was a fine, tall man, and surprisingly young. He leapt down from his sturdy pony and embraced Beledni heartily.

His name was Antal, and he and his horse company hailed from Igerov, a community in the far east of the southern oblast. Beledni knew him well. The companies had fought together in the pulk on several different campaigns. Beledni's great comradeship had in fact been with Antal's father, Gaspar. From the talk going on around him, Gerlach learned that Beledni and Gaspar had been friends and battle-brethren since their youths. Gaspar had died two summers before, and his horsemen divided into two warbands, each led by one of his sons. This explained why Antal looked too young to be a commander of horse. He treated Beledni like a favourite uncle.

Antal's horsemen, along with the company led by his brother Dmirov, had assembled with the pulk at Zhedevka, and been caught up in that great military disaster. They had braved a number of desperate escapades and managed to flee at last into the open country, first west and then north-east. Antal had come away with only forty of the seventy men he had started with. He had not seen Dmirov, nor any of his warband, since Zhedevka.

Noticing the strange rider and even stranger horse that carried the rota banner, Antal walked across to meet Gerlach. He yanked off his dusty gloves and clasped Gerlach's hands as Beledni made introductions.

'Vebla,' Beledni said, and Antal chuckled.

'Is your name?' the young commander asked.

'My name is Gerlach Heileman.'

'Good!' laughed Antal, as if the name 'vebla' was something better avoided.

'How long have you been here, at Leblya?' Gerlach wanted to know.

'Thirteen days,' Antal answered. His company had ridden there with all speed, hoping to congregate with other survivors of the battle. 'For eight days, no one come. Then lancers, Novgo's rota.'

Gerlach had to struggle to keep up with the exchange. 'Novgo?'

'Comrade rotamaster,' Beledni said. 'Of Dagnyper krug. Many good men raise wings with him.'

'Not so many,' said Antal sadly. 'Only five times five lancers of Novgo's rota live after Zhedevka.'

There was some quiet muttering and oaths of dismay from the lancers.

'Where are they now?' asked Gerlach.

'Kyazak come, same day Novgo's rota arrive. Great host, more than was here under today's sun.'

The Kul raiders had arrived from the south in huge numbers, either following the straggling survivors of Zhedevka, or happening on Leblya by pure unlucky chance. There were so many of them – 'covering steppe like flies on corpse' Antal said – that it was clear even as they approached that Leblya would not withstand the attack. Novgo, with what Beledni seemed to think was typically rash courage, had ridden all he had left of his rota out of Leblya and made a dash south, partly to warn any approaching companies that Leblya was no longer a safe haven, and partly to try to draw the kyazak away from the town.

A great proportion of the Kul had turned and chased Novgo's rota away across the grasslands. Neither rota nor enemy had been seen again.

The remaining Kul had laid siege to the town, and Antal's warriors had done their level best to defend the place. It was hard. Their supplies, especially of arrows, were limited, and the horse archers could not use their own strengths and face the raiders because they were woefully outnumbered. When Beledni's more sizeable rota appeared that morning and engaged the Kul, Antal had seized his chance, and led his archers out in a make or break raid to finish the siege.

It had paid off. Through strength and speed of horse, and the bonus of skilled archery, Beledni and Antal's companies had defeated a kyazak warband of much greater size.

In fact they had virtually annihilated them.

The Kislevites were all flushed with relief and victory. The thrill of battle still boiled excitedly inside them. But Gerlach couldn't help feel a little disappointment. He'd been dreaming of an allied host at Leblya, waiting to surge south and exact a bloody war-price on the Kurgan advance.

Instead, just one band, forty strong, of tired and ill-supplied horse archers, and word of a diminished lance company that had since disappeared.

He kept his thoughts to himself. The Kislevites were celebrating.

'I thought you would come today,' Antal told Beledni. 'I saw a shape in the sky that reminded me of you.'

'Yha! So I come, Antal Gasparitch! So I come!'

'I was not sure. Cloud look like you, but it came riding on strange white horse, which I know not your horse.' He smiled at Gerlach and pointed to Saksen. 'Now I understand.'

* * *

VI

THE ROTA HAD not come through unscathed. Two lancers – Ptor and Chagin – were dead, and Sorca, one of Beledni's veteran seniors, had an axe wound in his hip that was obviously mortal. But almost everyone had taken a nick, graze or cut of some kind. Mostly it was bruises and scrapes they didn't even remember getting. The worst of the minor wounds was a sword-cut along the side of young Kvetlai's hand and forearm. He showed the bloody gash off proudly.

The Kislevites retired into the town, where the inhabitants sent up a great roar and clangour with pots and pans and voices, hailing the victory and their deliverance. Antal's riders gathered up all the spent arrows they could find – even broken ones and kyazak shafts, for wood was so scarce – and rode in ahead of the lancers through the gatehouse. Ptor and Chagin were draped over their horses, and Beledni himself led Sorca, lolling in his saddle.

Many of the lancers raised their hands to acknowledge the cacophony. But Beledni did not seem to notice it. His entire concern was taken up with the dying friend and comrade riding slowly beside him.

VII

THE VICTORY FEAST that night was not grand, but generous considering the extent to which the siege had depleted Leblya's larders. Sad songs were sung to the memory of the fallen comrades, and the mood was sombre.

More miserable still was the talk. Gerlach heard a good many of the lancers, and the archers too, saying that the 'journey' was over, for this year at least. Though it was only early summer on the high steppes, and the war-season barely begun, the men seemed to agree that there was nothing left to be achieved this year. They would be better off returning to their stanitsa homes in time to help with the harvest and the winter slaughter.

Gerlach took himself apart from the others and sat alone. They had come into the ancient zal on the top of the great earthwork for the feast. It was immensely old. The roof had been replaced many times, and the body of the hall extended, but the basic inner frame and beam-work was original. It was hundreds of years old, perhaps thousands. In places, it was black from old fire damage – not the accumulation of cook-fire soot but real burn marks – and peppered with old indentations and nail holes.

He traced his fingertips over the pockmarked beam he sat against. The firelight caught the faintest traces of gold frayed into the worn timber, tiny pin-head scraps of it caught in the grain of wood, or hammered into empty nail marks.

These beams had been covered once, Gerlach realised. They had been clad in gold, wafer-thin foils of beaten gilt inscribed with the figures and symbols of their makers' divinity. These beams had stood since the time of the Scythians – since the earthwork itself had been raised. Zals had been built and razed and built again around their solid framework. The beams had worn each successive settlement's hall as a man wears a beshmet or pole staves support a canvas tent. They were older than the great cathedral temples and fortresses of his homeland.

So did great glory come and fade until it was scarcely visible any more. Cultures so rich and powerful that they could dominate the land and afford to wrap their buildings in gold leaf. But they had fled, and left only mounds, like graves, behind them.

Gerlach knew, in his heart, the Empire must surely fade too. He had grown up believing it to be permanent and eternal, by the grace of Sigmar, and pledged his life to maintaining that equilibrium. But it was for naught. The Empire would fall. Perhaps it had fallen already. Even if the great armies of his homeland had risen with effect and driven back the Northers this time, then it would be next year, or the year after that, or the one after that. But it would happen one day.

All any man could hope to do was delay the inevitable.

That was a calling he could believe in. To keep fighting the darkness so long as there was light to protect.

Vitali and Vaja came over to join him, worried that he had withdrawn from the krug. They brought koumiss, and were eager to celebrate their shared exploits on the field.

'We do war good together again, Vebla!' Vitali said.

Gerlach nodded and toasted them both with the fermented milk. They seemed inordinately proud of his accomplishments during the battle. He had kept the rota safe, the banner raised. He had also fought well, and taken the enemy's banner from them.

In truth, they had achieved far more than him. They had ridden loyally to keep him safe, and each of them had accounted for a great many more kyazak lives than Gerlach.

'Why Vebla face sad look it in?' Vaja asked.

'I hear the talk,' Gerlach answered the young lancer. 'You all talk of going home. As if you are done now.'

'Vebla will like much Yetchitch krug!' Vaja decided.

Vitali, as ever, seemed to grasp Gerlach's notion more soundly. 'You not want go, Vebla?' he asked.

Gerlach shook his head. 'Has Yetchitch ever been attacked? Not by kyazak, I mean. By Kurgan host, on a great invasion?'

They didn't think so, not in their lifetimes. Yetchitch was quite remote, and mainly had only bandits and raiders to fear.

'So you will ride home, and Yetchitch will be as you remember, and you will winter there and next spring, come back again to see what war there is to be fought, what glory to be found?'

'Yha!' said Vaja.

'My home is being attacked right now. Right this very minute. I am not done.'

'Shto?'

'Vebla is not yet done.'

VIII

THEIR FACES DARKENED as they thought about this. It was as hard for them to care about towns and villages to the south that they would never see, as it had been for Gerlach to give a damn about the oblast. Until, that is, he'd seen its grandeur and the spirit of its people. But for the first time, Vitali and Vaja seemed to sympathise. They had found affection and comradeship for Gerlach, and now they shared his unhappiness.

What divided the men of the Empire from the men of Kislev was Kislevite fatalism. Vitali and Vaja agreed the plight of Gerlach's home was a sad thing, but it was beyond them to do anything about it. Not quite 'of no matter', for they weren't that heartless, but far enough away for it to be a thing that made a man shrug and sigh. In Kislev, men believed they were made by fate. In the Empire, men believed they made their fates themselves.

Gerlach left them to their thoughts and their koumiss, and went to find Beledni, but the rotamaster was holding vigil with Sorca and was not to be disturbed. Gerlach walked through the hall, nodding to the men who offered him greetings. He saw Kvetlai. The boy had drunk too much, probably to dull the pain in his hand and arm, and was lolling pathetically by the fire.

Nearby, Gerlach found Maksim and Borodyn seated with Antal and the ataman of Leblya: a solid, portly elder called Sevhim.

They welcomed him and gave him a cup of kvass and a bowl of salt fish.

Antal was bright and curious, and asked Gerlach many questions about the Empire, a place he'd never visited. His thoughts ran away from him, beyond his broken grasp of Reikspiel, and Borodyn translated for him.

'I understand you're all thinking of going home,' Gerlach said at length, when he'd had enough of the questions.

Maksim nodded. He was chasing flecks of food out from between his teeth, and his working tongue bulged in his lean, drawn cheeks. 'Is of best we do this.'

'Is of best?'

Maksim shrugged.

'There is little to be gained, Vebla,' Borodyn answered instead. 'We have been bested and driven to flight. We have tried to... to regroup and make another chance for us, but...' he gestured at the hall around them, indicating Leblya itself, '...there is nothing.'

'I disagree,' said Gerlach.

'That is your privilege,' Borodyn accepted. 'Beledni rotamaster has tried hard. We rode to Dushyka, to Leblya, hunting for allies, for any remaining part of the pulk. Nothing, except for Antal and his brave riders.'

Antal smiled and nodded.

'So it is better to end and start again fresh and new than prolong this misadventure.'

'Beledni thinks this?'

'Beledni would have ridden home from Dushyka if not for you,' Maksim admitted.

'What? What does that mean?'

'This season is loss! Terrible loss!' Maksim snapped. 'Only because of Vebla did Beledni press on to Leblya. To see.'

'To see what?' demanded Gerlach.

'If pulk was gathered here,' said Antal.

Borodyn took a sip of kvass. 'Beledni rotamaster believes he owes a debt to you. To be fair, we all do. You took up the eagle-wing banner when it had fallen and carried it to safety. We all respect that.'

'Is why you carry rota,' growled Maksim.

'We all respect that,' repeated Borodyn, 'and none more so than Beledni. Most rotamasters would have turned their lancers homeward after a defeat like Zhedevka. But Beledni ordered us on here, to Leblya, because there was a chance the pulk had reassembled. If any great force had been here, we would have joined it, and gladly ridden south to help you get the vengeance you deserve. But it is not the case. Beledni has been more than fair to you. But he will not risk any more men.'

'I see. What about next year? When the Kurgan are so entrenched in the south and in the Empire there is no pulk left to join and no cause left to fight for?'

'Next year is next year,' said Maksim, tipping invisible dust out of his hand.

Gerlach got up angrily and walked away. Then he stopped, and looked back at the men.

'I have two questions,' he said. 'You are the riders of the dead, yha? Already mourned and given up by your krug?'

Borodyn and Maksim nodded at this.

'Then what lives are you risking?'

Borodyn smiled and translated. Both Maksim and Antal laughed.

'You do not understand, Vebla.'

'No, I suppose I don't. I suppose I don't understand the significance of the pictures Dazh puts in the sky, either. You saw Beledni, coming to help you on a white horse, didn't you?' He looked at Antal. The young man could only agree.

'Then what is Dazh telling you? To run away or heed the signs he puts in the sky to guide you?'

'Dazh tell us what he always tell us,' said Maksim, a little angry now. 'Follow Beledni. Follow rota. That is the only way.'

* * *

IX

At dawn, the rota buried its dead in the steppe.

It was one of the first truly warm days of summer and the heat began to rise even from the moment of daybreak.

The sky was blue and clear, and they could see for many leagues across the grassland. Skylarks were singing, far away up beyond the sight of man, and the air was droning with horseflies and the fizzles of newly hatched mosquitoes.

Beledni – his eyes red and his face drawn from too little sleep and too much drink – howled the names of Ptor, Chagin and Sorca at the rising sun, as if he hoped he could stop it from coming up.

Then Yevni blew his horn. The three horses took off from the gate of Leblya and ran away into the grass. Ptor and Chagin were bound in cloth and lashed over their saddles. Sorca, in the last hours of his life, was hunched over in his saddle, and pulling his dead comrades behind him.

Sorca had seen the same cloud shape for a second time. The three were riding away to wherever Demieter had gone.

The lancers, and mourners from Antal's company and the town, turned and went back inside the stockade, one by one.

Gerlach remained beside Beledni, the banner raised in his hand, until the three horses had become dots, and the dots themselves had receded into the dawn haze and were gone.

X

As they went back into the stanitsa, Gerlach tried to talk to Beledni, but the old rotamaster ignored him and disappeared into an izba to sleep.

Gerlach carefully planted the shaft of the banner in the earth of the inner yard, and dismounted to fetch some water and find something to breakfast on.

In the great zal, up on the mound, Kvetlai was sick. His wound had become infected, and was puffy and black. He was sweating and delirious. The men of the rota didn't seem to care. They brought Kvetlai water periodically, and Borodyn dressed his wound with salves, but their manner seemed dismissive.

Just after noon, with the sun at its highest and hottest, Gerlach saw Kvetlai stagger down across the yard and drag himself on to his horse. No one tried to obstruct him. He kicked his heels into his mare's ribs and bolted out of the gate and away across the steppe.

'Why didn't you stop him?' Gerlach demanded of Borodyn. 'His injury wasn't mortal, not like Sorca's!'

'It was full of poison. He had a fever.'

'But if you'd cared for him, he might have lived!'

'Dazh will care for him. Ursun will care. The steppe also. A sick warrior rides until the sickness sweats out of him. Kvetlai will return. Or Dazh will lead him on his journey.'

Gerlach turned away, disgusted. The Kislevite way doomed every man to fend for himself. It was as if riding answered every question of life and death. We are dying... ride away! We are defeated... ride away! We are sick... then ride away and see what fate provides! Is of no matter.

The only thing they cared about was the krug, and the only thing they followed was the rota.

Everything else was left in the hands of some distant god of wide, empty spaces who was too damn far away to hear.

XI

THE ONLY THING they followed was the rota. The banner.

Gerlach woke up in the still, cool hours before dawn. The hall fires were dying, and the whole of Leblya was asleep.

He had already decided to leave, to part company with the rota and head south, though he knew there was nothing a single man could hope to do.

Zhedevka had taught him that.

But his dream had given him a new idea.

He carried his armour and belongings out of the hall, careful not to wake the slumbering lancers, and got dressed in the yard. It was cold, and his breath smoked the air. The stars were still out, bright and proud in a canopy of charcoal grey and, in the east, the first glimmer of sunrise was showing.

Clad in his half-armour, he made Saksen ready, shushing the gelding's agitation with soft-spoken words and a gentle hand across its muzzle.

Gerlach walked Saksen out into the dry, bare yard. The first long, timid shadows of dawn were stretching out. He mounted up, and took a last look at the zal, perched on its Scythian mound like a crown.

The rota banner was sitting where he had placed it, base down in the hardpan. He plucked it up with his left hand, and then ducked both head and banner as he rode out under the open gate.

The steppe was violet in the half-light. The sky was mauve, splashed with yellow along the eastern horizon. It was growing warmer, and one by one, the stars were going out.

He turned Saksen south, raised the banner, and galloped away.

AACHDEN

I

It was now the early summer, the better part of three months since the unholy slaughter at Zhedevka in the Year That No One Forgets. The smoke of burning forests and blazing towns had clogged the northward sky permanently since the heart of spring.

The Kurgan horde had driven deeper into the south than they had ever done before. They had overwhelmed the borders of the Empire, setting proud cities like Erengrad to the torch along the way, and bathed their blades in the blood of good, pious folk. Some said the despoilers had reached as far as Middenheim, and thus all civilisation was at an end. Others vowed Karl Franz himself was riding at the head of the Empire's armies, praying to Sigmar for the chance to close with Archaon.

Archaon. That was a name made of darkness. Where it had first come from, no one could say. Spread by word of mouth, perhaps. Shrieked out in the dying breath of pitiful victims flayed by the Kurgan and swept south to sow terror instead of seeds that spring. Maybe it was heard in the chants of the encroaching hordes. Or perhaps it had just crept into the minds of kings and seers across the Old World in their nightmares.

Archaon was the name of the being who commanded the enemies of everything. The Lord of the End Times, greater even than Morkar or Asavar Kul. A man? Perhaps. A daemon? Quite possibly. Real? Well...

There are many to this day who believe Archaon was not a single being, but rather a fearsome being amalgamated from the confused identities of several Kurgan chieftains. Certainly, the Norther host itself was not one thing, but a union of many tribal armies and cult factions, each one ruled by a High Zar. Archaon was a mix of all of them, for the High Zars used his authority to reinforce their own considerable power, and attributed many of their conquests to his name.

But he was more than this, for he was real. Only a few hundred of the Kurgan knew that for sure, and only a few hundred men of the Empire had ever confirmed it by encountering him. Few survived to tell of it.

Archaon's invasion depended for its success on the High Zars who followed him, and on the zars under them. The North had sprouted a host of nigh on nineteen hundred thousand warriors, and no single commander could ever control a force that size – not even the disciplined military systems of the Empire.

Archaon, his name couched in infamy, relied on his lieutenants, the devoted High Zars, to marshal the several armies that collectively became his Great Horde.

Surtha Lenk was one of those High Zars.

Karl-Azytzeen met him face to face one morning that summer.

II

WEEKS EARLIER IN the pit of the Brunmarl playhouse, Karl had achieved more than he realised. At the time, all he knew was that he had slain two rivals whilst in the grip of a red rage. Beyond that bald fact, he wasn't sure of much at all. The men of Uldin's band had carried him from the pit, and shut him up in some dank stone room for the night.

He slept for what seemed like several years. When he woke up, the young shaman with the antler head-dress was prowling around him slowly, hunched low and muttering ugly words.

It was day. Light and rainwater seeped in through the broken roof.

The bolt was thrown back and Uldin came in. His head was bare and water ran off his bear-pelt and the short boar-spear he was carrying. He made a nod at the shaman, who bowed and scurried out.

'Skarkeetah says I should kill you,' Uldin announced.

'Then kill me,' Karl said indifferently. Uldin did not move.

Karl sat up and leant his aching back against the damp stone of the wall. 'I thought the slave lord believed me to be precious. To be touched by...' His voice trailed off. He could not bring himself to say the name.

Uldin ground his teeth thoughtfully. 'It is so. And that is why. He says a wise man in my position would kill you before you became too precious. Too... powerful.'

That made Karl smile. He was beaten, unarmed and half-naked in a dingy cell, and a Kurgan warlord with a spear was telling him he had enough power to pose a threat.

'Well, just how wise are you?' Karl sneered.

'Wise enough to appreciate value.'

'Because I won the fights? Saved your honour and your warband? Seems I got you a new shaman too.'

Uldin nodded slowly. 'When they saw the blue-eyed slave fight and win in the pit, many shamans yearned to join with my band and take Subotai's place. I chose Chegrume. He is a potent shaman, and sees special strength in you.'

'There's no mystery,' replied Karl. 'He knows I can read.'

'Words are power,' said Uldin.

'No, Kurgan. Knowledge is power. Words are just a way of getting it.'

Uldin took a few steps forward and crouched down in front of Karl. He lowered the spear and held it so that the tip was pressing sharply against Karl's chest.

'We put our mark on those men who impress us with their strength. Such men are useful in our challenges and devotions.'

'Better to waste the life of a useless slave in a sacrifice or a pit-fight than one of your own band, eh? I understand how it works. You collect up the best and the healthiest of the prisoners you take and squander them in your rituals becau–'

Uldin cut him off sharply, not even remotely interested. 'You faced me, Karl-Azytzeen, outside the zal at Zhedevka. You gave me this.' Uldin touched the scar on his shoulder where Karl's sabre had dug in. 'The first wound I have taken from an enemy warrior in eight summers.'

'My pleasure.' The spear tip dug a little harder.

'Then I had the best of you,' Uldin said.

'In the doorway. I remember.'

'I could have killed you.'

'I thought you had. I wish you had.'

'Tchar stayed my hand. Made me strike you with the flat of my blade. A man who can wound a zar is worth marking and keeping as a slave. Your life has belonged to me ever since. I could have ended it then, but I chose not to. I could end it now…'

Uldin gave the spear another little push and then took it away. 'But I choose not to. While you remember that power I have over you, you can do me no harm. You are no danger to me.'

Uldin slid a trophy ring off his arm and tossed it into Karl's lap. It was still warm. It had been worked into shape by one of the sword blades taken from the slaves in the pit the night before.

'Add to this, and my choice will not change.'

Uldin got up and walked out of the room. He left the door wide open.

After a while, Karl slipped the warm metal ring onto his right arm, and followed the zar into the daylight.

III

THE ZARS LED their warbands away from Brunmarl one by one. They headed west to join a massive host accreting around the ruins of Berdun. There, the numerous banners of the zars flocked around the great war standard of the High Zar himself: Surtha Lenk.

This Kurgan host was easily as large as the force that had taken Zhedevka, but it was only one of many that raged into the Empire as spring turned into summer. Surtha Lenk's horde sacked three towns in the Ostermark, and then forded the Talabec and drove on west into Ostland, where more towns perished to its fury.

Uldin's band saw little of the fighting. The host was so massive that often great parts of it were still arriving at a town by the time it had been razed by the front runners. Uldin chafed for glory. He wished for a battle where his band could take enough enemy heads to raise a skull-stack and earn him another victory mark on his cheek.

But by the time they reached Aachden, just eight days' march from Wolfenburg, with the Middle Mountains in sight, Karl had won two more trophy rings.

IV

THE LAST TIME Karl saw his fellow prisoners, who were still roped together and driven along with the wagons, they didn't recognise him. They probably wouldn't have greeted him even if they had.

Uldin's men let Karl keep the garments and armour pieces they had clad him in at Brunmarl. They gave him a sturdy spear with a black horsetail fixed behind the long tip, and an old brown mare without a saddle or a name. He rode in the band between the watchful eyes of Efgul and Hzaer the hornblower, and followed them into the fire.

V

AT AACHDEN, AN Imperial army had assembled to stop Surtha Lenk's horde. They occupied the upland fields of crops and pasture just north-east of the town, with a broadleaf forest to their north and the plain of the river Aach to their south. They were a great glittering mass in the summer light, like a patch of sea sparkling with the sun, fretted by banners of blue and gold, red and white. A huge force of professional soldiery, supported by significant sections of levies. They were dug in to deprive the host of any further advance, and to halt them dead before they reached Wolfenburg.

The countryside presented no obvious way around them, but then again going around an enemy was not the Kurgan way.

VI

ULDIN, HUNGRY FOR a share of victory, had steered his warband through to the leading edge of the Kurgan host. They had ridden overnight to get a good place for themselves, running their horses hard the moment word spread that the Empire had rallied to meet them at arms on the field at

Aachden. Karl wondered if his old nag would be able to keep up with the huge, black horses of the Kurgan riders, but it was indomitable and seemed to have fathomless stamina.

Chegrume, the shaman, rode with them on an ugly, ill-tempered tarpan. Its coat was brown, its mane and tail uncombed black, and its nature so foul that the antlered shaman had to tie himself to its back. He ran wild, weaving in and out of the galloping riders, chanting spells of fortitude and protection from metal.

Chegrume seemed a curious fellow to Karl. Not that all shamans weren't curious, given their calling. But he was young and fierce, more like a warrior than a witch priest. His youth troubled Karl too. He had supposed a shaman needed age to attain the feats of lore and wisdom necessary to his office. Subotai had been an older man, and Zar Blayda's wizard Ons Olker was not young. None of the shamans he had yet seen were younger than mature middle age.

But Chegrume was little more than a boy. It seemed as if he had been born with the arcane knowledge he needed. Or maybe acquiring that weight of lore so young had cost him something: his middle fingers, perhaps.

The day was clear and warm. The sky was blue. The weather paid no heed to the death about to take place, Karl thought.

The warband pushed their horses through the gathering press to win their ranking, as rival banner bearers, shaman and zars roared out reproachful challenges. But Uldin had chosen a place near to the lee of the river where bands of infantry spearmen had congregated, and none of them cared much to oppose five score warriors on warhorses.

The glittering army waited for them just over a league away. They had the advantage of height, for the gently rolling fields had a deceptive slope.

Breathing hard, their horses sweating and panting, the warband took its place and got its wind back. Men took off their helms and drank thirstily from skins, or daubed their faces and chests with pigment. Chegrume thumped up and down the serried rank, ululating and casting. Karl had the distinct feeling the shaman's frantic activity had less to do with magic and more to do with the fact his bastard tarpan would not stand still.

Karl sat on his mare with his spear across his iron-plated thighs and gazed at the army facing them. They were so close he could make out their banner colours and the details of their standards. He wondered whose companies they were, and what lord had command, and he tried to identify symbols he knew.

The main battle standard. A white skull with a garland wreath around it on a crimson field. That was…

To its left, a figure of death, armed with a lance and a black crossed white shield, mounted on a maned and speckled cat, walking through a flame. On the turquoise field behind it, a star with two burning tails swooped down. He knew that one, certainly. It was the… the…

Karl shivered despite the balmy heat of the morning. He knew none of them. He could not recognise a single design or emblem. Where had his memory of them gone?

'What's the matter, Karl-Azytzeen?' Efgul asked.

Karl looked round, as if blinking out of a dream. The hefty, hairy Kurgan was offering him a wineskin. Karl took it and drank deeply.

'You are afraid of the Empire?' Efgul added.

Karl shook his head. 'These last days, I have fought them already,' he said, and tapped the new-wrought rings on his arm.

'Not an army such as this,' Hzaer snarled from his other side. 'You must not shy. You are not of them any more.'

'If you shy,' Efgul said, 'the zar says we must kill you.'

'I will not.' Karl handed the skin to Hzaer, and the hornblower rotated his great brass carnyx back over his shoulder so it would not slide off while he was drinking.

'Yes, I do not think so, seh,' Efgul murmured, staring at Karl.

'I've come a long way,' Karl said to both of them and no one. 'A long and bloody way, and I can only go forward because going back now would be too hard.'

Efgul nodded, and buckled his houndskull helm into place.

'I don't recognise the emblems any more,' Karl confessed suddenly. 'Not one of them. The banners of my... of the Empire. I thought I knew them, but I can't place a single one.'

Hzaer grinned. His broken teeth made the grin a leer. 'That is Tchar's doing, Azytzeen,' he said.

'What is?'

'He favours you. Great Tchar has changed your mind to make it easier to forget. Give thanks for that.'

Karl supposed he did. Memory of his old life would make the life he had now far harder to endure.

Hooves thundered up. It was Uldin, on his great black steed. His wolf-mask helmet had been polished, and his pallasz was drawn.

'Word has been given!' he shouted to the hornblower. 'The High Zar has ordered we wait for the enemy to engage.'

'Engage?' Karl laughed. 'They've got the slope on their side and they're dug in. They're waiting for us to come to them.'

Uldin glared at him. 'They will not come?'

Karl snorted. Then, seeing the disapproving looks around him, he set his right hand across his heart and spoke more deferentially. 'They will not come. They'll do nothing if we sit here. Their aim is to block our advance and look! I believe that's what they're doing already, without lifting a finger.'

Uldin thought about this, his horse turning in circles.

Finally, he pointed at Karl and said, 'Come!'

* * *

VII

So it was that, on that morning in early summer, Karl-Azytzeen came face to face with Surtha Lenk.

The High Zar's pavilion was pitched behind the head of the ranked Kurgan mass. Its fabric was composed of tanned human hides, its guy ropes were plaited from sinew, and its posts calcified struts wrought from spines. It stank of decay and perfume.

Zar Uldin dismounted and pulled Karl off his mare. Karl scrambled and staggered as he was dragged towards the entrance of the battle tent.

Huge axemen with long horns rising from their heads blocked Uldin's path and it took a lot of talk to convince them to let him past. Only when Uldin had dragged Karl inside did Karl realise that the axemen at the door had not been wearing helmets. The tusk-horns sprouted directly from the bones of their distended skulls.

He felt sick.

But he was to feel sicker still, once he was inside. It was dark in the battle tent. Brass pendant lamps fumed out an acrid pall of incense. Things brushed against his skin like feathers and chittered in the dark.

The floor seemed to be composed of a carpet of snakes. Smooth, dry coils slipped around his feet.

'Welcome, Uldin,' a tiny voice said.

Uldin bowed. 'My lord.'

'Is this the changeling you have spoken of?'

'It is, lord seh.'

Karl glanced around. There were shadows everywhere, but none of them seemed like a person. He knew he had to keep his head bowed low.

'He smells of change. I like that. What did you call him?'

'Azytzeen,' Uldin said.

'Karl-Azytzeen,' Karl corrected.

'Oh! Spirited!' The miniscule voice moved closer. 'And why have you brought him here, Uldin?'

'He declares the enemy will not move, lord seh.'

A huge, armoured figure stood over Karl now, plated in crimson steel, more massive even than Hinn.

'Look at me, Azytzeen,' Surtha Lenk said.

Karl slowly turned his head up. Lenk was a giant three spans tall, plated in brass and iron.

Except he was not. A twisted, deformed thing, no bigger than a swaddling child, was strapped in a harness across the breast plate of the giant. It seemed to be all swollen face, with tiny, wasted, half-formed hands and feet sprouting from it. This was Lenk: a loathsome, slack face mottled with warts and suppurating blisters. One eye was very human and brown, the other, lower in the rugose flesh of the cheek, was swollen and glazed milky blue. The mighty horned helm of the giant carrying him had no visor piercings or eye-slits.

Karl could not stifle a gasp.

Surtha Lenk laughed. His little pink slit-mouth wobbled and let out a child's giggle.

'I find spirit usually ebbs at the sight of me. In return for my service, Tchar has been bounteous with his gifts. Am I not beautiful?'

Karl nodded.

'Nothing pleases the Eye of Tzeen so much as a man changed completely. Now... why will the enemy not move?'

'B-because they have the rising ground. They would rather deny us than battle us, so they will not give up their advantage by coming down the field to look for a fight. The basis of the Empire's might is the pike block. That strength is best used defensively. They... they will not come to us, and all the while we wait, they will stand there too, and the victory will be theirs without spill of blood, for their purpose will have been served.'

Karl's voice trailed off. Had he said too much? Too little? Surtha Lenk took another step forward, so Karl could feel the breath of the baby-thing on his face. The horned giant nursing it slid off his left gauntlet and reached out to stroke Karl's cheek with its bared fingers. The hand, though unnaturally large, looked human, but it moved as if the bones inside it were not solid. The palm and fingers writhed and curled fluidly like the feeling antlers of a slug.

Karl knew that it was the High Zar who was touching his face. The whole figure – giant and shrivelled thing combined – was Surtha Lenk.

'I have considered these things too,' Surtha Lenk whispered. 'I have fought the Old World before, and know something of its ways. My battle-shamans augur that a delay might spook the army before us, and trick them into rash action.'

The boneless hand withdrew. 'But Tchar speaks in you, and I am content to hear him. For I am restless and done with waiting. Spread word abroad. We will commence.'

The audience was apparently over. Uldin, plainly unnerved himself, hauled Karl out of the pavilion into the daylight.

Karl took a look back at the foul tent. He vowed he would never willingly go back inside it. He had imagined the High Zar to be that rare sort of man who commanded such power he could alter the face of the world and redirect the course of history. But he had imagined wrong. The High Zar was not any sort of man at all.

VIII

THE HORDE STIRRED. A clattering ripple ran through the dark ranks as spear shafts were raised and shields knocked together. Somewhere to the left line, kettledrums began a frenzied beating, then fell silent. Then they began again and did not stop.

Karl and the zar rode back to the warband. Uldin did not speak.

As they waited in rank, Karl suddenly felt cold, and the bright sunlight abruptly dimmed. The sky above Aachden and the enemy army was still clear and blue, but when he looked to his rear, he saw broad swathes of low dark cloud spoiling in from the east. The clouds were moving with visible speed, racing in to cover the heavens with a pitchy mantle. Spears of lightning blinked above the woodland to the east. Within minutes, the light had gone and the valley was muffled in a dead twilight. The first spats of rain began to fall, tapping off armour-iron and shield-wood. A vapour that was not quite a fog breathed over the land, making it harder to see.

Up the long slope of the field, the army of the Empire had become partially obscured. Storm clouds hovered above them too now, and there was no piece of summer blue left visible. An anxious murmur seemed to stiffen the silver-steel echelons of the Reik. Karl heard distant drums start up, and cymbals clash. He smelt gunpowder and hot pitch on the wet air.

Thunder boomed overhead, and the rain began to pelt torrentially. The vapour in the air thickened. Karl glanced down the wide front line of the horde, and realised it was moving. Not fast, but creeping forward, like spilled oil seeping across a floor.

Uldin called out, and they began to walk their horses. Berlas and the other archers slid their bows from their cases and nocked shafts to the strings.

Drums were thrashing a frenetic tempo that made the pulse rise in every man. Then the warhounds were let loose.

Karl saw them as they broke out from the rolling rank and began the chase up the slope of the field. They were dark and monstrous things, hundreds of them, loping and bounding and sending up a chilling howl.

The advance speed increased, as if the Kurgan were now keen to keep up with the dogs. Horns blew all through the host, and Hzaer blasted on his carnyx. They were cantering, with spearmen from the middle ranks running forward between the horses and baying like the hounds. The horde shook the ground as it flooded towards the standing army.

The pike walls came up, bristling in a thicket three men deep. Even to trained men, pole arms and pikes were aggravating weapons to handle. The great length of the shafts meant they wobbled under marching conditions and caused discomfort, and they were too long to be easily accommodated in close woodland or town streets. Sometimes it was even hard to find space enough to stack them out in an overnight camp.

But the nuisance they caused was worthwhile. With perfect drill, they made a lethal barrier that would stop even the heaviest cavalry. The hammer might be the symbol of the Empire, but the pike was the weapon on which its reputation was built.

As they broke into a gallop, Karl began to consider the odds. Uldin's warband was ferocious and fearless, but horse against pike had only one outcome. These pike men and halberdiers were ready and pitched square, unlike their poor brothers at Zhedevka. Kurgan blood was about to be spilled in great quantity.

And then it was spilled. There was a series of thunderclaps that was not thunder. The Imperial cannon, anchored in sets on either wing of the enemy's battle order, had fired. Pluming cones of yellow flame and mud spray burst up amongst the charging Kurgan. The bodies of men and horses were tossed into the air. Wood and steel and bone splintered. The huge shot from mortars dropped on the horde like rocks thrown from the heavens. Shrieking fire from the great cannon and the volley guns ripped horizontally down the field and tore into the front ranks.

Then the longbows, loosed from behind the pike wall, and a wave of white-feathered shafts arced over with a rasping hiss. Kurgan toppled and fell all around, struck through the helms and pauldrons and skewered from above by the long arrows. A heartbeat later, and the second wave hissed down, followed by the first massed volley of the arquebusiers and crossbowmen laced amongst the pike men in the wall. Karl felt a ball shot burn past his ear and a quarrel cracked into slivers as it came off the iron rim of his shield. To his left, one of Uldin's riders crashed over, horse and man together.

For a moment, Karl felt a twinge of martial pride for the culture that had raised him. The greatest army in the world. He would be content to die at its hands. He would ride his nameless nag into the pike wall and find his end.

The pike wall was right ahead now, and unmoving.

The hounds reached the pike wall. Hounds are not like horses, they do not quail and veer aside from obstruction. Whether this means horses are smarter than dogs, or dogs braver than horses, is hard to call. Hounds are unlike horses in other ways too: they are lower and smaller and fleeter, and much harder to strike with a pole blade four spans long. And they have the teeth of meat-eaters.

A few of the great hunting dogs were gashed and run through by the stalwart pikes. A few more were shot by handgun and crossbow and left yelping and lame on the mud. The bulk ran in under the pikes and into the men.

At once, the wall broke in several places. Men screamed and fell back, trying to dodge the ravening war-dogs. They crashed into the ranks behind them. Pikes dropped into the mire. Some parts of the rank unformed completely as frantic pike men turned their weapons too far and too suddenly to check the murderous hounds.

The Kurgan charge slammed into the Imperial front row and poured into the breaks and gaps. Men in white and red went down under the weight of horses or the thrust of horned spearmen. Once the enemy was in amongst them, the pike men were forced to abandon their shafts and equip themselves with hand weapons. They had no shields, and none of the Kurgans' momentum.

Karl crashed through beside Efgul, his mare snorting and squealing. Without saddle or stirrup, he had no brace to enable him to couch his spear, so he stabbed down with it, overarm. His first thrust went through a thigh, the second clean into the side of a sallet helm. Mud splashed everywhere, churned up by the chaos, and the roaring tumult was a concussive force. Efgul was hacking with his war-axe, cutting deeper into the slowly-giving resilience of the enemy file. All around Karl, the men of Uldin's warband, together with Kurgan spear and axe on foot, were striking and killing. A berdish axe smote down an arquebusier. A pallasz split a pike man. A crossbow bolt struck a Norther swordsman with such force his body slammed backwards and his round shield spun upwards into the air. Uldin's man Diormac caved skulls with his heavy flail, and his black warhorse kicked out its hooves. There was no room to move in the choking press, and no possibility of seeing further than a few spans in any direction.

Gathek, another of Uldin's men, suddenly rose above the turmoil of bodies. He was impaled on a pike that had lifted him, kicking, off his saddle. The pike shaft snapped, and Gathek's corpse fell back into the crush.

A sword struck against Karl's shield, and he wrenched round, burying his speartip in the swordsman's cuirass. It wedged fast, and was tugged from his hand. He was unarmed now, and forced to weather the assault of the Imperial infantry with only a shield. His only weapon was his horse, and he drove it forward, head down, so its lashing hooves would batter and break limbs.

The rain seemed as heavy as a waterfall now. Lightning seared the dark sky and whipped down into the earth, exploding the ground amongst the Empire's rear ranks. The storm, it seemed, fought for Surtha Lenk's cause too; it was repaying the bombardment of the Imperial cannon.

For a moment, Karl caught sight of other shapes through the rain and vapour. Giant shadows loomed above the height of the men: bestial nightmares that howled into the deluge and tore into the Imperial forces with talons and claws. One seemed to have wings that spread from its shoulders like sails. Another, too grotesque to comprehend, had a great bird's beak.

Karl's shield was half shredded now, and his mare's flanks were gashed and torn. He pushed on, trampling men underfoot, and at last broke clear into the field behind the Imperial array. Efgul, Yuskel and eight other riders came through with him, then came Lyr, Berlas and Uldin himself a moment later.

The men of the Empire were already fleeing. They could be seen scattering singly or in small groups down across the field in the direction of Aachden, weapons and armour thrown down in their wake. Loose war hounds were chasing some, and pulling those they caught down, screaming.

'Leave them!' Uldin bellowed. He swung the riders about as still more joined them, then drove in towards the enemy's rear ranks.

'Azytzeen!' Efgul shouted. He rode up close to Karl and gave him his saddle-sword, a falchion with a wooden grip and a billed tip. Karl took it and ran his horse after Uldin's. Hzaer's carnyx boomed.

The warband hurtled north, crossing the breaking flight of the Imperial bodies. They despatched those that came in reach as they thundered through. Karl tested Efgul's cutting sword on the head of a fleeing archer and found it was not wanting an edge.

An Imperial horse troop met the warband coming the other way. The Imperial commander had sent them to staunch the flow of deserters haemorrhaging from the back files. They were demilancers, their half-armour flashing and their cockades bobbing as they rode down the field, standing in their saddles. Most had lost their lances already, but they had sabres, and some had handguns.

Demilancers...

Karl-Azytzeen howled as he followed Uldin's charge into them. Warband and horse troop met head on, at full tilt, lashing past one another. Passing cuts from pallasz and war-axes struck demilancers off their geldings. Sabres and banging wheel-locks tumbled Kurgan riders out of their saddles.

Karl lost his shield to a pistol shot, and then swiped sideways with Efgul's sword, ripping a single, grievous wound through the neck of a lancer's troop horse and then through the ribcage of the lancer himself. Then he was fore-on to a demilancer who was intercepting him with sabre raised across the face at the charge position. Karl struck the blade aside, and they turned about each other, yanking back the heads of their steeds for another exchange. The sabre thrust at Karl, and he turned it aside again. Then he swung his steel down through the man's pauldron, shoulder and deep into his trunk. The demilancer convulsed, wailing, his blood spraying into the hard rain. Karl dragged his blade out, and the lancer was gone down into the waterlogged mud.

Karl glared around to engage again, horses and men crashed past him in all directions. There was a demilancer right upon him, coming from the hindquarters. This lancer had a wheel-lock raised stiffly in his left hand.

Karl saw the dog spark and the muzzle flash with fire and white smoke.

Then the shot split his head into pieces.

ZAMAK SPAYENYA

I

IN HINDSIGHT, PERHAPS it had not been the wisest thing to do.

After a day's straight gallop across the trackless steppe, Gerlach began to feel uneasy. There was nothing and no one out there. His two long rides with the rota, especially the trek to Leblya, had falsely inflated his confidence that he could cope out on the steppe and deal with its harsh extremes and painful solitude. He hadn't realised how much he had looked to the lancers for their support. And for their expertise.

He was, by the motion of the sun at least, heading due south. But after an hour or two it occurred to him that he could only presume south was the way to go. He had no specific knowledge of Leblya's relative location. Riding south might take him back to the Empire, but it could just as well carry him to the wilds of the Worlds Edge Mountains. He had no map, and no honed lore of the oblast. His course might run for days, for weeks, into nothing, unwittingly bypassing stanitsas just over the horizon that the lancers would have known to go to.

His hope had been to get a good start on the rota, and maybe outrun them for two or three days. Then, when they caught up with him, he would convince them to keep going with him into the south. If they didn't kill him, that is.

But there was no sign of riders behind him all the first day, and none on the second either.

The banner became too heavy to hold, and he was forced to ride with it cradled across his knees and saddlebow. He began to feel like a shameless thief, and dearly regretted taking it. Maybe if he had just ridden off, they would have followed him anyway. They seemed to care about his welfare. That made his crime seem worse. They had been good to him – staunch allies and generous comrades – and he had robbed them of their most precious artifact.

More than once he thought of turning back. He also considered leaving the rota somewhere for them to find. Scorching sunlit days turned to bitter oblast nights. The sun glared at him contemptuously, and the stars, in their multitude, mocked him.

The fourth day came and went, then the fifth. He had never been out of sight of other humans for so long. His only company was the passing clouds, but they seemed resentful, and chose not to show him any pictures he could read.

On the sixth morning, aching and anxious, he halted Saksen and stood for a long while, watching the northern horizon for signs of movement. Surely they would be coming close by now. He kept expecting to see them rise into view: heads, shoulders, horses, shimmering in the heat haze. Several times he thought he'd seen them, but it was just the light and space playing tricks on his tired mind.

He had brought some food and water, but nothing like enough for a trek of this magnitude. Vitali – and by Sigmar, he would have been overjoyed to see that smiling warrior again! – had showed him how to dig for water, and collect dew overnight in his armour plate and helm, but it was a meagre resource, and most of it went to his gelding. Saksen was strong, but he was also used to decent, regular fodder. He was a southerner, just like Gerlach, and was not built for these conditions. The troop horse had nothing of the stamina and resilience displayed by the robust steppe ponies the lancers rode. They seemed to fare without ready water, and greedily foraged on the tough grasses when rested at camp. Saksen appeared to find the grass indigestible. But when he was with the ponies, he had seemed content to follow their lead and graze. Gerlach could not make him eat the scrub, though he tried. Saksen was ailing.

Gerlach was ailing too. Thirst and hunger oppressed him physically, and he began to feel tormented by guilt and loneliness. He had ridden out of Leblya, intent on his scheme to draw the rota back to the war. That seemed inconsequential now. The entire fate of the Empire no longer mattered to him; he wondered why he had ever cared. Why had he been so reckless to involve himself in that faraway fight? Hadn't he realised where he was and how little he mattered?

In the late afternoon of the sixth day – maybe seventh, for he was no longer absolutely sure – he saw something in the grass ahead of him. It was nothing much, but in a place as blank and featureless, any deviation from the norm stood out.

They were bones. An untidy heap of scattered bones, old and stained pale yellow by the ministry of the wind and sun. For a while he stared at the remains, and eventually decided they belonged to a horse and a man. They had fallen here together, decayed and dried, until at last their loose bones had tumbled apart like pieces of a puzzle. How long had they been here? Years, certainly. Maybe decades, or even longer. Perhaps he was the first person to set eyes on them since the hour of their death.

They weren't the bones of a traveller, lost and killed by the brutal steppe, he decided. They were the bones of a rider who had chosen to gallop away from his life into the embrace of fate. Or the bones of a warrior who had been blessed with a steppe funeral.

As he rode away from them, a sick thought invaded his mind. Was it Sorca? Or Kvetlai? Or Ptor, or Chagin? How fast did the flies and ants and buzzards of the oblast strip a body? Were those bones merely days old?

And how long before he and Saksen formed a similar heap in another lonely spot?

No one had warned him about the sounds of the steppe. Riding with the men of the rota, he had not noticed them. But alone now, strange noises came to him above the thump of Saksen's hooves, the steady tinkling of the bit and harness, and the gentle rattle of his armour.

The open air uttered odd moans and long, distant wails that he presumed were the wind. Something invisible made strange clicks as loud as wheellocks being wound. A fretful buzzing sound came and went, growing louder and louder until he drew up to listen for it only to find that it had disappeared. There was an occasional sound of hooves that never came closer and the inexplicable rush of racing water.

At dusk each day, dull booms pealed across the steppe. He stopped and listened for them, trying to discern their source. There were no storm clouds so he knew it wasn't thunder. It sounded like a great drum, struck once every few minutes. He would wait and listen until his patience lapsed and then, as soon as he started off again, another boom would come.

There were sounds at night too: sharper wails, and strange hollow growls that seemed to circle about him in the dark. Sometimes he heard voices, so distinct that he called out to them. The moment he spoke, the voices died away. And sometimes, there was laughter.

But the daylight sounds were the worst. At night, he could imagine, with a creeping dread, that there were things in the blackness around him. But in the light, he could see for certain there were not.

Once, under the midday heat, he caught the sound of a metal hinge grinding as it swung to and fro. There was a beat behind it, like the repeating thunk of a hammer on a metal sheet.

He drew Saksen up, and the sound continued. It was coming from close by, just to his right. Saksen's ears flicked back and forth. The gelding heard it too.

Gerlach dismounted, and walked through the grass, tracking the noise. He had drawn his loaded handgun and was clutching it in his hand. With the wood and iron piece in his hand, he was at least guarded against evil spirits. The sound grew louder and more insistent. It seemed to emanate from a rock the size of a man's head that lay in the dust amongst other quartzy fragments.

He approached it, and gingerly bent down beside the rock. The shrieking hinge and hammer were so loud now, he felt like he was in a smithy. He circled the rock and the source of the sound remained stationary. Under the stone.

Gerlach reached down and lifted the rock up.

The hinge and the hammer stopped. A terrible, shrill whistling erupted out of the depression where the rock had sat. It sang up into the air and made him fall down in shock. The noise made Saksen start.

Then it stopped, and unnerving silence reasserted itself.

Gerlach threw the rock aside. He was shaking. When he looked up, Saksen, crazed and scared, was galloping away into the grass.

II

HE RAN AFTER his horse, calling its name as loudly as his parched throat could manage. Then he stopped and doubled back to retrieve the rota banner, which had fallen onto the ground when Saksen bolted. Dragging it with him, like a deranged fool, he ran after the swiftly disappearing gelding.

'Saksen! Saksen! In the name of Sigmar! Byeli-Saksen!'

The horse was gone. The buzzing returned.

Behind it, like wind through leaves, there was distant laughter.

III

HE TRUDGED FOR a long period of immeasurable time, limping against the shaft of the heavy banner. When the buzzing returned, harsh and rasping in his ears, he turned in a circle and yelled a challenge aloud.

'What are you? Where are you?'

The buzzing seemed to swoop at him, and he cried out in alarm and fired his pistol.

Silence. The white smoke of his shot billowed up into a little cloud that drifted away into the sunny air.

For a moment, the tiny cloud looked like a white horse at full gallop. Then it fumed away and dissolved into the steppe breeze.

IV

DUSK FELL. THE sky turned a dense, Imperial blue, like the air before a storm, and the grasslands went white. The wide landscape was luminous, and the heavens a dead, lightless gloom.

Gerlach saw a stark, white speck, motionless, a league ahead of him.

He stumbled on, hurrying towards it.

Saksen stood stock still, his reins trailing, his head up. His flanks were caked in dry salt. The gelding was looking south.

As Gerlach approached, Saksen turned his noble head once to look at his master, then resumed his vigil.

Gerlach cast down the banner and the spent pistol, and edged towards his horse, cooing softly and holding out his hands. He ripped up a handful of steppe grass, the greenest he could find, and offered it out.

'Byeli… Byeli… Byeli-Saksen. Steady now. Steady now, old friend….'

Saksen allowed him to get close, and even sniffed the grass, though he would not take it. Gerlach stroked and patted Saksen's neck and took hold of the loose reins.

'Byeli… Byeli-Saksen.'

Gerlach led Saksen back and collected the banner and the pistol. Saksen tugged impatiently, wanting to turn south again.

Gerlach mounted up. Once he had the advantage of saddle-height, he saw what lay in the distance.

A puff of dust, kicked up by horsemen.

Galvanised, Gerlach found his stirrups and kicked his heels.

'Yatsha!'

V

At first it seemed as if there were a half dozen riders, chasing north-east in the grey, fading light. But as he closed, Gerlach realised they were in fact one and five. One man was riding hard, pursued by five others.

Gerlach realised he could not hope to catch them. They were too far away, and running fast.

He reined up and raised the banner, planting its tip in the soil beside Saksen.

The chased rider saw it, and turned in towards Gerlach.

Gerlach primed his pistol, and slipped it into its case. Then he drew his sabre.

The lone rider was approaching, thrashing up a wake of dust with his furious gallop. A steppe horse. A rider in rough furs and leathers.

It was Kvetlai. And behind him came five Kul horsemen.

As soon as he recognised Kvetlai, Gerlach beckoned to him furiously. He didn't like the odds, but he was committed now. Five to one, or five to two if Kvetlai was able. Gerlach vowed he would make a good account of himself.

The riders came on.

As soon as he was close enough to identify Gerlach, Kvetlai started to yell, 'Vebla! Vebla! Yha!'

Gerlach smiled grimly. He waved Kvetlai on past him, and raised the wheel-lock, braced in both hands. He used his knees to keep Saksen at a steady halt.

Kvetlai swept past him, churning up a trail of dust and grit. The Kul horsemen were heartbeats away. Three had drawn swords, one an axe and a small shield. The closest, mailed in a low, frog-brow sallet, swung a flail.

Gerlach took aim. He was the target now. The Kul were riding him down and Kvetlai had disappeared somewhere behind him.

Four lengths away, Gerlach fired. His shot took the Kul with the flail in the neck and smashed him out of his saddle. His body slammed into the dust and rolled over and over as his empty horse rushed past Gerlach.

There was no time to reload. Gerlach cased his pistol and took up his sabre. He kicked Saksen forward and raised his blade crosswise to his face in the charge position. He galloped to greet the nearest Kul.

The horseman had a sword, and was swinging it in wild loops as he came on. Gerlach spurred Saksen abruptly to the man's off-side at the last moment, and thrust in across the saddle bow as they passed. The sabre came away bloody and the Kul screamed and fell forward over his mare's neck, dropping his blade.

The next two were on him, swordsman to the left and axe man to the right. Gerlach drove between them, and avoided both cutting slashes. Head low, Gerlach passed them, and met the tail-ender. Their swords struck and sent brief sparks up into the dark blue sky.

They both turned to re-engage.

The other two were turning as well, whooping and howling.

Gerlach went at the tail-ender and traded sword blows again. They had lost all momentum, and were saddle to saddle, hacking and blocking. The other two Kul were closing.

Gerlach split the air with his sabre, trying to drive off the tail-ender's blade. He was protecting both himself and Saksen, for the barbarian saw both as viable targets.

A fifth horseman appeared. Kvetlai raced back into the melee. He had no armour or troop weapons, but he had drawn his saddle-sword. It was really too long to use while riding, too clumsy for a mounted duel. But the Kul had their backs to him and Kvetlai's blade ripped through the axeman's spine.

The man fell and his horse came over with him in a flurry of dry soil. The Kul's round shield skidded away across the dust.

Gerlach locked his sabre with the blade of the Kul he was fighting, and turned the enemy's sword aside so hard the tip of it stabbed into his mount's neck. The horse shrieked and kicked back, bucking and throwing its rider. It charged away into the gathering night.

Gerlach rode forward as the thrown man began to pick himself up out of the grass and dust, and lopped his head off.

The remaining Kul rider stopped short. He lowered his dirty iron blade. Gerlach faced him, blood dripping off his raised sabre. Kvetlai closed in from behind.

With a terrified cry, the Kul took off, and rode away into the west.

Gerlach and Kvetlai sheathed their swords and trotted forward to meet each other. Gerlach held out his hand, but the young Kislevite hugged him instead.

'Vebla!' he declared. He declared a lot of other things too, but Gerlach did not understand. Kvetlai had the least Reikspiel of any lancer in Beledni's rota.

It made Gerlach smile. Starved of company, his first encounter was with a friend who spoke nothing of his tongue.

Gerlach took Kvetlai by the hands and examined his wound. The long gash on his hand and arm was oozing pink, but it was healing. Borodyn had been right. A lancer simply had to trust in Dazh and ride out until the poison sweated out of him. Kvetlai had got on his horse and healed himself.

What adventures he had experienced in the course of that healing, Gerlach did not know. He took up the banner, and tried to beckon Kvetlai.

'South!' Gerlach said, pointing. 'We must go south!'

'Nyeh!' Kvetlai said emphatically, and pointed west.

Gerlach was about to argue. Then he looked south. There were fires on the horizon. Torches clutched in the hands of six dozen horsemen. Kul horsemen.

Gerlach looked at Kvetlai and nodded. 'You're right. Let's head west.'

VI

THEY RODE INTO the west together, and into the deepening twilight. The fires followed them, flickering: bobbing specks against the almost-black land, like grounded stars. There were more than six dozen now, and they straggled right across the south-east skyline.

Kvetlai gabbled as they rode. He was excited and talkative. Though he knew Gerlach couldn't understand him, he didn't seem to care. It was of no matter. Just the sound of a voice pleased Gerlach. He recognised occasional words as they tumbled out of the young lancer's mouth. Kvetlai said 'pulk' several times, with emphasis.

'Pulk?' Gerlach asked.

'Shto?'

'Pulk?' Gerlach repeated, wishing he had a smattering of Kislevite. Kvetlai chattered something else, and Gerlach gave up.

They'd ridden for over an hour, and night had swallowed day. It was utterly black. The only way they could tell land from sky was the fact that above a certain line, there were stars. Except behind them, where low, yellow stars burned and moved.

Something vast rose before them, slowly and grandly. At first, Gerlach thought it was a rising moon, or that a piece of the bright moon had fallen onto the steppe. It was a great slab of white stone, ghostly in the starlight, at least a league across: a single, oblong crag sprouting from the flat vista of the steppe.

They approached it. It was hauntingly beautiful, and illuminated the steppe as the moon and star light reflected off its icy whiteness. It was also immense.

'Zamak Spayenya,' Kvetlai said.

They rode onto the lower slopes of clattering scree, weaving between slabs and blocks of skewed rock that time had sloughed from the high faces of the table mountain. The rocks had a warm, damp smell as if they still radiated the heat of the day. Kvetlai led Gerlach around the northern edge of the crag. He clearly knew this place. It was hardly surprising. This rock – this *Zamak Spayenya* – was so singular it had to be a well-known landmark of the endless grassland.

Still chatting cheerfully, Kvetlai located a narrow gorge in the side of the giant rock, and they rode down its steep defile, entering a cool darkness with only a ribbon of starry sky high above. The horses' hooves cracked and clicked on the bared, uprisen rock.

The slope grew steep and their mounts slowed. Kvetlai jumped down and motioned for Gerlach to do the same. They led the horses the rest of the way on foot.

The gorge opened out into a great bowl of space open to the sky. Echoes of their every move rolled around the sides. The bottom of the bowl was filled with black water, the moons and the stars reflected there in an unrippled mirror.

Kvetlai pulled off his saddlebags, pack roll and water skin, and let his pony loose. The steppe horse immediately went to the pool to drink and stirred circles out over the faces of the mirrored moons. Kvetlai joined it to replenish his water skin.

Gerlach slipped his saddle kit off Saksen's harness. The troop horse trotted over to slake its thirst the moment Gerlach slipped the reins.

Kvetlai splashed his face with water from the great cistern of rainfall, and then jumped up.

'Vebla!' he beckoned. Gerlach followed him. The boy clearly believed their horses would be safe here in this inner place.

Kvetlai clambered up the smooth, sloping surfaces of the inner rock, making his way into its upper levels. He stopped to help Gerlach with his kit, but respectfully refused to touch the rota banner Gerlach was lugging.

They left the pool basin behind them, and scaled the steep paths and slopes of scree up to the summit of the rock.

Gerlach looked out. The steppe lay below, spreading out into the dark. A cool wind ruffled his hair. This was higher than he had ever been – higher even than the steeple of the church at Talabheim. His brother had taken him up there when he was six or seven, and he'd gasped at the vista of streets and roofs and tiny people, and the pattern of fields and woods laid out beyond. Even though it was dark, this was somehow more impressive. An endless void spread out below him, and he was aware of a great depth of space. From up here, the steppe was not so much diminished as emphasised and increased.

He could no longer see the fires of the Kul.

Kvetlai took him to a deep cave high in the rock, the mouth of which overlooked the humbling emptiness. It was cool and dry inside. Kvetlai gleefully sat down in the dark and rummaged in his saddlebags. After a short time, he had coaxed to life a small fire, and fed it with pieces of animal bone that he had stockpiled for just such a purpose.

The fire rose, washing the smooth walls of the cave with shivering light. Gerlach divested himself of his kit and the heavier parts of his armour, and respectfully set the rota banner upright against the cave wall. Then he sat down opposite Kvetlai and warmed his hands at the fire.

Kvetlai recommenced his casual, unending chatter.

'Zamak Spayenya?' Gerlach asked, gesturing around them.

'Yha, Vebla! Yha!'

Kvetlai's saddlebags miraculously provided strips of dried salt-fish, wafer biscuits, lumps of cured pork and four eggs. The eggs had been hard boiled in vinegar to preserve them. Kvetlai showed Gerlach how to rub the eggs between his palms to crush off the shell. They had their water skins, and a small leather bottle of kvass that Kvetlai ceremonially unstoppered.

It was the best, most satisfying meal Gerlach Heileman would ever eat.

It grew colder as they settled back, passing the kvass between them. Kvetlai threw his last few bones onto the crackling fire, and the pieces of eggshell too. He was talking still, and from his tone, Gerlach realised Kvetlai was telling a formal tale, a traditional myth for the krug. Every now and then, apparently as part of the indecipherable story, he sat up and laughed a false, loud laugh at the shadows of the cave.

When he finished, he looked at Gerlach expectantly.

'Vebla gyavaryt,' he said.

'What?'

'Vebla... Vebla... you,' he said, nodding eagerly.

Gerlach realised it was his turn. He took a suck on his water skin and began: 'In the old times, there was a tribe of men that was called the Unberogen, and to them a child was born. His name was called Sigmar, and on the night of his birth, a star with two tails sailed across the sky...'

Gerlach told his story gently, and Kvetlai listened, rapt. Gerlach was reaching the famous part about the Black Fire Pass when something wailed in the dark and interrupted him. Kvetlai gave it no notice. Gerlach carried on, and then stopped again as the infernal buzzing and laughter that had stalked him on the steppe whispered past.

Kvetlai sat up straight and laughed his loud, false laugh at the shadows.

The noise faded.

The laughter came again, from the back of the cave, with a tiny hammer-beat mixed into it. Kvetlai turned and laughed in that direction. The sounds stopped.

Gerlach recommenced, but halted yet again as whispering voices chattered out of the jumping shadows at the edge of the fire. Kvetlai leaned over and laughed at them, making the voices ebb.

'Spirits... phantoms of the steppe?' Gerlach asked.

Kvetlai nodded, not knowing what he was nodding at.

'They have stalked me. I have been afraid of them.'

Sibilant whispers rushed in around the mouth of the cave. Kvetlai turned his head and laughed once more, hearty but false.

'Aha ha ha ha!'

'And laughing at them scares them away...' Gerlach breathed. He smiled. When a hinge began to squeak in the roof of the cave halfway through the tale of the mantling of Johan Helstrum, they both looked up and bawled out a roaring laugh.

'Ha ha ha ha!'

Kvetlai settled back. 'Johan,' he prompted. 'Johan...'

Gerlach grinned. 'As I was saying, Helstrum was thus the first of the line of Grand Theogonists...'

VII

KVETLAI WAS ASLEEP before the history of the Sigmarite Empire was done. Gerlach sat for a while, then took a burning rib out of the fire and wandered into the back of the cave. His eyes had not tricked him. There were markings on the white limestone walls.

Primitive markings, made with graphite and ochre dust. Men riding to the hunt, their charcoal-streaked javelins wounding leaping deer and elk. Crude though it was, the depiction of the horses was instantly recognisable. The low, brown shapes of hardy steppe ponies, with shaggy, black manes. The riders were drawn naked, simple and angular, but great eagle wings grew out of their backs.

Gerlach moved the light of the crisping bone further down the wall. Here were boars, and sheep. A great mound surrounded by horses that looked as if they had been raised stiff on stakes. A star with two streaming tails of fire. Horse warriors, clad in gold.

The gold was real foil leaf, tamped against the cave wall. Gerlach looked again, and realised he was not looking at horse warriors at all. The prancing figures were horse-and-man. The bodies of flying steeds, with the torsos of men growing out where the horse heads should have been. Their arms were spread wide, triumphant, brandishing recurve bows and charcoal-streak javelins.

The centaurs of myth. Men who were horses. Horses who were also men. Or, Gerlach thought, an ancient people whose lives had been so wholly dependent on the horse that there was no separating the two.

His bone-light went out. The ancient drawings vanished, as if they had galloped away into the shadows.

Gerlach crept back to the dying fire where Kvetlai slumbered.

He was about to sit down, when he heard a low, welling moan. He laughed at it, but it did not fade. He laughed again, louder and more vigorously, but the moan remained and rose as a whispering chatter.

It was coming from the mouth of the cave.

Gerlach walked to the opening and laughed wildly and loudly into the darkness. He heard the phantom laughter wash through the night and indignantly prepared to guffaw again to see it off.

A hand closed over his mouth, silencing him.

It was Kvetlai.

The lad pointed down the slope. Far below, around the skirts of the great rock, Kul torches were moving.

VIII

KVETLAI KICKED OUT the fire and then watched the cave mouth, his saddle-sword in his hand, as Gerlach dressed himself in the parts of his half-armour that he had taken off. Gerlach began to prime his wheel-lock too, but Kvetlai stopped him and patted his sword blade. His meaning was obvious. If they were going to live, they had to act quietly.

Gerlach put his handgun and its equipment aside, and followed Kvetlai out into the moonlight. He was holding his sabre, and drew his knife in the other hand.

There were flickering torch lights below them still, but other scads of flame could be seen moving up the rocks and along the gorges that cut into the table mountain.

The Kul were not moving directly towards them. There was a good chance these kyazak could spend the rest of the night searching the rock's mighty system of caves and ravines for them.

Gerlach and Kvetlai settled back in silence to wait it out, their swords gripped in their hands.

IX

THE MOONS ROSE and set. Voices and the occasional clatter of dislodged scree echoed down to them. They waited. Hours crawled by.

Below, the flames jiggled around the foot of the rock.

Gerlach woke up very suddenly. He had no idea how long he'd been asleep, but the sky was just beginning to turn pale. Kvetlai was sleeping, hunched against the far side of the cave mouth.

Gerlach was about to hiss his name when he saw they were not alone. A Kul warrior was softly approaching the lip of rock beyond the cave mouth. He could see the kyazak only as a dark shape with glittering eyes.

Gerlach waited, playing dead. Through half-shut lids, he watched the Kul coming closer. There was another one a short distance behind him. Gerlach's sabre had slid from his grasp while he slept, but the knife was still in his left hand. He kept still as the Kul crept up to him. The man had a short-hafted adze, and as he bent down, Gerlach heard him sniffing like a hunting dog.

Gerlach lunged, grabbing the Kul by the hair and ramming the knife up into his chest. The Kul squealed and struggled, but Gerlach kept him pinned. The second Kul at the edge of the rock-lip let out a guttural shout and raised a bow. The heavy arrow hissed as it flew, and splintered against the cave wall beside Gerlach's head. Gerlach fought to retain his grip on the first Kul, who was becoming limp and awfully heavy. He had to keep the man's body between him and the archer.

Running forward, the bowman fired again. The arrow smacked through the upper body of the corpse and travelled with such force that the head of it came through the other side, penetrated Gerlach's pauldron and stabbed a thumb's depth into his shoulder. Gerlach yelped out in pain. Before the archer could fire a third time, Kvetlai had sprung up and cut him through the ribs with his saddle-sword.

There was movement all around them as Kul scurried to close in on the source of the commotion. The flames of several torches showed close by. Kvetlai ran to one side of the rock-lip and hacked at another kyazak, sending his body slithering away down the sloping face. A fourth appeared, and Kvetlai turned to repel him. Their swords clattered against each other.

Having fought to hold on to his human shield, Gerlach now battled to rid himself of it. The man's deadweight pulled hard and painfully against the arrowhead and made Gerlach cry out again in frustrated anguish.

The arrow snapped, leaving a small, broken, finger length protruding from Gerlach's shoulder. The body fell away sideways, Gerlach's knife still wedged in its chest. Gerlach grabbed his sabre, pain flaming down his arm. Kyazak blood was all over his left hand and down his front.

Gerlach ran forward in time to contend with two more Kul sliding down the slope onto the rock-lip from the left side of the cave. He killed one with a swift thrust, and then battled with the other, who lunged and slashed at him with a short sword and a crackling torch. Gerlach's face was singed as the rushing flames jabbed at him.

Kvetlai had slain another Kul, and now struck out at more, moving so he was shoulder to shoulder with the demilancer. Gerlach finally managed to tear his sabre against the threatening torch and send it sparking and flaring down the incline. Then he overwhelmed the kyazak's untrained sword hand with three clean, proficient blows and finished him with a body-thrust.

Between them, with frantic effort, they killed or drove off the four Kul who had managed to get onto the rock-lip. Many more were approaching, from either side and below.

Kvetlai cried out something, and ransacked the body of the first kyazak he had taken – the archer who had gored Gerlach. He got the man's bow and his case of arrows, and began to fire them into the darkness. The spitting sounds of arrows were answered, more than once, by a cry of pain.

Dawn was on them. The sky had gone slate grey, and the crag side was slowly illuminating with watery light. The steppe below remained as dark as pitch right out to the line where it joined the cold, pale sky.

The kyazak rushed them again, from below and to the left, and it took all the effort and skill of the two men to hold them off. The Kul dropped back. To prepare bows, Gerlach thought.

Kvetlai called to him in this brief intermission and gestured upwards. Pausing only long enough for Gerlach to gather the banner, they began to scramble up the steep stone slope above the cave mouth, heading for the highest part of the crag. A few wayward arrows rattled off the rocks around them, and Kvetlai paused occasionally, legs spread and braced against the sharp incline, to loose an arrow or two back.

Gerlach concentrated on climbing and avoiding slithering back down to an ignominious doom. Half-armour was not made for such an activity, and the long, heavy banner was a downright hindrance. But he could not leave it for the filthy kyazak. He crawled up the hard, dry face of the rock, sometimes using the shaft of the banner as a prop. He was sweating freely. More arrows rushed up at them, striking the rock with brittle cracks or purring past their heads like bees.

They reached the top – a small platform of rock – just about the highest part of Zamak Spayenya. The limestone sloped away on all sides of it and to reach it any bandit would have to scale the open face as Gerlach and Kvetlai had done.

They sat down and recovered their breath. The waking day was much brighter now, and the light was falling with a silver radiance. A dawn breeze blew. They could see for many leagues in every direction. Gerlach could spot no sign of life except an eagle, gliding in the thermals a long way up.

They kept a careful watch over the edge of the platform. Some of the kyazak attempted to climb after them, and were dissuaded by a few arrows and hurled rocks. But all the Kul had to do was wait. It was already warm. The summer heat would make that exposed platform as hot as a griddle. Without water and cover, and with nowhere left to run, the two men would not last for any great time. From one side of the platform, it was possible to see down into the cool, shadowy basin in the heart of the crag where they had left their horses. They looked down at the pool and its tantalising promise of an end to thirst.

The silvery dawn became bright morning, blindingly white. The rising heat of noon broiled the sweat out of them. They became so torpid that one effort by the Kul to reach them almost succeeded. Gerlach only managed to knock the kyazak warriors back down the rock face using the pole of the banner as a makeshift spear.

The scalding heat did not seem to diminish as the long day ground on into the slow afternoon. Gerlach watched the smudges of cloud pass by overhead. They were meaningless, unformed, not even suggestive of character. But the gliding eagle returned, closer now, banking above them, and shortly after that a cloud appeared that was almost a circle or a ring.

'Krug,' Kvetlai said, his lips dry. He was watching the cloud.

Gerlach got to his feet.

'Shto, Vebla?' Kvetlai asked, supposing another rush of kyazak was coming. Gerlach slowly scanned the horizon, turning full circle. It had to be... it had to be...

Dazh did not send men messages lightly.

A tiny flash, out in the north-west, right at the very brink of the visible world.

'Kvetlai! Look there!' Gerlach pointed, and the boy stood up. Their movement at the edge of the platform provoked a couple of arrows up from below.

Kvetlai didn't seem to see, yet Gerlach was sure. The flash of sunlight on silver. But so far off, and perhaps moving away.

He grabbed up the banner and raised it as high as he could, holding the shaft by its very end in both hands and swinging the head so the banner cloth itself fluttered out in the high air. It was a huge effort, and he had to set it down every few moments to ease his arms. Every time he hoisted it up again, the Kul below loosed angry arrows and shouted curses and cat-calls. A few began to try climbing again. He waved the banner like a castaway mariner trying to hail a passing ship from a desert atoll. Gerlach's notion that the steppe was like a sea where its people lived like islanders now seemed desperately apt.

The distant flash was no longer visible, as if it had gone, or had never been there. A trick of the light, a trick of the eye.

Then Kvetlai called out, and pointed excitedly. A dot. Several dots in fact. A line of dots, moving gradually towards them.

Gerlach laughed out and set to waving the banner more vigorously.

The dots became shapes. The shapes became horsemen. Galloping horsemen, over fifty of them, clad in silver. Tall wings rose from their backs.

At some point, as the lancers raced closer, the kyazak saw them too. There was a round of hectic shouting from below the platform, and then the voices of the Norscya bandits receded. By the time the rota reached Zamak Spayenya, the bandit pack had fled, riding their ponies east into the steppe.

Gerlach and Kvetlai scrambled down from the platform, slithering most of the way. They gathered up what remained of their saddlebags and possessions from the cave where the looting Kul had scattered them, and climbed down into the shadows of the rainwater basin. Saksen and Kvetlai's horse had gone, but before they worried about that, the two men plunged into the pool to cool their baked, dry bodies and slake their thirst.

They emerged from the gorge into the sunlight. Their horses, either driven off by the Kul or simply fled away from them, were grazing in the scrub between the scattered boulders around the foot of the crag. Their ears twitched as they heard the drumming of hooves.

The rota appeared, riding around the bluff of Zamak Spayenya. Beledni was at their head. Kvetlai cried out and ran towards them as they reined to a halt.

Gerlach took a deep breath, lifted the banner, and walked after him.

* * *

X

THE MEN OF the rota were silent. Kvetlai was puzzled, not really sure what was going on or why Beledni rotamaster was glaring with such venom at the outlander they called 'Vebla'.

Beledni dismounted and walked towards Gerlach. Kvetlai went to him, and began a hasty account in Kislevite. Beledni ignored him and continued striding towards Gerlach. Then Kvetlai said something that made the rotamaster stop, turn back, and fire off a series of rapid questions.

Beledni finally silenced Kvetlai's eager answers with a curtly raised hand, and turned back to Gerlach. They stood face to face in the bright afternoon light, horseflies buzzing around them and the strong steppe wind ruffling the grass. Gerlach handed the banner to Beledni. He took it, and held it beside himself, upright in his left hand.

'Vebla steal rota banner,' he said at last. His eyes were dark and dangerous behind the visor of his szyszak.

'Yes,' Gerlach replied.

'Vebla steal rota banner so rota would follow him.'

'Yes, rotamaster.'

'Follow to find pulk. To find war.'

'Yes, rotamaster.'

'Even though Beledni rotamaster say nyeh.'

'Yha, rotamaster.'

They were not really questions. It was as if Beledni wanted to make sure he had the facts straight. He glanced up at the flapping banner for a moment, then looked back into Gerlach's face.

'Vebla save Kvetlai from kyazak.'

'We saved each other, rotamaster.'

'Kvetlai make ride to sweat out sickness. He not never come back, if Vebla not help him with kyazak.'

Gerlach shrugged.

'Kvetlai find pulk at Zoishenk.'

'What?'

'Kvetlai ride back to tell this to Beledni rotamaster.'

'I... I had no idea of this, rotamaster.'

Beledni nodded.

'Yetchitch rota go to Zoishenk now,' he said, briefly. With a casual movement, he handed the banner back to Gerlach and returned to his horse.

XI

THREE DAYS' RIDE into the south brought them to the cattle town of Zoishenk. It was larger than Leblya and Dushyka, larger than Zhedevka and Choika put together. It had a large livestock market and sat at the edge of a great grass plain on the banks of a wide, shallow river called the Tobol. The Tobol flowed down from some distant oblast mountains, and the locale of

Zoishenk was riven with a range of rocky hills and dense thorn-wood.

Riding out his sickness, deliriously sweating the poison from his wound, Kvetlai had come to Zoishenk almost by chance, and there found the masses of the Sanyza pulk. In the months following Zhedevka, the broken elements of the Kislevite pulk had assembled at Zoishenk instead of Leblya because of the threat of the kyazak bandit-army loose in the steppe to the north.

The stanitsa was teeming with soldiers. Almost seven hundred warriors were gathered there – three other rotas of winged lance, several bands of horse archers, and foot companies of pike and axe, along with the cruder assortments of levies and partisans. There was also the remainder of several Imperial pike companies that had fled Zhedevka and come here under the pulk's colours, combining their strengths to make one full regiment. Sanyza pulk – that is to say the army raised and recruited from the Sanyza area of the oblast – was under the command of the Boyarin Fyodor Kurkosk, a second cousin of the tzarina herself.

Additions and reinforcements – like Beledni's rota – were being added all the time, and scouts had been sent out to locate other scattered parts of the pulk and to drum up new support from the neighbouring regions. Word was that the Uskovic pulk, an army of much more considerable size, was already en route to join the Sanyza pulk. With those sort of numbers at his disposal, the boyarin would advance south, perhaps even as far as the Ostermark, and engage the Kurgan horde. By the end of the summer season, or by the start of the autumn, they would have joined with the foe and perhaps be driving him out of the Reik.

At long last, Gerlach had the chance to fight for his homeland, the chance he had been craving since the spring.

But Sigmar – or perhaps Dazh – had other plans for him.

By the time the rota reached Zoishenk, Gerlach was sick.

XII

NO ONE COULD say what filth had been caked on the tip of the kyazak arrow, and it had not helped that the barb had remained, lodged and festering, in Gerlach's shoulder for over a day. Borodyn had managed to dig it out with a flame-heated knife, but the wound was dirty. Gerlach became feverish, and his upper arm swelled so badly he could no longer wear armour around the limb. Defiantly, despite his progressively ailing state, he carried the banner all the way to Zoishenk. Vitali and Vaja were concerned he was about to pitch out of Saksen's saddle and they suggested Maksim should take the standard.

Once they had arrived at Zoishenk, Gerlach was carried to one of the livestock barns that had been converted into barracks for the pulk. He was laid out on a straw mattress. The flesh around his wound had gone black and the injury stank. He fell into a turbulent sleep, and did not regain consciousness for several days. Borodyn, Vaja, Vitali and Kvetlai took turns to watch him, spooning sips of gruel and water into his mouth and dressing his wound with salves of astringent herbs.

Like clouds across the steppe, fever dreams passed mysteriously through Gerlach's mind. In one, his father and brother came to him, both dressed in the full plate of the Order of the Red Shield, but neither would speak to him. In another, he lay helpless in long grass that knotted around him and held him down as Talabheim burned. Then he was running into the empty steppe at night, chasing a white horse that remained out of his reach. A blazing star with two long streamers of flame arching out behind it fell out of the night. The star flew at him. In its fiery heart was a staring blue eye ringed with writhing snakes.

Delirious, he became afraid. His dreaming mind recalled the fact that he and Kvetlai hadn't had time to blind the kyazaks they had killed at Zamak Spayenya. The spirits of the dead, loose in the darkness outside life, could see him and were coming to claim his soul. He cried out so fearfully and thrashed about so much, Vaja and Vitali had to hold him down for fear he would injure himself further.

After ten days, the death-fever broke. The fretful tremor left Gerlach and he woke suddenly, with apparent clarity, long enough to sip water and broth. Then he fell into a profound but untroubled sleep. Borodyn pronounced that Gerlach would live after all.

And he lived, but his recovery was slow. It took another week before he properly regained his senses, and another two before he could sit up unassisted. He was miserably weak and his undernourished flesh clung to his bones.

Well over a month after riding into Zoishenk, just as he was able to walk around for short periods, Maksim and Beledni came to him. They both looked serious and a little uncomfortable.

'What is it?' he asked.

'Beledni need your permission, Vebla,' said the rotamaster.

'For what?'

'For Maksim to carry rota banner,' Beledni said. Maksim made a little, respectful nod of his head.

'Why?'

'The boyarin has make decree. Pulk is to advance.'

'That's good! Good! I'm keen to get on myself, and–'

'Nyeh, Vebla.' Gerlach hadn't realised that Borodyn had been lurking in the shadows behind the lancers. 'You are not fit enough to walk across this room, let alone get up on a horse. You cannot come. You would not live a day.'

Gerlach shook his head fiercely.

'Is so, Vebla,' murmured the rotamaster. 'Beledni is sorry. You not come.'

Miserably disappointed, but knowing they were right, Gerlach looked away.

'Please to give Beledni permission for Maksim to carry rota banner,' Beledni said quietly.

'I give it,' Gerlach replied.

XIII

THE PULK DEPARTED at dawn the next day. Gerlach managed to get himself as far as the stable doorway to watch the army move out. Drums and horns sounded as the files marched out through the streets, and it was still possible to hear them a long time afterwards, as an echo from the valleys of the south.

XIV

GERLACH BATTLED TO bring himself back to fitness. He ate everything he could get hold of to rebuild his strength, and exercised his weak limbs to restore decent mobility. Three weeks after the pulk's departure, he was strong enough to walk and ride. He knew he was yet nothing like as strong as he had been, but it was enough. He gathered his possessions, collected some saddle supplies, and prepared to follow the pulk south.

It was late summer by then, hot and lazy. The days were drawing out and the land had become dry and dusty. The herders of Zoishenk were taking their grazing flocks higher into the foot hills to look for fresher pasture, and traders were arriving with harvested corn and grain from the farmlands in the south-east. The Tobol was now so parched by the high summer heat that its course was just a wide dusty track threaded by a feeble stream. Everywhere, the withered grass clicked with the sound of steppe crickets.

Then the pulk returned.

XV

THE BOYARIN'S ARMY had got as far south as Pradeshynya, contesting twice along the way with small warbands of raiders. At Pradeshynya, they sighted a massive host of raiders three or four times their size, undoubtedly the collective warbands of a significant High Zar. The pulk had withdrawn across the Tobol headwaters to avoid annihilation, and waited for the Uskovic pulk to arrive with reinforcements.

It never came. Whether it had been delayed, or annihilated, the men of Sanyza pulk could not know. The Boyarin decided to wait two more days, but in that time the enemy made its move. A host of warbands, a large chunk of the High Zar's horde, attacked the pulk across the Tobol salt-pan. It could have been a disaster, but the pulk was well prepared. The battle lasted for about five hours, right on into the late evening, whereupon the Kurgan fell back, badly mauled and suffering huge casualties at the hands of the resilient Kislevites. The withdrawal gave the boyarin a grace period to retreat back into the oblast before the entire horde massed and fell on them.

They were pursued for a time but, with a higher proportion of mounted troops than the Kurgan forces, the pulk outdistanced its adversaries.

Fyodor Kurkosk, in consultation with his commanders, was forced to make a hard decision. The summer was as good as over, and the hard weather of autumn and winter would be fast on them. The pulk would disband, and its constituent companies return to their own lands over winter. This gave them all time to recruit, resupply and raise more levies, and then build support from adjoining regions. Kurkosk decreed that the Sanyza pulk would reform at Zoishenk early after midwinter, preferably at the first thaw. With luck, it would be two or three times its current size. With more luck, it might be one of several pulks coordinated and drawn together over the winter season by the urgent efforts of the boyarin warlord and his officers.

Beledni's lancers were heading home into the steppe, to Yetchitch.

'You will come, Vebla, yha?' Vitali asked eagerly.

Gerlach had a poor choice. He could hardly ride south on his own into the enemy. And he didn't fancy staying alone in a cattle town for the winter. Besides, Zoishenk had become a place of repeatedly dashed hopes for him, and he was weary of it.

He would ride to Yetchitch with the rota. Even if it did feel like running away.

CHAMON DHAREK

I

'Give me a mirror,' Karl snapped.

'A…?'

'A looking glass,' said Karl. 'I know you have one. I've seen you using it in your doltish sorceries.'

Chegrume scowled for a moment. Then he reached into the roughly sewn pelts of his spirit-bag. 'It is not meant for looking in. Only for seeing in. Only shamans should–' The shaman shrugged. 'Perhaps one such as you might be permitted to use it.' He took the precious glass from the bag and held it out to Karl in his bony, long-nailed fingers.

Karl took it. It was an irregular piece of silver-backed glass fixed into a spoon-like paddle of fig wood. He held it up and stared into it.

It was the first time Karl had seen his own reflection since leaving the garrison at Vatzl, what seemed like years before. Karl Reiner Vollen no longer looked back at him.

The demilancer's pistol ball had struck him on the corner of the brow ridge over his left eye. The bone had shattered, and the whole area from the eyebrow down to the cheek was an ugly weal of distorted scar tissue. It was pinky-white and black-scabbed, but now, a week after the battle, the swelling was beginning to go down.

The injury had destroyed his left eye. Pain still throbbed in the dead socket, and he had a constant stabbing hurt in the skull above the eye. Chegrume had cleansed the wound and the ruined socket with hot iron and herbal tinctures. He had probably saved Karl's life from blood fever, but his face and sight would never be repaired.

Karl stared at his face for a long time. He was unshaven and his teeth were dirty. His black hair was so long now he wore it permanently in a tail. The three blue dots of Zar Uldin's mark looked like an old bruise on his right cheekbone.

He had been aware that all the Kurgan he had encountered since his wounding seemed to regard him with some measure of fear or apprehension, and averted their gaze whenever he was around. This seemed strange considering they were quite used to horrific injuries and mutilations. But they hadn't been showing revulsion.

Looking into the glass, Karl could plainly see what had scared them.

He had one eye. One blue eye. To make it worse, indelible powder burns from the injury had stained lines across his face, both over and under his good eye. The lines were twisted, and looked like snakes.

A single blue eye surrounded by snakes. No wonder no one dared look at him.

He handed the glass back to Chegrume.

'You should have let me die,' he told him.

II

SURTHA LENK'S HORDE had obliterated the army of the Reik outside Aachden. It was a notable victory. The town fell soon after, and many hundreds of its inhabitants, as well as men captured in battle, passed into the possession of the slave lord, Skarkeetah. Uldin, along with Blayda, Herfil and six other zars, had killed enough with his warband to earn the glory of a skull stack.

Chegrume had carved the new victory mark on Uldin's cheek. Four now, on that side.

Then Uldin gathered his warband for a victory feast – indeed all the bands in the High Zar's horde were celebrating the victory. Afterwards they would divide the spoils of war between them. Many trophy rings were made.

Wolfenburg lay close by. Uldin hoped to earn a fifth victory mark there before the last one had even scabbed over.

III

KARL-AZYTZEEN'S LEFT FOREARM was now wound with trophy rings from the elbow to the wrist, and there were three more around his right arm. Once he was well enough to walk, Uldin took him into a muddy field behind the ruins of Aachden and offered him his pick of the captured horses.

'I'll keep the one I have.'

'It is a poor thing, Karl-Azytzeen. Old and broken.'

'It serves me. It does not stop for anything. I will not trade it.'

Uldin shrugged. Even the zar refused to look directly at him. 'Then you should name it.' The Kurgan had no sentiment at all. They only gave a name to a thing when it became important. Most horses weren't named until they had carried their man through at least one battle.

'It doesn't need a name,' Karl replied. 'It is old, and has gone for this much of its life without one. It is simply my horse.' After this blunt dismissal, the men of the warband began to call the old nag Horse-of-Karl-Azytzeen.

'You are due a share of gold,' Uldin informed him.

'I have no use for gold. Give me a good fur and a saddle. I'm damned if I will fight on with a spear and no stirrups. And a decent sword.'

These things were provided within an hour, at the zar's orders. A good box-saddle with a brass harness, rowel spurs that Karl had nailed to his heavy boots, a heavy brown bear-pelt and a brooch to hold it. The brooch was Scythian gold, formed into the shape of a long-backed, leaping horse.

Uldin himself presented Karl with a sword. A superior pallasz, forged from steel rather than iron, with a straight bar guard and two hands of grip. Karl took a whetstone to its blade, and worked it until it was sharp enough to split a bough from a tree with one stroke, from either edge.

It was high summer, a time Karl had once particularly enjoyed. The weather was fine and warm, and the landscape – where it had not been touched and marred by the High Zar's massive host – was lush and green.

The horde left Aachden to rot and moved on to Wolfenburg.

IV

WOLFENBURG, THE GREAT sentinel city of Ostland's northern marches, lay in the foothills of the Middle Mountains amid vast blankets of forest. Even in the heat of summer, the mountains were white-capped and grim. Their huge blue-black shapes, fogged by cloud, dominated the skyline.

The city itself was a fortress town of ancient construction. Occupying a raised hillside above the river bend, it was well fortified with curtain walls and high, towered inner walls of great thickness. It had shut itself up in advance of the Northers' advance. Large tracts of forest outside the walls had been freshly cleared to remove available cover for an attacking force and to fill the city's stockpile of firewood.

The first warbands to reach the city made a hasty assault of the gatehouse and the south wall. But they were driven off, with costly losses, by vase-guns, hails of arrows, and scalding oil sluiced down through the murder holes above the gate.

The main part of the horde arrived and encamped around the city. More wood was cut, in great quantity, by berdish axe this time. This wood fed the camp-fires, and was also used to construct mobile shields that were pushed forward to allow the Kurgan archers with their powerful recurve bows to pepper the wall tops and the machicolations. Once the wagon train had arrived, the horde's sturdy old ballistae, trebuchets and catapults were trained on the city. The ballistae – essentially gigantic crossbows – launched savage bolts of iron-tipped hardwood two spans long at the walls. The trebuchets and catapults hurled rocks, weighted bales of burning straw, flasks of boiling oil and rotting human heads, collected from the field at Aachden expressly for the purpose.

The siege began in earnest. It was quite the dullest kind of war Karl had ever experienced. There was a feebly slow routine. The siege engines lobbed missiles at the wall, and the guns, slings and cannon of the town fired in reply, sometimes hurling the Kurgans' own projectiles back at them. This continued for days. Every few minutes there would be a sharp creak, a thump or a squeal of metal as one of the war machines fired. The drums beat continually.

The war bands were forced to bide their time. As horsemen, they had little part to play in this slow, erosive war.

Karl found himself gazing south-west across the forest for hours at a time. No more than fifteen days' good riding in that direction lay Talabheim, the home he could never now return to, unless it was to storm its noble walls and set its towers to burn.

V

THE SIEGE GROUND on for twelve weeks. There were a precious few bursts of activity. The Knights of the Order of the Silver Mountain, along with greatswords from the city garrison, made several sorties out of the gatehouse to harass the enemy. The warbands rode to meet them. Karl won two new trophy rings: one for a greatsword who almost filleted his horse, and another for a knight-at-arms whose silver plate-mail proved the sharpness of Karl's new pallasz beyond doubt.

Dismounted, Uldin's warband took part in most of the foot assaults against Wolfenburg's admirably solid walls. These usually happened at dusk or dawn. Covered by the hissing sheets of arrows sent up by the archers from behind the wooden screens, the Kurgan warriors charged the walls, hefting scaling ladders between them. Teams of straining warriors rolled up the massive timber ram under its protective portico of stretched animal hides.

The foot assaults were costly. Even if the ram reached the gates without being set ablaze, it failed to make a dent in the colossal doors. The scaling parties were decimated by the rains of arrows, rocks and pitch, or died from broken limbs and backs when their ladders were pushed away from the walls. Karl was grazed across the left shoulder by a crossbow bolt and his left hand was blistered with boiling oil. His wounds were typical of those received by the other men in the warband. Diormac lost an ear. Lyr was pinned through the leg by an Imperial arrow. Utz had his lower jaw smashed by a rock. He lived for two days, wailing and screaming, until Uldin could bear it no longer and cut his throat. Uldin was clearly upset about this, and openly blamed the High Zar for making one of his riders die ignominiously, out of the saddle. Surtha Lenk, opinion went, was not doing enough to finish this siege. There was dissent amongst the horde.

Karl filled his time between the brief periods of action helping Berlas and the other archers in the band to compose bows. It was a complex business, as the bows were fashioned from three parts. A central stave of maple or mulberry, woods which took glue well, was laminated with animal sinew on the back and horn on the front, in order to withstand the tension and compression. For special bows, Berlas used human sinew and bone. This stave, the grip, was fixed to the two arms of the bow, along which bone from longhorn cattle had been glued. Bone tips were attached, and the bows tied up tight against the shape they would be drawn to. Then the bow was left to dry, for weeks, or, if time permitted, months.

After that, more tendon sinew, beaten with a hammer into fibres, was applied in layers to the bow arms, and the bow was back-strung tightly again for more drying.

Dried, they were carefully warmed and then strung up the way they would be shot, ready for the tillering. This was a process of gentle filing and adjustment that ensured that the arms bent evenly at full draw for maximum accuracy.

Karl was not at all good at any of these stages, but Berlas was happy to have him handle each piece during the stages of construction, as if Karl's touch somehow conveyed a blessing on the weapons. They were valuable pieces, because of the effort of manufacture, and Berlas told him that, unlike swords, armour and horses, bows were never buried with the dead unless they were broken. It was too great a waste.

Once word spread that Karl was blessing bows, other men, some from rival warbands, came to him to have him touch bow components, arrowheads or even whetstones. He deeply resented the attention and what it implied, but he did not refuse any man.

Karl learned to shoot a bow. He had grasped basic archery skill using 'self' bows as a youth, but the recurve bow was a revelation. Each one imparted a draw equal to the body weight of a good-sized man with a simple, smooth pull, and suffered no stacking of power-weight at the release, as was the case with bows of a single piece of wood. He quickly found he was more accurate with the alien weapon than he had ever been with a longbow as a boy.

Berlas finessed his bow skill. He told Karl to forget the southern manner of drawing a bow with three fingers. Instead, the Kurgan drew with the thumb, and with the first three fingers locked over it. The thumb was guarded by a ring of bone or brass. Because of this, a Kurgan loosed his arrow from the right side of his bow, rather than the left as was the practice in the Empire. A recurve bow could send an arrow over three hundred spans, but was only considered accurate over forty-five bow lengths. Any target further than that was, in Berlas's expert opinion, a waste of arrows. However, an archer could shoot 'in arcade', which was to draw and loose upwards so that the dart came down on the target from an almost vertical angle. Unlike the Imperial toxophilists, who were infantry-based and could manage a long 'self' bow, the Kurgan needed a weapon they could fire easily from the saddle. Only the smooth-pulling recurve bows were effective in this respect.

Karl was practising arcade shots from the saddle in a tract of woodland away from the main force, when the riders came looking for him. It was the fourth month of the siege, and word had spread that the High Zar, aggrieved by the dissent showing in the horde, was intending to call up the powers of the Dark Gods and end the siege.

There were twenty riders, all from Surtha Lenk's bodyguard. One of the big men with bull horns sprouting obscenely out of his skull led them. He approached Karl and handed him a human skull that had been polished to a pearlescent finish. Karl took hold of it and then the horned man took it back. The gang of riders sped away after him.

Karl laughed. Now even the High Zar was looking to him to bless his instruments of war.

VI

THAT NIGHT, THE phosphorescent flickers of the Northland Lights danced above Wolfenburg. Then a winter storm came in, barging through the summer night. The tempest was ferocious. Thick frost covered the landscape and ice weighed down the thrashing trees. Lightning struck like repeated hammer blows against the city walls. It was so savage and unrelenting that the gatehouse collapsed.

Jeering and yelling, the Kurgan entered Wolfenburg, broke it open, and put everyone inside it to the sword.

VII

AT DAWN, AS the city burned, Uldin raised his skull-stack. His warband had done well, and the favour of the High Zar was upon them. Once Uldin had anointed the skull-pile with captive blood, he called for the mark to be made. Chegrume approached with the flint knife, but Uldin sent him back and called for Karl-Azytzeen.

Karl came forward and, under Chegrume's instruction, made the fifth victory mark on Uldin's cheek. At the last moment, he tossed the flint knife away and used Drogo Hance's true killer to slash the ritual mark on Uldin's face.

VIII

'WE'RE GOING NORTH,' Uldin told them. The truth was more complex than that. Autumn was upon them, and the leaves were just turning. Outriders reported a sizeable mass of enemy soldiers developing in the north, in the skirts of the Kislev oblast. Archaon wanted them denied, and Surtha Lenk's horde was the nearest.

Surtha Lenk summoned Uldin and made him a Hetzar, placing him in command of six warbands – his own, Zar Blayda's, Zar Herfil's, Zar Kreyya's, Zar Skolt's and Zar Tzagz's. As Hetzar, Uldin was to ride north and wipe out the harassing enemy. It was a great honour, though it was clear Uldin's warband had only been chosen because of Karl-Azytzeen. Blayda and Herfil were particularly enraged and resentful.

For the second time that year, Karl found himself advancing northwards into the fringes of the Kislevite oblast as part of a horse troop. The soft, decaying touch of autumn showed in the scenery, and the villages they passed through were either ruined by war or abandoned.

The air was turning colder, and it bore the smoky odour of leaf-fall. Dawns brought the first early frosts, and wet gales beat down for many of the days. For over two weeks, they didn't see another living soul in the woods, the fields, the pastures or the open grasses.

On the afternoon of the day they crossed the Lynsk, fording it where it was wide and shallow, they sighted riders on a stretch of open plain below forested uplands. They had left the broadleaf forests of the south behind them, and these woods were still green, despite the time of year. Fir trees, oblast pine and other evergreens formed a dark backdrop to the string of horsemen in the distance.

At first, they believed they had found the first traces of the rumoured Kislevite army they had been sent to quash. The warbands urgently readied themselves for battle.

But the riders were not Kislevites. They were kyazak horse bandits, probably Kul or Tahmak from the look of them. Efgul sneered to Karl. In his opinion, kyazak – Kul especially – were vermin and cowards. 'We have the numbers, Karl-Azytzeen,' he said. 'Mark my word, they will run before us.'

But in this, the hairy Northerner was wrong on two counts. The kyazak did not run at the sight of the Kurgan war company. And they had the numbers.

'They have put the lie to you, Efgul seh,' said Hzaer, riding on Karl's other side. The horse bandits were turning and riding down the plain towards Uldin's troop with mounting speed. Uldin had six warbands – almost four hundred horsemen – at his disposal, but the kyazak, who at first seemed to be just forty strong, quickly became a hundred, two hundred, five hundred. They came pouring out of the forest, joining the men already in the open.

Uldin roared a command, and Hzaer and the other carnyx-blowers blared out battle notes. The six standard bearers raised their banners, Yuskel hefting the largest of all. Uldin's standard of the gilded skulls and the one-eyed wolf face had been supplemented by huge elk antlers strung with bead-cords of human teeth to denote his status as Hetzar. The massed warriors immediately kicked forward into a hard gallop, drawing their weapons and shouting for blood.

Their warhorses at full stretch, the two cavalry hosts met and ran in amongst each other. The collective concussion was huge, as if the rival armies were like mountain rams slamming together and locking their horns. As the charge lines came together and overlapped, Karl was surrounded by a dizzying sequence of cracks, impacts and blows. The whole world shook and thrashed violently. Spear shafts snapped, shields shattered, bones broke. Horses went over and brought down the riders racing behind them. Men were smashed out of their seats. Karl's sword-arm already ached from the six or seven jarring blows he had landed.

All around them was a constant patter of wood splinters, metal shards, flecks of mud, beads of sweat and spats of blood. Their momentum robbed by the collision, the horse armies were now at a virtual standstill. Every man fought like a demented daemon in the saddle with those enemies within reach. Karl knew his pallasz had claimed the lives of at least four kyazak, but the combat was such a blur of overloaded sensations, he ultimately lost count.

Both forces sustained their battle-fury for over a quarter of an hour, but then the kyazak, who had taken the worst of it, lost spirit. Within minutes those that were still able to quit the plain had fled into the trees. The warbands of Zar Blayda and Zar Herfil broke away and chased the fleeing enemy, mercilessly hunting them into the depths of the forest. The remainder of Uldin's force rallied and pulled up, panting and shaken. The sheer effort of the brief but explosive battle had left many exhausted.

And many dead. Uldin's war-force had lost forty riders, with another dozen badly hurt. The kyazak had paid for defeat with above three hundred lives.

The Kurgan were shouting and singing their victory chants. Karl rode back into the line. Efgul, bleeding from a deep scratch across his chest, hooted and shook his fists in the air. Hzaer blew loud, discordant flourishes of triumph, even though a kyazak sword had taken the little finger of his right hand entirely away, and he was spattering blood with every movement he made. Apart from the gore of other men, Karl-Azytzeen was entirely unmarked.

After about two hours, Blayda and Herfil brought their hunting parties back and joined the victory. They had scalps and weapons for trophy rings, and news besides. They took the news to Uldin with not a little smug satisfaction.

They had encountered other riders in the forest, the advance parties of another Kurgan host. These men, who pledged allegiance to High Zar Okkodai Tarsus, said that north of the forests their High Zar had quelled the land with his mighty horde, and was now drawing south to swell the great army of Archaon. They had been driving the kyazak army before them, which explained why the horse bandits had attacked so desperately. Engaging four hundred Kurgan horse had seemed infinitely preferable to annihilation at the hands of a High Zar's ten thousand men.

There was more yet. Okkodai Tarsus had already beaten off the Kislevite army Uldin had been sent to find. This battle had taken place a week earlier, on the salt marshes of the Tobol, high in the north, and though inconclusive, it had ended the Kislevite threat. The army of the Gospodarinyi had scattered into the oblast, put into flight by the size of Okkodai Tarsus's great horde.

His glory denied him, Uldin flew into a dark rage. He had little stomach for the idea of returning to Surtha Lenk's side with no victory to show. To the dismay of Blayda and the other zars, he insisted they remain in the north, and push on to confirm the stories told by Okkodai Tarsus's men.

Besides, the oblast autumn could suddenly plunge into winter, almost overnight. Already there was the smell of snow in the air, and the cold Norscya winds were rising. Even if they turned back now, they were not likely to reach Ostland and the rest of the host before winter overtook them.

They rode north for another week and confirmed as best they could that no Kislevite army was lurking in the north country. Neither did they see a trace of Okkodai Tarsus's horde, which had swept away south and east in the direction of the Kislev capital.

As the first light snows of winter began to fall, Uldin led them west into the wild hill country north and east of Erengrad. They would go to Chamon Dharek, and spend winter there.

IX

CHAMON DHAREK WAS a remote place sacred to the Kurgan. It lay high up in the inhospitable hill country, a place of pilgrimage where the sons of the north might go to have their souls anointed by the gods, or where a warband might gather to shelter for the winter and make tribute to the great Shadow of the North. As was the case with many old and sacred places, the barriers between the mortal realm and the otherworld were thin at Chamon Dharek. The name meant the place of gold and darkness.

Chegrume the shaman was especially excited at the prospect. He had been to many shrines, but not this great and secret place in the west. 'A site of wonders and secrets!' he proclaimed, hungry with anticipation.

It took three weeks to reach it, the last stages spent trudging through drifting snow into the teeth of the blizzards that had conquered the ragged hills.

On the day they came to Chamon Dharek, the blizzards suspended their force and a red winter sun rose above the white blanket covering the hills. Chamon Dharek lay in a hidden valley, cut off from the world by a narrow pass. As they came out through the gates of the pass, many men stopped to gaze in wonder at the sacred place.

Karl-Azytzeen was one of them.

It was the largest kurgan grave mound Karl had yet seen: a towering rampart of earth now coated in fresh snow. At its base was a great hall of stone and timber, two granaries, and heavy-beamed barns for horses and chariots. Smaller shapes, perhaps standing stones, stood in a ring around the base of the mound, but they were so covered in snow it was impossible to say what they were.

At the crown of the ancient kurgan mound, a great bonfire blazed, despite the snow and the cold wind. Its flames leapt up beyond the height of many men, and licked up into the sky. The flames were white and blue, like burning ice.

In the sky above, the crackling, shimmering wonders of the Northland aurora made patterns and colours across the heavens.

X

THEY WERE NOT the first to arrive. Two other warbands, smaller than Hetzar Uldin's, had come to the place to spend the ice months feasting and worshipping. One was a band of Aeslings from the Norselands in the west – exceptionally tall men with cross-gaitered leggings, checkered surcoats and long, hooked axes. The other was a war party of Dolgans, nomad warriors from the Eastern Steppes. The Dolgans were kin to the Kurgan – indeed in the eyes of the south, the Dolgans were Kurgan. But there were differences that Karl could easily spot. Their style of armour and harness was lighter and favoured polished bronze and gold where the Kurgan used pitch-coated brass and iron. Their dialect was different too, not incomprehensible but, like the Aesling Norse, heavily accented.

Uldin's men put up their horses in the long stable barns, and went to the great hall. In that vast place, beneath the high, beamed ceiling, all the people who came to Chamon Dharek would live communally for the winter. Even with the addition of Uldin's three and a half hundred or so, there was more than enough space. The warm air was thick with fire smoke, and the smell of bodies and straw and wine. Lean hunting hounds trotted between the benches and across the unrolled rugs of the resting places.

Chamon Dharek had permanent residents of its own: a sect of priests who maintained the shrine all year round on behalf of the tribes of the north, and provided for any visitors. These priest-warriors defended the shrine from attack, maintained its stores, granaries and larders, and officiated at all the rites and ceremonies of the place. In return for their hospitality, any visiting warband was expected to leave a tribute of their war booty.

The sect were strange folk. The priest-warriors were heavily-built men, but the rest were women and young girls. All wore long robes as white as Skarkeetah's, and their heads were covered in pointed gold helms from the brims of which hung aventails of fine gold that entirely hid their faces. From the shape of their helms, Karl was sure they – like the massive brute Hinn – had skulls elongated by binding.

Uldin and his zars made representation to the priesthood, and paid their tribute of Kurgan gold and kyazak loot. Then Uldin met with the leaders of the Aeslings and the Dolgans, and partook of the ritual drink to pledge peace between their companies for the duration of the winter.

From the moment he entered the hall, Karl felt a tingling that warned him the air in this place was crawling with magical force. And from the moment he entered, he was the focus of great and apprehensive interest. The Aeslings, who wore heavy, studded collars to show their association with the death god, Kjorn, treated him with wary caution. The Dolgans however, who seemed to know much of the lore of Tchar, regarded him with awe.

Even the shrine-priests, who simply served and said little, seemed struck by him.

On the first night, they feasted all together, filling the hall to the rafters with a great din of singing and boasting and laughter. Only Chegrume was missing. He had hastened eagerly to the sacred shrine itself the moment they had arrived, and hadn't been seen since. Uldin, and others of the men, had already paid respectful visits to the shrine too, and most would visit every few days for the duration of their stay.

But the idea had not appealed to Karl. He was steeped in outland magic already, and had no wish to learn more about the tradition he had been made part of. Besides, the biting winter cold hurt the damaged part of his skull, and he preferred to stay in the heat of the hall.

The feast was generous and rich. Samogon and wine sweetened with honey was served in cups made out of hollowed, upturned human skulls. The insides of the head bowls were layered with gold.

'From the great mound,' Berlas said, seeing Karl was studying his cup. 'Drinking vessels made by the Scythians and hidden away under the earth in that mound.'

Karl raised his cup. Here was a skull whose owner had been dead twice as long as the Sigmarite Empire had existed.

At one of the feasting tables not so far away across the busy hall, Karl saw Zar Blayda in his scribed black wargear, drinking and laughing with the leader of the Aeslings. Where Uldin's warband followed Tchar, Blayda and his men favoured the bloody-handed god, Khar. The Aeslings' Kjorn was a different aspect of the same daemon-deity. The two warbands had much in common. Ons Olker, Blayda's tri-horned shaman, sat near to his zar. It was the first time Karl had seen him properly since becoming part of Uldin's warband. Where before Ons Olker had taken every opportunity to gaze malevolently at Karl, now he pointedly looked away. Like all the others, he was afraid of Karl's aspect, and dared not to look on it. Karl was quite sure he longed to.

'There is one to watch with a hand on your hilt,' Efgul muttered, chewing the meat of a mutton stick.

'The shaman?' Karl asked.

Efgul belched and wiped his hand across his mouth, distributing grease through his thick facial hair. 'Yes, him, Karl-Azytzeen. But more, his damned master.'

'Blayda.'

'Blayda, that's right, Karl seh. Blayda.' Efgul took a swig of samogon, and held the empty gilt skull out until it was refilled by one of the gold-masked priest-women.

'Blayda has ambition,' Hzaer said.

'Who doesn't?' laughed Berlas.

'Ambition to be High Zar one day,' Fegul One-Hand growled. 'Efgul seh is right. Blayda despises our lord for becoming Hetzar. Uldin seh is now an obstacle in his rising path.'

'He's nothing,' Yuskel the standard bearer declared. 'Uldin would take him to his grave, and he would never be warrior enough to challenge our High Zar.'

'Uldin would take him to his grave in a straight fight,' Karl said quietly. 'But Blayda seh will fight any way he can.'

The men around him fell silent and looked at Karl, until all of them realised they should not and hurriedly turned back to the food.

'You speak like you know him better than us, Karl seh,' Yuskel said.

'I do, in a way. Our zar... Hetzar now... is a fine man. A great warrior.'

They all gave a hearty cry and thumped their fists repeatedly on the feasting table.

'And a fair man,' Karl continued as the noise died down. 'Blayda is a... he is underhand. And the shaman. He has blood-tied me, for I did him offence.'

'What offence?' Diomac asked through a full mouth.

'I knocked in his head and put him on his arse,' said Karl.

The men laughed.

'He will not touch you now, Karl-Azytzeen,' said Yuskel firmly. 'Not now that...'

'Yuskel seh means,' said Efgul, 'that Ons Olker would have to look on you to strike you, and no bastard dares do that.'

The men laughed again, and thumped the table.

'Ons Olker might,' Karl said. 'He has a lot to be gained. Which of you doubt that our fine zar rose to favour because his warband contained a man touched by Tchar this way?' He put his hand up to his one good eye, and ran his fingertips along the powder-burn snakes. Not a man risked looking.

'And what might our fine zar become with Azytzeen at his right hand? I am the real threat to Blayda. Without me, Uldin might easily be overtaken as the High Zar's favourite. But with me alive and loyal to Uldin seh...'

Karl raised his skull cup and took a pledging drink. 'Which I am, let every man here know. With me alive, Blayda will never get a chance to rise in power and influence.'

The men nodded. None saw reason to deny the clear truth of Karl's remarks.

'So, though it might cost him his soul, Ons Olker will try. Before the winter is out. He will try, because he believes it is worth it to his zar. And he can always blame my death on the blood-tie I owe.'

'We will watch you, Karl-Azytzeen,' said Efgul suddenly, putting his hand over his heart.

'We will,' agreed Berlas and Fegul One-Hand nodded, doing the same.

'Ons Olker shaman will not get close to you while we are round you in the warband,' Yuskel declared, and the men raised their cups and drank a pledge, their hands making it heart-truth.

XI

LATER IN THE feast, as the merriment slowed with drunken torpor, Lyr and Sakondor brought a Dolgan over to Karl.

'His name is Broka,' Lyr said. 'He wishes very much to find the favour of Tchar, for his fortune has not been well. He seeks that favour from Karl-Azytzeen.'

The Dolgan, a powerful man in the gold and bronze wargear of a prominent warrior, got on his knees before Karl. He was very drunk, but there was a frightening earnestness in his tone.

'Give me the favour of fortune, Karl-Azytzeen. I beg of you,' he said in his thick, eastern accent. 'Give me the blessing of Tzeentch.'

'Who?' Karl said.

'It is the name they have for Tchar, Karl seh,' Sakondor whispered.

It was all too peculiar, and Karl felt uncomfortable being the centre of attention. He was about to deny the man and send him away, when the man changed Karl's mind by doing the one thing no one had done since Aachden.

He looked Karl directly in the face.

Karl stared at him, and then said, 'I think Tzeentch will favour you now.'

Tears welled in Broka's brown eyes, and he bent to kiss Karl's heavy boots before hurrying away.

The shrine-priests continued to serve wine and distribute food to those who still required it. Most of the warrior-priests had disappeared, and only the womenfolk remained... the youngest and most comely of them at that.

'Are they trying to tempt us?' Karl said.

'Of course,' Efgul slurred. 'They do not breed with their own kind here. It's a sacred thing. They keep their population alive by breeding with the best of the warriors who come to Chamon Dharek.'

'Indeed.'

'Just another pleasure and blessing of this holy place,' Berlas sniggered.

'I have a mind to sire me a splendid warrior-priest!' Efgul announced. 'What say you all?'

'I say,' announced Diormac, 'that you will whelp the hairiest warrior-priest of all time, Efgul seh.'

The men howled.

'And a fine thing that would be,' Efgul decided, taking a drink.

'You'd need to get the chance first, Efgul seh,' remarked Yuskel slyly. 'They only choose the best and the most propitious. I'd judge their interest is in one of us in particular.'

Karl realised Yuskel undoubtedly meant him.

He excused himself from the table, not because the idea didn't appeal to him but rather, in his drunken state, it did all too plainly. He walked around the hall, through the smoke, stepping over the bodies of some who had passed out, intending to go outside and clear his head. Music was playing, and some of the warriors were dancing with the women while their brethren clapped and chanted.

Moving through the crowded hall, he caught sight of a Kurgan warrior, one of Blayda's men, sitting alone with his back to a roof-post. The man's wargear was blackened with pitch and inscribed with gouged scrolls and spirals like a zar's, but Karl suddenly realised he knew him.

'Sir? Sir? It's me!'

'I know it is, Karl Reiner Vollen,' said von Margur. 'I've been watching you.'

Karl sat down beside the knight. Von Margur looked much more healthy and fit than he had the last time Karl had seen him. He was still quite blind apparently, his deadened eyes gazing into space. Von Margur smiled.

'It seems we have both changed our fortunes and remade ourselves.'

'You ride with Zar Blayda's company now, von Margur seh?' Karl asked.

'He saw favour in me, as Uldin did in you. Offered me the chance to renew my acquaintance with loyalty and courage. It was that or death. I find Tchar makes some choices infinitely simple.'

'I am pleased to see you, von Margur seh,' Karl said.

'Indeed so. Karl, please don't use that dog-speak "seh" thing. Around me. We are men of the Reik, and we should talk like men of the Reik.'

'I'm sorry–'

'Ha ha,' von Margur chuckled. 'You should hear your voice, Karl. So thick with the round vowels and hard gutturals of the Kurgan tongue. You speak their language like a native now.'

Karl halted. 'I am speaking the language of the beloved Reik, sir–' he began.

Von Margur shook his head and laughed. His broken eyes rolled in their sockets. 'No, Karl. I am speaking Reikspiel. You, I'm afraid, are speaking perfectly in the dialect of the Kurgan.'

Karl sat back beside the knight, stunned.

'Have you thought of escape?' von Margur said.

'I–' Karl bolted forward, afraid that someone might overhear.

'Of course not. It was foolish of me to suggest it,' von Margur said. 'Tchar has made too deep a mark on you. That eye. It's really something.'

'How c–' Karl began. 'Tchar has changed you too, I think, sir,' he ended up saying.

'Oh, he has, Karl,' sighed the blind knight. 'Oh, he most certainly has.'

Karl got up and excused himself. He needed to get outside into the cool air.

'It's good to see you, Karl,' said von Margur.

* * *

XII

THE WINTER PASSED by slowly. The warriors whiled away the short dark days with sleep, contests of strength and visits to the shrine. The nights were spent feasting and raising hell.

Chegrume was almost never seen. It seemed the young shaman had taken to living inside the shrine.

Karl passed his time talking with the men and practising his bowskill out in the snow on clear days. Berlas had given him a fine bow, one of the ones they had fashioned at Wolfenburg, now finished and strung. At nightfall, he joined the warband to feast and listen to their stories. On one occasion, Uldin held the whole hall rapt with a powerful account of an old Kurgan battle, the conclusion of which brought thunderous applause and a thumping of tables. The Aeslings sang their sad, keening sagas. The Dolgans danced their potentially lethal dance of swords.

From time to time, often when the samogon had the better of him, Karl gave in to the wordless advances of the silent priest-women. He never saw their faces or knew their names, for the chambers they led him to were always dark and thick with the same intoxicating smoke of burning seed-cases that Hinn had used back in the murdered Kislevite town whose name Karl had never learned. Karl would wake alone, in the cool, musky air of morning with his head full of half-remembered passions.

Some nights, he would feast with the Dolgans at their tables. They welcomed him as a brother... more than a brother, for they treated him with reverential respect. They told him of their god, Tzeentch, and how he ruled through change. Karl tried to explain that he found the ways strange and unsettling because of the world that he had come from. None of them seemed dismayed to discover he had been born a son of the enemy.

'All things change,' Broka told him. 'All things change, Karl-Azytzeen. The way we perceive the truth is dependent on context. We should never hold fast to a truth or a value because it might obscure our view of the truth of Tzeentch. That which changes grows ever stronger in the world. That which remains fixed is wasted away or broken down, for it cannot survive forever.'

It seemed an understandable philosophy for a nomadic tribe that was constantly moving and never established anything permanent. Karl liked Broka and the company of the Dolgans for their generosity and their freedom of expression. He was, however, alarmed to see that by this time – it was lately past midwinter – Broka's eyes had turned blue.

When he went out to practise drawing the bow, at least one of the warband went with him. It was usually Efgul, who always brought a flask of samogon, or Berlas or Hzaer. It seemed they were taking their pledge to guard him seriously.

There had been no sign of threat from Ons Olker, but then Uldin's band had purposefully had little to do with Blayda's company. Since the first night, Karl had not even spoken to von Margur. On the few occasions he had spied him, the knight had been aloof and remote.

Uldin chastised Karl for not visiting the shrine. The Hetzar seemed quite adamant about it, as if Karl's refusal augured badly for his band. Karl promised he would go to the shrine before the first thaw came and made it time to depart.

The year end was turning. As the long nights and quick days passed, the rainbow blooms of the aurora crackled through the sky above the eternal blue flame on the grave mound. Wolves howled in the snowbound forests surrounding Chamon Dharek.

Karl knew he would have to go to the shrine before he left this sacred place. The women had whispered it into his sleeping ear.

XIII

They had been feasting, yet again. The pleasures of unstinting food and drink were beginning to pall, and Karl had started to yearn for the clean, hard life in the saddle. At the feasting table, Lyr and Hzaer were speculating how long it would be before they departed from Chamon Dharek. A week, Lyr reckoned. Two, Hzaer insisted. Yuskel and Efgul announced between them that at least another moon would swell and slim before the snows thawed enough for decent riding.

'Karl-Azytzeen!' a voice hissed from behind them. It was Chegrume. The shaman was thin and sickly pale, and he was carefully averting his eyes from Karl's face.

'What?'

'It would be for the best if you came with me,' said Chegrume.

'I'm eating, witch-priest. Can't it wait?'

Chegrume shook his head. 'You must come now. Tchar wills it.'

'You had better do as he says, Karl seh,' Uldin growled from his seat down the table. 'I have learned to trust my shaman's instincts.'

Karl got up.

'Should I come with you, Karl seh?' asked Efgul.

Karl shook his head. He buckled his pallasz around his waist. 'I will be fine, Efgul seh. Eat well.'

'And take advantage of his absence to tup one of the women at last!' Fegul roared. 'He's had them to himself all winter!'

To the sound of their laughter, Karl followed the shaman out into the cold night outside the hall. He drew his bearskin around his shoulders and fastened the gold horse brooch firmly.

It had recently stopped snowing, and the air was clear. Stars, and the wavering, fuzzy light of the aurora, burned in the blackness above them.

'Where are we going?' Karl asked, his breath fuming the freezing air.

'The shrine,' Chegrume replied, beckoning him.

'No,' said Karl simply, turning back.

'You must! You must now! Tchar is close, oh, so close, and he has told me he is coming to bless you.'

'Tchar be damned! I don't want to.'

'He will make you whole again, Karl Reiner Vollen,' Chegrume said.

Karl took a flaming brand from a becket on the doorpost and followed the shaman around the vast hall towards the dark mass of the kurgan mound. Chegrume was shivering and hunched, his animal skins pulled tight around his thin shoulders, his bare feet sinking into the deep snow.

They trudged through the darkness. Karl had presumed they would climb up the hill to the flickering bale fire that lit the night, but instead Chegrume led him to an avenue of snow-covered shapes that led towards the base of the mound.

These were the same sort of shapes that stood in the ring around the man-made hill. As they passed between them, Karl raised his guttering torch, and saw that they were horses. Dead horses, waxed and mummified, mounted on heavy stakes to guard the tomb for the rest of time. The snow hung in heavy folds about their wizened carcasses, and hoar frost clung like glass to their drawn, snarling teeth.

Uldin had raised dead horses this way around Subotai's grave.

At the end of the icy colonnade of frozen horse-mummies, they came to a broad doorway in the base of the mound, an entrance propped open with a stone lintel. Torchlight crackled inside.

'What have you been doing in here?' Karl asked, his lips numb from the winter night's cold and tears freezing on to the tip of his nose.

'Learning, wondering, dreaming,' Chegrume said. He bowed his antlered head down under the lintel and went in. 'I came to the shrine of Chamon Dharek to learn and extend my power. The voices of the otherworld have been kind, and have blessed me in many ways. I have accepted power, Karl-Azytzeen. My efforts and ordeals in the cold have been rewarded. I have become one favoured by Tchar.'

Karl walked into the entrance tunnel behind the shaman. It was several measures warmer inside, out of the frost-wind, and the floor and walls were dry earth, lit by flaming, fluttering torches. The tunnel extended into the mound.

'I'm happy for you that you've found what you were looking for,' Karl called after Chegrume, who was hurrying ahead down the dry passage, his feet pattering on the floor. 'But why me?'

Chegrume turned back and beckoned Karl. 'Because Tchar wants you. He has set this time aside to meet with you.'

'I'm not sure I want to meet him at all,' Karl said.

'Don't!' said Chegrume, with a passion that startled Karl. 'Don't make him change his mind.'

Karl followed the lanky, antlered figure down the long tunnel into the belly of the kurgan. The air was hot and close, and stifled him with the heat of the torches. Forty-five bow-lengths in, at the extent of an accurate shot, the tunnel ended and gave out into a vast buried chamber. Its sides and floor were packed earth, and the walls curved over to form a domed ceiling.

Karl had never seen so much gold. Scythian gold, white and bright, in great profusion, spread about the place. Caskets, coffers, thrones, gorytos bow cases, helms, bridles, body armour for men and for horses. All of it was worked and decorated to the finest degree with Scythian emblems, and with intricate depictions of warriors in the saddle, chargers rising to lance, ibex and goat, ravens and eagles, swords and bows, and everywhere, everywhere, horses. The treasure of the ancient barrow glowed and twinkled in the torchlight. There was the wealth of nations in this one mound, and Karl was most amazed of all by the idea that it had never been plundered by the avaricious Kurgan and Norse who came to worship at the shrine.

They had seen it, been amongst it, but they had left it untouched. That told him of the reverence – and perhaps the terror – with which they regarded this place.

It had its guards. Warriors and servants sat or sprawled, or stood supported by stakes, all around the chamber. They had each been strangled and then mummified like the horses without. Husk-dry warriors sat on golden saddles, wearing golden armour. One, whose dead fist was raised on a stake, supported a mummified hawk with a golden hood over its desiccated eyes. Withered servants had been nailed and propped into kneeling poses of submission, their staked-up hands supporting golden platters on which the offerings had long since mouldered to dust, and gilded skull cups whose contents had evaporated before the coming of Sigmar. Emaciated concubines lay ready and eternally willing on golden bed frames, clad in dusty, rotting swathes of gold-shot silk. A wilting mummy clutched a golden carnyx, ready to blow it with his grinning, lipless mouth. Shrivelled warriors brandished swords and round shields with musty horse-tail decorations at their bosses. The warriors glared sightlessly into the gloom, sentries at the gates of the otherworld.

Karl walked forward slowly, gazing around at the extraordinary sight. He held his torch high above his head.

Chegrume had hurried to the centre of the chamber, where a great gilt altar was set on a heap of earth. Some kind of lustrous fire blazed within the golden altar, and the blue, green and white flames licked up out of it and raged up through a hole in the centre of the roof. The eternal fire on the mound top, Karl realised, came from within.

'Hurry! Hurry, Karl-Azytzeen!' Chegrume called. 'Tchar is close and he wishes to find you here.'

Karl joined the shaman at the foot of the altar. The flames had no heat to speak of. He felt greater warmth from the brand in his fist.

'Look into the flames,' Chegrume said. 'Look, and you will see.'

'See what?'

'You will see!' Chegrume insisted. He gestured to the blazing flames inside the gold coffer of the altar.

For the first time, Karl noticed the shaman's hands. Chegrume had suffered the loss of his middle fingers early in his life, and his hands had been like claws as a consequence.

Now, they were truly claws. The claws of a great bird. The outside fingers remaining on either hand had fused and become a lean, mobile claw, as had the index fingers and thumbs. The flesh had taken on the crumpled, scaly quality of a hawk's skin, and the nails had been replaced by dark, hooked talons. One of Chegrume's rewards had been to have his hands transformed into the feet of a bird of prey. Sallow brown feathers were growing in a fuzz out of his wrists and forearms.

Karl looked into the flames. He had no idea what to expect, so he was not disappointed. No great visitation came to him, no rush of otherworldy power, chorused by the clacking of immense avian beaks and the flapping of giant wings; no single, gazing eye.

No hissing voice of Tchar.

He pulled back and looked at the waiting shaman. The shaman grinned with joy.

'What was I supposed to see–' he began. And stopped. He could see. He could see out of both of his eyes.

Karl reached a hand up to his face and groped for the rough scar-tissue around his ruined eye socket. The rough knots of flesh were still there, but he could see, even when he closed his good eye.

Even when he put his palm over his lost eye.

He could see without eyes.

'Your glass!' he snapped, frightened. 'Give me your seeing glass.'

Chegrume reached his clumsy bird-hands into the spirit bag and brought out his seeing glass. Karl could not bear to touch the hooked talons as he took the object.

He gazed into the glass.

His face was as broken as he remembered it. Dark twists and folds of healed tissue surrounded and covered his left eye socket. But behind the thin coating of healed-over flesh, a hard blue light glowed and pulsed in his dead socket. It backlit the drawn skin so fiercely he could see traces of thin blood vessels in it, as a man sees against his eyelids when he turns his face to the sun, eyes closed.

'What have you done to me?' he said, stepping back off the altar mound and dropping the seeing glass.

'Nothing. I have done nothing–'

'What has Tchar done to me?' Karl hissed.

'Given you sight again,' Chegrume said.

Karl was about to reply when he froze and looked suddenly at the mouth of the chamber.

The flames flurried and blazed.

'What?' asked the shaman. 'What did you see?'

'You simple fool!' Karl spat, drawing his pallasz. 'You've played into their hands.'

'What? What do you mean, Karl-Azytzeen?'
'You've got me alone out here, shaman. It's what they've been waiting for.'
'Who?' Chegrume implored.
'Blayda and his shaman.'
'But... but they dare not even look on you, Karl-Azytzeen, chosen of Tchar! How could they hope to–'
A figure walked into the chamber, dressed in scribed-pitch wargear. His sword was drawn.
It was von Margur.
'Only those who cannot see would dare to strike at me,' Karl said to the shaman. 'It doesn't take the enlightenment of Tchar to work that out.'

XIV

'We don't have to do this, sir,' Karl said as he walked from the altar towards the knight, his pallasz raised.
'We do, Karl, I'm afraid,' said von Margur.
'Why?'
'Because you are much too dangerous to live. An abomination.'
'I see. In the slave-cages outside Zhedevka, you told me I would kill you. Doesn't that decide this fight before it starts?'
'I said you would make Uldin's fifth mark too,' von Margur said.
'I have done so.'
'And kill him.'
'He lives.'
'So what the sight shows us can be changed. Some things remain true and some things alter, thanks to the ebb and flow of Tchar's will. I will best you now and take your life.'
'Why, sir?'
'Because I am a spurred knight from a holy order, masterfully trained in swordsmanship, and you are nothing but a demilancer.'
'That's not what I meant.'
'Because you are an abhorrence to the world and I must be true to my oath as a knight of the Empire and rid mankind of you. You are an unwitting pawn of Khaos.'
'We are both pawns of Khaos,' Karl said. 'I just know it better than you. Do not force me to make true your prophecy. Back away, so we will not fight.'
Von Margur lifted his sword in both hands. His eyes rolled back into his skull as he swept his head around. He stroked his heavy sword about himself in a rushing figure of eight, expertly.
'Karl, you're wasting time,' he said. 'I know a Khaos bastard when I see one.'
'So do I,' said Karl-Azytzeen, closing his good eye.
Von Margur ran at him then, his sword whirring round. They met, and

their blades chimed together. Both men probed with blind vision to find a gap in each other's defence. Von Margur drove Karl backwards, then came down with a hammer blow that would have slit Karl from his pauldron to his hip. But Karl saw it was coming, and blocked, causing a shower of sparks. He lunged his heavy broadsword sidelong at von Margur's head.

The knight ducked away and circled, bringing his sword upright to defend against Karl's next crosswise stroke.

Parrying, von Margur danced back lightly, and swept his steel around to cut out Karl's belly. Karl deflected low, and shoved von Margur's sword back at him, following up with another strike towards the knight's head.

Von Margur saw that stroke's intent before it began, and landed a counter thrust that was bashed aside by the trophy rings on Karl's right forearm. It was then Karl noticed that both of von Margur's arms were solid with trophy rings from wrist to bicep.

Karl rounded and dug at von Margur with his blade tip. The knight denied this with a sure-handed parry, and then flew at Karl, his broadsword carving down at Karl's skull.

Karl stopped it dead, with another clink of sparks, then blocked and blocked again as von Margur hammered blow after vicious blow at him.

Backing up to give himself space, Karl then rejoined, his heavy, double-edged blade overlapping understrokes and overstrokes.

Von Margur stopped them all. He was more gifted than any sighted master of the heavy sword. This duel would be decided by the whim of Tchar alone, Karl knew. Which of his instruments did Tchar favour the most?

Von Margur cut at him, a slicing blow delivered to split Karl's head in two. But Karl had backed out of the lock, and threw his blade's tip up in a brutal slash.

The pallasz cut through von Margur's armpit and out of the opposite shoulder. It did this with such force of impact that the knight's turning sword flew out of his hand and winnowed away across the grave chamber, and struck a stake-raised set of golden horse armour before dropping to the ground. The two portions of von Margur fell on the dirt floor and a vast pool of steaming blood drained out of them.

Karl stared down at von Margur of Altdorf for a long time.

'Karl-Azytzeen?' Chegrume said softly, moving to approach him.

Karl ignored him and suddenly rushed into the treasure heaps on one side of the kurgan chamber. He threw aside golden chairs, stacks of gilded shields that fell with a crash, and coats of gilt mail so he could lunge into the shadows behind them. He stabbed once, and then again, as if jabbing at a rat. Then he pulled back with Ons Olker's naked, thrashing body impaled upon the length of his pallasz blade. Shell beads and necklaces of bone broke and scattered onto the chamber floor in the shaman's frenzy, and an awful gurgling wail shrilled out of the mouth-slit of the three-horned bull helm. More Scythian grave-goods crashed over as Ons Olker was dragged out of hiding.

Karl tipped his sword over, and let Ons Olker slide under his own weight off the razor-edged steel.

The shaman, convulsing, sprawled with a splash into the spreading lake of von Margur's lifeblood.

'I have done what I should have done at Zhedevka, Ons Olker,' Karl said. 'May you burn in the daemon pit.'

'Please, p-please, Azytzeen–' pleaded the shaman as he spasmed in his agonised death-throes, his roping guts coiling out of his ruptured torso, his drumming feet flecking blood into the air. 'P-please... say thee a fair word for m-my sake to Tchar–'

'Damn you,' Karl said.

Ons Olker twitched and shrieked his way to the end of his messy, painful death. When he finally fell silent, Karl looked at the doorway of the mound chamber. Chegrume followed his gaze, but could see nothing.

Karl raised his hand and pointed. 'Zar Blayda! I see you, you worm! I see you out there, cowering in the shadows!'

Blayda, clad in his black, inscribed armour, slowly stepped into the torch-glare of the chamber. He gazed down at the butchered bodies of von Margur and Ons Olker lying in the slick of stinking blood and sank to his knees with a moan of mortal dread.

'I submit to you, Karl-Azytzeen,' Blayda said, bowing his head. 'I submit.'

'Blayda...' Karl growled. 'Look at me. Look at my face.'

Hesitantly, terrified, Blayda looked up at Karl. He cried out at what he saw.

'Look at me. Look upon Tchar. Let what you see blind you forever. You will follow me until the end of all days.'

'Yes... yes! I will!' Blayda yelled, his left hand on his heart, and tears streaming from his eyes. A heart-truth.

Arrows thumped into his back, one after the other. The tips came out through his chest, one pinning his hand to his heart. Blayda pitched forward onto his face, transfixed and still kneeling.

Berlas, Diormac and Efgul burst into the tomb chamber, recurve bows drawn back and nocked with ready arrows. Behind them came Hzaer, Fegul One-Hand, Lyr, Sakondor, Yuskel, and many others, their sword blades dripping red-wet from the men of Blayda's band they had been forced to kill to gain entry to the mound.

His fellow riders had come to save him, as they had pledged. Karl-Azytzeen smiled.

'Aside! Get aside, you dogs!' a voice roared outside in the tunnel. 'Yuskel? Where are you?'

Uldin strode into the chamber, pushing violently through the gathered men and splashing into the great puddle of red. He glared down at the bodies, the blood and tumbled gold.

'What is this bloody crime, Berlas? What have you done, Diormac? A zar cut down, against the peace-pledge... and on sacred soil th–'

Uldin balked as he saw Karl clearly for the first time. He made a warding sign and, like Blayda, fell on his knees. Karl could see the Hetzar's scared eyes flashing through the slits of his wolf-mask helm.

'A Hetzar such as you should not bow to a man like me,' Karl insisted. 'My life has belonged to you since Zhedevka. You could have taken it, but you chose not to. You told me that all the while I remembered the power you had over my life, I was no danger to you. Get up, Hetzar Uldin.'

Uldin did so.

'I don't belong to you any more, Uldin. I am Tchar's now.'

'I know that,' Uldin said, his voice wavering slightly.

'And you should have listened to Skarkeetah slave lord's advice,' Karl said. He lashed out with his true killer, and the slim blade of Drogo Hance's dagger punched in through the sight-slit in Uldin's wolf mask, through his eye and deep into his brain.

Karl wrenched the knife out and Uldin fell onto his back, another bloody offering to the altar of Chamon Dharek littering the chamber floor.

Karl looked at the stunned faces of the men in the warband.

'Well?'

'Karl-Azytzeen!' Efgul yelled.

'Karl! Karl seh!' bellowed Hzaer and Yuskel.

'Zar!' Karl spat back at them, his ring-wrapped arms raised in triumph.

'Zar Azytzeen! Zar Azytzeen!' the men cried. 'Zar Azytzeen!'

VEBLA

I

They barely made it to Yetchitch before deep winter established its rule of raspotitsa. The word meant 'roadlessness', and referred to the period when the oblast succumbed to such a weight of snow that even the simplest of paths and tracks were lost and indecipherable.

All through the last week of their trek – the longest and most arduous Gerlach had undertaken – the snow fell, until the grass ocean of the steppe became a pure white flatness that hurt the eye.

They were in what Borodyn called the open steppe now. This great waste of plains extended across the north-east parts of the Kislev oblast, a higher and more open country than ever before. Gerlach had been awed by the vacant flatness of the steppe where Dushyka and Leblya and Zamak Spayenya lurked like little secrets, and could not imagine anywhere with a greater scale of emptiness. Level land and the surrounding horizon could surely only express so much.

But the open steppe was the wilderness's masterpiece. Even the lancers seemed humbled by its void. The sun and moons, as they cycled through the sky, appeared to have been reduced in size themselves so the landscape was vaster by comparison.

Through icy dawns and blizzarding days, they made their route, until thick snow reduced their pace to a trudge. Armour was too cold to wear, or even touch, for fear of flesh sticking fast to frozen metal. Huddled in layers of furs and beshmets, the men shivered into the frost-wind. Before departing Zoishenk, Beledni had obtained two coats for Gerlach: a sheepskin cloak, leggings and woollen hood-cap with a fur trim, all of which had seemed impractical purchases in the lazy heat of summer on the Tobol.

But Beledni knew what lay in the north to greet them.

In the final days, white hills and a hint of green forest could be glimpsed ahead of them through the fast-falling snow. This was the territory of Blindt, the hill country at the edge of the Sanyza region, the wooded highlands where Yetchitch lay.

The frozen mood of the rota thawed as they rode up at last into the deep pine forests. They began to sing krug songs with raw voices. The giant, black-trunked conifers rose around them, dusted with ice, and snowflakes fluttered down. They glimpsed elks, and flighty arctic foxes that pricked their ears at the sound of the men's voices and took away into the snow.

Gerlach could feel the rota's delight that home was close. He let Vaja and Vitali teach him the words to one of the songs, so he could join in. Their attempts were so confused, and so hindered by numb lips and muffles of fur, all three fell into uncontrollable laughter that rang out through the trees.

Ifan spied the lights of Yetchitch first and put up a cry. Yevni carefully warmed the mouthpiece of his horn, and blew a great blast that rolled away into echoes. A lonely horn sang back in reply from the stanitsa.

Yetchitch was a place the size of Dushyka. Thatched izbas huddled around a long zal, whose tiled roof was thick with snow except for the melt-hole around the chimney flue. The stanitsa had no defensive stockade, but was surrounded by a high fence of pine boards that acted as a barrier against the drifting snow. They walked their horses in through the fence gate and entered the yard.

The folk of Yetchitch flocked out in heavy clothes to greet them. There was no banging and clattering of pots, no ritual exchange of shared food and drink, just a warm, silent embrace of figures greeting lost sons. Parents and friends, siblings and, in some cases, children hurried through the snow to wrap their arms around their loved ones.

For a forlorn moment, Gerlach sat alone on Saksen, watching the wordless relief and joy, utterly ignored.

Eager boys led the horses away and the townsfolk gathered the weary, chilblained warriors into the warmth of the zal. A youth in furs, his top lip struggling to produce a moustache, came to Gerlach and greeted him with a nod as the demilancer dismounted. Other townsfolk grouped around, puzzled by the sight of a stranger holding the rota banner.

The youth held out his hand to take Gerlach's reins.

'What is his name?' he asked.

'He called Byeli-Saksen,' Gerlach answered in broken Kislevite. 'Take care him of good.'

The youth nodded solemnly, and led the tired troop-horse away with the rest.

The townsfolk grouped around Gerlach.

One of them, a thin, elderly woman, looked into his eyes. 'Why does Mikael Roussa not the carry banner?'

'Is dead he,' Gerlach said.

The woman frowned, as if this was not an answer. 'I know he is dead. Where is he?'

'At Zhedevka place, fell he,' Gerlach answered, wishing his fragile command of Kislevite was less basic.

The woman nodded at this, very matter-of-fact, and turned away. Other townsfolk closed around and put their arms around her heaving shoulders.

Beledni appeared. He took Gerlach by the sleeve and led him through the huddle of onlookers into the zal.

The sudden heat was shockingly fierce. Gerlach thought he would pass out. The hall was packed with the people of the stanitsa, many of whom were joking and laughing with the lancers, and feeding them hot staya as they helped them strip off their heavy travel garments.

Beledni took Gerlach to the end of the zal, and up onto a hardwood platform above the fire. This was the stage from which the village ataman presided over his people. The ataman himself, a middle-aged man with long, shaggy hair and the heavy upper body of a woodcutter, stepped up to join them with his esaul, who carried the ataman's bulava, the small mace that was his statement of power.

The ataman looked at Gerlach with a curious frown. Beledni turned to the assembled people and raised his stout arms for silence.

'This is Gerlach Heileman, of Talabheim!' he roared in Kislevite. 'The rota has braved much in this dark year, and lost many of our comrades. When Mikael Roussa fell down to his death, this brave man saved our banner, and for that duty, Beledni rotamaster has made him rota bearer!'

The townsfolk cheered out their approval.

Beledni tried to shush them a little. 'He is one of us now. He is of Yetchitch krug. Embrace him as a brother. We have called him Vebla!'

The people cheered again, though this time the applause was mixed with great laughter.

Gerlach looked at Beledni 'You make words kind, rotamaster,' he said, as best as he was able.

'Vebla deserve as much,' Beledni said, switching to his unpolished Reikspiel. 'Vebla deserve praise of krug. Now... Vebla give back rota banner to ataman.'

Gerlach turned to face the ataman and hand him the banner. Just before he let it go, Gerlach pulled it back and kissed the haft. The ataman took the banner, and carefully slipped the tip of its shaft down through a hole in the wooden stage so that it stood upright, watching over the zal. Then he crushed Gerlach to his chest in an enthusiastic bear-hug.

The people cheered again.

At the esaul's urgings, kvass and salt were brought out for the toasting. Gerlach made sure he knew where the nearest seat was.

II

They feasted well, slept and feasted again. The storerooms of Yetchitch, loaded with salt meat and cured pork from the autumn slaughter, yielded a plentiful supply of food, and there was a never-ending provision of kvass and koumiss.

Through the long nights of feasting, stories were traded. The lancers recounted the details of their adventures, their deaths and losses, their victories and escapes. The townsfolk and the families returned the favour with tales of the harvest, of animals sick or lost, of births and deaths and marriages. Music was played on the horsehead fiddle and the tambor.

Vitali proudly introduced Gerlach to his aged mother. Vaja showed off two little children he didn't look old enough to have sired. Mitri had Gerlach meet his plump, beautiful wife.

Kvetlai, nervous and hesitant, took Gerlach to meet the girl he was betrothed to marry. She was stunning and shy and, like Kvetlai, little more than a child. Her name was Lusha.

She had three sisters, and insisted they were all prettier than her. Her only brother, older than all the girls, had been Sorca.

When she saw the look of pained surprise on Gerlach's face, she told him, 'I have mourned him already. I mourned him when he went away.'

Mitri's wife, Darya, wanted to know why Gerlach did not shave his hair like the other warriors.

'A topknot and a moustache is so much more fetching,' she insisted.

'Men here, they not shave,' Gerlach said, pointing to the ataman and some of the other male townsfolk.

'They are not warriors!' she clucked.

III

The winter passed by. Maksim led a small band of men out from Yetchitch to recruit warriors from the other villages in the territory, hoping that the rotas of other stanitsas would be up to strength for the thaw.

Five youths from the Yetchitch krug had reached the age to join the rota. The men and the townsfolk spent one riotous, drunken night initiating them. This involved lewd drinking games, and the ceremonial shaving of their heads down to a tuft.

Beledni performed this duty with the sharpened tip of his own lance.

'Vebla not understand,' Gerlach said to Vitali, as they watched the shaving pantomime.

'We shave before battle, all of us,' Vitali said.

'This Vebla know. Vebla understand it nyeh.'

Vitali grinned his small-toothed grin. 'Before battle, we sharpen our swords and speartips. Make them trusty and sure. Then we shave our heads and cheeks and chins. If the rotamaster finds any men with stubble, he knows their edges are not battle-sharp.'

Gerlach sighed at the simplicity of it.

Heads pale and bare – and, in some cases, bleeding – the shivering, gawky supplicants stood straight as Beledni inspected them. Then he had each one touch the hem of the banner cloth on the stage and utter an oath of allegiance. Proud mothers wept.

The five boys were called Gennedy, Bodo, Xaver, Kubah and Valantin. Kubah was the youth who had come out on their arrival to lead Saksen away. He was, Gerlach learned, Beledni's own son. He could see it now. The familial similarity. Add a good few pounds, a few years and take away the front teeth…

Beledni then explained the philosophy of the last battle. Every battle, he told the boys, was the last. It was the one that would steal their life. If they treated any combat less seriously, they would surely die. A man of the rota fought every battle as though it was his very last.

Then Borodyn brought out their wings. Each one was fletched with the feathers of birds the youngsters had killed. Crow, crossbill, magpie, jay, kestrel. More illustrious plumes – eagle and hawk – would come later, once war skill had been tested.

These were the wings a rider needed to carry him up into the heavens to be with Dazh.

The laughter had died away. Everyone trooped out into the cold night, pulling on their outer garments and furs, and walked to a lamp-lit plot behind the zal. The snow had been cleared and five open graves were exposed, cut from the black earth.

The people of the stanitsa stood round as funeral prayers were said for the five boys. Their mothers and sisters cast dried summer flowers and the boy's shorn hair into the graves, and cried brokenly with loss. The boys were dead now, dead and passed away beyond the bosom of the family. They would be grieved now so that the grief could be set aside. No one would wait out the length of the year to hear news of their boy's fortune. They were dead, and gone to the fate of the rota.

They were, forever, riders of the dead.

IV

LATE IN THE midwinter, Gerlach had a vivid dream that woke him suddenly. He was lying in the zal, under furs, and sweating. All the men of the rota slept in the zal. Their family izbas had no beds for them now.

He found Borodyn sitting nearby, watching the great hearth crackle and spit.

'Vebla had dream,' Gerlach said, coming to sit by him.

'I suspected as much. We all have. I have seen it also in the stars. What did you see?'

'Vebla see–'

'In your own tongue, Vebla. I can manage that.'

Gerlach smiled. 'I saw a battle. A great field of men. Kurgan and the banners of Kislev, opposed. I had to ride out and fight their warlord.'

Borodyn horse master nodded. 'This I have seen, we all have seen. Dazh has written it in the krug of the sky.' He looked at Gerlach, his eyes reflecting the red sparks of the hearth.

'I thought you had come to us to save the banner. The rota banner. I thought that was why Dazh and Ursun had sent you. But that was just the start. The meeting point of Yetchitch rota and Gerlach-who-is-also-Vebla.'

'And now?'

'If the gods ride with you, you will fight the champion of Khaos.'

'Archaon? I will fight Archaon? Is that my destiny?'

Borodyn shrugged. 'Dreams don't lie, but they confuse. All I know is you are the one who will do battle with a great beast of Khaos. If you win, the oblast and your great Empire will live on. If you fail, and this monster beats you, then the Old World will sink away in a sea of blood. So, yes. I believe you are the warrior who will contest with Archaon, for no greater evil lives in the world.'

'Will I win?' Gerlach asked.

'The stars do not say, and neither do the dreams.'

'But will I win?' Gerlach insisted.

'Of course. You will have the rota of Yetchitch krug at your side.'

V

THE LAND WAS crusted with heavy snow, but the skies were clear and blue. Midwinter was behind them, and they were in that static place where the fallen cold simply lingered.

Gerlach went out into the town yard, and watched the boys of the stanitsa as they broke ponies to the snaffle bit. The rota supplicants, aloof in another part of the yard for they were boys no longer, were training the horses they would ride in Beledni's company. They were riding them in circles, reinless, and beating tambors, first one side of their mount's head and then the other. *Bang-bang! Bang-bang!*

Gerlach stood by the town fence, and watched the circling riders as he whetted the blade of the new spear Beledni had given him. Kubah was running his horse, trying to startle it with his hand-drum. He was a fine horseman, just like his father.

The next day was to be the wedding time of Kvetlai and Lusha. Gerlach had decided to shave for the occasion. He went into the zal, and ladled hot water out of the kettle-pan permanently fixed over the flames. Then he gingerly began to use the spear blade to shave his chin, his cheeks and his scalp, all except for his moustache and a long lock at his crown.

* * *

VI

EVERYONE GOT DRUNK at the rowdy wedding feast. The groom, his new white beshmet laced with feathers, insisted that Gerlach say a few words – a proposal loudly supported by Vaja and Vitali – and a few words was all the demilancer could manage. He spoke, in slurred, hopeless Kislevite, of Zamak Spayenya and Kvetlai's bravery, and then admired the beauty of the bride. The gathering cheered him anyway.

When he fell back into his seat, Mitri's wife stroked her hand across Gerlach's smooth scalp.

'Is better,' she decided.

The music swept up, and the feasting turned to dancing. Gerlach was dragged by the hand into the swirling bodies by Lexandra, one of the bride's sisters.

Lexandra was quite the most beautiful girl Gerlach had ever seen. As they danced, tight together, she giggled.

'You are Vebla.'

'And you are Lexandra.'

'Is not so funny. Vebla it is funny.'

'What does vebla mean? What does it mean, Lexandra? No one will tell me.'

'There is a ewe.'

'A ewe?'

'A mother sheep. It has lambs. Some are strong and big, others are small. Smallest of all, it fight hard against others, wanting milk. It... it annoying little beast, always in way, always underfoot, always begging for more, always needing care. It pushy and demanding.'

'And that is a vebla?'

'Pretty much so,' she said, and laughed so hard her head tipped back.

He whirled her around to the beat of the tambor. Her happy laughter would haunt him forever.

VII

A WEEK AFTER the wedding. The rota woke to the sound of Maksim bashing a ladle to and fro inside a brass potato pot.

He ignored their oaths and taunts and suggestions what he might do to himself.

'First thaw,' he said.

VIII

ACCEPTING THE ROTA banner from the ataman, Gerlach turned and walked out of the zal into the yard. Snow covered the ground, dense and crisp, but there was a smell of water in the air. The sky was greenish-blue above the pines.

The townsfolk clapped and yelled as Gerlach emerged. Over the winter, Borodyn had worked on Gerlach's battered, worn half-armour, and inlaid it with gold and silver chasing. A spike replaced the cockade of his troop helmet, and a veil of silver mesh hung down where his lobster tail had been. A lamellar coat clinked over his cuirass, right down to his hips, and furs were tied around his shoulders. Brackets on his backplate supported the frame of the tall wing of eagle feathers. It would take him a while to get used to the heart-shaped visor Borodyn had attached to the front of his helm. One had to look hard to discern that the basis of his helmet was an Imperial demilance burgonet and not a szyszak at all.

Lexandra ran out to him and gave him a ritual swig of koumiss and a heavy kiss that made the people roar. Gerlach held her close, then handed the banner to the waiting Kubah, splendid in his lancer wargear.

He leapt into Saksen's saddle from standing, to more appreciative whoops. Byeli-Saksen, fit and well-nourished, had been freshly dyed white and red, following the pattern the boys of Dushyka stanitsa had established. His mane and the tail that had been docked and bound as per cavalry rules had long since grown out to flowing length.

Kubah passed the banner back into Gerlach's hand. He hoisted it up, and Yevni blew the call to advance.

The fifty-three men of the rota, riders of the dead to a man, turned and galloped out of Yetchitch stanista and vanished into the forest.

The folk of the krug stood and waved until long after they were out of sight.

MAZHOROD

I

IN THE KISLEVITE tongue, it was called Mazhorod, but the Kurgan knew it as Khar'phak Aqshyek, for a great battle significant to them had once been fought there in a distant time. In summer, it was possible to walk the land thereabouts and find old arrowheads, shield bosses, bridle rings and other trinkets the ancient conflict had left behind in the soil. Mazhorod marked a decent fording place in the River Urskoy, a wide bank of shingle that slowed and lowered the old, broad river as it turned.

On either side of the crossing lay the spare, open country of a great plain, thinly populated with bent trees, gorse and steppe thistle. A high ridge of young mountains lay to the west, and a circuit of lower, rocky hills to the south-east.

It was barely spring. Snow still lay thick and heavy on the ground, and it would for six weeks more. But the thaw was on the land. The sky was a clear blue-white, and the air was clean and fresh. The Urskoy thundered along at its highest annual measure, swollen with melt water and riddled with shards of ice.

The year was still breathlessly young, but the fighting season had begun.

The rota's journey back down across the steppe to Zoishenk took three weeks longer than anticipated, even though Maksim's nose for the signs of thaw had got them into the saddle early. The snow that had drifted on the steppe during midwinter in the storming gales now formed deep dunes like a white desert. The riders had to wade many miles on foot, leading their mounts through cold, knee-deep snow.

When they reached Zoishenk, they found the Sanyza pulk had already formed and gone. Fyodor Kurkosk, the boyarin, had successfully used the winter to amass a considerable force four times the size of the diminished remnants that had gathered on the Tobol the previous summer. He was joined presently by the Uskovic pulk, also now of great size. Not wishing to delay any longer, and fritter away the early start they had got to the year, the boyarin had led his army south.

In the oblast that lay several hundred leagues west of Kislev itself – a land that had suffered under the predations of the Norscya hordes – the boyarin's force had encountered the roaming army of Okkodai Tarsus. The High Zar's cold, hungry mass of warriors was spreading west, summoned, it seemed, by Archaon, to support the crucial war now under way on the far side of the Middle Mountains.

The High Zar's horde was nearly twice the size of the boyarin's combined pulks. They met outside a thorn-wood at Krasicyno. For a while, it seemed as if the pulk's escape from Okkodai Tarsus on the salt-pan the previous year had been but a postponement of their destruction by his hand.

Until, that is, another army arrived. Moving up out of the south, an Imperial army from Stirland closed in on the High Zar's heels. Caught between Kislevite and Imperial armies at Krasicyno, the horde of Okkodai Tarsus was crushed, broken and put to flight in a battle that lasted two days.

Large portions of the Norscya horde, including the High Zar himself, survived and quit the field, but their further operation as a viable force was extinguished.

Jubilant, the combined army of allies turned west. They were one of the first forces from Kislev and the east to sweep back towards the Empire's heartland at that dark, needy time.

Others, led in part by the tzarina herself out of Kislev, were close behind.

Beledni's rota caught up with Fyodor Kurkosk's army at Mazhorod, bringing with them other late arrivals from Zoishenk. The mood was ebullient and confident.

Gerlach was not. That very fact enraged him. At last... at last! They were striking back and avenging the cruel wounds inflicted the previous summer. Everything he had been wishing for was now happening.

But now his midwinter dream, the memory and obscure meaning of it, was in the way.

'You be look happy, Vebla?' Vitali admonished him as they rode along together.

'Yha,' Vaja agreed. 'We war at ride. This what Vebla keep want, all through time. Ride at war, rota, Vebla say. Ride at war me with. Why you not ride at war me with? Like echo in cave. Now we ride at war you with and... hello! Vebla, he look like man who find piss in his cup.'

'I am content,' Gerlach said to them in their language. 'I am content we ride at war. Vebla just...'

'What Vebla just?' Vaja asked.

'It's the dream you had, isn't it?' Vitali said in Kislevite. 'The dream we all had.'

Gerlach nodded.

'It will come when it will come,' Vaja said sagely. He turned his hand, as if letting dust sprinkle out of it. 'Is of no matter.'

'I think,' Gerlach said, 'it might be of some matter.'

II

AT MAZHOROD, JUST before the crossing, scout riders ran back to the pulk. They had seen a great mass of the enemy coming eastwards towards them. Mazhorod would be their meeting point, their place of battle.

The boyarin camped the great pulk in the rocky hills south-east of the crossing. From there, they could see the whole plain, and the winding river. As night fell, they were able to view the torch fires of a massive Kurgan host on the far side of the Urskoy.

'Tomorrow, we fight,' Beledni told the rota as they gathered around the spitting fire of the krug. He had been summoned with the other company officers of the pulk to a meeting with the boyarin, and now he brought the import of that audience back to his men.

'They will try for the crossing, probably at dawn. The boyarin orders we take them as they come across. The river is deep. They will be vulnerable.'

The men cheered this. The skins of koumiss passed around the circle as men toasted victory. Beledni ordered them to shave.

Gerlach left the krug and walked out onto a jutting headland of rock. Around him, in the snowy gloom, the fires of the boyarin's great pulk flickered in the dark.

A few leagues away, on the other bank of the Urskoy – the river invisible now in the night – the fires of the enemy camp blazed on the plain.

'You are not shaving as I ordered,' Beledni said, appearing out of the night behind him.

'I will, rotamaster. Dutifully, before I sleep.'

'You have a trouble in your mind.'

Gerlach looked at the heavy, old rotamaster. 'You know about the dreams?'

'I have had them myself.'

'I find this frustrating,' Gerlach said, gesturing down at the lights of the Kurgan host. 'Dazh has told me I am to fight the great beast of Khaos, and that the future of great nations rests in my hands.'

'Yha.'

'Archaon, damned be his name, is the great beast, surely?'

'Beledni rotamaster would imagine so.'

'Well… he's not down there, is he? We have to break this host of Norscya tomorrow. And even if we win–'

'We will win, Vebla.'

'Of course. But even then, this great effort is just a step on the way for me. How many more armies must we break before I get to face the beast? How strong do I have to be?'

'Strong enough.'

Gerlach ran his hands back over his smooth, bald head and straightened his braided topknot. 'I hope so. It just seems I shouldn't be doing this. I should be somewhere else, where it matters.'

'This matters, Vebla. This matters. This, and then the next thing, and the next. It is a journey. And the journey is a–'

'Circle. I know. But how could my journey ever turn full circle and end up where Dazh says I should be? I've never met Archaon. I've never met any beast of Khaos. I think perhaps my journey is a straight line, whatever the Kislev philosophy thinks. And this fight we are preparing for is in my way.'

'You are Vebla,' Beledni said, switching to his broken Reikspiel. 'You nag and annoy. You worry at things. You not give up. You will find out the way your circle closes.'

Gerlach smiled. 'Can I tell you something, rotamaster?' he asked.

Beledni nodded.

'When I was a young man…' Gerlach began. 'Last year, in fact,' he added, making Beledni laugh. 'I believed I could single-handedly change the whole world. I rode out of Talabheim, so full of piss and vinegar, I was going to take on the night and overthrow it, all on my own. Be a champion of the Empire. Turn back the entire Norscya hordes with one flick of my blade.'

Gerlach looked up at the stars for a moment. 'My time spent with you, with the rota – out on the steppe – it changed my outlook. The wide oblast made me realise how small I was. How insignificant. Just a lone, little man in a huge world. It was… humbling.'

'The steppe is humbling to all,' conceded Beledni.

'Yha. And it was a long overdue lesson for a Vebla like me. Know my place. Be not so arrogant.'

'Whole year has not been wasted, then?' Beledni chuckled.

Gerlach laughed. 'But now, Dazh tells me I am not a little man after all. I am everything my puffed-up ego had me believe. So Dazh says.'

'Dazh, he shows us things that are significant,' Beledni nodded.

'Well, I have this destiny suddenly. One I'd cast aside because it was stupid. To be the man who single-handedly saved the world. To be the man who could face the beast of Khaos. To matter – really matter – in the scheme of things. And it's come too late, just when I realised I didn't matter after all.'

Beledni sat down on a rock. 'Dazh can really be a bastard like that,' he admitted. That made Gerlach laugh again.

'Every man matters,' Beledni said. 'How he lives, how he dies, what he does. The way he conducts his life, the manner of his passing from it. The krug turns and we take each day as it comes to us. If Dazh says you will find your beast of Khaos, you will find it. He will turn the world so it happens.'

'Will he?'

'Your dream was not a prophecy to make sense of. It was Dazh, warning you what was going to happen.'

III

THE WARBANDS OF Surtha Lenk's host massed on the west bank of the Urskoy as dawn came. They had been seething up into a frenzy since midnight, as the shamans blessed and praised them and screeched war-prayers amongst them.

In the weak, chilly light of dawn, the crossing seemed immeasurable. The Urskoy ran hard and frothy, glinting with broken pieces of ice. The horses would shy and refuse.

Carnyx horns blew loudly in the half-light. Though warriors in the warbands were disquieted, the zars and Hetzars were in no doubt. Archaon had ordered this. The Lord of the End Times had sent word to Surtha Lenk, ordering him east to deny the armies of the steppe. Archaon's eastern flank was exposed. The Lenk's horde was the measure of its urgent defence.

Those zars chosen by Surtha Lenk to lead the attack congregated on the foreshore of the crossing. Zar Herfil, Zar Skolt, Zar Bellicuz, Zar Narrhos, all massing horsemen, some nine hundred between them. Behind them advanced the foot troops, two thousand all told. In the feeble light, they could all see the Kislevites and the Sigmarite Imperials assembling to meet them on the other bank.

Zar Azytzeen led his horsemen up through the thick clot of readied warriors on the west shore. They parted as he approached at the head of his horse troop. He frightened them all. He was a stark figure, his arms wrapped in trophy rings, his head encased in a spiked gold war-helmet that some said had been taken from the barrow at Chamon Dharek. Others said it had been purpose-made to fit his head by the priest-smiths at that forbidden place. Whatever the truth, it was a chilling visage. The helm, beaten of white, Scythian gold, had only one eyeslit – on the right side. The rest of the half-visor was fashioned in the bas relief shape of a snake-fringed eye, with blue jade set into its pupil.

'We will make blood flow this day, Zar Azytzeen seh,' Yuskel said, spurring his braying black and white striped horse forward. The standard of Azytzeen's warband fluttered, upright in his thick hands.

'We will that, Yuskel seh,' said the zar.

* * *

IV

THE CARNYX BLEW. Surtha Lenk's host charged forward into the water, stumbling headlong through the heavy flow. Infantry came first, lifting high their shields and berdish axes. Behind them, the first of the horsemen dared the cold, fast river.

The great pulk waited for them, arms ready.

Kurgan men were swept over by the freezing melt-tide, their bodies washed away down stream. Horses fell numb and followed them, their riders tumbling and swirling after them.

But Surtha Lenk's force persevered by dint of sheer weight. The first foot warriors scrambled up on the east bank, and ran towards the patient enemy. Shortly after, the first of the riders made it across. Zar Herfil's band. Zar Skolt's.

The pulk waited until a significant mass of the enemy was across. An enemy that now had the river at its back and nowhere to run to.

Bone horns and clarions sounded. The pulk moved forward. The Stirland pike wall formed up to meet the attackers, while Imperial archers, on both sides of the river bend, punished the enemy that had cleared the crossing with a deluge of arrows. Men fell, left and right, impaled.

At the same time, a vast company of horse archers rode up along the bank from the south, and pelted the Kurgan struggling across the water. The effect was considerable. Hundreds of Kurgan died midstream, hailed on by a mass of Kislevite bows. Zar Herfil himself fell with an arrow through his skull, and Zar Skolt lurched off his whinnying horse, two Kislevite barbs sticking through his torso.

The great pulk sent up a huge roar of triumph, goading the enemy. The river and the pulk had combined to inflict terrible loss on the Kurgan.

On the western bank, Zar Azytzeen cursed aloud the names of the enemy gods, and blamed his own for their lack of support. Even his staunchest comrades blanched at this blasphemy.

'Tchar! Changer of ways! Why do you forsake us so?' Azytzeen bellowed into a dawn sky that was as blue as the eye of snakes. He took off his golden helmet so his sacred, ruined eye could glare up at the face of his god.

Perhaps Tchar was listening to his favoured son, or perhaps great Surtha Lenk had made similar entreaties with his sorcerous power. Whatever the cause, the sky grew darker suddenly. Marbled clouds of storm weather slid across the firmament and robbed away the daylight. Snow fell, at first, then hail too, ringing off the wargear of friend and foe alike. A savage chill cut the air, and the temperature dropped away sharply.

And the Urskoy at Mazhorod crossing froze solid.

The Kurgan yet to deploy from the west bank hesitated in bewilderment. The water had frozen so abruptly, so unnaturally that the warriors and horsemen still midstream were locked into it, some crushed by ice, others trapped and screaming. The eager spirit of the great pulk faltered and dimmed at the abnormal spectacle.

'Now! Now!' Zar Azytzeen roared, clamping his helm back over his head. 'Now, in the name of Archaon and Tchar!'

Hzaer blasted his carnyx, and the sounds was enthusiastically picked up and amplified by the hornblowers of other warbands. The bulk of the Kurgan horse horde thundered forward and clattered across the thick raft of ice, their hooves splintering fragments into the air like sapphires. Behind them, the foot warriors, the spearmen and the axemen, poured forward.

Azytzeen's warband was first on the shore. They charged through the scattering survivors of the first wave. At the sight of him, the front line of the Stirland pike wall broke in panic. The company of horse archers led by Dmirov, son of Gaspar, brother of Antal, was closest to the Kurgan horsemen. They had been harrying the Norscya who had made it to the shore. Dmirov turned his men and rode them full tilt into the oncoming riders.

Kislevite bows cracked and hissed, and arrows tore at the Northers. Warriors were struck from their saddles or fell with their slain or crippled warhorses.

The Kurgan had drawn their own bows. Berlas, Lyr, Diormac... every man including the zar himself, drew and shot, not once, but again and again, loading to the cord from the clutch of spare missiles they held between the fingers of their bowhands. Black shafts hailed into the oncoming Kislevites, volley after volley.

In seconds, dozens of them were down, rolling and flailing. By the time the two horse companies met, more of Dmirov's men were dead than alive.

Their arrows mostly spent, the Kurgan drew blades as they came level with the galloping steppe archers. Horses flashed past all around, but the heavy, armoured Northmen had much the better of it. Efgul took Dmirov's head without even slowing down. Sakondor slew the archers' banner bearer.

Then they were coming around and into the flank of the pulk, breaking it before them.

They were not alone. The other mounted warbands followed their Zars into the charge and drove into the facing and right-hand lines of the pulk. This sundering impact had scarcely been delivered when the Kurgan infantry followed.

The battle, so nearly won outright in its first moments, was now pitched and locked.

And fortune, in a manner that would please the eye of Tchar, was changing.

V

THE ROTA OF Yetchitch krug had been stationed on the right of the pulk, ready to sally out around the pike wall, when the river froze and the change began.

Beledni rose in the saddle and turned to the men. 'This is the last battle, remember! The only battle! Fight now as if it was your last stand, and it will not be so!'

At Beledni's fierce command, Yevni blew the charge, and the rota turned out, racing fast, lances couched. Two other rotas rose with them. It was a fine sight, a glorious sight. The gold and silver warriors, their tall wings fluttering, hammered through the snow cover with their banner tails flying from their lance tips.

A section of Kislev partisans, foot troops raised from the oblast, had just been split wide by the warband of Zar Kreyya and a wedge of Kurgan axemen. The galloping lancers came up into them like a golden tide.

None of foul Kreyya's men, armed as they were with axe and pallasz, had any reach to match the Kislevite lance. Spear-shafts shivered in lancers' hands, and they recoiled in their saddles and stirrups, as the long weapons cut into the Kurgan. Lances snapped and splintered on impact. Not a single one failed to wound or kill outright.

In one jarring moment of collision, the five new riders of the dead were baptised in battle, and claimed the honour of their first war-kill.

The zar's surviving men tried to break, but they were hemmed in by the now panicking infantry axemen around them. Kurgan began to kill Kurgan, involuntarily at first, as maddened horses trampled infantry. Kreyya, in his effort to ride clear, killed footmen in his path. Some of the terrified infantry turned their axes on the horsemen in a sick desperation to stay alive.

Most rota lances now had been dropped or broken. A few riders managed to keep hold of theirs and used them as they drove the charge home. Mitri left his, finally, through the chest of Kreyya's hornblower.

They took out their javelins, the shorter, throwing lances, and hurled them into the thick press. Vaja, just ahead of Gerlach, loosed his first javelin with such force it went through the shoulder armour of the fleeing zar. Kreyya screamed out, and fought to keep his warhorse upright. He managed to turn, in time to take Vaja's second javelin between the eyes.

The rotas had slaughtered Kreyya's warband and the infantry around it. Yevni blew his bone horn to raise the tempo again, and Beledni swung the krug around. There was another Kurgan warband closing in ahead.

And this one was already at full charge.

VI

YUSKEL HAD SIGHTED the rank position of the Kislevite boyarin, and yelled the fact to his zar. Roaring, Azytzeen pushed them forward. This was the kill he most wanted. The boyarin's head would be placed at the summit of his first skull stack to watch with burned-out sockets as Chegrume gave Zar Azytzeen his first victory mark. Then it would be cased in gold and set on the warband's standard.

Most of all, it would win Azytzeen favour with the High Zar. Then there would be no doubting the identity of Surtha Lenk's new favourite. He would be Hetzar Azytzeen, chief of chiefs.

A single line of Kislevite lancers stood between him and the boyarin's trabanten. The winged horsemen had just come through one fierce melee, and their lances and javelins were mostly spent. He would demolish them, take their heads, and cast the plucked feathers of their ridiculous wings into the hailstorm.

VII

AT FULL STRETCH, without hesitation, the warband of Zar Azytzeen and the rota of Yetchitch krug came across the snowfield at each other, and met head on.

VIII

'GREAT DAZH AND Sigmar preserve us all…' Gerlach gasped as he saw the beast that rode at the head of the enemy warband. The golden, one-eyed helm was wretched enough, but some obscene blue fire seemed to glow out from it, through the gold where there was no eye-slit. A daemon-thing, a creature stalking abroad, loosed by the otherworld. Gerlach could not imagine what foul hell had spawned that warrior.

But the blue and the gold had been shown to him by Dazh in his dreams, and he knew with utter certainty he was in the right place after all.

IX

THE WORLD BROKE, as if struck by a hammer. Kurgan warhorse and Kislevite chargers tore past each other. Confusion was all around them.

Confusion, and death.

Berlas loosed the last of his arrows. Mitri crashed over into the snow, his arms flung up, a black shaft slammed through his chest. Beledni rotamaster left Diormac dead in his wake, with a sword blow cleft through his helm. Maksim received a wound in his thigh from Efgul's axe blade as they swept past each other, and then met Sakondor face to face. Sakondor's pallasz took feathers from Maksim's wing. Maksim's sword took Sakondor's head off entirely.

Gennedy, youngest of the supplicants, hurled his last javelin but missed his mark. He screamed, briefly, as Lyr's sword felled him and his horse together.

Fegul One-Hand closed with Ifan, and they traded sword cuts, their horses turning around each other. Both landed wounding blows, but Fegul One-Hand's northern power broke Ifan's guard and split him through the chest. Fegul was whooping his victory when Kvetlai, with tears of rage in his eyes, rode by and silenced him forever with his shashka.

Vaja and Vitali, as ever a pair, flanked Gerlach as they came through the thickest part of the charging Kurgan line. Their swords hacked Northers off their mounts. They were closing tight on the foe's hideous standard and the brute on a striped horse-thing that carried it. Yevni and Kubah were hard at their backs.

Yuskel saw them coming, and raised his broadsword. Hzaer and Lyr plunged past him in defence. Hzaer thrust forward to reach the rota banner and kill its bearer, but Vitali locked with him and fought him saddle to saddle.

'Ride on!' Vaja shouted. 'Ride on, Vebla!' He was fending off Lyr's bill-tipped sword, his horse wounded and bleeding. Gerlach lurched Saksen on, trying to avoid the milling fighters around. Yevni and Kubah streaked past Gerlach and went straight for the enemy bearer. Kubah's sword tore through Yuskel's neck as he and Yevni flew by. Yuskel's striped beast brayed and kicked as Yuskel toppled from its back, and then ran. The warband's standard fell.

Yevni turned back, his horse's hooves slithering in the red-stained snow, trying to take the enemy standard as a trophy to break their morale.

Hzaer, in a hate-rage, wounded Vitali and broke off, covering the short distance to the fallen standard at a mad gallop. He struck Yevni off his mount with his first blow, and then hacked down into the head and shoulders of the fallen man as he tried to get up. Efgul appeared, took up the standard, and rode it clear.

Vaja saw all this as he stabbed his sword through Lyr's heart.

X

ZAR AZYTZEEN SAW the fluttering banner and the bearer on the red and white gelding. The Horse-of-Karl-Azytzeen shrilled as rowel spurs dug into its belly. It bolted forward. This was the one, Azytzeen knew. Even without the banner, this was the one. The inner sight Tchar had blessed him with was showing him that.

Gerlach saw the flash of gold and heard someone – Vaja or Vitali maybe – yelling his name in warning. The beast, the Khaos beast, that he had lost sight of in the mayhem of the horse fight, had reappeared now, and was riding him down.

That blue fire. Just the sight of it froze Gerlach's blood. As blue as the single blue eye he had seen in his fever-dreams. Not a prophecy at all. Just Dazh warning him what was coming.

His sabre was in his hand, his old demilance sabre. It did not seem weapon enough to fell a beast like this.

Gleaming riders suddenly rushed in and interposed themselves between the Khaos beast and the rota bearer. Beledni and Borodyn, rotamaster and horse master, side by side, confronting the charging zar. Neither one seemed remotely afraid.

Perhaps they should have been.

Zar Azytzeen's sword wounded Borodyn's mare so badly that it started to bolt, and then fell dead, throwing him to the ground. The fall, even onto snow, was so violent that Borodyn did not rise.

Beledni's shashka rang against the zar's pallasz. Sword masters both, they traded savage blow after blow, looking for the weaknesses in each other's guard.

Beledni found it, and struck in. His shashka broke against the warrior rings that cased the zar's right arm.

Zar Azytzeen swung his sword.

'Beledni!' Gerlach screamed. The rotamaster swayed for moment, then slipped gently out of his saddle.

Gerlach hurtled Saksen forward, screaming Beledni's name. He needed his sword now, and he needed his other hand on the reins to ride at such a rate. Without hesitation, he threw the rota banner into the snow and went straight at the murdering zar.

Azytzeen blinked at him. What he saw was a warrior, armed only with a cavalry sword, too deranged by anger and grief to be thinking clearly. It would be no effort to fend him off and kill him. That foolishly small sword...

A demilance sabre.

Karl-Azytzeen stared at the oncoming rider, and fixed him with the inner sight of Tchar.

He saw him, and knew him.

Gerlach Heileman. Why, of all the things Tchar had revealed to him, had this strange vision been left so late?

His great and bloody pallasz, rose in his hand for an easy kill. But he hesitated, for a second.

Gerlach's sabre, held at the charge position across his howling face, ripped down, tip-foremost, and ran through the zar's trunk, so deeply and so soundly the blade was snatched out of Gerlach's hand.

Gerlach pulled Saksen around for another pass. He drew his dagger in case the Khaos beast showed any signs of fighting on.

The zar lay on his back in the snow, dyeing it red. His golden helm had tumbled off.

The blue light had faded away completely.

He was dead.

Gerlach halted and gazed down. The zar's twisted face, ruined by scars, was somehow familiar to him.

Insanely, like the nonsense of a fever-dream, it was the face of Karl Reiner Vollen. But it was not. It was something that had once been called by that name. What had he become? What would he have become if Gerlach had not ended him here?

Gerlach shuddered, numb. If he had known for a moment the identity of his foe, perhaps he would have hesitated...

The sky was clearing as suddenly as it had gone black. In the wide plain, the great pulk, with renewed effort, was breaking the horde of Lenk and driving the remains of it back across a river that was in flood again.

Gerlach ignored his surroundings, caring little who won or lost now. He gathered up the fallen banner of the rota and walked to where Beledni lay. Borodyn, injured and in pain, knelt beside the rotamaster.

Gerlach crouched down too. There were tears in his eyes.

'Vebla not mourn. Is no time for grief,' Beledni sighed. 'Beledni rotamaster being dead for many years.'

Gerlach tried to stop his tears, but he could not manage it.

'You kill him, Vebla,' said Beledni. 'Like Dazh show you.'

'It was a circle, after all,' Gerlach said.

'Yha. Beledni rotamaster tell you this. But Vebla let banner fall.'

Gerlach shook his head and shrugged.

'Is of no matter,' he said.

PYRES

I

THEY BURIED BELEDNI and the other dead in the open steppe. The laden horses galloped away towards Dazh's fire. Gerlach hoped that when they ran out of earth to ride on, they would have wings to carry them onwards.

II

LATE IN THE spring, at Chamon Dharek, the last of the warband, who had fought to recover the body of their zar before fleeing the field at Mazhorod, laid him finally to rest.

They placed him in the golden mound, his wargear around him. Berlas laid a bow, unbroken, at his side.

The dauntless Horse-of-Karl-Azytzeen stood watch outside, its body stiff with fresh-hewn stakes, as the grave fires were lit. Hzaer blew a last, long blast upon his carnyx and Efgul shouted out the name.

'Azytzeen!'

III

THE SNOWS DEPARTED. The war across the world ground ever on. In the oblast, the spring freshened the land and clouds of mosquitoes rose from the melting ice. The rota lodged at Olcan Stanitsa to heal their wounds and recover their strength.

Gerlach had been unsettled for days. He was tired and longing for something he could not name.

Late one afternoon, as he stood in the yard and looked out across the steppe towards the reddening sky, he saw a cloud that looked like lambs suckling around a ewe, and knew that it was his time. That cloud had gone round the circle and now he had seen it twice. His journey was done.

He prepared Byeli-Saksen and put on his wargear. Vaja and Vitali sensed what was going on, but did not protest. They helped him don his gear. Gerlach gave the rota banner to Kubah.

'Guard him well,' he told Vaja and Vitali.

Then he rode out of the gates and into the steppe. Twilight was closing. Behind him, at the gateway of the stanitsa, Vaja and Vitali suddenly began shouting his name, as if they had changed their minds, and now hoped he would not ride away after all.

'Vebla!' they shouted, 'Vebla, yha!' over and over into the fading light. Gerlach did not look back. He rode towards the embrace of fate, and kept riding, until it was dark and the men, and the sound of their voices shouting his name, had faded entirely into the endless steppe.

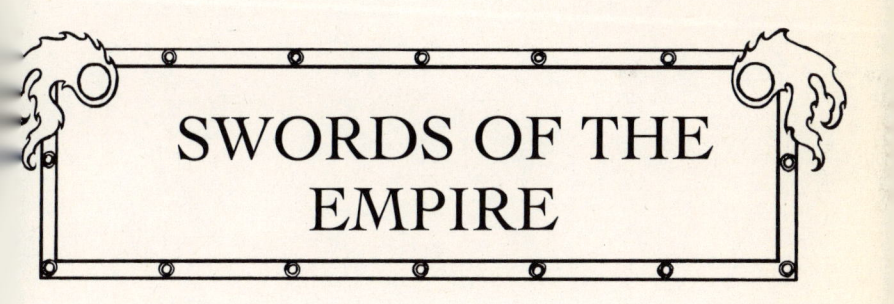

SWORDS OF THE EMPIRE

*'Two things that may be relied on– the swords of the Empire
and the snows of the North.'*

– Ostland proverb

I have known twenty-seven summers and twenty-six winters, and the winter that comes upon me now will be the hardest of all. With ample favour of fortune, we might weather these white months, but I have no wit to know for certain if fortune rides amongst my company in this extremity of the world. I doubt it greatly, for it has not shown us much of favour thus far along.

The provinces of the Empire wear winter like a heavy coat; they pull it around them in the latest part of the year and thuswise huddle within it, and cast it off again with a shrug at the first buds of spring. Not so here. This is the North, the high North, the wild, elder country. Here, winter comes from some profound source, and fills up the world from within, under the skin, freezing marrow to stone and slowing blood to glass. It is a foe of itself, and knows no quarter. Subarin has told me of it. He has described the cruel temper of the season, the furious storms, the aching arctic might. Men vanish, herds likewise, sometimes villages whole, lost overnight in the whiteness, marooned for months. And come the thaw, no sign remains, as if the poor, lonely places have been scraped from the hard ground by winter's sharp claws and cast into eternity.

Against such a sorry fate, I have guarded with this account. I have made it with haste, and for this reason I ask you to pardon kindly my mistakes. I am not a scribe, and my hands are not stained from the inkhorn. I am a soldier. I have rendered this in my best practice of penmanship on two tanned goat hides that in this country are employed in the part of vellum. The ink was purchased dearly at the cost of a company horse, and is the only flask of such hereabouts. It is poor stuff, weak and much more of water than of black. The wizard has ink bottles, of course, but I will not touch his belongings. When I have writ this out, I will roll the hides in a bag of pigskin, and bury it beneath a marked cairn of rocks here by the hillside trackway where, in spring, travellers may discover it. Such a discovery may be why you are reading this now. It is my hope that fortune will be with us, and that in spring, I will dig this up myself and convey it with all urgency back to the Reik. Either way, the matter of my account remains the same.

SIGMAR BLESS ME. I owned I was no scribe! I have just run my eyes back over the first part of my testament above, and damn myself at how badly I have commenced. I have run my heart ahead of my story, and scattered the facts heedless like a flock scattered by a wolf. Subarin tells me I can use the flat of a tanner's knife to scrape the hide clean and start again, but that seems a waste of such expensive ink. I will write on, and take heed of two lessons. Of the first, it is to cramp my hand smaller, for already I have occupied a whole shoulder of one hide with my words, and I fear the remainder of two goat-backs will not be adequate to contain this account. It is sobering indeed to realise that all that is important to me is to be measured out in goats.

Of the second, it is to start better. To make open the facts. First then, as I should have started, with my name. It is Jozef von Kassen. Let me make it again here, as I sign it – Jozef von Kassen – so that it vouches in my hand for the veracity of this account.

I have not goat enough to say more of myself in any length, and cannot set out the names of my family and lay down my lines of descent for fear of writing off the tail end of this hide onto the next. I will suffice with this: I am a knight of the Reiksguard, may Sigmar keep its light forever lit. It has been my signal honour to conduct, at the bidding of the Elector Counts, an expedition into the wastes that are known as Kislev, that is to say the barbarous sovereignty that is north of the Empire.

We left fair Altdorf on St Talve's Eve, he that is the patron saint of lambing. I had under my command twenty men at arms of the Reiksguard, all of horse with spears unto them, and including two handgunners. We made, as I may say, a sorry sight, for we had cast aside banners and decorations so as to pass unremarked upon in the isolate tracks beyond the Empire. This was on the advice of my masters. I myself had set aside my laurels, and my full plate, and even the barding of my steed. We wore simple half-plate, leather and cloaks, and some had hauberks of good chain. Had you come upon us in the driving rain, you would have mistaken us for brigands or a sell-sword company.

In this unseemly guise, we journeyed north, and performed our duty. To whit, this was to guard and escort a man of great worth. His name was Udo Jochrund, and he was a great wizard of the Order of the Wise, which is to say the Order of Light.

Like all mortal men, I am uncomfortable in the company of magic. It makes me to tremble, and turns my belly to acid. Sire Jochrund had the stuff around his person like a perfume. He was tall and slender, like the white aspens that grow in profusion in the lowlands of Kislev, his scalp shaved bald, with a great bounty of moustache and beard sweeping forth from his chin, cheeks and upper lip like a waterfall. This beard hair was dark, like charcoal, and seemed to clash at odds with the waxy pallor of his skin. His eyes, under bushy black brows, were brightly the colour of a harvest moon; that is like spun gold, like full-ripened corn, like a healthy gelding's urine. He wore long under-robes of earth-brown velvet, embroidered with many wondrous sigils and patterns in silver thread, and overtop he dressed in the long white caparison of his office and order. His hands were, in the most part of our adventure, gloved in glossy black leather, the rings worn glinting on the outside, and he carried the most curious carven staff, fully head-tall, worked in all intricacy to resemble a serpent coiled around a bough.

I have described him thus so you might know him by sight, but I have not described him at all. For it was in his manner that Udo Jochrund was known. Soft-voiced, let me start with that. Never a shout, never a bellow. His tone was as frail as a fallen leaf, dissolving in a trackway puddle, perfect in every detail yet insubstantial and fading like a spectre. Sometimes, from three furlongs distant, he had called to me, without any raising of his voice, and I had heard him most distinct. It was like he had quoth in my very head.

More so than his voice, his bearing. He was stiff and ungainly, gesturing in conversation with his elbows rather than his hands, as if he was afraid that more vital manners might cause his potent hands to write upon the air and manufacture magic unintended. More even than his voice, the smell of him. Like burned sugar-powder, but not rank. A sweet, sickly odour.

Sire Jochrund's mission was one of learning, as may be expected of an order whose purview is knowledge, and mine was to safeguard him. Before we set out, in the early part of spring, when I had been appointed to ride as his guard commander, he brought me to supper at his house. The food was ordinary, the atmosphere unnerving. By lamplight, in the late eve, his musty lodging was a place of jumping, darting shadows that could not be explained even by the flutter of the wicks.

I profess again, I am a soldier, nothing more or less, and have no sensibility for magic. I want no part of it, and would be glad never to have to acquaint myself with its actions. But yet, I am sanguine. Without the Colleges of Magic, and the martial magicians they have bred, our Empire would not stand today. In the van of every Imperial army stands a wizard from one or other order, bent to use his arcane might to achieve victory. Thus is the legacy of Teclis, who taught Magnus the Pious that magic was a necessary art, and one to be practised and honed, even in an honest and Sigmar-fearing country like ours.

At supper, in that haunted chamber, Sire Jochrund seemed to sense my distress, and made every effort to console my mind. He explained, in basic terms, the purposes of the Colleges of Magic, the nature of the eight orders, and the pertinence of his own, the first and most lauded order. Much of what he said I already knew, but it was the way he told it to me. He spoke, I suppose, as to a child eager to learn. I was transfixed by his voice, and by the way he kept on his glossy black gloves even when using the meat fork and tearing the soda-bread.

'I will explain the venture before us, von Kassen,' he declared, 'for I want you to understand it rightly, so that you will play your part unquestioningly. Magic is without—'

'Without what?' quoth I, in all innocence.

'Without us!' he cried with a tremendous laugh at the expense of my foolishness. 'It is all around us, it permeates the world, soaks into the fibres of the land. It is a fact of life. Deny it and you deny reality. The colleges do not create magic, they tap into it, harness it, use it, and direct it. Our skills are not those of creation, they are of comprehension.'

I nodded at that, though without much of the quality in question.

Then he bade me answer this: 'Why am I a wizard and you a soldier?'

I shook my poor head. Answers I had, in all truth, many, numbering amongst them merits of birth and demeanour, but the reply he was after was much simpler yet.

'Because you are trained in the use of horse and lance and sword, and I am trained in the use of the arcane.'

This much I had fathomed for myself. Then he said, 'Each order has unto itself its own discipline. For the Golden Order, alchemy. For the Grey Order, shadow. For the Amber Order, beastcraft… and such wise. The Light Order binds them all, for it is through us the knowing of their ways were divined. We scour and search, we find and collect, we catalogue and translate. We are the seekers of lore. We are the pathfinders of lost magics, or magics yet unknown to civilised man. And that is our endeavour now. A threat is rising in the North, von Kassen, a great and divisive threat that mayhap will tumble our proud Empire into dust.'

'May Sigmar guard us!' I said at once.

'May he indeed,' he agreed. 'But we may also guard ourselves. We have wrung the byways and remote villages of the Empire dry of lore, but in the realm of Kislev, rude magic abounds. Up in that great expanse are tiny communities and forgotten towns where shamans and wise-folk daily practise routines of lore and craft unknown to us. It may be that their very proximity to the wastes of Chaos means they are more connected to the source than us.'

At his mention of the word, I shuddered. He pulled aside his white robe and showed me an eight-pointed star sewn in silver on his tunic.

'Do you know this, von Kassen?'

I blanched and felt I should reach for my sword.

He saw me. He read me. He smiled. 'The octo-point star of Chaos. Eight fiery limbs, young man. Tell me... why are there eight Colleges of Magic?'

I stammered dumbly.

'Because,' he sighed, 'Chaos is the root of all magic. This much Teclis taught us. From their eight sorcerous winds, all magic derives. Be not afraid. Magic stems from Chaos, and is tainted by it, but it may be controlled and purified by a trained practitioner. Such is the purpose of the eight orders. And to discover such control is the purpose of the Light Order. In the scattered settlements of Kislev, in the tribal conclaves of the empty quarters, lore is waiting to be uncovered from the elders and shamans. Over the last nine years I have conducted seven missions to the North at the bidding of the elector counts. I tour the lonely stanitsas to learn new skills, new secrets, new crafts that have lain in their folk-rituals since the dawn of time.'

This, then, was our purpose. To ride north and protect Sire Jochrund as he sampled and collected, learning and borrowing and otherwise obtaining new rudiments of magic from the outlying barbarians so that the craft might be employed for the good of our Empire.

The wizard showed me the letters of permission and sealed charters from the princes that bade him do this thing. I needed no further convincing. In the Empty Quarter, this Imperial wizard might learn charms that could keep the Empire of Man standing for another thousand years, no matter what threat arose from the wild wastes.

We passed beyond the bounds of the Ostermark at the spring equinox, the rivers running hard and foamy with meltwater from the highlands. The air was brittle, like ice. Our convoy was as thus: twenty men at arms, shrouded in tan cloaks, myself, Sire Jochrund on his black gelding, besides a storewagon driven by the sire's apprentice, Sigert.

Rain beset us for the first month, then gales that rattled the moon on its hook. By the time the gales settled, we were far into Kislev itself, crossing the grasslands and the pine barrens from village to village. Time ground over and around, like a working millstone, slow, heavy and wearing. I had been in Kislev twice before, on military tours. I knew its vastness, the open flatness of its plains, the force of its winds. I felt them again on my face and wondered how many of them were driven by the eight winds of Chaos.

To a man birthed and raised in the forests and mountains of the Empire, Kislev is a formidable country. It has an expanse that I have not experienced anywhere else, nor can truly describe. The vast sky bends over it in supplication, where the sky in Imperial lands flutters above the peaks like a banner. Even in summer, sleet and hail come down from nowhere, horizontal. It stings the skin. The sun comes out, like a phantom, and chases down over distant hills. The nights seem long, breathless.

But I must confess, I like these wilds. The air is clear like crystal, the winds – whatever their origin – fresh and uplifting. Where there is flatness – the steppes, as they are called – there is total flatness, and nodding grasses nod forever to eternity. Where there are mountains, they rise suddenly, like giant's teeth, vast and snow-capped even in the heat of summer, colossal and overwhelming.

Through this, we tracked, following the wizard. I have not hide enough, nor ink enough, to remark upon all the particulars. We followed lonely drove tracks far up into the mountains. We came upon little places that had hidden themselves for ten thousand years. Stanitsas, they are called. Villages, in my tongue. Some perched on river bends, others hidden in secret, misty valleys. A few sat, proud and untamed, in the centre of vast steppe plains, like crowns discarded on the earth. One we came to was shrouded in an aspen forest. Another clung to a crag over the deepest gorge I have ever seen. Water tumbled below, as fulsome and fierce as the wizard's beard.

We spent a day at each, no more than two. The hospitality was astonishing. They lit their fires high and brought us in, and slaughtered a good many goats and hogs for spitting. We were given koumiss to drink – that is fermented mare's milk – as a welcoming gift from the ataman chiefs, and also stronger concoctions delivered with a pinch of salt. At every stop, the Kislevites knew how to drink and how to entertain.

At every village, Sire Jochrund withdrew with the esauls and the stanitsa shaman. He talked with them into the night, as moths braved the campfires in vast, dusty hosts. He learned. He collated.

On we went. The summer lengthened. A stanitsa greeted us, sparse on the plain, surrounded by eight sacred trees. Another, built on the summit of a granite crag like a tooth of the world, with steps hewn out of the living rock. Yet another, walled and discrete, surrounded at all sides by a lake of blue flowers, sprung from the dust, nodding in the breeze.

I remember telling Sire Jochrund that we should return. The summer was waning. Already, a taint of cold could be felt in the air.

He refused me, avowing that one last stop was in order. He'd learned such stuff at the last stanitsa (a walled township overlooking a gloomy vale), that he wanted to press on. Just a week more. Seven days.

That was when we came upon Kzarla. It lay beside a lake in the hills, and the lake lay in the ground like a black blade lying on grass.

But I forget myself! I must tell you of Subarin. And also of the fight. Ah, once more my story-wolf goes scattering my facts!

Fortune had been with us enough, at least, to keep fighting away. For the most part, at any rate. At Zhedevka, two of my men, whose names are – no, I will not name them. I punished them at the time. If this account is to be our last testament, I will not defame them with a slight injury. So let it be said that at Zhedevka, two of my party were embroiled in a tavern fight over some no-matter. In the elm brakes above Kacirk, where the grey Kislev sky seems to run unnaturally fast, and shushes through the swaying branches like a river torrent, we skirmished with some painted raiders who were swift discouraged by the use of handguns. Then at Vitzy, along the great shingle beaches of the river, we fought for an hour or so with robbers and bandits who came down out of the pine woods. There were above forty of them, and we traded steel with them all the way down to the stepping stone crossing where the river bends, at no loss of our own. We made account of four of them, and packed them off to their indifferent sky-god.

But that was all the bother for a long summer's riding, and grateful we were.

Until Svedora.

The wizard had made much of Svedora. It had been mentioned to him several times by the various elders and atamans he had interviewed during our trek, and he had made note of it at length in his chapbooks. It was a cattle town of some size, on the eastern slopes of the Czegniks, facing down across a wide valley girt with oak, myrtle and sandalwood towards the wide, mustard-yellow spring pastures by the reedy river.

Svedora was said to be a town steeped in magic – cattle magic, weather magic, old magic. We were told a shaman lived there still who knew much of the old ways.

I could feel Sire Jochrund's eagerness. Quite how much he had collected from the summer mission thus far I could not say. His chapbooks and scroll cases bulged, and he was forever writing. He had filled sacks with herbs and dried powders, flowers too, and had a little screw-press with which to flatten the blooms into perfect pictures of themselves. Bottles he had of tinctures given him by elders and wise men, and all other sundry totems and materials, all of which the sallow clerk Sigert catalogued and annotated.

Occasionally, most often after nightfall in our latest camp, I would observe the wizard striding out of the way to a field or spot nearby where he would perform – I believe in practise – rituals he had but recently learned. With what measure of success I cannot say. Once we heard a moaning in the dark that put the horses sore afeared; once he caused a blue flame to walk across the surface of a pool, and once he made a great dusty wind to blow up, and came back to us, his eyes reddened, cursing some nameless spirit for at least two days.

Sire Jochrund had his heart set on Svedora, even though on my map it lay a good three days further than I was happy to go. But on we went.

A great number of black starlings began to gather above us for the two days prior to our arrival at the stanitsa. A few at first, circling and twittering, then more, then more. We touched iron against ill-omen, and the wizard seemed bothered by the mob, but in the bracken fields below Svedora, with the walled town overlooking us, they departed most suddenly and flew off cheeping and piping into the western sky.

But our arrival had been noted, and a line of riders galloped out from the gatehouse and threaded a line of dust down the hill track towards us. I saw the flash of sunlight on speartips and armour.

I drew the company to a stand, and stretched them in a line abreast, alert but with weapons sheathed, with the wagon held to the rear. The riders came out of the trees and formed a matching line facing us at a distance of three furlongs.

Sigmar, but they were splendid. Thirty men in golden hauberks, and kettle-helms with nose-guards, decorated with bright jewellery, furs and expensive cloths. Upright from their backs rose the most remarkable wings of bright feathers, part of their decorative harness. Their horses were small, shaggy-maned creatures that had been painted shades of white, yellow, russet and pink. The men sported long, black moustaches and carried horse lances upright at their saddles. One held aloft a bright blue and white banner with a long swallowtail that turned and played in the wind like a water-snake.

They were not the enemy. They were a proud company of Kislevite lancers, of a type long renowned in the Empty Quarter. We however – travel-stained, dusty and displaying no flag or banner – resembled their traditional enemy, the plains bandit, all too well.

I left my spear standing tip-down in the dirt, and rode forward, gesturing to Schroder to do the same. Schroder was my first officer, and sergeant of the men-at-arms, a decent fellow from Ostland who had a useful measure of the Kislevite tongue. We covered the scrubby ground between the two facing lines, and after a moment, two riders broke from their formation and came towards us at a trot. I was encouraged to see they left their lances in the earth likeways.

Closer to, I was yet more transfixed by the ornate beauty of their armour. Gold, inlaid with turquoise and pieces of jet, and also a translucent orange gem called amber. Their horse armour was accoutred in jingling tassels and bead-ropes, and with medals or badges made of smoky silver inset with blue-glass stones. Their wings rose high above their backs, straight and true, formed of gilded wooden frames to which dyed eagle feathers had been expertly fletched. The valley wind rustled them and made the feathertips twitch, like the trim of a circling hawk. The brass nasal-guards of the riders' helms descended sharply almost to the lips, and gave them both a mean and snarling look.

Through Schroder, I greeted them, and made it as clear as I could our intentions were peaceful. They listened attentively, but made no change of expression, nor did they show any signs of comprehension. I produced the Imperial seal, and also my letters of permission, one of which was counter-sealed by the provost of the tzarina. The two men passed the items between themselves and muttered. Then one turned his painted pony smartly and raced off in the direction of their line, taking my letters and seal with him.

'Hie!' I exclaimed in consternation, and the rider who had stayed with us at once growled some caution, and drew his sabre enough that four fingers' width of blue-steel blade was visible outside its jewelled scabbard.

I raised my hands for peace and waited. The rider came clattering back, and brought with him another. This lancer was as finely amour-clad as the others, though he seemed at once to have some bearing the others did not quite possess.

'I have read your letters,' he said, using the language of the Reik perfectly.

'I would have ridden to you at once had I known. You carry no banner, and seemed to us to have the look of raiders.'

'Your pardon, sir,' I replied. 'We have sought to conduct our errand as anonymous travellers rather than as a mission of the Imperial crown.'

He nodded, and handed me back my belongings. 'These are unruly times. Welcome to Svedora, Sire von Kassen. I am named Subarin, of the rota of Svedora krug.'

A rota, as I had discovered earlier in the summer, was the Kislevite word for banner, and every town and stanitsa had its own. Around that banner, the town's band of lancers would form, their gathering known by the symbolic word 'krug', of which is meant 'circle'. A stanitsa's rota of lancers was sworn to protect both its own town and the community in the region round it. In return, the community of town and country funded the splendid armour and weapons of the riders. Settlements took special pride in this: a rota might be small or large, but it was always splendid. At times of great war, the rotas of all the towns in a region would form together into an army or 'pulk', supplemented by infantry and bowmen drawn from levies.

The Svedoran rota gallantly escorted my company up the trail and into the town itself. Subarin was not the 'rotamaster' – the honour of commanding the lancers fell to a slender, older man named Buryan. But Subarin – who, when he removed his helm, was revealed to be a commanding fellow with close-set green eyes that seemed quick and clever – was a man of education who had spent time in the Empire, and his fluency with my language accorded him the duty of dealing with Imperial matters.

Svedora had a commanding position above the valley, its size well disguised by the stands of myrtle and oak that lined the slopes. To its west, above the aspen-shingled roofs of the town, and the golden onion dome of its zal, the ragged foothills of the Czegniks rose away, half-hidden in garlands of cloud. The town, and its walls, were made of clay, baked into pink blocks that reminded my eye of the sugar and gelatine fancies they sometimes serve at court. The place was old indeed. On some walls were carvings, weathered by the fingers of time. They showed winged lancers with couched spears, men riding wolves, and nymphs of the myrtle woods.

The townsfolk came out, and made loud welcome, ringing handbells, chimes and tambors. We were greeted well, and fed, and our horses were cared for. One thing above all else that may be admired of the Kislevite: he values the horse, and knows its keeping.

We were presented to the ataman, and to sundry other estimable men, but the town's shaman we did not see. At length, Sire Jochrund and his clerk were taken to meet with the wise man in some secret place. They did not return until the next morning.

That night, I spoke with Subarin. 'Do you always ride out in full gear at the first sign of riders in the valley?' I asked of him.

'There had been auguries,' he said. 'Symbols in nature that the shaman warned us of. We thought evil rode with you.'

'Just magic,' I said.

He nodded, and swallowed a glass of samogon as a vouchsafe against ill-omen.

We spoke then of other matters, mostly of horses, in which Subarin took a particular interest. He made comment favourably on the warhorses my company rode, especially my own great destrier, all markedly larger beasts than the lancers' mounts. 'That was the first clue I had that you were not bandits… the size of your steeds. Only knights of the Empire and Bretonnia put the spur to warhorses of such measure.'

Subarin, it was revealed, owed his reputation and wealth to horse trading. He was esteemed across the region for his expertise in that wise, and the business had taken him as far as Middenheim in his younger days. He told me that night of the Kurgan, the ravagers who dwelt in the North. They too rode great warsteeds, he said, but there is no trade in them for they cannot be caught, let alone broken by civilised men.

At dawn, Sire Jochrund's clerk returned to us, his narrow eyes filled with sleep from a night spent in wakefulness. He told me (quite uncivilly, for he believed the eminence of his master bestowed some rank upon him also) that Sire Jochrund would be staying at this place for another two days, for he was engaged in great discourse with the wise man, and refused to be taken from it. To his sullen face, I told him that this was not to my liking. I had already urged the wizard that we should be commencing our return journey. Sigert shrugged, as if to dismiss me, and I urged him a second time to impress upon Sire Jochrund the gathering urgency of our departure. That morning, there had been frost upon the clay walls of Svedora, and a glassy cool in the air.

An hour or so presently, Sire Jochrund himself reappeared, and took me to one side for quiet words. There was an almost unseemly excitement about him, and his golden eyes darted all about. In his soft voice, he assured me we had to stay a while, for which news he was sorry.

'If we ride away now, Jozef, we risk losing the very worth of our mission. There is lore here, young man, that the Colleges of Magic must possess.'

He had begun to call me Jozef most frequently, as if I were his son, and perhaps it should have flattered me that he thought so. But it rankled me. I was ever courteous to him, calling him most formally 'Sire', yet he showed my office of knighthood no comparable respect.

Still, I consented to his wishes. I imagine it is hard for an ordinary mortal man, even a trained warrior of the Reik, to say no to a wizard, and to this soft-voiced, golden-eyed magician, it was impossible.

Sometimes, I fancied he had put some conjuration on me.

So, we waited for two days. The horses were glad of the rest, the men too. Some took the time to wash clothing or repair their wargear and trappings and resharpen their blades. Others shaved their cheeks and chins of beards that had grown on the journey. I did not. My hair, which usually I wore shaved up about the nape and ears, as is the custom beneath bascinet helms, had grown out, and my face was decorated with a bristle of beard. I had vowed not to cut nor trim the hair of my head until my return, as a mark of dedication to my mission, in Sigmar's name.

Subarin noticed that I was ill at ease and, in company of some of his fellow lancers, diverted my mind with hunting trips into the forest. We caught nothing but a few dapple-deer, for it was an excuse to ride free and fast, and forget troubles. The men of the rota had put off their fine armours, and dressed themselves in leathers and furs, but I noticed that Subarin still carried a fine saddle-sword, broad and straight, of the most exquisite damascened working, with all finery of lions and horsemen upon the golden scabbard. He saw me admire it, and showed it me, claiming it was many generations old, though the blade seemed new struck. A Scythian sword, he said, forged and owned by the great horse people that had once roamed these regions before the Gospodar khans led the Kislevite tribes to mastery of the land. Beside it, my Imperial blade seemed crude and dull.

In the landscape about Svedora, there were many curious places, shown to me by the worthy Subarin. A heathland upon which great stones stood in a ring, into which area no bird or animal made noise or motion. Other stones, graven with weather and lichen, had all but worn smooth, stood in glades of the woodland, and amongst the dense steppe thistles that choked the ravines of fast, falling streams.

In another place, very deep in the darkest belt of the woodland, my companions drew me to a ruinous tower that lingered amidst many tall maple trees. It was made of a black stone, finely dressed so as to be smooth, and was fully twenty horse lengths around about the base. At the height of a goodly oak, the tower was split asunder and broken, suggesting that once the tower had soared unto the sky. No fallen blocks or splinters of black stone remained around its base to attest to the disaster that had befallen it, nor did any of the fine maples grow within ten lengths of it, and further, no ivy or mosses lived upon its smooth, cyclopean walls. We rode about it thrice, widdershins as Subarin insisted, and I remarked that no door or window slit could be found in its sides. It was a mystery, he agreed, and it seemed that was why he had chosen to show it to me. None could say who had raised it, or when, or by what mischance it had come to be destroyed. When I asked him if any man had ever assayed to climb the walls and enter the tower through the broken top part, he laughed, as if such a thought was madness. I thanked him for showing me such a strange wonder, but were happy in my heart to ride away from that eerie glade.

In the early part of the morning of the third day, without reference to Sire Jochrund or his mealy-mouthed clerk, I roused the men and set the company for departure. All drawn up, we waited the length of an hour, and then, as I was about to send for the wizard, he appeared with Sigert in tow. His work in Svedora was done, he proclaimed, and for a moment, my heart was happy.

But then he gave me new instruction. From the wise man of Svedora, he had learned of a place called Kzarla, which lay up in the hills, and this place he now intended to visit also. His eagerness to reach Kzarla was even greater than it had been to come to Svedora. 'Seven days, Jozef, seven days there and back,' he told me, 'and then our work will be truly done!'

I made protest, but it was to no avail. We were to Kzarla bound, whatever I liked of it.

As we made to depart the gates of Svedora, the men of a mood quite downcast at the further travail, Subarin rode to us with two of his comrades. They were dressed in furs and cloaks for travel, but beneath wore the bright armour of their kind. Their lances and wings were wrapped in bundles across the backs of their steeds, and their golden spike-helms bounced at their waists. Subarin hailed me. At the advice of the town elders, he would ride in our company, so as to guide us directly to lonely Kzarla. This much he did to make as short as possible our journey, for he said the tracks of the hills were treacherous and befuddling to the newcomer. With his aid, we could make the ride as short as possible, and so speed the hour of our return. I thanked him for it, as did my sire the wizard.

They led us away from Svedora in the morning light, turning north and west into the ranges of the Czegniks, ascending steep tracks that wound between the stands of larches and mountain ash. The air was chill and damp, and there was no colour in the sky. Svedora's pink walls vanished below us in the mist, and above, the hills rose grey and severe, with the purple threat of greater summits beyond them.

The three Kislevites rode sure-footedly. Subarin's comrades were named Baibek and Markovo. Baibek was a small man with intense grey eyes, like a snow-owl, and his face was set always in a frown. Markovo was of larger build, with a wide jaw and half-shut eyes. He had a bright smile that he flashed like a sword blade.

Despite our guides, the going was slow, for the track was scarcely fit for our small wagon. We laboured in dim, tree-lined vales, and crawled up the black soil paths between rock crests, passing more than once marvellous cascades of water that fell in crashing, smoking streams into dark plunges below, bright as the girl's hair in the storybook.

Two days we laboured, up into the hills, passing so high above the table of the earth that we left all sign of trees behind. The hill country was heath and coarse grass, bramble and thistle, all swayed by the winds that blew down across these sloping pastures. Low cloud veiled the land, and brought rain and some little hail to us. Winter, I knew full well, was all but upon us.

Half a day from Kzarla, Subarin advised caution. Baibek had been riding ahead to scout the bleak country, and had returned with word that we were not the only riders abroad in the hills. From a distance, he had sighted a band of warriors on horseback, and counted forty shields. We paused, and made secure our armour, cinching it tight and placing helms upon our heads. We eased our swords in their sheaths, and made other preparation as necessary, then moved on again, following the track into a vale swirling with mist and vapour. Strange ringing and moaning came upon our ears, but Subarin told me this was but the echo of our traces and the song of the wind amongst the peaks.

Barely was I reassured than we were attacked.

They were, as I learned after, warriors of a brute-clan called the Kul, one of the many fraternities of Kurgan who claimed sovereignty of the North, and who knew only the worship of the feral gods and daemons in their savage minds. They thundered out upon us on their braying nags, full tilt, raising up a din of raw voices and furious howls. Each one of them was of mighty frame, dark-haired with unruly, matted locks, and they wore great pitch-black helms fixed most fearfully with horns and tusks. Beads and shells and also scalps and talismans rattled against their painted chests.

I gave sharp order and turned the company into their face, rising our pace to a counter-charge, for there was no wise of retreat or flight. I drew my sword and in we went, hooves clattering on the flinty soil, harnesses ringing. We shouted aloud the war cry of Sigmar to drown out their grim holler, and mingled with it I heard the battle call of the rota fly out from Subarin's lips. His glorious golden sword was flashing in his hand.

Such impact is made when charge meets charge. There are many distinct sounds of war – the clash of sword blades, the whistle of the axe, the thump of the arrow, the crack of gunpowder – but to my mind, there is no sound more true to the spirit of battle than the bone-shaking clash of riders crossing riders. It is the sound of knightly combat, where strength and skill are contended in equal measure. And it is not merely a sound. It is an uncommon jolt, a quake, like rocks smiting against one another, like a tree's trunk splitting, like a mountain falling down upon the flat earth.

Into their fury we raced, and that sound of impact was made. My blade was held out wide, and through it I felt the jar of collision, turning a rider back off his steed in a wild flailing that tossed broken tatters of his shield into the sky. Then another Kul went by at my left side, and down I sat so that my head might escape his swinging axe. To the right again, and a third raider, standing in his stirrups to stab at me with a pig-spear as he passed. He had not, I fancy, met a knight of the Reiksguard before, for there was a measure of surprise upon his horrid face as my sword broke his spear and clove in through his side to the breastbone, wrenching him off his horse in one action.

All around me, men were yelling and chargers snorting. The vale rang with the noise of traded blows. I heard the handgunners in my company volley their shots. Heavy crashes resounded as horses and men tumbled down. Two Kul spurred forward at me, both with swords, but I met them without falter, and did for one right swiftly, striking my blade across his neck.

The other lunged and made to cut me, and for his trouble I struck of his sword-arm at the joint, causing a goodly measure of hot blood to gout into the air. Schroder flew past me, with Konstanz, Lipfert and Brendel, all four furnished with spears they had couched point forward. Their course brought them hard into a quintet of Kul riders, and spear hafts clattered and snapped as three of the enemy were bowled over onto the ground. His spear lost, Schroder swept out his own sword, and laid about him, cutting the skull-top away from one passing Kul, so that his wretched body flopped sideways and was dragged by his frantic steed, plashing the liquor of his brain across the stones.

Near at hand, another Kul warrior, a very large creature with a ribbed hauberk of iron, was knocked from his saddle with mighty force as a javelin transfixed his torso through, front unto back. Markovo galloped past me, and I saw that it had been his sure hand that had launched the throwing spear to such fatal effect.

A further two Kul fell to my sword as I plunged into the thick of them, and a scrape I took across the left arm for my trouble. A third then, howling like a dog-fox, seemed hungry for my blade too, so I gave it him, and thank you kindly sir, and ripped out his lights with its sharpness before he could even bring his axe towards me.

I heard then a sharp cry aside me over the din of combat, and turned my head and horse in distress to see that Schroder had been cast off his steed onto the ground, with a wound upon his hip. Three of the enemy had dismounted in glee to rend him apart where he lay. I leapt from my own saddle, and ran in amongst them, killing two before they had even realised the peril at their heels. The third turned on me with his warsword, and met my blade with a loud chime of metal. Before I had yet finished him, more had run in, brandishing their filthy black swords and axes, howling for my blood and Schroder's. I put my will into my arm and my sword into their flesh, crashing them over, ripping them aside, striking them back so that, 'ere long, the ground was all of wringing wet with their heathen blood, and my vestments and armour were greatly besmirched too. Bodies piled around me, and it seemed the sight of such a number of their dead made them, in rage, strive yet more earnestly for my murder. All at once, a golden sword was cutting through their painted flesh and hairy backs, breaking spines and shattering jaws. Subarin, slight and small compared to the massive tribesmen, was yet making trophies of them, the splendid glitter of his armour seeming him to appear like a fine god amid the rude beasts.

Through force of arms, we cut our way to each other, breaking their shields and their hopes, and found, in the space of a heartbeat, the enemy had failed and fled. A dozen or so of the Kul galloped away up the valley in frantic flight, leaving a grievous number of their kin dead amongst the gorse and thistle, their horses scattering loose, bridles dragging.

I took quick account, and called the company to order, sending three men to round up my horse and the others that had gone free. Subarin, delighted by the victory, clapped his hands around my own, and all were bloody with our deeds.

Three men of my company were dead. I write their names here as memorial to their courage, for their lonely graves will like as not never be found in these remote hills. They were Mannfred Kruz of Altdorf, Lodmir Ameling, also of that town, and Sigmund Manhart of Talabec. Four more, including Schroder, had taken wounds, but none that could not be salved and bound so they might continue able.

The Kul dead, of which there were a great many, we left upon the cold earth, their split bodies steaming out their life-heat into the mountain air.

Lipfert brought my horse back to me, and as I rose into the saddle once more, I praised Subarin for his help, and also for the efforts of his comrades. He greatly surprised me by returning my praise tenfold. He had, it seemed, seen men of the Empire in battle, and these had not disgraced themselves, but he had never yet seen a knight of the Reiksguard in full fury. I believe I had impressed him greatly, and this made me feel pride in my rank and office, though I rued that he had not seen me girt in my full plate and caparison, for there is no finer sight in war than a knight of the Empire in his livery.

Thereafter, I rode to where the wagon stood. Sigert was pale of face, and was sipping wine from a flagon. Sire Jochrund dismounted and also praised me for my efforts, wishing that I communicate his gratitude to the company, and commiserating over the dead.

I felt foolish, but I questioned him. He was a great wizard, schooled in battle magic, yet he had not been able to intercede in this bloody fight. Could he not have conjured some marvelous spell that would have sent the Kul running, and spared our pains and our losses?

Sire Jochrund smiled, as if not slightly rebuked, and apologised, saying that he had been sleeping in the wagon when the attack began, and by the time he had roused, the fight was all around, with friend and foe intermingled in a terrible confusion. He had certain spells, but he feared to cast them lest their deadly enchantments smite down men of the company in error.

This seemed answer enough, though it did not please me. And he called me by the name of 'Jozef' again. We drew to order, and made on for Kzarla.

It was a dismal place, in a long valley high amongst the hills, remote and unked. It stood upon the shores of a long lake, where the waters were so cold and black, like obsidian glass, that there was no assaying its depth. The ibzas and halls of the town were dark and timber built, and the wood thereof must have been drawn up this distance from the lowlands under the hills. Kzarla was girt about by a picket of stakes, and also by a ditch and bank in the shape of a circle. As we approached the place, I spied what seemed to be an island in the lake, close to the shore where the village stood, and joined unto the shore by a causeway of stone and timber that seemed some three horse lengths long.

The rota of Kzarla came out to meet us. Three dozen men, in silver armour bright as the sky, their mail shirts fixed with ingots of polished jet. Their horses were tinted coal-black along the backs and powder white upon the legs and bellies, and silver bells had been threaded into the hair of their tails and manes. Each rider wore a black horsehair plume upon the spike of his silver helm. One carried the banner, fluttering upon a long pole, and this was a triangle of black with a key-patterned edge, with a silver circle in the centre. They seemed surprisingly prepared for battle, but if warbands of Kul and their ilk were haunting the highlands, then it was meet that they should be ready to drive them off.

They were a fierce sight, and had already drawn forth their shashkas, that is their war swords. Their painted horses pawed the ground, as if eager for the charge.

We came to a halt. Subarin nudged his mare forward, and gestured for me to accompany him.

'I will come also,' Sire Jochrund said, already astride his black steed.

Subarin nodded his assent, and the three of us rode across the lakeside heath towards the Kzarlan rota. None came out to meet us. They kept their line and waited until we had drawn up face to face. Only then, the wings of their line moved outwards, so that Subarin, the wizard and myself were flanked within a semicircle of silver-armoured riders.

Subarin dismounted and walked to their lead horseman, a tall grey-bearded warrior with silver wings rising from the cheek-guards of his helm. Subarin then made greeting, and the two conversed at length. I did not follow the words, but Subarin made courteous gesture over his shoulder at the pair of us, and the winged leader glanced our way, as if reviewing cattle he was being invited to purchase.

Then Subarin turned and beckoned. I thought he meant me, but he did not. He brought Sire Jochrund forward, and introductions were made. I sat alone, the eyes of the silver warriors upon me, to my disquiet.

The Kzarlan rotamaster – whose name I was to learn as Pyotr Gmelin – raised a polished bone horn and blew, and the strong, pure note was answered by two horns at the stanitsa fence. He motioned us to follow as he turned his rota at a swift trot towards the gate.

Subarin turned to me. 'Bring the company, Sire von Kassen. They will admit us to the krug.'

The summer's mission had shown me that there are few more honestly welcoming places in the world than a Kislevite stanitsa. The gathering of folk, the drumming and clapping, the unbidden food and hearty toasts. All who come to the krug are welcome guests for as long as they desire, no matter what their wealth or status.

But the Kzarlan welcome was a different matter. Villagers came out to stare upon us as we came in through the gate, but their faces were unfriendly and they made no clamour. Untethered goats ran to and fro across the black mud of the trackway. Eyes stared at us from the flaps of windows and doors. No one brought out flatbread, or pickled fish, or koumiss.

In a bare mud yard before the longhouse, the rota dismounted and led their horses away. The ataman, an old, robed man with a limp who leaned upon a gnarled stick, came out with his esaul and two swordsmen, and spoke with Subarin and Pyotr Gmelin. Then he hobbled down from the timber boarding, and solemnly greeted Sire Jochrund. Thereafter, he came to me, and placed his knobbly hands upon mine, and looked at me with rheumy eyes.

'Welcome,' he said.

I had the company make good the horses, and some modest fodder was brought. I went into the longhouse with Subarin, the wizard and his clerk at the invitation of the ataman. Pyotr Gmelin and four of his rota watched over us as we sat by the fire and took at last a little food and drink.

After some lengthy discussion, most all of which I could not follow, the shaman of Kzarla came forth from some secret chamber in the back of the longhouse. He was a shrivelled thing, with a weather-beaten face as lined and dry as a saddle kit. He wore hides all sewn along the edges, and marked with the figures of men and horses embroidered into the front of it. Beads hung around his thin neck in long strings. He carried a round tambor in one hand, and struck upon it slowly with a tasselled wooden rod as he walked around Sire Jochrund in wary circles. Then – once, I presume, the shaman's spirits were placated by the rite – the wise man and the wizard sat down apart from us and fell to talking.

I grew fatigued and walked beyond the walls of the longhouse, biding my time. I wandered along the boardwalk laid out above the silt at the back of the longhouse, and looked upon the causeway that led out to the island. It was a strange place: a mound of rock rising just above the surface of the black water, upon which some structure like a tent or a steppe yurt was raised. Its canvas sides were finely decorated with sewn patterns and shell beading. I wondered what it was for.

I saw the girl at that time. She came out of the yurt on the islet and walked back down the causeway towards me carrying a pot under one arm and a sheaf of herbs under the other. I had seen women in the stanitsa as we were riding in, but none so young or fair as this girl. Her skin was pale, and her long hair as shining and dark as the jet in the rota's armour.

She walked past me, her head straight as if to ignore me, but I saw her eyes dart my way in curiosity. Such a proud face. Such blue eyes!

Subarin came to find me, noticing the girl with an appreciative smile as he passed her.

'Your wizard and the shaman are set for a long night of talking. I think the shaman wishes to test your lord's prowess in the ways of magic before he allows his guard down. The ataman has said he will provide food tonight for your company, but after that, you and your men must withdraw from the stanitsa for the night.'

'Why?' I asked.

'It is a ritual time, preparing rites to announce the coming winter. No stranger may reside within the town ditch during such a sacred period.'

'Where are we supposed to stay?' I wondered, glancing at the sky which, already cold, was sharpening with the real bite of chill darkness.

Subarin pointed. At the far end of the stanitsa, outside the gateway and beyond the ditch, men of the village were raising a large yurt on the heathland. That was to be our accommodation.

'For all of us?' I asked.

Subarin nodded. 'Even myself and my comrades. Only your lord and his clerk are excepted, as a special case. Come, we must bring our horses out too.'

We set to it. Above, the night drew down, and the stars came out in the inky firmament. The glittering northern constellations of the gelding, the maiden, the kolter and the targette.

They fed us well, before a great fire, and entertained us with tunes upon the mandore, pibau and horse-head fiddle. Subarin brought the rotamaster Pyotr Gmelin to meet me. He had taken off his armour now, and wore wolf furs as grey as his beard. He poured fierce samogon into silver mazers for the three of us. Subarin had been commending my virtues as a warrior-knight to the noble rotamaster, and Pyotr Gmelin wanted to decide upon my merits for himself. He asked me, through Subarin's translations, various technical questions about swordsmanship, the use of horse companies in war, the couching of a spear, the functions of a shield, and thus like, and seemed suitably content by the answers I gave him.

'He contends,' Subarin said, 'that the true measure of an Empire knight is to see one in combat.'

'I trust that is not something that will be necessary,' I replied.

Then Pyotr Gmelin spoke further of the ill times that settled upon the land. In the opinion of all northern men, the dark was rising in the far wastelands. Kurgan, Kul, Norse and others of their feral kind, massing in their ghastly enclaves in numbers not seen for many lifetimes, preparing for a war upon the South. Next year, the year after perhaps, and there would be blood on the snows. Pyotr Gmelin mentioned a name – 'Archaeon' – and said that rumours had spoken of this being as the great leader, or Most High Zar, of the Chaos tribes. It is a name the south must learn, and soon, I am sure. It is a name Kislev and the Empire must watch for and guard against with all force of heart and arm and spirit.

I asked of Pyotr Gmelin about the island in the lake, of its purpose and means. It was, I discovered, the stanitsa's temple. They called it by its old name, a word not from the Gospodar tongue, but from the more ancient tribes. This word was 'cromlech', and it denoted an islet built not by nature but by the hand of man. In the distant past, 'before eight fathers' Pyotr Gmelin put it, which was a Kislevite saying that meant eight generations, but was used for any great passage of time, the cromlech at Kzarla had been built in the lake, perhaps by the Scythians, perhaps by the tribes that rode before the Scythians, perhaps even by the man-horses that came before all things in the dawn time. The folk of Kzarla had inherited the site, maintained it for as long as anyone could remember, and based all their seasonal magic upon it. Of this, he was not specific. He mentioned rites for fair weather, good crops, good fishing, rituals against ice, and against blizzard. But these, Pyotr Gmelin said, were matters for the shaman.

And for Sire Jochrund too, I now supposed.

They let us take koumiss and bread back to the yurt outside the fence, and bundles of arguls, that is dried animal dung, to feed a good fire. I posted watches outside through the night, against the chance the Kul should return.

After midnight, as the constellation of the ourga was dipping towards the mountain peaks, Schroder came to wake me. The first snows had come.

In the first light of day, the land and sky were white entire, and just the long shape of the lake showed black against the snow. The fall had ceased, having laid no more than a hand's depth, but it was still and bitter cold. Today, I knew, we must leave, tomorrow at the latest, or be forced to remain in Kzarla over the winter. For the sake of the men, I would not let the wizard gainsay me now. I pulled on my cloak and rode up into the stanitsa. Sire Jochrund, so Sigert told me when I found him, was out on the islet with the shaman, and could not be disturbed. I told the clerk my message, and stressed it was not for negotiation. Then I sat by the fire in the longhouse and waited. After a time, Sire Jochrund called for me, and I went out into the snow. The sun was now fuller and watery gold, the colour of the wizard's eyes, and the world gleamed so brightly as to pain my eyes.

Sire Jochrund stood by the landward end of the causeway, and I went to him. All about, the people of Kzarla were decorating the shore and the causeway with rushlights and braziers, and also traceries of chiming tin bells suspended from fishing poles. There was some ritual afoot.

Sire Jochrund took me calmly by the arm and, calling me 'Jozef' once again, assured me that all was well. Yes, he was aware that first snow had reached us. Yes, he knew we must make haste to go. He was all but done. Tomorrow we would ride, with no further delays. This was his promise. Tonight, the shaman was performing some winter ritual that Sire Jochrund most decidedly wished to witness. That would be the last part of the mission. Indeed, he was now in great haste to return to the bounds of the Empire.

He called Sigert up, and told him to begin packing the wagon, mentioning the items that must be left out for this last night. Sigert sniffed and nodded, rubbing his watering nose on his sleeve.

Reassured, at last, I returned to my horse, and rode back through the stanitsa to inform the company. As I passed through the streets thereof, I saw a curious thing.

It was the girl, the beautiful girl from the causeway. She had been dressed in a long blue shift of silk that seemed too slight for such a bitter day. Silver combs had been placed in her black tresses, and kohl applied around her eyes. About her shoulders, she was garlanded with strings of small white flowers, like moon drops or pfennig-worts. I wondered where such flowers had grown in the sparse cold hills.

Long ribbons of golden satin had been tied around her wrists, and by these lengths, she was being led through the town from ibza to ibza by the womenfolk of the village. The girl, I realised, was to play some role in the ritual to come, and this was part of her ceremonial preparation.

The womenfolk, old matrons mostly, were wrapped in skins and dark hooded tunics, their feet bound up in fur. They chattered and chided as they led the girl. Her feet were bare. I saw them beneath the hem of her shift as she walked unflinching through the crisp, snowy mud.

At each hut, she was greeted by the homeowner, who fed her a hunk of bread or a dry biscuit or a spoonful of meal, and also a bowl of mare's milk or koumiss. Her face was expressionless, as if she was dreaming, no smile and yet no frown. I found I was transfixed, in part by her beauty, and in part by her strangeness. As they led her on across my path, clucking to her and ringing little hand bells, she looked up at my face, and a tiny quizzical furrow made a little wrinkle between her eyebrows. There was a look – and then she had moved on. I rode to the yurt. Markovo was grilling a breakfast of fish and root pottage for the company over the fire. As we ate, we saw the Kzarla rota, in full gear, ride out from the gates, with Pyotr Gmelin at the head. They made off towards the west. The Kul warband, Baibek told us, had been sighted at dawn, in renewed force.

Night came. The rota had not returned. I stood in the doorway of the yurt, gazing out across the flatness of white that the full moons were illuminating like the finest bleached parchment. In nearby Kzarla, great fires had been banked up along the shores of the lake, burning away, it seemed to me, a whole winter's supply of arguls. Braziers and rush-lights glowed along the distant causeway, and out onto the islet, half seen to me beyond the stanitsa's fence. We could hear singing, and the beat of drums, also the clash of cymbals. The ritual had begun.

In the yurt, the company were all of readiness. Everything was packed, and they had donned their wargear, intending to sleep in it so that we could depart without delay at first light. By the firelight, they sat and waited, some drowsing, some occupied at dice or jacks. I had moved amongst them, making sure all was well, before withdrawing to the tent door.

The distant singing had turned to chanting. A sense of disquiet filled me. It seemed as if the world was skewing out of joint, like a sundial that has been turned so its gnomon reads not true the hour. There was magic upon the night air.

A screech-owl called, and made me start. Then, from the edges of my eye, I made of a motion out in the snowfield beyond where the company horses were tethered.

It was a dog-fox, its coat already white for winter, and it came padding in across the snow's blanket, tongue twitching, sniffing for scent so that steam showed at its snout.

I watched it as it scurried on towards the stanitsa, snuffling the ground as it went. Then, in a moment, it lay down flat upon its belly, and set its chin upon the ground, and there lay, looking towards the village and its fires, as if waiting. As if drawn to something as old and feral as itself.

Subarin came out to bring me a thimble cup of samogon. I swigged it against the cold, and then said:

'Do you see?'

He did not, for the fox had gone, but I told him of it and he shook his head. He could not explain it but he look toward the village as if resisting the impulse to go there.

'What is it?' I asked of him.

He was about to answer when we heard the sobbing. It was quite distinct, despite the uproar from the stanitsa, for it was closer at hand. Subarin and I exchanged glances, and then took off at once towards the gate.

Four or five of the womenfolk were crouched in the snow outside the ditch-fence, making a great show of sorrow. We came to them, and little sense could we make.

'They lament,' Subarin said, translating for me the best as he could understand their broken whimpers. 'They lament for tonight it must be really done and she will be gone from them.'

He looked at me. 'What might that mean?'

'Get the horses,' I said. 'Rouse the company and get the horses.'

He looked upon my visage for a moment, and then nodded, as if what he had seen there convinced him. He ran back across the snow towards the yurt.

Despite the prohibition on strangers, I hurried into the town. All activity was at the far end by the islet. The longhouse was a silhouette against the orange dance of the ritual fires. I ran on, along the boardwalk, and down towards the causeway.

The night was filled with flame and chanting. Sparks flew, and the foetid stench of burning dung was strong. Reflected flames fluttered out across the surface of the lake. The ruddy faces of all the villagers were about me in the smoky heat. My eyes watered. I pushed on.

I looked out towards the islet. My heart beat hard.

The tent upon the island had been taken down, revealing a stone block which looked to me like one of the heathen stones Subarin had shown to me in the forest around Svedora. This block reclined upon the platform of the cromlech, like an altar. Torches blazed around the rim of the islet, and by their light I saw the shaman capering about the stone. He was clad in a suit of bearskin, and had upon his scrawny head a crown of antlers and a mask of beaten silver. In his upraised right hand rattled a sistrum. In his upraised left glinted a silver dagger.

And on the stone, garlanded with flowers, lay the girl.

Then I saw Sire Jochrund, his long cloak billowing in the wind, walking out across the causeway towards the islet, with Sigert jumping and dancing like a court fool in his wake. The bastard clerk was stripped unto his breeks, and his puffy skin painted like a heathen. He was banging on a drum.

I refused to believe what I was seeing with my own eyes.

The crowd fell to a hush as Sire Jochrund – no, I will not write his name thuswise any more – as Jochrund reached the shaman and took from his hand the silver dagger. This was done with the exchange of many arcane speeches, accompanied by the beat of the clerk's infernal drum.

Jochrund raised the blade, and blessed it.

I had seen enough. I broke a path through the crowd and ran like a hare towards the causeway. A great cry went up from those about me, startled and alarmed. Two of the ataman's swordsmen rushed to arrest my path, but I knocked them down with my fists and laid them flat in the snow of the shore.

Then I was upon the causeway, and running still, my sword out in my hand. I bellowed the wizard's name, and cursed him in the power of holy Sigmar. He looked towards me, as if mystified to see me there. The shaman howled. Behind me, I could hear the raging tumult of the townsfolk.

I reached the islet.

'Jozef…' the wizard began. All I could see was the ritual dagger in his bare hand. Bare hand! All this time his cursed hands had been gloved and covered.

'Leave her!' I yelled.

The shaman screamed and – I'm quite certain – laid a curse on my soul that will last until the end of my days. He flew at me with a handaxe. I lashed out to meet him with my left hand, and caught him such a blow, his silver mask broke away and he went tumbling back off the platform's edge into the black water with a shriek and a flailing of limbs. He went under, and for an instance, I glimpsed his white form through the rippled water as it sank into the gloom. The shock of icy water had no doubt killed him in a second.

I cared not. I grabbed the girl up and dragged her backwards towards the causeway. She stumbled, as if sleeping, or drugged. Jochrund bellowed at me, using words I did not understand. I felt my hair stand up and my skin prickle. His clawing, bare hand gestured at me in intricate patterns, fluid and evil, and I knew that his magic was about to be unleashed upon my person. There was indeed a flash of green light, and smell like unto spoiled curds, but no great magical doom afflicted me.

Sigert, however, that base fool, had snatched up the silver dagger cast aside by his master, and came at me, cutting me deep across the meat of my right thigh with its razor edge. The pain was like a fire-burn. I yelled out, and my sword swung out instinctively, dividing Sigert's miserable head from his neck in a fountain of blood.

Holding the girl and limping, sword ready, I backed down the causeway towards the shore, as Jochrund, his face set all of manifest hatred, advanced after me. Glancing behind, I saw the shocked and frightened faces of a hundred villagers in the firelight. Shocked and frightened they might be, but still they blocked my line of escape.

'Jozef!' the wizard hissed, his hands circling and dancing once more.

'You will call me Sire von Kassen,' I corrected bluntly.

Jochrund spat and raised his hands above his head. Blue flame, like a crown of lightning, encircled them, gathering fury. I heard the thunder of hooves, the glorious sound of Sigmar's heavenly host come to carry me to my eternal slumber.

A golden javelin punched through Jochrund's left hip and threw him over onto the causeway. He screamed out an awful note of pain. The blue fire slipped off his hands like melting ice and dropped onto the lake, where it burned and spat malevolently like a marsh fire until it was spent.

I turned. The villagers were scattering in panic. The company was riding hard down the shore and along the boardwalk. At its head was Schroder, and Subarin, who was pulling a second throwing lance from his saddle boot.

'Come on! Come on, sire!' Schroder yelled. My horse's reins were pulling in his hand. I picked up the girl, as best as I could in spite my pain, and ran to my horse, throwing her up upon it and climbing up myself.

Then we rode. Down through the stanitsa of Kzarla, past the gates and the ditch, past our abandoned yurt, and into the darkness, kicking up snow and flints with our hooves.

Subarin led us to a hilltop where the remnants of a sunken mound formed a simple ditch which we might defend, and there we waited until the sun rose. Brendel bound my wound, and we lit a fire. It would be seen, I knew, but the biting night was too cold to bear. I moved the girl near the heat of it, and gave her water in her stupor, hoping she would rouse.

At length, as dawn filmed the east with a pearly glow, she woke, and began chattering with alarm and distress. Subarin came to her, for I was unable to calm her, and talked to her in soothing wise until she settled again.

He came to me then. 'She is chosen born.'

'What is meant by that?' I asked.

'Her lineage, Sire. It is born to supply the krug with offerings if the needs be.'

'You speak of it like it is human to do such a thing!'

Subarin smiled and shook his head. 'Only in these remote places do the oldest of old ways survive. This is as she has told it to me. At the coming of every winter, the folk of Kzarla krug make ceremony upon the islet. It is ritual and symbolic. A maiden is offered to the god of winter to make perforce the coming snows mild and not harsh.'

'A girl is slaughtered?'

'Not at all. A girl is offered. It is symbolic, as I said. There is a mumbled ritual involving the dagger, some flowers cast upon the water. She has done it three winters yet.'

'They do not kill her?'

'Of course not! Sire von Kassen, do you think we are barbarians out in these wilds?'

I made no answer.

'But the ceremony has its origins deep in the past, in other ages when men were not so fussy. The Scythians who raised that cromlech would indeed cut open a maiden every year-end and cast her body into the lake to fend off winter's cruelty. It is from that the Kzarla ritual derives.'

'So... what was that we saw?'

'She says, my friend, that your wizard had heard about the rite, and came to Kzarla to convince the shaman that it must be done the old way.'

'Why?'

'Because only a rite performed in the way of the old magic could enforce a true conjuration.'

I shook my poor, unknowing head. 'What?'

Subarin grinned. 'The folk of Kzarla perform the ritual symbolically every year. If it staves off winter's might, so much the good. But their Scythian forebears conducted the rite in all reality, with sacrifice, and conjured such magic as truly kept the force of winter at bay. Your lord–'

'My lord no longer!' I snarled.

'Mayhap. Your wizard persuaded the shaman, by means that cannot be known, that the rite should be performed actually this winter, as it was done in the old days. For a mild winter, he said, was the only thing that would safeguard Kislev and the Empire both.'

'He said that much? What did he mean?'

Subarin took out a skin of koumiss, and offered unto me the first draw. It warmed my bones greatly. He drank too, and then said:

'The girl says your wizard told the shaman a great threat is rising in the North. Its name is Archaeon, and beneath its fury, all of the kingdoms of the world might perish. But if the winter was mild, the armies of the Empire could advance early, prepared as they were, and lay waste to the Archaeon's hordes while they were still in their winter camps.'

'What is her name?'

'What, sire?'

'The girl. What is her name?'

'It is Mariya.'

THERE ARE NO such plans. As a knight of the Reiksguard, I would know, or at least have some inkling. Though the Empire is aware that a threat is rising in the wastes north of Kislev, it has made no plans to muster armies or draw them up to the Ostermark or the southern provinces of Kislev this year. There are no great regiments encamped upon the Linsk or the Upper Talabec in readiness for a sudden early thaw. If they move and muster, move and muster at all, it will be in the springtime, when the campaign season begins.

Jochrund was lying. A mild winter and early thaw would benefit only one side: the hosts of Chaos pouring down, early and unexpected, from the North.

This is the matter I must convey to you, and for which I have troubled to write this account. Heed it well, I beseech you. Be warned, be ready. Do not tarry. The North is coming. Archaeon is coming. Unless you prepare, the world will be set aflame. For Archaeon's talons are dug in everywhere, even into secret places, like the brittle soul of an Imperial wizard, whose villainy knows no bounds, and who would, corrupted by whatever means I know not, undermine the security of our realm, with a casting of rituals and a stab of silver.

As DAWN CAME up upon the terraces of our ancient fort, we saw the Kul. Four score and more besides, gathering at the foot of the slopes where the snow had drifted thick. They were ominous black shapes against the blazing white, furnished for war in pitch-black armour and iron. Their tattered banners flew and snapped in the wind. Drums beat. Jochrund had called them, I was sure. Cursed Jochrund had called them to his aid.

And I knew then why he had not interceded in the fight in the valley.

These animals were his kin.

Horn blew, and echoed down the vale. The Kul clattered their shields against their spear-hafts, and began to advance up the slopes towards us. Through a spyglass, I saw Jochrund – cursed wizard! – slumped as if ailing upon his steed, commanding the warriors on.

He wanted the girl. He wanted to finish his infernal rite and pave the way for Archaeon's victory.

I hallooed up my men, and Subarin and his two comrades stood with us. We had broke most of our spears in the battle before, so now we drew out our swords. Swords of the Empire, clean-forged and true. Subarin unsheathed his golden sword, and Baibek and Markovo slid out their sabres. Even with these fine blades, I doubted it would be enough.

Our breaths furled the high air. Hawks swooped about the hilltop in the brightness of the cold daylight. As the sun reached its quarter place, they came for us.

At ten paces, I had the handgunners fire, splitting bone and helmet cases, dropping brutes onto the slope. Then it was down to swords; swords and spears against the axes and blades and shields of the Kul.

I took off a skull clean at the jawline, and then ran another warrior through, ripping out my blade to meet the next and the next again, chopping aside venturing sword-points and shattering shields about their bosses. Cloven and bleeding, the bodies of Kul rolled and slithered down the steep slope of our makeshift fort. Markovo launched his last javelin, and impaled a horned foe who went cartwheeling down the hillside. Then he raised his sabre and slashed at neck and breastbone.

Baibek cut into sundry shields and took away a Kul's throat in a patter of blood, before smiting a skull-masked fighter through the chest. His blade stuck there, arrested by the breastbone, and he was still trying to free it when the boar-spears of the invaders stuck him through.

Konstanz died with an axe between his eyes and a Kul upon his sword, writhing. Zebluck was speared through the gut, and let out a great stain of blood upon the snow.

Mottsdan cut and hacked, and set forth upon the singing of a hymn, a verse of the Empire at full throat, which many others of the company joined with, and continued long after Mottsdan himself was cut asunder.

Lieber died upon a spear. Bahr, two dead by his sword, was ripped apart by an axe that struck him above the right hip.

Erhle, bloodied by a blow to the scalp, kept fighting until his own blood blinded him and Kul swords ripped through his vitals.

Kenserhaus brought down one Kul with his last spear and then took out his sword, but a heathen axe took his sword arm away at the wrist, and he fell back, weaponless, drenching himself with his own spurting blood, and fending off blows with his left arm, which shortly was chopped and splintered into pieces. Then he was finished, with a Kul sword through the heart and into the earth beneath.

Borchers, who was always of a fine spirit and indomitable heart, buried his sword in through the chest of a Kul warlord, who cut away his head with his dying spasm.

Then Schroder fell, a spear-point into his left eye, and died most pitiously with a terrible thrashing and screaming.

I killed the Kul spearman who had killed him, and then slashed my sword outwards through the thick hip of another Kul. A third I gashed across the eyes. I ran to find Mariya.

Behind the onslaught of tribesmen, I had seen Jochrund winding his way up the hill on his black steed, leaning over in the saddle from pain.

I found her, and dragged her to her feet. Her wild blue eyes told me there was nowhere left to run. The Kul were driving in now, over the ancient rampart mounds, putting the valiant company to the sword, even though the best part of their tribe lay dead upon the flanks of the hill.

Jochrund rode into view, backlit by the winter sun, and smiled as he saw me. His hands were bare. He conjured with them.

'Jozef,' he called, mocking, 'You have done enough.'

A bone horn blew. There was a sound like thunder. Hooves.

Behind the urgent pace of Pyotr Gmelin, the rota of Kzarla tore into the Kul pack from the rear. The silverclad lancers loosed their javelins first, then came in with their lances, after which, once the lances were shattered, they took out their sabres. Silver death, from out of the winter's heart, fell upon the Kul.

Kzarla had not been prepared to accept the true ritual. In the face of it, even the women had broken down. The stern and noble rota had been sent off on a false trail to keep it out of the way for the duration of the ceremony. That had been Jochrund's doing too.

Now they had come back.

I heard Subarin cry out in glee.

The fell wizard came upon me then, his crackling hands upraised, but I had learned from our last encounter. The girl was the key. Mariya was so pure, so signified in magic, so central to the rite, she was inured against all conjuration. I swept her up between myself and Jochrund, and when his fearsome spell spat down at me, her very presence cast its power aside, unworked.

He cursed me then, and made to do upon me another enchantment. But from his left hand side came Subarin, who cut the wizard's head in twain at the cheek bone with his golden Scythian sword. How meet that was, I thought. Jochrund had been hell-bent on reviving the old ways, and now a blade preserved from that ancient time had ended his wretched life.

> *I have writ enough. My goat hides are all but full, and there is just tinkering of my nib in the spent flask of ink. I am done, and my story told. I will bury it under the cairn as I have said, wrapped in pigskin, and hope that someone finds it.*
>
> *Or hope that I wake from winter and find it, and carry it forth. My country must know.*
>
> *The winter now sets in, and contains us at Kzarla. It will be a long winter. I have guaranteed as much.*
>
> *Signed and buried by my hand, that is Jozef von Kallen, Knight of the Reik.*

SHYI-ZAR

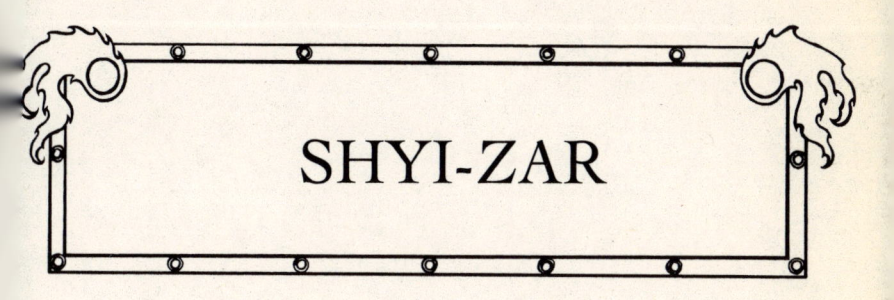

As High Zar Surtha Lenk gathers his Kurgan horde for their advance into south, the zars of his warbands compete with one another to gain the honoured and most prestigious rank of Shyi-Zar.

IT WAS DAWN in late winter. The sky was a blur of mauve darkness, broken in the east by a rind of approaching daylight, and the twin moons, like discs of fire-lit bone, were sinking to their setting places. A dawn like any other, thought Karthos, a cold and unforgiving sunrise, but his sorcerer said otherwise. This was an auspicious daybreak. A special time. A time that heralded the future.

Dutifully then, Karthos had woken the men early, kicking away their furs and growling their names. Sullen, they rose, and saw to the fire, which had sunk down to glowing embers in the last part of the night. Karthos took a swig of spirits to warm his belly. The warrior rings around his broad arms were as cold as ice upon his skin.

'What is he doing?' asked Odek. The sorcerer was now on the headland overlooking the camp, walking in slow circles around the goat he had brought with them from Kherdheg, murmuring words they couldn't hear. The goat, its headrope staked to the ground, was bleating.

'He's walking around that goat,' Karthos said. 'And talking to it.'

Odek grinned. 'With these eyes of mine, I see that much,' he said. He had ridden with the zar for nine seasons, and it was as much Karthos's phlegmatic humour and unfailing dryness that kept him loyal as it was the zar's potency in battle. He knew many Kurgan who followed their zars out of fear and duty, but he followed his out of respect and kinship. It was a bond that got as close to friendship as it was possible to get in the blighted North.

'I wondered... why?'

'I know you did,' nodded Karthos.

'So... why?'

Zar Karthos turned to his second-in-command. 'The sorcerer tells me this is a special time. Moonset.'

'The moons set every day.'

'Indeed. But this is a day amongst days. One moon sets, then the sun itself rises before the second moon can fall to its rest behind the plate of the world.'

'This he says?'

'This he says, and I doubt him not. It makes this time sacred. The light of the sun, he tells me, lets him see between the moons on this rare day. There are answers to be read there.'

'Including the answer that we want?'

'That,' replied the zar, 'is what I hope.'

The roused men had gathered by then, all ten of them. Koros Kyr, the standard bearer, Bereng, the horn-blower, T'nash He-Wolf, Odagidor, Lokas Long-ham, Aulkor, his brother Aulkmar, Gwul Gehar, Zbetz Red-fletch and Ffornesh the Dreamer. Furs and cloaks about their wide shoulders, they stood by the warmth of the spitting fire and watched the sorcerer at his rite.

One moon had set, its disc turning pale ivory then smoked silver as it slid down into the haze until it was out of sight. Then a band of flame lit the horizon, and the sun rose, heavy and copper, as if its furnaces had not yet been stoked up.

All of the warband knew the significance. This was Tchar's time. A time of change.

From the headland, the remaining moon behind his head like a halo, the sorcerer called to Karthos, and the zar hurried up the slope.

The sorcerer was called Ygdran Ygra. He was the oldest man Karthos had ever known, thin-limbed and spidery, his skin lined with age. He had been sorcerer to Karthos's father when Karthos's father had been zar.

'Take the blade,' Ygdran Ygra told Karthos. The proffered knife was a sharpened curve of moonstone instead of the sorcerer's usual silver dagger.

'Where must I strike?' asked Karthos. The goat bleated again, more shrill now.

Ygdran Ygra pinched at his own slack dewlap, and for a moment the zar thought he was being asked to butcher his sorcerer.

'The throat, zar, the throat,' the sorcerer instructed.

Karthos did as he was told. The goat ceased its noise. Ygdran Ygra had powdered the grass with chalk, and when the hot blood came out, steaming in the cold air, it ran and blotted amongst the white stalks.

'Good, good,' the sorcerer said, taking the slick blade back. He bent to read.

'Well?'

The sorcerer looked up at the zar. There was a curious fire in his milky blue eyes. 'You must pledge,' he said.

A smile ignited on Karthos's face. Down the slope, his men saw it, and started cheering and whooping even before he could relate the news.

Well-fed on goat meat, they broke camp and rode into the rising day. There was now an eagerness to the band that Karthos could feel. Sometimes a band dragged and lingered, unwilling, unfocused. But now they were fierce, and fired with a purpose. They were to pledge. Tchar had seen between the moons and licensed them. Lokas Long-ham and Ffornesh the Dreamer began to sing a war-song, full-voiced into the winter day.

This was how any zar wanted his warrior-pack. Vital, willing, indifferent to danger. Karthos was forced to gallop his steed hard to keep at the head of the charging group. He laughed into the cold wind.

They would follow him. Nothing would stand in his way. They would follow him to eternity.

At the next valley top, they reined in. Below, across a league of gorse heathland, lay the gathering place, staining the white sky with its smudges of smoke.

Zar Karthos raised his left hand, fingers splayed, the sign that meant, 'Let us ride'.

And down they went.

Around the ancient lightning tree that marked the gathering place, the horse clans had assembled in great numbers. Karthos had led his band to gatherings before, but the scale of this meeting took his breath away. He had not known so many men lived upon the plate of the world.

Perimeter fires had been set around the site, around the edges of the old circular ditch that had stood since before men had memories. Within, vast camps had sprung up. He saw the pitched standards of a score of warbands. Some he knew. That was Zar Herfil's, that was Zar Tzagz's, that Zar Uldin's. Kettle drums beat. Near to the lightning tree, the war tents of the High Zar's pavilion had been raised.

It was war then. That much was clear. Not just the seasonal rising of the clans, the annual gathering for raids down into the bloodless South.

The rumours and auguries had been true. Archaon had come, the deliverer, the striker-down of thrones and worlds. He had sent out his word, to transfix the hearts of the warrior bands, to make their very hairs stand up on end, to fire them for slaughter.

When had a High Zar last come forth for a gathering? When had a High Zar commended his clans unto himself for a spring driving? Not in Karthos's lifetime, nor in his worthy father's age either.

Zar Karthos felt his heartbeat rise, in time with the incessant drums. At long last, the promised age of conquest had come. The tempest of fire. The ending-of-times. The Storm of Chaos.

All along the borderlands now, as winter slackened its bite upon the world, high zars were marshalling their clans around them like this. Enra

Deathsword, Valmir Aesling, Sven Bloody Hand, Okkodai Tarsus, Zaros Bladeback, all answering the bidding of the strange and marvellous daemon-that-is-also-a-man Archaon.

The greatest of all Archaon's High Zars, Karthos believed, was Surtha Lenk, about whom this gathering now swelled. If any warlord might break open the boundaries of the feeble 'Empire' and strike down the tawdry crown of its so-called Emperor... what was given as his name now? Karl Franz? If any might strike down his crown and dash out his brains, it would be the great and malevolent Lenk.

Karthos's warband rode in through the gathering place. Koros Kyr held the skull standard high. Warriors turned to watch them pass by. Kul, Kurgan, Dolgan, Hastling... all manner of men, all manner of standards. Alien faces in strange wargears watched them go past.

'Be warned,' Odek muttered suddenly. Karthos had already seen the trouble. The banner of the bloody sword-blade on a red field. Zar Blayda's standard.

It was not true to say that no blood was lost between the zars. Far too much had been lost in their lingering clan-war.

Blayda, gaunt and tall in his pitched-black plate armour, etched with the details of his many victories, strode out onto the trackway into Karthos's path. Blayda's sorcerer, a capering, naked fool named Ons Olker, scampered around his master's heels.

Karthos dismounted and tossed his reins to Bereng. He marched through the trail's slush to face the black-armoured chieftain. Blayda drew his pallasz, the long tongue of the sword flashing in the rising sun.

Karthos did not reciprocate, though he heard Odek slide out his sword behind him.

'You know the law here,' Karthos said, staring at the visor slits of Blayda's ink-black helm.

'Do you need me to remind you?' Karthos added. 'In the gathering space of the High Zar, no clan shall fight with clan.'

Blayda lowered his sword. 'You are dung-eating scum, Karthos.'

He was being deliberately provocative. Karthos merely shrugged.

'I will wet my blade with your gut-blood and make you a notch upon my helm,' Blayda added, pointing at a part of his barbute that was not yet marked with an incised gash.

'Maybe. But not here,' Karthos replied.

Blayda raised his visor far enough to spit on Karthos's toes, then strode away, his leaping and cursing sorcerer in tow.

Karthos looked back at his clan. He raised his left hand, fingers splayed.

KOROS KYR PLANTED the spike of their standard into a patch of free ground and the warband settled. They were encamped not far from the pavilions of the High Zar. Water and burning wood was brought to them by the gathering's stewards, along with meat for cooking, wine, and grain for simmering.

Karthos had Odek, who was charged with the band's purse, pay them in decent gold.

T'nash came to the zar, suggesting they might also buy a decent fighter from the slavelord Skarkeetah so that they might undo Zar Blayda in formal combat.

Karthos shook his head. There were more important things afoot now.

The men of the warband were drinking wine as their food roasted and night fell. Attended by two of his band, Zar Skolt came to their camp site. He embraced Karthos like a brother, and they drank wine for a while, having many old victories to remember.

'Will you not fight Blayda?' asked Skolt. 'He yearns for it.'

Karthos shook his head. 'No, he may wait.'

'Besides,' said Odek. 'We are to be pledged.'

Zar Skolt sat up as if he had been stung. 'Is that true? Are you pledging?'

'The signs were good. My sorcerer has said it so. Not you?'

Skolt shook his head. 'My sorcerer saw no such good omens. Great Tchar, I envy you. Such an honour no warband could deny.'

'Who else may pledge?' Karthos asked.

Skolt shrugged. 'Uldin, I know. Herfil, Kreyya and Logar. And also Blayda.'

'Blayda?' mused Karthos. 'Indeed.'

ALL THROUGH THE first part of the night, despite a drizzling sleet that came in from the west, slaves worked in processions to build up the bonfires around the lightning tree at the heart of the gathering place. Great flames leapt up, so fierce that the sleet could not douse them. The hissing of steam filled the sacred place, like unseen snakes. The glow from the fires lit the tree from below, casting a moving amber light up its bald trunk and skeletal limbs. It illuminated the iron cages and gibbets hanging from the branches: offerings, sacrifices and the cadavers of enemies.

Gongs were struck to announce midnight and the time of pledging. Karthos went down to the ring of fire around the altar tree, where a great number of other zars and chieftains were assembling. None brought weapons to that hallowed earth. Herbs and seeds flung onto the fires filled the air with incense and heady smoke. Karthos felt his flesh sweat from the extreme heat. He saw Uldin, also Logar, and others he did not know. Blayda's grim black form was a shadow on the far side of the fire ring.

A hush fell. The High Zar had emerged from his pavilion, escorted by twenty white-robed warriors with horsehair crests. They carried bright lamps on long poles that bobbed like marsh fire as the procession approached.

Surtha Lenk was a monstrous giant of a man, clad in crimson armour. Karthos shuddered at the sight of him. Two goat-headed dwarfs scurried along at his heels. Karthos could not tell if they were children wearing goat-masks, or beastfolk enslaved to the High Zar's power. One carried a casket of jade and gold, the other carried Lenk's war sword. It was so large and heavy, the goat-thing was all but dragging it.

The zars parted, so that their master could reach the fire ring. Surtha Lenk stopped. The brass visor of his horned helm appeared to regard them all, yet to Karthos there seemed to be no eyeslits cut into it.

Lenk raised his massive arms, his huge hands outspread, cased in mail and thorny steel.

'You are to make the pledge,' he said. It was the first time Karthos had heard the High Zar's voice, and his guts turned to ice. It was slight and tiny, like a child's, yet it seemed to come from all around and drown out the crackle of the fire more easily than a bellowing roar.

'Tchar looks to you, warriors. This is holy change you undertake, beautiful to the Eye of Tzeen. Do you understand this pledge?'

'Lord seh!' the zars called out obediently.

One of the goat-things opened the casket and took something from it. Surtha Lenk received it and held it up for them all to see. It was a great claw of frightening dimensions, polished bone-white.

'Look upon it,' the High Zar whispered. 'The zar who brings its like back to me will be called shyi-zar, and he and his warrior band will be accorded the full honours of that title.'

The claw was put away again in its reliquary box. Surtha Lenk took his sword then, and held it upright before himself in one hand.

'Pledge!' he said.

One by one, the zars came to him, and slid their bared right hands down the edge of his warblade without any show of pain. Then each one turned and let the blood drip from their sliced palms into the fire.

Karthos did so in turn, not daring to show any pride by looking up at his master's hooked metal visage. He watched his own blood well up, black in the firelight, and heard the drops of it sizzle in the flames.

DAWN CAME, GREY and sunless, with sheeting rain and a savage wind that shook the hide tents and made the great lightning tree creak and moan. Karthos stretched out his left hand, fingers splayed. The warband left the gathering place.

They were not the first to depart. Some pledged bands, anxious to begin the task, had quit the camp before first light. Odek told his zar of the standards that were missing, Blayda's amongst them.

They crossed the heathlands to the west, into the driving rain, and then turned north, advancing into the haunted hills and miasmal valleys beyond. Here, the crests were granite, and the land suddenly shelved away into steep pine brakes of mist and darkness where the sun never touched, even in summer. They sighted another warband on a trail over to the west, but they were too far off to hail or identify.

Karthos had described the claw to his men, and much debate had followed as to its nature or origin. T'nash insisted it was in fact the tusk of a doombull, but the others shouted him down. It was the talon of a predator beast, a dragon's horn, a sliver fallen off the late moon and all other manner of things.

The sorcerer offered the soundest council. 'Let us not waste effort in fruitless searching, zar seh,' he ventured. 'Let us get truth, and use it.'

So they rode for Tehun Dhudek.

TEHUN DHUDEK WAS a fastness in the lonely hills that many men shunned for they feared it was cursed. But Ygdran Ygra, who knew more of the world's secrets than most men, had been there himself, and scoffed at the common rumours. 'A clan of sorcerers dwells there,' he informed the warband, 'and they have in them great powers of divination. If we please them with our offerings, they will tell us the true nature of the claw, and where we may find it.'

'But the curse...?' Aulkor said.

'Just stories spread by men who have been there to question the oracle and not liked the truth they have learned. To some men, the truth is a curse.'

Karthos hoped that would not be so for them.

THAT PART OF the hills was indeed lonely. The track wound up through the dismal cliffs of splintered granite, and along deep-cut ravines and narrow gorges. Their only company was a few bird flocks in the pale sky.

'Someone's been this way,' Odek said. There was horse dung on the scree of the trail, and it was not more than a day old.

'A lone rider?'

'No, zar seh. Look there, the soil of more than one animal. A warband, perhaps?'

'One with the same notion as us?'

They rode on a little way further, to the mouth of the sloping gorge that the sorcerer said led right to the fastness itself.

Odek looked round at Karthos sharply, but the zar had heard it too. Hooves, the shouts of men, carried down the gorge by the chill wind. And there, amongst it, the clash of blades.

Karthos drew his pallasz. Gripping it made pain flare in his hand, for though Ygdran Ygra had dressed his pledge-wound, his palm still throbbed.

His men needed no orders. Their weapons came out. Pallasz mostly: long, straight-bladed cleaver-swords. Lokas Long-ham had a horse-spear, and Gwul Gehar the waraxe he favoured. Zbetz Red-fletch and Aulkmar took out their recurve horse-bows and slipped on the bone rings of their thumb-guards.

Karthos raised his left hand, fingers splayed.

AT A FIRM gallop, Karthos led the way up the track and into Tehun Dhudek. The mouth of the ravine formed a gateway in a high ring-wall of dry stone construction that surrounded a flagged courtyard built upon a shelf in the cliff. The three longhouses of the fastness, along with an ancient and ragged tower, overlooked the courtyard from a promontory shelf, with stone steps running down to the floor of the yard itself.

Murder was underway here. Karthos counted at least nine Dolgan riders assaulting the place, hacking down the defenders with their hooked swords and adzes. The defenders were not warriors. They were shaman, acolytes and slaves, armed with poles and staves. The bodies of many, leaking blood, lay scattered around the gate-mouth and across the courtyard. A number of riderless horses milled around the yard.

'Bereng!' Karthos thundered, and the hornblower at his left side unloosed a mighty blast upon his carnyx that howled around the walled yard like a boom of echoing thunder.

The Dolgan warriors turned, amazed, enraged. Karthos saw their chieftain, a bearded and maned brute with arms wholly covered in warrior rings. Karthos did not know his name, or the name of his warband, for Kurgan and Dolgan were often strangers if not bitter foes except at times of gathering, but he knew the man's face. He had been at the fire-ring at midnight, pledging to the High Zar.

The Dolgans swept around to meet the Kurgan charge, kicking and slashing the fastness's defenders out of their way.

'Into them!' Karthos yelled.

The packs of riders met. Karthos's band had the advantage of surprise and momentum. Reins clamped between their teeth, Zbetz and Aulkmar loosed their first arrows. The shafts went buzzing across the walled yard. Aulkmar's struck a Dolgan through the chest and slammed him off his saddle. Zbetz sent another raider to his doom, a red-feathered arrow through his side.

Lokas Long-ham's spear shattered a Dolgan shield and transfixed the warrior holding it so that he was torn up out of his seat and off his horse. The spear went with him, wedged through his body, and Lokas let it go, reaching over to sweep his saddle-sword out of its long, leather scabbard as the next Dolgan flew at him.

Odek crossed blades with a particularly large Dolgan warrior, and they ripped their swords at one another, their terrified horses circling and stamping. T'nash He-Wolf felled one man cleanly, his pallasz windmilling, and then turned his steed's head hard to engage another.

Karthos, with Gwul Gehar at his right hand, went for the chieftain, but he had two heavy warriors in ringmail and over-plate as body guards. Their wild eyes flashed under the slits of their tusked helmets. They had swords and short, stabbing spears.

Karthos clashed with one, driving his pallasz at the Dolgan's badly timed sword swing, but the man's left hand came around to jab the stabbing spear at the Kurgan zar. Its iron tip glanced painfully off the banding of warrior rings around Karthos's right arm. Karthos, struggling to restrain his frantic horse with the power of his left arm, hacked backwards, and succeeded in breaking the spear haft and severing the thumb from the hand grasping it.

The Dolgan squealed, his maimed hand coming up in dismay, blood squirting from the wound. Better balanced in the saddle now, Karthos struck again, and the man barely got his sword up to block the blade.

From the corner of his eye, Karthos saw that the chieftain was coming for him too now, sword out, moving in from the left flank. Gwul was engaged with the other bodyguard, fighting the awkward, laboured rally that accompanied a duel of sword against axe.

Karthos snarled. He could not break from the bodyguard because the man, due to the pain and outrage of his hand wound, was hacking with a berserk frenzy. The zar could not disengage his blade in time to fend off the chieftain's attack.

The only option left was to avoid it. Karthos threw himself out of his saddle, crashing head-on into the injured bodyguard and tipping him and his horse right over. Men and horse sprawled on the cold flagstones of the yard, winded and stunned. Karthos heard Odagidor cry out his name, fearing his zar had fallen to a blade wound.

Wrestling, Karthos managed to pull free of the frantic bodyguard and regain his feet. The bodyguard had lost his sword, and clawed at Karthos's legs, painting him with crimson blood from his ruined hand. Karthos kicked him away and turned just in time to meet the downstroke of the bellowing Dolgan chief.

The Dolgan's hooked broadsword resounded off Karthos's pallasz with jarring force. The chieftain's bulky horse backed off a pace or two in alarm, and then came in again, and Karthos was forced to leap back to avoid the whistling blade. He was almost slammed off his feet by the tackling charge of the wounded bodyguard, who attacked him, screaming, with a bear-hug. Karthos's left hand was free, so he smacked it round and caught the bodyguard across the face with the iron rings of his warrior bands, breaking the enemy's nose in a spatter of blood. The Dolgan let go. Karthos grabbed him as he staggered, blinded by blood, and pulled him close as a shield, left arm locked around his throat.

The chieftain hacked again and disembowelled his own man. Karthos let the ruptured body topple away and ran across the flagstones to retrieve his horse.

Bereng's horn blew again. A few paces short of his twitchy steed, Karthos looked round. Nearly a dozen more Dolgan warriors were pouring down the steps on foot from the longhouses. That explained the riderless horses.

Karthos ran to meet them. Ffornash and Aulkor leapt from their horses to join with him. Odagidor remained in his saddle and came in close to the steps, scattering the foot soldiers with his hooves. There was a hissing sound, and one of the Dolgans coming down the steps sprawled backwards with a red-feathered arrow in his brow.

Karthos reached the lower steps, and swung his pallasz at the nearest Dolgan. This warrior had a long-hafted adze, and drove it down at the zar like a woodsman with a timber axe. Karthos side-stepped, and the man overbalanced from his desperate strike. Karthos's pallasz opened him from the hip to the armpit and scattered broken links of ringmail across the flagstones. The man fell onto the courtyard floor with bone-cracking force.

Ffornash the Dreamer had famed skill with the long-blade. He was a tall, lithe man who shunned armour because it slowed his limbs. Both fists around his sword grip, he danced up the steps, ducking an axe and sidestepping a stabbing spear, and sliced his silver sword back and forth, ripping through a neck and opening a Dolgan belly.

Aulkor broke a Dolgan sword against his heavy pallasz, and cut the man through to the breastbone with a side swing. But his blade was wedged. He tried to wrench it free as another Dolgan came down at him with an adze. Karthos flew forward with a howl, and ran the adze-wielder through before his blow could land. The Dolgan thumped away down the steps, his adze spinning free into the air as the dead hands released it.

'My thanks, zar seh,' Aulkor gasped, extracting his bloody sword at last.

Karthos did not reply. The fight was far from done. Now Odek, Odagidor and Gwul Gehar had joined them on foot, battling up the steps into the thick of the Dolgan pack. Another enemy fell and rolled heavily down the stone risers, hit by one of Aulkmar's arrows this time. The steps themselves had become slippery with blood. Dying men clawed at their ankles and shins. Karthos broke a shield away and then cut through the haft of an adze, then a forearm, then a throat. He was changing lives into death. Tchar would approve.

Fighting clear, he reached the top of the staircase. The only Dolgans there were corpses, transfixed by red and grey feathered arrows. He turned and looked back, in time to see the act that finished the fight.

Koros Kyr, still holding the warband's standard high, rode in hard and killed a Dolgan horseman with a wide blow of his pallasz. Then he reined hard around and removed the head of the Dolgan chief. It was a superb cut, all the power of the standard bearer's arm behind it. The brute's helmed head flew off in a mist of blood, and bounced and rolled like a cannonball on the flags. His horse took off, and carried the headless corpse out through the gate and away down the ravine.

Broken, the remaining Dolgans tried to flee, but there were Kurgan swords all around them. Gwul Gehar's waraxe finished two more. The few that made it to the gateway, wailing and screaming, were dropped hard by Zbetz and Aulkmar, who sat astride their tight-circling horses, loosing arrow after arrow.

Zar Karthos, spattered head to toe in gore, lowered his dripping pallasz and smiled. They had destroyed the Dolgan warband, and with no loss to themselves.

Tchar was evidently with them.

THE SORCERER CLAN of Tehun Dhudek had numbered sixteen, an extended family of sons and fathers and uncles. A further twenty acolytes had dwelt within the high stone walls, along with some thirty slaves and womenfolk.

Now only thirty lives remained all told, most of them the women, who had been hidden in the fastness caves when the raid began. The Dolgans had sought to learn the truths of the talon from the oracle by force of arms.

Ygdran Ygra had been right. The truth was sometimes a curse, for the Dolgans had found only death at Tehun Dhudek.

The survivors of the fastness clan regarded Karthos's warband with some wariness, fearing that they had exchanged one murdering pack for another. With his sorcerer, Karthos went to meet with the most senior of the surviving hetmen.

'We came to make fair offering in return for answers,' he told the old man squarely. 'We would not have resorted to violence. You need not fear us now.'

The old hetman sat on a clammy stone chair in the draughty hall of one of the longhouses. He had insisted on wearing a golden mask so that the Kurgan would not see his grief.

'What would you have given us, zar, as an offering?' one of his younger acolytes asked. This young man had a bandaged stump where his right hand had been struck off by the Dolgans. He clutched it against his chest like a newborn babe.

'Gold, fine stones from my war chest, salt-meat and wine. Whatever else pleased you that I could provide,' Karthos said.

'But now we have given you more than that,' said Ygdran Ygra. 'By force of arms and the sweat of toil, we have given you salvation from the Dolgans. What is that worth?'

Answers, it seemed. For two nights, Karthos's sorcerer was shut away in the furthest longhouse, probing the secrets of the clan's oracle. A great storm came up during that time, and hammered upon the doors and shutters. The warband sheltered in the first longhouse, their food and drink provided by the grateful clansfolk. The storm's rain put out the pyre of Dolgan bodies heaped in the yard before they were even half burned.

The storm cleared. A pale yellow light filled the sky above the fastness peaks. The mountain air was alive with the gurgle of water draining and running down the cliffs into the valleys far below.

Ygdran Ygra came out of seclusion, tired and hungry. He refused to speak until he had eaten a platter of pig's feet and drunk some watered ale besides. Karthos had never seen him so exhausted. For the first time, he looked his years, haggard and worn out.

'It will be quite a thing to do,' he said at last, his voice soft. He dabbed shiny spots of pig grease off his chin with a kerchief.

'How so?' Karthos asked, unplugging a wine flask and pouring himself a beakerful.

'I know where it is and what it is,' Ygdran Ygra replied. 'But now finding it is not the burden. Killing it is.' He shook his old head and tut-tutted.

'Even your father, Kelim Karthos, he who was zar before you, even he would have shrunk from this task.'

'Just tell me of it,' Karthos said.

'A heralder,' said the old sorcerer. 'Tchar wants us to take a heralder.'

KARTHOS FEARED THAT if he told the men, they would revolt and ride away. But they begged to know, and he could not keep it from them. So he sighed, sat down amongst them in the draughty longhouse, and blurted it out.

For a long moment, there was no sound except the moaning of the wind and no movement except the drift of the sunlight on the floor as clouds passed across the sky.

Then Ffornash the Dreamer let slip a low, sad chuckle, and Gwul Gehar spat in the hearth, and the brothers Aulkor and Aulkmar looked at one another and shuddered.

'So, not a doombull then?' asked T'nash He-Wolf.

Koros Kyr slapped him for his question, and the warband broke into laughter.

'You will ride with me?' Karthos asked.

'We are pledged, zar seh,' said Odek simply. 'Riding with you is what we do.'

IT TOOK FOUR days to reach the wastes. Four days' hard ride, and all of them fatigued and aching from the battle that, they were sure, only Tchar's will had seen them win so thoroughly. Odagidor suspected that Tchar had wanted them to crush the Dolgans because they were the ones who were destined to meet the pledge and take the shyi honour.

But Bereng muttered that they had been spared and granted victory only to give the heralder more blood to spill.

None of them had ever seen a heralder, except for Zbetz Red-fletch, who had been a child when one savaged his home village. He remembered little of it, except its ravening beak that had rent his father in two. He had been a young child. It had haunted his dreams ever since.

Lokas Long-ham said he thought he might once have seen one, circling in the heavens, high up, above Zamak Spayenya, many years before, when he had been riding with the warband of Zar Shevras. An eagle, the others said.

'With the body of a lion?' he replied.

'How could you tell if it was so far away?' asked Odagidor.

'Maybe it was an eagle,' Lokas said resignedly.

THE WASTES WERE cold and empty. Nothing living seemed to grow or thrive there. At all sides, the dry plains rolled away to the limits of the world, broken only by ridges of crusted rock and scattered boulders. The soil was as dry as dust, as white as a sorcerer's sacrificial chalk. The sky was dark, washed purple by the poisoned light. Thunder rumbled throughout the day, and around the hem of the horizon, slashes of lightning grazed the air and bit into the earth like bright and slender fangs.

The air smelled of decay. Wailing sounds echoed over the desolation, from no obvious source. Amongst the white dust, every few miles, gnawed bones protruded. Horse, man, man-beast.

ON THE FIFTH day out from Tehun Dhudek, Ygdran Ygra rose in his saddle and pointed.

'There! As the insight was given to me. An outfall of rock, spiked in three places, like the front part of a crown. Before it, a steep slope of rocks and stones. In the sky of the west, a crescent of clouds. This is the place.'

Karthos felt fear then, the turning of a long-standing worry into true fear. He sensed it settle upon his men too.

He drew a deep breath and raised his left hand out, fingers splayed.

They rode up into the flinty slope of stones. All of them carried long lances now, fashioned from the cold forests they had passed through to reach the open wastes. Swords would not be enough to do this deed.

According to Ygdran Ygra – and the lore of the Northlands – a heralder was a most feral beast, twisted from nature and combined by the mutable touch of Tchar into a chimera. It was in part a lion, but more massive than even the greatest hunting cats of the Taiga, but its head was that of an eagle or vicious prey bird, hugely beaked. It possessed wings. In the oldest of times, such animals had been plentiful and common, plaguing the realms of man, but they had faded away into the remote corners of the world. Some said the wizards and lords of the Empire had such creatures tamed as war-steeds.

They were called heralders, because their appearance was said to herald great events and moments of history. Ygdran Ygra feared the gods were playing with them. He had read the signs that they should pledge at a special dawn, a heralding moment. It was as if their path had been set from the start. Their doom too, perhaps.

In the language of the tribes, these rare beasts were called ghur-phaon, the essence of all beasts.

The warband moved up through the litter of rock, their horses' hooves causing stones to slip and patter away down the jumbled slope. Thunder rolled, distantly. There was an increased stench of death in the air, as if meat rotted close by. Karthos saw the rocks were splashed with great deposits of white dung, like birdlime, but far more prodigious.

'Caves,' said Odek.

His second-in-command was pointing to dark holes in the cliff face above them. Roosts indeed. This place felt like a lair.

Karthos lowered his lance and was about to call back to the band when a shrill cry cut the world apart. It was piercing, as loud as if an eagle had been perched upon his shoulder.

The ghur-phaon showed itself.

It had scented them, located them with its beady eyes perhaps. It came out of one of the deep caves and spread its fearful wings. They were mottled black and white, the lead feathers as long as a horse's back. It took to the air.

Zbetz Red-fletch screamed despite himself, his childhood horrors made flesh. All the horses reared, terrified, smelling the predator coming down upon them. Gwul Gehar was thrown down onto the stones, Lokas too, so hard his neck snapped like a twig. Aulkor's horse broke and ran, despite his best efforts to control it, and carried him away down the long scree slope.

'In Tchar's name...' Karthos heard Odek stammer.

The beast was huge. Its body massed the weight of six horses at least. It leapt into the air on lithe feline back limbs, its hide a mangy grey. A tail the length of the slave master's finest gang-lash whipped out behind it.

Karthos couldn't decide what was most terrifying: the width of the massive, beating wings or the horror of the ghur-phaon's foreparts. Its head, massive and distended, disproportionate to the limber body behind it, was the head of a vulture: a massive ivory beak like an ogre's waraxe, at the crest of which tiny, wild eyes gleamed. The beak clacked like swords striking together, and he saw a glimpse of a thin white tongue.

Around the head and back along the throat, the monster was fletched in black and white down, which became quite shaggy around its breast. Its forelimbs were not the nimble things of a cat. They were scaled bird's feet, huge and armoured in silver. Each of the three scale-encrusted toes on the forelimbs sported a long claw.

Just like the talon Karthos had seen the High Zar lift out of his box.

It came down upon them, keening into the dark sky, beak opened to rake them apart.

Zbetz Red-fletch fired off two arrows before it came upon them, but his darts seemed like tiny red flecks amongst its feathered breast. Aulkmar loosed one arrow of his own before his horse threw him. He broke his left forearm on the stones as he landed.

Odek, Ffornash and Bereng hurled their lances at it. All bounced off.

The creature landed amongst them, crashing out a blizzard of loose stones and chips in all directions. Koros Kyr and his horse were spilled over, and T'nash too, his horse ripped open by the ghur-phaon's talons. It lunged at Gwul Gehar's horse and bit it in two with a savage slash of its monstrous beak. The slope reeked of hot blood.

Odagidor charged into the side of it, the tip of his lance digging deep. It recoiled and lashed out. Odagidor's horse lost its head from the muzzle to the eyes and toppled. Odagidor had his spear shattered and his left arm removed at the elbow. Gwul tried to drag him clear, both of them sprayed with the blood pumping from Odagidor's stump.

Odek tried to recover his spear, but the vast, flapping wings smashed him over. Zbetz fired an arrow that struck the ghur-phaon in the throat. Enraged, it surged forward across the loose stones and seized Zbetz by the right hand and forearm, lifting him off his horse and shaking him in its beak.

Screaming in pain, Zbetz flew through the air, his arm shredded.

Karthos raised his lance and spurred his horse on, keeping the tip of his weapon low. The monster's claws had just ripped Aulkor in half at the waist.

Karthos plunged the lance into the beast's upper body from the side, pushing it in with all the force he could muster. The ghur-phaon started to bleat and wail, its body thrashing. It almost tore the lance out of Karthos's hands.

Odek ran to him, and T'nash and Koros Kyr, and they all put their muscles into it, grabbing the shaft and pushing it home.

The ghur-phaon screamed.

'Hold it here!' Karthos yelled, and let go of the lance. He drew his pallasz and ran towards the snapping head of the monster. Double-handed, above his head, he swung the sword down and cut wide its neck, casting scads of down into the air. Blood engulfed him like a mountain torrent.

He sank to his knees.

'Zar seh... it's dead,' Odek said.

Karthos nodded, and went to one of the outstretched forepaws. With a cry, he struck at it, and then raised the bloody claw in his hand.

AULKOR, ODAGIDOR, ZBETZ and Lokas were dead. Their mangled and twisted bodies were bound up and thrown across the backs of riderless horses. Almost every warrior was bruised and hurt. Aulkmar's arm was shattered, but he complained only for his dead brother.

THE MOONS WERE setting. They rode back along the trackway towards the gathering place. Flies buzzed around the dead strung from their spare horses.

Twenty strong, Zar Blayda's warband rode out into their path. Their swords were drawn.

Karthos simply raised the talon in his hand. Dried blood clotted its thickness.

'Want to try for it?' he hissed.

Blayda turned his band back and rode away.

THE RING FIRE around the tree was lit. The bands had gathered.

Karthos led his warband up to the pavilion to claim his honour. Drums beat all around them.

'Have you fulfilled the deed?' Surtha Lenk said as he emerged from his tent.

Karthos showed the High Zar the talon.

'You know what this means?'

'It means that my warband and I have done what is necessary. We have made your pledge. We must be granted with the honour of shyi-zar.'

'Shyi-zar. Death zar. You understand what it is I want from you?'

'Yes, lord seh. You ride to war. Should you fall there, you need the best warriors to ride ahead of you into the afterworld, to prepare your place and guard you when you arrive. This is the duty of the shyi-zar. This honour amongst honours I claim for my warband.'

Surtha Lenk nodded.

'Thank you. Ride on to battle, Shyi-zar Karthos,' he said.

And with the ghur-phaon talon, he cut Karthos's throat, and Odek's, and those of all the others, every single soul of them willing.

Slaves and sorcerers banked the ring fires up until the lightning tree was awash with firelight. Slaughtered, gutted and stuffed, the warsteeds were set upon poles, facing east, and the riders of the warband placed upon them, similarly supported.

They had achieved the highest honour, the duty of preparing the way for their High Zar in the afterworld.

Karthos, Odek, Koros Kyr with his standard, Bereng with his carnyx, T'nash, Odagidor and the rest of them.

They would ride into eternity and make it ready.

Karthos's left arm was splinted up on a pole. Raised, outstretched.

Fingers splayed.

THE WARHAMMER

VILGRIM THE AGONIST RAISES THE WARHAMMER HIGH. HIS GRIP IS TIGHT AND TRUE.
HIS RIDERS SEE IT AND THEY ROAR OUT THEIR BATTLE-CHANT.
THERE WILL BE BLOOD ON THE FIELDS OF OSTLITZ BEFORE NIGHTFALL.
THE WARHAMMER
Script: Dan Abnett • Art: Colin MacNeil
Letters: Fiona Stephenson

THEN VILGRIM GIVES THE WORD--
WASTE THIS PLACE!
--AND THE DEATH OF THE NORTHERN IMPERIAL BURG OSTLITZ BEGINS.
GREAT GODS! THEY'RE COMING FROM THE FLANK!
THEY'RE COMING FROM THE FLANK! TURN THE GUNS! TURN THE BLOODY GUNS, FOR PITY'S SAKE!

THE AGONIST. THE THRICE-DAMNED AGONIST.
HOW DOES HE DO THAT? HOW DOES HE ALWAYS KNOW?
ALWAYS, HE STRIKES WHERE THE DEFENCES ARE WEAKEST. LIKE A BLOODY CHARM.
IT WAS THE SAME AT MERLINGE... OOTBURG... NADEL... EVERY DAMN ONE OF HIS RAIDS.
SIGMAR'S BONES, GENERAL! WE'RE ALL AWARE OF HIS MURDEROUS CRIMES!
DO SOMETHING! YOU MUST DO SOMETHING!
WHAT, EXACTLY, BURGOMEISTER KNITTEL? TURN BACK THE CLOCK?
WE HAD FOUR DAYS TO PREPARE! OUR SCOUTS SAID HE WAS COMING FROM THE NORTHEAST AND WE LAID OUR CANNON AND MORTARS ACCORDINGLY!
NOW HE COMES UPON US FROM THE WEST! THE WEST! AS IF BY SOME SORCERY HE KNOWS EXACTLY WHERE TO STRIKE TO DRAW THE MOST BLOOD!
IF THE CREWS CAN TURN THE GUNS IN TIME, PERHAPS...
A-ARE YOU SAYING WE'RE ALL GOING TO DIE?
MY DEAR BURGOMEISTER...

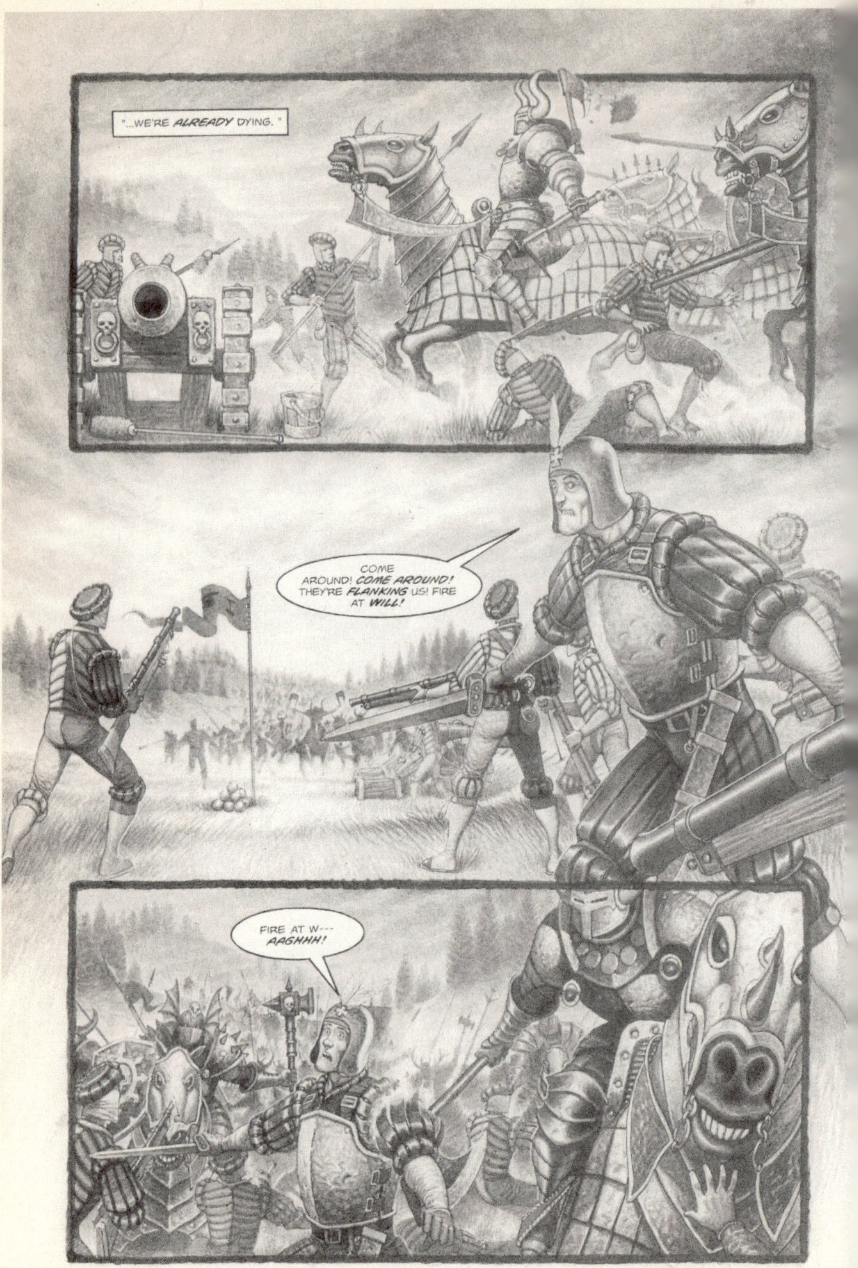
"...WE'RE ALREADY DYING."
COME AROUND! COME AROUND! THEY'RE FLANKING US! FIRE AT WILL!
FIRE AT W--- AAGHHH!

PUT YOUR BACKS INTO IT! ROLL THEM ROUND!
JODL! COVER THE GUNS! BUY THEM WHAT LITTLE TIME YOU CAN!
YOU HEARD THE SERGEANT, MEN...
...HOLD THE LINE AND GIVE THEM HELL!

THE AGONIST.

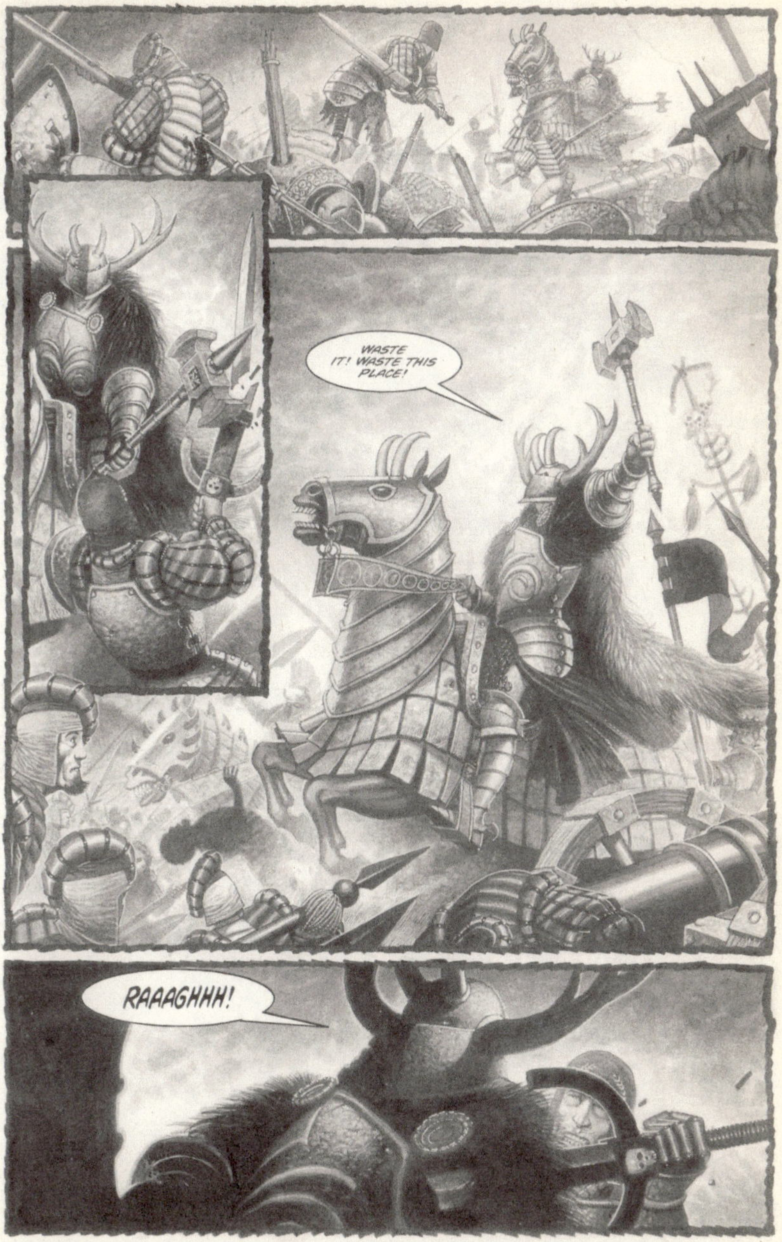
WASTE IT! WASTE THIS PLACE!
RAAAGHHH!

WARM.

THE HAMMER *THROBS* WITH HEAT, WAR-HEAT. *BATTLE-HEAT.*

FOR A *SECOND*, HE WONDERS IF IT IS CURSED.

BUT THERE'S NO TIME TO THINK ABOUT *THAT*.

IT'S NOT A CURSE. HE KNOWS THAT NOW WITH COMPLETE CERTAINTY.
IT'S SIMPLY A HUNGER FOR GLORY. THE WARHAMMER YEARNS ONLY FOR TRIUMPH IN THE HEAT OF WAR.
AND IF THE HANDS THAT CLASP IT ARE WORTHY ENOUGH, TRIUMPH IS EXACTLY WHERE IT WILL TAKE THEM.
THE AGONIST IS DEAD! THE AGONIST IS DEAD!
PRAISE SIGMAR! PRAISE SIGMAR THIS DAY!
THEY'RE BROKEN, BURGOMEISTER! THE FOE IS TURNING!
I DON'T KNOW HOW IN THE NAME OF BLOODY FATE IT HAPPENED, BUT WE'VE GOT THEM ON THE RUN!
BLESSED SIGMAR MUST LOVE OSTLITZ, BURGOMEISTER. THEY'VE FINALLY ENDED THE AGONIST'S RUN OF LUCK...

"...AND GIVEN HIS GOOD FORTUNE TO *US!*"

THE MEN OF OSTLITZ SING OUT THE *VICTORY HYMN* OF THE EMPIRE.

GERD JODL RAISES THE WARHAMMER HIGH. HIS GRIP IS *TIGHT* AND *TRUE*.

THE BEGINNING...

THE WARHAMMER

Script: Dan Abnett • Art: Paul Jeacock
Letters: Fiona Stephenson

PART TWO

> AT THEM! AT THEM! SONS OF THE EMPIRE, BREAK THEIR LINE!

THERE IS *THUNDER*, BUT IT IS THE THUNDER OF STORMING *HOOVES*. THE SKY WEEPS. THE SOIL SHUDDERS.

JODL, THE *FEARLESS* FEELS NOTHING EXCEPT THE WARHAMMER'S HUNGER.

IT'S A HUNGER FOR GLORY, A THIRST FOR VICTORY.

AN INSATIABLE DESIRE TO BE THE WEAPON OF A *CHAMPION*.

BREAK THEIR LINE!
AND BREAK THEIR THRICE-DAMNED BACKS!
'GENERAL? THE LEFT FLANK HAS CHARGED, SIR.'
WHAT? SIGMAR'S TEETH! I DON'T BELIEVE THIS!
WHAT IS THAT FOOL JODL DOING? I TOLD HIM TO HOLD!
WHAT DO WE DO, SIR?
WE'VE NO BLOODY CHOICE, MAN! THAT GLORY-HOUND HAS FORCED OUR HAND! IF WE LEAVE HIM TO IT, IT'LL BREAK OUR RANK FORMATION WIDE OPEN!
SOUND THE ADVANCE! ENGAGE!

WELL?
THE ENEMY HAS WITHDRAWN NORTH OF THE RIVER, BUT THEY'RE HARDLY BROKEN. WE'VE LOST PERHAPS FOUR SCORE MEN.
DAMN IT ALL!
THE CAMPAIGN SEASON'S NEARLY OVER. ANOTHER WEEK AND THE WEATHER WILL DRIVE US BACK FOR THE WINTER.
THIS SHOULD HAVE BEEN AN END TO IT TODAY! A ROUT! A SLAUGHTER! WE PREPARED SO CAREFULLY...
...AND NOW THE FOE SLIPS AWAY, ALL BUT INTACT, WITH A WHOLE WINTER TO REPAIR HIS STRENGTH.
COME THE SPRING, HE'LL BE BACK, RAIDING WORSE THAN EVER!
DAMN GERD JODL! DAMN HIM TO HELL!
BUT... HE'S THE BEST WE HAVE, SIR!
YES HE IS! TEN SUMMERS GONE, HE WON THE FIELD AT OSTLITZ AND I THANKED SIGMAR FOR HIM!
OH, HE'S BRAVE! BRAVEST MAN I EVER SAW! BUT HE KNOWS NO PRUDENCE! NO STRATAGEMS!
IF HE SO MUCH AS SMELLS A FIGHT, HE'S IN IT! BOUND THE GLORY AND DAMN THE CONSEQUENCES!
YOU KNOW WHAT HE IS, THAT JODL THE FEARLESS?
A LIABILITY.

MALBURG, ON THE TALABEC, SIX WEEKS LATER...
HE'S HERE.
VERY WELL. I TRUST YOU'VE MADE HIM COMFORTABLE AND QUARTERED HIS TROOPS?
YES, MILORD. IS IT TRUE WHAT THEY SAY?
I DON'T KNOW. WHAT DO THEY SAY?
THAT HE'S OUT OF FAVOUR, DISGRACED. THAT HE'S ONLY BEEN SENT TO US BECAUSE THEY DON'T KNOW WHAT ELSE TO DO WITH HIM.
THAT'S JUST TATTLE. WE ASKED FOR HELP, THEY'VE SENT THE BEST. MALBURG DESERVES THAT, DOESN'T IT?
WE ASKED FOR A CHAMPION, REMEMBER? NOT A GLORIFIED RAT-CATCHER.
HOW DO I LOOK?
HERR JODL! IT IS A PRIVILEGE AND A PLEASURE! ALL MALBURG WELCOMES YOU! WE ARE HONOURED THAT YOU DIGNIFY US WITH YOUR AID.

THE HONOUR'S MINE, LORD. THE FIGHTING SEASON'S OVER FOR THE YEAR, AND GENERAL WISCH SUGGESTED I MIGHT BE OF USE HERE.
SPLENDID. AND HOW WENT THE SEASON?
WHY? WHAT HAVE YOU HEARD?
NOTHING, HERR JODL! I WAS SIMPLY ASKING.
IT WENT WELL ENOUGH, BUT IT LACKED...
...GLORY. THERE IS PRECIOUS LITTLE FIRE IN MEN'S BLOOD THESE DAYS.
THEY EXPECT VICTORY, BUT THEY NEVER TAKE THE RISKS THAT WILL SECURE IT.
THEY'LL BE CRUSHED WITHIN A WEEK.
THEY, HERR JODL?
I WAS JUST THINKING ALOUD, LORD.
NOW AS TO YOUR PROBLEM... THE VERMIN... REST ASSURED...

...KNEE DEEP IN ORDURE! THAT'S OUR REWARD!
TRAIPSING ABOUT IN THE SEWERS, HUNTING FOR RATS...
RAT-KIN.
WHATEVER! THIS IS WHAT WE GET FOR BEING OLD FEARLESS'S TROOP! KNEE DEEP IN SEWAGE!
THIS IS AN HONOUR.
DID ME TELL YOU THAT? DID HE?
TELL ME, DOES THIS SMELL LIKE AN HONOUR TO YOU?
EVERY OTHER BLOODY SOLDIER IN THE EMPIRE GETS TO BILLET OUT THE WINTER, FEAST LIKE A PIG AND DRINK LIKE FISH.
BUT NOT US, OH NO! BECAUSE WE'RE JODL THE FEARLESS'S MEN, AND JODL THE FEARLESS WANTS TO KEEP GOING, WANTS TO KEEP WINNING, WANTS TO SNIFF OUT ANOTHER FIGHT.
TELL YOU WHAT, BOYS, HE'S SNIFFED OUT SOMETHING. AND I WANT A TRANSFER TO ANOTHER BRIGADE.
SHUT UP. HE'S COMING.
ANYTHING?
NOT A SIGN, SIR. NO TRACE OF A LAIR.

SHOULD WE CALL IT A DAY, SIR?
NO! THEY'RE JUST HIDING FROM US. THERE'S A VICTORY TO BE HAD DOWN HERE, THE HAMMER PROMI-
THE HAMMER WHAT, SIR?
NOTHING. I MEANT TO SAY... I CAN FEEL VICTORY, WAITING FOR US. YOU WANT VICTORY, DON'T YOU?
OH, YES, SIR...
...THEN COME ON!
ACTUALLY, I SHOULD HAVE SAID 'WHAT I WANT IS A WARM BED, A FLAGON OF ALE AND A LUSTY GIRL WITH NO SENSE OF SMELL'.
FUNNY HOW YOU ALWAYS THINK OF THE REALLY WITTY ANSWERS WHEN IT'S TOO LATE, EH?
HINZ? WHERE'D YOU GO? HINZ?
OH SIGMAR'S BONES...

SKAVEN! SKAVEN!
THEY'RE BLOODY EVERYW-GGLLRKK!
BLADES OUT! WE'RE AMBUSHED!
THEY COME LIKE A TIDE. GNASHING TEETH, SCRABBLING CLAWS, SHRILL CRIES.
THEY COME FROM EVERYWHERE.

AGHHH!
NO!
NOOOOO!
THEY'RE ALL OVER HIM.
JODL THE FEARLESS FEELS FEAR FOR THE FIRST TIME.
BECAUSE AT LAST HE TRULY UNDERSTANDS THE WARHAMMER'S HUNGER.

IT'S SO SIMPLE, SO PURE.
IT'S A HUNGER FOR GLORY. A THIRST FOR VICTORY.
AN INSATIABLE DESIRE TO BE THE WEAPON OF A CHAMPION.
ANY CHAMPION.
END

THE WARHAMMER

Script: Dan Abnett • Art: Adrian Smith
Letters: Fiona Stephenson

PART THREE

FIRST, THERE WAS *WRYTH*.

WRYTH WARBITE, BLACK OF PELT, BRIGHT OF EYE, UNDER THE MAN-TOWN OF MARHEIM, WHERE THE LIGHT DECAYS.

HE FOUND IT. *HE* WON IT. A *FIGHT-TROPHY*.

IT *SMELLED* VALUABLE. IT WAS QUITE THE *FINEST* PIECE OF MAN-MAKING HE'D *EVER* GOT HIS PAWS ON.

WRYTH WARBITE CALLED IT A SHRILL SOUND THAT MEANS 'FATE-BREAKER' IN THE MAN-TONGUE.

HE KNEW HE COULD TAKE THIS PIECE OF FINE MAN-MAKING AND *UN-MAKE* MEN WITH IT.

AND A *LOT* MORE BESIDES.

HE WOULD UN-MAKE HIS *DESTINY*, UNDER THE MAN-TOWN OF MARHEIM, WHERE THE LIGHT DECAYS.

NO *LONGER* WOULD HE BE WRYTH WARBITE, CLAN CHAMPION OF REEKILL, BONDKIN OF CLANLORD GREE.

CLAN CUSTOM SAID THAT WRYTH SHOULD MAKE AN *OFFERING* OF THE FIGHT-TROPHY TO HIS GREAT CLANLORD.

WRYTH DECIDED TO *UN-MAKE* THAT CUSTOM...

...AS SOON AS HE'D *FINISHED* UN-MAKING CLANLORD GREE.

AND SO *HE* WAS CLANLORD, UNDER THE MAN-TOWN OF MARHEIM, WHERE THE LIGHT DECAYS.

NEXT, THERE WAS *SKUR*.

SKUR JAGEARED, YELLOW OF TOOTH AND LONG OF FLANK, IN THE MARSHES OF THE TALABEC, WHERE THE WATERS FUME.

HE WAS PLEDGED TO *SERVE* THE NEW CLANLORD OF THE REEKILL.

AND SO HE *DID*, WITH FURY AND VIGOUR, FOR SEVEN MAN YEARS.

BUT ALL THE WHILE, HIS GAZE *LINGERED*, LONGINGLY, ON FATE-BREAKER, GREAT FIGHT-TROPHY, CLAN-LORD'S WEAPON.

WISHING IT WAS HIS, AND HIS ALONE, IN THE MARSHES OF THE TALABEC, WHERE THE WATERS FUME.

UNDER WRYTH CLANLORD, THE REEKILL MADE *WAR* UPON THE NIGHT GOBLINS OF THE BURNING EYE.

FATE-BREAKER *BROKE* THE GOBLINS' FATE.

AND CLAN REEKILL FEASTED WELL, AND DRANK TO THE *EXPANSION* OF THEIR SUBTERRANEAN TERRITORY.

BUT SKUR JAGEARED DID NOT TOUCH A *DROP*.

SO *CLEAR HEADED* WAS HE WHEN DRUNKEN STUPOR CLAIMED THE REST.

AND WRYTH HE *UN-MADE*.

NOW *SKUR* WAS CLANLORD OF THE REEKILL, IN THE MARSHES OF THE TALABEC, WHERE THE WATERS FUME.

NEXT CAME *GNAASH*.

GNAASH ONE-EYE, DARK OF MANE AND QUICK OF PAW, IN THE STONE-CUT BURROWS BENEATH THE MOUNTAINS, WHERE NO LIGHT FALLS.

GNAASH WAS LORD OF *CLAN RYPP*, PRAISE BE THE HORNED RAT.

FOR FORTY MAN-YEARS, UNDER SKUR, CLAN REEKILL *GOUGED* AND *RAIDED* INTO CLAN RYPP UNDER-LAND, AND RYPP *RESISTED*.

SPIES TOLD GNAASH OF THE GREAT FIGHT-TROPHY HIS ENEMY LORD WIELDED.

FATE-BREAKER. BACK-CRACKER. RAT-MASHER.

GNAASH KNEW VICTORY WOULD NOT BE HIS UNLESS HE HAD FATE-BREAKER FOR *HIMSELF*.

HE PRAYED, BY THE LORDS OF DECAY, *HOW* HE PRAYED!

AND GREAT GIFTS AND BRIBES HE MADE TO THE RATKIN *WARLOCKS*, FEARED BY ALL.

MAGICK THEY WOVE FOR HIM. *PLAGUE* MAGICK. *DECAY* MAGICK.

SKUR OF THE REEKILL, AND HIS CHAMPIONS, WERE LURED INTO A TRAP.

GNAASH *BAITED* IT HIMSELF.

GREAT RAT-TRAP, BORN OF FETID MAGICKS, WEAVING *SHADOWS* IN THE STONE-CUT BURROWS BENEATH THE MOUNTAINS, WHERE NO LIGHT FALLS.

HERE SKUR BREATHED HIS LAST AND WAS UN-MADE.

AND GNAASH OF THE RYP TOOK *OWNERSHIP* OF FATE-BREAKER.

IN HIS TRIUMPH, HE UN-MADE ITS OLD NAME AND CALLED IT A SHRILL SOUND THAT MEANS 'SHADOW-PRIZE' IN THE MAN-TONGUE.

AND *SEVENTY* MAN-YEARS HE RULED, SHADOW-PRIZE IN HIS PAW.

THEN THERE WAS *SKEEL*.

SKEEL WAS A BASTARD-HEIR OF GNAASH, NOT EVEN *WHELPED* WHEN GNAASH TOOK SHADOW PRIZE FROM SKUR.

SKEEL BYBLOW, BROWN OF PELT AND RED OF EYE, AT THE WORLD'S EDGE WHERE ONLY SILENCE ECHOES.

POWER HE DREAMED OF, HIS YOUNG HEART GREEDY.

WITH STORIES OF *RUNT-MAN GOLD*, HE TEMPTED GNAASH DEEP INTO THE VAULTS OF THE MOUNTAINS.

AND THERE HE TURNED UPON HIS *SIRE*.

AND *TOOK* SHADOW-PRIZE, AND *TOOK* THE TITLE CLANLORD.

HOWEVER *BRIEFLY*.

AND IN DARKNESS AND IN DUST THEY LAY, UN-MADE, FOR A *HUNDRED* YEARS, AT THE WORLD'S EDGE WHERE ONLY SILENCE ECHOES.

WHAT'S THIS? WHAT'S *THIS*, I SAY?

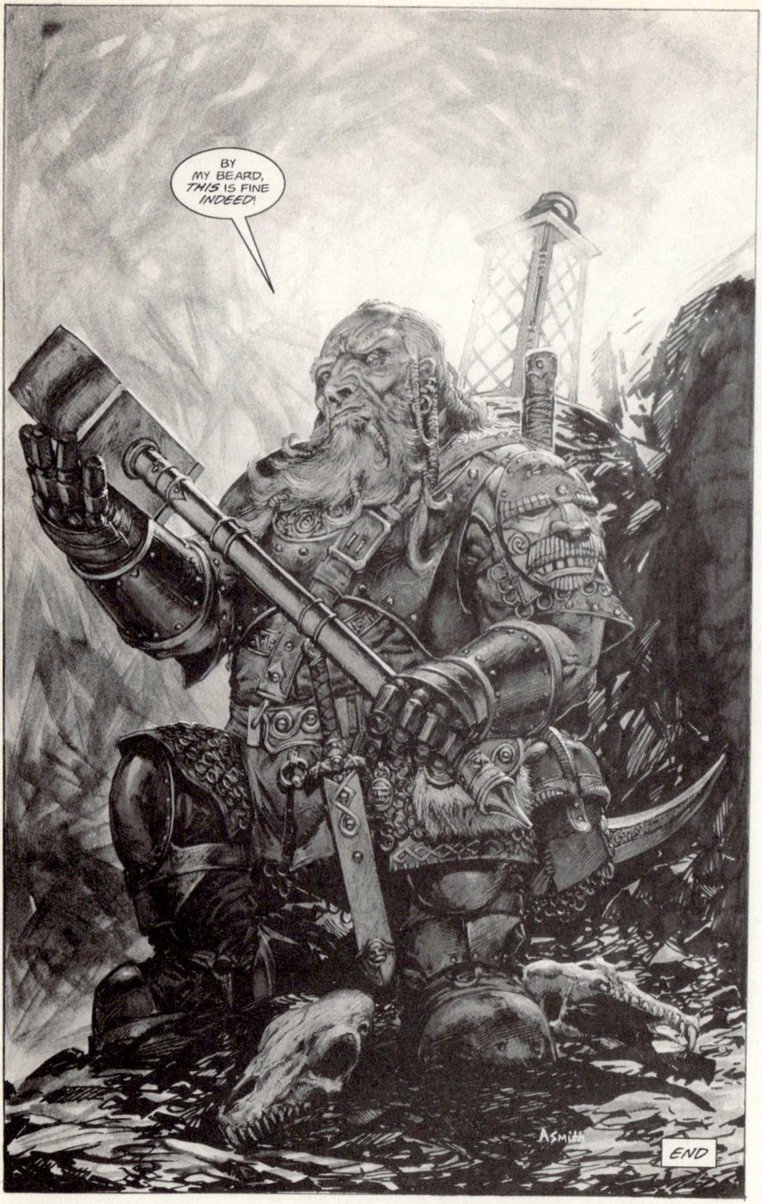
BY MY BEARD, THIS IS FINE INDEED!
ASmith
END

ABOUT THE AUTHOR

Dan Abnett is a novelist and award-winning comic book writer. He has written over thirty-five novels, including the acclaimed Gaunt's Ghosts series, the Eisenhorn and Ravenor trilogies and, with Mike Lee, the Darkblade cycle. His novels *Horus Rising* and *Legion* (both for the Black Library) and his Torchwood novel *Border Princes* (for the BBC) were all bestsellers. His novel *Triumff*, for Angry Robot, was published in 2009 and nominated for the British Fantasy Society Award for Best Novel. He lives and works in Maidstone, Kent.

Dan's blog and website can be found *www.danabnett.com*
Follow him on Twitter @*VincentAbnett*.

WULFRIK
Read an exclusive extract from the Warhammer Heroes novel, *Wulfrik*, by C. L. Werner

WULFRIK'S FIST CLENCHED tighter about the hilt of his sword. A Norscan did not fear death in the same way the weak southlings did. To die in battle was the greatest triumph most Norscans aspired to, a glorious death with blade in hand and his wounds to the fore. An end to make both gods and ancestors proud.

It was that promise which drew men to his banner, which made warriors from across Norsca and beyond flock to his side. Wulfrik felt no guilt when such men fell, for he knew that in their deaths they found the glory they desired. This time, however, there was guilt in his breast, the sharp stab of shame in his heart. The men he had left behind, strewn across the landscape like so much carrion, they had not died the glorious death of warriors. They had been felled like dumb beasts, struck down by elven arrows, killed before they could even see the enemy.

He had watched men die before in such cruel fashion, but always there had been reason for their deaths. This time, that reason was a lie – a lie that Wulfrik had insisted on believing. He had led them to this slaughter. The shame of their deaths was his. It was his punishment for trying to defy the will of the gods.

Wulfrik reached a hand to his thigh, ripping from his flesh the barbed arrow that had struck his leg. He threw back his shaggy head, roaring in pain as the missile was torn free. Contemptuously he snapped the shaft and threw the pieces to the ground. Again he threw back his head and roared, but this time it was a cry of challenge, not pain. Let the filthy elves come! He would face them and show them a finish even their cold hearts would remember!

A strong hand closed upon his shoulder. Like his namesake, Wulfrik spun about, snapping his fangs and striking out with his sword. A tall blond Norscan dodged back as the other warrior blindly lashed out at him, falling into a fighting crouch as he fell back. There was hate in the blond giant's eyes as he met the furious gaze of Wulfrik, but it was tempered by the man's own sense of shame.

'We can't make a stand here,' the huscarl said. 'They will cut us down as they did the others.'

Wulfrik sneered at the cowardly words of his comrade. Alone of his crew, the treacherous Broendulf had survived. 'If it is a choice between arrows in my belly or a knife in my back, I charge the bowmen and damn their sires with my dying breath!'

Broendulf's face flushed crimson as the champion spoke. For an instant, he considered answering Wulfrik's challenge. Among the Sarls, Broendulf had always been known for his sharp wits. They did not desert him now.

'If we die here, who is left to avenge your crew?' Broendulf asked. He saw doubt flash through Wulfrik's eyes. Emboldened, he pressed the point with words that were hateful to him even as they left his tongue. 'If you die here, who is there to protect Hjordis from her father?'

Wulfrik continued to glare at Broendulf. 'After the traitor is dead, we will finish this thing between us,' he growled. 'Hjordis is mine!'

Broendulf answered the champion with a cold smile. 'As you say, we will finish this thing between us. But not here.'

An arrow sizzled through the chill morning air, passing so near to Wulfrik's head that it disturbed his mane of crimson hair. The champion paused only long enough to spit in the direction of the unseen archer, then turned and began running across the barren ground, weaving from side to side in an effort to foil the aim of his enemies. Other arrows followed the first, rattling against the stones, striking sparks from the iron heels of the Norscans' boots.

Even with a half-dozen wounds peppering the champion's body, it was an effort for Broendulf to match Wulfrik's pace. However much he hated the man, Broendulf could not control the awe he felt in his presence. Wulfrik was truly a warrior who had been chosen by the gods; no simple mortal could match his endurance. He was like one of the bronze machine-beasts of the dawi zharr, untiring, indefatigable. Broendulf counted himself among the strongest warriors of all the Sarls, but beside Wulfrik, he felt as puny as a southling priest.

The cries of their pursuers grew nearer now. It was difficult to tell from the strange, almost melodious tones of elven speech, but there seemed a trace of panic in their voices. Wulfrik allowed himself a grim smile. The elves were afraid the men were going to escape. He allowed himself to concentrate on the cries. Even the curse of the gods had its blessings. For Wulfrik, that blessing was the Gift of Tongues. By focussing his mind, he could understand the speech of any creature, no matter how strange. Often he would use this eerie talent only to challenge his foes in words they could understand, but it had its other uses.

As he listened to the cries of the elves, Wulfrik's smile dropped. They were not afraid the men would escape. The elves were only afraid they would not be able to catch them alive. During the chase it seemed they had decided that the rest of the Norscans had died too swiftly. With Wulfrik and Broendulf, the elves intended to take their time.

Humans were not the only creatures who had a concept of revenge.

The cause for the elves' concern thrust itself upon Wulfrik with such suddenness that he nearly pitched over the edge. The northman charged across the rocky grade, unheeding of its gradual rise, unaware of the jagged cut that had sheared away its side as cleanly as though by the Blood God's axe. His feet teetering upon the crumbling lip of the cliff, he watched pebbles kicked up by his approach sail out into empty air. For an instant he stared into the dark waters of the sea, watching its waves smash against the breakers far below. Then Wulfrik regained his balance and steadied himself at the edge of the cliff.

The craggy shoreline stretched away in either direction as far as Wulfrik's keen gaze could see, rising from the blue sea like a great white wall. Mammoth rocks, curled and twisted by the ravages of brine and wind, leered from the depths, huddling about the feet of the cliffs like a mob of mongrel half-kin. Faintly, the northman could see the distant shores of barrier islands, their bleak stone shores little more than a black smear upon the horizon. Wulfrik scowled at the forbidding islands. If half the tales told in the sagas were true, there would be no respite from his enemies even if he could reach the forsaken spits of rock.

Broendulf was beside him a moment later, gasping for breath and staring with horror at the angry sea below. 'Where's the ship?' he moaned, gesturing at the breakers with his axe.

Wulfrik pointed to a jumble of shattered wreckage being pounded against the rocks. 'It seems our anchorage wasn't as secure as I thought,' he growled. Suddenly the champion's eyes went wide with shock. 'Mermedus's rutting eel!' he exclaimed as he spotted the thing slithering across the ship's broken hull.

A long, lean coil of scaly flesh slowly crushed the planks of the longship beneath its bulk. Azure above and with a white belly below, the monstrous serpent blended almost perfectly with the waves that crashed against it, only the contrast between itself and the wreck in its grasp allowing the men on the cliff above to see it. Here, both Norscans knew, was the killer of their ship, the monster whose thoughtless act of destruction had obliterated the greatest longship ever built by mortal hands.

More pointedly, the merwyrm had left them stranded, denied their only hope of escape from the trap they had been led into.

'What do we do now?' Broendulf raged, smashing his fist against his side in impotent fury. Another arrow clattered off the stones near his feet.

Wulfrik smiled coldly at the blond Sarl. 'The dragon or the elves,' he told Broendulf. 'The gods leave us small choice, but at least the serpent won't make a game of killing us.'

Wulfrik did not wait to see what effect, if any, his logic had upon the other Norscan. Clenching the blade of his sword between his fangs, the warrior flung himself over the side of the cliff.